"BEHIND US!" he yelled, instinctively. He wasn't fast enough still proved sufficient to save his b back of his neck, found the steel bracer of his right arm instead. There was nothing he could do about the momentum of the wolf's leap, though, and the animal's body slammed into his, hitting him with a hundred-and-fifty-some-odd pounds of unstoppable force. He had only a glimpse of whitish, dirty fur before he was flying off his saddle sideways, hitting the frozen ground with a hard *thud* that knocked the torch from his left hand and Ahna from his lap.

The wolf, though, stayed atop him.

It was a vicious thing, unlike any animal he had ever seen. Even sandcats were quick to strike and retreat, calculating their movements and attacks. The wolf, rather than backing off now that it had vulnerable prey on the ground, never let go of the bracer, wrenching Raz's arm about so powerfully he felt his elbow strain under the pressure. They rolled once, twice, three times down the hill, and only then did Raz understand what the creature was doing.

It was keeping him down until the others arrived to help.

Everything clicked into place, and Raz moved with all the haste and skill of a cornered killer. Dropping the gladius he'd managed to hold onto in his pinned right hand, he sliced at the animal's neck with claws of his left, intent on freeing himself. Thick, knotted hair foiled the blow, though, and so Raz drew his whole hand back, clenching the gauntlet into a steel fist.

The punch broke the animal's neck with a *snap*.

It fell limp off his arm with a pitiful yelp of pain, jaw slackening abruptly. Raz didn't pause, though, whirling around to meet the assault he knew was coming head on. The four wolves on the left seemed to have gone around the hill, likely trying to take the Priests from the flank.

The three on the right, though, were already on him.

With a roar that might have shaken the snow from the trees around him, Raz lanced forward. As the first wolf leapt for him with a snarl, going for the throat, Raz snatched it out of the air by the neck with one hand and slammed it to the ground. The other two came from either side of him, and he leapt back and away, abandoning his hope of gutting the pinned one before it could get back on its feet.

He did, though, manage to draw the war-ax from his belt.

"COME ON!" he screamed, his wings spreading to their fullest extent, ripping his hood back so his crest flared like a blade over his head as the wolf he'd downed managed to scramble up and join the others. "COME AND GET ME!"

The beasts obliged.

Winter's King
Book Three of *The Wings of War* series
Bryce O'Connor

ISBN: 0-9988106-3-0
ISBN-13: 978-0-9988106-3-8
Edited by Vince Connors and Isaure de Buron
Map by Bryce O'Connor

Cover Art by Andreas Zafiratos
Cover Design by Bryce O'Connor & Andreas Zafiratos

WINTER'S KING

BRYCE O'CONNOR

For my Bonne Maman
who was so often the keystone
to a childhood full of wonder.

ACKNOWLEDGMENTS

As ever, I will always thank my family first for all their support. My mother and father, Vince and Isaure, who took it a step further this time around by doing almost all the essential editing of *Winter King*'s final draft, and my sister Sabine, who is still making me look bad in the smarts department.

Next again to Joe Jackson, author of *The Eve of Redemption* series, for his continued (and indispensable) help cleaning up the final submission of the book. Check out his own awesome writings on his site (https://citaria.wordpress.com) or reach out to him directly with business inquiries regarding read-throughs, editing, and developmental feedback at: shoelessauthor@gmail.com

As always to Dan, Bev, Gary, and Barb, for taking me in so many times over the years and helping me become a better writer in so many way.

To Kate, for still and ever putting up with me. You are literally crazy. How do you do it? Like seriously?

Again to my unbelievable cover artist Andreas Zafiratos, who all agree has surpassed himself this time around. *Winter's King* is my favorite cover to date. See more of his work at www.facebook.com/artofalbinoz or contact him with business inquiries directly at andreaszafeiratos@gmail.com. Yes, the last name is different. Take it up with him, ha!

Again to the myriad of authors and writers who continue to inspired me as a creator, whose worlds I borrow and steal from without hesitation or remorse. Thank you all.

A new one. To the team over at Bungie and Activision for cobbling together the amazing bundle of fun that is Destiny. I have been playing since week 1, and Trials with my friends is still my favorite place to escape to when I need a break from writing and the real world. Can't wait for D2!!!

To my alpha and beta readers, as well as my review team! Without you, NONE of the books I have published thus far would be half as good as they ended up:

Her Majesty Ashley Klimek, Ruth C. Jones (ruthiejones.com), Simon "Mort" Evans (who is definitely on the team!), Emi-Jo Smith, Emi-Jo Smith, Adam Siefertson, TuFF GoNG, Larry Payton, Patrick "biker dude" Anguish, David Lubkin, Fuchsia Aurelius, Todd Ponto, Adarsh Venkatesh, Cat Zablocki, Jerri-Lee 'Sprinkles' Bickley, Nicholas Rocan, Master Seamen Walsh, Emily-Ann, Chris G, Ares Wolfe, Bruce L Hevener, *Drake Vato,* Jonathan Williamson, Professor Ethan L. Alderman, Devin Fuoco, Devin Fuoco, Mr. Derek E. Larson, MMus, Med, Noel Townsend, Harley Strutton queen of literature, Peter "Hutch" Hutchinson, M.B.Schroeder, David Haselden, and Elise Woodfolk

If you are interested in joining the beta group and getting early access to the books, reach out to me at: bryce@bryceoconnorbooks.com.

And, forever and always, to you readers. Ironically there isn't enough ink in the world to spell out how grateful I am to you. As I get nearer and nearer to being a full-time writer, I can't help but wonder at this journey you have taken me on. You are the gas in the engine of an interstellar flight, rocketing me into the sky with every page you turn. Thank you all, endlessly and then some.

WINTER'S KING

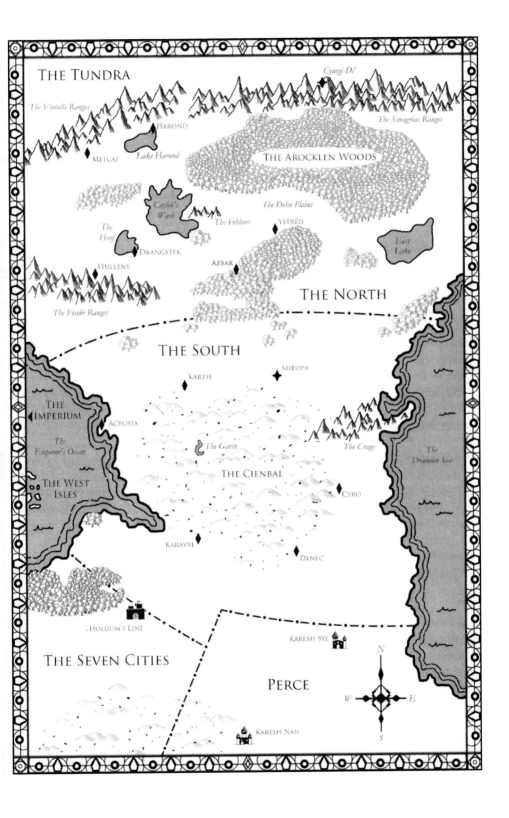

THE TUNDRA

The Vietalis Ranges

Cyurgi Di'

The Saragrias Ranges

HAROND

METCAF

Lake Harond

THE AROCKLEN WOODS

Cayleb's Wash

The Dehn Plains

The Fehlons

YSTRÉD

The Hoof

DRANGSTEK

AZBAR

East Lake

STULLENS

THE NORTH

The Fissúr Ranges

THE SOUTH

KARTH

MIROPA

THE IMPERIUM

ACROSIA

The Emperor's Ocean

The Garin

The Crags

THE CIENBAL

The Dramion Sea

THE WEST ISLES

CYRO

KARAVYL

DYNEC

HOLDUM'S LINE

KARESH SYL

THE SEVEN CITIES

PERCE

N

W   E

S

KARESH NAN

861 v.S.

PROLOGUE

"The Stone Gods—it is commonly believed among those of academia—were a theology born of the forces of nature whose brutality mankind, despite all his potential wickedness, can hardly compare to. Mountain lightning storms, blizzards which leave the world only shades of white, avalanches that descend to bury men alive. It seems logical, when considering this, the deities born of such worship could only be as cruel as the events they were meant to emulate…"

—from the libraries of Cyurgi' Di

Egard Rost shook in his worn boots as he approached the wide leather tent staked out at the top of the hill before him. It loomed out of the dark at him and his paired escorts, illuminated by braziers set on either side of the entrance and by the glow of a hundred cooking fires ablaze about the camp at his back. Above and beyond it, the trees of the Arocklen Woods towered overhead, glowing a dim blue as the ice and snow piled in the thick branches reflected the sheen of the moon and stars somewhere far above them.

Egard knew he had no real reason to fear the place, just as he had no real reason to fear for his life. He was valuable, and these nightly visitations to Grahst's tent were a small price to pay for the general's protection.

Even so, as the man over his left shoulder shoved him towards the front flaps once they'd crested the hill, Egard couldn't help but swallow, the chafed skin of his throat rubbing against the heavy loop of thick, patterned steel that encircled his neck.

He might be valuable, but a slave will always feel fear when within reach of the whip…

Egard moved haltingly forward, spreading the leathers that kept out the cold air of the Woods, and stepped inside. The general's tent was nothing overtly impressive. Grahst had packed light, favoring speed over comfort as the vanguard under his command moved quickly east with each passing day. Still, it was spacious, warm and bright, the smoke from the foursome of torches set in each corner dragged up and away through ventilating holes in the peaks of the ceiling. Most of the ground about Egard's feet was the grass of the forest floor, but to his right a number of pelts had been piled, forming a makeshift bed.

And there, seated upon it, his sword across his knees and an oil cloth in hand, sat Kareth Grahst.

The youngest general of the Kayle's army did not even raise his eyes to his visitor, finishing the meticulous task of caring for his blade. Egard, in turn, said nothing, watching his master warily as the Sigûrth shined the steel, checking his reflection in the sheen of the metal. Grahst was a large man, even by the standards of the mountain tribes, with the thick arms and legs of one born to swing a sword. He had dark blue eyes, much like his cousin's, but Grahst's hair was blonde rather than brown. It was braided in the same fashion as all of his clan, beaded and ringed with baubles and trinkets, as Egard had been forced to do with his own hair. A smile played at the general's lips even as he continued to work his weapon, like he were amused by something.

Of course he is, Egard thought with a chill. *He's amused by me.*

Kareth Grahst would have been considered a cruel man in the world outside his mountains. He enjoyed exerting control where he could, thrived on rising above and stomping down on the men below. From killing to pillaging to raping to enslavement, the general drew passion from blood and violence, excitement from battle and death. In the world outside his mountains, he would have been an exile, cast out as savage and wicked.

Amongst his own, though, such qualities only made him *strong.*

When Grahst was finally tired of playing his little game of making Egard wait on him, he set aside the sword. His blue eyes came up slowly, settling on his property's wan brown ones, and immediately Egard felt his heartbeat pick up.

"Van ys, skav."

The general spoke in the rolling, rough mountain tongue, but Egard understood it perfectly. In a different life he had been a man of another place, another god and purpose, and he had spent much time dealing with both the mountain clans and the civil government of Metcaf, the valley town east of Harond.

When Metcaf had fallen under the boot of the Kayle, though, Egard had only been among the more valuable pieces of loot.

Come here, slave, Grahst had said.

And Egard did as commanded.

He approached, stepping onto the furs, then brought himself down to sit across from the general. Grahst continued to watch him all the while, the maddening smile still hinted at on his face.

Egard had a feeling the danger was only real when the man smiled in full.

For a few seconds, the pair looked at each other. Egard knew what was expected of him, but he waited for his master to give him the command. It was his small defiance, the only rebellion he could manage without risking losing a finger, or more.

"*Eysi*," Grahst said eventually, eyes narrowing.

Begin.

And so Egard brought up his hands, willing the flames to come.

The magic poured into his palms and over his fingers like liquid, licking upwards from his skin in tendrils of white fire that danced and spat back and forth. With nothing more than thought he crafted the simple spells, his will causing the flames to shift and grow, then shrink and separate. It formed patterns over his hands and wrists, and he turned them slowly, allowing the fire to move across his knuckles like living ivory spikes.

All the while, Grahst watched with wide eyes.

There was no hunger in that gaze, surprisingly. Egard had thought, on the first night he had been summoned to the general's tent and told to perform his spells, that Grahst was somehow after the power. He had thought the general desired the magics, desired the strength they could bring him.

Instead, he had only watched, studying the fire like a man studies a battlefield.

Which is exactly what he's doing, Egard thought to himself.

He had considered, more than once, bringing the full force of his magic to bear as he'd sat there, alone with the general. He had considered demonstrating the potency of a stunning spell, then later even wondered if he had it within him to kill the cruel man. He had made plans, formed ideas, crafted escape routes in his mind and told himself he was waiting for the right opportunity.

In the end, though, Egard had proven himself too much of a coward to go through with any of them. The laws of his old faith had bound him, and his fear of being caught—or worse, trying and failing to strike down Grahst himself—had paralyzed his hopes and dreams of freedom.

Not to mention that he would be alone in the Woods, among the wolves and bears and winter snows…

Egard continued to provide his magical game of show for some time, as he'd expected to. Every evening it was the same: arrive, demonstrate the powers of his old god, then work late into the night on Kareth's mastery of the Common Tongue. This last part was the true purpose of the nightly visits, of course. Ever since he'd found out that the Kayle had been having *his* slaves teach him the language of the greater world, Grahst had taken the interest on with fervor. He had always emulated his cousin in that fashion, lesser man that he was, though Gûlraht Baoill's slaves were all young women he had dragged from the burning skeletons of Metcaf and Harond, not a single beaten, defeated man like Egard.

Eventually, the general had had enough of the magics. He held up a hand, and Egard ceased the show at once, waiting. It was always Grahst who began their conversation, but it often took him some time to find the words and wrap his tongue around their strange pronunciations.

"Tonight," he finally got out, "you teach of the faith. Teach many words, as many as can remember."

Egard nodded.

"Do well more, and perhaps a slave I make you not, one day," Grahst continued.

And he said it with a smile.

I

"By the vast majority of those familiar with his legends, Raz i'Syul Arro is a misunderstood soul. To that greater populace, the unstudied masses who repeat the tales of the Monster to each other around the campfire flames, Arro embodies nothing more than righteous violence. He was a being of savage morality, the creature spat forth by whatever gods laid claim to his world to cleanse it of the filth that festered upon their creation. To these people, those enthusiastically retelling of his conquests in raised voices under waving arms, Arro's path left behind nothing but justly charred earth. To these people, he was a paladin of virtuous fury, untouched by anything but the burning vengeance that drove him through his crusade against the evils of the Common Age.
It is only those few of us who've looked deeper, who have sought out the truths that time has so casually cast aside, that ache with some echo of the sorrow and suffering the Monster of Karth must have carried with him for the better part of his life…"

—*Born of the Dahgün Bone*, author unknown

It defies all reason, the way winter can be so quiet. When the winds die and nothing is left of the storm but still-falling snow, sound seems to vanish altogether from the world. What remains is not true silence, per se—there is an inexplicable heaviness to the air, a denseness that bears down upon the ears—but it is as close as one can come in all the noise and vigor that is life.

And it is more than enough to pull an already feverish mind towards madness.

It was on this cusp that Raz i'Syul Arro was hovering. His whole body was simultaneously wracked with cold and yet burning up from the inside. He'd been on horseback for three days straight, barely pausing to let the animal rest and graze on what little grass could be found along the clearer bases of the trees that lined their northbound road. He himself had no appetite. It had fled from him much like his awareness of time, leaving only an unrelenting thirst he kept sated with the snow that fell thickly upon his hunched shoulders.

That, and the pulsing sensation of bone-deep agony lancing through his back with every wheezing breath he took.

It was an unfamiliar sensation for Raz. This was illness, he'd realized, true disease. He'd seen it before, but never experienced it. He'd always caught the summer colds less often than the rest of his cousins growing up, and—even when they did find a way into his chest—his body very often fought the ailments off far quicker than the other Arros.

Not this time, though. This time, the infection had taken firm hold of his flesh, and appeared to have no intention of letting go.

When he'd first started to fall ill, Raz had cursed the names of the men who had put him in this predicament. In particular he'd held himself together for a while by wishing every malediction on Quin Tern—the Azbar councilman who'd had him stand against a small army of mercenaries for Tern's own pleasure—and Sury Atheus—the West Isler who'd driven a blade through his back in the process. But Atheus was dead and Tern not far behind if he wasn't already, and Raz's mind had long since slipped away from anger towards thoughts not so firmly anchored in reality.

Slumped over the neck of the horse trudging along beneath him through the snow, Raz's amber eyes gazed unfocused upon the road ahead. Though some sane part of his conscience knew well that there was nothing there, the rest had long since betrayed him to the fever. At first they had been nothing but shapes, dark splotches against the snow. Over the course of the last day or so, however, the shadows had taken form, and now Raz watched as the distinct pair gallivanted around him and his horse. The siblings' laughter seemed to echo through the hollows of his mind as he watched them duck and dodge between the trees, crossing back and forth before him, chasing one another through the snow. They seemed happy, now, free of the burdens that had weighed on them in life. Out here, in the woods beyond the binding walls of Azbar, they had finally shed all worries and cares, and for the first time Raz got to see the pair in truth for the children they were.

It was an odd comfort, a sense of pseudo-tranquility, witnessing the dead in the peace that follows life.

One of the shades strayed closer, and as she grew more distinct in proximity Raz extended out a shaking, tentative hand. The girl stood on tiptoes in the snow to reach up for his clawed fingers. Raz hoped, for what felt the hundredth time that day, that when they met he would feel the pressure of her skin through the gauntlet, the softness of a child's touch against the leather.

When her fingers found his, though, they passed through steel and flesh like smoke.

"Lueski…" Raz mumbled dully, turning as the horse moved on so as to watch the smiling girl, her blue eyes bright behind a loose curtain of black hair. "Lueski… I'm so sorry."

The shade didn't respond, though. She only giggled, then skipped up ahead to rejoin her brother.

The rest of the day kept on like this, with Raz feeling himself falling further and further into the fever. By nightfall he had begun seeing other things among the woods, some as pleasant as the vision of the Koyt children, some far less so. At times the snow would melt abruptly around him to reveal the dense greenery of the forest that hid beneath winter's coat, reminding him briefly of the utter wonder he had felt when he'd first reached the North after his flight from the fringe cities far to the south. At other times his fitful dozing would be disturbed by ghastly sights, ghosts of the dead that haunted him from beneath the trees, their bodies mangled, just as he'd left them. Krom Ayzenbas' tattooed chest was ripped open so that his ribs looked to form the petals of some grisly flower. Ergoin Sass did nothing to replace the entrails spilling out upon the ground about his feet, fallen and hanging from the great gash across his midriff. The eight final champions of the Arena took turns in their appearances, their bodies painted with blood and gore, all sporting the ugly wounds that had claimed their lives.

The final ghost to appear in the last of the Sun's dying light was that of Quin Tern himself, his face and hands blackened by frostbite, gleaming eyes following Raz cruelly from the shadows as the horse kept on.

Night came, and for the first time in days the snows finally abated. Storm clouds gave way to a shockingly clear sky, and if Raz had been of a mind to look up he might have been reminded of evenings spent as a child, sitting atop the roof of his parents' wagon, attempting to memorize the intricate constellations that patterned Her Stars. As it was, though, all Raz knew was that, as the Moon rose, the grisly visions faded, shying away from Her gaze. Only Lueski and Arrun were left to keep his company, ambling along on either side of his horse. Several times he fell into bouts of slumber in the saddle, only to be jolted into wakefulness as the animal snorted or shifted abruptly beneath him. He wanted to stop, wanted to make camp and light himself the largest fire the world would ever see. He tried to convince himself several times that it was the prudent move, the right choice to make. Maybe warmth and rest were what he needed to rid himself of this sickness. Maybe the flames would burn the malady right out of his chest.

But no. In the end, he knew better. He was starting to taste the infection on his breath, now, a sort of rotten, sickly sweet flavor with every exhale. It was in his lungs, he knew, and there was nothing he could do about it.

Nothing, that is, except forge forward, and pray in irony to the Twins that he would come across the faithful of another god before it was too late.

And so Raz kept ahorse, ignoring the ache of his back and the pain of his legs for doing so. He was mercifully spared the chafing suffered by man, the saddle finding little to rub away against the slick scales of his dark skin, but it was a silver lining he found only in passing, his mind intent on the visions, the fever, and a single burning recollection.

The northbound road for Ystréa, he quoted to himself as the morning Sun blazed orange and pink over the trees to his right. *I've only to stay on the northbound road for Ystréd.*

The trouble lay in that Raz had no good sense of where, exactly, Ystréd was, much less how far he had to continue his trek through the snow to reach it. It was only one among many questions he was kicking himself for not discovering an answer for sooner, at the very least before he made this hasty flight northward once more.

Again, though, there was nothing to be done about it. Raz had long since given up on the hope of making out markers along the road. Anything shorter than a signpost was well buried beneath the snow by now. He held out on the chance that he might cross paths with a traveler willing to lend a hand—or at least assure him he was on the right path— but Raz had his doubts anyone but he could be foolish enough to brave the wrath of the freeze come in full.

All that was left to him was to keep going, and hope by the Sun and Moon and all Her Stars that he didn't come across a fork in the road.

With the morning light, the specters returned, but Raz was too worn and weak to be bothered by their grim spectacle today. He barely noticed the dead as his horse ambled on, just as he barely noticed the animal itself meander back and forth casually across the road, wandering around in search of what grass it could scrounge beneath the snow.

Noon came and went, the clear sky refusing to betray the world once more to the grey clouds of winter just yet. Soon after—at least to Raz's mind—the Sun had begun to dip downward, and the somber yellows and reds of dusk gave way minute by minute to the night.

It was as the last vestiges of this sunset faded, bowing graciously to the overwhelming darkness, that Raz heard the unmistakable sounds of man.

At first he didn't allow himself to hope, chalking the noise up to nothing more than an added element of his hallucinations. Head bowed beneath his hood and eyes only half open, he kept on, lost to the sway of the horse. As the sounds grew louder though, Raz forced himself to look up, gritting sharp teeth at the burning ache that ripped through his back at the motion.

It was only when he made out the glow of flames, firelight dancing through the pines a little ways off the road to his right, that Raz realized what he was seeing.

For the first time in days, a little of his strength returned to him. Holding tight to Ahna with one hand, the dviassegai still balanced across his thighs, he pulled his horse's reins around with the other to line the mount up with the light, kicking it into a trot through the snow. As the horse stepped off the clearer path into the woods, the dull thump of

11

hooves through fresh snow was replaced by the crunch of iron shoes breaking through packed ice and frozen underbrush. As they got closer Raz could make out voices, the distinct sound of at least four or five men. By the time he pulled his horse into the firelight, laughter and the vulgar lyrics of some raunchy evening ballad were clear over the strumming of a lyre in minimally skilled hands.

All of it stopped, though, as Raz and his horse lumbered to a halt among the festivities.

It was a small camp, by any standard. Five men sat around a hearty fire in a space between the trees, the ground around them roughly cleared. Back behind them, a little deeper into the woods, Raz saw the silhouettes of horses, their forms draped with thick blankets to ward off the cold of the night. They were moving around a small, open-air cart, laden with what looked to be packs, food, and spare bedrolls.

Raz would have taken the group for travelling merchants, perhaps intent on making Azbar and its newly booming economy while they still could, except that each of the men had a sword either looped around their waist or sitting within easy reach.

There was a pause as the five men stared in complete shock up at Raz. Whatever they'd had planned for the evening, it certainly did not seem to have involved a half-dead, half-frozen atherian ambling suddenly into their midst. Raz did his best to meet their gazes, noting through his fevered haze the scars many sported across weathered faces, as well as the thick leather and iron armor they wore even as they settled in for the evening. Had he been in his right mind, he might also have noted the tension that fell slowly upon the group, and the inching of hands towards hilts.

"Ystréd," Raz croaked, wincing at the harshness of his voice and the jolt of pain that stabbed at his throat and lungs as he spoke. "Take me— Take me to Ystréd."

Not one of the men did more than blink. A few eyes darted around him, as though expecting further company to follow Raz through the dark, but as a whole they said nothing.

"You will be compensated," Raz wheezed. "My friends... My friends will see to it."

Still nothing.

At last, something like apprehension tugged its way to the forefront of Raz's thoughts, instinct managing a small cry of warning through the fog of sickness.

Raz, already bordering on delirium, had no trouble brushing the suspicion aside.

"Please." His voice sounded like cracking branches, rough and sharp from disuse. "Ystréd. Take me to Yst—"

WHAM.

Something hard and heavy collided with the back of Raz's head through his hood, and stars exploded across his vision. At once what little strength had been left in his limbs deserted him, and he crumpled, sliding sideways off the saddle. He hit the ground with a clattering *crunch* of flesh and steel against frozen earth, Ahna's heavy haft falling atop him. His horse, unsure of what had happened to its rider, screamed and reared, coming down so close to his head Raz felt the thump of hooves against ground on his face.

"Dammit it all, Kisser!" a man's rough voice roared, and a form leapt up from the fire to dart across Raz's darkening vision. "Get the horse away from 'im! Here!" The man grabbed the reins of Raz's mount and shushed the animal, trying to calm it as it reared again. "Shhh. *Shhhh*, boy! It's all right. Calm, boy. Caaaalm."

The horse's panic subsided slowly, and eventually it allowed itself to be led away, apparently in the direction of the others and the cart. At the same time, Raz felt a boot come down on his shoulder and shove him over.

A face appeared, and it took a moment for Raz to realize that this one was younger and less harsh than the five he'd seen before. The boy had curly brown hair set over hazel eyes, and thick scruff of the same color that lent itself well to his looks.

"Lifegiver's saggy tits," he hissed, looking down on Raz. "You've got to be shitting me."

Another face appeared, then another. Before long five heads were hovering, blurry and spinning, above Raz. He lay beneath them, shivering and weak, barely aware of the words exchanged and the happenings around him.

"S'not possible..." one voice said.

"It is!" another nearly squealed in excitement. "It's him! It's *him*!"

"What in the blazes is the lizard doing all the way out here?" a third demanded.

"Don't know, don't care," the young one called Kisser appeared to reply. "Don't look like much, though, do he?"

"An' small wonder."

This last voice was the first Raz had heard, the one who had yelled to have Kisser get the horse away from him. As he watched, the five heads Raz could see shifted to make room for a sixth, and the way they fell silent was enough to tell him, even in his delusionary state, that this was the one in charge.

"See the blood?" the man asked, pointing a fuzzy hand at the left side of Raz's chest. "See the shivering? This one's got one foot up Laor's arse.

Strip him of his weapons and tie him up, then get him closer to the fire before he dies of the cold."

"Eh?" Kisser looked up in surprise. "We're not gonna kill him?"

"Kill him? And give his head enough time to rot 'afore we can get it south? How much do you think an empty atherian skull will be worth to the Mahsadën? Don't be an idiot. Now *get to it*!"

At once the other five jumped to follow the orders, bending down around Raz. When he felt rough hands move across his body and armor, he realized he was losing the fight to keep his eyes open. As he finally fell into the black, giving in to the fever and the blow to the head, the last thing he saw was a single face, clear and terrifying in a way none of the others had been, staring down at him.

Quin Tern's hungry leer was filled with unbridled glee, framed grimly against the frostbitten flesh of his dead features.

II

"It is said that, in his later years, the Lifetaker came to develop a deep regret for the blood spilled by his hands. I am relieved to discover this, for I admit to great consternation upon the discovery that my position among the Laorin was once filled by what some history books have dubbed 'the single greatest killer to have walked tall in the Common Age.' It appears, however, that my concerns were premature. Though his time as High Priest was short, the impacts of his life cannot be denied, for they ripple into the peace we witness even today, some four hundred years after his time."

—Kalun Vos, High Priest of Cyurgi' Di, c.390 a.S

There was a brief knock on the room door, and Talo Brahnt was plucked from his thoughts as he jumped at the sound. He sat at a small, lopsided escritoire set up in front of the diamond-paned window of his and Carro's small room. Before him, pinned flat by several unlit candles and his inkwell, a blank piece of parchment lay waiting for the stroke of the quill he had ready in his right hand. He'd been intent on penning up a letter to Kal Yu'ri, High Priest of the small Laorin temple in Azbar, hoping to get news of how Raz i'Syul Arro was faring in their absence. Talo was quite sure that—though the atherian may not have said so outright—he had been sorry to see the Priests leave, their attentions drawn away from the plight of the Arena by more pressing matters closer to home. It was this thought that had carried Talo away, dragging him into reminiscence of how he'd asked Arro to join him and Carro on their trek northward, and how the man had—with surprising conviction—refused.

And so Talo found himself staring off into a clear morning sky, a rare sight so many weeks into the freeze, with a quill suspended uselessly over still blank parchment.

Suspended, that is, until he had flinched and flung dark ink everywhere.

"*Damn!*" Talo cursed, leaping up from his chair and dropping the quill onto the desk, plucking at the sleeve of his white High Priest's robe, now blotched with mismatched black spots. As he did so, the door behind him creaked open slowly, and Carro al'Dor poked his head into the room.

"Road workers say they should have the way north clear by the end of the day. You're sure you want to wait and—*What did you do to those robes?*"

Talo quailed as the big man stormed into the room. Though Carro was well known as a wise and gentle man at heart, he had all the features and bearing of the Sigûrth father who had raped his mother and abandoned her with an unwanted child. He was as tall as Talo—his head barely fitting an inch or so below the frame of the door—but whereas Talo kept his peppered beard cropped and his straight silver-brown hair in a long tail down his back, Carro had taken on some of the cultural traditions of his ancestral people. His blond beard was bushy and braided, tied off with bands of metal and carved wood that had grown in multitude as the years passed. Similar rings were knotted into the dreads and braids of his thick, wild hair. Despite the white robes of his faith, any who did not know Carro al'Dor well always had a hard time believing he was a Priest of the Lifegiver, much less a skilled healer and among the best scribes the Laorin had to offer the world.

At that moment, Talo couldn't blame them. All of the fierceness of his clan heritage was painted clear in Carro's blue eyes as he stalked forward, glaring at the splotches along the stained sleeve.

"How is it," he growled, grabbing Talo's arm to pull the ink spots up to his nose and exam them, "that you manage to do *this* not half a day after I wash our clothes!"

"Don't blame me!" Talo exclaimed, trying to tug himself free. "Next time don't come barging into a room when a man has finally found some peace and quiet for a change!"

"Some day we are going to have a discussion regarding the definition of 'barging,' handsome," Carro retorted with a snort, dabbing a finger on the largest of the blotches and rubbing the wet ink between thumb and forefinger. "Hmm, still damp. Shouldn't be too much trouble…"

Moving his hand so that his palm hovered about half an inch over Talo's sleeve, Carro ran it along the length of the High Priest's arm. There was a dim glow of white light, and Carro pulled away to reveal nothing but faint discolorations where moments before had been a pattern of black splots.

"Better, but I'll have to work out the rest once we get home," Carro mumbled, examining his work. Then he looked up at Talo again. "Now, did you hear what I said?"

"Roads will be clear by afternoon," Talo repeated with a nod, pulling at his sleeve to examine it himself. "Good. We can leave then. This damn storm didn't seem ready to ever give up. Let's hope we don't get caught in anything like that for the rest of our trip."

"Let's hope," Carro said with a nod, crossing his arms. "But why wait for the afternoon? If we leave now we'll have a full day of riding before we lose any light, instead of just a few hours. I could have the stable boy—"

"Not worth it," Talo cut across him, returning to the desk, intent on putting away the parchment and ink. He would draft the letter later, he decided. "If the way isn't cleared, we won't be more than a few hours on the road before the snow gets too deep to do more than walk. Leave the workers to their labors. What little time we lose will be worth minimizing the risk of laming the horses."

"If you're sure," Carro grumbled, turning to ease himself down on the closest corner of the room's single bed before giving Talo a sidelong look. "I'm not convince you're not delaying on purpose, though…"

"To what end?" Talo asked with feigned sweetness, crossing his arms as he prepared for the accusation he knew full well was coming.

"Arro," Carro huffed, waving a hand aimlessly towards the southern wall of the room, the direction they had come from Azbar. "I can't help but consider you might be slowing us down deliberately, hoping he'll have changed his mind. Even if he did, he would have been a fool to try the roads through that storm! We're lucky we made it to Ystréd without much trouble as it was, and the atherian trying to do the same would be—!"

"I'm not waiting for anything, Carro."

Carro paused in his half-hearted rant, watching Talo closely.

"I admit I held out some hope on our way here," the High Priest said with a shrug. "I won't deny it. But it's dissipated. Two days waiting out the snow here, and another four on the road before that… If Arro had wanted to catch up to us by now, I'm sure he would have. Even bringing along the Koyts. One way or another, the man would have made it into town at least, and that alone would have made enough noise to reach us within the hour. No, I hold no delusions. Arro made his choice, and it's time I respected it."

Despite all this, Carro was still watching him suspiciously.

"So you're not delaying us?" the Priest asked after a moment. "There's nothing holding you back?"

Talo sighed. "By 'holding me back,' do you mean something other than the fact that we left Azbar in the hands of its lunatic chairman and his twisted council? Or abandoned our goal of taking the Arena down completely? Or left Arro to fend for himself, as well as Arrun and Lueski?" He grimaced. "No. No, obviously there's nothing holding me back. Nothing at all."

He'd done his best to leach the bitterness from the words, but even as he said them Talo knew he hadn't succeeded. He watched Carro's face tighten, then soften. Pushing himself back up onto his feet, the Priest moved until they stood barely a foot away from each other. Talo tensed as Carro's big hands came to rest gently on either side of his crossed arms.

"I'm sorry," the Priest said softly, meeting his gaze. "I know this isn't what you wanted. Hell, it's not how *I* planned on things going either. But Syrah made it clear we are needed home, Talo…"

Again, Talo sighed. "I know," he said, relieved to hear his voice calm. "This mess with Baoill is going to be a thorn in our side, I can feel it."

"Gûlraht Baoill may be the very least of your problems if we don't get back to the Citadel in the next fortnight," Carro chuckled. "Forget the thorn. Syrah might just have your head and be done with it."

"Would save me some trouble in the long run…" Talo grumbled in reply. "The Kayle has twenty-five thousand at his disposal, and Ystréd and Azbar are right in his warpath."

"*If* he keeps heading south," Carro said with a shrug. "I'll bet anything Ystréd is scouting the Woods constantly, and if we haven't heard anything yet it might mean Baoill's halted his march. The Arocklen offers his army food, shelter, and warmth through the freeze. It's not a bad place to winter before picking things up again come spring."

"Even if that's true, it doesn't change the fact that the valley towns will have to deal with him one way or the other."

"All the more reason to get you home, then," Carro said with a nod.

In response, Talo frowned. After a moment he turned away from the Priest to lean over the escritoire and reach up, pushing open the windows across from him. The clear day hadn't chased away the bite of the freeze, and cold air spilled into the room, washing over both of them.

They were on the top floor of Ystréd's small temple, in the room Atler—the High Priestess of the local chapter—kept for travelling Laorin and guests. It wasn't an impressive chamber by any means, but it was comfortable despite the bed and the desk taking up much of the floor, and a good deal more comfortable than the night they'd spent at The Red Bear almost two months back, when they'd been making for Azbar. When they'd realized the snows weren't going to let up anytime soon, Talo and Carro had opted for the hospitality of the faith rather than a quick stay in the local inn.

The building across from them was constructed of the same dark timber and grey granite as a majority of the rest of the city's residences, lumber and quarried stone from the rich woodlands that made up much of the North. The street below was cobbled and clean, swept clear of snow through the night. As he watched, a party of roughened men passed below on horseback, towing a small cart behind them whose contents were hidden below a layer of heavy pelts. At one end of the road, a couple were arguing about something as they walked, barely distinguishable under all their furs. At the other, a group of children were laughing and bombarding each other with snowballs, scooping the stuff from every surface and ledge that hadn't yet been wiped clean. Their joy should have been infectious.

Instead, it only deepened Talo's frown.

"They aren't ready," he grunted over his shoulder. Behind him, he heard Carro sigh, then the creak of the bed as the man got to his feet again. A big hand came to rest on Talo's arm.

"You know this and I know this, love, but there's nothing to be done about it now," Carro said softly. "Focus on the task at hand. Syrah already has the council primed for action against the Kayle. The remaining valley towns will jump at your word. We can unify them."

"Even Baoill won't be able to do much against the combined forces of Azbar, Drangstek, and Stullens, not to mention whatever Ystréd itself can afford to throw into the mix," Talo said with a nod. "Still… I hate the idea of war."

"Then don't let it come to that. The Kayle isn't stupid. If he sees defeat on the horizon, he won't dare continue his campaign."

"No, he's not," Talo mumbled resentfully. "In fact, he's smart enough to know his time to strike is limited, I think. I'm surprised we've heard nothing from him. It worries me…"

Carro was about to respond when another knock came through the door, interrupting him.

"Come in," he said, letting his hand drop from Talo's shoulder and looking around.

The door opened slowly, and a small boy in acolyte's robes peeked his head into the room, looking rather anxious at the prospect of being sent to speak with the temple's distinguished guests all on his own.

"The High Priestess bids you join her to break fast, sirs," he squeaked, flushing a violent shade of red.

"Tell Tana we will be down shortly, thank you," Carro said with a smile. The crimson in the boy's face only deepened, though, and after a brief nod he vanished, leaving the door to hang open in his hasty attempt to escape his embarrassment.

Carro chuckled, then turned back to Talo.

"Coming?" he asked.

Talo nodded, but didn't move, his mind elsewhere as he continued to look up at the blue sky above, thoughts hovering over the doubts and feelings he couldn't shake off, telling him that something wasn't right.

He dragged himself out of his worry, though, when Carro's gentle fingers took his chin and turned his head to face him.

"There's nothing to be done right now," Carro said with a sad smile. "Agonizing over Baoill and his plans will do no more than turn your hair white, and I'm not ready for that just yet. I'm still getting used to the silver."

Talo snorted, but reached up and took Carro's hands in his.

"Chances are I won't live long enough for you to worry about that," he joked, managing a half smile as he stepped past his lover, intent on the scent of fresh bread he could suddenly make out, wafting through the open door.

III

Kisser was not in a good mood.

There were any number of reasons for his temper—such as hating the fact that the rest of the group had ever started calling him "Kisser" in the first place, or that he'd been stuck carrying the Monster's gear so it wouldn't be in reach if the atherian decided to suddenly wake—but at the moment his ire was distinct and direct. It was so pointed, in fact, that he was almost surprised Garth hadn't felt his eyes boring hatefully into his back.

Look at him, strutting around like he's come to lay his claim on the world, Kisser fumed, as he'd done constantly for the last half-day.

He was getting used to being discounted, even ignored. Garth Ve'Set and his band had taken Kisser in on a whim more than anything, impressed by the con he'd been running on women—and the occasional man—back in Stullens, wooing and seducing them before disappearing into the night with any valuables they'd been foolish enough to let him get his hands on. Garth had apparently hoped his group would have a use for Kisser's good looks and silver tongue, but a mercenary's life doesn't often parallel the social setting and environments needed to pull off such tricks, nor did it often entail the patience that was just as essential.

Before long, Kisser had found himself fallen from Garth's favorite prospect to not much more than a minor nuisance to the group as a whole.

Still, it wasn't any of them who brought the Monster down.

Kisser glanced into the cart that rumbled along the cobblestone to his left. Every spare pelt they had had been laid out carefully like a blanket, hiding the shivering form of Raz i'Syul Arro completely from view. After Kisser had hit him from behind, the atherian proved to be a docile prisoner. Whether it was the blow or the sickness that seemed to be wracking his body, the Monster had been out cold through their night of travel, and now well into the morning. Even after they made it to Ystréd, trading the comparative smoothness of the snow and dirt for the uneven clattering of stone roads, the beast had done little more than give muffled groans through the pelts.

Kisser looked up at the buildings around them. Ystréd was a small town by most Northern standards, home to less than a hundred thousand people. Its walls were dwarfed by the towering bastions of Stullens and Drangstek to the west, and even more so by Azbar's to the south. Even the recent additions and fortifications—cobbled together fervently following the sacking of Metcaf and Harond by the mountain tribes' new Kayle—didn't do much to add confidence to the sight of barely ten feet of mortared slate and marble.

Still, it was a quiet town, edging the hills of the Dehn Plains, and Kisser was pleased to be back. They hadn't stayed long after their last arrival, even though they'd intended to weather out the winter within the city. The band had just finished laying claim to an old abandoned house in the slums, in fact, when Garth came back from the markets with eyes all aglitter and bearing news from Azbar.

And so they'd set off again, this time southward, dreaming of claiming the great bounty on the Monster's head for themselves.

And then he stumbles right into camp, half dead in the snow.

Kisser couldn't figure out how he felt about the situation, exactly. Part of him was seething at the fact that not one among the group had acknowledged that it had been *he* who had brought the Monster down, but a larger part was endlessly stunned that he'd had the opportunity in the first place. What in the Lifegiver's name the lizard had been doing so far from Azbar's Arena in the middle of the freeze was beyond any of them, and i'Syul himself wasn't about to give up any hints to the condition of his affairs.

Even as he thought this, Kisser caught Garth glancing over his shoulder, eyeing the cart nervously.

"Where is this place, Les?" he asked in an aggravated tone, his patience apparently wearing thin.

Beside him, Les Woyt inclined his head to the left, northward.

"Jus' around the bend," he said. "Sven'll be there, you'll see. Cheapest we'll find, and a copper or two extra should convince him ta' keep his mouth shut until we can make south again."

Garth nodded once, but otherwise didn't reply. Kisser felt his anger boil upward again.

A physician. They were carting around ten thousand gold pieces worth of dead weight, looking for a physician. Kisser had tried to argue with Garth that they didn't *need* the atherian alive, that whatever was left of his head would be more than enough for the Mahsadën, so long as they took the infamous Ahna with them, and maybe a wing too. The man would hear none of it, though, and all Kisser had earned himself was a cuffing.

Garth wasn't a stupid man, but his ambition could make him foolish, like asking Kisser to join them in the first place: rash, and done without thinking it all through. He wanted to drag the Monster back in one piece, wanted to present the beast *alive* to the šef of the Southern fringe cities. He'd convinced the others easily enough, quashing any reservations the four might have had with promises of fame and glory, of the contracts the news of their successful capture of the Monster would earn them, and of the mountains of gold they would win.

Kisser wanted none of it. Even if Garth stiffed him of a fair share of the bounty, a thousand or so Southern gold crowns was more money than he had a sense of what to do with. He could stop scamming, at the very least. Maybe even buy himself an apprenticeship with one of the valley towns' theater groups, and give a stab at making an honest living of his life.

And Garth, in his infinitely idiotic wisdom, was risking all of that.

"There."

Les was pointing to a narrow two-story building, squashed between a pair of larger houses. It wasn't in any terrible state of disrepair, but the broken roof slats they could see beneath the piled snow and rickety state of the door didn't speak much to the success—or skills—of whatever physician held practice there.

Garth pulled his horse around, and everyone followed suit behind him. Kisser cursed as the great two-headed spear shifted in its place across his lap and nearly slid to the ground. The weight of the thing had made his legs go numb more than once during the ride to Ystréd, and he was good and ready to be rid of it, if only for a time.

"Everyone, off," Garth barked, swinging himself down from his saddle and landing with a crunch in the thin layer of ice and snow that patterned parts of the road. "Les, go make sure yer man's awake. The rest of ya', help Kisser."

Veret, Mihk, and Albur, the other three men in Garth's little entourage, grumbled at the orders, but did as they were told. Together they slid Ahna off his thighs, huffing and grunting under her top-heavy mass despite their number. Kisser gave his legs a minute to regain feeling, watching the threesome struggle to hide the spear under the cart before he dismounted. He was careful, swinging himself off, not to catch his boots on the handles of i'Syul's gladius and ax, slung from the saddle, nor on the wicked tips of the clawed gauntlets they'd shoved on either side in traveling pouches.

The rest of the armor Garth had left on the beast, hoping the padding and leathers would help keep him warm long enough to make it to the city.

There was a creak of old hinges, and Kisser looked around. The door of the building had been pulled partially open and the head of an aged, thin man with lank grey hair appeared around its edge. He exchanged a few words with Les, and Kisser saw the man raise a brow in what was either suspicion or disbelief. Regardless of whatever had been said, though, he nodded, opening the door wide.

"Give us a moment," Kisser heard the man say, and he stepped away from the door, reappearing a few seconds later throwing a heavy cloak over his narrow shoulders.

"Damn freeze'll be the death of us all," the physician—Sven, if Kisser had heard correctly—grumbled, stepping out into the cold, his breath misting in the air as he spoke. "Now show me this 'special patient' of yours, before I decide to go back to my warmth and fire."

"Over here," Garth said, crossing in front of him and leading the man towards the cart. When Sven had shuffled his way over, cursing the ice and snow and their whole party for pulling him out from the warmth of his home, Garth reached down and lifted the corner of the layered pelts.

Kisser couldn't see the atherian from where he stood, but he didn't have to. He knew the Monster was a thing to behold, even out cold and senseless. The dark sleekness of his scaled skin, the bunched ripples of lithe muscle beneath it. The lizard's stupor did nothing, either, to hide the scattered, half-finger long teeth that jutted up and down between his lips, nor the wicked edge of his clawed fingers and vibrant red of his ears and wings.

And, judging by the physician's gasp of horrified wonder, the old man hadn't missed any of those things.

There was a brief pause during which the man gaped in open astonishment at the figure beneath the furs, clearly incapable of doing anything else. Then, oddly, he glanced up at Garth and the rest of them, eyeing each one briefly as though sizing them up.

"Get any ideas about claimin' the bounty for yerself, *Sven*," Garth growled in a throaty whisper, placing his hand pointedly on the hilt of the long knife thrust into the front of his belt, "and they won't even bother *trying* to count how many parts they find you in. Crystal?"

The old man's eyes grew wide, eyeing the hand, and he nodded. "Get him inside," he hissed. "Quickly, before someone sees him. I'll go clear the table."

It took four of them, including Kisser, to drag i'Syul off the cart and carry him across the small yard, his wings dragging over the ground and snow. The curses started when they had to maneuver their way through the door of the physician's home, huffing and straining under the weight of the Monster. Sven led them first right, around the door, then down a narrow hallway that opened into what once had been some sort of living space, now converted into a passing excuse for doctor's quarters. The desk against one wall was buried under mountains of books and piled papers, similar articles spilling onto the floor and over every surface of the room. Wooden and metal models of limbs and torsos were everywhere, along with carefully painted depictions of the internal workings of the human body, organs, and bones. A well-fed fire rippled in a wide, soot-stained hearth along the back wall, filling the room with blissful warmth. In the middle of the floor was a hip-high, wide timber table, nicked and stained in places with what Kisser would have guessed was wine were it not for the assortment of wicked looking instruments laid out on a cloth atop a wooden gurney nearby.

It was towards this table that the physician led them, indicating its cleared surface as he moved out of their way.

"Up here," he told them. "Gentle now. Man looks well on his way already without you lot banging him around."

"Ain't no man at all," Albur said as he huffed, heaving i'Syul up onto the table as indicated.

"As you say, as you say," Sven responded dismissively, not really listening. Instead he moved forward again, shooing Veret away unceremoniously before leaning over the atherian.

"Fever," he mumbled to himself as he worked, his mottled hands poking and fumbling over every inch of the Monster. "Wasn't joking about the 'on his way' part, it seems. Where'd all this blood come from?" He paused to examine the sticky redness that spread along the lizard's left side, causing the furs of his wide mantle to cling to the leather straps and exposed skin. "Wounded, obviously. But where?"

"Back," Garth barked. He'd come in with Les behind the other four as they carried the atherian in, and now leaned in the doorframe of the room. "Got a look at it when we was strippin' 'im of his sword."

"Back?" The old man blinked at Garth, then down at his patient again. "He'll need to be flipped. I need to see it."

Albur and Veret glanced at Garth for confirmation. When he nodded, they moved forward to roll the atherian up on his right side. The mantle rolled with him, requiring the physician to retrieve one of his instruments from the gurney. It was a slim silver blade, almost too narrow to withstand any kind of pressure, but it made quick work of the furs and shirt beneath, and when he was done the old man tossed the ruined cloak and cloth aside.

"Aaahh…" he breathed, leaning forward to get a closer look. Kisser for one, did the opposite, pulling away from the table and covering his nose with a hand.

He'd smelled rot before, on the wasted food of wealthier men he had scavenged as a kid. He'd even known infection, when a former slum rat friend of his had lost his hand to a dog, and passed a week later as the sickness spread like black snakes through his blood. The sweet, sour stink had been the same, then.

The scent of a creeping, ugly death.

"Urgh," Veret muttered, turning his head away from the putrid gash along the left side of the atherian's spine and looking suddenly queasy. "Bastard's done for, Garth. Someone run 'im through. Take his head off and let's be done with it."

"Not just yet."

All eyes turned to the physician, who was still inspecting the wound carefully, his nose so close to the rotten hole of flesh that Kisser couldn't understand how he could stand it. After a moment, though, he stood straight and looked around at Garth.

"It won't be easy, but we can still save him. I've got medicines and herbs that will stop the infection, and a friend of mine is a truly gifted surgeon. She'll be able to cut away whatever is already lost, as well as pack the wound. I'd say he'd need at least a week or two of rest after, but given your gentleman's apparent hurry I could forgive your departure so long as you give me a day to make sure the wound stays clean."

"You daft, ol' man?" Veret growled at him, letting the atherian roll onto his back again. "Ain't no savin' this one. Rot's got in his lungs, I'm sure of it."

"Oh, you *are*, are you?" Sven asked him sarcastically. "Then tell me, friend, where you studied your medicine. I'd be delighted to know."

That shut the sellsword up. Veret retreated into silent sulkiness, walking away from the table to prop himself up against the edge of the desk. The physician smirked in silent triumph, then turned back to Garth.

"What will it be?"

Everyone turned to look at the bandleader, awaiting his answer. Garth seemed uncertain, taking in the atherian with pallid eyes, contemplating the unconscious man's form.

"Do it, if ya' can," he said after a moment. "Ain't gonna pay ya' until it's done, though. No use wastin' coin on a dead man. And you'll do it on yer own. Don't want more people knowing about this than have to, so yer friend can stay pretty and quiet somewhere else."

"Without her, your prize is done for," the physician said with narrowed eyes, lifting a hand to wave it about at the room. "Look at this place, this *dump*. You think I earned all this with skilled hands and a steady grasp? I'm used to people saying they'll pay after, 'cause they know half the time they'll walk out worse than when they came in. Either you let me bring her in, or the only thing of your beast you'll be carrying south"—he tapped i'Syul's muscled shoulder with a finger—"will be bones."

Again, Garth hesitated. Kisser wanted to roll his eyes, just as—he was pleased to see—Veret seemed inclined to do. Still, they both stayed quiet.

"...How do I know yer woman will keep 'er trap shut?" Garth finally asked. "How do I know she won't make a play 'erself, eh? Ten thousand crowns is a lot of money, old man."

"It is," the physician agreed, "but that's the last thing she's like to do, trust me. She'll play by your rules. She has reasons enough not to draw any unwanted attention, especially from the Southern lords."

Garth frowned.

Then he stepped away from the doorframe, indicating the hall behind him with a jerk of his head. "Fetch her," he said. "And be quick about it. Albur will be going with you, just to make sure neither of you get any ideas of your own."

If the woman noticed the lecherous stares she was getting from the men that surrounded her, she certainly pretended not to. Not surprising, either, as she was more than likely used to such attentions by now. When Sven had returned, Albur in tow, Kisser had found himself having a hard time keeping his eyes off the newcomer with them.

He had his doubts the woman was anything more than modestly pretty where she came from, but up in the North her eccentricities were rare, almost exotic. Her skin had clearly paled over time, but it was still a good deal darker than that of any of the men around her, save the atherian. Her hair was pitch too, almost inky black, and it made her stand out in a world of fair and brown-haired women. Her eyes, though, were what really set the woman apart. Blue and green and hazel were colors of the North, colors of the earth and sky and snow and mountains. They could be captivating in their own right, of course, but they were also common.

The grey of the surgeon's, though, was rare. This far north, nosing with the Dehn, such eyes were sparingly seen. They were things of the border towns and trade roads, and occasionally of Azbar.

They were the grey of old mortar and mudbrick, the grey of colored cloth bleached by the scorching god of the desert.

They were the grey of a true Southerner.

"Where in the Lifegiver's name did the old man find this one?" Kisser had muttered under his breath to Mihk, who'd been standing next to him when the group had returned. The older man hadn't said anything in reply, though he rarely did. This time, however, his silence was more likely the symptom of distraction than any sullen temperament.

She was wearing the typical garbs of a Northerner, all leather wrappings and fur, and Kisser found his head suddenly filled with twirling images of dancing women in silks and light clothes, all bare legs and tanned skin. He felt an odd disappointment—and suspected he wasn't the only one—that the woman seemed to have acclimated well to the Northern cold, but the knowledge that more of her alluring figure was hidden under the ugly pelts and layers needed to weather the freeze was almost disheartening.

"Her Stars," the surgeon had said, a leather bag swinging from one hand as she paused in the doorway, entering the room behind Albur and the old physician, eyes on the atherian shivering on the table. "Raz i'Syul."

For a long moment she'd stared at the man in what was almost terrified reverence. Then her eyes lifted to meet Sven's, who had moved to stand over the Monster, and the physician gave her a small nod.

"I won't be able to do much more than mix a draft of pomatus and trelec seed to help with the pain and infection, at least for now," he said, then looked over his shoulder at Veret. "Flip him over, if you please. She'll need to see the wound."

Veret mumbled something under his breath, but did as requested. With Albur's help, he rolled i'Syul over onto his stomach, the man's steel armor grating against itself as he crashed down onto the table again.

The surgeon moved forward then, apparently as uncaring of the infected stench as Sven was. Placing her bag on the floor by the table, she leaned over the Monster. When she saw the pus-lined hole left by some blade or another, she frowned.

"Forceps, Sven," she said, reaching up to peel away some of what was left the of the atherian's shirt from around the wound. "And boiling water, as soon as you can."

The old man nodded, picking up an odd, bent rod with two flattened ends that looked to pinch together with the right amount of pressure. Handing it to the woman, he hurried off, disappearing down another hall at the back of the room. There was a clatter of metal, and after a minute the man reappeared with a heavy pot.

"Here," he said, shoving the pot into Les' hands. "Fill this with snow—*clean* snow---and bring it back. Be careful not to dump it all over my floor, mind you."

Les looked annoyed, but glanced at Garth, who gestured to the front door with another tilt of his head. Sighing, Les turned and headed outside.

"Can ya' save him?" Garth asked, turning his attention back on the woman. For a moment she didn't say anything, using the "forceps"—as she'd called them—to tug at the edges of the wound, peering at its fleshy walls.

27

"Likely, yes," she said finally. "But not with the tools I have here. Sven has the means to suture and pack the wound, but not what I need to clean it and cut away the rotten flesh."

Garth's eyes narrowed, and he pushed himself off the doorframe.

"What's in the bag, then, if ya' didn't bring yer tools?" he asked her accusingly, pointing at the leather sack at her feet.

In response the woman put down the forceps and bent to pick up the bag. Setting it on the table, she popped the clasp, reaching in to pull out a thick roll of clean gauze.

"Wrappings and extra medicines," she said, using her other hand to pull out a couple of vials with some sort of powdered herb in them. "I misunderstood. I was under the impression Sven was looking for help with a fresher wound. My tools are in my offices at my home, though. I can leave and be back within a half-hour, if I can borrow a horse."

"Ha!" Garth laughed. "Like I would let ya' take one of ours on yer own. Veret will go with you." He nodded in Veret's direction, and the man leapt to at once, clearly eager to get out of the physician's house.

The surgeon looked over his shoulder at him, and Kisser got the distinct impression she was almost sizing the man up.

"Fine," she said, just as Les came lumbering down the hall, the pot the old man had given him filled to the brim with clean slush. "In the meantime you can have your men assist Sven in setting the water to boil, as well as cutting the rest of the clothes from Arro's back. I want everything ready to start when I return."

Garth scowled, but shrugged. "If it's what ya' need." Then he looked at Veret. "Get her pretty little arse on a horse. And make sure she don't lame one of our animals, or it's on you."

Veret nodded, squeezing past Les and his load and making for the main door.

As she made to pass into the hall behind him, though, Garth grabbed the woman by the arm and jerked her closer.

"I'll tell you the same thing I told the doctor," he breathed into her ear. "You even *think* of making a play for the bounty yerself, and I'll drag ya' back South right along with i'Syul's head in a basket. I get the feeling that's not something ya' want, is it girly?"

For the first time, Kisser caught a glimpse of what might have been fear on what he could see of the woman's face, and he thought Garth had hit his mark.

Then it was gone, and she pulled her arm roughly from his grasp.

"No, it's not," she snapped. "And if you were brighter than a snuffed candle you'd figure that's the same reason I've got no interest in this damn bounty you're drooling over. I'll save your prize, you'll pay Sven and I, and you'll get the hell out of our city."

"Ooh," Garth said, following her with his eyes as she stalked passed. "I *like* a girl with fire. What's yer name, woman? After our little trip southward I might have to come back and pay ya' a visit. I'll be a rich man, ya' know…"

At the door, the woman paused. Then she turned and gave the man a venomous smile.

"You would be surprised how certain I am that that will *never* happen, sellsword," she said with all the false sweetness the world had to offer. "But if it makes you feel better, it's Evalyn, though most just call me Eva."

IV

"No man, I feel certain, has brushed the other side of the veil as often as I, in my years. At first I had only myself to count on when it came to avoiding that door that separates life and death, our world from the next. As the years passed, though, that changed, until I one day realized there would always be one hand or another behind me, ready to pull me back from the brink."

—Raz i'Syul Arro

"Remind me to sign you up for Priest Enot's manners lessons when we get back to the Citadel," Carro muttered sidelong to Talo. "One would think each and every one of these people had personally offended you, at the rate you're ignoring them."

Talo started, and looked up from his plate. He'd let his mind wander off again, this time preoccupied with thoughts and theories regarding Gûlraht Baoill.

They were sitting side by side at the misshapen oak table that took up much of the temple's small dining hall. The other seats were occupied by a combination of the Priests, Priestesses, and acolytes that called Ystréd home, while yet others were scurrying about around them, squeezing past chairs and each other as they went about their morning chores. Across from them sat High Priestess Tana Atler, a portly young woman who'd come into the position somewhat abruptly the year before, when her former Priest-Mentor had abdicated the mantle to her and left to travel the Northern lands as a member of the wandering faith. Still, it was Talo's understanding that she adapted well to the responsibilities, despite her youth, and the thought pleased him.

It was something of a matter of pride, seeing the younger generation he had helped Eret Ta'hir sculpt so aptly shoulder the responsibilities their elders no longer could.

Atler was currently involved in a conversation with an older acolyte sitting beside her, but even as he watched them Talo saw her glance up at him curiously, almost worryingly. Up and down the table, in fact, many of the temple's residents were casting underhanded looks in his direction, some kindly concerned like Atler's, others openly annoyed.

Clearly his unconscious absence had not gone unnoticed.

"Sorry," he said quietly to Carro, picking up a piece of bread from his plate—now cold and rapidly hardening—and requesting the berry spread at his lover's opposite elbow with a gesture. "The Kayle just doesn't seem to want to leave me."

"More like you don't seem to want to leave him," Carro said with a snort, sliding the spread over.

"A distinct possibility." Talo nodded, dipping a knife into the preserves and lathering his bread.

"Did you sleep well, you two?"

Talo looked up. Atler was watching him with a sort of amused twinkle in her eye.

"Very," Talo said with a small smile, careful not to drip berry on the table as he broke the bread into two halves. "Though Carro here would have me believe it's not the first time you've asked that."

Atler returned the smile. "It's possible it's the second or third attempt. I don't take offense though. Usually our residents find breakfast more interesting than I, so the fact that you didn't seem keen on either made me feel a little better about myself."

"I apologize." Talo frowned, still holding both halves of the bread in each hand. "I've had a bit more on my mind than usual, of late."

"More than most of us, I'm sure," Atler nodded as Talo took a bite. "This business with the tribes... I can't say I'm looking forward to the fallout."

"Our hope is to avoid getting to that point," Carro said, letting Talo chew. "A council of Cyurgi' Di's most venerated faithful have been assessing the situation for several weeks now. One of them has had significant experience with the Sigûrth clan directly, in fact, and is advising all action taken thus far."

"Syrah Brahnt," Atler said with a nod. "We certainly know of her. A pity the treaties she managed to establish didn't hold in the end. Your daughter, I assume?" She looked back at Talo.

Talo swallowed and chuckled. "Something like that. Syrah was given to the faith fairly young, and eventually came under my tutelage. She was in Stullens when Drangstek was razed, twenty or so years ago."

"Poor girl," Atler said sadly. "I imagine it's not easy, seeing one's greatest accomplishment ripped away like that."

"No," Talo said with a sigh, the Arena flitting painfully across his thoughts. "It's certainly not, but we haven't had much opportunity to speak to her about it, unfortunately. Birds aren't very conducive to addressing such matters and, since the magics can't cross that distance, we're left with struggling to get home in the middle of the damn freeze."

"I certainly don't envy you," Atler said with a soft laugh, getting up to allow one of the Priests milling around them to take her seat. "I've never braved our winters myself. Ystréd has been my family's home for as many generations as we can count back, and I plan to keep it that way."

Let us pray you have that opportunity, then, Talo thought privately as the woman walked away, making for the kitchens.

They ate the rest of their meal in relative silence, occasionally exchanging small talk with some of the older members of the temple and answering enthusiastic questions from the acolytes about Cyurgi' Di and all the fabled wonders of the High Citadel and the Arocklen Woods along the feet of the Saragrias. Talo had to admit to himself, by the time they took their leave of the table—he leaning heavily on Carro's arm to stand up—that it was nice to be among members of the faith again who had little more on their minds than the day's chores and their duties to the town. He and Carro's time in Azbar had been spent with the Laorin as well, but it had been a frantic few weeks, filled with planning and deliberation and sneaking about the city to meet with Arro as often as possible. There had been little peace in the stay, and even less joy. In fact, he hadn't even realized how much he missed the community he and Carro had left behind in the Citadel until the storms had forced them to pause in Ystréd these last couple of days. He almost laughed to himself, remembering how, even before they'd arrived in Azbar, he and Carro had been discussing the possible abdication of his own High Priest's mantle and returning to a life of wandering, just as Atler's mentor had.

I would miss this all too much, Talo thought to himself, looking over his shoulder as Carro led him to the stairs, watching the late risers take their newly vacated seats at the breakfast table. *Maybe not at first, but certainly in the long run.*

They had just taken their first few steps upwards, intent on heading back to their room to prepare for their afternoon departure, when the brief peace of the morning was broken by the scream of horses.

"What was that?" Carro demanded, half turning to look at the temple's wide main door, shut tight against the cold. Around them, the rest of the Laorin had paused in whatever they were doing, lifting heads at the abrupt sound. For a moment the morning was quiet again.

Then they heard the shouts.

"... Help! Help... me!"

The distant pleas were those of a woman, Talo realized, growing steadily closer, and even as he thought this he began to make out the hard beat of hooves against cobblestone.

"What's going on?"

Atler had reappeared. Before anyone could answer her, though, the shouts started again, closing rapidly now.

"... the door! Please...! OPEN THE DOOR!"

There was a frozen silence, Atler looking suddenly tense and unsure.

Talo decided it was time to step in.

"Open the door!" he boomed, pulling himself free of Carro's grasp and hobbling his way back down the stairs as fast as he could. "All acolytes, out. *NOW!*"

The faithful of Ystréd seemed at a loss as to what to do, looking between Talo and their own High Priestess.

Fortunately, Atler was fairly quick to recover her senses.

"As he says!" she shouted, hurrying forward. "Acolytes out! All others, behind High Priest Brahnt and myself. Doren,"—she pointed at a young man in a corner of the room—"my staff, if you please. Kerren,"—she looked to a pair of women near the front of the room, their arms full of firewood they'd apparently been splintering for kindling in one of the temple's side rooms—"you and Hemma get that door open! Quickly now!"

All hesitation vanished from the room. At once the Laorin leapt into action, doing as instructed. In a blink the two women had the front door flung open, just in time for Talo to limp his way outside, Atler and Carro right behind him. Even in the fury of the moment the cold hit them like a solid blow, making them blink away sudden tears as an icy wind tore at their robes and the exposed skin of their faces.

The temple was on the border of Ystréd's middle and upper class quarters, a squat little two-story building flanked by the taller structures all around. The road, running east to west in front of the temple, had been cleared of the offending snow. Even the vestiges of the great storm that had hammered them over the last several days were starting to melt away under the merciful appearance of the sun.

Good thing, too, because icy stone would have made poor footing for the pair of riders barreling towards them from the left.

At first Talo thought the two figures were together, the foremost of them—a dark skinned woman in traditional Northern garb—having been the one who must have shouted. As they got closer, though, he saw that the woman's expression was desperate, her frightened gaze only breaking from them to peer back at the man following close behind her.

A man, Talo realized as he saw the glint of steel in the sunlight, riding with bare sword in hand.

"Carro, get the girl!" he yelled over his shoulder, limping into the road as fast as his knee would allow him. "Atler, go with him, and help with the horses! Let me handle the rider!"

If the High Priestess had any problem with taking orders, she didn't voice it. Instead he heard both of them step out behind him, ready to follow his instructions. Before them the horses still hammered onward, but Talo caught the woman's eye and waved to the side with one hand, hoping she would catch his meaning. She did, pulling her mount to the other side of the road.

Leaving the man behind her suddenly very much exposed.

It was a simple spell, amongst the first taught to budding acolytes, but it was one Talo had found served many uses over the years. Calling on the gifts Laor had lent him, Talo drew a breath. Then, focusing the magic into the motion, he stepped forward with one foot, thrusting an open palm forward before him.

There was a flash of white. The air in front of Talo shimmered in a rapidly widening pattern. Like an invisible wave crashing across the road, what snow was left between the cracks in the cobblestones and roofs around them was suddenly thrown up and away, shoved by an intangible force.

When the wave collided with the rider and his mount, it stopped them almost dead.

The horse screamed as its headlong charge was abruptly cut short, its body moving for a moment as though suddenly submerged in water. The man, too, seemed all at once to flounder against a thickening of the air, shouting in alarm as his body tumbled off the back of his saddle in an almost gentle arc, his sword slipping as though in slow motion from his hand.

Then the magic passed, and he hit the ground with a *crunch* of leather and iron armor against stone.

One horse galloped by Talo's right, rider in tow, followed a few seconds later by the second, stumbling and tripping in the confusion of attempting to adjust to the shift in momentum it had inexplicably experienced.

Talo didn't watch them pass, his eyes staying on the man left behind in the road some twenty feet away.

The now-horseless swordsman had clearly been winded by the fall, coughing and groaning as he rolled himself onto his side, one hand scrounging about for his blade. When he didn't find it within easy reach, he started cursing under his breath, forcing himself onto one knee and drawing a long knife from his belt.

He'd just gotten to his feet, and was turning to face the temple, when Talo's second wave of magic blew him away again, blasting him another ten feet down the road.

This time the man didn't get up again, knocked unconscious by the crushing force of the strike.

When he was certain the attacker had been taken care of, Talo finally relaxed a little. Standing straight, he turned to see how Carro and Atler had fared. The High Priestess had her hands full with the swordsman's animal, the horse rearing and squealing in fear, driven to its wit's end by the chase and its rider's sudden unsaddling. She'd managed to catch it by the reins, and was doing her best to calm it while simultaneously avoiding the creature's kicking legs.

"Shh!" she was saying, holding a hand up in an attempt to seem as non-threatening as possible. "Shh, boy! You're all right. It's all right."

Behind her, Carro was in the process of assisting the woman down off her own horse. She was shivering, clearly shaken by the ordeal, but she accepted his hand without hesitation, allowing herself to be half-helped, half-carried to the ground.

"Are you hurt?" Carro was asking her as she dismounted. "What happened? Why was that man chasing you?"

"Give her a moment, Carro," Talo said, limping his way over to them. "She can talk when she's ready."

The woman nodded at that, head bowed beneath the hood of her fur cloak. One hand was clasped against her chest, the other resting on her horse's shoulder for support. She was taking slow, shaking breaths, trying—and apparently failing—to calm herself.

"It's done, miss," Talo said gently, coming to stand before her. "He won't be waking for a while, I think, much less trying to come after you again."

"Y-you're sure?" she asked shakily, still not raising her head. "You're absolutely sure?"

"I've yet to know anyone who can stand for long after one of Talo's spells," Carro told her with chuckle. "Let alone two. You're quite safe, my dear."

The woman nodded at that. Then, after a moment, she took a final deep breath and looked up.

The first thing Talo realized was that she was—very, *very* clearly—*not* a native member of the Northern realms. If her tanned skin—somewhat more ashen than the skin of the true desert dwellers he remembered from his trip into the sand plains so many years ago—wasn't enough, the faded grey of her eyes spelled it out absolutely.

The second thing he realized was that those same eyes had lost none of the panic they had held before he'd stopped the man who'd so clearly been intent on killing her.

"Thank you," she whispered. "A-All of you." She looked between Carro and Atler, who had finally calmed the panicking horse and was stroking its muzzle nearby. "I-I don't know what I would have done if… I have no idea of how to even start repaying you."

"You can start by telling us who you are, and explaining why that man"—Talo threw a thumb over his shoulder to indicate the prone figure, now attracting something of a crowd twenty feet down the road— "seemed so adamant on having your head. He doesn't have the uniform of the town guard, and you don't look like much of a killer or a thief, so I have my doubts it was a justified pursuit."

"E-Eva" she said shakily, glancing behind Talo at the unconscious form. "My name is Eva. And that man—V-Veret, I think his name was—

was supposed to make sure I didn't run for it. When I did, he drew his s-sword and…"

She shivered, pausing. Then she looked up again, her voice stronger, though her face was still lined in desperation.

"It doesn't *matter*, though," she hissed, stepping away from her horse towards Talo. "Please. I need your help. My friend needs your help. I'd heard the Laorin would aid those in need. It's why I ran for the temple."

"You've heard right," Carro said, moving to stand by Talo. "But the faith isn't one to jump into a situation it knows nothing about. Come inside and you'll be able to tell us what we can do for—"

"There isn't *time*!" Eva practically screamed, hands balled into fearful fists at her side. "*Please*. They're going to kill him, if he doesn't die on his own first. I can't save him. I'm not even sure *you* can. But *please! Help him!* I owe him everything!"

Talo and Carro exchanged a curious glance.

"We can try," Talo said calmly. "But my friend is right, miss. You need to tell us *something*, anything that might give us an idea of who it is we would be helping."

"A friend is in need," Eva hissed shakily. "Taken prisoner, and dying even as we speak. Isn't that enough?"

"I wish it were," Talo told her just as the Priest Atler had called Doren finally appeared in the temple door, her staff in one hand. "But we've known people who've chosen to dive headlong into such situations, and barely lived to regret it. You need to tell us everything you can, and be quick about it."

"I *can't!*" The woman's voice was panicked, the delay in their assistance obviously causing her great distress. "We don't have time, I'm telling you! Please! I owe him my life. *Please!*"

She looked desperately between the two Priests, who stood silently, watching her expectantly.

"I can't," she repeated after a moment, tears welling in her grey eyes. "I *can't.* If you knew… If you knew, you might not come…"

"Knew what, woman?" Carro asked her, his patience apparently wearing a little thin. Talo shot him a disapproving look, which he returned in equal measure.

Enough is enough, it said.

Before them, the Southerner hesitated, clearly struggling with herself, the part that was unwilling to give the Priests what they wanted battling with the side that wanted so desperately to enlist their aid.

After a time, though, she seemed to crumple, the will to fight fleeing with each passing second.

"My friend…" she began in a hoarse whisper, eyes on the ground at the Priests' feet. "He's not really… He's not exactly…"

Eva paused, forcing to take a deep breath. Then she looked up and met Talo's eyes with newfound determination.

"He's not... human."

The cold of the winter was abruptly nothing to Talo. It might have been full of summer warmth, in fact, compared to the wash of ice that arched its way down his spine and into every limb. He looked around, dumbfounded, at Carro, whose own shock seemed enough to make him have a hard time tearing his eyes away from the dark skinned woman.

"Arro is *here?*" the Priest finally managed to sputter. "He's *here?* In Ystréd?"

It was Eva's turn to stare, looking up at the big man, obviously taken aback.

"You know him?" she demanded, gaping at Carro. "But how could you—?"

"Arro?" Atler interrupted, still off to the side with the horses. "Raz i'Syul Arro? What in the Lifegiver's name is that beast doing here?"

"He's *not* a beast!" Eva whirled on the High Priestess, suddenly irate. "You can't know—you can't *imagine* what he's been through, what he's done! You have *no* idea what he is!"

"We do."

Talo had regained some of the feeling in his limbs. The shock of the news had yet to settle, but he'd deal with it as it came. He met the Southerner's eyes as she turned again to face him, suddenly understanding the desperation he saw there.

"Carro and I know him well enough, Eva. We know there's more to him than 'the Monster'. Right now, though, you're right. It doesn't matter. Right now, you just need to tell us *where he is.*"

V

"There are words that describe those of our faith well, or so we like to imagine. Kind, gentle, compassionate, supportive. These are warm words, words of hope and light and ardor. These are words meant to instill and support peace, to cultivate a love for Laor in all His magnificence, and to breed respect among men for all other men. No one, though, pauses to consider the other words that fit the Laorin just as well. Words such as powerful. As hard. As cunning.
Words such as fearsome."

—private journal of Eret Ta'hir

Kisser was relieved, looking around, that he wasn't the only one getting nervous. Albur had pulled out a narrow knife from his boot and was cleaning his fingernails with it. Mihk sat on a rickety stool in the far corner, his knee bouncing beneath him. Les had long since returned from the kitchen where he'd left the physician Sven to melt and boil the snow, and was now standing by the atherian's wheezing form, staring at Arro blankly, his thoughts on other things.

Even Garth, still waiting by the door, couldn't help glancing at the room window every minute or so.

"Where are they?" he finally demanded, peeling himself off the doorframe and striding into the room proper. "Veret should'a had the bitch back twenty minutes ago!"

No one answered him—not wanting to give the man a target to vent his wrath on—which didn't improve Garth's mood in the least. Naturally, therefore, his ire found its usual mark.

"Kisser!" he bellowed, turning to glare at the young man. "Get off yer ass and drag the old man out 'a the kitchen. I wanna know what that Eva woman is up to!"

Kisser grit his teeth against a response and slid off the counter he'd seated himself atop. Picking his way through the clutter, he made for the back of the room towards the hall down which he assumed the kitchen had to be. Even as he turned the corner he heard Garth shift his wrath on Albur, yelling something about the state of the man's filthy hands.

Kisser sighed and kept walking. The back hallway, already a narrow space, was all the more restricted by a set of broad windowed cabinets along the right wall, their wooden shelves sagging sadly under the weight of yet more books and oddities, including what looked to be the better half of a human skull. Slipping his way past, Kisser found a closed door at the end of the hall. Grabbing the handle, he pried it open to peer into the room beyond.

"Garth says he wants you, old man!" he started. "He's not happy about—!"

Kisser stopped midsentence, freezing with one hand still on the door handle.

The kitchen was a typical thing, a cramped space taken up mostly by a small table and single rickety chair in the middle of the room. A line of old stone counters adorned the two walls opposite, all of which were also littered with various objects ranging from old scrolls to knives to scraps of bread and other forgotten foods. An open fireplace of brick and mortar stood to Kisser's left, wide and shallow, over which all manner of pans and kettles could be suspended. The iron pot Les had packed with snow was at that moment hung over a bed of smoking coals, in fact, the water Sven had been supposedly boiling having long since evaporated.

Of the man himself, Kisser saw nothing more than the cracked opening of a narrow back door, left ajar in a rushed escaped.

"Shit…"

For a brief moment Kisser considered running after the man, hoping to track him down and gain himself some credit in the eyes of Garth's group. When he realized that he had no idea how long the physician had been gone, though, the desire to give chase morphed rapidly into a wish to flee through the door himself, to escape Garth's fury and the others' harpings and taunts.

Thinking better of it, though, Kisser opted instead to whirl around and scramble back to the main room, where the rest of the group still waited.

"If Veret's tryin' ta' pull something, I'll gut him," Garth was muttering to himself, pacing back and forth in front of the window as Kisser got over the tall stacks of yellowed parchment that partially blocked the hallway. "He'd better be dead, or dying in a ditch somewhere."

"He's gone."

All eyes shifted to Kisser, who felt weak and shaky as Garth's mean gaze met his.

"What did you say?" the man spat, stopping his striding.

"He's gone," Kisser said again, abruptly aware of the others in the room leering at him as well. "Sven. He ran for it. Through a back door."

There was a tense few seconds in which Garth merely stared at Kisser, his right hand twitching by his side as though itching to go for the hilt of the sword on his hip. When he did move, though, it wasn't towards the younger man.

In two steps Garth was in front of Les. His fist collided with the side of the man's face so hard Les fell sideways into the table on which the

Monster still lay, then to the floor where he rolled and moaned, clutching at what was at least a few broken teeth.

"There was a back door?" Garth howled, kicking the fallen man in the ribs as he twisted. "A *back door*, Les? And you didn't think ta' stay and watch 'im? Bloody. Fucking. IDIOT!"

These last words were punctuated with a stomp of Garth's boot across Les' legs and body. No one moved to stop the group leader as he took his frustration out on the poor man at his feet, having no interest in shifting Garth's attention to themselves. Once he'd had enough, Garth stood over Les, breathing hard.

When his eyes moved, they fell on the leather bag the woman Eva had left at the edge of the table to his left.

Stepping over, he grabbed the bag in both hands and pulled it open roughly, peering inside. Whatever he saw only spiked his fury, though, because he screamed in frustration and upended the bag over Les, who covered his face and curled into a ball as the contents tumbled down onto his head and shoulders. The wrappings and medicine vials the Southerner had pulled out to show them came first, bouncing and rolling over the floor.

Then a dozen slim silver instruments—the tools of the surgeon's trade—fell out after them.

"Bitch!" Mihk cursed from the corner, jumping to his feet.

"We've been had," Garth said through angry breaths. "Kisser, Albur, get this *idiot*,"—he gave Les another kick for good measure—"on his feet. Mihk, get the horses ready."

"What about Veret?" Kisser asked, smart enough to already be moving towards Les as he did so.

"Like I said," Garth grumbled, turning to face the table and drawing his blade. "Dead or dying, most like."

With that, he brought the sword up high in both hands, ready to bring it down with all his might on the Raz i'Syul's neck.

"STOP!"

To a one, each of them froze and whirled towards the back of the room. A great bear of a man was stepping over the parchments piled across the entrance of the hallway that led to the kitchen. He leaned heavily on a tall silvery staff in his left hand, and seemed to be favoring one leg more than the other. His trimmed beard was more grey than brown, and the hood of his white robes was pulled up over his head, a single narrow strip of black arching back along its crest. Kisser knew what those cloths meant—as did any man of the North—and he grew suddenly nervous. The Priests and Priestesses of Laor were forbidden from killing, but that didn't mean they weren't formidable in their own way.

When the newcomer managed to steady himself on both feet, he regarded the room with sharp blue eyes that revealed none of the weakness his limp might suggest. When they found Garth, they fell to the sword, now hanging tensed at the man's side.

"I won't permit you to kill this man," the Priest said, indicating the atherian with a wave of his free hand as he looked back up to meet Garth's angry gaze levelly. "Raz i'Syul is under the protection of the faith. Harm him in any way, and I will give you great cause to regret it."

"This ain't yer business, High Priest," Garth said, and Kisser abruptly recalled what the black stripe along the top and back of the Priest's robes denoted. "This *thing* here"—he jabbed the point of his sword in Arro's direction—"is worth more than any a' us will make in a lifetime, dead or alive. And, as I don't much feel like haulin' all that weight halfway across the world right now, dead it is."

"I wouldn't recommend that."

At the second voice, Kisser and the others spun to face the front of the room, where another man was ducking under the stoop of the door. He, too, wore the white robes of the faith, though they lacked the black stripe of office that the first man's had. Beyond that, whereas the High Priest before them looked more troublesome than dangerous, *this* man had the unmistakable look of a menacing character. As tall as his partner, a mane of braided blond hair dominated the man's shoulders, peeking out from either side of the hood he, too, had pulled up over his head. Rings of wood and metal shifted in dreaded locks, just like the ornaments that decorated his plated beard.

There's mountain man blood in this one, Kisser thought to himself, unconsciously taking a step back.

The second stranger noted the motion, his own staff shifting in his hand as he turned his head to regard Kisser with the clear blue eyes that ran common among the Northern people.

Whatever they saw, there, the man kept to himself.

"Just two of ya'?" Garth scoffed, shifting so he could keep both Laorin in his range of vision. "Think tha's enough to make us run off?"

"Two is more than enough," the High Priest said calmly, lifting his free hand before him. There was a flash of white, and a glimmer of pale ivory flames blinked into existence, hovering over his gloved palm. "That being said, I'd like to avoid a fight. My friend"—he nodded to the other Priest—"isn't a fan of violence, you see."

Kisser glanced at the blond man, and indeed saw an odd sort of queasiness flash across the man's face. Garth must have seen it too, because he started to chuckle.

"Craven!" He laughed, taking a step towards the High Priest. "Bastard's a coward! He don't have what it takes to tussle with us."

"If that is your choice, you should know he doesn't have to 'tussle' with any of you at all," the first man responded, and the flame in his palm suddenly began to burn with a new intensity. "He just has to keep you from getting away."

And with that he sent the fire streaking towards them, aiming right for Garth with a flick of his wrist.

Garth cursed and leapt out of the way, intending to dodge the light. Before it could whizz past him, though, the magic exploded with a *whoosh* of flames, and a blinding flash filled the room, bright as the sun over freshly fallen snow. Kisser was abruptly thieved of his sight, his vision going completely white, and he cursed as he struggled to unsheathe the knife he kept in one boot. He wasn't the only one, apparently. All around him other voices were swearing, and he could make out the familiar scrape of swords and axes being drawn from their sheaths.

Among the ring of metal, however, came a distinctly different sound. A dull *thump thump thump*, like the chorus made by a maid as she beat dust from a rug.

When something collided with Kisser's abdomen, cold and hard and driven with incredible strength, he had just enough time to register that the sound was that of the High Priest's steel staff pounding into flesh. Then another blow took him in the temple, and the white of his vision blinked to black.

Talo took down the man directly in front of him first, the one he'd been exchanging words with, assuming him to be the leader. His own sight was only mildly affected by the flash spell, the brunt of the blinding light blocked by tightly shut eyes and a raised hand at the last moment. As soon as the spell burned itself out, he'd been moving.

The first blow caught the blinded man across the wrist of his sword hand, the second coming around so fast to catch the man in the chest that he didn't have time to do more than grunt in pain as his blade dropped from limp fingers. The next two strikes were practiced hits to the gut and knee, bringing the man down to a kneel.

Then the blunt end of Talo's staff caught him directly between the eyes, knocking him unconscious to the floor.

All in about four seconds.

Talo didn't have time to thrill in the momentary pleasure of finding the rhythm of battle once again, though. Three other men still stood, floundering about with fists and weapons as they screamed in surprise and anger, rubbing at their eyes with free hands in a vain attempt to rid themselves of the offending blindness. Three paces to the left, a young man was drawing a knife from his boot, cursing to himself and blinking rapidly as he looked around in sightless panic.

Talo was on him in a blink, practiced blows to his stomach and the side of his head laying the mercenary out cold.

By then, though, sight had begun to return to the eyes of the last two men. They stood on the other side of the table upon which Raz i'Syul lay sprawled unconscious on his stomach with one arm hanging off the edge. Talo rushed to meet them, hoping to catch at least one of the pair off guard, but the messiness of the room played against him. He was forced to watch his step even as he bulled forward, nearly stumbling over the clutter more than once. He reached the two men just in time for them to wheel on him, weapons at the ready.

But Talo didn't slow.

The steel staff in his hands snaked out in a silver blur, going for the small point between the abdomen and chest of the first man where even a moderate jab of pressure would leave him winded. The blow struck true, but jarred as it hit hollowly against the iron chest piece that must have been hidden beneath the mercenary's thin fur and leather armor. Only Talo's years in the pits of Azbar saved him then—or at least his left hand—as he twisted away from a savage uppercut blow from the man's own sword. He felt the wind from the blade whisk against his face, and almost fell backwards as he stumbled over a small pile of books that shifted under his back foot. It gave the second man enough time to rush forward, bellowing as he raised a long-handled ax above his head in one hand, long knife in the other.

Talo let go of his staff all together, his hand whipping out in practiced patterns to grab the charging man's wrists before the weapons could find their mark. Then, with a twist of his body, he used his opponent's own momentum to flip him around and over, swinging him sideways and diagonally by the arms much like a woodcutter might swing his ax at the trunk of a tree.

The man hit the room's small desk with a *crash*, flipping the thing on its side even as he tumbled over it, and didn't rise again.

Not pausing, Talo spun about to meet the last man, expecting another rush. Instead, he found the sellsword scrambling away from him, tripping over the jumbled riff raff in his rush for the front hall.

"Get outta' my way!" he heard the man snarl, brandishing his sword at Carro, who stood in the way of the man's escape.

In response, Carro wrenched an arm back, paused, then punched the man square in the face with a fist roughly the size and weight of a set of bricks.

43

"Sorry," Talo heard him mumble in earnest over the uneven noises of yet another limp form falling back into the mess.

There was a moment of quiet, the only sounds coming from the wind as it whistled through a couple of loose panes in the wide window over Talo's shoulder. He looked around the room, unwilling to let his guard down just yet as he eyed the other men scattered about the floor, waiting for someone to groan and push themselves to their feet.

Eventually, though, he relaxed, and looked around at Carro.

"You alright?" Talo asked him. The Priest nodded, carefully avoiding glancing down at the blood on his hands as he looked about desperately for something to wipe it off with, his face tinged green.

"Swell," he said queasily as he finally tugged a dirty old cloth from beneath of sheaf of old papers, sending them tumbling to the floor. "You?"

Talo gave a pained grunt in response. As the adrenaline of the fight faded, a throbbing ache was already blooming in his bad knee, building quickly.

"Let's just say it's going to be a long time before I stop regretting this," he groaned, hobbling over to lean against the corner of the now upturned desk. Carro started towards him at once, but Talo raised a hand to stop him.

"I'll live," he said through gritted teeth, then waved at Arro, still prostrated over the table. "See to him. I'll tell Eva and Atler it's safe."

Carro hesitated only for a moment, then nodded his understanding. As the Priest used his long legs to clamber over the stacks of book and papers and random oddities, Talo lifted the index finger of his free hand and started moving it in concise circles through the air. At once, light trailed across the space he was tracing, solidifying from a bare glow until it hung like white silk suspended around his digit. Then, with a flick, he sent the messenger spell off, slipping across the mess of the floor, down the hall, and under the lip of the front door.

"How's the boy?" he asked Carro, clenching his jaw against a wave of pain as he pushed himself off the desk and limped to where his staff lay. By the table, Carro was bent to examine the atherian's back, one hand pressing the side of his hood over his nose and mouth. Talo was about to ask him what was the matter when he caught a hint of the stench.

"Infected," Carro told him unnecessarily, voice muffled behind the cloth, just as the door down the hall opened and Eva stepped inside, High Priestess Atler right behind her. "Awfully, too. Someone almost ran him through."

"He's lucky to be alive." Eva breathed in relief, looking around at the men strewn about the room. "Another few inches and the blade would have found heart."

"He's made of hardier stuff than the rest of us, thank Laor," Talo told her with a grunt as he finally managed to lift his staff awkwardly from the floor. By the table, Eva nodded.

"I once saw him take a kick that might have caved in the chest of another man," she said, her hand reaching out to rest on Arro's upturned forearm. "Two, actually. When he saved me from some bitch woman slaver. The blows broke a few of his ribs, but even then barely a week went by before it was like nothing had happened."

"Well whatever advantage his body might grant him, it's losing now," Carro said, still leaning over the atherian. "We need to do something about this, before it's too late."

"What do you need?" Eva asked at once.

Leaving the healers to their discussion, Talo tried to catch Atler's eye. The poor woman was staring at the prone form of the atherian, though, as she had been from the moment she'd stepped into the room. There was a measured dose of awe in her gaze, the amazement of bearing witness to something wonderful and terrifying. Even as he watched, Talo saw her take in the sheen of sleek, scaled skin, then the breadth of sunset wings, one of them pinned under the man when he'd been rolled.

When her eyes found the claws of his long fingers, the dark talons on his feet, and the white teeth protruding up and down from between his lips, though, some of that awe turned to fear.

"There's nothing to be afraid of," Talo told her gently, coming to stand beside her. "A kind soul hidden in a harsh vessel, I promise you."

Atler nodded her understanding, but still didn't look away. She'd ridden hard with them, leaving the temple workings to her Priests and Priestesses, and had listened intently to Eva's shouted story as they barreled through the streets, never saying a word. Talo was unsure what impact the tale had on the woman, but as he saw her eyes flick up to the Southerner's face, softening at the intense concern that painted Eva's tanned features, he allowed himself to hope it had weighed her opinion for the better.

"Is he going to live?" she asked quietly, not wanting to interrupt Carro and Eva's conversation.

Talo nodded. "Carro knows what he's doing, and so—I think we can assume—does our Southern friend. If Arro was beyond saving, they would have said so."

Atler hesitated, obviously torn, still watching Eva's face.

"Good," she said after a moment.

Talo nodded, allowing the High Priestess a minute of quiet observance as the healers plied their trade, Eva picking her tools up from the ground and Carro sterilizing them quickly with a flash of magic. When they got to work on the atherian himself, though, Talo nudged the woman to get her attention, then nodded at the men strewn about the room.

"How about we make sure they don't wake up before the guard arrives, hm?"

It was a chore, an hour or so later, moving Arro's sleeping form from the house back to the cart Talo assumed the mercenaries had used to smuggle him into the city in the first place. Not for the first time, as he watched Carro—hefting the atherian's body under the arms—and the two women—each straining under the weight of a massive leg—Talo wished Laor had granted his faithful the magics to dispel weight. It would certainly save them all a lot of sweat and trouble during the gathering season at the apex of every summer when the Laorin descended from the High Citadel to stock their stores in preparation for the winter.

Though, he had to admit, there was something oddly hilarious about watching Carro, with all his bulk, heaving and hoing and going red in the face under Arro's mass.

Piling the heavy pelts under and atop the atherian's freshly bandaged body, they hitched the cart to Carro's saddle before retrieving all of Arro's gear from one of the horses tied down nearby. Next, they heaved Ahna out from where she'd been stowed between the wheels of the cart itself, and tucked her in beside her master. This done, they finally set off at a steady pace, careful not to jostle the slumbering man any more than necessary. After a time, Atler split off from them, searching out a patrol of Ystréd's city guard, prepared with a well-rehearsed tale about how men had broken into the home of one of their faithful, and how she and some of her Laorin had been forced to subdue them.

Eva assured them all she would be able to find Sven in time to get the story straight with him, too.

When they arrived back at the temple, Talo enlisted the help of a half-dozen of the strongest Priests and Priestess who'd come out to greet them, giving quiet orders even as he accepted Carro's help in dismounting his horse. Together the men and women lifted Arro, still hidden under the furs, and carried him into the temple proper. Once inside, Talo had several of the acolytes close the wide double doors behind them.

Any witnesses on the street would assume the Laorin were prepping some poor unfortunate for the pyre, or something like that.

"Doren." Talo caught the arm of a passing Priest he recognized—the man Atler had asked to fetch her staff for her earlier in the day—as Arro's still-covered form was set down carefully on the floor of the common hall. "Have a room prepared, preferably on the bottom floor, with a fireplace if possible. Also, see how well the kitchens are stocked with meat. Anything will do."

If the Priest found either of the requests odd, he didn't say. Instead he nodded, then set off at a trot to see to the arrangements.

"How's he doing?" Talo asked Carro as the big man bent down to pull the topmost furs off Arro's face. There was a collective gasp from the gathered Laorin as the Monster of Karth was revealed—if not in all his glory. Talo ignored them.

"Better, I think," Carro said, placing a big hand on the atherian's head, between his spined ears. "He's cooler than he was, but I don't know what fever would look like with him, or when it would break." He looked around at Eva. "Any thoughts?"

The Southerner shook her head. "Atherian are slaves in the lands past the fringe cities, in Perce and the Seven Cities, but in the South we rarely see them. I wouldn't know any better than you."

Carro sighed, but nodded, getting to his feet again and glancing at Talo. "Nothing to do but wait and pray and hope for the best, love."

Talo nodded, then motioned for Carro to follow him. Stepping away from crowd and leaving Eva to tend to Arro, the pair ducked into the relative solitude of a far corner, bending their heads together.

"Carro…" Talo started, glancing back at the atherian. "Where are the children? Where are Arrun and Lueski?"

Carro frowned, then looked back at the atherian as though expecting to see the Koyts standing over him worriedly. "I… don't know," he said slowly, his face suddenly dark. "He wouldn't have left them, would he?"

"To fend for themselves? No." Talo shook his head.

"Maybe he had no choice. Those men brought him here, which implies he was on the road heading to Ystréd, and well on the way or they'd have gone to Azbar."

"Maybe…" Talo said with a frown. "I don't like it. Something's off. Something's wrong."

Sadly, all Carro could do was nod in agreement.

VI

"They called her 'the White Witch,' which must have seemed fitting enough in the eyes of the masses. Amongst the wild tribes of the Northern mountains, those of sickly and infirm birth are often given to the elements, left for the cold and wind to swallow and forget, sacrifices to the Stone Gods in a plea to keep their people strong. An albino moving among them, a woman grown and powerful in her own right, must have seemed near blasphemy to many. One could almost imagine the sight as a spit in the face of the divine, a literal act of defiance in the refusal to bow to the weakness that bleached her body, a refusal to accept fate and die."

— *The Atherian*, by Jûn fi'Surr

"What are we going to do?"

"They're coming here? *Here?*"

"Damn savages, all of them."

"We can't be sure. No one can be sure. They can't be coming here, can they?

"Why can't they leave us be?"

From her place at the end of one of the eight long tables that took up the great width of the dining hall, Syrah Brahnt let out a frustrated sigh, shoving her plate of peppered venison, black beans, and spiced potatoes away from her. It had been three days since Jofrey told the Citadel's council of their suspicions, and in that time rumors had spread like wildfire. Voices whispered and gossiped all around, reaching Syrah even in her secluded corner, as distant from the main body of late evening diners as she had managed to get.

Told him not to include Petrük, Syrah thought bitterly, resting her elbows on the table and leaning forward to rub her temples with pale fingers. *The old bitch can't help but cause a stir.*

It hadn't been Jofrey's intention to hide the truth from the Laorin, of course. He would have told the residents of the Citadel eventually, or at least would have had the other members of the council spread the news. The plan, however, had been to first verify what they could, and perhaps avoid needless panic. Instead, a loose tongue—one Syrah was quite sure belonged to an insufferable old hag of a woman—had let slip the news.

Gûlraht Baoill, the self-proclaimed Kayle of nearly *all* the northern range clans, was marching on Cyurgi' Di at the head of twenty-five thousand strong.

Small wonder people are frightened.

Syrah glanced over her shoulder into the packed table behind her. Most of the faces she could see were intent on their conversation, men and women of all ranks trading rumors and theories over the table like fast flowing currency. Not for the first time—despite Jofrey's placations—she cursed her former Priest-Mentor for his foolish amble south, leaving the High Citadel to deal with the newly rising Arenas in some of the lower valley towns.

If Talo had stayed, *he* would have known what to do. If he had acted befittingly of his post as High Priest, *he* would have been here to deal with this crisis.

Instead, he'd left Jofrey and Syrah to handle the mess.

Syrah sighed again, forcing the anger to wane. It wasn't really Talo's fault he was gone, as Jofrey reminded her over and over again every time she brought it up. No one could have expected Baoill's meteoric rise to power, nor the violent path he would carve across the base of the Vietalis ranges as he razed the valley cities of Metcaf and Harond. The situation in Azbar might be minute in the face of the eminent threat of the Kayle's new army, but at the time the plea sent by Kal Yu'ri—the High Priest of Azbar's small temple—had certainly seemed worth addressing. Even Syrah had ended up giving Talo her blessing to go, wanting him to recover a little of the peace of mind she'd seen the man lose the moment he'd received Yu'ri's letter.

She knew well what it was like to see the victories of hard years and even harder labor ripped away and trampled on.

"Mistress Brahnt?"

Syrah sat up, turning to look around as the voice spoke from over her shoulder. Behind her, a young girl stood in acolyte's robes, extra furs pulled around her collar to ward off the chill that always managed to seep into the halls of the Citadel despite the heated steam that ran through pipes in the walls and floors around them.

"Yes?" Syrah replied, eyeing the girl. She didn't recognize her, though that was hardly surprising. The Citadel was the largest of Laor's temples, home to thousands of all ages. Dozens more arrived every summer, some converts and some born to the faith, delivered by parents or travelling Priests and Priestess, or else arriving on foot, managing the harrowing climb up the mountain path all on their own.

The girl flushed as she met Syrah's pink eyes. "Priest al'Sen wishes you to join him in the High Priest's quarters," she managed to get out, speaking in a rush. "He thought I might find you here and... here you are." She let the hesitant finish trail awkwardly.

"Here I am, yes," Syrah said with a forced smile, waving at the plate of food she'd pushed aside. "And, as you can see, I haven't finished eating yet. Please tell Jofrey I'll attend him in the morning."

She liked the man plenty, but the throb between her temples the rumormongers had left her with was rapidly draining any will she might have had to deal with anything else that evening.

Maybe I'll drag Reyn away from the practice chambers early, she thought privately, a different sort of hunger suddenly filling the void left by her lost appetite as she thought of the man's broad shoulders and muscled arms. *There's more than one way to cure a headache...*

"Begging your pardon, ma'am," the girl squeaked, cutting across Syrah's daydreaming, "but he made it seem very, very important."

That got Syrah to pause. "How do you mean?" she asked with a frown.

"He told me to find you, and told me that if I didn't to 'knock on every bloody door in the Citadel' until I did."

Another pause.

"Shit," Syrah muttered finally under her breath, not liking the possible implications of such pressing summons.

"S-Sorry?" the girl asked nervously.

"Nothing worth repeating," Syrah told her, pushing herself away from the table and standing up. "Are you hungry?"

The acolyte hesitated, then nodded.

"Good, then that's yours," Syrah told her, heating her abandoned dinner with a wave of her hand and a flash of magic before stepping over the bench she'd been sitting on. "I get the feeling I won't have time to come back for it tonight."

Not waiting for the girl to respond, she brushed past her, heading for the hall's arched entryway.

Despite the urgency in her step, Syrah couldn't help but feel relieved as she left the brightness and noise of the dining hall, the ache behind her sensitive eyes fading a little in the dimmer lights of the High Citadel's tunnel halls. Candles and oil lamps stood in little alcoves dug into the brick and earthen walls, or else hung from old chains above her head, flickering weird shadows about as she passed. There was a comfort to the space, a sense of home and safety that all the adventures she'd had couldn't really compensate for. She'd loved travelling the Northern lands, and had her doubts she was ready to settle down just yet, but there was certainly something about the rough-hewn brick around her and the smoothed stone beneath her feet that drew her in, making her eternally question any notion that she would ever want to leave.

This place, this vast, titanic keep crafted by ancient men for a war that never seemed to have come, was more a home to her than any place she could fathom actually existed out there in the great vastness of the world.

Syrah nodded to the men and women she passed as she walked, briefly greeting the Priests and Priestesses she knew and bestowing quick smiles on the acolytes who gave her small bows, moving aside to let her by. She was a known face in these halls, the former acolyte of the High Priest of Cyurgi' Di himself, the youngest member of the Citadel's council, and the woman who had brought some peace to the endless war between the valley towns and the mountain tribes.

A peace that seemed to have vanished even before the inked signatures had a chance to dry on the parchment of the treaties.

Reaching the plain wooden door of the High Priest's quarters, Syrah didn't even bother knocking. Lifting the handle, she let herself into the circular room, closing the door again behind her as she slid inside, looking around.

When Talo had departed for Azbar, taking Carro with him, he'd left Jofrey al'Sen empowered with the responsibilities of the High Priest's mantle, and the man had adapted well to the weight of the position. He still slept in his own quarters a few halls down, but had taken to using Talo's chambers as his study and place of meeting, putting the wide L-shaped escritoire in the middle of the room to good use. The shelves and shelves of books that lined almost every inch of the rounded walls not occupied by arched windows or the headboard of the room's wide bed had proven invaluable as well, as some of the tomes—which Syrah suspected were Carro's, given his bastard's curiosity for his father culture—had helped to fill in gaps in the Laorin's knowledge of the mountain tribes that Syrah herself hadn't been able to.

Three men stood by the desk in the center of the room, pausing in their discussion when they heard the door open behind them. One was Jofrey, a small man in his fifties, sporting a greying beard that reached the top of his chest, blue eyes crinkled around the edges from laughing and smiling and squinting through his crystal spectacles at too many letters into the darker hours of too many nights. He wore stained grey pants and a loose cotton shirt—a far sight different from the usual refinement he cut in the crisp white of his Priest's robes—and Syrah felt an involuntary chill run down her spine as she realized he'd been roused from his bed.

Whatever had happened, it had been important enough to wake him from what rare sleep he got these days...

Of the other two, Syrah only recognized them vaguely. They were men of the cloth, residents of the High Citadel, but you wouldn't have thought so given the image they cut now. Bedecked from head to toe in pelts and thick wool overcoats and pants, the men looked like they would have fit more at home with the mountain men that were causing such a stir than among the faithful of the keep. The fur stuck to them in clumps, thick and drenched with what she assumed was melted snow, and they had the miserable air about them of men stuck too long in out in the freeze.

"Syrah," Jofrey greeted her with a tired smile as she approached them. "Good. Sona managed to find you then. I hoped she would."

"You seemed to have made it very clear that it was in everyone's best interest she did," Syrah told him with a nod, coming to stand opposite him, between the two nameless Priests.

"I did indeed," he mumbled, half listening as he glanced to the man on Syrah's right. "Have you met Priest Loben? Or," he waved to the man on Syrah's left, "Priest Derro?"

"We haven't had the pleasure, no," Syrah replied, nodding to each of the Priests in turn. "We've come across each other in passing, I'm sure, but nothing more."

"Always busy running around, eh?" Loben, the one on her right, jested with a strained grin. He had a pinched, ungraciously framed face, but his smile was friendly, if stressed. "I remember you as a girl, much the same. Always running around with Reyn Hartlet and the rest of your little friends. My son, Bellen, was in some of your classes, in fact."

"I remember Bellen." Syrah perked up. "He helped me get through arithmetics! I never had much of a mind for numbers, sadly."

"And you never had much of a mind for company either, it seems," the other man, Priest Derro, grumbled from her left. "What in the Lifegiver's name possessed you to get involved with the savages, woman? I would think someone cut from Brahnt's cloth would never have been so foolhardy."

There was a thick silence as Syrah turned slowly to look Derro in the face. He was a short, rotund man, barely an inch taller than she, with beady eyes that glared at her with zealous confidence and foolish judgment. His pudgy face looked as though it were usually clean-shaven, but had taken on the shadow of several days of stubble, now sprouting in patches around his flabby neck, weak chin, and thin lips like dying grass on dry soil.

"What 'possessed me'"—she rolled the phrase pointedly as she replied—"were the vows we made to do what we can for *all* people, sir. Not just those whose accessibility happens to be within stone's throw of a well-laden table."

The remark struck the fat man as intended, and he flushed, opening his mouth to respond.

Jofrey, however, beat him to it.

"Derro, keep your opinions to yourself," he said sharply, the tired man replaced suddenly by the striking presence of the interim High Priest. "The news you both bring is enough to swallow tonight, and I need none of your ugly comments to spice my meal, *thank you very much*."

"What news?" Syrah asked quickly, deciding to do her part in bringing the conversation back to the subject at hand as she looked between Jofrey and Priest Loben.

"Mountain men," Loben said in mumbled answer. "At the base of the pass."

In response to this, Derro snorted. "So Loben *thinks*," he grumbled. "Six days we've camped at the bottom of those damn stairs, with this one"—he waved an impatient hand at the taller Priest—"jumping at every stray flutter of leaves and flick in the shadows. Spends most of his time shaking in his boots, muttering about wolves and ursali. Now it's the damn Kayle himself."

"Camped?" Syrah repeated, confused.

"Loben and Derro are two of ten," Jofrey told her with a nod. "I sent a group of our more experienced through the storms, to guard the mountain pass, with provisions for two weeks. If the Kayle is indeed coming here, the progress of the bulk of his army will be slow. It was my hope, though, that eyes and ears in the Woods might be able to warn us of any scouting parties he may have sent ahead."

"Wise," Syrah said with a nod before looking back at Loben. "And?"

Loben bit his lip nervously, giving a sidelong look at Derro, who opened his mouth to say something more.

He hadn't quite gotten it out before Syrah lifted an angry finger, not even turning to look at him.

"When it's your turn to speak, sir, you will be told," she spat, before addressing Loben kindly again. "Now... What did you see?"

The Priest chewed on his lip a moment more, then found his voice as he shrugged. "I... can't be sure," he said. "Men. I know that. I was a ways into the Arocklen, heading west, when I saw them. At first I thought they were just wolves, or something likewise, so I conjured flames to scare them off. When the light hit them, though, they were *men*."

"Or hallucinations," Derro muttered.

Syrah ignored him. "What did they look like?" she pressed Loben. "Describe them."

"Thin," the Priest said at once, more eager now that he knew Syrah wasn't going to shun his story right out the gate. "Bearded. With dirty faces and animal skulls atop their heads, or on their shoulders."

Syrah cursed internally.

"Goatmen," she told the group, though she turned to look at Jofrey in particular. "The Gähs. Of all the tribes, they are the least fond of blood and battles. They prefer hunting and animal sacrifices to please their gods. Loben probably frightened them as much as they did him. They're superb woodsmen and trackers, though. It makes sense that Baoill would use them as scouts." She frowned. "It also means that the Kayle will have found the mountain path, if he didn't know where it was already. They'll have followed Loben back easily enough, and then it's only a matter of time before word gets back to the main army, even if they are weeks out."

She paused, struck by a sudden concerning thought. The worry must have crossed her face, because Jofrey's eyes narrowed.

"What is it?" he asked her.

Syrah didn't respond for a few seconds, mentally going over the possibilities and probabilities.

"... I can't say for sure," she said slowly, "but if Baoill's bothered to send scouts *this* far ahead, it's possible he's sent a vanguard as well..."

That didn't settle well with anyone, though Derro managed to speak first. "A *vanguard*?" His round face blanched. Apparently he no longer doubted that his companion had seen what he'd claimed. "Of what? More of these Goatmen?"

"Doubtful." Syrah shook her head, still thinking. "The Gähs clan isn't one for open war. They're archers, cutthroats at best. If the Kayle intends to start his siege as early as possible, he'll have sent others as a first onslaught. If he's conquered the eastern tribes, he might take advantage of their knowledge of the terrain. Maybe Sefi or Velkrin. In that case, though, he'll be delayed. My bet would be on the Kregoan, or the Amreht. He might even send the Sigûrth, if he thinks he can spare them."

"And that would be... bad?" Derro asked, the hesitation in the question spelling out all too clearly how much he did *not*, in fact, want to hear the answer.

"Any and all of them," Syrah said with a nod. "The Goatmen are an exception in their relative docility. The rest of the clans have a saying: *Garros es Feys es Kayle, da brán ed brún.* 'Glory to Gods and King, by blood and bone.'"

She let the portent of the words weigh down on the three men.

Finally, Jofrey spoke. "So..." he started slowly. "The war reaches us at last."

Syrah nodded. "I would pull the rest of your scouts back, at least far enough up the path to make for an easy escape if need be. The Goatmen won't want for open battle, but they'll come crawling out of the trees in the night if the Kayle wants your men dead. Don't give them the opportunity."

"Agreed." Jofrey looked between Derro and Loben. "See to it."

The two men nodded, both pale in the face. Giving a brief bow to both Syrah and Jofrey—though Derro's tilt to Syrah was more a convulsive twitch than any sort of respectful gesture—they turned and hurried off.

After the door had swung shut behind them, Jofrey sighed, leaning back to rest on the edge of the desk behind him and rubbing his eyes with a thumb and the bent knuckle of his forefinger.

"A siege," he muttered, chuckling into his hand darkly. "A bloody siege. I tell you, Syrah, of all the things I've seen in my life—and I've seen a damn few things, believe it or not—*this* is not something I'd ever have expected to bear witness to."

"That makes you and a couple thousand others, in this place," Syrah said with a dry chuckle, crossing her arms. "Do we have the provisions to make it through the winter?"

Jofrey nodded, though he still frowned. "Well enough, though we'll be surviving off nothing more than gruel if the valley towns don't come to our aid in time. If they don't come at all, we won't make it beyond the first month of summer."

"Cheerful," Syrah grumbled.

Jofrey shrugged. "Realistic. If it comes to it, we'll need to know where our weaknesses are."

"I supposed," Syrah said with a huff, reaching up to push a lock of white hair behind her ear. "Still, let's hope it doesn't come to that. You've sent birds out to the towns?"

"The very night you made out the Kayle's plan." Jofrey nodded. "And a few more the morning after for good measure. We've done all we can, at this point."

Syrah frowned, suddenly thinking hard. "Not quite."

Jofrey cocked a brow at that. "Explain." He leaned towards her, his curiosity piqued.

"The vanguard," she told him. "If they come, and they're western tribes, then there's a good chance I've worked with their people. If they were part of the main host I doubt I would have much of a chance to talk any sort of sense into them while they were under Baoill's thumb, but separate from the army they might not be so unified…"

"Go on," Jofrey said with a slow nod, indicated he followed so far.

"So…" Syrah started, forming the idea as she spoke. "If we could disrupt the front line of the Kayle's attack, it would mean a lot of trouble for him when he'd arrive. No siege, no camps, and less soldiers."

Jofrey fell into contemplation, his eyes on the floor as he thought, one hand absent-mindedly stroking his beard.

"A punishing strike," he agreed after a moment.

"Very. It would make it harder for the Kayle to establish a foothold in the Woods, much less along the path or at the gates of the Citadel. If we can disband whatever spearhead he sends—or even disrupt it—we could delay him weeks, and at the very least a few days. It might make all the difference, in the end."

"So you want me to... what? Give you permission to meet their vanguard head on?"

Syrah smiled. "Just give me permission to craft a white flag from some old bed sheets."

Jofrey sighed, and returned to rubbing his eyes tiredly.

"I get the distinct feeling," he said eventually, "that it wouldn't matter in the least whether or not I give you my blessing to do anything."

Syrah laughed, shrugging. "If it makes you feel better," she said with a sly smile, "it wouldn't have mattered if Talo had been here either."

VII

"We talked of many things, into the dark hours of just as many nights. We talked of the past, of the future, of the present. We talked of politics and wars, of people and places and things. We talked about dreams, aspirations, and the direction in which life had taken us. When we talked about what we wished for, though, what our greatest desires really were, at the core of all things, Raz would always go quiet. Then he would tell me of what he missed most about an old life, of the warm comforts of home, love, and family."

—Syrah Brahnt

As Raz came to, the first thing he was aware of was that he was floating. A softness enveloped him, a silken gentleness, like the clouds themselves had been stitched tightly together to wrap around him in a soft cocoon.

The second thing he was aware of was the horrible, bone-deep ache of his back, chest, and head.

Raz groaned, fidgeting in discomfort. From somewhere nearby he heard a gasp, then the scrape of what sounded like wood on wood as a chair was pushed back when someone hurriedly stood up. He was aware of their presence above him, of a body leaning over him, and the cloud shifting around him.

No, he realized. *Not a cloud. A bed.*

Raz cracked his eyes open slowly, marveling at how even this small motion made his head throb, the painful pressure behind his eyes that accented several days of dehydration, sickness, and what he suspected was very callous treatment.

"Ooowwwwwe," was all he could manage through gritted teeth.

At this some of the tension faded from the blurry outline of the worrying figure hovering over him, and there was a light, feminine snigger.

"Raz i'Syul Arro, groaning like a child. Now I really *have* seen it all."

Raz's eyes flew open at the sound of the familiar voice, and he rapidly tried to blink away the sleep. Slowly the faded silhouette solidified, forming itself into a pretty Southern woman bedecked in light Northern fashion, a grey blanket pulled over her white wool shirt in an attempt to ward off what chill the roaring fire in the hearth on the far wall hadn't been able to chase away.

"*Eva?*" Raz croaked through a dry throat, not believing his eyes. In response, the woman smiled broadly.

"In the flesh." She gave him a little nod. "And very glad to see you back among the living."

"But...how? What...?" Raz couldn't keep his questions in order, taking his eyes off the former slave to look around the room, wincing as the motion shot pain up his spine and into his neck. It was a sparse chamber, with plain plank floors and walls of plaster and stone. Above his head, heavy crossbeams lined the ceiling, supporting what he assumed to be at least one other floor to the building.

"Go easy," Eva said, sitting down on the edge of the bed and resting a hand atop his where it lay beneath the covers. "You're safe. We have all the time to talk."

Raz calmed at the pressure of her hand on his, forcing himself to relax, feeling the ache in his back ebb as he let himself sink fully into the pillow behind his head.

"I can't remember the last time I slept in a bed," he said, feeling the plushness of the feather filled mattress beneath his shoulders and fingers.

"You've been busy, I hear," Eva said with a laugh. "Challenging the Mahsadën can't have left you with much opportunity to frequent the better inns and taverns on your way up here."

"It didn't leave much opportunity for sleep at all, much less anything else," Raz said with a smirk. Then his face sobered, and he contemplated Eva carefully, studying her face.

"I want you to tell me everything that's happened since you left the South," he said finally, calmer this time. "First, though... I don't remember much, after the road. I remember the men, and every now and then what I think was the bumping of a cart..."

"Mercenaries had you," Eva said with a frown. "Possibly split off from one of the valley towns' militaries. It happens, and only moreso since word spread about your open invitation in the Arena. I don't know how they got you, but it seems they wanted you alive. Badly enough even to break for Ystréd and ferret out someone who would patch you up without too many questions."

"And that person happened to be *you?*" Raz demanded doubtfully.

Eva shook her head. "No. They took you to an acquaintance of mine, a hack named Sven. Terrible physician, but a decent man overall, and he owed me a few favors given the number of times I've come to the rescue for him when he's botched up. When he saw you he found a way to let me know you were in the city."

"Why?" Raz asked, still confused. "How did he know that—?"

"That I'd want to find you?" Eva finished for him. "Like I said, he's a good enough man, when it comes down to it. After you got the others and me out of Miropa, we made north as fast as possible, just as you'd said. Made it as far as Azbar without trouble, but..." She trailed off.

"You found trouble there," Raz finished darkly, nodding. "Not surprising. What happened?"

Eva looked as though it was a painful memory, grimacing as she spoke. "The city guard let us in without issue, but within a few nights Tym and his idiot friend Dayle got into a brawl at one of the local pubs. Before any of us could do anything, the guard had swooped in and thrown everyone in irons, the two of them included."

She sighed sadly. There might not have been any love lost between herself and the men, but Raz could imagine what happened next wasn't anything they deserved.

"They were thrown in the pit," he said stoically, pulling his hand gently out from beneath the covers to place it atop of Eva's. "I'm sorry, Eva."

The woman shrugged. "Nothing any of us could do about it. Didn't even have time to get to the town hall and make a plea to the Chairman and his council before Tym and Dayle were dead."

Raz nodded from the pillow. "If it makes you feel better, the Chairman got his due, in the end."

Eva's eyes widened at that. Then she allowed herself a hard smirk. "Gone the same way as the Mahsadën, has he?"

"The Mahsadën had it easy in comparison," Raz replied, though he didn't smile. "There are some lines that even slavers hesitate to cross. Tern didn't, and he paid for it."

Eva's brow furrowed at the words, but she didn't voice her curiosity. Raz suspected the edge with which he'd spoken had been enough to imply it was nothing he wanted to discuss.

"Well," she continued as though there had been no pause in the conversation, "after what happened to Tym and Dayle, the rest of us decided it was time to go our separate ways. The Azbar guard were looking for any excuse to add to the fodder of the Arena, and we knew some of them had seen us all arrive together. A few stayed, promising to keep as far from the eyes of the law as possible, but most made west for the larger valley towns of Drangstek and Stullens, or south again for some of the smaller border towns."

"But you came further north?"

Eva nodded. "I wanted to be as far from the South as I could get. I would have made for the High Citadel itself, if I could, but the Twins might frown on me pretending to pray to another god." She laughed at the joke, though Raz didn't follow.

"Anyways," she said after a moment, "Ystréd is as far as I got. I was on my own, and didn't have a clue what I was supposed to do next. I couldn't bring myself to beg, even though I was sleeping on the streets with all the other tramps. I was this close"—she held up the thumb and forefinger of her free hand, peering through the tiny space between them at Raz—"to selling myself to one of the slum brothels when I met Sven. During the summer he trades tonics and salves to the beggars and vagrants for what coppers or food they can scrounge together during the day. It's not pretty work, but it keeps him fed and many of the slum dwellers from dying of infection and diseases, even if he is as shitty a doctor as they come."

Raz snorted at that, gritting his teeth as the action jolted a sharp burning pain in his back.

"Seems he did a fair enough job on me," he managed to wheeze out eventually. "Last I remember I was close enough to dying to start seeing ghosts."

Eva smirked. "If Sven had gotten his hands on you, you'd probably have been worse off, and he knows it. No, you're alive because it turns out I'm a damn sight better with a scalpel than I ever thought I could be, and your Priest friends"—she waved at the door of the room—"have powers unlike anything I've ever seen."

"Priest?" Raz asked, confused. "Did Brahnt find—?"

"Getting to that!" Eva cut across him, obviously enjoying the recounting of her adventures over the last months. "As I was saying, Sven took me in and got me back on my feet in exchange for my help when necessary. I made him a better healer, and he made sure I didn't starve to death, or die beaten and raped in some snowy back alley of the city. After a while I started making waves of my own, treating the more gruesome injuries the idiot gangs and criminal rings of this place manage to make each other suffer, the stuff Sven would never have gone near." She laughed. "They call me 'the Carver' if you can believe it."

"I can," Raz chuckled in a pained way. "Feels like you carved half my back right out of me."

Eva punched him in the chest, making him wince.

"So," she kept on, failing to hide a smile, "when you landed on his table, Sven knew enough about you and I both to put two and two together, and he convinced the men who'd brought you to him to loop me in. Apparently their leader thought you were worth a lot more alive than dead. As soon as I could, I made a run for this place." She waved a hand about her to indicate the room. "And—as it turns out—I wasn't the only one looking for you."

"Lucky me." Raz coughed. "I imagine I'd be in chains and halfway back to Miropa by now if that hadn't been the case."

"Probably not, actually," Eva said with a mockingly casual shrug. "Apparently your friend—the High Priest, I think—put down the mercenaries as they were bringing the sword down on your head. So... you'd just be dead."

"Oh, well that's pleasant," Raz said with a grunt. "Is that the bedside manner you keep for all your patients, 'Carver'?"

Eva winked. "Only the ones I like. Now—" she removed her hand from under his and stood up, patting out the wrinkles of her shirt and pants—"unless I'm much mistaken, there are a couple individuals who would appreciate it if I didn't keep the fact that you've woken up from them any longer. One has been so on edge to leave the city you'd think the place was about to burn to the ground or something."

Raz chuckled again. "al'Dor," he said with a nod. "Don't judge him too harshly. He never seemed a man capable of anything more than the best intentions."

"Well his anxiety is making *me* anxious," Eva said with a little pout before making for the door. "I'll fetch them, and you can tell him so."

"Tell him yourself!" Raz did his best to yell after her as the woman left the room. When she was gone, he rolled his head back to the opposite wall, in which was inlaid a narrow window of cheap glass panes, the kind that distorted the light and made it hard to see through.

Despite this, Raz stilled as he made out the snow falling outside once again.

A darkness started to creep back into him as the blurred, shifting white descended against a grey sky. For a few minutes, as Eva had been recounting her stories, Raz had forgotten it all, lost in a sort of reminiscent comfort. Now, though, as the woman's warmth left the room, leaving him only with the chill of the winter he could see through the window, the weight of everything came crashing down once again.

His fever might have broken, but even in lucidity Raz thought he could see the outline of children against the glass, laughing and playing in the snow.

Hearing movement in the hall, Raz turned his head back to the door in time to see it pushed open. Two men entered, the first leaning on the arm of the other with his left hand, his heavy steel staff in his right. As he watched a smiling Talo Brahnt and stern-faced Carro al'Dor make their way slowly into his room—followed again by Eva, as well as a woman he didn't recognize—Raz couldn't help but grin a little.

"I'm told I have you to thank for saving my neck," he said, speaking to Brahnt as the High Priest accepted al'Dor's help in easing himself down into a wooden chair on the left side of the bed. As always he favored the bad leg that had plagued him for what Raz was sure was much longer than they'd known each other.

"Quite," Brahnt chuckled, leaning forward in his chair to get closer to the bed. "Though don't be fooled into thinking it was a selfless act. Syrah would have me murdered in my sleep if she found out I'd allowed some ratty sellsword to kill you off."

He reached out his free hand, then—the one not still wrapped around his staff for support—and rested it on Raz's exposed shoulder.

"It's good to see you again, boy," he said with deep sincerity, blue eyes shining as he spoke. "I admit my hopes weren't high that our paths would cross again after Carro and I left Azbar."

Raz nodded, but said nothing, feeling the darkness claim a little bit more of his mood as the memories of his flight from Quin Tern's city reluctantly re-emerged.

"How are you feeling?" al'Dor asked sympathetically after a moment. There was, perhaps, not as much of the almost-fatherly affection in his words that Brahnt managed, but the concern was genuine.

"Ask me in a day or two," Raz groaned, straightening himself up slowly until he half-sat, half-leaned with his bare back against the plain wood of the wall at the head of the bed, his wings falling to either side. "I feel like I've been speared and tossed around by a bull elephant."

"A what?" the strange woman asked curiously. She was bedecked in the same robes as Brahnt, white with a single black line down the apex of the hood and back, and stood with the sort of nervous authority exuded by those not yet used to their station.

"Big Southern animal," Eva told her, bringing her hands up to her mouth and extending her index fingers. "Tusks the size of your arm."

"Oh," the woman—whom Raz deduced likely to be the leader of Ystréd's Laorin flock, as Kal Yu'ri had been of Azbar's—responded with wide eyes, and she said no more.

"Arro," Brahnt said, seeing Raz's eyes on her, "this is Tana Atler, High Priestess of the Laorin temple of Ystréd."

"Where I assume I'm currently claiming someone's room and bed," Raz said with a nod at the woman. "You have my thanks, High Priestess. I'll do my best to be out of your home as soon as possible."

Atler seemed unable to responded, her eyes still wide as they met his. After an awkward moment of silence, Eva made an effort to nudge the woman, but Raz smiled and waved her away.

"I understand your shock," he said with as much of a laugh as his mending wound would allow. "I don't imagine you see much of my kind this far into the North."

At that, the High Priestess seemed to find her voice.

"That-That's one way to put it," she squeaked, before continuing in a rush. "Of course, any friend of Talo's is a friend of ours. You're welcome to stay as long as you need. Are you hungry? There's pork left from the evening meal, though it was a bit dry. I'll have Doren bring you up extra furs, too. Talo says you're not much for the cold, and the weather is only going to get…"

She mumbled to a halt as al'Dor coughed pointedly, but Raz just kept smiling.

"And he's right, but I'll make out fine with the fire and what you've been able to provide me with already." He waved a hand at the bed and the blanket that still covered the lower half his body. "Again, though, you have my thanks."

Atler nodded but said nothing more this time, her face red with awe and embarrassment.

"Arro," Brahnt spoke from beside him. "Can you tell us what happened? How you ended up in the hands of those men? And that wound… Did they do that?"

"Getting captured wasn't my intention, if that's what you mean," Raz told him, reaching up to rub the back of his head unconsciously as he remembered the blow that had taken him by surprise. "And no. The blade that did that belonged to a man dead a good three or four days before I was stupid enough to get myself caught."

Beside Brahnt, al'Dor winced, but Raz ignored him, continuing.

"I was making my way here, I think. At least, that's what I set out to do from Azbar. A day or so in, though, and it's not so clear. The wound got infected—"

"You think?" Eva asked sarcastically from the back of the room.

"—and things went downhill fast," Raz kept on, disregarding her, too. "By the time I found their camp, I was in bad shape. *Really* bad shape. I think I remember asking them to take me to Ystréd. Tried to tell them to take me to you, actually, if memory serves. Instead, one of them snuck up from behind and got the drop on me. From there… well, from what Eva says, you actually probably know better than I."

"And Azbar?" al'Dor asked him, arms crossed as he hovered behind Brahnt's shoulder. "What of the Arena? And the Koyts?"

The name chilled Raz to the bone, hearing it from another's mouth. It was as though the realization that the children had not been his alone to remember, to suffer the memories, was turning his blood to ice. He couldn't speak, couldn't even breathe. There was no anger directed at the Priest, but Raz stared up at him from his place on the bed, mouth hanging open, unable to answer.

There was only emptiness.

"Raz…" Brahnt started gently, half reaching out, as though wanting to touch Raz's arm again. "Raz… Where are Arrun and Lueski?"

Slowly, Raz's amber eyes moved from al'Dor's dark blue ones to the ice-chip irises of Brahnt's.

Then they moved again, to the back of the room, where Eva and Atler still stood.

Talo got the message.

"Ladies, if you could give us a moment," he said, looking around at the two women.

Atler nodded at once, but Eva seemed hesitant, eyes on Raz as though seeking acknowledgment that this was what he wanted. When he did nothing but meet her gaze, she took it as silent confirmation and followed the High Priestess out the door.

When it had closed behind them, Raz turned to look out the window again.

For a long time he said nothing, watching the flakes fall against the rapidly coming night outside. Someone had lit a lantern below the lip of the glass, so that it almost looked as though the snow were falling into distorted flames, swallowed by the light and heat.

As the lives of the small and innocent are swallowed by those of the cruel and ambitious, he thought to himself.

Neither of the Priests spoke up behind him, giving him his moment. By the time he was able to form the words, Raz had no doubt Brahnt and al'Dor had developed their own suspicions based on nothing more than his silence.

"The Koyts are dead," he managed finally to get out. He still refused to look away from the window, as though not seeing the men's faces would make their reactions less raw for him. "Tern killed Arrun, or had him killed, rather. When she saw what had been done to her brother, Lueski took her own life."

Though he couldn't see the Priests, their responses to this announcement turned out to be nothing he could escape. Brahnt let out a noise somewhere between a pained grunt and a moan, and al'Dor gasped before letting a dark "No..." slip his lips. Their genuine shock caused a well of emotion to build up inside Raz, and not for the first time in his life he was grateful that the Sun hadn't born him into the world with the ability to shed tears.

He gave the men a minute of their own privacy, letting them come to terms with the news. It wasn't until his keen ears made out the steadying of Brahnt's angry breathing that he finally looked around.

al'Dor—the only man in the room with much of a soul left to him, Raz believed—was red-eyed and white-faced despite never actually having met the children. Talo, on the other hand, was obviously fighting to control the rising tide of fury and sadness that Raz was all too familiar with. He had spent the few days before his descent into delirium fighting it off himself.

"What of Tern?" Brahnt eventually managed in a tone of forced calm. "The Arena?"

"The Arena stands," Raz said darkly. "Though very likely under new management, by now."

He let the meaning of the words sink in, watching as al'Dor turned even paler and Brahnt achieved a sort of violent calmness, barely able to hold back a cold half-smile. Raz chose very deliberately not to spell out the details of Tern's end. The Laorin were an odd breed, capable of violence and—according to the Grandmother—even cruelty, but they stood firm by the cardinal rule of their order: that no death ever be dealt by the hands of the faithful, even in self-defense. The Laorin believed life to be the greatest gift their god, Laor, had granted man, and so to take it away was just as much the greatest form of blasphemy, a direct spitting into the face of the creator Himself.

While Brahnt, Yu'ri, and—as far as he knew—al'Dor had tolerated Raz's methods of doling out his own forms of justice, he didn't feel the need to weigh down their consciences with unnecessary details.

"We can only hope Rhen will be given the reign of the place, then," Brahnt said thoughtfully, all too obviously trying to steer his thoughts anywhere from the Koyts. "If the council is allowed to take over, things won't be much improved."

"Short of burning the whole damn place to the ground, the Doctore would be the best option," Raz agreed with a sigh, happy to take the opportunity the High Priest was offering them all. "I realize, looking back, that she deserved more credit than I ever gave her."

"Good people can be found in the strangest of places," al'Dor said, nodding solemnly. Brahnt and Raz returned the gesture simultaneously.

"Have you heard more of the mountain man?" Raz asked after a pause. "Baoill, was it?"

The question seemed to take the Priests by surprise, because they blinked. Raz shrugged.

"You made him seem like trouble enough to keep tabs on," he explained simply.

"*More* than enough," Brahnt muttered. "But no. Nothing of import, at least. Rumors that he's only a few miles north of us circulate about as much as rumors that he's not pushing southward at all. It's typical, for the time of year. The storms too often cut the valley towns off from each other, as well as any eyes they might have out in the world. The temple here is even smaller than Azbar's, too, so there's no guarantee if Ystréd's governing council *did* happen to know something that we'd hear about it."

He stopped, eyeing Raz with a cocked eye, as though suddenly suspecting something.

"Why do you ask?"

Because there are bad men in the world, Raz wanted to reply, thinking of something Alyssa Rhen had told him while keeping him from getting himself killed that day on the frozen pit floor of the Arena.

Instead, he said only, "Because I've never had much taste for men who build their power on the pain and suffering of others."

al'Dor chuckled at that. "Too true and then some. And it's about time that *someone*—" he looked pointedly down at Brahnt, "—did something about it."

"Carro has been sour company since I insisted we wait until you woke before setting off," Brahnt said, speaking to Raz but shooting his partner a falsely sweet smile over his shoulder. "He thinks every day we spend here is another day we let the Kayle dig his fingers into the Arocklen."

"He might not be far off the truth," Raz said, watching Brahnt carefully. "But what do you think?"

"I think some things are worth sticking around for. Some opportunities require delay and compromise."

Raz nodded, but said nothing more, waiting for the question he knew was coming.

When Brahnt met his gaze, it was with a burning intensity that Raz couldn't help himself from emulating, feeling it rouse up a vengeful anger within, the flickers of the justified rage that had made ash of the Mahsadën, the champions of the Arena, and Quin Tern himself.

"Raz," Brahnt began, leaning forward again so that their eyes were perfectly level. "Gûlraht Baoill is a plague. He's a tyrant and a murderer and a slaver. He places no value on human life, and has no respect for my god, your gods, or any gods that do not insist on blood and sacrifice as proof of devotion. He has burned the old and infirm alive, and impaled children—still breathing—along the walls of his conquered cities as a warning to his enemies."

He paused, letting his words settle in.

"You left Azbar for a reason. You followed us *for a reason*. You know this man, or at least know his kind, and I don't imagine it takes much for you to sum up what this new Kayle is capable of, what he will do if left unchecked."

Another pause. Then he asked the question.

"Will you help us?"

The last time the Priest has asked this of him, Raz had turned him down, summoning every reason he could to convince himself that he was not suited for what Brahnt wanted from him. He'd insisted he was of more value in Azbar, where he could champion the people of the city and keep his charges safe.

Now, though, the Koyts were dead, and the people he had been trying so desperately to shield from the cruelty of the world had cheered along with Quin Tern when Arrun's head had rolled across the frozen mud and snow of the pit floor.

This time, Raz just nodded.

VIII

It was two days before Raz could get out of bed on his own again, and another two before he was well enough to travel. He'd insisted he was fine as soon as he'd been able to stand but—to his surprise—it was Carro al'Dor who had shouted him down.

"You'll be fine when *I* say you're fine, and not a damned second before," the man had told him fiercely, shoving him back onto the edge of the bed unceremoniously. "In the meantime, sit down, shut up, and let us take care of that wound."

As big as the Priest was, he was still an easy head shorter than Raz. Still, Raz had allowed him do as he insisted, letting the man clean the laceration, apply the ointments he and Eva prepared, and cast his healing spells before packing it with clean bandages.

Some fights, Jarden Arro had once said long ago, *are best avoided.*

By the time the fifth day rose a grey dawn, dark clouds lumbering threateningly over the world like angry giants of smoke and wind, Raz was sick enough of being cooped up that he would have set off *on foot* if someone had given him so much as the opportunity. Fortunately, there turned out to be no need. Tana Atler's Priests and Priestesses had claimed the mercenaries' horses from the city guard as reward for the Laorin's intervention, stabling them around the back of the temple. Raz watched through his bedroom window as al'Dor went about prepping the animals for their departure, foggy breath billowing out from beneath the white hood he'd pulled over his mane of beaded blond hair. The Priest had been at it for the last half-hour, lashing everything from food to bedding to rope and spare clothes off either side of three saddles.

Water was the only thing he didn't pack. There was never any shortage of snow to melt along the road.

"You're sure you won't come with us?" Raz asked aloud.

From her place beside him, Eva nodded her head, also looking down at al'Dor's warped form through the cheap glass.

"I've got a place here," she said. "And Sven is going to need help going underground. Can't assume the sellswords will rot for too long in the city lockups, and when they get out they'll be after blood."

Raz only grunted in reply, not convinced.

Eva smiled. "I'll be fine." She reached up to rest a hand on the bandages over his left shoulder. "And it's not like you need me anymore to take care of you out there."

Raz said nothing again. It was true, despite his reservations. Once the infection that had slowly been eating away at him had been eradicated, his body had responded with its usual fervor. The wound in his back was still tender, but raw pink flesh had replaced the hole the West Isler Sury Atheus had carved into him with his narrow blade.

Raz doubted he would ever be rid of the scar, but it beat the alternative.

Still, he was far from fighting fit just yet. The healing muscle was stiff and sore, and he still had trouble moving his left arm without significant pain throughout his back. He kept it in a black cotton sling, tied behind his neck like a necklace, and had had to suffer the indignity of relying on Eva for help getting his shirt and cloak on for the past two mornings.

"It's not *me* I'm worried about," Raz finally said, still watching the Priest laboring away below. "Ystréd isn't as safe as you think. If even half of what the Priests say is true, then falling across the path of this 'Baoill' character will be trouble."

"And *if* he shows up at our doorstep, I'll find a way to sneak away, just like the good little fugitive I am," Eva said, looking around and flashing him an exaggerated smile.

Raz turned to glare down at her intently, wanting to make her realize how little amusement he found in the possibility of the Kayle's arrival at the city gates.

It didn't work.

"Relax," the woman said, patting him on the shoulder before letting her hand fall. "In this weather it will be months before he could make it this far south. Just like it will be months before I can leave. Even *if* I planned on running—and I don't—what good would it do me? Where am I supposed to go?"

"North. With us. As I've been telling you for four days."

"And for four days I've been telling you I won't leave. So stop trying." Eva looked up at him, then, her eyes softened. "I have people here who need me. And, in a lot of ways, I need them. I can't just leave."

The words hit Raz hard, but he didn't let her see it. They summarized everything he had told Brahnt when he'd first refused to leave Azbar.

He didn't like it, but he understood.

An hour later, Raz stepped back out into the cold for the first time in days, Eva at his side and Ahna—her blades hidden in their usual leather sack—thrown over one shoulder. A heavy traveling bag filled with his armor and other weapons hung from her end. He marveled as always—and as he seemed incapable of stopping himself from doing—at the bite of the air. The chill had deepened even in the week he'd been unconscious and recuperating, but beneath the heavy sown furs a few of the temple's more talented seamstresses had put together for him, he hardly felt it. The thick, tan and brown pelts spilled heavily across his shoulders, falling around him and making Raz feel rather like a moving, furry hill. They covered him nearly completely, even hiding—when his hands were by his side—the clawed steel fingers of his gauntlets, the only gloves any of them had been able to find that fit him.

Jerr's work continued to remain unparalleled.

The Laorin had done much better than just providing him with the massive mantle, though. They'd fashioned him boots, of a sort, more furs bound in thick leather, which shielded his shins and feet a great deal better than the makeshift wraps he'd made of his old cloak that had barely kept his toes from falling off on his feverish ride north. His claws protruded from slits in the skins, and the bottoms of the boots had been stitched together with the paw pads of some larger animal, hopefully improving his purchase on ice and snow. He'd have to watch where he stepped, and try to keep the insides as dry as possible, but the boots were a fine gift, and when Raz had received them he'd given Atler an appreciative nod, which the High Priestess returned in kind. It softened a little of the budding apprehension Raz was beginning to feel, knowing now where their true destination was.

Cyurgi' Di, the High Citadel, the greatest pillar of Laorin faith in the world.

A place Raz didn't expect to find many kindred spirits…

"Ready, lad?"

Raz turned back to the open double doors of the temple to see al'Dor standing in the opening, one last pack thrown over his shoulder. Behind him, Brahnt was sharing a few finals words with Atler, leaning heavily on his staff as always.

In answer, Raz nodded to the Priest. He was turning to face Eva again, intent on imploring her one final time to come with them, when the woman wrapped her arms around his waist, squeezing him tight.

"Safe travels, you," she mumbled into the furs. "And thank you. For everything."

"I think that's *my* line," Raz said with a chuckle, easing Ahna against the nearby wall so he could return the hug with his good hand.

"Maybe," Eva said, pulling away and wiping her eyes with the back of her glove before smiling up at him. "But, I never really got to say it the last time, and I think I owed you the favor anyway."

Raz returned the smile, reaching up to put his clawed right hand on her head, pushing it about in a brotherly fashion.

"Take care of yourself," he said. "Stay safe."

Eva nodded, but said nothing more as Raz turned away to face the road. al'Dor was watching him expectantly, the bag he'd been carrying already hanging from the side of the saddle of his hefty grey mare. From the temple, the *thump* of steel on wood came, and Brahnt joined them outside.

69

"Best we're off," he said to Raz as he passed. "I can't pretend we haven't delayed too long already. Have you said your farewells?"

"Yes," Raz said, not looking back at Eva as he retrieved Ahna from her place on the wall and heaved her and the bag back onto his shoulder. "Lead the way."

Brahnt did so, limping out into the road until al'Dor met him, taking the High Priest's free arm and helping him to the brown spotted mare beside his own mount.

The last animal remaining stood separate, and was a far cry different from the docile pair the Priests had selected for themselves. A massive black stallion, maybe seventeen hands tall, it snorted temperamentally as Raz looked over at it, meeting his eye defiantly, daring him to approach. Raz had rarely seen a specimen of the same size, and only then as sleek creatures of preened elegance, kept as badges of luxury by some of the wealthier clients—and targets—he'd had in Miropa. It stomped and hoofed at the ground, shaking its great head and bobbing it up in down in challenge.

"Had to trade for that one," Atler said, stepping out of the temple last to stand beside Raz. "Wasn't hard, actually. Apparently no one wanted to go near him."

"Wonder why," Raz muttered sarcastically. He'd just taken a step towards the horse when Atler stopped him.

"Arro, a moment," she said. Raz turned to look back at her, but the woman wasn't watching him. Instead, her eyes were on Brahnt and al'Dor, the latter boosting the former up into his saddle.

"I need you to understand something," she said, still not taking her eyes off the pair. "Talo has told me enough of your story to convince me you bare no ill intentions towards him or any of our faith, but I'm not so convinced that your presence among us won't bear poor results regardless. That man"—she indicated Brahnt with a tilt of her head—"is arguably the most important leader of our people, and therefore the most important part of the Laorin's stand against Baoill, and all men like him."

At last, she turned to Raz.

"I need you to understand," she said again, "that you don't just travel with a man of importance. You travel with a man who *understands* evil, who has lived it, breathed it. Many of our faith—myself included, I'm afraid—have led sheltered lives. The Laorin are powerful, it's true. We have numbers, magic and influence. But we have no *plan*, no greater purpose beyond spreading His word and His light to those in need. Talo does, or at the very least has the ability to marshal the faith and the valley towns to *some* purpose, whatever it may be."

She took a deep breath, as though attempting to conquer some fear. "If Talo was willing to wait so long, to sacrifice so much precious time to have you with him, I have to believe there is a reason. Still... please... understand what I am telling you. Understand what he is. And understand that you are a danger to him."

"I know."

The response took Atler by obvious surprise, but Raz didn't let her cut in as he continued.

"I do understand," he said, also watching the Priests as Brahnt successfully swung his bad leg over the saddle. "Maybe I don't yet appreciate the full value he has to you—much less to the North as a whole—but I'm certainly aware that my presence around him and al'Dor isn't conducive to their safety. Miropa still has a bounty on my head, not to mention whatever the council of Azbar has probably thrown into the pile by now. I would be surprised if we so much as manage to get out of the city without any trouble."

His gauntleted hand tightened around Ahna's handle reflexively. "And yet, he wants me with him. I'm not sure to what end, or honestly what sort of help I can be in whatever shit storm it is he's riding the three of us into, but I believe as you do: there is a reason. I may not know what it is—hell, I'm not convinced *he* knows what it is—but it's there, carved out either by my gods or yours."

He held the High Priestess' gaze firmly, letting her see the resolution there. "I am part of this now, despite either of our reservations, and I don't think there's anything to be done but wait and see how the cards fall."

Atler's face turned somber at that. "His life is worth more than yours," she said, her voice hardening. "And you owe it to him, if it comes to that."

Raz nodded once. "If it comes to that."

Then he stepped away from the woman, neither glancing back at her nor at Eva over his other shoulder, and made for the stallion.

The animal watched him approach almost imperiously, one dark eye taking him in as Raz moved in a slow arch around it, careful to stay in easy view the entire time. When he stood fifteen feet from its right shoulder, he eased Ahna and his pack down to the ground.

Then, careful to stay low and as small as he could manage, he edged forward, slowly advancing until he was only a few feet away from the horse. As it dragged an iron shoe over the ground in warning, Raz worked his right gauntlet off awkwardly with his left hand—a tough job given the sling. When he managed it, he reached out, leaving his bare palm up, and waited.

It was several seconds before the stallion showed any interest, and another long few before it made its move. In that time Raz could feel the cold and wind start to numb his long fingers, digging down to the bone, but he suffered the discomfort. His patience paid off when the horse turned towards him, taking a few plodding steps in his direction to snort at his scaled skin, first from a little distance, then closer as it made out nothing threatening.

"Good man," Raz said in a soothing voice—or as soothing as his voice could get. "That's it. We can be friends, can't we?"

The horse—as horses are like to do—ignored him. Instead it kept snuffling at his hand, then at the furs hanging over him. As it moved up his arm Raz reached out to carefully place a few fingers on the bulge of the stallion's shoulder. When it didn't protest, he slowly slid his palm down the animal's hide, going with the grain of the hair.

Eventually he made it up the horse's neck and mane, until finally his hand was petting along the dark ridge of its muzzle.

"Good man," Raz said again to the now-calm animal.

After that it took a little effort for him to figure out how to mount one handed, but he managed, finally balancing Ahna and his things precariously across the saddle before putting one foot in the stirrup and heaving himself up using the pommel. Once he settled, the dviassegai now balanced more comfortably across his lap, he took hold of the reins and turned the stallion about.

Brahnt and al'Dor were both waiting for him, looking on with bemused expressions.

"Problem?" he asked, heeling over to them.

al'Dor shook his head. "Just surprised to see you handle a horse so well."

"We were betting what part of you the thing was going to take a chunk out of first," Brahnt joked, grinning.

Raz managed to give them a crooked smile in return. "Rhen said the same thing when she got me out of Azbar. You forget I spent my childhood with the desert caravans of the Cienbal. I could break and ride you two into the ground, if it came to it."

"Let's hope it doesn't," al'Dor grumbled, eyeing Raz's stallion as it huffed at his mare.

Then, with nothing more than a last grateful incline of his head in Atler and Eva's direction, the Priest turned his mount about and started west down the road. Brahnt paused long enough to raise a hand in farewell to the two women and shout his thanks before kicking his horse into a trot to catch up with his partner.

Raz took the longest, unable to help himself from looking back at Eva. He had no other words for her, and nor—it seemed—did she for him. Still, it was a long moment before he raised his own hand, watching her return the gesture with a sad smile.

Then Raz wheeled the stallion about, urging it down the road with a flick of the reins and a shouted "*hyah!*"

"Gale."

The name came to Raz not long after, riding in silence between the two Priests, and he wasn't sure he'd meant to say it out loud. Still, both men turned inward to look at him. al'Dor looked a little confused, but Brahnt seemed to know where Raz's head was at.

"The horse?" he asked, and Raz nodded.

"It was the name of my father's horse, when I was a boy," he said, passing the reins to his bad hand long enough to pat the side of the stallion's neck. "The beast I learned to ride on, in fact."

"*That* must have been a sight," al'Dor chuckled, surprising Raz with the humor.

Apparently getting back on the road was doing much to lift the man's spirits.

"It was," Raz said. "Apart from the fact that Gale was hell-bent on not having a scaly little bastard like me on his back, Father always said I had about as much interest in riding as 'the sands did in turning to snow.'" He laughed. "Oh, the irony…"

"What was your father's name?" Brahnt asked him. "I never found out."

"Agais," Raz told him at once, amazed when he realized this was, perhaps, the first time he'd spoken the name aloud in years. "My mother was Grea, and my sister was Ahna."

"Ahna?" al'Dor asked curiously as they took a corner between the buildings. "Ahna, as in…?"

He let the question hang in the air between them, glancing down at the dviassegai's hidden blades, suspended over the cobblestone as the haft remained balanced across Raz's thigh.

"The very same," Raz said, pulling Gale back to fall in behind the Priests as they entered the more trafficked lanes of the main fairway, which would take them straight to Ystréd's west gate.

He thought al'Dor may have mumbled something in response to this revelation, but ignored it, preferring to keep the good-natured Priest he was seeing for the first time to the stern and anxious man he'd been dealing with over the last few days. Raz also decided it was time to focus on other things as, looking around, he watched their presence being noted by the crowd of riders, pedestrians, and beggars that ringed them on all sides.

Brahnt had assured him that getting to the gate wouldn't be an issue, so long as he stuck close to them. Sure enough, no one seemed inclined on bothering their party as they clopped along down the road, moving with the crowd. Indeed, while most of the eyes that peered in their direction were first drawn to Raz, poorly hidden despite the heavy furs, it was only briefly. Then the stares would shift, flicking between Brahnt and al'Dor, often lingering on the black line along the back of the High Priest's white cloak before looking away again.

Influence, Raz thought, remembering what Atler said and impressed by the deference. In truth, while he could begrudgingly admit to himself that he had developed a certain esteem for the Priests—particularly Brahnt—Raz had never seen much to indicate the Laorin held any sort of sway in the North. Azbar had been his only example to go by but—seeing this new response to the white robes—the people of that particular city were rapidly proving poor models for how most of the populace reacted to the Laorin. Indeed, some of the people milling about them made it a point to press closer to al'Dor and Brahnt, reaching out to touch their horses and legs as they passed, and smiling as the men rapidly traced a sort of half circle and horizontal line across their foreheads, like a rising sun.

Fortunately, the masses seemed smart enough to give Raz a wide berth.

It continued like this, the three of them moving at a crawling pace, for nearly half a mile. At last, just as Raz was starting to feel a familiar headache return as the people pressed in on all sides, the gate came into view. It was a sad thing, more of a glorified hole in the low ten-foot wall than anything else, but it served its current purpose well enough. People came and went from either side of the road, and as they got closer Raz made out a trio of men in uniform directing the traffic with practiced signals, controlling the comings and goings that were undoubtedly spiking with the temporary taming of the winter storms.

When one the guards caught sight of *him* though, his signals stopped, and he froze.

It was then that Raz started to feel uneasy. He watched the man as they approached, keeping one eye on him and only barely listening to Talo's and Carro's exchanges on either side. The guard went back to his duties, but he couldn't seem to help glancing around every few seconds, as though to make sure Raz was still making his way along the road.

Raz's suspicions came to fruition just as he and the Priests reached the gate, making to follow the wagon that had fallen in in front of them. The guard he had been eyeing stepped across their path sharply, blocking their way to the rolling snow-covered hills that could be seen beyond the wall.

"Halt!" the man shouted, throwing one hand up and placing the other on the hilt of his sword. "You, biggun"—he pointed a finger at Raz—"show yerself. *Now.*"

"Is that really necessary?" Brahnt asked in reply from slightly in front and to the left of Raz, his horse sidestepping nervously at the sudden stop.

"What's going on?" One of the other guardsmen—an officer, judging by the metallic patch on his shirt—had walked over to see what the fuss was about. "Wetts, why are these people stopped?"

Then he noticed what little of Raz's face wasn't hidden beneath the hood of fur mantle, and his eyes grew wide.

"Sir, it's *him*," the guard called Wetts said unnecessarily, his voice pitching into an excited squeak, his eyes never leaving Raz's. "It's him. It's the Monster!"

Though the travelers around them had certainly already been aware of Raz's presence among their throng, the energy that had been tempered by Brahnt and al'Dor's places on either side of him was quickly rising with the guard's blatant audacity. Whispers soon built into shouts, and everywhere people were craning up on their toes to see what was happening, or else peering around wagon covers and over high carts.

"Lieutenant," Brahnt spoke to the officer, obviously having a better understanding of the patch on his breast than Raz did, "this doesn't concern the city guard. My *friend*—" he said the word pointedly, accenting it with a gesture towards Raz so that there was *absolutely* no mistaking the line Wetts and his commander were toeing "—travels with me on Laorin business, and makes for Cyurgi' Di."

The name of the Citadel drew more whispers from the crowd, if less than Raz's byname had. Through the hum of a hundred voices, Raz made out several mentions of "High Priest" and "Talo Brahnt" and even "Lifetaker…"

To his credit, the lieutenant seemed to keep a good head on his shoulders, and after a moment's hesitation he nodded.

"Move along," he said briskly, stepping aside and waving them through. "Wetts, get out of the way."

The younger guardsman looked almost horrified, whipping around to look at his commander.

"Wha'? But there's fifteen *thousand* gold on his head!"

Most unfortunately the idiot didn't bother to keep his voice down, and Raz felt a wave of furor welling up in the crowd, a sudden, boiling hunger erupting from what had been nothing more than awe and curiosity. Almost instinctively he reached back down for Ahna's shaft, wondering in the back of his mind how long he would last, one-handed against a mob of hungry and greedy peasants.

"I said *move*, Wetts," the lieutenant snarled, fixing the man with an angry glare.

For a moment, Wetts looked on, stunned. Then, finally, he stepped aside, red in the face.

"My thanks," Brahnt said to the officer, tipping him an appreciative gesture with one hand, after which he kicked his horse between the two men and on through the gate.

Raz was next, but he urged Gale through more slowly, keeping a subtle eye on Wetts, who stood to his right. The man's hand had never left the hilt of his sword, and he seemed to be building himself up for something, staring at the ground with wide eyes and shaking like he were trying to draw every ounce of strength and bravery from the deepest part of his soul.

Raz knew what the man was going to do, even if Brahnt and the lieutenant didn't. Therefore, when Wetts ripped the blade from its sheath and leapt forward at him, howling like a madman, he almost sighed in exasperation.

Twisting Ahna's haft in his hands and throwing her weight forward with a quick shift of his hips, the blunt side of her heavy steel end caught the guard beneath his raised arm. The blow certainly didn't kill him, but it launched him sideways, causing the man to career into Gale's muscled shoulder.

The stallion barely seemed to notice.

"Raz, *no!*" Brahnt shouted, and Raz heard the High Priest's mare whinny as she was brought about.

"Relax, old man," Raz growled back calmly, letting Ahna's weighted tip slide to the muddy ground as he threw a leg off his saddle. "I'm not gonna hurt the idiot."

He noted both Brahnt and al'Dor's silence as he stepped down, feeling his claws and boots find good grip despite the slush. Moving around Ahna's diagonal haft, he squatted down beside Wetts, who seemed to have been dazed by his collision with the horse. He was having trouble pushing himself into a sitting position, his eyes a little lost until they took in Raz's form so close to him.

Letting his dark red wings peek out several feet to either side of him beneath the mantle, Raz spoke.

"Listen here, shit-for-brains." Raz picked up the man's sword with his good hand, lifting it out of the mud. "I'm hurt, I'm tired, and I'm out of patience when it comes to every crook and two-bit fool who thinks my head is their ticket to wealth and glory."

He flipped the sword over in his hand and, aiming carefully, drove half the blade into the hard earth, right between Wett's sprawled legs, inches from his groin.

"I've killed a dozen bastards for every time you've pissed the bed," Raz snarled, slowly pulling the hilt of the sword sideways, careful not to show so much as a flicker of the strain it took. "I've cut and sliced and murdered my way through more men and women than I think your dull little mind is able to fathom. *So*, next time you decide you want a shot at taking me on"—there was the tinkle of cracking metal—"think better of it."

The iron sword broke with a pinging screech, scattering silvery shards in the muck and leaving the better part of the blade buried in the mud.

Getting to his feet, Raz tossed the hilt of the weapon aside and turned around, fearing no reaction from Wetts as he did. The guard was practically catatonic, wide eyes on shattered metal protruding from the ground not a half a hand from the seam of his pants. As Raz took hold of the pommel, pulling himself up awkwardly back into the saddle, he wrinkled his snout at the sudden stench.

Ironically, the man had wet himself.

"A bit much, wouldn't you say?" al'Dor asked him under his breath, passing his mare around Gale and reaching out to help Raz pull Ahna back across his lap.

"Not in the least." Raz shook his head, then tilted it over his shoulder to indicate the thick line of people and draft animals behind them. "We weren't so far off from being the center of some *very* unfortunate attention. Now look at them."

The Priest's brows creased, and he looked around. The palpable aura of greed Raz had felt had cooled as suddenly as it had arisen, and it must have shown in the shocked and frightened faces of the people, because al'Dor's eyes went wide.

"I thought you'd prefer scare tactics to my… uh… usual methods," Raz said with a shrug as the man returned his attention to the road, both of them heeling their mounts into trots, approaching Brahnt side by side.

There was a moment in which al'Dor looked at him thoughtfully, the sudden wind of the outside world kicking the braids of his blonde hair and beard about his face.

Then he smiled and, without a word, reached out to clap Raz once on the back before spurring his horse into a half gallop along the cleared north road.

IX

"While it is generally believed that the wars of 861 and 862v.S resulted in a total forfeiture of peace between the valley towns and mountain clans, this is one of those facts sadly so often 'lost to history.' Indeed, while the burning of Metcaf and Harond certainly took their toll on many potential truces at the time, the treaties previously established by the Laorin Priestess Syrah Brahnt—perhaps best known for her mitigating influence on the Dragon of the North—were used as templates by the Peacekeeper over the next decade, eventually manifesting into the near-total integration of the valley and tribal cultures."

—*The North: Ancient Tradition and Culture*, by Agor Kehn

They arrived, like shadows of the falling snow itself, melting out of the trees in one uniform, semicircular line. Syrah saw the goat skulls of the Gähs, the reddened faces of Amreht, painted in animal blood, and the scarred cheeks and pierced noses of the Kregoan. She also saw a few white-painted foreheads of the Sefi, the heavy necklaces of human bones that adorned the necks of the Velkrin, and a scattering of other tribal markers she didn't recognize.

She suspected the worst, though, when a small pack broke off from the rest of the Kayle's vanguard, wading quickly through the shin-deep snow. Syrah and her small retinue of Priests and Priestesses stood in a defensive staggering at the base of the mountain pass, below a long strip of white cloth that whipped and snapped on its birch pole in the indecisive wind of the blizzard.

Her fears were confirmed as the mountain men grew closer, and she saw that they bore no other markings than the bones and beads entwined in their thick hair and beards.

Sigûrth, she thought, succeeding in masking the chill that ran down her spine as the men stopped half-a-dozen paces away. Several of the ten others on either side of her didn't fare so well at keeping their composure. She heard whispering mounting around her, and Priest Derro—the viperous coward—even took a step back in fright.

Her job was only getting harder by the second, she realized.

For a long time only the creak of trees and the fluctuating shriek of the storm against the mountain broke the tense silence between the two parties. When it threatened to become a full minute, Syrah decided it was time to speak.

"Ahd, vér üd'gen," she greeted them in their own tongue. *"Garros es dü Kayle."*

Hail, honored guests. Glory be to your king.

She had hoped—no, *expected*—the formal, honorary salute to at least draw the appropriate formal response, as was custom among the tribes. It was considered a near-unparalleled insult not to acknowledge the greeting of another man or woman, an insult reserved only for cowards and blasphemers.

And, so, when Syrah received nothing but the glare of cold eyes from beneath wind-twisted hoods thrown up against the snow, she knew exactly where she stood.

Regardless, after long seconds she decided to try again.

"*Ka vred es üi-karyn?*" she asked them with a polite smile. "*Üi-trebs nast brán dü.*"

What brings you to our mountains? My people have drawn no blood from you.

That brought something out of the Sigûrth. One man, at the very center of the group, grabbed the individual next to him by the back of the neck and forced him abruptly to his knees. Then he squatted beside the kneeling figure, pale blue eyes never leaving Syrah's as he murmured into his ear and reached out to pull the hood from the other's head.

"Lifegiver's mercy..." Syrah heard Priest Loben gasp from somewhere to her left.

The face beneath the hood, Syrah realized, was not that of a Sigûrth. It wasn't even that of a tribesman. Rather, it was a gaunter, lighter face with the narrow tendencies of the valley towns. The man's hair and beard were long and dark, beaded with wood, bone, and metal in the same fashion as those standing around him. There was, however, one great difference. A solid loop of thick, silvery steel that wound all the way around his neck, heavy and etched with patterns all too familiar to Syrah.

They were the same etchings that decorated the staffs she and the others were currently without...

"Laor's mercy..." someone else gasped from behind her. "He's a bloody *Priest.*"

Before anyone could say anything more, though, the captive Priest began to speak.

"My name," he rasped out in a broken voice, "is Egard Rost. I was once a Priest of Laor, as you are. A man of the cloth, residing in the temple of Harond. Now I have seen the brighter light, and have abandoned my false faith in favor of a greater devotion and truth. Them of Stone crafted the world in their great hands, just as they crafted the men of the mountains from rock and ice, making them stronger than any other."

As Egard Rost spoke the words, Syrah could hear the shivering in his voice, an anguished sort of shake that had nothing to do with the cold.

"I now act," Rost continued loudly as the storm picked up, kicking the loose snow around them in gusts, "as the voice of my lord and master, the mighty Kareth Grahst, warrior beyond all others, and cousin to the Kayle himself, greatest leader of men."

The former Priest nearly choked on the words, but kept going. "It is my master's first wish that your Witch"—he indicated Syrah with a hand—"be made silent, and cease to befoul the word of the Gods with her wicked tongue. It is then my master's second wish that you all"—he gestured at the line as a whole—"take a willful knee to him, and accept servitude in exchange for your lives."

Syrah bristled at that.

"'In exchange for our lives'?" she demanded in the Common Tongue, barely keeping the fury from her voice as she continued to glare at the man called Kareth Grahst, whose eyes had still never left hers. "We meet here, beneath a flag of truce, and this *brute*"—she waved an angry hand at the Sigûrth—"has the gall to speak of murder?"

There was a brief pause as Rost translated the words back to Grahst over his shoulder. The mountain man smiled cruelly, putting a big hand on the back of Rost's neck and whispering a response in his ear.

Still not once looking away from Syrah.

"We do not recognize your flag, Witch," Rost yelled over the wind. "We do not recognize your rights, your customs, and we certainly do not recognize the frail deity you so pathetically kneel before. We are men of the Stone Gods, and your beliefs mean little and less to us."

Syrah felt her temper boil at the words, but she forced herself to stay calm. She was not there to stoke the fires of this aggression, after all, despite the fact that every fiber of her being seemed to be urging her to do so. She'd come with a purpose, and had every intention of seeing it to the end, suffering any abuse along the way.

With stressed determination she stepped forward, weaving her fingers into a rapid rune before pulling at the collar of her robes to drag them down her neck. There was the barest pulse of white, and when next she spoke Syrah felt her words rip painfully from her throat, magnified tenfold so as to be clear to every man and woman within a hundred yards.

"*Why have you come?*" she began, speaking the mountain tongue, disregarding the irate grimaces on the Sigûrths' faces as she ignored Grahst's demands with obvious deliberation. Instead, she looked around at the others, the rest of the clansmen who stood in well-practiced formation around her. There were hundreds of them, possibly even as many as a half-a-thousand—she couldn't be sure through the snow and trees.

"*I do not ask this man'*—she nodded in Grahst's direction—"*why you have come, because I know his reasons. He comes with the hammer of war in hand, intent on nothing but the destruction of a people of peace. He comes desiring only blood and the spoils of battle, caring nothing of the cost of it, so long as he is satisfied. Do you think I mean my cost, though? Do you think I mean my home, my future, my life? No...."* Syrah shook her head, seeking the eyes of as many of the tribesmen as she could, from every clan she could make among them. *"Those learned among you will know that death does not carry the fear for me that it does for most men. My god is lord of all life, constantly tending to the circle of creation, replacing those of good heart, soul, and mind back into the world so as to continue bettering it for eternity. With my death comes only my rebirth and, so, I do not fear it."*

Syrah could only pray the bravado in her voice hid the quiver that might have revealed the lie for what it was.

"The cost I refer to is not one I must pay. It is not one of my faith, or my people. It is a cost you must pay, and have already begun to. I ask again: why have you come? Winter blooms in full, and yet you have left your wives to fend for themselves against the cold. The storms have come, and yet you have left your children to die, buried and forgotten beneath the snows. Why? Why, I ask you, have you abandoned your homes, deserted your lands, and forsaken your families?"

Now she was starting to hear a murmur from the warriors. An angry one. It wasn't the one she intended to leave them with, but it was the place she needed to start.

Anger often left the mind open to more penetrating suggestions.

"Is it because you chose to leave?" Syrah pressed on, still looking about. *"Is it because you desired war and blood and death? Did you wake one morning suddenly so riddled with a lust for the sword that you took arms with the first war-band you came across? Were you so intent on murder that you simply had no choice but to leave your people to their fate? ...I think not."*

She paused a moment, letting her words sink into the tribesmen, smiling internally as many angry faces became steadily confused. She began to touch on the resentment she hoped—by the Lifegiver—existed amongst some of them.

"You were not given a choice. You were not granted your right to refuse, to live life peaceably with your people. You were torn from that peace, friends. You were ripped from your beds, pulled from your homes and temples by a tyrant, a conqueror who deigned not offer any option but his sword, his army, and his goals."

Syrah narrowed her eyes, locking onto the gaze of one man in particular, an Amreht who stood flanked on either side by others of his clan. This man's face was pure fury behind streaked blood paint, and Syrah wasn't so sure it was directed at her anymore.

She had touched a nerve. She was getting somewhere.

"You fight. I understand that. You are men of the mountains. Men of battle and blood and of the Stone Gods. But who do you fight for? Who do you kill and die for? Is it for you? For your family, your friends? Or have you become nothing more than the edge of another's sword? Do you, men of the mountains, greatest of the world's warriors,

take pride in being wielded by another, like a borrowed ax or—worse yet—a stolen one?"

The reaction was almost palpable now, like the rumbling of a distant avalanche at the very edge of one's hearing. Among the Amreht it was greatest—Gûlraht Baoill's conquest of their tribe had been particularly brutal—but they weren't the only ones appearing to suffer discontent. Many of the Kregoan had dark looks on their scarred faces, and among the Sefi and the Velkrin—newest to have been brought into the fold—disquiet glances passed from warrior to warrior. Syrah was surprised, looking for their reaction, to see that only a few of the Goatmen remained, and many of those that did were in the act of slowly slinking back into the Woods while the Sigûrth had their backs turned.

As though reading signs of danger around them…

Syrah could barely gain control of the victorious grin that played at her lips as she watched her practiced words, rehearsed a hundred times with Jofrey, start to take their effect. The vanguard was crumbling, just as they'd hoped.

"We have come to you in peace, unarmed and unarmored, in the hopes of waking you into the reality of your bondage—no, your slavery. Your Kayle claims to want to take the North for his people, to seize the world for the good of the clans, and yet which of his acts prove him worthy of being the lord he claims? His burning of your homes? His butchering of your children? His conquering of your kin? You, the warriors of the mountains, have long practiced the tradition of taking prisoners as your slaves, returning them to the tribe to be distributed and put to task. Tell me, then… How is what has happened to you any different? You were challenged, beaten, and taken hostage. Yes, instead of a hoe or sewing needles you were handed your swords and axes and hammers. Yes, instead of the fields you were sent to war. And yes, instead of a steel collar"—she gestured to the metal ring around Egard Rost's neck—*"you were told to wear the symbols of your tribes with pride. But how, in the end, does it amount to anything different? How—?"*

'AAAAARRRRGH!'

Syrah's words were cut short by an anguished shriek of pain and horror. She stared, wide eyed, at the grouped Sigûrth men, as did every other soul within the clearing's boundaries. Taking advantage of Syrah's own call to observe the slave collar around the former Priest's throat, Kareth Grahst had decided to seize the opportunity to break the spell she was spinning with her words. The moment she had pointed out Rost, Grahst had pushed himself to his feet, pulled the man up by the back of his robes, and drawn a long broadsword from where it had been hidden beneath his furs on his hip.

Then, without a moment's pause, he'd run it through the man's lower back.

Rost screamed, twisting and thrashing in pain, slicing his own hand to the bone as he grabbed at the bloody blade protruding more than a foot out of his stomach. Grahst, after he was sure every eye was on the slave, withdrew the sword, then plunged it back in, this time forcing the steel through the lower part of Rost's gut.

Again and again Grahst impaled the man, metal penetrating flesh with a wet, sucking *sthuck* each time, careful not to pierce lung or diaphragm so as to ensure Rost would keep screaming. Again and again he ran him through, shoving the sword between skin and bone and muscle with such savage fury that soon the front of Rost's abdomen was a tattered mess, too damaged to hold his entrails and organs in, and they began to spill out even through what was left of his shirt and fur cloak. Grahst had stabbed the man at least a half dozen times before he finally stopped screaming, and it was another three before he stopped moving altogether. When this happened, Grahst threw the body to the ground and fell to one knee beside it, grabbing the twitching man's hair with his free hand and lifting the sword high with the other.

With two savage chops, blood flicking across the settling snow in scattered lines, Grahst severed Egard Rost's head as he lay dying in the snow.

Throughout this entire ordeal, Syrah had stood paralyzed, unable to so much as twitch a finger as she watched the murder. Around her the other Laorin—all as equally numbed by horrified fascination—had done the same. Like her, none of them had ever witnessed such barbaric cruelty. Syrah had seen death in her day. Terrible deaths. But those had been passings of illness and injury. Even working on both sides of the battle line between the valley towns and the Sigûrth, Syrah had never seen such gruesome and callous disregard for life as what Kareth Grahst had just forced them all to bear witness to.

And she had once seen Raz i'Syul Arro kill four men in as many breaths…

Someone—Syrah wasn't sure who—was vomiting behind her.

"The Sigûrth say you silent… you silent."

A cold, unlike anything Syrah had ever known, washed down her back at the words. Kareth Grahst spoke the Common Tongue with a deep, booming tenor which carried over the wind, his words broken and heavily accented. He was getting back on his feet, attempting to wipe away some of the blood splattered across his face with the back of his sword hand as he did, Rost's head in the other.

And he was still smiling.

"You silent," Grahst repeated, starting in her direction, "and you listen. Words, not enough. Bravery, not enough. The White *Wyth* takes the Sigûrth's traditions, takes the Sigûrth's life ways. The White *Wyth* comes, tells Sigûrth to bow to the *vrek*"—he spat the slur the mountain men had for the people of the valley towns even through curved lips—"tells them bow must, or death. Tell them to peace make, or death. *Wyth* speaks of dying children, dying families, dying tribes. But words, not enough."

No more than two strides away, the Sigûrth tossed Egard Rost's head at Syrah's feet.

"Blood, enough."

Syrah forced herself not to look down, forced herself not to imagine the scream that must be frozen into Rost's pale, narrow features. Instead she held Grahst's gaze, praying so hard to the Lifegiver for the strength to keep doing so that she was amazed no one could hear her pleas.

"I came to your lands as a servant of your people," she said firmly, lifting her head proudly despite the shake in her legs. "It was my wish to see them through the freeze, nothing more. If the 'bowing' you're referring to is a reference to the late Kayle accepting the help from—"

"SPEAK OF EMREHT, YOU WILL NOT!"

Syrah stopped abruptly, surprised as, for the first time, Grahst lost his smile. The confident, leisurely grin was suddenly replaced by a snarl of fury, twisting his blood-smeared, bearded face into a wrathful, wide-eyed glare.

It took Syrah a moment to make the connection.

"Grahst..." she said slowly, the realization dawning on her. "Grahst... You're his *son*!"

The smile returned to the mountain man's face, but it was as hard and cold as the stone of the stairs behind Syrah and her entourage.

"Son, his," he confirmed with a nod. "My *haro*, Emreht Grahst was, for shame of it."

"Shame?" Syrah demanded, feeling the anger seethe again within her. "*Shame*? You stand here, in the shadow of the man who butchered your father for his crown, spreading his evil and misery and chaos, and you have the balls to accuse *Emreht* of acting shamefully? It was your father's decisions that allowed you to survive the last freeze, Grahst. It was his level-headedness—largely lacking in his offspring, it seems—that stopped the bloodshed for the first time in hundreds of years. Emreht didn't like it, but he did what was needed of him to ensure the safety and strength of his people. He was a true leader. He was a—"

"*Welkin*," Grahst finished for her, obviously hard-pressed to keep the smile up. "Coward. Shame to Sigûrth. Shame to Gods of Stone. Shame to himself. Shame to family. We of Stone, not cowards. Not *welkin*. The storms, we survive. The winter—the *Kerr'ël*—we survive. Of the *vrek*, we need nothing. Emreht is shame."

"Fool," Syrah managed to say through clenched teeth. "Beast. Animal. The world has no use for men who seek nothing but violence when there could be harmony, war when there could be peace. You create your own hardships. You kill your own children."

"Children, then, not blessed," Grahst said with a shrug.

Syrah glowered at him for a moment, tempering her desire to fling faith at him, to pound Laor's will into his thick, dirty skull.

But shitting on their beliefs was not going to win her back any momentum in this fight.

"*You pray to hard gods, Kareth Grahst,*" she said finally, switching back to the tribal dialect. "*I can see why the men of Stone have been made so strong.*"

"*Cease your desperate flattery, Witch,*" one of the other Sigûrth shouted in turn. "*It won't save you now.*"

Grahst put a hand up without turning around, as though to silence the interrupter.

"*Indeea,*" he boomed, speaking in his native tongue as well. "*It is time to forgo your foolish hope of seeding our ranks with mutiny, woman. My men may not be traditionally 'loyal,' just as you suspect, but there are other ways to guarantee the obedience of even clans as vicious as the Amreht and Kregoan.*"

"*Bastara,*" Syrah snapped. "*What did you do?*"

"*Shall we just say,*" Grahst said with a wicked tilt of his head, hand still up in the air, "*that none of them want to discover that their children weren't blessed by the Gods...*"

Syrah felt her hands shake, though she knew her anger was only partially directed at the Sigûrth. She felt stupid, almost pathetic. Of *course* a man like Gûlraht Baoill would have crafted himself an insurance policy. His army was made of men who likely hated him. Of course he would guarantee himself a way to control them.

"Syrah?"

Syrah turned to see one of the Priestesses, Sehne, looking at her with terrified eyes, and she realized she'd been silent for several long seconds.

"Syrah... W-what is it?" the Priestess asked her shakily. "What is he saying?"

Syrah opened her mouth to answer, but no words offered themselves in adequate response.

"Nothing," she finally said, her eyes moving over the rest of her group. "At least nothing worth listening to. We're leaving. It's time we got word back to Jofrey. Get the others ready to—"

"*No.*"

Grahst's sharp interruption cut across Syrah's orders, and she half turned to look at him, frowning. The man was still smiling, but there was something infinitely crueler about the sudden glee in his face.

And he was still holding that damn hand up, like a child with a question...

"We're leaving," she said again, in his tongue this time, in case he'd misunderstood. *"You've made your point, and I've failed in making mine. The flag of truce guarantees us safe passage. We'll return to the Citadel, and you can freeze your bloody damn arse off down here until your master arrives."*

Grahst's face only stretched with further pleasure. *"You came into our homes, Witch, preaching of your god and his ways. You spat on our traditions, stomped on our beliefs. Our customs were nothing more than an annoyance to you, to be followed out of courtesy rather than any true respect. You treaded your muddy boots all over our culture, and yet you expect us to recognize your laws? Your formalities? HA."* The man's laugh was bitter and hard. *"No, Witch. No. Unfortunately for you, my 'master,' as you call him, would take great pleasure in making some points to you himself. I have my orders, and we already told you—"*

Syrah realized what was about to happen before the man had said the words, and she felt that cruel cold wash over her again as her eyes shot up to Grahst's raised hand in sudden realization.

"—we don't recognize your flag."

The hand dropped, chopping earthward in a signaling stroke.

"LOOK OUT!" Syrah yelled in the Common Tongue, whirling around. "BEHIND—!"

She didn't get to finish the sentence. There was a *thump*, and a dark form landed in front of her, cutting her off from the others and bulling her back with a narrow shoulder pauldroned by the skull of some feline animal. Syrah stumbled and tripped over the uneven ground beneath the snow, tumbling down and landing hard on her back. Scrambling onto her feet quickly, she rushed forward, back into the fray.

The Goatmen of Gähs, the scrawny wild men she'd thought had fled from Grahst's company at her spurring words, were dropping down from where they'd slunk up into the cliffs above them. With great leaps and howls of the hunt, an easy score of them rained upon the ten Laorin huddled together at the base of the pass, killing two before anyone had time to react, cut down by bone knives and stone-headed hatchets. One other—Loben, she thought—fell as Syrah shouted for *"STAFFS!"*, his scream cutting through the sudden din of the battle. Derro, at the center of the group, extended his arms before him and pulled his hands inward, as though coaxing some imperceptible form into a loose embrace. Then he thrust his open palms skyward.

From beneath the snow at their feet, ten steel staffs leapt upright to stand, momentarily suspended, throughout the chaos.

Syrah plucked hers out of the air, and years of training and skills coursed back into her limbs. Taking a running leap and pulsing a touch of magic into her back foot, she shot over the seven remaining Priests and Priestesses to land right in the middle of the Goatmen, taking them utterly by surprise. With a scream of rage she lifted her staff high, then drove it downward into the frozen earth, pouring as much power into the blow as she could manage.

A concussive blast rocked the air, blowing the snow in a ten-foot radius around Syrah away in a perfect circle. The Goatmen outside of that range stumbled and tripped, knocked about by the invisible discharge of force.

The half-dozen *inside* were thrown fifteen feet up and away by the shockwave.

Not waiting for her enemy to recover, Syrah pounced on the fallen men like a wolf among wounded animals. By the time the Gähs had recovered their footing she'd broken a jaw, an arm, and knocked one less fortunate out completely. Her staff twisted about in her hands like an extension of herself, working more like a lash of supple leather than the hardened steel of Cyurgi' Di's forges. It dealt out blows in rapid succession, forming a cage of silver around her that none of the thin, dirty men could penetrate. Every now and then she would summon up a little speck of light and throw it with precise deliberation out into the melee, looking to stun anyone that wore furs and bones. These spells the Gähs generally dodged with ease, but the magics kept the men on their toes and were getting more and more difficult to avoid as the other Laorin began to find the rhythm of battle around her. It wasn't long before the remaining Priests and Priestesses were joining Syrah to form a defensive ring, each protecting the others' backs.

They were only six, now...

But six was enough. About fifteen Goatmen still encircled them, their beady eyes peering through dirty hair. The mountain men howled like a pack as they circled in staggered directions, some around to the right, others to the left, and all alternatingly dashing in for feigned jabs at hands and legs and faces. It made for a confusing tactic, forcing the Laorin to watch every one of their opponents rather than just one at a time. Any wrong move would leave them exposed from some angle or another, and their precarious stalemate would shatter. Syrah felt herself start to sweat as she recognized the tactic. It was how the Goatmen hunted.

And she and the others had just become the prey.

"Watch for the rush," she said over her shoulder, just loudly enough to ensure that everyone could hear. "They're going to come all at once. Be ready."

No one said anything, but she heard the sound of shifting snow and muttered prayers as bodies tensed and magic was drawn from the ether. Syrah readied her own spells, feeling power course through her arms and legs, bolstering them for the fight. She could see the tension altering the

Gähs, see them shift slightly in preparation as if some silent signal was given.

They looked just about ready to pounce when howled words shattered the taut silence that had momentarily gripped the battlefield.

"DA BRÁN ED BRÚN!"

Syrah's attention snapped around, but too late. The Sigûrth, Kareth Grahst at their head, split through the ring of Gähs, the Goatmen leaping back and away at the warcry. The Laorin—having been too preoccupied with the immediate danger—were suddenly hit by the spearhead formation of a dozen true tribal warriors, steel flashing and teeth bared in violent excitement. They struck head on, trusting in the overwhelming force of their charge—and the sheer mass of their leather and fur-clad bodies—to carry through whatever the Priests and Priestesses could throw at them.

They weren't wrong.

Syrah felt her grip on the magics wink out as she lost her concentration, the casted strength she'd been building up in her body vanishing in an instant. At the same time, she saw Kareth bring his sword down on Sehne, the heavy blade smashing through her hastily raised block and catching her squarely in the head.

The woman's skull split with a *crack*, like a log under a woodsman's ax.

Rage and fear burned through Syrah, helping her find and draw from her gifts again in panicked heaves of power. She shot a trifecta of stunning spells at the Sigûrth even as she ducked under the horizontal swing of a heavy warhammer, and didn't see if they made their marks or not. Dodging a second swing, she tucked her staff under one arm and thrust the open palm of her other hand in the direction of her attacker, a massive man in black furs with a myriad of silver bangles in his blonde hair. It was a move Talo had drilled into her, and the practice yielded instant results. The blast that erupted from between Syrah's fingers caught the mountain man a direct blow, bowling him backwards and sending him tumbling and bouncing a half-dozen yards. Another man stepped in to replace the first, the paired hatchets he hefted in each hand already slick with the blood of some unfortunate or another. Syrah didn't have time to summon another spell before he was on her, and she had to dance out of the way, ducking, somersaulting, and spinning from under the Sigûrth's heavy blows. When she'd gained just enough distance to recover herself she shifted the momentum and met the man head on, surprising him with the abrupt change in pattern. Working this to her advantage, Syrah made quick work of the Sigûrth, breaking a wrist with a swift downward cross-strike before snapping her body back, reversing the staff up, right into the mountain warrior's temple.

Steel hit hair and bone with a *thunk*, and the man went stiff, toppling over sideways, out cold. Breathing heavily, Syrah turned towards the rest of the fight, looking to assist whatever comrades might still be left standing.

She didn't so much as get to take a step before she found Kareth Grahst himself blocking her way, his leering grin bearing down even as his blade snaked in—deftly handled despite his bulk—and dealt her a shallow slash across the ribs.

A blooming pain seared through the left side of Syrah's chest. She stumbled backwards, desperately avoiding another quick jab from Grahst's sword. The next one she parried away with her staff, and the next, but the fourth punched through her defenses, leaving her robes hanging loose at one shoulder where a narrow cut marked an upwards slant of weeping red across her collarbone.

Grahst, though, had no intention of letting up.

He worked her back relentlessly, nearly running her through when she tripped and scrambled to her feet as her heels found the first step up the pass. He kept his blade moving, dealing her superficial strikes when he could, but mostly just bearing his sword down on the steel of her staff as she frantically deflected his attacks. Syrah had always considered herself a good fighter, a natural combatant. She'd shamed most of her classmates in the Citadel, and held her own out in the world without much effort more than once.

Now, though, she saw for the first time what *true* skill was. Rather than talent and teaching, Grahst's bladework was the result of need and hardship, an expertise gained only from living by the sword since he was old enough to wield it. There was almost nothing she could do. Had he left her even a moment to recover she might have been able to blind him with a flash of magic, or blast the ice and snow out from under him, but Grahst was all too clearly aware of this. His attacks were preemptively relentless, a vicious series of cuts and thrusts that kept her attention completely devoted to blocking, dodging, and parrying his blade.

Syrah didn't know what scared her more, in that moment: the fact that the mountain man could have killed her a half dozen times already, or that he hadn't with obvious intent...

Their fight was a long, drawn out ordeal, with Syrah taking every opportunity she could to free a hand for a spell or sneak her staff in to deal her own counterblows. Each time she attempted either of these things, though, she was forced to take the defense once more as Grahst's strikes increased in speed and strength. Despite her training, her will, and what magic she'd managed to passively pull into her failing limbs, eventually Syrah felt fatigue set in. At first the burning pain in her shoulders and hands was slow to build, but before long she felt her reactions slowing, her blocks weakening. Eventually, the only thing left to happen did.

One slashing downswing, driven as hard as Grahst could manage, ripped the staff from Syrah's weak, numb hands to send it spinning and pinging down the stone stairs.

Quick paired blows to the shoulder and outside of her left thigh with the flat of the Sigûrth's blade took Syrah to the ground, sending her sprawling to her side in the snow. From there, she struggled to get up, her gasps billowing out like plumes of smoke as she fought to catch her breath, but another hit to her arm sent her down again with a cry.

Twice more she tried to rise, and twice more Grahst put her back on the ground.

It was only after she'd laid there for a time, her breast heaving and the exposed skin beneath her slashed robes burning against the wind and wetness of the snow, that Grahst bent down. Syrah screamed as his thick fingers entwined themselves in her white hair, pulling her forcefully up onto her knees. She clawed at the hand that held her up, feeling her scalp stretch to the point of tearing under the excruciating tension, and she screamed louder.

"SILENCE, WITCH!"

Syrah was thrown forward violently, Grahst shoving her back down the stairs he'd forced her up. She barely managed to get her hands out in front of her before she hit the stone, though she still felt her lip split and some jagged edge beneath the snow catch the flesh above her right eye, ripping through her brow. When she stopped tumbling, spilling out before the first of the steps, Syrah curled up, shivering and struggling with all that was left of her strength not to sob in pain, exhaustion, and fright.

There was the crunch of approaching feet over the ice, and Grahst's big hand took her by the already-tearing neckline of her white robes, half-lifting her from the ground.

"See for yourself," the Sigûrth breathed into her face, still grinning maniacally and sheathing his sword at his side as he squatted beside her, *"what your false god has given leave to. See for yourself what he has deemed a worthy end for his oh-so-noble warriors."* He grabbed her by the jaw, pinching the lower half of her face between thumb and fingers, and forced her head around.

Syrah's wretched shriek came out in an agonized moan through the man's hand.

There, at the base of the stairs, what was left of the Priests and Priestesses Jofrey had entrusted with guarding the mountain pass lay like a red stain on the whiteness of the world. Nothing moved among the remains except the vulturish Goatmen, darting from corpse to corpse in search of anything of value or interest. The sheer strength of the mountain men was evidenced by the scattered limbs, hands, and heads that lay around and within the area of the bodies, the trampled battlefield dyed with pooling and splattered blood. Few of the corpses were left intact, and even those were savaged and disfigured by great slashes and the ugly crush of bones that left faces unrecognizable. It looked rather like one of the Stone Gods themselves had reached out and struck the place where the Laorin had stood with some great hammer, smashing the bodies of the faithful beyond all recognition.

And then, as though in an effort to completely wipe their memory from the world, Syrah watched the falling snows rapidly begin to hide what was left of her companions from all mortal eyes.

"*Take their heads up the pass and throw them at the keep's gates!*" Grahst roared, releasing Syrah's face roughly and letting her slim, beaten form hang from one hand at his side as he pushed himself to his feet. "*Let them see what they can come to expect!*"

There was a unanimous roar of approval from the rest of the vanguard, even those hundreds not of the Sigûrth tribe, and the closest to the Laorin's corpses set about their orders with enthusiasm. Syrah found herself utterly numb, her head and arms hanging limply, her legs curled beneath her, refusing to follow her desperate desire for them to leap into action, to tear her away from Grahst's hold and fly her up the stairs, back to the safety of the Citadel.

Instead, she managed only to shed a single tear from her right eye, which stung as it trailed downward along her cheekbone, pulled sideways by the lopsided tilt of her head.

She felt Grahst's gaze fall once more upon her.

"*Now, White Witch,*" the man said, and she could hear his smile in his voice, "*let's see how long it takes us to strip you of that defiant pride of yours.*"

Then, raising his free hand, he dealt her a massive blow with the hard leather back of his gauntlet, and Syrah plummeted into darkness.

X

"I admit—with no small amount of shame—the cruel delight I experienced when I realized Raz i'Syul Arro's purpose among us. Our trust in the Lifegiver comes with the sacrifice of never—or at least never again—claiming another's life. To most this seems a small, trivial part of the vows, an afterthought of amusement associated with the absurdity of the notion. To most, Laor might as well have demanded that they never fly, or never breathe beneath the water, or never craft mountains with their bare hands. To a few, though, that sacrifice was larger. In Talo's case it was the ending of a chapter in his life, a final farewell to the Lifetaker and all his vicious glory. To others, it was a welcome abandonment, a forgoing of the ugliest—if fortunately only occasional—necessity of a hard life. For me, though… For me the vow to leave my hands unbloodied has been a much, much larger offering. It was a talent for murder, after all, that lent itself to the excitement of my youth. A gift for killing. The haggling over price, the hunt, the act… I lived for every moment of it. It was difficult, therefore, to give up that greatest part of myself when I discovered that with age sometimes came a conscience, and with a conscience came a burning, brutal desire for absolution.

And so, again, I admit my delight—and my shame—when I realized Raz i'Syul Arro's purpose among us."

—from the journals of Jofrey al'Sen

Jofrey sat for a long time in the semi-darkness of the High Priest's rooms, his head in his hands, his elbows leaning against the marbled pine surface of the L-shaped desk he sat behind. The council, gathered before him, stood in complete silence, having just heard his grave news and witnessed the bloody wicker baskets and their contents, provided as proof.

The reddish stains, black streaks in the dim light of the candles, still blemished the stone floor between the desk and the grouped Priests and Priestesses.

"What are we going to do?"

It was Aster Re'het, the youngest of the remaining council, who gathered the courage to ask the question, and it came out in an all too terrified whisper.

Jofrey gave her the only answer he could.

"Laor only knows."

For once, no one spoke a word in support or anger. Even Valaria Petrük and her lapdog, the deceptively bitter Behn Argo, had nothing to add to Jofrey's response, no scathing retorts to follow up with in quick succession. The contents of the baskets had banished all feuds from the chamber, sucked all grudges and bad blood away, at least for a time.

And all it took was the imminent threat on all our lives, Jofrey thought ironically, not looking up from the desk.

"You're certain Syrah wasn't among them?" Cullen Brern, the Citadel's master-at-arms, ventured to ask.

"I am," Jofrey said with a nod, finally lifting his head to meet their gazes. "Even those I couldn't identify lacked white hair. Whether that means she's been captured, or simply that there wasn't enough left of her to throw in a basket, I couldn't say."

"That's awfully callous, Jofrey," Kallet Brern said quietly from beside his brother. "Shouldn't we do something? Shouldn't we—?"

"Shouldn't we what, Brern?" Priest Argo cut in bitingly, finally seeming to find his voice. "Gather a search party? Send someone looking? You'll have about as much of a chance of success as you would suing the savages for peace! Brahnt is dead, and if she's not, we should all pray to the Lifegiver she isn't long for this world."

Ordinarily Jofrey would have silenced the man, but he had neither the energy nor the desire to do so. It so happened that he agreed with the angry old Priest—almost too enthusiastically, if truth be told—and it pained him deeply.

Among the mountain clans, the Sigûrth in particular were not known for treating their prisoners and slaves with anything close to what a civil soul would call dignity…

"Still…" old Benala Forn in turn spoke up from between the Brern brothers and Aster. "Is there nothing to be done? Send word to the valley towns, perhaps?"

"Syrah saw to that some time ago, and again more recently," Jofrey said with a sigh, reclining to rest against the back of his chair, finally looking up at the dark ceiling in thought. "Her first letters warned of the burning of Harond, and of Baoill's eastward march into the Arocklen. The next birds were sent no more than two weeks past, when word came from Ystréd's advanced scouts that the Kayle's armies hadn't pushed south through the tree line as we expected, but rather seemed to have continued deeper into the Woods…"

"Making for the pass…" Priest Elber finished, standing beside the chair that had been dragged back for Jerrom Eyr, the oldest of their party.

"Exactly," Jofrey said with a nod.

"Then there's nothing to be done." Petrük had, at last, recovered some of her coldness. "We have our reserves, and we can ward the gates. We'll outlast them. If they're committed to laying siege to the Citadel, it won't be long before their supplies run short, and they'll be forced to make a move. By then the towns will have gathered in force, and the whole ugly matter will be put to an end."

"Possible," Jofrey admitted with a shrug. "But unlikely. The tribes are accustomed to life in the ranges, where there is only ever little in the way of food. If provisions can be found in the Woods, the Kayle's men will find them, and make them last."

"Or they'll just start eating each other, as is undoubtedly their custom," Argo muttered quietly.

"As for the valley towns," Jofrey continued, ignoring the man, "I find I have little faith in the prospect of a rapid coalition of forces. Drangstek and Stullen's march north in the hopes of assisting Harond was one thing. The first two have close geographical and economic ties, the latter of which they shared with Harond and Metcaf, before their sackings. But Azbar's trade is mostly self-sufficient, and Ystréd is too far removed to have more than minimal interaction with the western towns. While the Kayle persists to show no deliberate interest in the continued razing of the North's remaining municipalities, I find it hard to believe any of the valley towns will be keen on doing anything more than hunkering down and taking advantage of the freeze to fortify their own defenses…"

There was a long silence as Jofrey's words rang true.

"Laor have mercy," Jerrom managed in a frail, breathy voice. "Laor have mercy on us all…"

"So then what *is* the plan?" Kallet asked, his voice tinged with frustration and the very beginnings of anger. "Are we meant to sit here, stuffed away in our halls and just—?"

BANG!

To a one, every member of the council jumped as the door to the chambers slammed open and a broad youth stumbled in, heaving and gasping. He'd clearly sprinted to reach them, and as Jofrey recognized the shoulder-length blond hair of his former acolyte, he instantly understood why.

"Reyn!" Cullen—the young Priest's superior in the practice chambers—exclaimed, fuming. "What in the *blazes* do you think you're doing? This is a meeting of council! Remove yourself, before—!"

Reyn Hartlet cut across his master without so much as sparing him a glance. "Is it true?" he demanded, his eyes only on Jofrey, shoulders shivering from the strain of the run and whatever emotions were crashing down on him. "Is it? Is she…? Is Syrah…?"

He left the question unfinished, unable to say the words. The Citadel's master-at-arms was about to berate him again, but Jofrey stopped him with a shake of his head.

"Leave him, Cullen," he said sadly. "Syrah is… important to him."

Cullen Brern fell silent, and Jofrey pushed himself to his feet.

"Reyn," he said quietly. "To answer you... We don't know. I don't want to offer you false hope, but I won't hide from you that Syrah wasn't among the dead left at the Citadel gates."

"So she could be alive!" Reyn exclaimed fiercely. "Syrah could be alive out there. She could need help. What's being done? Do you need volunteers? I'll go! I'll take anyone willing and—!"

"You'll go nowhere, *boy*," Petrük interrupted him haughtily. "And nothing is being *done* because there is nothing to bloody well *do*. Were you a member of this council then you would have been privy to that debate, which has already occurred. However, as you are *not*, then there is no reason for us to—"

"I said *leave him*," Jofrey snarled, slamming a fist down on the desk and nearly upturning the inkwell sitting in the top right corner.

The woman shut up at once, eyes wide at the surprising outburst of anger. Jofrey didn't care. Jofrey didn't give a *shit*. In the mood he was in, the bitch could choke on her own tongue and he didn't feel he'd be able to convince himself to help her.

"Reyn," he said, speaking firmly and meeting his former student's gaze. "I'm sorry. I'm loath to ask you to leave, but it's true that there are things to be discussed in which your involvement cannot be permitted at this time. I *swear to you* that if news of Syrah reaches us, or if we vote that something is to be done, I will personally make sure you—"

"*If* you vote?" Reyn howled, grief and rage spilling into the words. "IF you vote? How can you—? How could you—? It's SYRAH, dammit! How can you even CONSIDER leaving her to those men?"

"Right now, as much as it pains me to admit it, we have no choice. We don't know if she's alive, but we *do* know that the enemy at the bottom of that pass numbered enough to slaughter ten of our own, all experienced and well trained in the use of their gifts. We cannot afford—"

"*You* cannot afford," Reyn howled, face contorting in disgusted fury. "*You* cannot afford the lives, Jofrey. And I wonder why? Is it perhaps because you know it's on *your* head that those lives rest? That the blood is on *your* hands?"

"*Reyn! Enough*, I say!" Cullen tried to cut in again, but the young Priest didn't seem to hear the master-at-arms' outcry.

"Sending a handful of our own to guard the stairs," he spat, his livid blue eyes almost bulging as he stared at Jofrey. "Sending them into the Woods in the middle of the freeze, to watch the pass, like *dogs*. How did you think it was going to end, hm? How did you think that would turn out? Or did you think at all? Maybe you believed word wouldn't get out, that people wouldn't discover that you'd sent the men and women under your care to *die*. But people know. Families were told. Friends were told. And now people *know*, Jofrey. If Talo were here—"

"TALO. ISN'T. *HERE!*"

Jofrey punctuated every word with purpose, finishing the last with a slam of his open hand on the desk, so hard he did, this time, upturn the inkwell. To a one every Priest and Priestesses in the room jumped again, taken aback by the atypical outburst. Jofrey, though, had reached the end of his line.

"Look around!" he bellowed at Reyn, waving a hand about the room. "Look around, before you choose to continue down this path, before you choose to continue playing the insolent brat! Talo Brahnt is not here! Were he here, then yes, perhaps those men and women wouldn't have died on the pass! Yes, perhaps Syrah wouldn't have fooled him into thinking this was an opportunity to weaken the enemy's offense! But he's not here, and instead of Talo you have an old man who can do only what he believes is best and who has faith in those around him, as I did in Syrah."

He leaned against the desk with one hand, bringing his other up to rub his eyes. "Furthermore, *Reyn Hartlei*, you not only insult me but EMBARRASS YOURSELF with your childish screeching and casting of blame! You imply that I don't care for the men and women of this Citadel. You imply that I didn't—don't!—care for Syrah! I'll allow your grief, longing, and *adolescent* lust some leeway, but I *draw the line* at your insinuations of callousness, at your suggestion that I lack compassion. I do not lack compassion. I do not lack in any form the emotions that have taken control of your tongue, Reyn, nor do I believe I feel in any way less for Syrah's loss than you do. I simply do not have the LUXURY OF ALLOWING IT TO SWAY MY ABILITY TO PROTECT THE PEOPLE UNDER MY CARE!"

He dropped his hand and met Reyn's eyes again. The young man had gone stiff, though the anger had not yet left the handsome frame of his face.

"So," Jofrey continued, "if you're quite done with your infantile tantrum, you will leave us. You will return to your work, and allow the council to stop wasting its time on this *pointless discussion*. I said I would keep you informed, and I will. You have my word."

At last, Reyn's composure seemed to collapse in on itself. He sagged, his eyes never leaving Jofrey's, but the wrathful fire that had shone so brightly was extinguished. Instead, he looked nothing short of desolate, a sad outline of the strong youth that had stood in his place not a minute before.

"But..." he croaked quietly. "But... Syrah. What about... about Syrah?"

There was a silence.

"Come on, lad," Cullen Brern said gruffly, though his voice was kind. Moving beside Reyn he put a heavy, hard hand on the young Priest's shoulder and gently coaxed him around. Then the pair left the room, Brern leading his charge before him like one might guide the blind.

"Good riddance," Argo grumbled once the door had closed behind the pair, turning back to Jofrey. "And well said. I'd had about enough of—"

"Another word, Priest Argo, and I will demonstrate exactly how much *I* have had of *you*," Jofrey growled, his eyes not leaving the spot where Reyn had just been standing.

Argo almost choked on his words, flushing a vivid-reddish purple in fury, but something in the glassy gaze behind Jofrey's spectacles stopped him short of blurting out a blistering reply.

For a long time after that, they all stood quiet, watching Jofrey think. So intent was he on his own planning that the man hardly noticed a few of the council start to whisper amongst themselves, or hear the storm howling against the round wall of the room.

There were pieces in play on this board, Jofrey realized. Pieces no one was considering, and ones the Kayle could know nothing about. Though he had no faith in any alliance being hastened together at his behest—or even at the need of the Laorin as a whole—there was one individual who might have that ability, one man who might be able to galvanize the valley towns into rendering aid.

And Talo Brahnt wasn't stuck inside the walls of the Citadel...

It was Reyn's outburst that had brought on the realization. No, Talo was indeed too far removed to have had any chance of influencing the day's events, but the more Jofrey considered it, the more he saw a greater hand in the High Priest's sudden trek southward. Perhaps it was the Lifegiver's will that had taken the man beyond the Woods, taken him beyond the pass and behind the enemy line. Talo *had* to be returning soon. They'd sent a half-dozen letters to Azbar, some to the city's council, some to Kal Yu'ri, the local temple's own High Priest, and some to Talo himself. He was *bound* to have received word one way or another, even if a few of the birds had gotten themselves caught in the storms.

And if he was on his way...

"We will do as Priestess Petrük recommends." Jofrey spoke to the room, silencing all whispered conversations at once. "I know it might not be the popular opinion"—he raised a hand to stop Kallet and Forn from interrupting him—"but after some deliberation I find it to be the most prudent."

"But the mountain men will outlast us!" Re'het said in surprise. "You said so yourself! We've only the reserves to last us the winter, and that's a tenuous guarantee at best. We'd have to start rationing now, and if something should happen to the store… Lifegiver save us."

"You're correct," Jofrey acknowledged the young woman's concerns with a nod, "and I hold to that same unease, but I'm not sure it will come to that. We forget: Talo will be on his way back…"

At once the council began to murmur. Like Jofrey, it seemed the sudden reminder brought to mind other realizations, new options to consider.

"He'll be coming from the south," Priest Elber said thoughtfully. "He'll chance on the vanguard—or perhaps the majority of the Kayle's army, depending on the timeline—and come upon them from behind."

"Do we expect him to attack them outright?" Petrük asked scornfully, wrinkling her upper lip as though she were the only one to whom such an idea was ludicrous. "Because he *will* be alone. It's not as though Carro has ever been much use in a fight."

"Of *course* not," old Jerrom rasped impatiently from his chair, coughing between sentences. "Talo won't be fool enough to give them the opportunity. He and Carro will be ahorse—there's no other way through the Woods this time of year. If he rides hard, he could be back in Ystréd within a fortnight. From there he could rouse all the temples of the North."

"Not to mention Ystréd itself," Elber offered. "The town has always been friendly to us."

"*And* whoever else doesn't want to let the Kayle dig himself in too deep in the east," Re'het added, smacking her fist into her open palm in realization. "It might not be the conjoined forces of the valley towns—"

"But it'll sure as hell be a pack to contend with," Kallet finished her thought, smirking the foolhardy smile of a suddenly-confident man. "Five, maybe ten thousand? It won't be enough to challenge the Kayle himself, but it might be enough for Talo to draw attention away from the Citadel, at least for a time."

"Time we will use to our advantage, whenever that may be." Jofrey leaned over the desk, extending both arms and placing the tips of all ten fingers on the wood. "We won't *need* to weather the winter. Even in the freeze, with travel slowed by the snow, it won't be more than three months, four at most."

"*If* Brahnt is returning, and *if* he bothers with seeking help at all," Priest Argo grumbled nastily, casting a doubtful glance across the council. "Who is to say he won't save his own skin?"

"Don't be a fool, Behn," Petrük told him coolly, giving him a sidelong look. "Even you and I can't argue that to be the case."

The older Priest flushed an embarrassed pink, and fell silent again.

"Are we all in agreement, then?" Jofrey asked the group, meeting each gaze one after the other. Most nodded at once. Jerrom and Elber took a moment of reflection before doing so, as well as Petrük and Argo—though Jofrey suspected their delay was more out of stubborn willfulness than any thoughtful deliberation.

"Unanimous," Jofrey said with a nod after the old Priestess had finally indicated her agreement, feeling a sort of chilly relief fall over him as the plan settled into place. "In that case: Petrük, get me the most recent census of our residents. Re'het, wake some of your older acolytes and make me a detailed inventory of what *exactly* comprises our winter reserves. Argo, go with her, and see to it that we've enough of everything else we might need. Wood, blankets, medicine, everything. Kallet, fetch your brother, and return here. I'll need his input on the readiness of our Priests, and yours on the state of the furnaces. Elber and Forn, take as many of the most gifted you can find and set to casting the wards. And Jerrom... Go to bed. In the morning, help with the spellwork."

The orders were given, and each member of the council hurried off to their own tasks, leaving one after the other out the room door. When they were all gone, Jofrey sat down heavily, falling back against the chair as the rush of strength and confidence he'd momentarily found drained away. Suddenly he felt cold, shivering despite the warmth of the chamber, and turned to look out the diamond-paned window into the night. The storm raged, ever present even in the darkness, melting slush streaking the glass like grey paint against a black canvas. It had started to hail, the ice striking the window with staggered *pink pink pinks* that were rapidly intensifying in both volume and frequency. By morning Jofrey suspected the air itself would be nothing more than a churning white sea falling ever downward.

His greatest fear, though, was that the storm that assaulted them from above was nothing as compared to that which threatened them from below.

Lifegiver, he prayed, closing his eyes and seeking out the power that lay behind the raging wind outside, *lend us your strength. See us through this, so that we might know another cold winter, another cruel storm. See us through this, so that your greatest Gift is not extinguished from these halls that have, for so many of us, been a home when no other place could satisfy.*

When he was done, Jofrey sat for another minute, listening to the groan of the coming blizzard.

Then he got up, and set off to prepare Cyurgi' Di for war.

XI

"Despite breathtaking mountain ranges, magnificent coastal seascapes, and even the wondrous dark reaches of the Arocklen Woods, the Dehn Plains are perhaps the most enchanting of the Northern lands. A sprawling sight dancing with rolling hills of grass and flowers in the summer months, it is no less beautiful in the freeze. A singular lolling slate of white against the swirling grey of storm clouds in the heavens above, one feels almost suspended over an angry ocean, churning and calling out its hunger with thunder and wind. There are times, in fact, when it is difficult to keep at bay the irrational fear of falling up up up into those ravenous dark waters..."

—*The Eloquent's Guide to Northern Geography,* author unknown

Raz barely kept his feet, all strength drained from him as he stared out at the queer reflection of a world he had so long ago left far behind.

He stood along the precipice of the tallest hill he'd been able to find in the dark within easy walk of their small camp, having just crested its highest ridge. Ahna was at his side, hanging loose from one hand with her blades sinking down into the foot of snow that surrounded him, and the thick hood of his heavy furs was pulled up so that only his snout suffered the abuse of the buffeting, biting gales. Above him the sky was streaked with the white of thin clouds against the interlacing colors of dawn, themselves shifting like water as the Sun began to show itself over the eastern edge of the world. For a time, it seemed, they were going to get a reprieve from the storms that had dogged them for the last week, slowing their horses and making it impossible to bear witness to the scenery about them.

Now, though, for the first time in what seemed like a small eternity, the day was clear, and Raz reached up with his free hand to pull his fur hood slowly down, not wanting so much as a strand of hair between his amber eyes and the quiet country spread out before him.

"By the Sun..." he whispered hoarsely.

Time, by its own strange plans, had returned him to the desert. Instead of sand there was snow, and instead of devouring heat there was nothing but a cruel, cutting chill, but in all other respects it was as though the Cienbal had painted itself across the land, drawing inspiration from Raz's own memories. The sway of the earth, up and down like the fluttering of cloth left to dry in a lazy breeze. Lines on lines of distant hills layered atop themselves, so that the horizon was interrupted by the bump and sway of the earth. There were even edges along the ridges of those hills where snow had caved under its own weight, tumbling into the valleys in small avalanches just as the sands had from atop the dunes. Icy wisps flicked like lines of smoke over the otherwise perfect stillness, pale and white rather than the reddish brown of dust, but carried off by the wind all the same.

Even had Raz found more words to express his awe, he would have tamed them in reverence.

For a long time he stood alone atop that hill, shin deep in the snow, welcoming the steadily brightening light of the Sun that marked the new day. al'Dor's woven magic—reworked every other day or so—held in Raz's boots, keeping his feet and legs warm and dry, and the thickness of the furs did the rest. His ears, vulnerable to the cold in their bareness, ached before long, but he ignored the pain, allowing the delicate membranes to stiffen and eventually go numb.

The memory was worth suffering for, if even just a little.

The Sun had risen in truth when Raz decided it was time to return. The oranges and yellows of the early morning were rapidly giving way to clear, calm blue as he turned and made his descent carefully down the hill, digging his claws into the hardened earth and dead grass he could feel beneath the white. Ahna he threw over one shoulder, shifting to step sideways down the slope, trying not to slip as he moved.

About five minutes later he found the road again—visible only by his own tracks along a winding path of suspicious flatness between the hills—and followed it north. Soon he came to a particularly sharp bend and, still following the trail of his boots and tail, made his way up and over the outcroppings of rock that had sheltered their little party for the night. Coming to the stone's edge Raz leapt down, spreading his wings momentarily to slow his twenty-foot fall, and landed lightly in the shallower snow at the mouth of their little hollow.

The shelter—which he'd found them the afternoon before when the storm had become too violent to brave any longer—was mostly of natural creation, a sort of divot in the earth beneath an overhanging ledge of slate and loose roots. Icicles, hung suspended over their heads when they'd first entered, were now long melted away within the heat of the complex protective wards the two Priests had spent nearly an hour working around the little nook and their horses. Even now the magic cut an odd line against the earth, the invisible, shifting sphere of warmth made distinct by a circular line of ice in the snow, the other side of which revealed brown grass and damp earth.

Stepping into the ward, Raz felt the tension of the cold leave his neck and shoulders, and he sighed audibly. Leaning Ahna against the earthen wall to his left, he smirked down at the pair of men still sleeping soundly beneath the low ceiling of stone, their bedrolls pulled close together, hands laying only inches apart atop their shared furs.

When they'd first set off, Raz wasn't quite sure what to make of the men's relationship, being largely unfamiliar with such romances. Similar inclinations existed in the South, of course, but were largely shunned, or kept very quiet. The only remotely similar comparisons he'd been able to make had been the comforts some men discreetly bought from others of the same sex in brothels and whorehouses in and about the South's fringe cities, or the predatory perversions animals like Ergoin Sass had harbored for younger boys.

Rapidly though, he'd realized such comparisons couldn't have hit further from the mark.

At first he'd found it odd, being around the lovers in their element, enjoying the relative seclusion the road allowed from what he imagined were very busy lives. Raz had felt uncomfortable in his own skin, watching the pair, not quite sure how to act around them, or what to say. Quickly he'd learned, though, that there was no special way to act, no secret to keeping himself from interrupting or offending their relationship. They were simply two people, very much fond of one another, and with no desire or need to hide it from the world. Soon after he'd realized this, Raz had learned to take the relationship in stride, even going so far as to tease the Priests as one might tease young lovers caught in their shyness.

"Oy!" Raz shouted, shoving Brahnt's exposed shoulder with a clawed foot. "Lovebirds! Time we're off! Sun's been up long enough as is!"

The Priest jerked awake, bleary eyes blinking open as he lifted his head to look about before squinting at the brightness of the Sun reflected off the snow outside the hollow. He grumbled, rolling himself onto one side and reaching up with both hands to rub at his face, muttering something about "mouthy reptiles" and "lizard soup for breakfast."

Raz grinned, turning away to ready Gale and perform his morning exercises in the warmth of the Sun as al'Dor awoke in turn, yawning and stretching his wide frame to its full extent. The man called out "Morning!" after him, and Raz raised a hand in reply without looking back.

"Storm's finally gone and blown itself out," he heard Brahnt say, huffing and grunting as he struggled to get his feet on his bad knee. "Laor's mercy... Carro, come see. Come *see*, dammit!"

There was the grind of stone and earth, followed by the *crunch* of snow caving underfoot.

"Oh my..." Raz heard the Priest breathe out in wonder after a short inhaled gasp of awe, and he knew the men were taking in the Dehn in all its wintery wonder.

"It's a better view from the hills," he called back over his shoulder as he hefted his saddle up with his good arm from where it had been draped over a small boulder by the entrance overnight, at the edges of the sphere of magical heat. "Go. I'll get the horses bridled."

Amusingly, neither of the Priests had to be told twice. They set off as soon as they'd finished scrambling to get their boots on, Brahnt leaning on al'Dor and his staff as usual, making use of the path Raz had already cut around the outcropping and wading their way through the snow in the direction he'd gone not an hour before. They took their time, which Raz neither minded nor intended to blame them for. Apart from having a good understanding of the sobering wonderment both men had to be experiencing, the solitude let him get Gale and the two mares ready in quick succession. The horses, originally skittish around him, had become accustomed to Raz's form and presence within a few days, and even tilted their broad heads into him now in appeals for pats and scratches, which he obliged. After this, Raz set about his new morning ritual: working the cold out of stiff and sore muscles.

The ache in his back hand't completely dissipated even after a week of travel, but it was far removed from the piercing discomfort it had been when they'd left the stunted walls of Ystréd behind in favor of the northern road. The makeshift sling Eva had supplied him with had been discarded three days prior, and Raz had since been working to recover the surprising amount of strength and dexterity that had wasted away during his illness and subsequent recuperation. Using his tail to clear himself a rough circle in the sunniest—and therefore warmest—spot he could find, Raz began with general stretching and flexing of the larger muscles in his legs, arms, chest, and back. Once he'd sufficiently warmed up, he drew the gladius from over his shoulder with his right hand and plucked the war-ax from his belt with his left. For a minute or two he went through the motions, building up a burn in his hands, wrists, and forearms with the slow, deliberate manipulations of the weapons' weights.

Then, allowing himself a steady ramping up in speed and strength, Raz began to dance.

He moved with all the efficiency a life of the sword had managed to instill in him. The edges of his blades whistled as they cut the air in everything from long arcs to short, complex maneuvers kept tight to the body. His legs glided beneath him like liquid, his footwork carrying his weight back and forth, twisting his bulk about effortlessly even as he started moving faster and faster. Within a minute Raz was in full swing of the battle trance, spinning and jumping and somersaulting and pirouetting in order to dart and dodge out of the way of imaginary blows dispensed by invisible foes. Before long he lost himself completely, allowing instinct and experience to take control bit by bit, brushing away the pain between his shoulder blades until he felt it no more, ignoring fatigue and the burn of tiring muscles until they ached no more. Silently he waged war against his thoughts, kicking up snow and ice to glimmer in the air of the bright morning, settling around him like a drifting rain of shattered glass as he moved.

It was almost a half hour before the Priests returned, coming back around on the path, by which time Raz had long since built himself up and burned himself out, dancing until he could dance no more. They found him on his knees in the middle of his crude little circle, heaving in gasps of icy air, sword and ax limp in each hand, their blades resting against the ground.

They didn't offer any comment on his position, just as he didn't offer any comment on the sort of stupefied reverence plastered across al'Dor's blonde bearded face that said that he—like Raz—had been hard pressed to turn away from the majestic, untouched perfection of the Dehn.

After a hurried breakfast of dried bread and salted beef softened with melted snow, they wasted no time on their departure. From horseback Brahnt dispelled the wards with a few waves of his hand and a flash of white light, then brought his mount around and led them back around the outcropping towards the road. Once they'd returned to the path, the three men slipped into their habit of riding abreast, Raz and al'Dor flanking Brahnt on the left and right respectively. The going was slow, none of them willing to push their horses into more than a steady trot over the treacherously hidden earth, but it was still faster than anything they'd managed in most of the week prior. Today, at least, vertical sleet wasn't cutting at their hands and faces, nor was the wind buffeting them about so much that they kept running either into each other or off the road entirely. Even the Priests' quick wards and warming spells, cast periodically throughout the day, never held up long against the blizzard's constant battery, and a majority of their time had been spent hunched and miserable in their saddles, only looking up every few minutes to ensure they hadn't strayed far from each other or the road.

Now, though—while the cold kept slipping through the thinnest layers of their furs and cloaks and their lips were still cracked from the dryness of the air—the mood of the journey could not have been more different. After days of near-constant silence as they rode—not counting the sporadic yelling at each other over the storm to check they were still heading in the right direction—the three companions found themselves overjoyed with the prospect of distraction and discussion. Even Raz had grown tired of the pseudo-solitude, and took advantage of the clear day to strike up a conversation as soon as they found a steady pace.

"How much farther do we have?" he asked as they led the horses down a sharp incline in the road, one after the other. "Not that I haven't thoroughly enjoyed myself the last few days, but if we get caught in another storm like that I'm turning tail and making for the South again, bounty be damned."

Behind him, al'Dor chuckled. "A ways, yet. Another week at least, likely two. And I'm surprised you weren't warned before making the trek up. If it's sand and sunlight you were hoping for, you certainly picked the wrong direction."

"Oh, I was warned," Raz grumbled unwillingly, taking his habitual spot by Brahnt's left again as the road widened once more. "I just apparently couldn't quite fathom the extent of the natural disaster I was willfully wading into…"

"Speak for yourself," Brahnt himself said, lifting a gloved hand from where it kept his staff balanced across his legs to scratch at his snow-flecked beard. "I've been in your lands, too, Arro, and I'll take the cold and all its little bastard friends over the sweltering misery you Southerners call the 'cooler seasons' any day, and then some. Cooler, my foot! If it'd gotten any hotter I was afraid the bricks that held the roof up over our head were going to start melting."

Raz scoffed. "Then don't visit the fringe cities in the summer, old man. The days are so hot that women cook their meat on the underside of iron pots left in the Sun. The slummers become more of a nuisance by fighting amongst themselves for shade and water than they ever do just picking pockets and begging for scraps. In the desert, sarydâ wrap the hilts of their weapons in rough cloth, because the pommels and cross guards become so heated they've been known to sear the skin right from the hand."

"You make my point for me," Brahnt laughed, ending his scratching and waving his hand about at the Dehn. "Are you really going to insist you prefer that place's searing misery to this?"

Raz opened his mouth to retort, all too intent on defending his homeland, but stopped abruptly. Turning, he looked over the sweeping, smooth white bouncing of the Plains.

He decided silence was the more dignified response.

"Exactly," Brahnt said with a smile. "Though truth be told, lad, these hills aren't the most fascinating thing I hope to show you on this trip. Look north." He nodded in the direction they were headed.

Raz looked around, peering into the distance. It took him a moment to make out what he believed the Priest was referring to.

Then he whistled.

There, only outlines even to Raz's keen eyes, the blue and white shadow of mountains cut across the horizon. Like the jagged, broken teeth of some great old wolf they jutted up from the earth into the sky. It wasn't the first time Raz had made out such things, of course. He'd seen the Crags that dipped into the eastern stretches of the Cienbal on multiple occasions, though never from up close. Regardless, those reddish, arid ranges held little comparison to the titans that rose in either direction—even so indistinctly at this distance—like a line of giant soldiers as far as the eye could see. Their wide, interlocking bases were mixed in and lost to one another, steep, angular slopes mostly hidden among the clouds. Despite this, Raz could most distinctly make out the start of peaks, highlighted against the heavens because of the greyish-white tinge of eternal snow.

"The Saragrias?" he asked, drawing from what little the Priest had told him of their destination, and still squinting as he tried to make out more of the ragged contours.

Beside him, both Brahnt and al'Dor blinked and turned to stare at him, the latter leaning around the former to do so.

"You can see the ranges?" he asked in astonishment. In response, Raz nodded.

"Impressive," Brahnt said with his own whistle of appreciation. "But no. As neither Carro nor I can see the mountains as of yet, I was actually speaking of something a little more earthbound. Look down a little, nearer the base of the peaks."

Raz did as instructed, and this time he noticed a thick band of black lining most of the horizon, so obvious he was surprised it wasn't the first thing he noticed.

Not as surprised, though, as when he made out the trunks and swaying canopy of thousands upon thousands of trees.

"A forest!" he exclaimed, barely able to keep the glee out of his voice. He'd long since fallen in love with the sprawling woodlands surrounding Azbar, many miles to the south.

"The Arocklen Woods," al'Dor agreed with a nod, "though I wish we were intending to traverse it by way of the summer roads. The pines can be cruel in winter."

"Have you ever done so?" Raz asked curiously, though his eyes never left the distant tree line. "Either of you?"

"Braved the Woods in the middle of the freeze?" al'Dor asked with a snort. "Not I. I've barely ever left the Citadel once the snows come, and I hadn't planned on doing so this year either. Someone, though"—he gave Brahnt a sidelong look—"thought it best to give me the opportunity."

Brahnt smiled, but otherwise didn't acknowledge the humorous barb.

"I have," he said in response to Raz's question, slowing his mare down slightly as they reached a wide wooden bridge suspended over a narrow stream that cut a thin line through the snow to their left. "Only once, though, when I brought Syrah from the western towns as a girl to join the faith."

Raz was quiet, and Brahnt took the silent hint to continue.

"In my younger days, in the decade or two after I first received my staff, I made my own attempts to work out a peace between the valley towns and mountain tribes. I never had as much success as Syrah—though there's irony in that now, come to think of it—but what small victories I managed lent me enough credit in the eyes of both people to work as a sort of liaison, when the need arose."

He frowned, and Raz could tell he was dredging up old memories with all this talk.

"Baoill isn't the first act of war the people of the towns have suffered at the hands of the mountain men. About twenty years ago one of the western municipalities, the city of Drangstek, was razed to the ground by a clan from the Fissür ranges to the south. Fortunately the attack was one of brute force, the armies spotted miles off, and Drangstek managed to evacuate a majority of its population before the worst befell them. Most fled to Stullens, a neighboring valley town, but four hundred thousand can't settle well within walls meant to harbor only half that number, and other problems arose. Sickness, starvation, violence... Before long Stullens and Drangstek both were calling for aid from the faith, and we responded in turn. I was one of many to make the pilgrimage, hoping my diplomatic credit might serve purpose."

The frown turned into a crooked smile of amusement.

"I wasn't long in leaving, though. Once the tribes had left the bones of the city, most of Drangstek's people flocked back and started to rebuild. Stullens found its peace again, the plagues died off, and crime fell. As I wasn't needed, I made for the Citadel."

"Though not alone," al'Dor said slyly from beside him.

"Oh no," Brahnt chortled. "No, not alone. Though by the end of our journey I might have wished half a hundred times that I *had* left the little brat back in Stullens."

"Syrah?" Raz asked.

He barely had time to realize it was the first time he'd ever said her name aloud before Brahnt answered.

"Syrah," he confirmed. "The youngest of a family with too many mouths to feed. Her parents had approached me more than once, begging that I might take at least one of their children into the faith. At first I refused, but after a time they convinced me to at least meet the children. When I saw Syrah... well..."

"Life could have been hard for her," Raz finished for him, nodding and thinking of what he could remember of the woman, recalling her colorless, smooth skin, and the pretty shine of her rose-colored eyes. "It can be difficult, being different..."

"Especially when the choice is starvation, the faith, or an over-packed orphanage. And so... I took her, and the tale only gets duller from there."

"Oh I don't know about *that*!" al'Dor offered up. "Young Syrah was anything but dull, if I recall. She had you fretting about after her like a worried old woman from day one. Always off, scampering about with the other children, convincing them to get themselves into trouble. I thought Talo was going to lose his hair by the end of the first year, if he didn't pull it out first. She was a troublemaker, that one."

"She was a child," Brahnt retorted, speaking with a note of pride that reminded Raz of how he'd sometimes overheard his own father talk of him. "It wasn't more than a week before she'd made friends—"

"Built a gang," al'Dor muttered.

"—and went about her business doing all it is that children do."

"Causing mayhem and disaster and getting under everyone's feet."

"Well *either way*," Brahnt said firmly, giving his lover a hard sidelong glance, "the fact remains that she grew up well enough, and made something of herself."

al'Dor smiled. "Oh you know I'm only teasing. I love Syrah like a daughter, and I certainly won't say she doesn't deserve the praise. It's a pity Baoill came to power when he did. If the treaties she'd worked out with the Sigûrth had held for any amount of time, she'd have made history."

"She made history either way," Talo said, still sounding a little irritated. "The fact that any Kayle at all—even the former Kayle—was willing to put his name to a true peace is unprecedented. All *I* ever managed to do was build accords for truces, and establish a trade route between the Fissür and Stullens that didn't last more than two summers. Syrah's successes are of a different caliber."

"I'm not arguing that, handsome. I'm merely addressing the unfortunate circumstances. If Baoill hadn't risen so quickly—"

"Then someone else would have. The new Kayle isn't a coincidence, he's a complexity of Syrah's success. If anything, the desperation with which he amassed his forces seems to me only to indicate *exactly* how much of a threat he saw in her. You're not giving her the credit she—"

"She sounds like an incredible woman."

Brahnt stumbled over his words as Raz spoke, interrupting their argument, and both he and al'Dor seemed suddenly to remember that they weren't alone on the road. The High Priest coughed in embarrassment and al'Dor leaned around him again, a little pink in the face, to address Raz.

"She is, and I would never say it any other way." He gave Brahnt a quick glare. "In fact... you remind me a bit of her, Arro."

That took Raz by surprise, and he blinked before looking around at the blond man.

"*Me?*" he asked with a confused laugh, utterly unable to keep the disbelief out of his voice. "I don't think I've ever heard of anyone I would *less* relate to. You make this woman sound—"

"Dependable?" Brahnt asked him as they took a bend in the road and found themselves fighting their way uphill. "Driven? Caring?"

Raz scowled at him, though he didn't miss the attempted compliment.

"Peaceful," he said simply, tugging on Gale's reins to keep the stallion from aggressively overtaking the more plodding mares. "I was going to say 'peaceful.'"

"Ha!" Brahnt turned to al'Dor as though looking for someone to share a joke with. "'Peaceful,' he says! 'Peaceful'!"

And then the High Priest was laughing in truth, the sound dampened by the heavy snow.

"If someone wants to explain the joke to me?" Raz muttered, looking between the two men.

It was al'Dor who answered him, though he too couldn't seem to help from smiling at Brahnt's continued guffaws.

"Syrah is… interesting. I fear we've painted a poor picture for you, lad. She's not some nun who's locked herself in a tower to pore over old scriptures and offer wisdom via letters and birds. She's… direct."

"She's *fiery!*" Brahnt said loudly, still chortling. "Peaceful, my ass! Syrah's got a tongue like a lash, mind like a razor, and fists like stone— though that last one she might have got from me. Oh she can be all prim and proper when need be, but give her half a chance and she'll put you in your place, Arro, mark my words."

Raz couldn't help it. He was suddenly very much intrigued.

He was remembering, as it happened, the first time he had *really* seen Syrah Brahnt. Though he'd put eyes on her in the Karthian markets, he'd thought her likely mad then, all covered up in silks and leathers that must have felt like an oven in the Southern sun. No, the first time he'd truly taken her in had been some minutes later, in the moments after he'd butchered the men who'd snatched her off the street, intending to sell her off at a good price.

He had a better memory than most men, but even he was surprised to realize he remembered every detail of the moment.

Her face had been clearly comely, despite the bruising around one eye. Torn robes revealed the almost luminescent skin of one shoulder, hinting at indecency, and yet despite this she'd stood tall and composed, demanding his attention with a commanding presence. Her voice had been smooth, clear as crystal, cutting through the battle fog and bloodlust to rip Raz back from the edge of murderous instinct as she vied for the life of one of her would-be kidnappers.

That was what he remembered the best out of all of it. The abrupt, precise return to his senses, pulling him firmly back from the edge of the abyss that had since become a constant stain upon his soul.

Whether it had been the circumstance, the timing, or just the woman herself, no one and nothing had ever been able to pull Raz back from the edge with such absolute force.

He realized suddenly that he'd been silent for almost a minute, and he looked up sharply. Brahnt and al'Dor were watching him, rolling along with the gait of their horses, matching grins adorning both bearded faces.

"What?" Raz demanded defensively.

"Oh, nothing, boy," Brahnt said, the grin not falling from his face. "It's just like Carro says, though, isn't it? You're a bit like her. A good bit like her."

Raz decided not to respond, which only earned him a chuckle from the two older men.

The rest of the day's ride kept on and completed in pleasant fashion, the Priests catching up on conversation lost to the storm and telling him all about the Laorin, the Citadel, and the North as a whole. They made good time, as well, after crossing paths with what looked to be a patrol of Ystréd scouts returning from reconnaissance. Brahnt and al'Dor did nothing more than give the dozen mounted soldiers polite nods as they passed, not wanting to draw attention to Raz's presence, but as soon as they could they set their mounts along the clearer trampled path left by the south-bound horses, almost doubling their pace. By nightfall, in fact, Brahnt said they weren't more than a few hours ride from the edge of Arocklen, and that they'd reach the tree line by mid-morning the following day.

Despite this, despite the wondrous curiosity he held for the coming Woods, despite the magnificence of the Dehn under the bright, welcoming light of the Moon and Her Stars, and despite the stories of magic and intrigue the Priests had filled the day with, Raz dreamt of no such things that night.

Rather, for the first time in his life, a woman filled Raz's dreams. A human woman, pretty and smiling, her skin as gentle and pale as the snow that fell around her, her white, braided hair spilling about her shoulder, and her eyes filled with a rose fire that burned with such hope and warmth that it stole Raz's breath away.

XII

"I know nothing of fear, nothing of terror. No, this is not a boast, though it may be an exaggeration. I am familiar with both emotions of course, and would be a fool and a braggart to say otherwise. What I mean to say, rather, is that my experience with fear and terror are mere shadows in comparison to what I know is possible, to what I have witnessed in the eyes of too many I have come across. Those cursed souls made to suffer in the Cages. Children convinced they were destined for slaughter in the pits of the Arena. Slaves in Perce, atherian and human alike, passed like currency from one set of hands to another, not knowing which are crueler. No, I know nothing of terror, nor do I have any wish to educate myself in its secrets."

—the Dragon of the North

At first, Syrah thought the boot that woke her from her fitful sleep seemed oddly gentle, the blow it dealt her thigh muffled and dull. As she jerked up and away, however, she realized the lack of pain had nothing to do with any peculiar mercy from the wearer, but rather from the distinct numbness that layered her skin like a blanket. The chill of the hour was so deep, so tangible that the air itself seemed to have taken on a new texture, a sharp, harsh grit that bit at her dry tongue and throat and stung her chapped lips.

"*Ras, Wyth.*"

A hard voice, speaking the harsh enunciations of the mountain tongue.

Rise, Witch.

It took a moment for Syrah to get her bearings. She lay atop a layer of dirty furs, tucked in the corner of a small tent, numb arms awkwardly pinned under her body. A thin, ragged blanket had been thrown atop her, but the worn threading did even less to keep her warm then the ripped fabric of her Priestess' robes. There was no fire in the tent—nor any place to build one, it seemed—the only light offered coming from the torch the man who'd woken her held low and to the side, keeping the flames away from the thick cloth canvas and revealing a plethora of bags, crates, baskets, and leather traveling sacks piled about the floor.

Syrah saw none of it, her eyes fixed on the tribesman standing above her. Sigûrth, she could tell by the braided hair. The hand not holding his torch was clasped tight around the hilt of a short-sword, bared steel feebly glinting in the flames.

And he was alone.

Syrah moved instinctively, planning to take full advantage of her enemy's solitude while she could. She didn't know where she was, but she doubted she'd ended up anywhere she wanted to stay for even a moment longer than she had to. There might not be another such chance, and hesitation was 'a good way to a bad death,' as Talo had drilled into her head. Leaping up, she started to draw the magics into her hand, intending to hit the man with a paralyzing blast that would lay him out for hours.

Things could have gone much better.

Instead of landing on her feet, something snapped taught about Syrah's ankles, sending her tumbling back down towards the cold furs. At the same time, another something caught around her wrists behind her back, preventing her from throwing her arms up to stop herself, much less strike with the intended spell.

It was only after Syrah had landed painfully, half on her shoulder and half on the cut right side of her face, that she realized she'd been chained.

As panic began to set in, Syrah looked down to see the iron manacles clamped about her feet, their insides lined with thick straw so the metal wouldn't frostbite the skin of her shins through the leather of her boots. Beginning to regain some sensation in her fingers, she felt around to discover that her hands were similarly bound.

Rapidly, the panic turned into anger.

"Cowards!" she snarled, whipping her body around and kicking out at the man with both legs, trying to catch him in the knees. "Craven! Fucking ball-less sacks of…"

Syrah let out a flow of curses in every language she knew, which was quite a few. The Sigûrth, for his part, didn't so much as blink at the berating, nor did he seem much bothered by the clumsy attack. Stepping aside easily, he brought the flat of his short-sword down hard across Syrah's thighs. Instantly her screams of fury turned into a wail of pain, and she rolled over, away from him. Despite this, the man struck her twice more with the steel, once across the side of her leg, then again across her upper arm and chest.

This last blow knocked the wind out of Syrah, and she gasped and wheezed even as she heard the man sheath his blade and bend over her.

"*I said RISE, Witch!*" he hissed into her ear, grabbing her firmly under her throbbing arm and hauling her to her feet.

Syrah stood as directed, or attempted to. Almost immediately she stumbled and fell as the chains tangled between her feet, and at once the Sigûrth brought her up again roughly. From there she was half-led, half-dragged out of the tent, pulled through the heavy hanging leathers that made up the entranceway.

As the sting of the winter air hit her in full, Syrah looked around with equal parts awe and fear.

The Woods' gnarled trunks towered up around them like dark sentinels, holding up the denseness of the canopy that formed an almost-

112

impervious ceiling of branches, spiny leaves, and layered snow several meters above their heads. Ordinarily it would have been pitch black there beneath the trees—despite Syrah not actually knowing what the time was—but the Woods were alight with an eerie orange glow, a ghostly reflection of a hundred small camp fires scattered out before her in all directions. The flames reflected across snow-strewn ground, and again off the bluish canopy high above where the worst of the storms had built up in the branches. They even shone off the trees, in patched lines where moisture had frozen over bark, leaving thin sheens of ice.

Despite her personal predicament, a small part of Syrah became immeasurably saddened by the sight. She had failed.

Gûlraht Baoill's vanguard had successfully entrenched itself in the Arocklen.

"*Move, woman,*" her escort snapped, pulling her along again. This time Syrah did a better job of keeping up with him, adapting to the distance her legs could make with every step. She only tripped a few more times on the uneven floor of the forest as she was led by the arm through the camp. All manner of faces turned in her direction as they walked, but only the Sigûrth they passed jeered and threw whatever was at hand in her direction.

The rest of the tribes seemed distinctly more sober. While there was no pity in the blue eyes that she caught as they passed, nor was there shared any of the pleasure and amusement that struck the Kayle's clan.

They walked for only a few minutes, winding their way through the encampment. Syrah didn't ask where she was being led. She had her suspicions, and they were rapidly confirmed as yet another grouping of tents —much smaller—appeared atop a hill as they came around a particularly thick set of trees. The mountain man beside her didn't slow as they took the incline of the earth, and twice more Syrah fell, though she kept her curses to herself.

Or at least kept them for Grahst, when she saw him.

Soon Syrah could make out the roaring laughter of a dozen men, as well as the hearty smells of meat and bread and ale. As they stepped between the first row of tents the air steadily lost its chilly edge, warming until they passed into the bright glow of a wide, low fire in the middle of a flattened clearing. Lounging and sitting around the heavy stones that caged the flames, Grahst's favorites were talking and joking, some arguing, some playing with dice, and some digging into heavy haunches of deer and elk meat, the carcasses strung up in the dark beyond the fires. Grahst himself was at the head of the circle, seated atop the stump of an old tree over which someone had thrown what look like a wolf pelt.

It had been Syrah's hope and intention to meet the man eye to eye. To face and challenge him, at least in defiance. Grahst had robbed her of her courage during their fight, ripped it from her as no other man had ever been able to do so before, and she had silently sworn to herself that it would not happen again.

Unfortunately, her plan was thrown to the wind when the man who'd taken her from the tent planted a heavy boot in her back and shoved her forward into the group.

Syrah didn't have a prayer of keeping her feet. Even if the log that tripped her up—upon which sat a pair of conversing Sigûrth—hadn't been there, the chains around her ankles would have done her in. As it was, Syrah barely managed to take two stumbling steps before her shins caught the wood and she fell heavily directly into the middle of the clearing.

And directly at Kareth Grahst's feet.

A roar of laughter went up around her. They howled and jeered, laughing as Syrah struggled to get herself up, to lift herself from the ground.

"No." Grahst's voice cut across her efforts. "*Stay there, Witch.*"

There was a shuffle of approaching feet, then a boot dealt Syrah a hard kick that doubled her up, forcing her to curl around herself on her side, hacking and heaving. Another gale of amusement arose, and Syrah felt the fear start to creep back up her spine.

Still, she refused to go down so easily.

Fighting the nauseous throbs emanating from where the blow had landed in her gut, Syrah slowly began to edge herself up again, leveraging her body awkwardly on a bent elbow. She was allowed to attain her knees on this attempt, and looked up just in time to see Grahst give a nod to the man standing over her, the one who'd escorted her to the camp.

This time a fist caught her in the side of the face.

Syrah went down again, tumbling to the ground where she groaned, helpless to stop the sounds as pain radiated from her stomach and head simultaneously.

Through the fog, she heard shouts of "*More! More!*" in the mountain tongue.

"*Enough fun, Krehni,*" Grahst said. "*Get her up.*"

Hard hands grabbed her by the front of her torn robes, and Syrah was hauled up onto her knees again. The world spun for several seconds at the motion, and Syrah bowed and sucked in air as she fought the queasiness that ripped through her. Her hair was falling loose of her braids, tumbling over her ears and face. She could feel her left eye start to swell from where she'd been hit, and the cut above her right had opened again. Blood dripped to the ground before her, and it was a long time before Syrah gathered the strength to look up and gaze into the face of a demon.

Grahst met her stare levelly.

"*You're brave, Witch,*" he said softly, and Syrah realized that the cacophony of noise about the fire had deadened, all attentions fixed on them. "*A fool, yes. But also brave. Like my father, in fact. I've thought about what you said, considered your words. In the end… I think you may have been right.*"

Syrah didn't respond to him, watching the man lean forward, eyes fixed—as always—on hers.

"*My father was brave, as you insisted. For many years, and as many winters he was brave. I saw him fight men and animals alike with no more fear than stone itself. I saw him meet every provocation without doubt, without concern for his own life. He could have drafted a champion to fight in his place to face my cousin, when Gûlraht challenged him. He could have, but he didn't. Rather, he faced a man half again as strong, half again as fast, and half again as young as he in the circle.*"

Grahst's eyes narrowed. "*Bravery killed my father, Witch. Bravery spilled his blood and ended his life. Bravery is what made him a fool.*"

He paused, letting the words ring clear.

"*With that in mind…*" he continued evenly, "*I wonder if you will prove yourself to be just as much a fool.*"

"*The only thing I intend to prove, Grahst,*" Syrah replied in the man's own tongue, so that the others seated around them could make no mistake to the meaning of her words, "*is that—as much of a fool as he may or may not have been—you will never be a glint of the man your father was. Whereas he sought to save his people from sacrifice and bloodshed at his own expense, you seek to thrust them into war and suffering for your own pleasure. Whereas he built, you destroy. Whereas—*"

"*I seek no such thing for my people, Witch! I seek glory for them. I seek victory. Blood and life are sacrifices, I'll give you that, but much must be sacrificed in war. Much must be sacrificed for the betterment of my people.*"

He smiled, then, and it was a reflection of the cruel smile Syrah had seen play upon his face only moments before he'd butchered Egard Rost and thrown the former Priest's head at her feet.

The fear deepened within her, hardening to ice.

"*But you call me destroyer,*" he purred, as though enjoying the title. "*Yes… Yes, I don't believe I can argue that. I do destroy. I destroy that which stands in the way of the rising of my King and our people. I destroy that which hinders the glory of myself and my men. I destroy that which seeks to seed the mind of those devout to the Stone Gods with treacherous filth and flawed faiths. I destroy all this—*" his eyes suddenly gleamed with wicked excitement "*—just as my King will destroy the nest of vipers that thrives upon the mountains above us.*"

"*The Lifegiver hears your pompous bleating as you and I might hear the screeching of bickering rats in the wall,*" Syrah spat. "*The High Citadel is beyond you, Grahst. It is beyond you, your men, and even your King.*"

"*Perhaps it is,*" Grahst said with a slow nod and a conceding motion of his hand. "*And yet, perhaps not. Perhaps—for example—if I and my men had the means in our possession by which to could gather information, our chance would be greater. Significantly greater."*

Syrah felt her heart sink at the words, realizing what Grahst meant.

"Perhaps—again, just for example—if I and my men had someone within our reach who knew all there is to know of this 'High Citadel' and all its holdings, then conquering it might not be such a challenge after all."

His grin widened, and he rested his chin on a fist as he watched her. *"My King is going to kill you, Witch. There is nothing and no one who can stop it— not that any here wish a different fate for the likes of you. He's going to kill you, and he's going to do it the moment he arrives. You will die, in this dark place. Your life will end here, beneath the bleakness of these trees. But there are things that can change..."*

Syrah felt herself paling at the words, but in the pause that followed she refused to voice the question she knew Grahst wanted her to ask, requesting what *could* be changed. Instead, she just continued to glare at him.

After a time, Grahst seemed to realize he wasn't going to win this small battle, and he continued. *"There is the question of how you will die, of course. There are quick ways, even among the Sigûrth. Gûlraht could claim your head with one blow, if he so desires, or perhaps one of the more zealous of our clan might be convinced to fall upon you and slit your throat in the night. These are peaceful ways to pass, Witch, and you know this. You know too, that there are other ways. My King might bind you to a tree at the edge of camp, leaving you for the Stone Gods and the wolves that prowl the Woods at night. He may have you slain in the ways of old, flayed alive until you die from shock and pain upon the rack. He may even make it as slow a death as possible, smothering you beneath a plank of wood upon which just enough stone will be added that it takes you hours—or even days—to suffocate."*

He raised an eyebrow. *"But in talking of time, you must also know that it could be more than a fortnight before Gûlraht reaches us with the bulk of our army. A fortnight before he arrives, and a fortnight during which my men and I—"* he waved his other hand and looked about at the half-dozen that surrounded the fire *"—do with you as we see fit... Or not."*

He looked back at Syrah, still ever smiling. *"Do you understand what I mean, Witch? Do you understand what I imply, woman?"*

Syrah had thought she understood, but the way in which he said this last word left her with no doubt.

She could feel what little bravery she had left slipping rapidly way, and she scrambled to hold onto it, praying silently to the Lifegiver for strength.

Grahst took her silence as understanding.

"Gooa," he said, slapping his knee as though they had just hammered out an excellent business deal. *"Then let us begin... How many of your 'Priests' man this Citadel of yours?"*

Syrah set her jaw, held his gaze, and said nothing.

After several seconds, Grahst lost a little of his smile. Looking away from her he glanced at the man still standing over her left shoulder—Krehnt, he had called him—and gave a small nod.

Without so much as a hesitation in which to give Syrah a chance to prepare herself, Krehnt stooped down, grabbed the smallest finger of Syrah's right hand, and broke it with a twisting *snap*.

Syrah screamed, partially collapsing as agony ripped through her, lancing into every limb and digging into her mind. She barely kept to her knees, head touching the cold earth as she continued to shriek, writhing in pain.

"*Let's try again!*" she heard Grahst shout over her howling. "*How MANY, Witch?*"

It took all the strength she had for Syrah to roll her head to one side, and her words came through teeth grit in pain.

"More than you can handle, *vrek*," she said in the Common Tongue. Though she thought it likely Grahst knew enough of the language to have understood everything, the slur, at least, was not lost upon the rest of the group. Several men roared in fury, a couple even reaching for sword and ax handles, leering in her direction.

Grahst held them up with a raised hand, but he, too, seemed to have lost much of the cruel amusement that had toyed across his face before she'd spoken.

"*You are dangerously close to sealing your own fate*, woman." He said the word carefully again, as though attempting once more to remind her of certain vulnerabilities.

Then he managed to smile again, though it was somewhat more forced than usual. "*Perhaps I am asking too much too soon*," he said, almost politely. "*Krehnt, help her up again.*"

Syrah yelled again as Krehnt's fingers dug into her hair, pulling her back up into a kneeling position. When he let go, she half slumped, shivering in pain, her right hand still feeling as though it had been lit afire. She did her best to calm herself, did her best to draw out the magics within to heal what damage she could.

The pain began to subside.

"*Let's try something else*," Grahst was saying, leaning back and running a hand through his beaded beard in false pensiveness. "*Something simple… Ah! I know. Why don't you tell me what sort of stores you've gathered up in your keep? How long can your faithful sustain themselves holed up within their walls? A month, a year?*"

Syrah was fighting to calm her breathing. The throbbing in her hand was tempered enough now to allow her to think straight, and she prepared herself, drawing the spell into her palms in anticipation.

When Krehnt went for another finger, she would make sure to leave him with a scar he'd never forget her by.

"Long enough for Laor's wrath to wipe you and your *friends* from this life and the next," she finally answered, baring her teeth at Grahst.

Once more there was a pause in which Grahst grew momentarily still. Then, again, he nodded to Krehnt, and Syrah readied a blast of fire from her good hand.

Only Krehnt didn't go for her fingers. Instead, quick as a flash, he drew a knife from his belt, grabbed the bottom of Syrah's right ear, and preceded to cut off the better part of the flesh he had pinched between his fingers.

This time Syrah only heard herself scream from some far-off place. The pain and shock snaked into her mind, devouring every sense as metal sawed through tissue, and within seconds everything went black and she knew herself to be falling.

She couldn't have been out very long, because she felt Krehnt's hand in her hair once more, and she was already on her knees again before she came fully to. She didn't have any more sound to give the pain, instead losing herself in a sort of numbness that enveloped her body, mind, and soul.

Only when a gentle finger tilted her chin up did Syrah lift her eyes from the ground.

Grahst had moved from his place on the stump, and was on one knee before her. If that wasn't terrifying enough, the other men around the fire had moved closer, surrounding them in a dark, seething huddle. She could smell them, now, could make out the stench of weeks of hard road on unwashed bodies.

It made Syrah feel ill.

"*I tell you for your own sake,*" Grahst said, almost kindly, keen blue eyes cruelly soft as they met hers, "*that this will be your last chance. My King will take your Citadel, with or without your help. It is your last opportunity to save yourself many days in which you will wish very desperately that you had made a different choice. Do you understand?*"

Syrah only stared numbly back at him, and again he took this as a sign of her grasp on the situation.

He nodded. "*Very well. I'll ask the same question again. What sort of stores do your Priests have in reserve?*"

For a long time Syrah continued to stare at him, half lost to the pain in her hand, head, and body, and half preparing herself, conquering the cold and fear with thoughts of Talo, Carro, Jofrey, Reyn, and every other person she had ever loved or cared for high up above them, safe in the Citadel.

Then she drew in a quick breath, and spit in Kareth Grahst's face.

Instantly there was a seething roar, and Syrah felt a dozen hands make to reach for her, their owners howling in rage.

Once more, though, Grahst stopped them.

"NO!"

The hands froze and retreated, and Syrah glared defiantly at the man kneeling before her, watching him wipe the spittle from his nose and cheek with the back of his hand.

"*I admit to disappointment, Witch. I had hoped you wouldn't turn out to be the same type of fool as my father. As it stands, though, you've made your choice. Now... you have another.*"

In a blur Grahst's right hand plucked the knife Krehnt had used to cut off the lower half of her ear from her torturer's grasp. In the same motion, Grahst's left hand wrapped around her throat, swinging her bodily down and slamming her sideways to the ground before twisting her painfully onto her back.

Syrah had just enough time to gasp in pain when she realized the tip of the bloody knife was suspended over her right eye.

"*Your choice, Witch, is this: your eye, or your virtues. Choose.*"

Cold fire rushed through Syrah, a pure wash of terror and desperation. She couldn't move, couldn't think. All of a sudden the only thing Syrah was capable of was reliving the last time she had felt such fear, under the hungry gazes of a band of slavers in a dirty little abandoned hut at the edge of hot market road.

It was all she could do, and Syrah Brahnt would regret this hesitation for the rest of her life.

"*Another silence?*" Grahst asked harshly. "*Very well. Then I'll have both.*"

And then Syrah felt the blade dig into the jagged cut above her eye, scraping against the bone as Grahst dragged it downward in quick precision.

She had just enough time to become aware of the explosion of inexplicable agony, just enough time to become aware that half of her vision had gone suddenly dark, when she felt innumerable fingers tearing at her already shredded robes.

Despite this, Syrah only started to scream when she felt the sting of the cool air against her bare breasts, and the wrenching of her legs as they were forced apart by strong, unyielding hands.

XIII

"It saddens me to this day, her terror of the forests. Some have been fool enough to call her agitation 'irrational' in my presence, even 'juvenile.' They refuse to see the pain in her, as she cowers there beneath the trees. They refuse to see the torment reliving certain memories forces her to experience once again. It has often taken her own hand on my arm to keep me from teaching those ignorant men a hard and harsh lesson. Still... despite my own understanding, it saddens me. For—when all the lands of the world are there to be judged—is there really any place more wondrous than the grand woodlands of the Northern ranges?"

—the Dragon of the North

As he'd stood upon that hill, overlooking the magnificence of the Dehn Plains, the place had done something to Raz. He'd been given a glimpse of an old life, a life of sands and family, of heat—despite the bitter cold—and Sun. It had been a breathtaking experience, and one he knew he would often revisit when in need of a good memory to draw warmth from.

Not as often, though, Raz told himself, the first coherent thought he'd had in a full minute, *as I'll revisit this.*

It had started to snow again, the flurries growing steadily heavier since they'd left their camp that morning. Now, three or four hours later, the Sun was little more than a distinct patch of mild brightness against a darkened sky, and the air was thick with tumbling white. Behind them the rolling land of the Dehn was swallowed up by the building storm, the horizon blurred as land melded with snow and sky.

And before them, towering with a sort of menacing welcome, the Arocklen Woods drew Raz's eyes as though he'd been enchanted.

The tree line started abruptly, marked by barely fifty paces of steadily thickening trunks before the darkness beneath the canopy became so dense even Raz couldn't make out a thing from this distance. Most of the forest consisted of evergreens, of firs and pines of various kinds mixed with the towering outlines of larger cedars and bulky hollies. The right halves of their bluish and green foliage were caked with snow as the winds blew hard from the east, giving them an almost painted look as they swayed. While the staggered runts at the very edges of the Woods weren't much bigger than the scattered trees they'd seen over the course of the morning—their lowest branches barely high enough for Raz to crouch under comfortably—the forest built itself up like the angle of a mountain, and by the time the Sun became blocked beneath the canopy Raz doubted he could have reached the bottom branches of the shortest pines even with Ahna held to her extent.

The tallest, it looked like, had trunks that towered twenty or thirty feet before whatever god had crafted the Arocklen even thought of branches.

The ground too, changed rather abruptly. Whereas Gale—snorting and stomping impatiently beneath Raz—stood now in a solid foot-and-a-half of fresh powder and packed ice, as the trees thickened so too did the snows thin. Not fifty yards ahead of where he and the Priests sat mounted at the very edge of the Woods, Raz was almost positive he could make out undergrowth, browned in the cold, and clear, hard earth. The terrain was abruptly different as well. For the last half-mile of their trek they'd left the hills of the Dehn behind—as well as whatever relative shelter had been offered from the wind—and moved onto nearly flat land. Within the trees, though, the earth started to take on a carved, jagged appearance, rolling and jutting up and down and out in patches of rocky outcroppings, grassy inclines and dips, and moss-covered, earthen walls.

"Told you it was a sight."

Raz blinked and turned to look over his shoulder. Brahnt was gazing at the tree line as well, blue eyes taking in the Woods from beneath the raised hood of his High Priest's robe. On his other side, al'Dor was doing the same, even raising a big gloved hand to block the flurries from his face. Both men's beards were caked with snow, their noses red from the wind and cold. Raz, too, felt numbness across his protruding snout, but the ride had kept him otherwise warm and he was getting slowly used to the icy temperament of the freeze.

"That you did," he responded, looking back around at the Woods. "I admit, I don't know what I'm keener on doing: plunging headfirst in, or turning tail to run."

al'Dor, overhearing this, snorted.

"You're a braver man then I if you're even considering the former!" he shouted as the wind picked up momentarily. "The Arocklen in the summer is one thing. All greenery and warmth and sunlight pouring through the canopy overhead. This, though—" he waved a hand at the foreboding mouth of the forest before them "—this makes me feel like I'm about to step willfully into the belly of the beast."

Brahnt, for his part, became unusually somber at the words, and Raz glanced at him.

"He's not so far off the mark, is he?" he asked quietly, so that only the High Priest could hear.

Brahnt gave a small shake of his head as he heeled his mare forward. "No, he's not. This forest isn't somewhere I would really ever wish to be, this time of year. Stay vigilant, Arro."

"Was planning on it," Raz replied, pressing Gale forward to keep up with the man. "Your 'Kayle' is somewhere about in there. What are the chances we come across him, or his men?"

"Hopefully slim. Baoill entered the woods far to the north, and even farther west. If his goal is to make for Ystréd then Azbar, pushing east into the trees would slow him down significantly given the breadth of his army. He's probably keeping to the western edge of the Woods, using it for cover so he can make *some* progress south over the course of the winter and push out into the Dehn as soon as the snows clear."

Brahnt frowned, then, pulling his horse around so as not to collide with the branches of the first of the trees. "Still… We'll take the trails east a bit, before making for Cyurgi' Di."

"Just in case?" Raz muttered just as they reached the shade of the true Woods.

Brahnt nodded. "Just in case."

"What are you two mumbling about over there?" al'Dor asked them, his words taking on a suddenly crisp tenor that almost irritated Raz's sensitive ears after so many days in the muffling snow.

"Nothing, handsome," Brahnt said quickly, throwing him a smile. "Arro is asking me about Syrah again."

Raz rolled his eyes. It had become a running joke all morning between the two men. Apparently he'd revealed more interest than he'd intended as they'd spoken the afternoon before, and the Priests had taken it in full stride, making suggestive comments and teasing winks whenever they had the opportunity. Privately, Raz didn't mind. He'd grown fond of the pair very much despite his initial reservations, and he thought they were due their amusement. It made it hard, though, to question them about the woman.

And Raz certainly wanted to.

He had yet to pin down exactly from where his curiosity—no, Raz admitted to himself—his *interest*, bloomed. He'd always wondered, on the occasions he'd dwelled on that fateful day, what her name was, and what business she'd been about to be wandering Karth's markets on her own. He'd always pondered if she'd ever made it back home to the North, or even out of Karth. That, though, had been just about the extent of his concerns.

Now… Now there was something else bouncing about inside his mind, and Raz couldn't put his finger on it.

He suspected that his intrigue had much to do with the way he had met Syrah Brahnt, and the way they had parted. He suspected, too, that it had much to do with the events that had followed in quick succession. Syrah—if the title could be truly given to any one thing—had been the catalyst of the eruption that had torn his life apart, turned it upside down and inside out. *She* had been the trigger. *She* had been both the fuse *and* the lighting spark.

And yet, not a single ounce of Raz could cast the blame on her.

That, in and of itself, had been curious to him. All his adult life he had been quick to lay the blame on those responsible for the cruelties of the world, placing it at his own feet and at the feet of others in equal measure. When one drove towards madness and murder, Raz had always found it simple to shape his understanding of a man—or woman—by the sins that rested upon their shoulders. It made it easy for him to do what he had to do, to wipe the filth from the face of the earth.

But Syrah Brahnt, he'd found, could bear no such outline in his mind. He'd tried, just out of curiosity. He'd *tried* to get angry, *tried* to blame and to hate her, *tried* to destroy the notion of the woman that the Priests were building for him.

He'd failed abysmally.

A shadow caught his eye, darting between the trunks of two trees to his left. Raz glanced in its direction, but found it only to be a trick of the limited light against the underbrush. Still, the motion made him think of the shades that had dogged his steps to Ystréd, and Lueski Koyt leapt suddenly to the forefront of his mind.

In the bright blue of her eyes, hidden beneath a waterfall of black hair, Raz suddenly found the answer.

I care.

The realization slipped across Raz's thoughts like a breeze. Perhaps it was just the fact that the concept was unfamiliar to him, or at least long removed and sequestered to another life. Whatever it was, he was surprised by how long it had taken the understanding to fall into place. He remembered again the first time he had met Syrah, then the first time he had learned her name, in the Koyts' little home in Azbar. He had fallen asleep that night thinking of that name.

As he had fallen asleep last night to dreams of the woman she had become.

I care, he thought again.

And of course he cared. Syrah Brahnt was perhaps the only bright thing to have come from the darkness that was the end of that part of Raz's life. The death of the Arros, the loss of his mother and father and sister... For the first time—the idea striking Raz like a punch in the chin—he realized that it had not been for nothing.

Something had come from that loss. *Something* had come from that sacrifice. From the outside, it might not seem like much, but to Raz it meant everything.

Syrah had survived.

Of course he cared.

The clarity didn't bear with it any joy, but it did bring a sort of peace to Raz. As though some tiny part of the fires that burned within him had winked out, their angry heat no longer needed. For some inexplicable reason, Raz felt suddenly less alone in the world. It turned out he hadn't lost everything that night, as he'd always thought. He'd lost much, yes, but not everything. The girl had lived. She had survived and thrived, growing into a woman that her adopted father was proud of and her people seemed to have great love and respect for.

Syrah was what he had sacrificed for. Syrah was what was left to him.

And in that moment, as the light of the sky faded into blackness through the trees behind him, Raz decided he would tell her that, give her that knowledge—that honor—if it was the last thing he did in this world.

Crack.

Raz jerked out of his reverie, right hand flying to the handle of the gladius over his shoulder, looking around with teeth bared as his crest flared instinctively against the back of his hood. To his right Brahnt and al'Dor stared, just as surprised by his response as he had been by the sound.

In al'Dor's hand was a thick length of dead wood, torn from the upward jutting skeleton of a fallen branch they had ridden by.

"Easy, lad," the Priest said with a nervous smile, raising his other hand in a calming sign. "No need to get all worked up."

Raz stared at the splintered wood for another second.

Then he released the sword.

"Sorry," he said, returning the hand to Ahna's shaft, making sure she was still balanced over his thighs. "I was… elsewhere."

"Well don't fall asleep on us just yet," al'Dor said, examining the branch in his hand for splinters. "This may be the one part of the trip I'll be happy to have those blades of yours with us. Wolves are scared of two things. Steel—" he grabbed the shattered end of the wood with his other hand "—and fire."

There was a flash of white light, and the end of the branch was suddenly engulfed in a layer of flickering ivory flames that emanated a soft, gentle glow which nonetheless penetrated the darkness for twenty paces in every direction.

Raz blinked in momentary blindness as his eyes adjusted to this new source of light, and when he'd regained his vision he saw that al'Dor had passed the makeshift torch along to Brahnt, who was now holding it out for him to take.

"Are we sure that's smart?" he asked. "Fire is going to make us easy enough to track in this dark."

"And fire is also going to make it easy enough not to kill our horses." Brahnt smirked. "Even you won't be able to see much once we lose what little sunlight we have left." He jerked his head over his shoulder, indicating the fading daylight.

Raz hesitated, but eventually reached out to take the torch.

"Thanks," he said, turning about to raise the white flames high, examining his surroundings in detail now even as al'Dor broke off from them in search of more fallen branches.

The trees rose around and above them like a thousand twisted pillars holding up a ceiling of glimmering ice and shadows high above their heads. The trunks curved and bent around themselves, as though refusing to grow according to nature's dictation. A few scattered saplings and younger trees were spread between the older evergreens that made up the majority of the Woods, but these slimmer specimens stood sad, dwarfed compared to the thickness of the elders that rose up about them like angry parents over small children. The narrowest of the great trees Raz saw might have taken two men to reach completely around, fingers barely touching.

The widest would have taken ten.

Raz was also taken aback to notice life among the stillness. Snow foxes darted across their path more than once, little more than a blur of white fur that made the mares nicker and shy when it happened. Big, furry variations of what Raz had learned were squirrels scampered regularly up and down the trees, black eyes glinting in the light of the three torches they now carried. Once or twice Raz even saw the white upturned tail and slim legs of another creature, catching a glimpse of them darting off further into the Woods, frightened by the light and horses.

He fought off the welling sadness as he remembered a night some months ago now, just as the freeze began to fall across the land, where a boy had taught him the name "deer" as his little sister fell asleep, head in his lap…

Despite this, Raz was pleased to see the animals. It gave the otherwise still Woods a soul-like quality, speaking to something hidden deeper within the stillness of the gnarled pines. He could imagine, to some extent, the verdure of which al'Dor had spoken, during the warmer months of summer. He tried to take his memories of his first week in Northern land, lost among the thinner woods along the border of the North and South, and apply them to his current surroundings. He found himself imagining a world of light and color and life, the brown of the moss replaced with vibrant rust and green, with flowers growing in lines and patches along where the Sun managed to peek through during the day. At night, he crafted himself a quiet world of singing insects and cool, soft grass, upon which one could lay to study Her Stars through the branches. In comparison, looking at the cold world about him, Raz thought suddenly of tombstones, cold and hard and angry in winter.

The idea made him shiver, and he was unable to stop himself swinging the torch around to glance behind their little party, peering into the dark. The Sun was gone completely now, and Raz realized he was less comfortable with the prospect than he'd expected. It wasn't the claustrophobia, that discomfort and anxiety that had sometimes plagued him in the market streets of the fringe cities. Rather, it was the base feeling that no one was watching over him now. Not the Sun, not the Moon, not Her Stars, and not even the Arros.

He was alone.

Well… not completely.

Raz brought his attention back around to face the trail. He'd fallen behind the Priests a little, Gale slowing down when Raz had turned, as though sensing his rider's hesitation. The Priests were having another one of their amusing tiffs, apparently arguing about what their first meal would be when they finally reached the High Citadel.

"*Lamb?*" al'Dor was demanding shrilly, as though genuinely offended by the prospect. "Three weeks we'll have been on this damn road, up to our end in snow, and all you can come up with is *lamb?*"

"*With* spiced apple slices, thickened garlic broth, and cranberry and nut bread." Brahnt sniffed indignantly at his lover as they dipped down along a steep embankment, making to cross a frozen stream that twisted its way through the trees. "Give me some credit."

al'Dor only muttered something in reply, making Raz smile from behind the pair.

Losing the Koyts had ripped a hole in him, one that was far come from healing. The children had once more given Raz things he had long assumed he would forever be without. Kindness, love, family. They had broken his conceived notion that his path in the world was one best walked alone, best kept in the shadows.

And then they'd been torn away, and the hatred and rage that had bloomed in Raz from that act had ripped great gauges in the delicate fabric of the new reality he had started to discover for himself.

Now, though, Raz could feel those holes slowly stitching themselves back together. He had friends in the world, he knew now. Watching the broad backs of Talo Brahnt and Carro al'Dor, Raz couldn't help but thank the Sun for sending the men to him, carrying with them the strength he had needed to quite literally get back on his feet.

Heeling Gale forward, Raz made to catch up to the pair, joining in the conversation.

XIV

"To this day the Stone Gods hold a place in the culture of the world. Though their faith has largely faded in the last centuries—as the customs of the valley towns and mountain tribes became steadily integrated over time—it is not uncommon to see traces of the old deities in modern spiritual arts. Wood and bone carvings often adorn hearths and tables, believed to bring strength and protection to a household. Murals and motifs can be seen as bas-relief and friezes on walls, columns, and in the accents of a home. It is my understanding that many of these depictions are, in fact, misinterpreted representations of the Lifegiver, a generally faceless ideal until the end of the first century b.S., over which period this bastardization seems to have taken place. Only in the far north, past the Saragrias and Vietalis ranges, do the old ways of the Stone Gods still hold sway. There, in the Tundra, it is said there still exists a civilization of men as brutal and savage as the Kayles of old, as wicked as the goa-kings who'd ruled the mountain tribes with a bloody, iron fist. It is a small wonder we, of the modern era, have not pushed beyond the mountains, nor that those who try so rarely return..."

—*The North: Ancient Tradition and Culture,* by Agor Kehn

They charged Gûlraht in pairs, as instructed. The blades and axes they hefted were of dulled wood and leather—because Gûlraht was no fool—but the men wielded them expertly, as they had wielded steel and iron from birth. They did not give their Kayle respite between attacks, did not offer him a moment to catch his breath between groups. They fought viciously, as though their life depended on it.

The Kayle was not known to look favorably upon weakness.

Gûlraht himself had no weapons. His massive two-handed great-ax, handed down to him by his father as he died, lay propped against the creaking trunk of a tree nearby, surrounded by mountain men and looking as though it meant to join them in spectating the fights. He had only his fists to defend himself with, clenched before his weathered face in a defensive stance. He watched as the first two men rushed him, howling their battle cries as they came.

They didn't last long.

The first went down in an instant as Gûlraht dodged nimbly towards the swing of his wooden ax, bringing himself into the space between blade and body in which a weapon becomes almost useless. A strike to the gut doubled the man over, his nose breaking with a *crunch* as it found the Kayle's knee, brought up swiftly to meet his face.

Gûlraht made sure to temper the blow. There was no use in killing able-bodied men just for his pleasure.

As the man tumbled to the ground, groaning in pain and clutching at his nose, Gûlraht spun in time to throw himself clear of a swinging blade, the blunted tip missing his bulk by a hair's breadth. For several seconds he was put on the defensive again, kept at bay by the combined strength and skill of his opponent, the sword *whooshing* through the air in complicated patterns.

He would have to find a use for this one…

But Gûlraht was of an altogether different breed of warrior. He had been taught to kill as every young man of the mountain clans was taught. He had been taught to bathe in the blood and glory of his enemy, to draw out their weaknesses, to exploit all things about a man that can be exploited. He was of the mountains, as hard and unyielding as stone itself.

Gûlraht, though, had learned other lessons too, as he grew. He'd learned long ago that he did not see as other men saw, did not think as other men thought. His mind was faster, sharper. His mind was steeled, keen to the world.

His mind was crueler.

And his mind had led him to understand that survival, above all else, was key. Survival by strength, by sacrifice, or by any other means necessary.

In this situation, survival by the icy dirt he managed to shovel onto the edge of his foot, kicking it up into the face of the sword-wielding soldier as a cross-swing went up and wide, barely missing Gûlraht's thigh.

The man cried out, blinded by the spray of earth and snow, one hand leaving the sword hilt and flying to his eyes. It was an instinctive move, an ingrained response to which humans had no defense or override.

And it was all Gûlraht needed.

He closed the space between them in a blink. He did not lean on theatrics, did not flourish his strength and skills for those that watched from the trees. He was there to keep his body strong and limber, there for his evening ritual of breaking the monotony of the march that pressed them ever deeper into the dark of the Arocklen, following Grahst and the vanguard.

And he was there to prove that challenging him—as he had challenged Emreht Grahst, and as any man of mountain blood had the right to do—was a fool's move.

Gûlraht downed his opponent in one blow, his right fist catching him in the side of the head and laying him out flat, slamming him down into the hard, cold earth.

He didn't get up again.

Once more, Gûlraht spun around, though, not relishing in his victory just yet. Two more were already charging him, rushing him together. Both swung swords this time, and one bore a light hide shield on his left arm.

They pressed him side by side, yelling their taunts, blades thrust out before them.

Amusingly, they didn't even last half as long.

Gûlraht saw the opening, and took it. The men were too close together, the fear of their Kayle leading them to fight pressed practically up against the other, shoulder to shoulder. It was a technique that worked well for shield walls, or for spearmen and pike wielders.

It did not work so well here.

Gûlraht took the simple path. Letting the pair come to him, he waited until the last possible moment, allowing the swords within a foot, wooden edges glowing in the light of the torches held by many of the observers among the trees. When he judged the timing to be right, he twisted his bulk and ducked, sliding barely under the points that had been aimed at his body, the largest target available. The obvious attack suddenly robbed from them, neither man reacted quickly enough, too concerned with striking the other as their momentum carried them forward, right into the Kayle.

Powerful legs propelled Gûlraht's mass upward, both hands reaching up to either side. There were twin "*urks*" of choked breath as the two men found themselves each caught by the throat, their legs failing and tripping up beneath them as their charge was cut short.

With a roar and the ripple of straining muscle, Gûlraht lifted both men a foot into the air behind the impetus of his lunge, swords and the shield tumbling from desperate hands to grasp and claw at his arms.

Then he brought the men down to slam them, too, back into the ground.

One laid there, coughing and hacking as he strained to gain back the breath that had been knocked out from him. The other was out cold. Yet again Gûlraht sprang up and spun about, ready for the third pair. These two wielded the mock replacements for a long hammer and spear, hefting them up as they shouted and rushed forward. Gûlraht was about to spring forward to meet them, looking to down the hammer-wielder with a quick blow before he managed to get his heavier weapon into a defensive position, when a voice cut through the fight.

"*MY KAYLE!*"

At once the two men froze in their tracks. Gûlraht for his part, halted his lunge, taking a few loping steps before he could stop. He turned around slowly, feeling the anger boil up inside of him at the intrusion.

"*Agor,*" he breathed, his voice a menacing rumble as he looked upon the man who had shouted over the fight, "*it's a special sort of fool who interrupts me without—*"

But then Gûlraht stopped.

Agor Vareks was not the oldest of his generals but, among men who often lived short lives, he was old enough. Black, dreaded hair framed a wind-beaten face, streaks of grey and silver twisting through it. Gold and wooden beads were thick among the braids, and the narrow bones of some wildcat plated his beard to hang just past his chest. He stood tall despite his fifty or so years, maybe half-a-head more than most of the men lingering around the trampled ring.

Still, even Agor looked up to Gûlraht, who stood two-head taller than *him*.

But Gûlraht was not looking down at the general, now. His dark eyes had skipped right over the man, darting from him to the smaller, slighter figure standing to his left. Dirt and filth lined the man's cheeks and hair, light leather armor streaked with red and green paints over black fur. He was slim, built for speed and silence, and his pale eyes darted about nervously from beneath a wolf-skull helm, taking in the Kayle, the men being helped up behind him, and the hundred shadows of the warriors among the trees.

Gûlraht had thousands of the Gähs among his forces. He had ensured the submission of their tribes before pushing east through the valley towns of Metcaf and Harond, along the tip of the Saragrias Ranges, and into the Aroclen Woods. The Goatmen were agile, adapting well to the forest and its hills, and had provided the backbone of his scouting forces, managing the terrain better than the heavier, bulkier men of the other tribes. Hundreds came and went from the front line every day, providing reports, identifying shelter and water sources, and directing the hunters and foragers into the trees to gather food and supplies when possible. Gûlraht didn't know them all. He barely knew any of them, truth be told, and wasn't bothered by the fact.

But this one, he *did* know...

"*Elrös,*" he said by way of greeting, hiding his surprise. "*I hope for your sake Kareth knows you've left the vanguard...*"

Elrös of the Grasses bobbed his head skittishly, apparently finding it hard to meet Gûlraht's eyes.

"He does, my Kayle," the man said, wringing thin hands over each other. "*Grahst sent me himself, in fact. I come bearing news, you see...*"

That caught Gûlraht's attention, and he looked down upon the man with narrowed eyes. Originally one of a dozen chieftains of the Gähs' individual clans, Elrös had been quickest to bend the knee when the new Kayle came over the mountains with an army some fifteen thousand strong. As a reward, he had been allowed to keep his life.

Most of the others, Gûlraht had executed himself.

Elrös had proven himself a useful ally in the end, demonstrating keen wit and intuition when it came to managing the Woods, even through the freeze. When Kareth Grahst had taken the advanced guard—some five hundred lightly supplied warriors—Gûlraht had given him the Goatman and his score of troops to command, hoping it would lend well to Grahst's speed.

Now, though, Elrös of the Grasses had returned, and Gûlraht admitted to himself he couldn't begin to guess why.

"*Report,*" he said shortly, crossing muscled arms over one another and glowering down at the Goatman.

Elrös, in turn, seemed to shrink down into himself.

"*My Kayle,*" he practically squeaked when he spoke now, "*the information I bring is best to be heard in private.*" His eyes darted to Agor. "*Grahst made it clear, my Kayle. I'm to deliver my news to you, and only you.*"

Impatience pinched at Gûlraht, but he brushed it aside, frowning. His cousin was a vicious, quick-tempered man, but he wasn't stupid. If Kareth thought the particulars of Elrös' report were best revealed behind closed doors, then he would have cause.

Something has happened, Gûlraht thought, still looking down on the Goatman imperiously. *Something Kareth believes I will need to consider before acting.*

"*Agor,*" Gûlraht said without taking his eyes off of Elrös. The elder general looked up. "*Take him to my tent. I'll be there shortly. Let no one speak to him until I arrive.*" He shot the old man a glaring look. "*That includes you.*"

If Agor Vareks was offended by the suggestion, he didn't show it. He nodded briefly, then took Elrös of the Grasses by the shoulder and spun him around. Gûlraht watched them go.

What could have happened?

A quarter-hour later Gûlraht had dismissed the spectators, following their torchlight back towards the camp. In one hand he carried his great ax, allowing the familiar weight of the weapon to settle his mind. His thoughts—as thoughts are wont to do given any opportunity—flit about to every worst possible scenario. Had the valley towns mustered their forces already? Had the Laorin proved more vicious than anticipated? Had some disaster befallen the front line?

As he arrived among the first row of tents, Gûlraht brushed the concerns aside. He ignored the frightened glances cast his way by the camp slaves as they scurried from his path, just as he ignored the monotonous lip service and bows of the men about him. He was Kayle. He was a god among lessers.

And he had neither the time nor the patience for the weaker rabble, the fodder with which he would feed his battles and please Them of Stone.

Still, as he hiked his way up to the lip of the cliff ledge that overlooked the east camp, even the Kayle took pause to bask in the magnificence of the sight.

Before him the Woods opened up like some vast, endless chamber. Crooked trunks reached up to support a glittering ceiling of ice, branches twisting through the packed snow like black veins. From his place along the ridge, looking down into the great space beneath the canopy created by the massive trees, Gûlraht felt almost as though he were peering from atop a staircase into an immense, columned room.

A room filled with noise, smoke, and the burning orange glow of thousands upon thousands of cooking fires.

Tents of leather and cloth and fur pelts extended for as far as the eye could see, disappearing and reappearing as the land dipped and cut away into itself. Dotted spots of light marked groupings of companions, shield-brothers and clanmates, and shapes shifted about and between them like ants. The camp hummed with the low mélange of hundreds of conversations and arguments, and beneath the buzz Gûlraht could make out the sharp shouts of orders being given to the evening's watch and the departing night patrols. The heavy hammering of metal reached his ears, and looking off to his left he made out the deeper shine of the forge fires as the dozen smiths they had brought with them began their nightly duties of repairing gear damaged in the march. The thick wafting of hot food floated up to him as Gûlraht stood over his army, mixing with the stench of a thousand unwashed bodies and the mess of human waste that was an unavoidable byproduct of so many men grouped together in one place.

Gûlraht didn't mind.

To him, it was the same as the smell of oil and steel and blood that meant battle was on the horizon.

Turning north, Gûlraht walked until he found a narrow trail that led down the cliff wall, descending some twenty feet until he reached the lower ground. Starting to pick his way through the camp, he again ignored the looks and shouts he received from his soldiers and their slaves, moving past them, a hulking giant among weaker, undeserving men.

It was another ten minutes or so before Gûlraht managed to make his way through the camp. His own tent stood erect at the eastern-most edge of the army, the frontline of the march. It was a plain thing, no different than the thousands of others he had just left behind, though it was somewhat larger. He'd done away with the extravagant, chambered pavilion of cotton and silk that had been Emreht's home during times of war and raiding. It had made Gûlraht feel pampered, and the pointless lavishness seemed little more than a good reason for his men to see him as unable to bear the difficulties of the world.

A man weathered the elements and laughed in their faces, just as he laughed in the face of death when it tried again and again to claim him. A man did not turn his back to the wind and curl up pitifully until the storm was at an end.

And so Gûlraht had burned the damn thing, and kept his old tent instead.

A group of slaves, all women of the valley towns, were scurrying about when he arrived, most tending to a large fire and the skewers of meat and roots suspended over it. Two were lugging heavy buckets of water they would use later for baths, dumping them into a wide barrel brought close to the flames so its contents could heat while Gûlraht ate.

The bath was for the women. Gûlraht couldn't care less what sort of filth and stench he accumulated on the march, but even *he* couldn't deny the preferred appeal of a clean, well-scrubbed girl to entertain him before he slept...

The Kayle didn't do more than glance at any one of the women now, though. He would pick one later, if he was in the mood. For the moment, he had more pressing matters to attend to.

Moving past the fire, Gûlraht pulled open the sown bear hides used as a door and stepped into the relative warmth of the tent.

Agor and Elrös of the Grasses were there, as expected, waiting for him. Two other men accompanied the pair, standing opposite them on the other side of a shallow iron brazier filled with a carefully tended bed of smokeless, glowing embers. Gûlraht did not nod to the newcomers, having suspected they might make themselves known. Erek Rathst and Rako the Calm—or Rako the Soft, as most of the army was more like to call him when his back was turned—were the last of his generals. Erek was a younger man, around the same age as Kareth, and he shared Gûlraht's cousin's penchant for battle, though not so much of his wild temperament. Rako, on the other hand, was Gûlraht's uncle, and the oldest of his advisors. He was a thinning, whining shadow of a once powerful warrior who spent most of their meetings seeking to pacify the younger men, trying to convince them to temper their bloodlust with kind words and contemplation. Gûlraht had taken him into his fold purely to satisfy the older generations of the Sigûrth, many of whom had stood by and cheered—or at the very least done nothing to stop it—as Emreht Grahst had signed away their traditions and lifestyle with nothing more than a flourish of ink.

Erek, Gûlraht would have summoned himself. Rako, on the other hand...

"They were here when we arrived," Agor said with an apologizing shrug as Gûlraht shot him a pointed glare. *"I didn't send for anyone."*

"We received word that there was a runner from the front line," Erek said at once, light blue eyes taking in every inch of Elrös with a fiery interest.

"Out," Gûlraht said by way of response. *"All of you."*

Rako, standing slightly behind Erek, cleared his throat.

"My Kayle," he started, his monotonous, placating tone grating immediately on Gûlraht's already faltering patience, *"we are aware of the Gähs' hesitancy to speak with anyone but yourself, but might not it be more prudent to—?"*

"I did not ask for your opinion, Rako." Gûlraht met the man's watery eyes with cold intensity. *"I merely commanded you to get out. Now."*

Rako the Calm blinked indignantly but, before he could open his mouth to argue further, Erek had put a hand on his shoulder and started pressing him towards the entrance. The younger general nodded to his Kayle as they moved around him.

"We'll wait outside," he said simply before pulling aside the bear hides and guiding Rako through with a firm hand.

Gûlraht didn't respond, his gaze fixed on the Goatman as Agor followed the other two, stepping back out into the night.

The moment the tent flap was closed, Gûlraht leaned forward, towering over the man.

"Now…" he said, his tone venomously calm. *"Speak."*

"My Kayle," Elrös started at once with a nervous nod, *"Grahst first wishes me to inform you that the vanguard has encamped along the base of the great stair leading to the false faith's great hall, a place they call the* 'Citadel.'" He made a poor pronunciation of the Common word. *"My Goatmen are searching the mountains as we speak, but when I left, five nights past, no evidence of a second path or escape had been found. We believe we have them locked within their walls."*

He paused here, as though wanting to give his Kayle an opportunity to respond, but Gûlraht said nothing. He just watched and waited for the Goatman to continue with dark, unblinking eyes.

"They were expecting us," Elrös eventually continued, taking the hint. *"One of their priests came upon a scouting party. When he ran, they were able to follow him to the stairs. Several days later, upon the arrival of the main advance, we found a small group of the false-god's preachers waiting for us, carrying their white standard of peace."*

Gûlraht almost snorted at that, but refrained. *Another one of their inexplicable habits,* he thought to himself. At both Metcaf and Harond, great men of the town had ridden out to meet him, bearing a white "flag of truce," as they called it. They'd come right up to the front line of his army, shouting nonsense in their foul language, attempting to settle terms and sue for peace.

Both times, Gûlraht had Gähs archers shoot down the men and their horses.

"They attempted to break morale and alienate the clans from your Sigûrth. My Kayle was wise to leave many of his own men back in the villages of the conquered clans. Very wise."

Gûlraht frowned at the reminder. It was a tasteless act, a cruel measure to put to his own people, but it was necessary for the time being.

"What did Kareth do?" he asked, speaking for the first time since Elrös had started talking. The Gähs, in turn, smiled with surprising cruelty.

"He mirrors well your strength, my Kayle. He broke the false-prophets' spell by executing one of his own slaves before them. It broke them, in their weakness, to witness the man's death. Before that, though, Grahst had me take my men into the cliffs, slipping behind the priests."

All nervousness vanished momentarily from the man now, his eyes gleaming with violent excitement.

"We fell on them like a howling storm, and the Stone Gods will be long pleased with the swiftness of the battle that followed."

In the ensuing silence Gûlraht continued to stare down at the man, unmoving. Slowly Elrös' fearful timidity returned to him, and he began to shrink into himself once more, as though cowering in place beneath the Kayle's presence.

"Is that all?"

Gûlraht felt his temper spiking once more as he asked the question. If Grahst had sent the Goatman away just to revel in the glory of this miniscule victory, then Gûlraht would have words for his cousin when they met in two weeks.

In the meantime, he would have more than words for the unfortunate messenger.

"Is that all?" he asked again, his rumbling voice rising. *"Is that everything you have brought me, Goatman? If so, consider me unimpressed. You've interrupted my evening rituals and forced me to dismiss my generals, all to give Kareth his moment of—!"*

"There is more, my King!" Elrös practically squealed, cringing in truth now as he recoiled from Gûlraht's titanic presence. *"There is more! One of the false-prophets was kept alive, my King. She was kept alive for you! She is—!"*

"I've more slaves than I know what to do with AS IS, GOATMAN!" Gûlraht roared, letting the fury loose as he took a step towards the trembling Gähs. *"WHAT AM I TO DO WITH SOME WHORE PRIESTESS OF A LYING GOD?"*

"SHE IS THE WITCH!" Elrös howled in terror, scrambling away from his Kayle. *"GRAHST SAYS THE WOMAN IS THE WHITE WITCH!"*

For one of the few times in his life, Gûlraht's wrath vanished in an instant.

He stood frozen, hands at his sides, clenched into fists that had been more than ready to pummel the offending Gähs into a painful death. He looked down at the man, now, stunned.

"*What did you say?*" he hissed.

"*The White Witch, my Kayle!*" Elrös practically sobbed, crouched on the floor of the tent now, open hands held above his head as though to shield himself from the coming blow. "*Grahst swears by the Gods that he has captured the Witch! He says the false-prophets wanted to send a delegate who spoke our language, who knew our culture. He says they must have thought it the best chance they had to fracture our front line.*"

"*And so they sent the Witch,*" Gûlraht murmured in disbelief.

It only took a few moments for his mind to make sense of the logic. From the outside, it seemed like a foolish play. The Laorin had practically fed the woman right to them, given the Sigûrth exactly what they wanted. After some consideration, however, to the followers of the false-god, it must have seemed like *exactly* the right move to make. The woman—*Brahnt*, he thought with a private snarl, recalling her name—had a reputation among many of the mountain clans, and not by the "Witch" moniker he and his Sigûrth knew her as. She was better known for the help she'd given the sick, and for the food she had brought for the starving. She'd shown them how to tend to the injured, improve their halls and homes, and even shown them how to farm some meager bounty from what little fertile earth could be found among the mountains. To those clans, those weaker, pathetic tribes who had been unable to gain the favor of the Stone Gods and had instead turned to the Priestess for help, Syrah Brahnt had been a grain of light in a hard life.

Suddenly, Gûlraht was no longer so aggrieved that he had kept so many of his Sigûrth among the villages of the conquered clans. He wondered suddenly what would have happened if he hadn't, if he had not left the threat of danger over the homes and families of his soldiers. He wondered what sort of damage the passionate words of the Witch could have done to his front line.

Yes, the Laorin had not been fools. They had done what they thought best, given all the information they had.

And it had blown up in their faces.

Abruptly, suddenly, Gûlraht smiled. It was a monstrous, hard grimace, ecstatic with cruel energy as the Kayle realized what this meant. He thought suddenly of the Witch in iron shackles, beaten and bloody, held captive by his men in the vanguard.

Gûlraht could only hope Kareth wasn't fool enough to kill her before he could get his hands on her himself...

Reaching down quickly, Gûlraht heaved Elrös of the Grasses up by the sides of his leather cuirass. The man looked practically petrified, twitching in his Kayle's massive hands as though terrified to move, and yet desperately wanting to run away.

"*This, Goatman,*" Gûlraht breathed into his face, still smiling maniacally, "*is great,* great *news.*"

He set the man down on his feet, and Elrös was left standing, wolf-skull helm askew, looking very confused.

"*M-my Kayle?*" he asked tentatively, as though suspecting some ploy at his expense.

Gûlraht, though, wasn't paying much attention to him anymore. He had turned, stepping away from the Gähs to stare, transfixed, into the swirling red and orange of the embers in the brazier.

"*Fetch my generals,*" he said to the air, though Elrös knew it was he who was being addressed. The man waited tentatively for further instruction, but when none came he nodded, gave a shaking bow, and made for the tent's entrance.

"*Elrös.*"

The Goatman nearly jumped out of his armor as Gûlraht, still looking into the coals, called after him.

"*Y-yes, my Kayle?*" he asked, trying to control his voice as his heart pounded fearfully in his chest.

"*Take a girl for your bed tonight. You've done well.*"

At that, Elrös brightened significantly.

"*Yes, my Kayle!*" he said gleefully, and Gûlraht could hear the wicked smile return. "*Thank you!*"

And then he was gone, sweeping between the pelts back out into the Woods, going about the Kayle's orders. Soon after, Agor, Erek, and Rako reentered the tent. For a time they stood silent, and Gûlraht ignored the feeling of their eyes on his broad back. He was too filled with murderous, palpable fire, too preoccupied with the shufflings of his own thoughts. For almost a full minute he stood not facing them, both parties silent.

Then he spoke.

"*Kareth has the Witch.*"

The generals, like he, stood in stunned speechlessness for a time.

"*What?*" Agor finally demanded, as though he hadn't heard properly. To his left, Erek said nothing, fierce gaze riveted. To his right, though, Rako shook himself free of the shock, pulling himself up to stand with a dignified air Gûlraht had never liked.

"*She'll be of great use to you in the coming battle, my King,*" he said quickly. "*We should dispatch the Goatman back to your cousin at once, and ensure she is being treated well. She could prove a valuable hostage, which we could exchange for—*"

"We will exchange her for NOTHING," Gûlraht snarled, whirling on the older man. *"And I don't give a shit what Kareth does to her in the meantime, so long as she's still alive by the time we reach the siege line. The Witch is MINE!"*

He spoke with such ferocity that even the old general didn't raise his voice to question him.

"I'll tear the bitch limb from limb," he continued in a growl, his fingers twitching unconsciously at his sides. *"I'll rip her apart with my own hands, and I'll make her beg me to do it. She tried to take everything from us. She tried to take our culture, our traditions. She tried to bend our will to hers, tried to draw us away from the Stone Gods."* He glowered at Rako with dark, hungry eyes. *"I hold no place for such blasphemy in my heart, and I recommend you seek to quench yours."*

He turned to Argo.

"Tell the men to enjoy their last night of leisure," he commanded. *"Come first light, we march at double pace. I want my hands around the bitch's throat within the fortnight."*

Argo smiled in anticipation, bowing briefly.

"As you command, my King," he said at once, then turned and hurried out the tent's entrance.

"Erek," Gûlraht turned to the younger of the remaining generals, *"have a unit of our remaining Gähs ready to leave ahead of us with Elrös, come morning. They're to bolster Kareth's troops, and to relay a message to my cousin."*

Erek smirked.

"The Witch is to live?" he guessed.

Gûlraht nodded. *"Kareth can do as he pleases with her, but if she dies before I arrive, I'll treat him to whatever abuses he had her suffer, and then kill him myself."*

"It will be done," Erek said, and he followed Agor out of the tent.

"And I, my King?" Rako asked after he'd gone. *"How might I serve your will, in this victory?"*

In response, Gûlraht sneered down at the man.

"You, Rako? Why you have the most important task of them all..." He pointed to the light of the fire that outlined the bearskin flaps of the entrance. *"When you leave, send my girls to me. There will be no lesson in tongues, tonight, and it turns out I may just be in the mood for two or three of them after all..."*

XV

"I've come to understand that the North is a place of lies, of wicked dangerous secrets. Masked by the presumed safety of timber and granite walls, corruption and greed strangle the valley towns. Hidden behind the beauty of the land, creatures of the dark prowl the shadows. In the South, at least, the risks we face were in open knowledge, if not brought up in polite conversation. Here in this cold realm, however, I have rapidly grown frightened of discovering what wonders may or may not exist in the world around me. For, with each new stone I turn over, it seems a dozen venomous things crawl out into the open."

—*Evalyn Zall, the Carver of Ystréd*

For over a week Raz and the Priests wound their way east then north through the Arocklen Woods, following a twisting trail that snaked between the trees, a barely distinct path of worn earth cutting through limp and frozen undergrowth. Several times a day all three were forced to dismount, leading the horses by hand up and down steep inclines of unstable earth and roots, or along treacherous ledges of ground and stone slickened with ice where trickles of water seeped along their surfaces during the summer. They only stopped briefly at midday—or what they best guessed to be midday—for a rest and a meal, and once or twice when the opportunity to hunt presented itself. Raz had been impressed when the Priests had deftly set a trap for a large antlered animal they'd told him was an "elk"—similar to a deer, but bigger and darker-haired—instructing him to get behind the creature and chase it towards them. It had been difficult to move quietly through the woods guided by little more than glints of light through the branches above, but he'd managed, darting out at the animal from the left. The elk had screamed and turn to careen eastward through the trees.

It had barely made it twenty feet before two points of ivory light— ghostly mirages in the semi-darkness, guided by skilled hands—caught the creature from either side.

They'd eaten well that night, and every day thereafter.

Evenings were a pleasant affair that had rapidly evolved into habit. When the very last hints of the Sun's light faded, winking out the slim rays that occasionally managed to cut their way through the canopy, they would call a halt and go about making camp. Raz would set off into the trees in search of firewood, leaving the Priests to start the spellwork of warding whatever little nook they had found for shelter. There was little snow in the Arocklen—aside from occasional tumbling chunks that dislodged without warning from above, often taking branches and bark with them as they fell earthward with echoing *cracks*—and even less wind, so the wards weren't as elaborate as those they'd used when crossing the Dehn. It took only about a half hour for the sphere of warmth to be cast and bound, which was ideal. It offered Raz a chance to find his solitude again, to bask in discreet wonder at the scenery of the Woods as he went about taking his war-ax to logs and dead branches in the pallid darkness under the glow of the Moon through the ice above. He thought, too, that the two men enjoyed this time, giving them at least a brief period of privacy every day without his constant presence.

They had no tents, trusting in the land and the Laorin's magics to shelter them as needed. They often spent nights lounging on pelts and bedrolls spread over cleared ground, making conversation about everything and nothing, or else taking in the dancing show of guttering shadows above them, projected onto the packed snow and branches by the evening's fire. It was warm and comfortable there, within their little bubble of magical heat beneath the trees, and Raz had long since allowed himself to be enraptured by the majesty of the forest. He would rise earlier than the men every morning, as he always did. After stealing a bite or two of elk meat to break his fast—thawed and seared over the embers of the prior night's fire—he'd take Ahna and his other weapons into the trees, walking through the diminishing dark until he found any space wide enough to exercise in. He'd go through his morning routine, working his body until he was on his knees, heaving in breaths of icy air and letting them out again in billowing jets of steam, like the flaming breaths of the mythical dahgün. Then he would sit for a time, taking in the morning and the Woods and the uneven pattern of the land spreading out before him through the dawn.

Sometimes he sat for so long that the cold would start digging into his bones, and he'd have to warm himself up all over again.

So it was for a week, with Brahnt and al'Dor growing more and more cheerful with every passing day. Raz couldn't blame them. It must have been a pleasant prospect, returning to Cyurgi' Di after nearly three months of absence. His initial apprehension had budded into intrigue over the last few days, and from there even into anticipation. After the wonder of the Woods, Raz was starting to become curious as to what sort of place the High Citadel really was to enact such hope and excitement from the Laorin. The men had tried to describe it to him time and time again, but no words seemed to do the place true justice, and Brahnt always resigned himself to simply saying "You'll see for yourself, soon enough."

Now, Raz couldn't convince himself one way or the other that he wasn't looking forward to it.

The anticipation came to an abrupt end as evening fell on their ninth day within the Arocklen.

Raz smelled them before he made out the sounds of their approach. The stench of wet fur was the first warning, but as he became aware of their presence he started to weed other things from the air. A tired breeze, sneaking its way through the trees, brought with it the taste of rot and decay. There was a putrid, iron scent there, too, edging the stink of the approaching beasts.

Blood. And death.

"... and so it was around 740v.S. that the border actually became a marked distinction," al'Dor was telling Raz while Brahnt busied himself ahead of them, knocking snow out of his boots as they rode. "Before that, there were disputes regarding taxation and—"

"Something's out there."

al'Dor tripped over his words as Raz cut him off. Raz himself was peering west through the trees, down along the leaf-strewn hill whose crest the trail had followed for the last quarter-mile. He was trying to see through the gloom, but the brightness of the torches they still held in their hands was blinding him beyond anything more than fifty feet.

"What did you say?"

Brahnt had heard him, and was pulling his mare to a halt ahead. Gale and al'Dor's horses stopped in turn, though Gale huffed in annoyance as he was suddenly brought to a standstill.

"There's something out there," Raz said again, switching his torch to his left hand and drawing the gladius with his right. The metal hissed out of its sheath, the sound ringing eerily through the Woods. He raised the flames high, but could see nothing else. "Some*things*. I can hear them. Can you give me more light?"

At once Talo took his hand from his horse's reins and lifted it slowly overhead, palm up. As he did, the orbs of white flames that crowned their torches expanded and roared, growing until they tripled in size. The sudden bloom of light hurt Raz's eyes, but he squinted through the dark, his gaze trailing the edges of the illuminated ring, now extending some hundred feet in all directions.

At first he saw nothing more than the detail of the Woods below. A few dead trees had fallen along the side of the hill, or else come to rest against their living counterparts, propped up at odd angles. Clear glimmers reflected from yet more patches of ice where trails of water might otherwise have flowed free down the slope. A massive boulder, about as tall as Raz and half again as long, sat at the very base of the incline, nestled into the angled earth and covered in mismatched patches of encrusted white lichen and brown moss.

On either side this rock, about ten feet in each direction, paired eyes glinted and blinked, shining in the light of the flames.

"WOLVES!" Brahnt shouted, and the hand he had used to brighten the torches was suddenly alight with fire. His own torch he flung down the hill, its flames dimming slightly as they lost the spurring of his magic. It landed ten feet from the mossy bolder, though, and the light was still more than strong enough to banish the dark around it.

Raz felt his grip tighten involuntarily on the handle of his gladius as the animals were revealed.

He had had a concept of what "wolves" were. Arrun had given him a description once, and al'Dor had expanded on it not a few days before at Raz's request. He knew what a dog was. He'd played with his fair share of them growing up along the shores of the Garin, kept as pets or guard animals by some of the various trading clans. He'd thought of a wolf as a large, hairier version of a dog, roaming about in packs.

This last detail was the only one that did the beasts justice.

There were seven of them that they could see. Three along the right side of the hill's bottom, four to the left. They were massive creatures compared to the slight image Raz had composed in his head, ranging from four to five feet from heads to haunches, and the largest likely weighing around two hundred pounds. Their fur was white and grey, so matted and dirty in places that it stuck up frozen in the air. Their muzzles and fore chests were all a unanimous shade of reddish brown, stained time after time with the blood of the kill. To a one they stood stock still, bodies parallel to the trail, heads turned upwards to look up the hill, teeth bared.

Raz was about to demand what the Priests wanted to do, seeking out some guidance in the situation, when he caught the delicate crunch of leaves from the right.

"BEHIND US!" he yelled, whirling and bringing the gladius up instinctively. He wasn't fast enough to deal a killing blow, but his reflexes still proved sufficient to save his life as yellowish fangs, intended for the back of his neck, found the steel bracer of his right arm instead. There was nothing he could do about the momentum of the wolf's leap, though, and the animal's body slammed into his, hitting him with a hundred-and-fifty-some-odd pounds of unstoppable force. He had only a glimpse of whitish, dirty fur before he was flying off his saddle sideways, hitting the frozen ground with a hard *thud* that knocked the torch from his left hand and Ahna from his lap.

The wolf, though, stayed atop him.

It was a vicious thing, unlike any animal he had ever seen. Even sandcats were quick to strike and retreat, calculating their movements and attacks. The wolf, rather than backing off now that it had vulnerable prey on the ground, never let go of the bracer, wrenching Raz's arm about so powerfully he felt his elbow strain under the pressure. They rolled once, twice, three times down the hill, and only then did Raz understand what the creature was doing.

It was keeping him down until the others arrived to help.

Everything clicked into place, and Raz moved with all the haste and skill of a cornered killer. Dropping the gladius he'd managed to hold onto in his pinned right hand, he sliced at the animal's neck with claws of his left, intent on freeing himself. Thick, knotted hair foiled the blow, though, and so Raz drew his whole hand back, clenching the gauntlet into a steel fist.

The punch broke the animal's neck with a *snap*.

It fell limp off his arm with a pitiful yelp of pain, jaw slackening abruptly. Raz didn't pause, though, whirling around to meet the assault he knew was coming head on. The four wolves on the left seemed to have gone around the hill, likely trying to take the Priests from the flank.

The three on the right, though, were already on him.

With a roar that might have shaken the snow from the trees around him, Raz lanced forward. As the first wolf leapt for him with a snarl, going for the throat, Raz snatched it out of the air by the neck with one hand and slammed it to the ground. The other two came from either side of him, and he leapt back and away, abandoning his hope of gutting the pinned one before it could get back on its feet.

He did, though, manage to draw the war-ax from his belt.

"COME ON!" he screamed, his wings spreading to their fullest extent, ripping his hood back so his crest flared like a blade over his head as the wolf he'd downed managed to scramble up and join the others. "COME AND GET ME!"

The beasts obliged.

They rushed him head-on now, not splitting up this time. One went for his face, but the others stayed low, darting at his legs. Dropping under the leaping one, Raz's struck at the closest of the bottom two, looking to plant his ax between its eyes. The animal was too quick, though, dodging away.

But simultaneously abandoning its companion.

Momentarily free of all other distractions, Raz's full attention snapped onto the third wolf just as it reached him. He was too slow to stop the bite, too slow to keep it from latching crushing jaws around his left thigh, but his thick furs and the leather wrappings he dressed his legs in every day kept the teeth from piercing flesh.

Instead of taking him down, the wolf found itself on the end of a massive kick from Raz's armored right leg.

Ribs cracked audibly, and the wolf screeched as it was sent flying down the hill, tumbling to rest against the boulder where it stayed, whimpering and kicking its legs. Without pausing Raz spun to face the remaining two animals. The wolves changed tactics yet again, circling him slowly in opposite directions, keeping their distance and threatening him with throaty, angry growls all the while. He returned the threats with his own snarls, doing his best as long as he could to keep both in view, knowing they would attack as soon as they were on either side of him.

He didn't give them the chance.

With a howl Raz threw himself at the closest animal before it could bunch up for the pounce. Its companion rushed in the moment he started to move, probably hoping to leap onto his back and pull him down, but even the wolves of the North couldn't keep pace with Raz i'Syul Arro in his element.

He caught the wolf he'd launched himself at barely, seizing it by the scruff of the neck with a clawed hand as it tried to leap away. It howled in pain, thrashing in his grip and trying to get its teeth around to gnash at his arm, but only long enough for the ax to flash up.

Then it fell, and the animal sagged in Raz's hand as blood and brain spilled over the steel of his fingers.

Upon seeing this, the last wolf did the only smart thing it could. Turning tail, it bolted back into the Woods, yelping as it ran.

Breathing hard, Raz let the carcass fall from his grasp. Heaving himself around he scrambled up the hill towards the flashing light of magic and the shapes of rearing horses at its crest, snatching his gladius from the ground as he did. When he reached the top he found Brahnt and al'Dor in the full swing of battle, and Raz couldn't help but pause in stunned amazement.

The Priests were standing in a *ring* of fire.

They had encircled themselves and the two remaining mounts in what could only be described as a halo of flame. al'Dor seemed to be the one maintaining the spell, standing at its center between a panicking Gale and Brahnt's spotted mare, arms held out before him and face twisted in concentration. Brahnt himself was at the very edge of the ring, alternately striking out with his staff and launching handfuls of flame at the dark shapes that seemed to be attempting to get past the fire. A half-dozen wolves circled the men, looking for a way in.

Several paces down the path, al'Dor's horse lay still, obviously dead, neck and abdomen torn open by teeth and claws to spill hot blood and organs over the leafy, snow-speckled ground.

"WHAT ABOUT ARRO?" al'Dor was screaming, twisting his hands in intricate runes as he worked the magic. "TALO! WHERE IS RAZ?"

"JUST KEEP THE WARD UP!" the High Priest yelled in return. "RAZ CAN TAKE CARE OF HIMSELF! JUST *KEEP THE WARD UP!*"

At the words, Raz came to his senses.

And decided it was time to make his presence known.

With another roaring warcry the Monster of Karth barreled into the side of the pack, taking them completely unaware. Using his gladius and ax to devastating effect he cut down two before any of the others had a chance to turn and face him. The last four collapsed inward at once, attacking from either side of the ring. One he killed as it hurled itself at him, sliding on wet leaves under its leaping form and splitting it through the chest. Another died in similar fashion, flipped over by a kick and gutted by the flashing sword.

The other two were never given the opportunity to try their luck. By the time Raz had turned around they were smoldering husks, smoke wafting from the gaps between exposed bone and sizzling muscle that marked where Brahnt's fire had taken them in the sides.

No one relaxed.

"Are they gone?" Brahnt yelled over the roar of the spell, eyes darting between the trees. Raz didn't reply, doing the same. His nose was useless, foiled by the stench of the dead animals scattered about his feet, as were his ears, deafened by the screams of Gale and the one mare they were left with, coupled with the snap and whoosh of the flames.

Still, his eyes were sharp in the light of the fire, and after a minute he flicked his gladius clean of blood, sliding it back into it sheath with a *click* over his shoulder.

"They're gone!" he shouted in confirmation, and almost at once the ward fell. He turned in time to see al'Dor stumble onto all fours, heaving.

"Laor's mercy," the Priest said. "I don't think I could have held much longer."

"You did well," Brahnt told him, extinguishing the flames he'd still been holding in his right hand and limping over to the blond man. "Are you alright? Can you stand?"

al'Dor shook his head. "Maybe in a minute. Just-just give me a minute."

Raz let Brahnt tend to the Priest, moving forward with raised hands—one still holding the bloody war-ax—in the hope of soothing Gale. The stallion was huffing and screaming, stamping the ground in fear, dark eyes rolling about. Tossing the ax aside, Raz approached him slowly, inch by inch, speaking to the animal all the while in gentle tones.

"Easy, boy," he said, stepping closer and keeping low. "Eeeasy. Shh."

It took some time, but he eventually managed to get ahold of the horse's reins, and within a minute Gale calmed, pressing himself into

Raz's stroking hands as though taking comfort from the act. After this, Brahnt's mare—which seemed to have been considering bolting off through the trees—did the same, coming about and bobbing her head to snort at the still bodies of the wolves.

"Everyone all right?" Raz asked after he was sure the animals weren't going to make a run for it, turning to look at the Priests. al'Dor had found his feet, leaning on Brahnt's arm for a change, and he still looked shaken.

"Lifegiver's *balls*," he cursed, lifting his head to look about, his face blanched. "Where did they come from? Where did they *come from*?"

"Everywhere," Raz answered him, moving back to pick up his discarded ax and starting to work the hardened, frozen blood off the blade with a steel claw. "They're pack hunters. We have wild dogs in the desert, and it's much the same. They attack from as many angles as they can because they know it's almost impossible to defend every direction."

"Bloody lucky we had you then, huh?" al'Dor said with a strained, wheezing laugh. "Lifegiver's balls. Lifegiver's *balls*!"

"Calm down, Carro," Brahnt told him quietly. "You're in shock. It's to be expected. Breathe. Breathe. There you go…" He looked up at Raz as some color started to return to al'Dor's face. "Are we sure they're gone? Can you hear anything else?"

Raz turned his head back to the trees, ears spreading to their fullest extent. After a few seconds, he shook his head.

"Nothing, but we should get moving all the same." He frowned down at the carcasses of the wolves, then up the path to where al'Dor's horse lay, still now against the swaying of the trees. "Something is bound to come along, and we should be well clear of this place when it does."

Brahnt nodded, holding al'Dor up.

"We only have two horses now, though," he said. "How are we—?"

"I can walk." Raz indicated the blond Priest. "Get him onto Gale. I'll help you onto your mare. Quickly, though. It's not safe here."

And he meant it, too. The stink of the wolves was rapidly becoming overpowered by the rich scent of blood and charred meat. The Priests probably didn't notice, but Raz did, and it put him on edge. His mind started playing tricks on him, twisting the sound of the wind into the faint snuffling of some larger animal…

Nothing moved in the woods, though, and he brushed the sensation aside.

Still, they had to get going.

Slipping the war-ax into its loop on his belt, Raz moved to help Brahnt get al'Dor up into Gale's saddle. The black stallion didn't like having the unfamiliar weight on its back, and made it known, but a few reassuring words from Raz were enough to make the animal tolerate his new rider, at least for a time. After that, Raz took a knee to boost Brahnt and his bad leg up onto his own mount, hefting the Priest's staff up after him.

Lastly, once both men were settled, Raz picked one of the still-burning torches up from the ground and held it aloft, peering down the hill for the glint of steel. Finding it, he eased himself carefully down the incline.

Dislodging Ahna from where she'd gotten tangled in a thick patch of damp roots, he returned to the Laorin.

As he crested the hill for the last time, Raz thought again that he could make out a low sniffing of some kind, almost like the snorting the horses made when they were impatient. He paused, listening hard. When nothing came of it, though, he pushed the sensation off again as a product of his own anxiety and desire to get moving again as soon as possible.

Setting Ahna over one shoulder, he took hold of Gale's bridle and started off, heading north again, leading their party up the path, around the body of the dead horse, and through the trees once more.

Had he not been in such a rush to leave, Raz might have noticed something odd about the scene they were leaving behind. For one thing, he might have found it strange that the wolf he had kicked down the hill, the one who's ribs he had broken, was utterly silent, no longer whimpering in pain. Perhaps he might have let this go, crediting it to shock or death from internal bleeding and injury.

Still, had Raz noticed this, it's likely he would have at least paused to look down the hill, to see if the wolf had perhaps made its escape and should be watched for, in case it wanted to try its luck again.

And if Raz had looked down the hill, he might have noticed that the moss-covered bolder—the one he'd sent the wolf sailing into—had shifted slightly, turning to silence the whimpering animal as it lay helpless on the ground nearby.

But Raz didn't look down the hill, and so Raz didn't see the thing he'd assumed to be made of stone and moss become roused from its winter slumber by the scent of blood. He didn't see the creature rise onto four great paws, pale teeth reddened as they dragged the dead wolf up by its throat.

And he didn't see the thing as it started to move, lumbering its way to the top of the hill to sniff at the air and peer with black eyes northward, up the path.

XVI

It took the better part of two hours before Raz was able to shed the anxiety that had dogged their little group. The attack had left al'Dor understandably shaken, and the man's fear-filled silence had done nothing to help Raz and Brahnt forgo their own concerns as they traveled, the two of them conversing in quiet tones all the while.

"We're not far, now," Brahnt had said in an attempt to reassure them, shortly after they'd escaped the hill. "A day, if that. We'll manage without one horse."

"We can make it less if we travel through the night," Raz had replied. "Would we be able to get there by morning?"

"Possibly," the High Priest had told him without hesitation, seeing the wisdom in the concept. "Mid-day at the latest."

"Then we'll do that." Raz had nodded. "I won't have us making camp so close to that mess."

Brahnt hadn't raised a concern, and al'Dor was in no state to do so, and so the matter had been considered settled. Now, though, two hours later, Raz was starting to question the decision. For a time the Woods around them had taken on a sinister air, a creeping gloom that had turned the dark beauty of the place into a foreboding ocean of unknown dangers and wicked secrets. He had been reminded again of tombstones, looking at the great pines and firs and cedars that curled up over the trail like the ribs of some dead giant, and he wondered abruptly how many bones of how many travelers were scattered among these trees, fallen prey to the wolves, or to the cold, or to any other number of perils the place hid behind its thick veil of wonder.

But slowly, as they put mile after mile of distance between themselves and the bloody hill, Raz walking quickly along between the horses, his reality shifted back to a level place. Fear was replaced by calm, doubt by relief, and the pounding of his heart by acute, sudden fatigue.

Raz's pace began to slow, and within twenty minutes he was leading Gale along the path at a plodding cadence, the rhythmic bobbing of the stallion's head in his left hand doing nothing to help the weariness. Brahnt had long since replaced the torches they'd abandoned with the bodies of the wolves, but the bouncing light was dim, and it wasn't long before Raz found himself hard-pressed to keep his eyes on the trees. He wouldn't fall asleep, he knew that. Raz had spent too many late nights out on the roofs of Miropa, tracking and hunting his marks, to believe he could actually nod off.

Still, being tired meant he wasn't alert.

"al'Dor," Raz said suddenly, intent on striking up a conversation in an attempt to keep himself awake as he shrugged his hood off to let the cold air bite at his ears and face for a bit.

The Priest, slumped in the saddle over Raz's left shoulder, didn't respond. Looking around, Raz saw with some amusement that the older man had himself fallen fast asleep, swaying gently with the rocking of Gale's body, his torch held slack in one hand.

"Let him be, lad."

Turning to his right, Raz watched Brahnt bring his mare up alongside them, his own torch held high, eyes bright in the faded light. They were turned now on al'Dor, and Raz was almost embarrassed to see the fondness in that gaze.

"He's had a rough experience," Brahnt continued. "As long as I've known him, Carro has never been one for fighting. He's a gentle man, more inclined to books than bloodshed."

Raz nodded, having deduced as much some time ago.

"He held his own, all the same," he said, shifting Ahna more comfortably on his shoulder before glancing back around at the Priest.

"I think you'll find the Laorin a strange breed, Raz," Brahnt said, and Raz didn't miss the familiarity he used. "Most are a docile people, having sought out Laor and His gifts in the hopes of leading a peaceful life in the service of His light. They aren't quick to strike, aren't quick to raise the sword, or to cry for blood." Brahnt smiled, looking forward, above the trail, as though he could see the mountains through the trees. "They are kind. Hardworking. They live for others, and live to *love* others. There are exceptions, of course, individuals whose integrity I have questioned, as well as their place in His plan, but at the end of the day the Laorin as a whole are a people for the people. A chalice from which we strive to let other people draw strength from."

He reached out, without looking down from the trees, to rest a big hand gently on the forearm of his sleeping partner.

"To manage that, though," he continued, "they have to *be* strong. They have to *be* that source of power, of light and warmth. The Laorin are gentle Raz, but they are capable of great, *great* things."

Raz didn't say anything. Brahnt's words were making him recall, once again, a pale skinned girl, her white hair falling out of its braids to tumble about her shoulders between the torn fabrics of her gown. She had stood so tall, so fiercely, as she brought him back from the edge.

And she had fallen, so fragile and so light, into his arms when the moment for greatness had passed.

"I think they'll like you."

At that, Raz blinked and looked around. Brahnt was smiling down on him, taking him in with piercing eyes, as though sizing him up for some task or another.

"What's that supposed to mean?" Raz asked. Behind him, al'Dor snorted in his sleep.

"It means," Brahnt said, "that I have a feeling I won't regret having dragged you along on this little adventure, lad. There's something in you, some fire I wouldn't even begin to know how to put out. I'm not fool enough to try to convince you that it's Laor's light that makes you burn so bright. I know you wouldn't believe it, and I'm not sure I do either."

He paused, frowning a little, his eyes suddenly taking on a perplexed expression. "Truth be told, there's something darker, fiercer, about the fire inside you. Something consuming. Something—"

"Demented," Raz finished for him quietly. "Don't go too far down that road, Brahnt. Puzzle out what my soul looks like, and you won't like what you find."

To his surprise, the older man laughed.

"You're a fool, Raz, and I'm glad for it," Brahnt said, still chuckling. "You *still* think it's evil, this weight you carry around with you?"

"Shouldn't I?" Raz was suddenly irritated. "You've been down my road. You've been where I stand. You've lived with blood on your hands and you—"

"I have *never* been where you stand, boy."

The calmness of the words took Raz by surprise.

"I have never been where you stand," Brahnt said, quietly, and his eyes once again rose to look up the path, "and I don't think I could ever be where you stand. What do you see, when you look at me, Raz?"

Raz paused at that, confused.

How was he supposed to answer that?

"What do you see?" Brahnt repeated, his tone suddenly firm, as though Raz were one of his acolytes and he was *expected* to answer promptly.

Raz hesitated.

Then he spoke.

"Goodness," he told the man, turning to look at the trail too. "Purity. A wall, incapable of being swayed, no matter the force set upon it."

Talo chuckled. "And how," he asked, "do you think Carro sees me?" He waved a hand at the sleeping Priest. "Or Syrah? Or the rest of the Laorin under my care."

"The same," Raz told him, this time immediately.

"And you'd be right." Talo sighed. "And yet... You are all so, so wrong..."

Raz frowned, but didn't turn to look at Brahnt as the man continued.

"You give me far too much credit, boy," he said. "You honor me far too greatly by telling me I have been where you have been, that I have stood in your shoes. We've both seen blood, I'll grant you that, but there are types of violence in this world, Raz, *variations* of cruelty, with equally varying results."

He paused, then brought a hand up and, with a short flash of white, conjured a handful of flames of the kind he had used to battle the wolves.

"You see yourself as evil? And I as good? You see yourself as a demented creature, and I as a wall? Tell me, Raz... what did you take from the world?"

Again, Raz said nothing, perplexed once more by the question.

"No answer? I didn't think so, because you have no answer to give. You're not even sure what I'm talking about. *I'll* give you the answer, though: nothing. You took nothing from the world, even as you fell, Raz. You shed no blood that did not need to be spilt, took no life that should have been spared. And when you fell it was not because you took too much, but because something was *taken from you*. You fell when your family burned, when your life was turned to ash and ruin. You fell when beasts dressed in the skins of men came out of the night to steal from you everything that made you an Arro."

Raz bristled at the mention of his family, but as he looked back, he saw that Brahnt's eyes were on the ivory flames cupped in one hand.

And the look they held told Raz that the man was far, far away...

"I *took*, Raz," Brahnt kept on quietly. "I took, and never gave. I killed, and never spared. I was literally known for it, knows as the Life*taker*. It brought me joy, brought me fame, brought me wealth. I took and I took and I took and I never, *ever* gave. I laughed and spat in the faces of men who tried to tell me what I was. I chased them out of town when they called me 'monster.' Those that wouldn't leave, I killed, to the great amusement of a bloodthirsty crowd."

"They called you 'monster'?"

Raz couldn't help but ask the question. It had chilled him, hearing it.

"Aye, they did, though not of the fashion they call you the same. They called me 'monster,' and I relished it, bathed in it. And *took* from it everything I could."

Brahnt closed his eyes, and Raz thought he saw a wetness shine along the lashes of his eyes.

"I rose, eventually. I saved myself from the creature I had become, through much help from people I had once threatened and shunned. I have since done my best to atone, done my best to replace what was destroyed. But I took much, Raz, *much*. But you—" he looked down to meet Raz's amber eyes "—you have only ever tried to *give*. So... never tell me I have stood where you have stood."

151

Raz thought that was an exaggeration. He had, after all, spent more years than he cared to consider doing nothing but taking, nothing but killing and murdering.

"I know what you're thinking," Brahnt said with a chuckle at Raz's silence.

"Do you?" Raz asked him doubtfully.

"You think I'm giving you too much credit. You think I don't know where you have been, or what you have done."

"It's possible."

"Perhaps," Brahnt conceded with a shrug. "And you *are* a killer, boy. I won't pretend it's otherwise. But if you think it's impossible to be a killer without sacrificing the heart, than you are a fool just as much. Do you remember the story of the dahgün?"

"'There are those that fight to end the fight,'" Raz quoted with a nod. "Or something like that. I remember."

"Then you will figure out what I mean by 'take'—and what I mean by 'give'—eventually," Brahnt said with a shrug.

Raz grimaced in queer amusement. "Maybe. Still don't know what it has to do with the Laorin liking me, though."

For a time, Brahnt just looked down at the flames in his hands.

Then he bent down, and held them out to Raz.

"Here," he said simply. "Take them."

Raz blinked. "Huh?"

"Take them," Brahnt said again, sounding as though he were hard pressed not to roll his eyes. "They won't hurt you."

"How do you know?" Raz grumbled, taking a small step sideways, closer to Gale and away from the flames.

"They won't," was all Brahnt said.

Raz looked between the man and his magic, hesitating for a long time. He felt stupid, his primal, human fear of fire mixing with the obvious reality that the High Priest clearly had control over the flames.

Essentially, it came down to whether or not he trusted the man.

At that thought, Raz held out his hand.

Brahnt was about to give them to him, making to pour the magic into Raz's outstretched palm like one might pour water from one hand to the other, when Raz's ears twitched.

He spun around, Ahna flying into his grasp. Behind him the flames tumbling to the forest floor. They winked out in spattered blinks of white light as the horses kept walking, leaving Raz to stand along the trail.

"What is it?" Brahnt asked in an urgent whisper, suddenly alert. Beside him al'Dor stirred, rising from his slumber as Gale stopped suddenly beneath him.

"What-What's happened?" he mumbled loudly, blinking away sleep and looking around. "What's going—?"

Brahnt shut him up with a hand over his mouth, muffling the question.

"Raz?" the High Priest asked, barely loud enough to hear.

Raz didn't answer him. He was listening, sifting through the sounds of the Woods, trying to make the noise out again. He was *sure* he had heard it this time. It wasn't a figment of his imagination, no trick played on him by his own mind while amongst the blood and stench of the dead wolves. He had heard it this time.

And he heard it again.

A snuffling, grumbling noise, from somewhere off to their left.

And it was getting closer.

"*Raz,*" Brahnt said insistently. "What is it? Do you need more light?"

Raz was about to answer him, telling him to brighten the flames again, when another noise came. From the depths of the darkness, rising like an angry storm from the shadows, a deep, throaty grumble broke through the quiet of the night. Slowly it grew louder, and as it did Raz made out another sound, steady at first, then coming fast and faster.

The *thump* of earth, coupled with the *crunch* of ice and leaves.

The grumble built into a huffing growl, staggered with the steps, and then into a thunderous, bellowing roar that made Raz's ears ring as—for the first time in his life—he began to fall back.

He did so, because Raz could see now the thing that had lain hidden in the dark. He could see the size of it, see its lumbering silhouette charging through the trees.

Charging, unstoppable and terrible in its might, right at them.

"Run," he said over his shoulder, taking another step back, then another.

Then he turned around, breaking into a panicked sprint back towards the Priests.

"Run!" he screamed. "RUN!"

XVII

Only twice in his life could Raz remember ever running as fast and hard as he did now. The first time had been nearly a decade ago, when he'd heard the screams of his family lifted up into the night sky on the rising glow of his burning home. The second had only been a few weeks back, when he'd watched Lueski slit her own throat on the harsh edge of Azzeki Koro's dark blade and he'd caught her before she'd hit the ground.

Then, though, he had been running *towards* something. There is an inexplicable pull, in that situation, a distinct, indefinable desire that draws one to new speeds in the desperate haste to be there, to be where they are so hopelessly needed.

It is an altogether different feeling to run *from* something, Raz discovered.

He had known fear before. He was confident in his skills, confident in his strength and his speed, but only a fool faces death without blinking. Raz had known fear, had felt it creep along his spine when he'd understood the situation was dire. It had been a small thing, though, the hint of an itch on his mind that was easily disregarded.

There was no ignoring what he felt now.

The terror was so real it was practically tangible. It clung to his neck and back, grasped at his chest as he ran. Raz could feel it on his skin, feel it in his *mouth*. It gripped him so absolutely it was like he had been submerged, been shoved beneath a black tide of dread. It ripped at him, clawing at his skin, building up as a dark ache in his chest.

And it pushed him with rough, cruel hands as he and the Priests barreled their way through the Woods.

Trees whipped by, the branches of the shorter saplings whizzing above their heads. Raz could hear the thunder of the horses' hooves as they ran, charging heedlessly through underbrush, down slick hills, and over icy streams that glimmered beneath the light of Talo's single torch. They crashed through bushes and leapt over rocks and roots, twisting around the great trunks that rose above them like indifferent gods, taking in the fear of the mortals scurrying about their feet without so much as a twitch of interest or empathy. Together they careened, unconcerned with the direction or the distance, every thought focused only on being rid of the angry, looming shadow that lurched in their wake, pursuing them with alarming speed.

And then, all of a sudden it seemed, Raz was running alone.

He would never recall, looking back later, when he became separated from the Priests. He didn't know if it was he who had taken a different path, or them. He eventually suspected that it was he who had strayed, falling behind the faster horses, unstoppable in their panic, and failing to follow them around a turn or losing them in the brushwood. Whatever the case, all Raz knew at the time was that in one moment the dark silhouettes of the horses seemed to be only a short way ahead of him, the animals screaming in fear.

And then he was running alone through the Woods.

For almost half a minute after this realization, though, Raz still didn't stop. The terror still gripped him, stroking the skin of his neck like some wicked lover. It drove him ever forward, propelling him over crevices in great leaps, or else sent him vaulting over mossy stones and fallen logs. It whispered in his ears while he fled, teasing him with images of the terrible thing that had followed them from the hill.

Run, the voice said. *Run*.

It took losing Ahna to bring Raz back to his senses.

It happened in a blink. Abruptly, materializing out of the limited light of the Moon through the ice above, the earth dropped away as if it had been torn away by some titan's hand, the forest floor breaking off at a ledge before sloping severely downward. Without so much as a pause, Raz launched himself off the ridge of upward jutting earth, aiming for the massive trunk of a fallen tree that extended from the very base of the tall hill he would have otherwise had to slide down. He landed hard on the rotten bark and started moving forward again at once, intending to run the length of the trunk all the way to the flatter ground below.

He did not expect Ahna's head to get caught in the tangles of a dead branch that jutted out from the old trunk, just to the left of where he landed.

In his frenzied, panicked mindset, all Raz felt was a massive tug on his left hand, the one that had gripped Ahna so tightly as he ran. In the next instant the dviassegai was torn from his grasp and Raz—suddenly off-balanced by the abrupt loss of her weight—only managed a few stumbling steps before he plummeted off the side of the tree, tumbling to the ground some seven or eight feet below. He hit the hill with a *crash*, his armor crunching against the frozen earth before he started falling, rolling and tumbling down the incline. He grunted and winced as he fell, cursing and trying his damnedest to get his feet under him. He couldn't manage it, though, the impetus of his mad flight through the Woods sending him head-over-heels, kicking up earth and ice and leaves around him as he spilled headlong downward. For ten long seconds Raz could do nothing more than swear and roar and pray to the Twins that he wasn't going to break his neck against some boulder or root.

Then, at long last, Raz's tumbling form reached the bottom of the hill and he spilled out onto his back, wings and limbs flopping around him to lay stiff against the icy ground.

For a while Raz just laid there, breathing hard, staring up at the dimmest blue light that was the canopy high, high above him. He listened, straining his ears as hard as he could, waiting for the expected sound of the beast's screaming roar that meant it was lumbering down the hill after him. He *knew* he would hear it, *knew* the thing was coming for him. The terror wouldn't allow him to conceive it any other way, wouldn't allow him to pause and seek out rationality. It tore at him, wrenching at his chest as his heart pounded so hard it hurt.

But nothing came. After thirty seconds Raz began to calm, feeling his breathing start to slow. Another half-minute and the world around him fell into clarity, no longer dimmed by the fear-induced tunnel vision that had driven him headlong through the trees.

Soon after that, Raz forced himself to sit up, groaning as the muscles of his back—stiffened by the beating of the hill and the coolness of the ground—stretched and ached in protest. His groan seemed to echo through the gnarled evergreens looming around him as he rolled himself onto one knee.

And it made him realize, once more, that he was alone.

Raz froze, looking up suddenly. Again he listened, this time seeking out the voices of the Priests, or at least the whinnying of the horses or the pounding of their iron shoes against the hardened floor of the forest. The fear hadn't dissipated completely yet, but it had removed itself enough to allow Raz to focus on other things, on other sounds.

Sounds that were just as absent as those of the beast.

"Shit," Raz hissed, shoving himself up onto his feet with another grunt. His head spun, and he stumbled over roots to a nearby fir, resting a hand against it and supporting himself as he closed his eyes, waiting for the dizziness to pass. When it did, Raz looked up again, feeling things fall into place, and starting to assess his situation.

He'd managed to keep the gladius, somehow. He checked it, half-drawing it and rattling the blade in its sheath before snapping it down again, satisfied the sword was in one piece. His ax, too, he still had, safely snug in the loop on his belt. His knife, though, was gone, lost in the tumbling fall.

As was Ahna…

"*Shit!*" Raz groaned again, scrambling back towards the massive form of the fallen tree. "Shit, shit, *shit!*"

The leviathan was barely more than a silhouette in the dark. So little light penetrated the trees here that even Raz could barely see more than a few feet before him.

Despite this, it didn't stop him from clambering up onto the trunk, then rushing up its length back towards the top of the hill, using his steel claws and lithe tail as anchors as he climbed.

156

He found her waiting right where he'd lost her. He thanked every god in the book when he made out the barest outline of the dviassegai's twin blades, caught in the Y-shaped split of branches that had torn her from his grasp. He pulled himself up the last few feet carefully, claws digging into the soft, decaying wood beneath him, not wanting to risk dislodging her head from the branches.

"Sorry, sis," he muttered as he freed her gently, sliding her out of her perch.

Once he was sure the weapon was undamaged, Raz eased himself onto his feet, clawed toes gripping bark and splinters well enough for him to find good purchase despite the slope. Looking up again, Raz could make out the ledge he had leapt from. There seemed to be a bit more light the further he went up the hill, and after a moment's hesitation Raz began to climb, one foot carefully after the other, up the trunk. When he reached the top, the wood beneath him tapering to a rotten stub of moss and wilting mushrooms, he paused again, listening.

Nothing. Not a sound or hint of the Priests, nor of the thing that had been chasing them. The Woods were quiet save for the creaks of the trees and the rustling of branches overhead. Raz was alone among the pines, lost in the steeps of the forest.

"Shit."

Help wasn't long in arriving.

Raz had just finished heaving himself back up onto the apex of the ridge, leaping after Ahna, who he had tossed up first. He'd almost failed in his jump for the lip, some four or five feet in front and above his head, the darkness making it hard to see where he could grab and where he could push himself up over the torn earth with his feet. In the end he'd managed it, though, hauling his bulk onto the forest floor and shoving himself back to his feet with a grunt.

He had just recovered Ahna, half-hidden in the underbrush, when a pale glow bloomed through the trees far to his left, distinct in its white, dancing rays that spilled in flickering lines through the trunks as it approached.

Magic.

Brahnt, Raz thought in relief, thinking of the torch the High Priest had managed to hold onto. Starting towards the light, though, Raz frowned as he realized that this glow was an unfamiliar one, too dim and gentle to be cast by the rippling flames of the Laorin's fire spells. It was moving, also, in an odd way. It seemed to flow, almost, weaving its way through the

Woods, drifting hither and to, an indistinct orb of light dancing back and forth across Raz's vision.

Whatever it was, it wasn't the Priests.

But it seemed to be searching…

"Here!" Raz yelled, not hesitating, hastening towards the spell. As soon as his voice broke the relative silence of the dark he saw the light stop then shift direction, making directly for him at alarming speed.

It was twenty feet away when he finally saw what it was.

It looked like a strip of silk, fraying tail washing back and forth lazily behind it as it moved. Like a stroke of white painted by some arcane brush in midair, the spell slipped over the brush and between the trees, illuminating the Woods for several feet in all directions as it moved. When it came to a stop before Raz it floated before him, like the white silk had been suspended in water, twisting slowly about in some intangible current.

Raz paused, unsure of what to do. When the spell made no indication of resolving on its own, though, nor any effort to move or guide him through the trees, he slowly reached out a hand.

The magic descended, as though drawn to him, to settle and hang across his palm.

As it faded, he was made to understand the message. No words came to him. No disembodied voice of Brahnt's or al'Dor's or any other sorts. Instead a feeling enveloped him, an absolute understanding of what he had to do.

Follow, the feeling said. *Hurry*.

As the message was relayed the magic subsided, the silk fading in a glister of white until Raz was left holding an empty hand out into the air. Despite this, the light it had radiated lingered, existing without source, without center.

But when the light moved, pulled back through the trees in the direction it had come, Raz chased after it with all haste.

For nearly a minute he ran flat out, following the glowing orb of magic. He was experiencing the pull again, the desperate need to be in a place. He didn't know exactly why, this time, but the feeling the messenger spell had given him had left little doubt that there was no time to waste. He rushed deeper into the Woods, his path illuminated now by the light. He leapt over fallen branches, dashed around trees and sprinted up and down the rolls and break of the land. His clawed feet pounded the frozen earth, the feeling of desperation growing with every second.

And then the magic faded, melting into the greater glow of a much brighter light as Raz charged between two massive trunks and found himself hurtling into thigh-deep snow beneath the inky black of the night sky.

XVIII

The clearing was a shocking sight after so many days beneath the sheltering boughs of the Arocklen. It seemed so strange, so out of place, taking Raz by such surprise he might as well have looked up to see two Moons arching above him in the night. About fifty paces across, it was an oblong space, borders edged by the Woods, as though the trees stood sentinel about the place. A single pine, small but knotted in a way that spoke of great age and beauty, stood slightly decentered, raised up on what seemed to be an odd mound of earth beneath the snow.

For a moment Raz could give no reason for the existence of the place. It made no sense, in the lushness of the forest, for such a gap in the greenery to exist.

Then his feet cut down through the thinner snow at the very edge of the clearing, and he felt his claws clack and slip against a cold hardness he was all too familiar with. He had learned the feel of it beneath his feet, practicing in the Arena, had memorized where the muddy puddles turned to deathtraps as winter came.

Beneath the snow was solid, ungiving ice.

A lake.

Raz's shock at the prospect nearly tripped him up, but he caught himself before stumbling. As he plowed over the ice though, barreling through the snow, any worries he might have had for his footing vanished. There was no room for such concern, as he looked past the single tree sitting atop what must have been its own tiny island.

Because there, playing against the white and black of snow and Woods, terror itself had manifested from the darkness of the night.

Brahnt's mare was down, body and throat torn and shredded, half buried against a backdrop of splattered and pooling red. The old High Priest himself stood his ground as best he could, slowed by the snow and his bad knee, his steel staff held defensively before him with one hand, the other aglow with the white flames of his faith. al'Dor, still mounted atop Gale, circled around behind him, supporting as best he could as the stallion kicked and reared in fright. As he hurtled towards them, moving in great, bounding leaps through powder, Raz watched the pair dance skillfully, striking out at the hulking form of their opponent, fighting to keep it at bay.

"Sun take me…" he couldn't help but swear as he took in the animal.

The ursalus was massive, gargantuan. Even on all fours it couldn't have been more than half-a-foot shorter than him, its thick brown and white fur dirty and frozen into patches, as the wolves' had been. It was a feral giant, yellowed teeth the length of a man's finger, grey claws twice that size. Hungry black eyes gleamed in the white flames the Priests were throwing at it, reflecting more hunger than pain. As powerful as they were combined, it seemed the two men were struggling to do more than keep the creature at bay, their magics and Brahnt's staff barely enough to stop it from charging.

It was just as Raz reached the tree between them, though, that those minor defenses failed.

"Back, beast! BACK!"

Talo knew Carro was drawing strength from his fear as he guided Gale with his knees behind him, the white flames in the Priest's hands flaring as he slung a ball of fire directly at the bear. It caught the animal in the shoulder, searing the fur and skin but otherwise doing little to press it back. Instead it roared, swiping at the air. Taking advantage as it settled again on all fours, Talo jumped forward between the paws, smashing the creature across the face with his staff and shooting three consecutive bolts as he threw himself back over the snow and out of range again.

The magic fizzled and died in the same way, winking out in a tendril of smoke over the animal's thick, patchy hide.

"Lifegiver's mercy," Talo muttered, more in anger than in prayer as he pushed himself to his feet, ignoring the screaming pain in his bad knee that was building even through the adrenaline of the fight.

He'd only ever seen a few ursali in his life, and he'd been careful to avoid them every time. Even those, though, as big as they'd been, were nothing in comparison to the size of the beast before them now. He'd heard the females could grow to massive proportions—a 'small house' had been the exact terminology, in fact—but he'd paid the legends no attention.

Now, though, he was wishing he had.

He stumbled back as the bear pushed forward. Summoning another ball of flame, he threw it half-desperately, catching the animal a lucky blow in the head. The beast screamed, taking several steps back, but didn't retreat further. Instead it paused a little ways away, already devouring the two men with dark eyes that were aged with vicious intelligence. Turning slightly, it circled them, moving like a cat through the thick snow.

More like a wolf, Talo corrected himself, thinking of the pack they'd left dead on the hill as he watched the animal move. For its huge form the bear moved fluidly, almost gracefully. It was the king of predators, the master of the Woods.

And clearly it didn't like intruders.

160

"It's too big!" Carro shouted from behind him, drawing more flames into his hands. "Talo, we have to run!"

"Where to?" Talo snapped over his shoulder, not looking away from the ursalus' black eyes. "With one horse? We wouldn't make it ten feet. There's nowhere to go!"

It was true, and they both knew it. They'd tried to escape, tried to flee when Raz had screamed for them to run. Talo had gotten a glimpse of the beast as it came crashing out of the woods onto the path not twenty feet behind the atherian as he sprinted in their direction. Carro had been frozen in shock, but fortunately Gale—apparently smarter than his rider in that moment—had screamed and bolted at once.

Talo and his mare had been no more than a moment behind.

They'd galloped for what seemed like hours. It probably hadn't been more than two to three minutes really, but the perception of how long their flight lasted was skewed by the terror of knowing what was following them. Talo had felt so small, so insignificant as he ran. His own strengths and abilities seemed to vanish from his mind compared to the sheer, terrible power that lumbered along in their wake. At some point—though he wasn't sure exactly when—they had lost Raz, the man falling behind as their horses bolted wildly through the trees, their way lit by the torch. There had been an instant, when he'd realized their loss, that he'd wanted to turn around, to pull his mare about.

But the silhouette of the bear had still been behind them, crashing through the forest after the part of their split group that had the most meat to offer, and Talo hadn't been able to do more than cast a messenger spell to seek the atherian out on its own.

Eventually they'd broken through the trees, smashing into the snow bank of the clearing. At first they'd managed fine, the horses handling the snow without issue, Talo's mare following Gale's trail as the stallion cleared a path with his powerful legs.

But then the mare had slipped, and it was only after Talo had been thrown from the saddle, landing on his back in the snow in time to see the great bear descend on the poor, terrified horse, that he had realized they'd been charging over the slick ice of a frozen lake.

After that, it had been nothing but a battle to survive.

Talo fell back as the bear dashed forward, great drifts of snow flying into the air on either side of it as it reared up to strike out at him. He brought the full weight of his staff down with both hands, but the outstretched paw he'd been aiming for was already out of the way and the steel sunk harmlessly into the snow. Pulling it free, he resumed a defensive stance, listening to Gale shuffling nervously behind him and watching the bear continue its prowling circle.

"Come get me, you wicked bitch," he muttered under his breath. For a second the great animal paused, almost as though it were taking in his words.

Then the bear pounced.

Talo threw himself out of the way again, but by the time he'd clambered to his feet it was too late to see the trap. The ursalus had gotten smart to their tactics, had figured out they'd only keep beating it back if it attacked him head on with Carro pouring fire down on it from above. Instead of charging again, the beast sprang to the side, around Talo, flanking the more unsuspecting prey.

Gale screamed and reared, kicking out as the bear leapt for him.

"Carro!" Talo yelled as his lover tumbled off the back of the saddle. He ran forward, stumbling through the snow as the ursalus swiped at the stallion, catching the horse a bloody blow in the shoulder. Gale screamed again, stumbling sideways and nearly falling over on the uneven slickness of the snow and the ice beneath. He gained his footing at the last moment, three hooves finding firmness in the packed white.

The last came down right on Carro's left arm as he struggled to stand, trying to get out from beneath the horse.

There was a *crack* of breaking bone, and all Talo could hear after that were the screams.

"CARRO! *NO!*"

The fires that gathered in Talo's hands then were like none he'd ever summoned before, fed by terror, rage, and desperation. They boiled up his arms and into his palms, building such frightening heat that the snow around him began to melt in a hiss of steam, though he felt none of it himself. Bringing both hands over his head, the spells crackled and sparked as they touched, molding into a single molten ball of fire.

Then he flung the combined spell with all his might at the lumbering ursalus, launching it just as the beast made to lunge at Carro and Gale once again.

The snow beneath the flames melted to ice as it traced a wide path through the night. It caught the bear squarely in the side, and the explosion knocked Talo back a step despite his distance. The ursalus, in turn, roared as it was blasted sideways, slipping and falling as the concussive force rocked its body and blew a twenty-foot radius of snow clear of the shining ice. The reek of burned fur and seared fat filled the air, grey smoke wafting upwards in smoldering twirls. Breathing hard, Talo watched the bear hack and wheeze, snarling in wild rage as it struggled back onto its feet. He was just starting to gather the magics again, drawing another balled inferno from Carro's continued screams, when the bear turned on him, black eyes shining with pain and hate.

Then it was charging him, lurching with terrifying speed, great claws dragging it over the newly exposed ice with deadly efficiency. Drawing his arms up again, Talo felt the glowing inferno pulse and grow between his hands, expanding under the desperate call for power he bellowed silently to the Lifegiver. When the orb of crackling red plasma was thrice the size of his head, Talo took careful aim, eyeing the space between the bear's eyes as a hunter would sight an arrow.

When the perfect moment came, he threw.

He threw, and he missed.

The flames scorched more fur, barely missing the bear as it dodged out of the way. Talo had only enough time to feel his heart skip a single beat, throbbing in spasmed terror, when the great beast was in front of him. The bear reared back on its hind legs, suddenly little more than a massive shadow as it towered, nearly ten feet tall, over his comparatively pitiful frame.

The last thing Talo saw before a great, clawed paw caught him squarely in the chest was a glint of steel. There was a blur of a dark figure launching itself through the air, a murderous, vicious roar that sounded more animal than man.

And then, with a crash of crushing agony, the world went black.

Raz collided with the bear's massive shoulder just as it dealt Brahnt a blow worthy of a giant. Raz screamed as he leapt, launching himself off the packed snow, unable to do more than bring Ahna's points up like a hunting spear in his desperation to get to the animal.

He was too late, though, and the clawed paw took Brahnt in the chest just as the dviassegai pierced the beast's side, Raz's weight slamming into the animal after it.

He didn't see the High Priest fly through the air, didn't hear the *thump* of his landing. By the time Raz had shoved himself away from the bear, tearing Ahna free and leaping clear as it screamed in pain and fell sideways, twisting onto all fours again, all Raz saw was Brahnt's still form sprawled out some fifteen feet away at the edge of the island and the lone, twisted pine that crowned it.

He didn't even have a moment to cry out to the man. He would have liked to, would have liked to run to him in the same way al'Dor was now, the old Priest stumbling and tripping through the snow, left arm clutched to his chest as he scrambled to reach Talo. Raz would have liked to drop Ahna and make a mad dash in the same direction, slipping and stumbling over the slickness of the twenty-foot circle of ice he now stood in.

But Raz could do no such thing. Raz, in fact, could barely afford to do more than glance in Brahnt's direction.

Because Raz had succeeded in drawing the attention of the beast.

Slowly, in a calculating, terrifying manner, the bear turned, shifting its bulk fluidly over the frozen lake. It was smoking, patches of seared fur and raw skin marking where the Priests' spells had landed, and Raz wrinkled his snout at the stench of charred flesh that corrupted the otherwise crispness of the cool night. He crouched, readying Ahna in an aggressive position, arms flexed and coiled as he brought her up, her tips dyed red by blood that was already freezing.

Raz spoke no words, then. There were no taunts to be given, no threats to be made. The beast before him was a creature of utter ferocity, pure power and violent, murderous hunger. He had its attention, he knew. One horse was dead, the Priests were dealt with, and the remaining stallion posed no danger. The ursalus had only one threat left before it could treat itself to the feast of flesh that had so foolishly wandered across its path. There was only one small bit of trouble to attend to, and then it would descend on the dead and dying around it, gorging itself for as long as it could before trudging off, back into the Woods, to resume its winter rest.

Like hell you will, Raz thought, setting his legs, digging his claws down and listening to the gentle crack of ice beneath his feet.

And then he and Ahna were moving like the wind.

He charged under the glow of the Moon and Her Stars, his howling cry echoing into the night, the dviassegai's blades flashing. The bear, not to be outdone, leapt forward, pounding over the frozen lake towards him, bellowing out its own thundering roar. They met halfway, and would have collided in a crunch of flesh and metal if Raz didn't leap up at the last second, sailing over the charging beast and swinging Ahna under him like a scythe.

Blood sprayed over the ice. The bear screamed in pain again, stumbling and tripping over its front right paw, weakened by the sudden severing of the muscles along the inside of its shoulder. Raz didn't give the animal time to recover, though, twisting even as he landed, slamming a clawed hand down to stop himself sliding further, and launching himself back again. The bear had only half-turned to meet him when he collided with it, driving the entirety of Ahna's blades into its side, deep into flesh and organs. The animal gave a deep, retching hack. Blood poured from its mouth, pooling onto the ice and staining its yellow teeth and the white fur of its chin and muzzle.

But this beast, it seemed, was made of tougher stuff than man. It twisted to finish the turn, wrenching Raz right along with it as he tried to hold onto Ahna's haft. His grip failed him, though, and he was thrown half-a-dozen feet, sliding several more before his steel claws drew him to a screeching halt where he managed to flip himself onto his feet. He made to draw his gladius and ax but realized that this time, in his tumble, the sword had been knocked free of its sheath. He found it quickly, shining against the ice between he and the bear, who stood huffing and panting as blood continued to ooze from its jaws, waiting for him to move. Ahna protruded from its left side, all six feet of her haft extending outward, awkward and rigid.

Pulling the war-ax from its loop, Raz ran.

And again, the bear rushed to meet him.

Raz reached the gladius first, throwing himself to his knees and scooping the blade up by the handle in his right hand. Hammered steel knee caps met ice, and with a screaming whine Raz slid forward with astounding speed, right past the beast. The move took the animal by surprise, just as he'd hoped, and he bent himself backwards under the swipe of its right paw, too slow and too late to catch him now.

His ax was quicker, burying itself into the thick muscle of the ursalus' neck before getting caught on collarbone and jerking from Raz's hand. The gladius flashed too, though, catching it in the right side and cleaving the animal open again through thick skin and matted fur.

Raz shoved himself onto his feet just before he collided with the thicker snow that surrounded their small battleground. He whirled to meet the bear. The wound leaked beneath where the war-ax now sat wedged just to the side of its throat. Despite this, despite the limp it had every time it put weight onto its right front leg, or Ahna and the ax sticking out from it, or the raw patches from where the magic had burned into it, the bear seemed to have no intent on slowing down. It gave another rumbling growl as it turned on him yet again, and this time the thing didn't wait to see what Raz would do. It lunged forward, snarling and spitting blood.

With no time to think of another move, Raz did the only thing left to him. Bringing the gladius up, he charged to meet the bear, and this time they slammed right into each other.

Raz lost the battle of the masses, just as he knew he would. He kept his feet, though, the flat of his gladius lodged into the crook of the bear's shoulder, blade supported against his own upper arm like a shield even as he was pushed back with astounding force. The claws protruding from his fur boots screeched once again, cutting furrows in the ice as the bear pressed into him, trying to knock him down. As soon as it began to slow, intending to change tactics when it realized its prey wasn't so easily leveled, Raz's hand snapped out to seize a fistful of greyish hair on the animal's shoulder. Using it for leverage, he vaulted over the ursalus' paw just as it drew back to swipe at him yet again.

Landing lightly at its side, confusing the bear with his sudden disappearance from its sight, Raz began his rain of death.

For a long time Raz made no big moves with the gladius, using the narrow sword's lightness and speed to his advantage as he dealt the bear cut after cut about its head, neck, and front legs. There was no opportunity for risk in this dance, no slack to be given or chance to be taken. Raz was done for if he took so much as a single blow by those great claws, and he knew it. The sheer power backing every one of the bear's moves, the weight behind its lunging attacks, were no less fearsome than a battering ram. Raz could not make mistakes. There was no leeway or latitude to give this battle. He dodged every strike the bear made at him, making sure to dig his claws into the scarred ice each time he shifted his feet. He never attacked unless his footing was true, never darted in for a slash or stab unless he knew the opening was there. A hundred times his blade lashed in, and a hundred times he darted, rolled, and leapt away from grey claws and blood-stained teeth. The duel dragged on, Raz's breath coming in ragged heaves of rolling vapor, illuminated thickly in the Moon's light so that it looked like smoke. When he tired too much he retreated, always giving himself the moment's reprieve he needed to keep from tripping up, keep from making a mistake.

And so, when the opportunity for the killing blow arrived, Raz was ready to throw all of his strength into it.

The chance came abruptly, brought on by the bear's wounds and its own exhaustion. Raz had just dealt the beast a nasty slash across the muzzle, barely missing one of its gleaming black eyes, and it roared, utterly enraged. Shoving itself onto its hind legs, the bear lunged down at Raz from above, as though intent on crushing him with the sheer force of its weight. Raz barely got out of the way in time, flinging himself sideways and dragging himself across the ragged ice with steel claws. The bear fell all the same, though, slamming both paws down exactly on the spot he had just been.

The right leg, though, weakened by the very first crippling blow Raz had dealt, crumpled and collapsed beneath it under the force of its falling body. With a *crash* Raz feared might actually break the ice, the bear smashed onto its side, roaring as it fell. For a moment it lay, suddenly exposed, paws clawing at the air as it tried to get back up.

A moment was all Raz i'Syul Arro had ever needed.

He was on the bear in a flash, lancing forward, bringing the gladius down at a savage angle just as the animal managed to roll itself onto all fours again. Piercing steel, stained with icy rivulets of red, cut high into the side of the bear's neck. Raz had gone for the spine, seeking the delicate nerves at the base of the brain.

He had aimed true.

The ursalus spasmed as though struck by a cannon ball, and it let out a garbled scream of pain. The gladius slipped further in, and the bear seemed to lose control of its right legs, collapsing and rolling halfway onto its side. Raz held onto the blade, gripping it like a handle as it was dragged along with the beast, using the weapon to pull himself right up onto the bear's massive furred body. Letting go he stepped sideways, grabbed Ahna with both hands, and wrenched her free of the creature's ribs.

As the ursalus gave a final, furious scream, blood pouring once more from its mouth, Raz matched the sound with his own roar. At the same time he leapt, launching himself as high into the air as he could, twisting as he did. The night air whipped around him, the Moon illuminating the crimson ice that marked their battlefield like some violent painting of red and blue. For half a moment he hung suspended, howling as he brought Ahna up and over his head with both hands.

Then he fell, driving the dviassegai's twin blades downward like some beastly woodsman's ax.

They caught the bear in the neck, between the edge of its blood-caked jaw and the place from which the gladius protruded from its spine. Unstoppable behind the force of the weapon's fall, steel cleaved through fur, flesh, and bone, severing all in one blow. Chips of ice flew in all directions as Ahna crashed into the frozen lake beneath the bear, flung like shards of shattered red glass, wet and glistening.

Then the ursalus' head tumbled free of its huge, beaten body, and the bear was finally silent.

At once Raz fell to his knees, heaving in gulps of cold air as he tried to catch his breath. Dragging Ahna back towards him, he lifted her up with a grunt and set her points into the ice, using her to support his weight as his limbs shook. For a long time he stayed there, feeling his mind catch up to his body, hearing the world around him settle and return from the distant place it had faded to as he fought.

"Talo. Talo! No... Please. Talo..."

The words, pitiful and quiet, reached him as the calmness of the winter night fell over Raz once again. Slowly, viscerally afraid of what he would see, he raised his head and looked to the center of the lake. A furrow in the snow, streaked dark with blood, led from where he knew the man's body had lain. It climbed up, onto the slow incline of the tiny island, and under the branches of the pine, twisting and swaying in the wind.

There, bathed in white gold light as al'Dor worked some great magic with one hand over his broken form, Talo Brahnt sat propped up against the trunk of the ancient tree.

"Talo, please." al'Dor was whispering through streaks of glistening tears. "*Please*. Don't leave me..."

Raz got up slowly, using Ahna to haul himself to his feet. It seemed that the Woods themselves grew still in reverence as he began to walk, unsteady on shaking legs, letting the dviassegai fall to the ice behind him. As though the wind were bowing its head in sadness, a clear silence gripped the clearing. It wasn't the muffled, oppressing dullness of snow, nor the eerie emptiness of the Woods. This was a stillness of the world itself, a calming of spirit and soul and elements.

An elegy of the very land.

Raz made his way steadily through the snow, not feeling its cool chill against the steel of his armor, nor the resistance of its weight as he walked. He reached the edge of the island and climbed, claws gripping as they found stiff earth. Gently he pushed aside the boughs of the old pine and bent to pass beneath them.

All the while, he never looked away from the broad, broken body of Talo Brahnt.

The man lived yet, by some cruel miracle. He was seated, his back against the trunk, arms hanging limply at his side. His eyes were half open, watching al'Dor work with his good hand, and there was a sad sort of smile on his lips as he witnessed the desperate need with which the Priest wove his magics.

Lips that bubbled with hardening blood.

The man was a mess. One shoulder looked out of place, either dislocated or broken high up on the arm. The left side of his face was lacerated and bruised, as though it had found some rock beneath the snow when he was thrown, and Raz realized with shocked anguish that he could see the streak of pale bone behind cut skin and torn, silver brown hair. Blood dripped from his ears and nose, and Raz followed the trails down, along his neck, past his collarbone, and on to the real damage.

al'Dor had managed to tear open the front of the High Priest's robes, revealing what had only a few minutes before been the strong figure of a once powerful man. Silvery blade scars crossed each other over Brahnt's skin, leaving a latticework of pale lines through thick grey chest hair. Other marks were dispersed about as well, the writhing patches of long-healed burns, the lumped, purplish scars of past puncture wounds. Talo Brahnt's body told a violent story of a different life, one lived by the sword rather than by the faith.

And now it looked as though it would have fit better as a sad fate found at the end of that old path...

Brahnt breathed in shallow, wheezing swallows even as he watched his partner work. Nothing moved except the bruised skin of his abdomen, almost every rib broken and splintered, some even protruding through bloody holes from his sides, ugly reminders of the great wound. His thick robes had foiled the cruel edge of the bear's claws, it seemed, but all the same four dark, discolored streaks ran the diagonal length of his chest, from right shoulder to left hip. The center of this area, where the sternum of the ribcage was, seemed oddly dented, almost caved in.

His chest had been crushed.

"Brahnt…" was all Raz managed to say as he fell to one knee opposite al'Dor.

At his name, the High Priest slowly turned his head. His sad smile seemed only to grow as he met Raz's amber eyes, revealing bloodstained teeth.

"I-I'm afraid," he wheezed in inhaling gasps, "that this is… this is where we part ways… lad…"

On his right side, al'Dor started to sob.

"Shh, h-handsome," Brahnt said, rolling his head back to look at the Priest and trying to raise a hand to reach the man. "Shh. There's nothing… nothing to be afraid of now."

"No," al'Dor said as he cried, ignoring the outstretched arm while his right hand continued over the man's body, his left clutched awkwardly to his chest, twisted in an odd way. "No, no, no …"

With every word, the magic he was working seemed to intensify in strength. Raz watched, half horrified, half mesmerized, as slow moving tendrils of golden light, like captured lightning, shivered over the skin of Brahnt's chest.

"Enough, C-Carro," Brahnt said weakly, coughing blood and trying again to reach for him. "Please… Enough…"

al'Dor only gave a jerking, denying shake of his head, and again ignored the plea, continuing to work his spells.

It was Raz who stopped him.

Gently he reached out and took al'Dor's right hand in his, halting its motions. The Priest made a feeble attempt to pull away as the magic sputtered out and died, but it was a half-hearted try, and after a moment he stopped even these minimal struggles, his sobs becoming deeper and harder. Raz guided his hand, then, pulling it to the side slowly until it settled atop Brahnt's.

al'Dor's knuckles turned white as he clutched at his lover's fingers, interlacing them in his.

It was darker now, but the Moon was bright above, slipping through the branches to illuminate and reflect off the snow and ground about them. Raz watched Brahnt continue to gaze at al'Dor for a moment, then turn his head once again to face him.

"I never… never got to ex-explain," the High Priest wheezed quietly.

"Explain what?" Raz asked him gently, meeting the man's gaze as bravely as he could.

"Why they'll… like you. Why our p-people will… will like you."

With what seemed like a great effort, Brahnt lifted his left hand up, bringing it to chest level. There was a dim flash of white, and their little shelter beneath the tree was suddenly bright with ivory light.

Once again, Brahnt held the flames out to him.

"Take th-them."

Raz shook his head, reaching out to put a hand on the man's shoulder carefully.

"Save your strength, Brahnt," he started. "You need to—"

"Take them, you b-bloody fool," the man growled weakly as blood began to stream from his lips.

Raz hesitated, eyes moving to the flames.

"Take them, Raz."

It was Carro who said it. The Priest didn't look up from where his eyes were fixed on the ground beneath his knees, left arm still clutched to his chest, right hand still clinging to Brahnt's.

Raz reached out.

This time the flames fell into his palm as Brahnt poured them shakily into the cup of his fingers. Raz jerked reflexively as the magic settled into the leather of his gauntlet, bearing with it a sort of ethereal weight, like the better part of his arm had been submerged in a pool of water. It didn't burn though, as he was frightened it might. Instead the fire flickered warmly in his hand, reflecting in white and red shivers against the bloodied steel of his claws.

"All f-fire... can burn, boy," Brahnt croaked, and Raz clung to his every word as he gazed into the flames. "Ours burns... ours burns at our c-command. Ours burns... at our bidding."

The hand that had conjured the magic moved to settle on Raz's forearm.

"Your fire... burns t-too. Your fire burns... burns hotter than ours, and more savagely. Your fire is... darker, d-deeper. But Raz... it does not consume you."

At that, Raz tore his eyes away to look at Brahnt.

"It could... c-could have," the High Priest continued in a rasp. "Maybe... it did, once. But it does not consume you. You... *You* control *it*, now. *You* c-command *it*. There is... is violence in the world, Raz. We... the Laorin know this. And we hate it, yes... but we kn-know it."

Raz felt the man's fingers twitch against the steel of his bracers, and knew he was trying to squeeze his arm through the gauntlet.

"Consider for a moment... what you are. Consider what you... r-represent. You are the world's violence, Raz. You... you are death, and blood. You are... are the darkness to our l-light. And yet... you are light itself, as well. You are... kind. You... you are c-caring. You seek to protect, seek to... shield the world. Syrah... Lueski and Arrun... Me. You are... a s-sword, Raz. You are a bloody... sword. But you are a sword raised in the... the defense of all."

Brahnt's gaze took on an almost pleading cast, making it clear how much he needed Raz to hear his words.

"They will... will like you for that, l-lad. They will... love you, for that. They will love you, because your fire... your f-fire does not consume you. Do you... understand?"

For a long time, Raz only looked at the man. He had no way to convey how carefully he had listened, how passionately he had heard this final message.

In the end, he simply nodded.

It seemed enough for the High Priest, who smiled and let the magic fade from Raz's hand.

"G-good," the man said through the newly restored dark, coughing again and spraying more blood down his front. "Now, on the t-topic of... of swords... Do you have yours?"

Raz felt a chill crawl down his spine, but he didn't voice the fear. He just shook his head.

"Be a friend and... and g-get it. Give Carro and I... a moment."

At once, Raz got to his feet. Turning, he ducked under the edge of the tree, onto the snow, and into the full light of the night sky once again. For a time he stood there, looking up at the Moon and Her Stars, offering up a prayer for the strength he would need.

Then he started down the island's embankment, back onto the ice, and made for the still outline of the ursalus, a great shape of indistinct black against a backdrop of bluish ice.

He returned a few minutes later, having taken his time to extract the gladius from where it sat, buried nearly to the hilt above the stump of the bear's neck, and cleaning it against the animal's matted fur. When he stepped under the branches again, he averted his eyes from the men for a second, allowing them to finish a private moment. When he looked back, al'Dor was wiping red from his lips and beard, and the blood was smeared about Brahnt's mouth.

The High Priest turned his eyes on Raz again, and Raz felt the great emptiness that had become his heart expand and swallow every part of him as he saw that the man had tears in his eyes.

Raz knelt down beside him, blade hanging from his side.

"What-what's that for?" Carro asked, his voice hoarse and braking, eyes on the gladius.

Raz couldn't answer him.

"It's... m-mercy," Brahnt wheezed, squeezing the Priest's hand. "It's... kindness, Carro. Please... let him be..."

al'Dor's eyes, red and raw with tears, widened in sudden realization. For a second Raz thought the man was going to throw himself at him, or cast some blasting spell that would send him flying back out into the snow. He at least thought the Priest would howl his denials, shaking his head and sobbing in refusal to accept what was to be done.

al'Dor, though, demonstrated a strength Raz had only seen hints of in the time he had known him. Instead of speaking, the man's eyes moved from the sword to Brahnt's tearful face, then down to the terrifying image that remained of his body. He was a healer, Raz realized. He must have known—of all the people beneath that tree—what Brahnt's wounds meant. Lungs filling with blood. The slow constriction of the heart and the arteries around it. The pain of broken bones and ruptured organs…

A stillness overtook al'Dor, broken only by the redoubling of his clinging to the High Priest's right hand.

Then he nodded.

Raz looked to Brahnt.

"Are you ready?" he asked him quietly. For a long few seconds the old man didn't say anything, his eyes on al'Dor. When he finally rolled his head over the tree to look at Raz, he blinked rapidly, as though trying to chase away the fear that was threatening to overcome him.

"I am," he said after a moment, in as strong a voice as he could manage.

Taking the sword in his left hand, Raz grasped the man's shoulder with his right.

"You will be missed, my friend," he whispered hoarsely.

Brahnt swallowed and nodded. "Tell Syrah… when you see her. Tell her I will always… always be there."

"I will," Raz promised, bringing the blade so that the point hovered, unwavering, over the man's heart.

One last time, Talo turned his head to meet al'Dor's gaze, his hand tightening in the Priest's.

"I love you," he said. "Remember me."

Then the blade slipped forward, sliding between broken ribs, and Talo Brahnt, High Priest of Cyurgi' Di, died with a single, quiet exhalation of relief as pain and fear left him forever.

XIX

"Even in death, some souls leave an intangible mark on the world. It is impossible not to feel them there, feel their presence just beyond the veil that separates the living from those already risen into the arms of the Lifegiver. Though I pray the loved ones I've lost have long since returned to the world in Laor's infinite circle of rebirth, I cannot help but feel that some part of each of them remains yet with me, suspended between this old life I was a part of and the new one they must now enjoy. It is painful to feel that presence and the constant reminder it bears to mind, and yet it is simultaneously wondrously consoling to know that they are—even in some small way—still there to watch over and guide me..."

—private journal of Eret Ta'hir

Syrah awoke with a start, shivering violently as her body tried and failed to ward off the winter night. At first the overwhelming fear returned, the crushing terror that consumed her every time she heard booted feet crunching against the icy leaves outside. She lay beneath her thin blanket once more, coughing and shaking against the hard ground through the furs beneath her, numbing the pain of her healing finger and bloody ear.

The cold was going to kill her.

Syrah knew it, *had* known it for many nights now. The winter was too cruel, beating what little magical warmth she was able to cast about herself with her hands chained behind her back. At first it had been a frightening prospect, a horrifying realization that had kept her up for many days without sleep, chasing away every form of fatigue. Eventually, though, she'd started praying for the nights to grow colder, for the freeze to come and deliver her from her torment, and Syrah had found herself sleeping with ease.

Dreams, after all, were the only escape left to her...

The irons that bound her wrists and ankles clinked in the dark as Syrah maneuvered herself up with difficulty, listening with dreadful trepidation for whatever it was that had awoken her. It wouldn't have been the first time Kareth Grahst's men descended on her in the late hours of the night, drunk and violent in their lust. She'd always heard them coming, when she hadn't been able to sleep, but the last time it had happened had been after she'd rediscovered the momentary peace of slumber, and they had only left her in the earliest hours of the morning, sobbing into the furs.

Now though, no sound came. Syrah's left eye blinked against the glow of the ever-burning fires lingering teasingly around the edges of the tent flaps, her blinded right crudely wrapped in a bandage that had long since grown dark and dirty. Men's voices could be heard, but they were far off in the direction of the camp.

What was it, then, that had woken her?

For a long moment, Syrah couldn't puzzle it out. There seemed to be no reason for her sudden stirring. No cause for it. Nothing moved about the tent, man or wind or tree or animal, and nothing hinted of coming trouble.

After a minute or two, though, Syrah's fear subsided, and the fading of that feeling allowed her to become steadily aware of a pain, deep and aching, that had rooted itself like some wicked flower in her heart.

Something had happened.

Syrah didn't know what. There was no hint, no sign. Nothing was granted to her but a chasm of emptiness that ripped through her chest, opening her up and swallowing her whole from the inside out.

Somewhere, somehow, something had happened...

Slowly, Syrah let herself down again, easing back onto the furs. For a time she lay there, bathing in the painful wash of the mysterious agony.

Then she began to sob softly, and it was hours before she finally cried herself to sleep again.

XX

"It is a fascinating thing, to compare the great religions and gods of our world. While the concept of omnipotence is a ludicrous ideal in dire need of further examination by the masses, one should never pass up the opportunity to study the theologies of the land and draw one's own conclusions regarding potential differences and relations. On the one hand, for example, the Laorin believe whole-heartedly that only the foulest of souls do not return to the world after death. On the other, the Southern followers of the Twins seek out their ancestors in the night sky, believing them ever-present in the heavens. Is it not incredible how two people, divided by such drastic beliefs, manage somehow to coexist?"

—*A Comprehensive Overview of Modern Theology*, Jek Bor'ht

Raz watched the ritual in sad, silent wonderment.

He stood on the frozen surface of the lake, not a foot or two beyond the short embankment of the little island. The steel of Ahna's blades, slung over one shoulder, glimmered in the somber light of the morning Sun, faint behind the thick rolling storm clouds that had drawn over the world as midnight came and went. The snows had started just as dawn broke, flickering down from the heavens to cling against the thick furs Raz still had drawn over his leathers and armor.

It caught, too, in the overhanging branches that shielded the unmoving form of Talo Brahnt, his eyes closed and his face peaceful, still propped against the trunk of the old tree that was his last and final companion in death.

al'Dor stood above Raz, just outside the boughs, sharing a last, lingering moment with his lover as he gazed through the dance of the spiny leaves. He had been there, hovering beyond the shelter of the branches, for a long time now, offering silent prayers to his Lifegiver.

Raz didn't rush him.

At last, after what must have been a quarter hour, and just as Raz was starting to feel the cold finally get to him through his furs, the Priest moved. Raz watched, amazed, as the man slowly raised his right hand, his left arm now strapped to his chest by a crude sling. Over several seconds, a white light spilled outward to outline the fingers of his upturned hand. It didn't burn beneath flame, as much of the magic Raz had thus far seen entailed. Rather, the light shimmered skyward, like some beacon calling home the souls of the departed.

There was a *clink* and the scrape of shifting metal, and Raz's eyes moved in time to see the glint of silver steel beneath the tree. Slowly, steadily, as though drawn up by careful hands invisible to the eye, Talo's staff lifted itself from the ground where it had lain beside its master. It took several seconds, turning as it rose, but eventually the staff hung perpendicular to the ground, hovering over a point in the earth just to the right of the High Priest's body.

For another long moment al'Dor stood there, and Raz watched in silence as the smothered desire to weep shook the man's body, hand still upheld. He seemed to be preparing himself, bracing his composure for a single, final goodbye.

Then there was a flash of light, and the steel staff smashed downward in a single, smooth, lancing fall. It crashed into the frozen earth with a mighty *crack* of breaking and shifting ground, and bits of dirt and frost-tipped grass were thrown into the air. Raz was forced to shield his face with the hand holding Ahna's haft as a stone whipped past his chin, thunking off the metal of his pauldron beneath the furs.

When he looked up again, a thin, silver mist lingered around the base of the steel, the staff itself standing erect and straight, like a narrow tower watching eternally over the final resting place of its fallen master.

al'Dor let his hand fall, and it seemed then that he crumpled into himself. So bad was the shaking of his body that for a moment Raz thought the man would tumble to his knees and start sobbing once more, as he had for much of the night. The Priest, though, only took the time he needed to calm himself. Eventually he straightened, took a long, deep breath, and turned slowly away from the shaded resting place of his better half.

When his eyes met Raz's, they were red and swollen, but dry.

"His staff will stand forever in that earth," the man said, starting to move carefully down the incline towards where Raz stood on the snow and ice. "Even you couldn't pull it out now."

"Then it will mark the final rest of a great man," Raz said with a nod, reaching out to hand the Priest his own steel staff—which he had been holding in his left hand—and help the man step off the island and onto the frozen lake. "I'm so sorry, al'Dor. I wish… I wish I could have made it…"

He had wanted to say it sooner. He had wanted to say it all night, as he made camp along the edge of the trees that surrounded the clearing, building himself and an injured Gale a fire to keep warm by. He hadn't slept at all, of course, his body and mind too drunk on the shock and grief that kept his thoughts from settling enough to allow him to drift off.

He wouldn't have been able to sleep anyways, though. The Priest's piercing wails of loss, echoing across the lake from where he had stayed with the body of his lover until dawn finally came, were like the haunting screams of some heartbroken ghost through the trees.

al'Dor sighed at his words.

"That makes two of us, boy," he said sadly as he found his footing on the ice and started making for the Woods. "But I don't blame you. I don't think anyone could blame you." He gave Raz a sidelong look, though, walking beside him. "But after all this, if you don't stop calling me 'al'Dor' I'll be sure to find *something* to blame you for."

Raz couldn't help it. He cracked a gloomy smile.

"As you wish, Carro."

They moved slowly, as they left the lake. The lacerations across Gale's right shoulder turned out to be shallow, but they left the horse with a mild limp even after Carro had tended to them as best he could, and Raz was too tired now to have to keep pace with a trotting horse regardless. They chose to walk, at least for a time, giving the animal a rest from his two-week chore of bearing a rider. Furthermore, neither Raz nor Carro was in any hurry to leave Talo behind for good. They took their time packing up, all the haste they'd carried for a fortnight drained away.

When they finally departed, it was a painful, silent going.

For a long time they walked, neither man speaking as they kept their eyes on the ground, moving east and north under the light of the single torch they'd cobbled together after Raz found a suitable heft of dead wood and Carro lit it with his good hand. They'd lost the trail in their mad dash the evening before, fleeing its guidance as the terrifying form of the ursalus had descended on them from behind. They'd run west, though— that, Raz had been able to deduce—and together they'd both agreed that an east-by-north plot would eventually take them back to the trail. Worst case scenario, even if they missed it they would reach the foot of the ranges by no later than mid-afternoon, and from there Carro would be able to guide them to the mountain path.

That was the only time they spoke for nearly an hour, until Carro's agitated voice grated across the relative quiet of the winter woodland.

"What are we bloody well going to do?"

Raz looked up, jerked from his private thoughts at the question. They were deep in the Woods, now, the last true light of the cloud-veiled Sun having long faded behind them. They trekked once more between the bent behemoths of the forest, guiding Gale across the meandering terrain of the broken hills and thick underbrush beneath the trees.

"About what?" Raz asked, completely at a loss as to what the man was talking about.

It was Carro's turn to start. Apparently the question hadn't been intended to be voiced aloud, or at the very least hadn't been directed at

Raz. The Priest looked at him, his blue eyes no longer red and irritated, but rather lined now with a different sort of worry.

After a second, Carro seemed to decide the conversation was no longer worth partaking in alone.

"The Kayle," he said in an anxious tone. "What are we going to do?"

Raz frowned. He'd forgotten entirely about the mountain man, Baoill. For much of their journey through the Woods, in fact, the man had been a mostly unmentioned topic, as though Talo had wanted one last moment of peace before arriving a Cyurgi' Di.

Now that he contemplated the original purpose of their passage north, though… Raz could see the problem.

"Was Talo so integral to the Laorin's plan on dealing with him?" he asked.

Instantly Carro blanched, and Raz realized his mistake.

"I'm sorry, Carro," he said quickly. "That was insensitive of me. I shouldn't have—"

"I-It's fine," the Priest said, cutting him off in a shaking voice and looking away. "We don't have time for grief right now." He took a moment, breathing deeply again and closing his eyes.

"He was," he said eventually. "At least, in a way. Unless Syrah and the council have thought of something either T-Tal—" he tripped over the man's name, choking on it.

He threw a hand up, though, as Raz made to duck under Gale's neck and reached out to console him.

"No *time* for grief," he repeated, this time with a note of anger that transitioned into firmness as he started again. "Unless Syrah and the council have thought of something either Talo or I haven't, as far as we know the Citadel has no set plan. Talo was the one we would have relied on to *make* the plans, truth be told. He had the most experience with the mountain tribes—apart from Syrah—and by far the greatest rapport with the valley towns. He would have played negotiator and, if that failed, herald to the towns, communicating and coordinating their people. If anything, we were returning home to start building off whatever Syrah and Jofrey will hopefully have managed to start in our absence…"

Raz's frown deepened, but he nodded. He'd been aware of this, generally. And it didn't bode well at all…

"What about Syrah?" he asked. "Would she be able to manage the same role?"

Carro looked skeptical, and shrugged. "One day, most certainly. *This* day, though… Syrah is brilliant, and she's strong. She'll be of enormous value one way or the other, but spearheading a response to Gûlraht Baoill's madness… I have my doubts. She's impetuous, even rash. She'll grow out of it, given time, but for the moment she lacks the experience of the older members of the Citadel's council."

"Then one amongst you will have to fill the role Talo would have taken."

"Yes…" Carro agreed slowly, stepping closer to Gale so as to avoid a thick hedge of spiny shrubbery as they walked. "But none amongst us have near the same pull with the valley towns as Talo did."

"The individual might matter little, if Baoill's intent is to raze the North," Raz said. "Your god seems to have a firm place in the hearts of many up here, and the Kayle has already burned two cities to the ground if my understanding is correct. The Laorin taking a stand against the tribes might be enough on its own, giving the remaining municipalities a standard to gather around."

"You would think so," Carro said with a sigh, "but again, I have my doubts. For one the valley towns aren't as tightly knit as you might think. They're not like your desert cities, interwoven with each other in some way, whether it be commerce or politics—or even your 'Mahsadën.' It's been a hard enough trek for the three of us to…"

He trailed off quietly for a moment, and Raz let him take his time as he saw tears well unbidden in the man's eyes. After a few seconds, Carro regained control of himself.

"It's been a hard enough trek for us," he kept on, ducking under tendrils of browned, leafy vines that hung from the lowest branches of an old spruce. "And we had horses. Imagine trying to get a trading caravan through the freeze. The winter essentially cut the towns off from each other for most of the year. Even when a message *must* be relayed, it's common practice to send three, even four birds into the storms, as there's always a chance they won't find their destination." He shook his head. "There's no guarantee the towns would—or even could—come to each other's defense."

"Some did," Raz pressed, thinking back to what Talo and Carro had told him as they'd caught him up on the situation in the days before they'd departed Ystréd. "Stullens, was it? And another… Drak-something?"

"Drangstek." Carro nodded. "It's true, they did, after Metcaf came under attack, but Stullens and Drangstek are close—closer even than Azbar and Ystréd—and it was the very earliest weeks of the freeze when their combined forces pushed north. Beyond that, Stullens and Drangstek had more ties to Metcaf and Harond than typical. Drangstek and Harond were both fishing communities. They traded boat timber, metals, tools, and even workmen on a regular basis. Stullens and Metcaf benefitted from their respective proximity. In comparison, Ystréd is a tiny municipality, too far away to be worth any notice, and Azbar is the opposite, a titan of commerce, capable of complete independence from Northern trading due to its general monopoly on border exchange."

He grimaced at some thought. "I wouldn't be surprised if Quin Tern made an attempt to unite the forces of the other towns to him, while he lived. It might have been worth the attempt."

Raz spat in the grass. "Tern was smart enough to make the attempt, but cruel and greedy enough to have then used the army to his advantage. I can practically *guarantee* he would have left Ystréd to its fate to start with, as it's further north than Azbar and in the direct path of the Kayle's march south. I admit I hope your council doesn't intend to use another town as a sacrificial pawn in its plans."

"I can think of one or two members who might consider it." Carro grimaced. "But the majority? No. It would never be allowed. Still, that brings me to my other concern: even if the towns would be willing to band together and form a standing force capable of stopping the Kayle, the Laorin wouldn't be the ones to raise the 'banner,' as you called it. The Priests and Priestesses of Laor won't fight the Kayle. They can't. You know this."

Raz raised a brow at that. "All I know is that you can't kill," he said, crouching and leaping the eight-foot span of a wide frozen stream as Carro began crossing the uneven ice carefully, Gale following dutifully behind. "What was it that Talo intended to do, then? When you said he would be herald to the towns, coordinating them?"

"He would have been the intermediary," Carro responded, reaching the far side of the stream and leaning his staff against a nearby tree momentarily to turn around and guide the stallion the last few feet by the reins. "The peacekeeper, for lack of a better word. The Laorin might take the side of the valley towns in this war against the Kayle, given Baoill's atrocities, but they are absolutely neutral when it comes to matters between the towns themselves. Talo would have been the arbiter, the known and respected face and name, who could ensure the fairness of whatever pacts and alliances had to be formed. He would have eventually drafted the Priests and Priestesses as well, but as healers and negotiators, not as soldiers. War is unavoidable, in this world. We of the faith will struggle mightily to ensure that Laor's great gift of life is not spat on by man, but when we inevitably fail in this task it is up to us to take on the secondary duty of saving as many as can be saved. Syrah and Talo weren't the only ones to have worked with the mountain clans in their day. Others have as well—if with less success—and were taught the tribal tongue by the clans. Even more—myself included—have a good grasp of the mountain tongue gained through practice. We can serve as translators, as mediators between forces seeking terms, or surrender. Important roles in a war between people who don't have a common language."

180

Raz didn't disagree. He had an odd thought, in fact, at the Priest's words. It rose, as abrupt as a snake preparing to strike.

"A pity no one has thought of that to the south," he muttered as they took a decline of hard, mossy-eaten earth.

"Why is that?" Carro asked curiously, using his staff to steady himself as he descended uneasily down the hill.

Raz shrugged. "The atherian. The others of my kind. Southerners themselves don't keep them, but plenty are enslaved all the same and carried off down to Perce and the Seven Cities." He grit his teeth in sudden anger. "I hate slavers."

"A barbaric practice," Carro agreed with a sort of tired resignation. Then, out of nowhere, he gave a mirthless laugh.

"What's so funny?" Raz asked him.

"I was going to joke," the Priest said, still smirking wryly as they reached flat ground again, "that if you find some way of ridding us of this damn Kayle, oh great 'Scourge of the South,' that I'll bloody well make it my life's purpose to learn the lizard-kind language for you."

Raz chuckled. "You volunteering to be my… 'arbiter,' was it?"

The Priest smiled, the first real one he'd managed all morning. It was a hard grin, lined with sadness and grief, but there was at least some small hint of true amusement there.

"Raz i'Syul Arro. You find a way to free the North of Gûlraht Baoill, and Lifegiver take me if I don't volunteer to be anything you damn well need, boy."

XXI

They spent a pleasant morning joking and devising cruel ways to rid themselves of the offending Kayle—or as pleasant as they could manage while trying to shed the weight of Talo's death, even for a time. They'd eventually concluded there was realistically nothing either of them could do or come up with in their present situation, trekking steadily northeast through the Woods, and so their conversation took the amusing turn towards venting their grief and frustration in Gûlraht Baoill's unfortunate direction. With some coaxing—or perhaps just succumbing to the need to think of anything but the man he had been forced to leave behind on that frozen lake—Carro had shed what remained of the stiff shell of authority and piousness he had held since Raz had met him. Though this may have been due to the Priest's need to simply confide in someone—even if that someone was the Monster of Karth—Raz came to suspect, as the morning went on, that he had finally won the man over entirely in some form or another. Maybe when the head of the great ursalus had fallen to the ice.

Or maybe it had been when Raz's blade had ended Talo's pain with a merciful rapidity Carro could never have managed...

Regardless, the man that emerged—though obviously heavy with sadness and sorrow—turned out to be an excellent travelling companion, capable of crassness and amusingly vindictive thoughts Raz would not have credited him with the day before. When Carro had suggested tying the Kayle up, dropping him up to his neck in a barrel of water, and letting it freeze overnight outside before seeing how far the man would bounce down the side of the mountain, Raz had actually laughed aloud. The sound, so odd to his own ears, had frightened a pair of ravens slumbering on a branch high above them and sent them off with shrill repeated caws that imitated dull, fading echoes as the birds sped off southward through the trees.

They continued on like this for several hours, content in the distraction from less pleasant ponderings. They became so engrossed, in fact, in a particular conversation in which Carro was giving Raz his most blatant opinion of some of the members of the High Citadel's council, that Raz almost missed the first true patches of dim light that cut down through the canopy of the Woods. When he noticed them, though, he saw too that the snow—only frosting or thinly layered on the forest floor over the past ten-day—was growing steadily thicker as they walked. Within a quarter hour, in fact, it was piling up in heavy mounds beneath trees that seemed to be shrinking before their very eyes the further they pressed. For several minutes Raz was taken by the bizarre impression of sudden, immense growth, as though he and Carro were sprouting to gigantic proportions with every step they took. The blue-green evergreens of the Arocklen had towered over them so absolutely for so long that seeing these odd, diminutive specimens start to surround them was as incredible an experience as entering the Woods in the first place, if less mystifying.

And then they stepped out of the final edge of the forest, and Raz's awareness of his own size and meaning was flipped yet again on its head.

They'd missed the trail, he realized at once. At some point, likely distracted by conversation, he, Carro, and Gale had crossed the narrow strip of worn earth, already hard to make out in the undergrowth and frost of winter. They'd continued on—very likely too far east now—until the Arocklen came to an end, spilling them out once more into knee-high snow, the sky a blur of greyish-white as more fell heavily around them. There was no wind for the moment, though, and so the flakes descended in lazy, enticing patterns, accentuating the sparse examples of trees that still lay before them, jutting from stony ground at increasingly higher points as the ground rose in a steady incline, steeper and steeper until Raz felt the earth were trying to fold over itself.

When he looked up upon the Saragrias Ranges in all their colossal glory, Raz forgot any forged concept he'd ever had of his own worth in the world.

He had been aware of their presence since before they'd entered the Woods, of course. Though Talo and Carro had never been able to make the ranges out, Raz's sharp eyes had trailed their outline often for the final hours before reaching the tree line. He'd wondered—offhandedly, at the time—what manner of creation could be so large as to tower imperiously over the earth. It had been a question born of impressed curiosity.

Now, it was a question reincarnated from shocking wonder that oddly toed the line of something very much like fear.

The mountains were prodigious crafts of some god or another. That was the only way Raz could categorize them so that the Saragrias became fathomable. He didn't know what or whose gods, but he didn't really care one way or the other. They rose—even more teeth-like now that he could see them up close—to pierce the very sky. The lowest peaks among them he could just make out through the snow, scraping at the storm clouds as a far-off wind blew powdered white streams from their cliffs and into the air in constant, tumbling currents. Their sides, pockmarked with ledges and pockets of huddled pines, swooped upward and overhead, grey against the contrast of dark stone and snow. High, high above, white capped the very top of each, like a series of wintery crowns that gave the ranges nothing short of the bearing of kingly titans suspended over an endless empire.

But that was only the smallest of them. The largest, thrusting up from the land here and there between the bands of the mountains that seemed to extend ever northward, did not toy with the sky as their shorter cousins did. Rather, those colossi, behemoths of stone and earth, were *swallowed* by the heavens, their great peaks sometimes vanishing into the clouds long before Raz could make out so much as a hint of capping snow. Lacking their white crowns, Raz couldn't help but wonder if their heights ascended into a world beyond the one he knew so well. Did they thrust all the way up into the night sky, perhaps? Did they rise to stand as proud sentries for the Moon's nightly traverse?

For the first time in what would become a great many times, Raz pondered if climbing to the top of the greatest of those peaks might allow him a glimpse of the souls that had long left him for the brightness of Her Stars...

"Well... Unfortunate, but I guess it can't be helped."

Raz blinked, tearing his eyes from the mountains to look around at Carro. The man was gazing up at the line of the Saragrias as well, but with such an utter lack of awe that shocked Raz so deeply, it almost made him sad.

"W-What's that?" he asked faintly, struggling to pull his mind back from the tops of the Saragrias and down to the real world. Carro looked around at him, brows furrowed in concern.

"You alright, boy?"

Raz nodded, getting a grip on himself. "What's unfortunate?" he asked again, extinguishing his torch in the snow so he could put a hand out to pat Gale's neck as the horse limped closer to him.

In truth he did it more to support himself than anything, feeling slightly dizzy standing there in the shadow of the mountains.

Carro watched him a moment longer, the look not leaving his face. Eventually, though, he answered. "We're too far east. We'll need to double back. Not for long, though. I know this place. We're within the harvest radius, so we're not far."

"The what?" Raz asked.

"The harvest radius," Carro repeated, turning around already and making back towards the trees. "Each summer, the residents of the Citadel descend every few days to forage and hunt for food. In a couple of months the Woods supply most of our needs for the freeze, though game gets scarce quickly. The harvest radius is just the space of several miles about the base of the pass where this happens."

"Clever," Raz responded, giving the mountains one last long look before grabbing the doused torch from the snow again and following the Priest back into the relative cover of the trees. He didn't know if he felt safer, hidden beneath the branches, or saddened as they moved away from the ranges. "I hadn't considered that. I suppose it can't be easy to grow food through such a winter."

"We make do with hardier varieties," Carro told him as the light began to fade overhead. "The kitchens plant potatoes and some other vegetables indoors. Enough to last the freeze. Game is dressed and frozen in outer rooms and sheds, ones that aren't heated. It's hard, some years, but we make it through without anyone starving."

"Indoors?" Raz asked, equal parts perplexed and intrigued at the multitude of particulars Carro had just revealed. "You can farm without the Sun? And unheated? What do you mean? Come to think of it, how *do* you live up there without every one of you freezing your balls off through the winter?"

Carro chuckled. "With a lot of effort and even more help from the gifts Laor has granted us. Planting is simple enough. We can manage the soil and water on our own, but for light we have to rely on the magics. Heat, though, is more complicated..."

For the next half hour or so Raz listened in rapt attention as Carro began to tell him of all the marvels of Cyrugi' Di that Talo had never seen to reveal. He described the great system of copper piping that channeled steam and hot air through the walls and floor of the Citadel throughout the year, fed by massive furnaces in the bowels of the temple. He talked of the wonders of the library, making it out to be a cavernous expanse of endless knowledge, all bathed in the painted history of the faith across its grand domed ceiling. He told Raz about the classrooms, the practice chambers, the dormitories, and the dining hall where men and women of all ranks and ages ate and conversed together when time allowed. He even spoke of Priest-Mentors, of the ceremonies of consecration, of graduating from the position of acolyte and earning one's staff, as well as the rare ritual of Breaking—the process in which a member of the faith was stripped of their powers and cast out, leaving them marked with a great scar across their face.

This last bit of information had tugged at Raz's memory, though he didn't quite know why.

"Why would a Priest be Broken?" he asked—his first question since Carro had started on about the Citadel and the faith. "Is it a sacrifice? Or—?"

"No sacrifice," Carro answered him, scowling a little at the suggestion. "Laor requires no such barbaric offerings, like those demanded by the Stone Gods. No... Breaking of Priests, Priestesses, or even acolytes only occurs under one circumstance: the throwing aside of vows, the violation of our most cardinal principal."

Raz understood at once.

"Killers," he said tonelessly.

"Killers," Carro repeated in agreement. "Or those of the faith who—through action or inaction—knowingly partake in the deliberate death of another…"

He trailed off, and Raz noticed that the man had suddenly paled.

"What is it?" he asked, concerned.

"Nothing," Carro said quickly, seeming to shake off some overbearing thought. "Nothing worth dwelling on, at the very least." He licked his lips. "As I was saying, Breaking is our faith's most extreme form of punishment. I've only witnessed it once, performed on a girl only a few years older than Syrah. Her powers were ripped from her, she was relieved of her acolyte's robes, and then carted to Ystréd within a week. There she was left with the gold for food and lodging for a single night."

"Harsh," Raz said, impressed by the unmerciful nature of the act. "I wouldn't have expected it from your kind."

"The Laorin have no clemency for betrayers of the faith," Carro said, his voice hard as they pushed through a particularly heavy thicket of underbrush. "Least of all heartless, cruel creatures like Lazura. Do you know what she did? She—*mmmph!*"

Raz practically lifted Carro off his feet, the hand that had been holding the torch wrapped firmly about the Priest's mouth, the torch itself falling with a *hiss* against the icy ground. As the man struggled in his arms, his shouts of surprise and pain as his broken arm was pressed against his body muffled by the leather and steel of Raz's gauntlet, Raz stomped out the flames with the pads of one fur boot and dragged Carro back into the bushes. He ran into Gale's chest as he backed up, the stallion fortunately having not pressed through behind them yet, and the animal nickered loudly in surprise.

"Shhhh," Raz hissed to both of them, eyes wide as he willed them to adjust quickly to the limited light of the Woods.

At once Carro stopped struggling, recognizing the tension in Raz's bearing. Raz let him go, and the Priest blinked the pained watering of his eyes away as they crouched in the dark in front of the horse.

"What is it?" he asked in a shrill whisper, sounding suddenly terrified. "Another bear? Laor have mercy, not another b—"

Raz stopped him again, this time with a single finger raised to his lips. He was listening once more. This time, though, it wasn't an animal he was worried about.

Raz had discerned two very distinct things as they'd shoved their way through the hedge they now crouched behind. The first: they'd found the path. It trailed, a narrow band of pale dirt through the cool lushness of the Woods, off right and left, north and south respectively. Carro had been correct in the end, they *had* been close, and clearly hadn't overshot the path by much, as they'd only been walking west again for about twenty minutes.

The second thing, though, had been the distinct and unmistakable sound of men's voices.

Whether it was too many days with only the Priests—*now Priest*, Raz thought sadly—for company, or the fact that Talo had put him on edge when they'd first crossed the Arocklen's borders, it hadn't taken more than an instant for Raz to realize that the voices had not been speaking in the Common Tongue. Rather, the sharp, garbled words he'd made out had been in a guttural, rough language, one he did not recognize. Couple that with the grind and clink of shifting leather and metal plating, and Raz deduced quickly who the voices had belonged to.

"I think your mountain men are here."

He said the words very quietly, as though the softness of them would somehow diminish Carro's reaction. It did no such thing, of course, and the Priest's sudden intake of breath sounded howlingly loud to Raz's sharp ears.

"*Shhh*," he said again, more urgently. "*Quiet*. They're coming."

And indeed they were. Raz rather thought it was Gale, huffing and stomping behind them, who had gotten them caught. He and Carro's voices might have been lost to the wind and creak of trees, but the horse's nicker would have been distinct. Even as he thought this, the barest hint of firelight dug its way through the darkness to their right, north along the trail. The voices had stopped, but the sound of feet and the grind of armor were more and more distinct.

Raz thought fast. There was no time to drill Carro on what could be expected if they were caught, or what the best course of action was to ensure that that *didn't* happen. He had to act, and he had to act *now*.

His grip tightened around Ahna's haft as he made his decision.

"Carro, I'm going to leave you."

Beside him, the Priest's eyes grew even wider. He opened his mouth to protest, but Raz cut him off.

"You need to *trust me*," he said quickly, already getting up. "I'll be back. We don't know how many there are and we don't know what they'll do if they find us, but neither do we have the time to debate it. I'll be *right back*."

He was in the process of turning north, intent on dashing through the flickering shadows of the trees as the torchlight grew ever nearer from the same direction, when Carro grabbed the loose furs of his leg. He whirled, about to hiss in fury at the man, but stopped.

Carro was not looking at him in fear, now. No, that wasn't true. He *was* looking at Raz in fear, but it was a different kind of fear. There was a strength in the scared complexion of this face, a rigidity in his composure.

Raz had seen it before, this impressive—almost irritating—countenance, this bravery in the face of terror.

He had seen it in the bearing of Syrah Brahnt, so many years ago, as she had vied for the life of a dying slaver.

"Don't kill them," Carro said, the quiet demand somewhere between an order and a plea. "*Please*, Raz. Don't kill them. I don't want—I *can't* let another... another be..."

He trailed off. Raz hesitated. He only half understood what Carro was talking about, for one thing, and the last time he had bowed to such a request the results had been hellish.

But, in the end, he nodded. Bending down he eased Ahna gently to the ground just as the light flared in truth around the trees, sneaking through the thicket that hid them both in a mosaic of brightness.

Then Raz bolted right, running through the dark.

He moved fast, but not far, whispering between the warped trunks like some demon of the night. He hadn't gone more than a dozen yards before he caught a glimpse of the men through the forest, running along the trail in the other direction. He took two more bounding strides, then spun and slipped left to the edge of the path, looking south.

They were only two. The pair wore worn leather armor supplemented with iron plating in various forms and places, and from behind Raz was momentarily taken by how they could have almost been Carro and Talo. They were large, heavily muscled men, both with dirty wild hair—one blond and the other light brown—and as they looked around, searching for the source of whatever sound had alerted them, Raz saw decorative scars tracing lines through thick beards and up along their cheeks. Both carried torches aloft, their other hands hefting heavy axes at the ready.

As he darted across the path Raz hoped, for a moment, that the men would run right past the thicket behind which Carro crouched and Gale stood. He kept an eye on them as he moved, quiet as a shadow, back in their direction, now on the opposite side of the trail. It seemed luck wasn't about to favor him, though, and as one of the men shouted, practically skidding to a halt in front of the brush, Raz realized with an angry rush that while he and Carro had been well enough hidden, the stallion probably towered in perfectly plain view.

By that point, though, he was even with them, and just when the two mountain men whirled in the horse's direction, Raz's great outline flickered against the canopy as he leapt out from the darkness behind them with a snarl like a wild animal.

It was a short, brutal fight. One man caught a mailed fist in the side of the head as he turned towards this new sound, the other yelling in surprise when Raz's tail swept his thick legs out from under him. The first went down at once, body going limp as wet paper, ax and torch tumbling from useless fingers. The second hit the ground with a muffled *thud* and the crunch of leather and iron, but didn't get so much as a chance to start heaving himself back up before Raz was over him. He had only the briefest moment to look up, blue eyes wide as a clawed foot rose up before his eyes.

"*Dahgün,*" he breathed in quiet shock, staring up into Raz's face, illuminated beneath his hood by the two torches lying flickering beside the trail.

Then Raz's foot came down, slamming the man's head into the ground behind it.

There was a moment of silence as the forest around them settled, the Woods taking as much notice of the scuffle as it might have the falling of a single flake of snow.

Then Carro came tumbling out of the brush.

"*Dammit,* Raz!" he grumbled, hurrying over the man whose head Raz had just pounded into the earth.

"They're *fine,*" Raz said in exasperation. "I pulled my punches. They'll wake up in a bit, though with a hell of a headache to remember me by."

"This one is bleeding, though!" Carro exclaimed, shuffling over to the first man, on his side on the path.

"Huh, so he is," Raz said, taking a cursory peek at the mountain man's face over the Priest's shoulder. The pointed steel edge of the gauntlet's knuckles had ripped open the skin beneath his left eye, and it was bleeding profusely. Raz was about to voice some quip about "just adding to the scars," when Carro started twisting his right hand over the man's face. He watched the Priest work his magic again, fascinated by the golden, dancing lines of the healing spell. He stood witness, awed into silence, as the cut sealed itself before his very eyes, the loose fold of broken skin piecing itself back together again as though by—well, as though by magic.

"Amazing," he heard himself mutter.

Carro finished his work, the gold light fading abruptly, and reached up to wipe sweat from his brow.

"You Priests really go the distance," Raz muttered, crossing his arms and shoving the man Carro had just tended to over on his back with a foot. "Waste of your gift, if you ask me."

Carro sighed. "Why am I not in the least bit surprised to hear you say that?"

Then he frowned down at the mountain man, taking in the scars of his face and what—Raz realized only now that he was closer—appeared to be a thick, vertical piercing of some ashen bone through the man's nose.

"*Are* they mountain men?" Raz asked tentatively. He had assumed—and was fairly sure he was correct—but it didn't hurt to ask.

Carro nodded. "Kregoan, the both of them," he said, glancing at the other unconscious form behind them as well. "One of the western tribes, of the Vietalis."

"Then they're your Kayle's men," Raz said, frowning. "Unless there's another reason members of the western ranges would be wandering the Arocklen in the middle of the freeze...?"

Again, Carro nodded.

"They're Baoill's, without a doubt," he concurred. "But what in the Lifegiver's name they're doing this far east, I haven't got a bloody damn clue. Scouts, maybe?"

Raz shook his head. "Not likely. Scouts would travel lighter." He kicked the iron plating on the closest man's armor for emphasis. "And they'd have supplies, maybe even mounts. These don't strike me as the 'scouting' type, anyway..."

"You're not wrong there," Carro mumbled, looking suddenly more troubled. "Kregoan are among the more savage of the tribes. Other clans are better suited for reconnaissance. So again: what *the hell* are they doing here?"

Raz hesitated. For a moment he thought of not telling the Priest what he was afraid the men might have been. He considered every possibility that came to mind, starting with deserters and ending with the most obvious choice. Deserters would have run *from* the sound of people, rather than towards them. Patrols—if the mountain men were pushing units this far into the Woods—would have had more men and been better stocked.

These two, though, were paired, armed, without supplies, and carrying torches...

"Carro..." he said slowly, looking north up the path, along the route they were meant to take. "I think these are sentries."

XXII

"Laor take me…" Carro choked in a shocked whisper.

Raz considered muttering his own curses, but decided to let the Priest have his moment. In truth, he was more concerned with taking stock of the scene that lay beneath them, sprawling out from the base of the hill whose topmost lip they now crouched behind, a nightmare bathed in a bright orange glow beneath the trees.

Hundreds of tents were staked sidelong across the broken terrain of the Woods, thrown up in any space that allowed for their width. They extended as far as Raz could see between the trees, illuminating the Arocklen with the dancing light of cooking fires that made the icy canopy above gleam and shimmer like a ceiling of solid crystal. Smoke hung thick in the air, an angry haze creeping across the forest when it was unable to escape upwards. The smell of the last ten-day, usually the crisp, clean scent of the evergreens and snow and wind, vanished in a curdling stench of fire and leather and piss.

And through it all, little more than black silhouettes against the flames, dozens on dozens of men were moving about the camp, their voices and the sound of their day's endeavors winding their way up the hill with ease.

"He's here," Carro breathed in horror from beside Raz. "He's *here.*"

"He's not."

The Priest blinked and looked around at Raz, who hadn't taken his eyes off the camp.

"What do you mean?" the man demanded in near desperation. "Are you not seeing what I'm seeing? That's the Kayle's army! He came east. Lifegiver's tits, why would he—?"

"He's not here," Raz insisted, reaching up to pull back the furs of his hood, freeing his ears. "At least, I don't think so. And that's not the whole of his army. I don't think there can be more than a thousand down there, probably less."

He couldn't get a physical count, given that the tents stretched further into the Woods than he could make out, but it was the noise that gave it away. The camp raised a ruckus, true enough, but it was the din of hundreds, not thousands. Raz had heard the voices of thousands, listened to them ringing out around him as he stood among the dead in the pit of the Arena.

Even among the Woods, the full mass of Gûlraht Baoill's army would have existed in a constant, ebbing roar of sound.

"Not here?" Carro asked softly, clearly having trouble wrapping his head around everything he was seeing. "But then… Where—What is…? I don't understand… Why are *they* here?"

At that, Raz frowned. Of the pair of them, he didn't remotely think it likely to be *he* would be the one to have a better idea of why the Kayle would have a contingent of his greater force camped along the base of the Citadel's mountain path. He didn't have a damn clue what the man was thinking, or if this was even part of Baoill's plan at all. Maybe this was a mutinied unit, pressing further eastward in order to escape the wrath of their former commander. No… too much of a coincidence. With hundreds on hundreds of square miles, it was just too unlikely such absconders would just *happen* to have settled along the bottom of the stairs. It was all the more likely they had been ordered here, ordered to set up camp, almost like they were—

It hit Raz like a bolt in the head.

"It's a siege," he muttered in realization. Carro turned to look at him again, confused.

"A-A siege?" he asked hesitantly, not comprehending. "I'm not follow—"

Then he stopped, eyes growing wide.

"Oh no… the stairs. They're trying to block the stairs."

"Is there another way to or from the Citadel?" Raz asked him quickly, peering back down at the camp.

Carro shook his head, his voice strained as he spoke. "Cyurgi' Di was initially built as a fortress to guard against some unknown enemy come from the Tundra, to the north of the mountains. There would never have been a need for a secondary escape if they were only defending the one direction."

"The Citadel wasn't built by the Laorin?"

"No." Again, the Priest shook his head. "No one is actually sure who built it, but it wasn't the faith. We've just occupied it for as long as there's been written record."

"And whoever built it never thought they'd need to defend from the south," Raz muttered, finishing the thought. "This is bad. It's definitely a blockade. This must be some kind of advance guard, meant to keep the Laorin in place until the larger body of the army arrives."

"But why?" Carro hissed, his good hand shaking as it clung to the steel of his staff, lying on the ground before him. "Why attack the Citadel? What good does it do them?"

Possibly quite a lot, Raz thought privately. If everything Carro had said about the Laorin was true, then crippling the faith would be like cutting the head off the snake. Eliminating the influence of the Lifegiver—and his followers' ability to band the valley towns—didn't seem like such a terrible move to make…

Maybe that's all this was. Instead of a vanguard, maybe this smaller force was merely a detachment of the army on assignment, aiming to disrupt the activities of Cyurgi' Di.

Still... something felt off...

"Stop thinking strategically," he told Carro. "Is there a reason the mountain men would want to starve the Laorin out? *Any* reason."

Carro, surprisingly, snorted.

"If we're ignoring military value, then there are a thousand and more," he said. "Most of the tribes are devout to their Stone Gods. Many *despise* the Lifegiver, and those that spread His light even more. Syrah once told me that Baoill threatened her life when—"

For the second time, Carro froze. This time his eyes were blank, drawn back to some memory, some fragment of thought as something clicked.

"What?" Raz demanded in a hiss. "What is it?"

For another moment Carro said nothing. He just stared emptily at Raz's chest, piecing together whatever was going on in his mind.

"Syrah," he finally said. "They... They might be here for Syrah..."

That sent a chill down Raz's spine he neither liked, nor fully understood. Carro's words were simultaneously frightening, confusing, and infuriating.

He didn't completely know why, but Raz was sure of one single, absolute fact: he'd be *damned* if the mountain brutes thought they could lay a finger on the white-haired woman.

"Why?" he asked. "Why would they be after her?"

"I'm not sure *they* are," Carro said, indicating the camp with an awkward shift of his broken arm. "Not personally, at least. But Baoill... Baoill might very well be. After Syrah returned from the Vietalis Ranges, she told us stories of the Sigûrth. She said even more in the letter she sent after the fall of Harond. It was part of her plea for us to return home..."

He paused, still gathering his thoughts.

"Baoill *hated* her," he said uneasily. "He despised the work she was doing, accused her of attempting to rob the tribe of its culture, the people of their gods. Syrah even said he suggested more than once she be made a prisoner, and treated to the old ways of execution."

"Which were?"

Carro turned slightly green and shivered. "Too unpleasant to describe. Needless to say, if the new Kayle has a grudge..."

"He may act on it, now that he has the means," Raz said with a nod. "Two birds with one stone."

Carro looked confused at that, and Raz sighed.

"He pays back an old enemy, and handicaps the one institution that may prove to be a major threat to his crusade in the immediate future," he explained, voicing his earlier thoughts. "If the Laorin *really* have—or had—the ability to marshal the remaining valley towns, then by marching on the Citadel the Kayle has the opportunity to get his hands on Syrah *and* remove a majority of the faith's influence in one go." He looked back down at the camp. "All in all, I think your Kayle is one clever bastard."

Carro continued to watch him, the look on his face equal parts impressed and terrified.

"Apparently he's not the only one," he muttered after a time, finally looking away.

"Hmm?" Raz asked, not taking his eyes from the milling throng of mountain warriors moving about their cooking fires, shouting to each other and shifting as patrols and sentries came and went.

"Nothing," the Priest said shakily. "But I'd like to get moving. Staying here makes me nervous."

"Is our goal still the stairs?"

Carro stopped, half stooped as he'd been making to stand and turn away from the firelight.

"Of course," he said, his tone almost accusing in his surprise. "Did you think there was another option?"

Raz said nothing for several seconds, still not looking away from the glow of the camp.

"It's going to be risky," he spoke up finally. "This changes things, Carro. Getting to the stairs isn't going to be a simple matter of finding them and making the climb. There are bound to be men watching the base of the path, and even if we *do* get past them, what have we accomplished? Nothing more than getting us stuck in the Citadel with the rest of your people. It's not the smart play. We would be better off turning around and making back for Ystréd."

"Ystréd?" Carro demanded shrilly, looking suddenly furious. "*Ystréa?* And what are we going to do there? How does turning and running help those trapped atop the mountain?"

"How does getting trapped up there with them help them?" Raz retorted. "It doesn't. We have nothing with us that will be of use, no information that might solve their predicament. They must know they're trapped, by now. They know the Kayle's men are waiting for them at the bottom of the stairs. But if we turn around and make back for the valley towns, we *do* have information. We can tell them that we think the Kayle isn't actually pushing south. We can tell them they have time to prepare, to gather an army and launch a counterassault before Baoill even has a chance to make for Ystréd. We could—"

"Leave my people to *die*," Carro cut across him in a harsh, hissed whisper, his face still set in fury. "You're suggesting we abandon the faithful, suggesting we sacrifice them to their fate in order to buy the rest of the North a few months of time to prepare."

Raz was taken aback. "That's not what I'm saying. I just think we—"

"No, you're not *thinking*," Carro spat. "You're not *thinking* at all. If we leave now, we sentence the men and women of the Citadel to nothing more than a delayed death. By the time we reach Ystréd again—in the full freeze, mind you—contact the valley towns—again, in the full freeze, which I've already told you is difficult enough as is—and marshal them to our banner, it would be summer at minimum. And that's *if* Talo had been with us!"

He calmed suddenly, as he spoke his lover's name. For a moment, pain and sadness replaced anger, and his body seemed to sag as his gaze fell to the ground. When he spoke again, it was with a softer, kinder tone.

"I'm sorry, Raz. I know you don't have an ideal grasp on all the players in this game, so this time I need *you* to trust *me*. I understand the logic of your idea, but it won't work. There are too many factors, and I don't have the pull Talo did with the towns. The best we could hope to do is get back to Atler and have her petition Ystréd's High Court to reach out to the other municipalities, and you can be damn sure no one will answer—at least not in time." He sighed. "I know there's probably nothing we can do. I know it's a fool's errand, but I know the only life I would be saving by turning around now is my own. Worst of all—" he looked up at Raz, his face pained but composed "—I know I can't do anything alone."

Raz watched him carefully, taking in the man and processing his words. There was truth there, Raz conceded. He *didn't* know all the factors, and he just couldn't imagine Carro letting emotion cloud his judgment in this crucial moment. If he said Raz's plan was scrap, then it was scrap. If he said leaving now was equivalent to condemning the residents of the Citadel to their fate, then he meant it.

And that, Raz told himself as the dreamt image of a dancing woman crept among his thoughts again, *is unacceptable.*

As the self-preserving wedge of himself screamed in frustration, Raz knew he had made his decision.

"Alright," he said simply. Carro blinked in surprise again.

Then he looked suddenly hopeful.

"Al-Alright?" he asked tentatively, eyes brightening.

"Alright," Raz repeated with a nod. "I'll help. Moon knows I've been dodging Her long enough as it is. Might as well keep gambling. But it's one thing to knock out a pair of distracted sentries in the half-dark, Carro. It's another entirely to take on whatever guard the commander of this—" he waved down at the tents "—has undoubtedly posted. We're already going to have to go around the edge of the camp to even *get* to the path.

After that… I have no idea what's waiting for us, but whatever it is there's a good chance we're going to have to fight our way through."

Carro's face lost its hopefulness, looking suddenly green again, but when he opened his mouth to speak, Raz cut him off.

"Don't bother asking me not to kill, Carro. I've done your Lifegiver one favor already today. I intend to do him—and Talo—another by getting your neck up to the Citadel in one piece, if I can manage it. To do that, I can't keep playing the saint. I'll do what needs doing, despite your hounding."

"You can't," Carro pleaded. "*Please*, Raz. You *can't*. They're people. They've been granted life by something far beyond you and I. They have families. Children. Please. You ca—"

"I can, and I will," Raz growled, edging away from the hill and getting to his feet, lifting Ahna back over his shoulder from where she'd lain crossways on the ground before him. "You can't win this one, Carro. I *know* they have families. I *know* they have children. If that were enough to stop death—even enough to stop cruelty—then the world would have no use for people like me. Maybe it would be better for it, and maybe not. Either way, you have a choice. I'm not giving you an ultimatum. It's simply the reality of your situation: either you accept my help in every form it comes and we have a shot at actually making it to your High Citadel, or we turn back."

"Before you say anything," he continued quickly, interrupting Carro's angry spluttering as he started to reply, "consider the consequences: if we make it up the stairs, you have a chance to help your people. If you're thinking of leaving me here, ask yourself if you can get to the path on your own. If not, then it's worse than if we had made for Ystréd again. I die—likely to this damned cold—you die, and the Laorin die in their fortress on the mountain, with no chance of anyone sending help. Personally I think we're all fucked either way, but that's my business."

Carro's face was deathly white. "Th-they could send letters," he stuttered. "Syrah and the council can plead for assistance on their own! I'm sure they have already!"

"And to what end? You've done your best to convince me that Talo was the only true solution the Laorin had to this mess. Talo is gone, Carro. I'm sorry, but he's gone. So what good will inked words from some nameless Priest or Priestess do your people now?"

Carro was quivering. Not out of anger, Raz knew, but out of horror. He was at an impasse with his own ethics. Whatever direction he chose, death awaited. It was the inevitable difficulty of holding true to a code, of wielding iron morals.

And it had been the undoing of more than one man who'd been unable to bend his rules in order to make a decision.

196

Carro seemed to be fighting that exact struggle. He was shaking, a permanent expression of hopelessness imprinted across his features. He looked practically on the very edge of going mad, like he'd been handed a blade and told to murder one of his children.

After a while, Raz decided to throw him some rope.

"Your lover had to make a similar decision, not so long ago, Carro," he said kindly, taking a step forward. "In Azbar. Talo had to choose in the space of a very short time whether he would lend me—me, the bloody, savage Monster of Karth, the murderous Scourge of the South—his aid, and the faith's aid. He had the same struggle, with the devil of my persuading logic sitting on one shoulder and the godly words of Kal Yu'ri on the other. He had to make a choice, and do you know what he said?"

Slowly, Carro shook his head, his blue eyes shining in the orange glow reflecting off the icy canopy above them.

"He said, 'Until the day comes when He sees fit to end all wars, the Lifegiver is not unaware that violence will exist among His flock.' He spoke of the difference between a life taken, and a life given, and said that if any were to ask him what he would prefer—the death of less or the death of more—then it would be an easy answer to give. He said that, when your Lifegiver saw fit to give him the opportunity to save those he could, he would take it. Even if that opportunity was me."

It was all true. They were the words that had convinced Raz that Talo was a man worth respecting, a man worth following, and they were the words he had kept with him ever since that day in the Koyts' cramped home.

"I need you to take the opportunity that is me, Carro," he said finally. "I need you to accept that the world is not black and white, and that there are times when the only path that can be taken is the better of two *shitty* opportunities. I need you to pick the lesser of the evils, as Talo did before you."

The words struck Carro hard. Raz could see that. The shaking had ended, but the man seemed also to have stopped breathing, like the disclosure of Talo's actions had shaken something loose within him and he were struggling to replace it.

When he moved again, he surprised Raz by giving a slow, unsound laugh.

"That sounds like Talo," he said wearily. "To a letter, that sounds just like him. I always envied him that ability. That strength…"

"And you were one of many," Raz told him. "But you have a chance now to borrow some of it for a purpose."

Carro nodded slowly.

"You've backed me into a corner, Raz," he said with a twisted grimace, looking down at the camp below them. "I'm not sure I like it."

"I told you, I'm giving you no ultimatum. These are simply the facts of the situation."

Carro nodded again. "I suppose so. Still... I don't like it."

"No one would. It doesn't change the fact that you need to make a choice..."

Carro gave a pained, warped sort of smile.

"Aye, that I do..." he said almost inaudibly, as though speaking to himself. "And if that's the case, I might have an idea. Let's go find out if there really *is* a difference between less and more."

XXIII

Raz was not a fan of Carro's plan.

He'd been thoroughly impressed with it, at first, as the Priest explained, outlining the concept to him on their brisk walk back along the path, Gale plodding along at their back after they'd retrieved him from where he'd been hidden among the trees. When they'd gotten to *his* role in the scheme, though, Raz had bristled.

"You want me to *what?*"

"Not *actually*," Carro had told him in a huff. The man seemed to have found a bit of his old self now that they'd made a decision. "You'll just need to pretend. Your hands won't even be bound."

It didn't make Raz feel any better. Still, as he hadn't been able to come up with anything better—mostly, he thought, because he knew shit-all about what they were getting themselves into—he went with it. It was several minutes of rapid walking later, therefore, that they arrived at their initial destination.

They'd snuffed out the torches the sentries had been carrying and dragged the unconscious forms behind the thickets along the left side of the path, out of easy view. By the time they returned, one of the mountain men was slowly coming to, groaning and blinking as he attempted to clear his head.

Quick as a snake Raz fell to one knee beside him, drew his gladius, and slammed the sword's pommel down between the man's eyes, knocking him out cold once more.

"What?" Raz asked innocently as Carro caught up to him and gave him a scathing look.

The Priest had seemed to decide that silence was the best punishment, and set about his task without so much as a word to Raz.

It took a while for them to make their preparations. They began by selecting the larger of the two men—the one closer to Carro's size—and stripping him of his armor, leathers, and most of his furs. Raz would have taken him down to his loincloth and let him freeze, but Carro's withering warnings of where he'd light his magical fires next time resulted in the man being left in a thick shirt, heavy cotton pants, and socks.

He'd probably catch a cold, but it was doubtful he'd die before he or his companion woke up.

This done, they moved north up the path again, then off into the Woods to get Carro dressed. It was tedious work, requiring the man to change first into the lighter traveler's attire he'd apparently worn most of the way to Azbar when they'd left the Citadel at summer's end, then don the heavier leather and iron armor they'd scavenged off the sentry. Both he and Raz shared in a number of curses throughout this process, Carro because the bulky layers stank and his broken arm made him grunt in pain every time it shifted, and Raz because he was so accustomed to the exquisite work of Allihmad Jerr that he had practically forgotten how much of a headache it could be to strap a man into armor. At last, though, they managed, and eventually Carro stood, huffing and wheezing, looking very much the part of a true mountain man in weathered gear, his blond, braided hair and beard touching it all off nicely.

Next came Ahna and Carro's staff. Raz had always done his best to keep the dviassegai easily accessible, but after some deliberation they concluded it was neither likely nor practical for the plan at hand. In the end Raz had covered her blades with her old leather sack, then—with much help from Carro and *no* help from the horse—strapped her and the staff lengthwise along Gale's left side. They'd shifted as much other weight as they could to the animal's right, including Raz's gladius and war-ax, and eventually seemed to find a good balance.

Barring a deliberate inspection, Ahna and the steel staff could now pass as a pair of plain spears, and Gale as the well-armed charger of a mountain warrior.

At last it was Raz's turn. Grumbling all the while, he used a good length of browning vine he managed to pull down from a nearby sapling to wrap his heavy furs tightly about his hands and wrists. This served the dual purpose of hiding the steel of his gauntlets and making it look as though his hands—when held close together—had been bound. Once he'd managed this he pulled his tail in and about his waist, then tucked his wings in as tight as they would go. Drawing his hood up as high as he could over his face, Raz did a final check to make sure his gladius and ax were within easy reach, hanging off Gale's saddle behind Carro's thigh, having helped the man clambered up onto the horse a minute earlier.

Then Raz reached up and, with a scowl he couldn't help, grabbed the back-most saddle straps, keeping his wrists close together.

In the space of twenty minutes, Carro al'Dor and Raz i'Syul Arro, Priest of Laor and the infamous Monster of Karth, had become nothing more than a tribesman dragging along a vanquished, enslaved prisoner.

"Did I mention how much I *really* don't like this?" Raz asked for the fourth time as they started to walk north and west again, back towards the mountain men's camp, Gale limping steadily along. He wasn't sure if it was just in his head, but he thought the bare skin of the twin scars that encircled his wrists beneath his gauntlets was itching suddenly. "I mean I really, *really* don't like this."

"Well next time *you* can come up with a plan," Carro snapped under his breath. "Now be quiet. We'll be there soon."

Indeed, it wasn't more than a minute before the orange glow of the fires made itself known through the Woods once more. Together Raz and

Carro carved a careful route, aiming to get as close as they could while keeping to the very edges of the eastern side of the encampment. A majority of the activity they had been able to make out from the top of the hill seemed to have been limited to the center, south, west, and north. The east side, along which they aimed to trail, had looked to be where the Kayle's men stored their supplies, equipment, foodstuffs, and other such materials. There were a couple of tents, but Raz hadn't seen much activity going in and out of them, and he thought it likely they were just more storage areas.

If they could keep out of the light, they might just be able to make it all the way around without getting spotted.

They had debated taking a wide route and making for the base of the stairs at an angle, avoiding the mountain men altogether. Raz had nixed this, though, arguing that approaching the path indirectly would only be more suspicious, and give whatever guard had been posted there further time to make out the inconsistencies in their—and especially Raz's—disguise. He'd also vetoed avoiding the base of the path altogether and climbing the mountain from a different angle, or at least meeting with the stairs at another point. He'd pointed out that, if it were possible to manage the mountain face without taking the stairs, the Laorin would have very likely done so a long time ago. The sides of the Saragrias Ranges were simply too steep and too rocky for Carro to handle, and Raz didn't know how much he trusted Gale's footing in the depths of the snow already, injured as he was...

In the end, the direct route was their only option, and so Raz and Carro found themselves creeping along the edge of the camp, doing their utmost to stay out of the light and away from the eyes of the more active areas to their left.

For what seemed like an eternity they moved along, Carro doing his best to sit tall and proud in the saddle, trying to look the victorious warrior, and Raz working hard on seeming the cowering prisoner of war, stumbling along beside the horse. Neither were very convincing, but it proved an irrelevant concern for the time being. Not a soul moved among the stacked storage and narrow tents they crept along. They seemed to have punched a hole in the sentry line when Raz had knocked the two men they'd left back along the path unconscious, and were now reaping their reward. The majority of sound and voices Raz could make out were at least fifty or so yards away, well into the ranks of the camp.

And praise the Sun for that, he thought, giving silent thanks. He had thought the dark and his boots might hide his feet well enough—the only part of him there was nothing he could do to disguise—but the light of the cooking fire was bright, to the point where anyone passing by would likely not have been fooled. All they had to do was get through the trees and into the snow, and he would be much less likely to be—

Raz froze. A sound had reached his ears, muffled and horrifying. He stood in the semi-darkness, eyes scanning the boxes and barrels alongside him through the fur that hung over his face. After a moment they fell on a wide, patched canvas tent some thirty feet ahead, and the sound seemed to grow more distinct as he realized the source.

He heard, in a furious, billowing thrall of rage, the unmistakable grunts and heavy breathing of a man in pleasure. This would have been unremarkable, perhaps, except for the fact that there seemed to be more than one male voice coming from within. At least another, maybe two, were present, laughing and talking in the strange, guttural speech of the mountains.

And underlying it all, limited and muted behind the noise of the man's exertion and his companion's voiced amusement, were the distinct, pitiful whimpers of a woman, gagged and held against her will, struggling and fighting to be free of the hands and gazes that undoubtedly held her firm.

"Raz!"

Raz's conscience ripped back into place so abruptly it left him reeling. He realized that he had stopped moving, transfixed by the sounds. Carro and Gale, unaware that he had let go of the saddle straps, had continued on a dozen feet, ambling slowly across the uneven ground. The Priest was looking around him in alarm, turned about in the saddle.

"What are you doing?" the man demanded in an urgent whisper.

Raz, in answer, put a finger to his lips with one hand, then pointed towards the tent with another. Carro whirled about as though expecting to see a patrol closing in on them, or perhaps some solitary drunkard who had wandered off to relieve himself in the trees.

Then Raz saw the Priest stiffen, and he knew the man could make out the sounds of the woman's struggles as well.

Raz crept forward, doubly careful to stay quiet now, until he caught up with Carro and the horse. He paused for a moment, struggling with himself, the anger flaring in him as he continued to listen.

Losing the battle, he reached up and began drawing the gladius from its sheath, steel scraping quietly like cold vengeance.

He was taken completely by surprise when Carro stopped him, one big hand reaching back to close around his wrist.

Raz snarled his frustration at the act, but the Priest ignored him. He hadn't even looked away from the tent, and had reacted only to the sound of the sword being drawn. For a long time he stared at the leather canvas that only partially muffled the assault, and Raz could feel the tension in Carro's body as thick fingers twitched about his gauntlet.

202

Finally, the man turned around, his face sad and tense.

"Can you stop them?" he asked, his voice chokingly hoarse.

Raz nodded.

"Without alerting the others?"

At that, Raz hesitated. He turned his attention back on the tent, listening again. He was sure, now, that there were at least three men within. More might even be outside, waiting their turn. Pushing aside the violent emotions that welled up within him at that thought, Raz forced himself to consider the surroundings, assessing all the elements. There were three, maybe more. The rest of the Kayle's men seemed to be congregated closer to the center of the camp, but it was doubtful they were *all* there. Someone was bound to hear a scuffle, and Raz couldn't guarantee no one would have time to shout an alarm before he got to them. Even the woman, whoever she was, was a risk, as it wouldn't have been the first time a girl had screamed at the sight of his face...

Slowly, feeling as though every muscle in his body were fighting the motion, Raz shook his head.

Carro's grip tightened, and it was a few seconds before he spoke.

"'The lesser of the evils,'" he quoted, his voice breaking. "Getting ourselves killed serves no one. Not even that poor girl."

For a long time Raz didn't move, the gladius still half drawn from where it hung behind Carro's thigh.

Then, slowly, he sheathed it again, releasing the hilt with a massive effort. He didn't say a word as he wrapped his hands around the saddle straps again, and he didn't look away from the tent until they had long passed it, Carro heeling Gale into a slow trot northward, keeping to the camp's edge all the while.

The muffled sounds of the woman's plaintive, wretched wailing dogged Raz unforgivingly.

It wasn't more than two minutes before they traded the last of the tents for the shadows again, and another couple before the trees began to thin, snow starting to pile thicker and thicker along the forest floor once more. They'd managed to sneak in and out of the encampment without running into so much as a soul, and Raz breathed a tiny bit easier as his booted feet became lost in the piling white. He offered up another brief thanks to the Sun, squinting up at its pale outline against the overcast sky as the canopy gapped and thinned.

Then he turned his gaze earthward again, keeping his face well shaded beneath his hood, eyes skimming the rapidly brightening edge of the Woods that opened up before them, marking the end of the trees.

As they stepped out into the open air for what Raz hoped would be the last time in a good long while, he forced himself not to look up and gape at the harsh angles of the Saragrias again. He kept his head resolutely tucked in mock defeat, no longer struggling to fake a stumbling gait as his shorter legs slipped and caught in the snows that Gale's long limbs made easy work of. He studied the scene before him carefully, peering once more from between the long hairs of the furs that hid his face. He couldn't see much at first, most everything being a distorted jumble of white and grey of snow and earth and granite, but with patient study he eventually made out what he assumed to be their goal. Straight ahead of them a gap existed in the boulders and trees of the rapidly inclining mountain face. It wasn't a massive space—probably about a dozen feet wide—but it was distinct against the otherwise rough-hewn rock that marked the ranges. Past this opening, Raz was barely able to make out staggered shelvings in the heavy snow, rising and twisting up and off to the left.

The stairs, he realized with amazement, unable to help himself and tilting his chin up just a fraction, trying to follow the path as high as it went. The steps curved around themselves several times within his limited vision, then were lost in the slope of the earth and the scattered patches of stunted, bent spruces and firs that dotted the peaks.

It took Carro's sharp inhale of alarm to bring Raz's attention back to their base, and he cursed silently.

Damn...

Scattered about the bottom of the stairway, lounging in a wide space that seemed to have been periodically cleared of snow, the dark outlines of no less than a full score of armed men contrasted sharply with the white and grey of the scene. Raz sized them all up, watching the group take note of the horse, its rider, and the apparently unfortunate soul being dragged along towards them. He wasn't surprised, of course. He had hoped whoever was in command of the Kayle's men now laying siege to the Citadel might have been fool enough to leave only a light guard on the stairs, but it had been a dubious wish. It made sense to secure the one avenue by which the Laorin could possibly escape. While twenty men weren't enough to hold back an onslaught from above if the Priests and Priestesses decided to make a play for their freedom, it was more than sufficient to secure the path long enough for the rest of the advance guard to be summoned. The outcroppings and boulders on either side of the stairs provided plenty of cover from whatever magic or weaponry the Laorin might have been able to hurl from higher up, and as several of the men got to their feet Raz saw more than one bow slung behind backs and over shoulders. They were crude looking weapons, worn and well used, but the slim men who carried them—bedecked in thin leathers and dark furs adorned with what seemed to be at least one animal skull of some kind or another—looked well versed in their use.

They came ready, Raz thought, impressed as he watched the rest of the sentries stand up and turn to face him and Carro. *They could easily defend the path long enough to keep the Laorin from getting too far down ana—*

Raz's thoughts were interrupted by a sudden, alarming notion. They were more than halfway to the base of the stairs now, less than thirty feet from the first steps. The plan had been for Carro to hail whoever guarded the path with a raised hand, then tell them Raz was a deserter dragged along for their entertainment—a phrase Carro had been practicing under his breath in the mountain tongue over and over the last few minutes. The hope was that he would be able to "kick" Raz into the middle of them, and from there the Monster of Karth would be allowed to wreak all the havoc of his profession while Carro cleared a path through on Gale. The bows posed an issue to this, obviously, as the Priest would be a large, slow target atop the horse as they struggled up the first curve in the snowy path.

But that wasn't the concern that had blared so loudly across Raz's concentration. Rather, what made him uneasy was not what the bowmen would do once the Priest broke through, but rather what they were doing now. Instead of regarding Carro with enthusiasm—or at the very least watching him with curiosity, as Raz had assumed they would—the sentries' faces were rapidly shifting from surprise to suspicion, and then on to alarm. As he watched, Raz saw bows being unslung, along with swords and axes drawn from the sheaths and belt loops of the larger men all about the archers. For a moment Raz was confused, wondering what about Carro's disguise was causing such disquiet.

Then, as he followed the men's eyes, he realized the mistake he and the Priest had made. The massive, seventeen-hands mistake they had made.

When they'd been spying on the camp, Raz had heard many things. Voices, laughter, clinking tankards, shouted orders, arguments, the hammering of metal, the shuffling of boots, the crunching break of wood and the crackle of flames. He had been so focused on making out what he *could* hear, in fact, that he hadn't bother at all to pause and consider what he *couldn't* hear.

Like the whinnying and neighs that usually accompanied any larger force of men.

"Horses," he hissed in horrified shock.

Above, Carro—who had been doing his best to maintain the pose of a proud warrior—jumped and looked down.

"What?" he gasped.

Raz had already given himself away, letting go of the saddle straps and tearing his gladius and war-ax free of their loops, when he answered.

"Horses, Carro!" he yelled, already sprinting forward, plowing as fast as he could in great leaps through the heavy snow. "They don't have horses!"

XXIV

They'd been less than fifteen feet away when Raz started his mad dash for the stairs. Their plan was shit now, he knew, and as he ran he heard the mountain men begin to shout, rattled by his sudden charge. He watched as the quickest of the bowmen raised his weapon, arrow drawn and nocked in rapid succession. As Gale screamed in sudden fear behind him, Raz cocked his left arm back and hurled the war ax.

It was a throw made more out of desperation than anything else, and the weapon went wide of its mark, hitting stone and clattering harmlessly away. Still, it was enough to shake the mountain man's concentration, and he yelled some curse as he leapt sideways, his own arrow disappearing into the snow somewhere off to Raz's right.

He might have only his gladius, now, but the move had given Raz the seconds he needed to close the distance, hurtling through the ice and slush before blowing out of the bank onto the cleared ground of the path's base. With a snarling roar he barreled forward, going for the second of what looked to be four archers. The sound seemed to strike pure terror into the men, and for three shocking seconds a majority of them appeared paralyzed, blue eyes gaping at Raz's massive form as he descended on them. In the blink it took him to reach the first of his victims, Raz couldn't understand what had gripped them so suddenly.

The gladius had long fallen, in fact, hacking a diagonal slash through the man's bow, leather, and breastbone, when Raz heard the word once again.

"*Dahgün...*" came the terrified whisper.

This time, the name registered. It hadn't made an impression the first time, when the scarred mountain man he'd knocked unconscious had gasped it in shock at the sight of his face. Now, though, as Raz turned and crashed right into the middle of the tribesmen, gladius sweeping left and right as he howled like some demon born of the winter storms, Raz recalled.

Dahgün, he remembered.

Dragon.

In his desperate rush to keep from being pinned down in the snow between the trees and the stairway, Raz had forgotten all about keeping his wings tight to his back and his tail hidden. As he careened around the shocked group—sword cutting into armor and flesh wherever it found an opening—they whipped and snapped around him, crunching into bodies and throwing men off their feet. Black, scaled muscle collided with iron and fur. Leathery sunset membrane buffeted heads and faces, blinding men and sending them screaming back in fear. Against twenty Raz should have been overwhelmed, and he knew it. His goal had been to push

207

through, not into, to draw attention so that Carro could drive Gale at any opening that made itself available between the sentries. When the mountain men had frozen, though, struck still by the terrifying apparition of his winged form, Raz had adapted.

And now, as blood streaked the frosted stone beneath his clawed feet, he realized with sudden astounding elation that he was *winning*.

By the time the men shook off their fear, it was too late. Four lay dead—including two bowmen—and another two were screaming their life away as they writhed about on the ground, clutching at a punctured abdomen and a mangled leg. Fourteen still stood, but even as he threw himself backward, avoiding the horizontal slash of a heavy claymore, Raz saw the horror reflected in their eyes. He had seen fear in his life. He'd seen it pooled in the gaze of every man and woman he had ever killed, drowning them in the moments before death. Fear of him, fear of death, fear of pain and the unknown.

But the terror that held the mountain men, it seemed, was of a different order altogether. Raz couldn't quite grasp it, as he lunged between two larger men to impale a third bowman through the gut, the thinner man's bear-skull helm leering ironically as he died. This was a different dread than anything he had yet come across.

They fear the dragon, he mused, darting back out of the ring he'd dived into, dealing one man a great, hacking slash across the face as he retreated.

Then let's give them a dragon.

Somersaulting sideways, his clawed hand getting a good grip against the cleared ground, Raz launched himself back again, well away from the twelve left. As they began to turn on him, starting to rush him as a group, Raz reached up and threw back the hood of his robes. Cold air bit at his reptilian features, a mild wind chilling his black snout and white teeth. Still, taking a lunging step forward—like the warning feign of a snake— Raz flared his neck crest up over his head, spread his ears to their extent, and let loose a thundering, howling scream that seemed to shake the very earth beneath his feet.

The sound crashed over the mountain men like one of the Laorin's blasting spells. Many had stumbled when he'd revealed his face, howling in fear at the sight. As the rumbling cry hit them, like the defiant roar of some terrifying animal, to a one they hesitated, blood rushing from already pale faces. Leaping on the opportunity, Raz lunged at the closest man, smashing aside a desperate, terrified swing of the man's ax and cutting him down with a vicious two-handed upward slash.

Then he heard the clop of hooves on stone, and help arrived in a flash of magic.

Raz had just whirled to face his next opponent, bloody gladius raised high, when white fire erupted outward from the ground at his feet. It bloomed in an imperfect wedge before him, racing across the stone to lick at boots and furs, singeing hair and catching on cloth where it could. At once the remaining mountain men began to yell in fear, screaming again about the "*Dahgün! Dahgün!*"

Over the crackle of the white flames, Raz heard the *clang* of steel hitting stone. Almost immediately there was another *clang*, then another, and through the shimmer of the magic Raz watched as the men began to fall back, empty hands raised against the sudden, crushing heat. In their delirium the men of the tribes didn't have a prayer against this last great proof of power. With pitching wails of fear that echoed upwards, reverberating against the slopes of the mountains, the path's sentries ran, scrambling in all directions through the snow, desperate to get away from Raz and the mocking bite of the flames.

It was only after the last of them was finally gone, sprinting back into the cover of the Woods, that Raz looked over his shoulder.

Carro was still atop Gale, right hand outstretched as he held the spell, left awkwardly wrapped about the stallion's reins despite being slung across his chest. He looked strained and pale, shifting with the horse at the edge of the cleared stone. Raz had been so preoccupied with the fight that he hadn't kept track of the Priest, more concerned with the archers and keeping himself in one piece.

The mountain men, however, seemed to have done the same, and Carro had taken full advantage, slinking close enough to be of assistance.

Raz grinned at him, flicking his gladius free of most of the blood as he turned. "Couldn't have asked for better timing."

"I thought you could use the help," Carro grumbled back, letting his hand drop. At once, the fires dissipated in fading crackles. "Didn't think it would work *that* well, though."

"They were calling me 'dahgün,'" Raz said with a shrug. "I think you just helped prove a point, in their eyes."

"Ah," Carro said in understanding. "Well if they thought you were suddenly breathing fire, that'll certainly do it. They're a superstitious people. I doubt they have any more of an idea of what true dragons might have looked like than we do."

"Apparently wings, teeth, and claws were the only obligatory requirements," Raz replied, turning back to examine the aftermath of the sentries' retreat.

While the Priest's magic hadn't done more than scorch the armor of the dead, it had left the ground cracked and charred. Smoke wisped upwards from burned grass that had been hiding beneath what ice and snow the mountain men hadn't been able to clear, and steam rose from blackened stone slats that marked the start of the stairs. Atop one of these, the war ax lay innocently, awaiting its retrieval. Raz hurried over to pluck it from the ground, stowing it in its customary loop at his hip before sheathing the gladius over his shoulder.

He'd clean the rest of the blood off later.

"We need to get moving," Carro said, as though echoing Raz's thoughts. "Those men will be back with reinforcements inside of ten minutes."

"Less, probably." Raz looked up the imposing streak of white and grey against the mountain face that was the snow-covered stairway. "But you're right. Will you be able to manage on Gale?"

"Not a good idea."

There was a *thump*, and Raz turned to see that the Priest had slid himself—somewhat clumsily given his one working arm—out of the saddle. He, too, was eyeing the stairway.

"Better to go on foot," Carro continued, leading Gale over. "The path is only going to become more treacherous as we get higher."

"Can we lead him up?" Raz asked in concern, taking the stallion's reins as Carro struggled to slide his staff free from where it lay strapped atop Ahna.

Carro nodded. "It won't be easy, but we'll manage. Mind you I haven't got a clue how in Laor's name we'll get him back down, but it's either we take him or we leave him."

"We take him," Raz said without hesitating, stroking the stallion's muzzle absently as he eyed the path again.

"Aye, I thought you'd say that," Carro said with half a smile. Then he frowned, looking around at the scattered dead that littered the blackened ground, their forms already frosted with wind-blown snow.

"Can I..." he started uneasily. "Can I have a moment...? To send them off?"

Raz paused, looking over his shoulder at the still line of the Woods that encircled them.

Then he nodded.

"Pray quickly, Priest," he said, reaching out to grip the man's shoulder briefly before starting for the steps, Gale in tow. "Time is not on our side."

XXV

"It is the opinion of many a learned man that the Laorin's magical 'gifts —whom the faith believe to this day were granted to their founding members by their benevolent Lifegiver—would be more aptly classified as a sort of unorthodox art. Their abilities, while limited, are varied and adaptable, allowing the use of the base, simpler spells to be worked and molded into more complex creations. One such scholar—the famed author Agor Kehn—claims to have been fortunate enough to observe this phenomenon while traveling along the Northern roads, doing research for a book. Caught in a summer storm, Kehn asserts to have stumbled across a wandering Priest who offered to conjure up a ward to shield them both from the rain and wind. In great detail Kehn would later put to ink a description of watching in amazement as the man twisted magics of warmth and protection about a 'messenger spell,' encasing them in a comfortable shell that would warn the Priest if anyone should disturb them while they slept. Kehn would go on, some time later, to make comment on this experience, finishing his retelling with a literary flourish in which he compared the Priest's spellwork as 'akin to a master painter's combination of essential colors into a creation of endless magnificence...'"

—*Legends Beyond the Border*, by Zyryl Vahs

The first ward triggered silently, alerting Priest Elber just as he was seating himself along one of the long benches that adorned the great hall's leftmost table. The magic pulsed and ran over his skin like a shiver, tingling up his arms and into his back. He froze, almost dropping the sparse plate of seared venison, salted potatoes, and toasted grains that were the paltry rations of the midday meal. His appetite—ignored well past noon as he'd diligently made his daily exam of the spells that surrounded the Citadel—was suddenly forgotten. He shot up straight again, looking about for Benala Forn, whom he was sure he'd seen upon first entering the hall.

Sure enough, the old Priestess was there, clambering to her feet two tables over even as her eyes met his, wrinkled face tight and pale.

She sensed it too.

And the woman wasn't the only one. Throughout the rows of late lunchers, several among the faithful had stiffened suddenly, jolting up from their meals or away from conversations. Elber recognized them as a scattering of the Priests and Priestesses he and Forn had selected to help them craft the wards, after Jofrey had put them in charge of the Citadel's first lines of defense.

"Damn..." Elber cursed under his breath.

211

Then he dropped his plate roughly onto the table, ignoring it as much of the food bounced and spilled onto the roughened wood, and took a rapid path through the diners back towards the hall's wide entrance.

"Did you feel it?" Forn asked him, her wise, kindly voice sounding uncommonly edged with what might have been fear.

Elber nodded. "I did. Let's hope Jofrey is in Talo's quarters. He'll want to know something is coming up the path..."

Jofrey, lamentably, was not in the High Priest's quarters, nor was he in his own smaller chambers when they went looking there. Eventually a young Priestess was able to tell them that she had seen him in the library, tucked away in a secluded corner that the other men, women, and children had been giving a wide berth all morning.

They'd thanked her, then hurried off.

Five minutes later they reached the huge, ornately crafted door of the library, its layered wood paneling overlapping and tucking into itself to form a maze of fascinating, abstract geometries. Elber and Forn didn't look up as they entered the expansive room that formed what was arguably the single greatest marvel in the entirety of the Citadel. Both council members had spent more decades serving Laor within the walls of Cyurgi' Di than either cared to count, and so the awe that struck all newly indoctrinated when entering the vaulted chambers had long since worn away. There had been a time, perhaps, when Elber and Forn had felt the warm, blossoming magnificence of the place, radiating about them from the thousand upon thousands of cloth and leather-bound texts that sat patiently on ring after ring of ancient bookcases. Perhaps then they might even have been tempted to raise their eyes skyward to the incredible painted murals of the faith's history that adorned the domed ceiling, or inward to the great raised grate through which the fiery glow of the temple's furnaces could be seen a dozen floors below.

As it was, though, Elber and Forn saw none of this, each scanning one side of the library only for a sign of Jofrey al'Sen. It took them a minute, but eventually Forn caught sight of him—indeed seated behind a narrow student's desk in a far corner of the room—and she tugged on Elber's sleeve, indicating the interim High Priest with a silent jerk of her head.

Quickly, they hurried over.

They were ten feet away when Jofrey seemed to take notice. He began to look up, a scowl darkening his aged face.

"If it's not important," he started crossly, "I'd very much prefer not to be bothered right n—"

He cut himself short, seeing who it was that was interrupting what looked to be a very thorough study of any book within the library that might make mention of the mountain clans. As he and Forn came to a stop to hover over the narrow desk and its occupant, Elber saw copies of such tomes as *Cultural Clashes of the Common Age* and *A Study of Mythos: the North*. The text Jofrey was now perusing, in fact, looked to be the fragile, two-hundred-year-old journal of Priest Gálos Br'hest, a former chieftain of a small Saragrias tribe whose remnants had been rapidly swallowed by the larger clans after Br'hest's voluntary conversion to the Laorin way.

Elber allowed himself a moment to pity Jofrey. After no news of Syrah's condition in over a week, most of the council assumed her dead. Jofrey, however, had refused to give up on the woman, and spent every moment of what little spare time was afforded to him collecting any scrap of information he could on the tribes, hoping to find an avenue of negotiation.

As far as he knew, Elber did not believe the man had had any success.

And we have bigger things to worry about, now.

"The first ward has been breached," Forn said quietly, not waiting for Jofrey to question why it was they had sought him out. "Elber and I were both alerted."

Elber nodded in confirmation. "Several of the men and women we recruited to assist us in the spellwork seemed to have experienced the same warning," he said in a low tone. "I'm sure Jerrom will say the same, if we can find him."

For a few seconds Jofrey's strained face became suddenly tighter, the implications of this information bearing down on him all at once. Quickly, though, he composed himself, closing Gálos Br'hest's journal with a *snap* and pushing himself to his feet. Waving a hand to catch the attention of a passing library attendant, he gestured the acolyte over.

"Have these brought to the High Priest's quarters," Jofrey told the girl, indicating the journal and a half-dozen other books piled to one side of the desk. "I will complete my perusal of them there. The rest can be returned to their shelves, if you please."

The acolyte bobbed her head once, moving to obey even as Jofrey indicated for Elber and Forn to follow him. He started for the library door immediately, cutting through the shelves and readers with long, quick strides. As they made it into the hall, Jofrey didn't stop walking.

He did, however, give the pair behind him a glance over his shoulder. "Explain."

"It happened about twenty minutes ago," Forn began at once. "The first ward extends as close to the base of the stairs as we could manage.

The edge that crosses the path is about an hour up from the bottom of the mountains."

"And someone triggered it?" Jofrey asked, eyes set resolutely forward as they continued through the Citadel halls. "Do we know who? Or how many?"

Men and women of all ranks and studies moved out of their way as the three of them hurried by, pulling aside children and the unwary to leave the way unhindered for the interim High Priest and the council members.

"No," Elber answered with a shake of his head. "The ward is far overextended as is. We can't even tell you if it was broken along the stairway, at least for the time being. It's the first line of the defense, a warning toll. *If* something is indeed coming up the mountain path it's going to be a while before we know what."

"How long?"

"Assuming it takes them the usual half-day or so to climb, several hours," Forn replied. "Likely more, as the steps are well-choked by snow. The second ward extends halfway down the stairs. The third is halfway again to that."

"And they'll be able to tell us from where they're coming?" Jofrey asked, leading them around a sharp turn down the incline of a long ramp, their shadows flickering against the wall to their left, cast by the scattered blue and white candles set in small alcoves in the stone to their right.

"Yes, the second will tell us from where," Elber said in agreement. "The third what, and how many. There are a fourth and fifth, layered over one another along the very top of the stairs. They'll blind anyone who steps onto the outer courtyard beyond the gate, and set fire to the stone. We crafted the spells carefully. The magics will burn through leather and fur and scald the skin. Anyone would be fool to brave the flames."

Jofrey waved the details aside.

"The outer wards," he said with the air of a man fixed on a single problem. "I think it's safe to assume that the snows will slow anyone witless enough to make the ascent. That means we can't expect to glean any more information until after sunset, and that's *if* they push through the night."

"That would be imprudent," Elber said thoughtfully. "Traveling by torchlight would be beyond dangerous this time of year. Footing is already precarious without reflections on the ice, not to mention the risk of the flames going out if there's a strong enough wind."

"Agreed," Jofrey said with a nod as the hall opened up into a larger corridor they all recognized. "All the same, we shouldn't assume anything. If the tribes are making a play they would want to move fast. They aren't aware we know they're coming, and the risk of a few dozen lost to the mountain may seem worth the advantage of surprise. If the Kayle is sending an offensive force he will likely march them straight, without pause."

"Why would he attack, though?" Forn asked. "He has us trapped. All he has to do is stay put along the base of the path."

Jofrey frowned. "I don't know. Baoill seems more than patient enough to wait out our stores, but there might be other factors at play. The most obvious reason I can think of is that he doesn't want to give the other valley towns time to form an alliance. I imagine he ideally wants to push south as soon as possible. Laor knows if that's even the entirety of his army down there. It might just be a contingent, tasked specifically with ensuring we stayed holed up."

"All the more reason *not* to press," Forn kept on. "They risk losing their advantage, trapped on the path."

"Unless they don't stick to the stairs…" Elber said darkly. "They're mountain men. The slopes are their homes. Just because *we* don't have a prayer of managing the mountain faces doesn't mean *they* can't."

A collective shiver passed through all three of them at that thought, each imagining the disaster of the Citadel surrounded, encircled by ten thousand campfires scattered among the cliffs.

"It's a moot point," Forn said eventually. "There's nothing we can do either way. In a few hours we'll know what's coming, and from where. All we can do is wait."

"No," Jofrey disagreed. "That's not *all* we can do."

He stopped them, at last, in front of a large, well-known archway. Every acolyte, for as long it took for them to be granted their staffs, spent a portion of every waking day within the honeycomb of halls and rooms beyond.

The practice chambers of Cyurgi' Di, after all, were where every future Priest and Priestess came to understand the dangers of the world, and learned to defend themselves accordingly with every advantage at their disposal.

Without another word Jofrey turned and stepped under the archway, hastening down the main hallway as Elber and Forn followed dutifully behind. To their left and right, doors and other vaulted openings entered onto rooms of various shapes and sizes, some full of practicing acolytes under the watchful eye of older instructors, some with a scattering of Priests and Priestesses busy keeping their skills sharp, and some dark and empty. Quickly the maze of spaces filled with the sounds of mock battle, shouted directions mixing with the *booms* and *cracks* of magic and the clang of steel on steel. Heat expelled itself from rooms here and there, following flashes of white that flared like thunderless lightning. There was the *crunch* of breaking wood, and Elber caught a glimpse of a group of students practicing shaping their gifts into forceful discharges, using the created spells to throw the abused forms of straw and timber dummies across the floor, sometimes smashing them against the far wall.

"Too much force, Ela," he heard an instructor say kindly as they passed. "You'll kill someone with a blast like that."

After a minute or so of winding their way in and about the chambers, peeking through every door they came across, Jofrey finally stopped. Together the three stood outside the entrance to a massive arched space, the ceiling and walls illuminated by a trio of simple hanging braziers that were suspended in a staggered pattern from the timber beaming. Below these, evenly spaced over the wide stone floor, a dozen or so pairs of men and women were sparring, apparently alternating between using their staffs and choosing from a multitude of dulled iron replicas that had been forged in the image of the weapons all Laorin might eventually face out in the violent world of man. They wielded them in practiced engagements, reviewing well-learned techniques and strategies of defense against the various instruments of war, combining unarmed combat, the steel staffs, and imitated motions of spellcasting to feign the disarming and incapacitation of their opponents. Along the walls, shouting encouragements and feedback, several instructors in sleeveless cloth tunics paced back and forth, their gazes shifting from pair to pair.

It was towards one of these men that Jofrey moved, signaling Elber and Forn to stay put. As they waited patiently, watching some of the sparrers look up in surprise at the appearance of the interim High Priest, Elber thought he saw one of the other instructors staring in their direction.

He turned to meet the man's gaze, but Reyn Hartlet looked away quickly, returning to his work.

Half a minute later Jofrey returned, Cullen Brern in tow. The Citadel's master-at-arms looked as though the last ten-day had not been easy on him. There were bags under his eyes, and his usually rigid form seemed oddly diminished, as though exhaustion were pulling him down into a slouch.

"What's going on?" he asked Elber and Forn. "Jofrey says the first ward was triggered?"

As one the two nodded, and Elber let Forn relay once again what they had already told Jofrey.

"Lifegiver's saggy *fucking* balls," Brern swore, reaching up to wipe a sweating brow with the back of one hand as he stared at the floor, taking in this new information. "This could be bad. If the Kayle is pushing for the Citadel…"

"We don't know what he's doing," Jofrey said firmly. "We shouldn't assume a full assault without more information. It could be a scouting party, or even envoys."

"Is there a chance it might be Talo and Carro?" the master-at-arms asked. "Maybe they snuck past Baoill's camp, somehow?"

That struck Elber. It was a thought he hadn't given the slightest consideration.

Jofrey, though, shook his head.

"We've discussed this. If Talo saw the predicament the Citadel is in, I can't imagine he would be so foolish as to try and sneak past the Kayle's forces just to join us in this mess. He alone has the clout right now to get us the assistance we need from the towns. It's my genuine hope that Talo is already on his way back to Ystréd as we speak, and hopefully working on a plan that *doesn't* end in our starvation come the summer months."

There was a momentary silence, which no one dared fill with the doubts that flashed across each of their minds.

"Then the Kayle's men it is," Brern said with a sigh. "What are our options?"

"I suggested we wait," Forn offered tentatively. "The second ward will tell us if something is approaching from the path, as I said. Jofrey seems to have a different idea, though…"

Jofrey nodded. "I'm not sure we can afford to be patient, given our predicament. The highest wards offer us some passive defense, but it's limited, and the magics will drain quickly if Baoill keeps pushing forward." He looked at Brern. "My thought is that we could use something else to a much greater advantage: the path itself."

To Elber's mild amusement, the master-at-arms didn't look the least bit surprised by this suggestion.

"Aye, I've had the same notion, of late," the man said, looking pensive. "The rules of engagement against a foe that is larger and more powerful than you are simple. First: run. Avoid the fight. Failing this: limit the opponent's movement and ability to use their greater strength to their advantage. Similar tactics apply to the concept of great numbers, rather than greater strength."

"Trap them along the path," Elber said, catching on. "Make it impossible for them to use the sheer mass of the army against us."

"Precisely," Brern said as Jofrey nodded to him, indicating he should continue the explanation. "It wouldn't take much to push them back, truth be told. Even less to stall them. There are half-a-hundred positions along the steps where twenty unassuming soldiers could arguable hold off ten times their number just by using the high ground to their advantage. Priests and Priestesses wielding magic… A handful would do." He frowned suddenly. "It wouldn't last forever, mind. As far as the tribes go,

I doubt they'd be as hard-pressed as we are to handle the mountains if they have to."

"We had the same thought," Jofrey said quickly. "We don't like it, but forcing the Kayle's men to manage and attack from rougher terrain is a victory in and of itself when compared to simply allowing them to flood the courtyard from the stairs, isn't it?"

"It is," Brern agreed, bushy eyebrows rising in realization. "*Quite* a win, in fact. Forcing them into the cliffs would have a hefty impact on morale, I imagine. Even if they're accustomed to it, I can't believe the mountain men would prefer to lay their siege among the storm and rocks compared to the relative shelter of the Arocklen and the ease of the mountain path."

"So we do what?" Forn asked, seemingly a little lost. "Attack them before they attack us?"

"Something like that..." Jofrey paused, thinking. "I don't think there's any need to prepare a full assault just yet. Still, assuming your ward was indeed triggered along the path, it would be better to inform ourselves as soon as possible, rather than wait for the other spells to go off. Ideally we could send a group small enough to move undetected, but large enough to provide the firepower necessary to slow down any assault."

"A dozen would do it," Brern said gruffly, crossing his arms and jerking his head over his shoulder into the room Jofrey had pulled them out of. "And I could have them ready in the matter of a quarter-hour."

"Good," Jofrey said. "Then take what you need. If someone is coming up the path, find them. If it's an envoy, or a parley group, relay it to us with a messenger spell and return. Leave them be. If the Kayle is attacking, inform us the same way, and we will send reinforcements with all haste."

Brern nodded his head briefly.

"I'll make a call for volunteers right away," he said, letting his arms fall and making to turn back into the practice chamber. "I can't imagine it will take long to—"

"I volunteer," a young man's voice interrupted him, and Reyn Hartlet stepped out from around the corner of the wall behind which he had snuck, undetected, to eavesdrop.

"Dammit, Reyn!" Brern yelped, startling involuntarily. The younger Priest had stepped directly into his path. "That's the *second* time you've barged in on—!"

"Let him be, Brern."

Jofrey's voice was firm, his eyes on his former student. The master-at-arms fell silent at once.

"Reyn," he said—too gently, in Elber's opinion—, "I won't have you turning this into some witch hunt. This is a discreet mission, we're speaking of. Combat is a *last resort*. Do you understand?"

Reyn's posture stiffened, but he nodded.

"I understand," he said, his voice hard. "I still volunteer."

"Then it's up to your superior," Jofrey replied, looking to Brern again. "Assuming he's willing to take the command, of course."

"Like it crossed my mind not to," the master-at-arms snorted, his eyes still on Reyn. "But aye, I'll have him. He's a hardheaded fool, sometimes, but there's no better fighter. I might just need him, if things go bad."

He stepped forward suddenly, bringing himself nose to nose with the younger man. Both stood tall, within an inch of each other, but Brern's heavy brown beard and broader shoulders won out against Reyn's clean-shaven good looks and muscled build.

"You hear that, Hartlet?" he breathed into the Priest's face. "I'm giving you a chance to show us all you can control yourself. Think you can manage it, for once?"

Reyn's face stayed tense, but he nodded at once.

"Yes," he said quickly. "I swear it."

"Good," Brern said. "Then make yourself useful—" he jerked his head to indicate the other pairs still sparring behind the Priest "—and start gathering the rest. I want another ten. The best you can find."

Reyn nodded again, looking a little relieved to have been accepted. He was about to turn back, moving to follow Brern's instructions, when he paused.

Looking back, he gave the four of them a brief, rigid bow, eyes on one in particular.

"Thank you, Jofrey," he said to his former Priest-Mentor.

Then he was off, booming voice already calling for a halt to the mock combat and requesting that all eyes fall on him.

"Sure that was a good idea?" Elber asked Jofrey and Brern as they watched the thirty Priests and Priestesses start to migrate towards Reyn Hartlet, now standing along one wall. "He's been hot-headed ever since Syrah was killed."

Jofrey stiffened at the comment, but made no reply. The master-at-arms, though, scratched at his beard.

"He's a good lad," he said. "He's just got nowhere to put the anger. Letting him out of these damn halls for a night will do him a world of good."

No one said anything to that, but as Brern stepped back into the chamber, moving to add his voice to Reyn's, Elber thought he heard the aging Priest add a grumbled "Hopefully…" under his breath.

XXVI

"When you pause to think about it, there is really no greater madness in the world than the Citadel path. Six thousand crafted steps, twisting their way up the sheer sides of the Saragrias Ranges? What sort of devil possessed the maniac who looked at that mountain and thought 'Hmm... Yes. This looks like an excellent spot for a stairway'?"

—Talo Brahnt, after a few too many drinks

Damn these stairs!

Raz—though he would never say so aloud—prided himself on his physique. On the one hand his body was the tool by which he plied his trade, the one instrument he would never be able to do without. On the other, his lithe frame, strength, and speed made up much of the thread from which his infamy had been spun, woven into the subliminal fright behind every mention of the Monster of Karth, the Scourge of the South. It was a legend that had won him a solitude he had enjoyed for so many years, a peace and quietness he had started to miss again after the deaths of Lueski and Arrun.

At the moment, though, Raz himself felt his own understanding of that legend tatter and fray, imagining what he looked like now.

He was *hanging* onto Ahna. Not resting on. Not helping himself with. *Hanging.* With both hands he clung to her haft, feeling his arms burn every time he wrenched her pointed tip out of the packed snow to plunge it back in one or two steps ahead of him. His legs were long past such pain, the thick, bone-deep ache of fatigue having dissipated into resolute, sluggish numbness around the third hour of their ascent. His breath came in heaving billows, his lungs screaming from a combination of the thinning atmosphere and icy temperature of the air that was only getting colder as they climbed. *This*, however, was the one thing that didn't bother Raz. He welcomed the chill that filled his chest with every gasped inhalation, cooling him from the inside out. Despite the frigid winter evening, for once Raz was boiling beneath his furs, burning up as his body worked to carry him along the stairs step by step by step.

Never again, he thought to himself, looking up to see where Carro had gotten off to. *Never, EVER, again.*

The old Priest was, as always, well ahead of him. Almost from the moment they had started their climb the man had fallen into a sad, sullen silence, and Raz had given him his space. It was the first time since the previous night Carro had had any opportunity to be alone with his wandering mind, and Raz rather thought the man could use some time to himself.

He's alone, Raz thought sadly as he lifted Ahna yet again from the snow and shoved her back down again on the next step. *That's a feeling we know well, isn't it, sis?*

The thought of Talo's death had dredged up other memories with it, and Raz had taken his own time to let the darkness of the last few weeks sink in just a little bit, just enough to allow himself to feel what he knew needed to be felt. He remembered the horror of Arrun's head as Quin Tern kicked it over the frosted pit floor of the Arena. He remembered watching Lueski's mind crumble in silence as she looked down on what was left of her brother, watching her reach up and slice her own throat on the blade already held to her neck.

As he remembered holding her, cradling her small hands against his chest while she died miserably in his arms, the little girl's last words echoed up through his memories, as though the gusting mountain wind had carried it from the emptiness that extended infinitely outward, grey and subdued, to Raz's left.

"I'll miss you," she had said, just before grabbing for the blade.

I miss you too, Raz thought sadly, feeling the scrabbling claws of sorrow dig in and pull his heart towards the ground.

Raz turned the feeling into anger, though, and used it to fuel the endless upward climb long after his body had had enough. He drew from the rage, pulling from it like water miraculously drawn from a well that had long since gone dry.

And so went their ascent, for the larger part of four hours, until the dim light of the Sun began to fade. Carro led the way, guiding Gale along by reins clutched in the hand slung across his chest, the steel staff in the other feeling about the snow and stone for good footing. Raz followed behind, simultaneously cursing the ache and fatigue of a body unaccustomed to this particular sort of strain and basking in the wallowing, pensive freedom the climb allowed him. The going was slow, but neither man complained, content in their own thoughts and in their own company. They might have found each other to be surprisingly pleasant company—especially since the tragedy of the previous night—but neither was upset to have some time to themselves.

Despite this, Raz was more than a little relieved when he looked up to see Carro waving to him with his staff from above a bend in the path, thirty feet off and a dozen feet above his head. The Priest seemed to be shouting something, but as the winds whipped back and forth through Raz's steel and furs even he couldn't make out the words.

"Hold on!" he shouted back, motioning that he was on his way. "I'm coming!"

A minute or two later Raz had managed a rapid double turn in the path, catching up to the Priest, who stood overlooking the great plummet that dropped away before them. The world far below was a dim wash of green and white, the Arocklen spreading out across the earth beneath a layer of mists and low-hanging clouds, darkening quickly in the fading hour.

"Are we stopping?" Raz wheezed, almost desperately, as he finally came to a halt beside Carro.

"It's about that time." Carro nodded and indicated the path in front of them, which continued flat for a ways before curving around an edge in the rock. "There's an alcove carved into the mountain, about a hundred feet past that bend. It's a resting spot for pilgrims and traveling Priests."

Raz didn't respond, focusing on catching his breath. He had seen such breaks in the path, flattened and cleared portions of stone cut around the steps or into the mountain. He figured they would camp for the night in such a place, given that the snows were slowing them down so much, and he hoped silently the walls of the alcove were high enough to keep out the mountain winds.

At Raz's silence, Carro looked over at him curiously. The Priest took him in with concern, eyeing his heaving chest and his legs, which Raz realized—to his great chagrin—were shaking under his own weight.

Abruptly, Carro flushed as though in embarrassment, eyes widening.

"What?" Raz asked, looking down at himself, confused.

"Uh…" Carro began, sounding like he didn't know how to start, an uncomfortable, awkward smile coming across his lips. "Well, I… I seem to have forgotten…"

"Forgotten?" Raz demanded, suddenly concerned. Had they left something important behind? "Forgotten what?"

Carro hesitated. Then, in response, he set his staff against the wall to their right, turned, and pressed his now-free hand to Raz's chest.

Almost immediately Raz felt strength flush back into his limbs, warmth rushing through him and chasing off the aches and pains of the afternoon's climb like hounds running off an unwanted intruder. Within seconds he felt almost completely rejuvenated, his breath coming easier, his posture straightening as the fatigue vanished.

In an odd combination of gratitude and fury, he stared at Carro.

"MAGIC?" he demanded, his voice a shriek of incredulity. "You've been using *MAGIC* to help you climb?"

"Of course," Carro grumbled, looking sheepish as he pulled his hand away. "How do you think we manage the stairs every other day during the harvest season? I was wondering why you were so far behind…"

"I was behind because *someone* forgot that my gods *didn't* leave me with the miraculous gift of *sorcery*," Raz spluttered, still utterly bewildered that he had not, in fact, had to have suffered through the last four hours in utter misery.

"Sorry," Carro mumbled, not facing Raz as he picked up his staff again. "I was... elsewhere."

As he watched the Priest turn to stare off once more at the darkening grey line of the horizon, Raz felt his anger leave him. Carro was lost in his own thoughts again, a small, heartbroken frown barely visible through the snow that caked his blonde beard.

Raz knew whom it was the man was thinking of.

"Come on," Raz said gruffly, stepping past the Priest and plucking the reins from his bad hand as he did. "No use standing out here in the snow and wind."

It was a minute or two later—Raz leading the way this time—that the alcove Carro had described finally came into view. As they rounded the corner in the mountainside, Raz saw that the path extended even and straight before them for another twenty-five yards or so, then sloped upwards once again as the stairs resumed their winding climb through the cliffs. About a dozen steps above them, a ragged, worn slice of solid rock had been cut right out of the wall of the path, leaving an opening about five feet wide through which a man and—thankfully—a horse could easily fit. Pulling Gale along carefully behind him, Raz made his way forward along the last flat lane of the path, then up the stairs. He suffered a brief moment of subconscious confusion as his mind fought to cope with a sudden, unnatural lack of fatigue at the climb, his legs abruptly carrying him strongly and surely up the steps, one after another. Getting over this, though, Raz made his way upward, then turned to lead Gale through the rift in the wall.

At once the wind dulled. Raz found himself in a wide, circular niche carved out of the rock by what could only have been magic. The alcove was open to the elements, its walls extending no more than five or six feet above his head, but it shielded them well enough from the buffets of whatever storm might be brewing around them, and once they cleared the snow from the ground it would be plenty dry. Even as he thought this, in fact, Raz felt a pleasant warmth spread about his feet, and he turned to see that Carro had followed him and Gale promptly through the wall. The Priest was already at work, moving his staff gently through the air before him in a complicated series of motions, winding each into the other. As he did, Raz felt the heat around his legs intensify, and he recognized the spell as one similar to the casted warmth Carro and Talo would sometimes take turns weaving over their little party as they'd pushed north, across the Dehn, and into the relative shelter of the Woods.

The snow melted quickly, crunching and sinking into itself as it turned first to water then trickling fog. For several minutes Raz did nothing more than watch, leading Gale around the wall of the alcove to stand beside Carro as the Priest worked, his staff moving in constant fluidity. When the last of the piled snow was gone, revealing dry, uneven slate beneath, Carro heaved a heavy sigh and stepped deeper into the space.

"I'll get the wards up, if you would be so kind as to start making camp."

Raz nodded, and before long the pair had settled into an old routine that—nevertheless—felt uncomfortably lopsided without the presence of the third man now missing from their company.

A half hour later they were sitting across from each other, silently watching the pitch and dance of the hearty white fire Carro had summoned into existence in the center of the alcove. The heat the magic gave off was unneeded—the protective barriers the Priest had managed to eventually cast offered plenty—but nonetheless Raz reveled in its waves, extending his wings out and around the flames to bath in the arcane warmth. One hand was resting against the coolness of the stone beneath him, the other holding his gladius suspended over the fire, turning it every now and then so that the thin strips of meat impaled along the length of its steel cooked evenly. It was fortunate they were so close to the Citadel, Raz told himself. He wasn't sure their remaining elk and venison would have lasted more than another two, maybe three meals.

"How do you do it, Raz?"

Raz blinked at the sudden question, lifting his eyes to look at Carro across the flames. The man wasn't looking at him, his gaze on the twisting light of the fire. He had a lost, empty look about him, like a man who'd woken up to a world he knew nothing about.

"Do what?" Raz asked, though he thought he could guess where the conversation was about to take them.

"Carry this," Carro told him quietly. "Bear this... this weight." His hood was pulled down, and the snow had melted out of his beard and hair. He looked as old as Raz had ever seen him look, staring off, blind to the light and stone and sky around him.

For several heartbeats Raz didn't respond. He knew what the Priest was looking for, of course, but he suspected the man wouldn't like the answer.

"I don't," he said finally, retracting the gladius from over the flames as the meat started to sizzle and pop. "Or rather, I didn't."

Carro looked up at that, eyeing him curiously.

"Caring for another," Raz kept on, "comes with risks, Carro. Sharing your soul means giving a part of yourself to another, leaving it exposed, vulnerable. I don't doubt you are aware of this, in your own way, but age does not always equal experience in such matters. When grief—true grief, the kind that only the theft of a life can elicit—takes us… different people cope in different ways."

"What do you mean?" Carro asked, almost desperately.

Raz sighed, waving the gladius about him slowly to cool the food. "I mean that death is a meteor, and the impact it has on us is relevant to our preparation for it. As a beloved elder succumbs to old age, we see the meteor far off in the night sky, and have all the time in the world to brace ourselves for it. When illness strikes suddenly, we catch a glimpse of death's coming, and have at least a moment to ready for the fall."

He set the sword down carefully, the still-warm tip propped up on his knee so that the meat wouldn't become soiled against the ground.

"But when life is snatched away—when death comes so suddenly it leaves again in a blink—there is no preparation for the pain. There is no bracing for the impact."

Across the fire, Carro nodded slowly, his face darkened by shadows that played against the lines of his brow and cheeks.

"What do you do, then?" he mumbled. "When the meteor strikes, what do you do? How do you bear it?"

Again, Raz paused.

And again, he decided to answer honestly.

"I don't," he repeated quietly. "I didn't. When I lost my family, Carro, I spent the next week in madness. I didn't eat, I didn't sleep… I just hunted. I existed as some vicious phantom of myself, some bloodthirsty, ephemeral projection of everything that eventually led the Mahsadën to extend me their hand, led the spectators of the Arena to cheer me as their hero, their bloody champion. I didn't bear the weight, Carro. I let it crush me, let it break me. I let the weight mold me, until eventually what I was mirrored the moniker of 'Monster' all too well." He held the Priest's gaze firmly. "I'm sorry, but I'm not the one to ask such a question to. I was young, foolish, and I had the opportunity for an outlet, for vengeance."

"I wish I had that outlet," Carro said in a broken voice. "I wish I had a way to—"

"No," Raz said harshly, sweeping a hand before him in anger. "That is *not* what you want, Priest. I may not be able to tell you *how* to bear the pain you now carry, and I'm truly sorry for that, but I *am* the one to tell you that—above all else—you *must* bear it. No matter what. Let it weigh you down, let it shape you, and you will be looking down a very dark path, Carro. A path that leads nowhere good."

"A path you know well?" Carro asked.

Raz gave a hard, unwilling smile. "All too well, yes. And I can tell you with resounding conviction that it is not a road you will do well on. That trail is more shadow than light, more blood than life. Your Lifegiver does not exist down that path. His warmth does not penetrate the cold of that way."

He reached down, tugging a steaming slice of venison from the blade. Juice dripped from the meat over the ground as Raz reached over and around the fire, leaning forward to offer Carro the food.

"You," he said, kindly now, watching the Priest eye the meat with disinterest, "are best suited for the harder path, my friend. I caved, and I fell. Talo said that the fires I carry with me don't consume me, but they *dia*. Once, they *dia*. They burned so hot I forgot what it was to live, what it was to care. I spilled as much blood in a week as any five of the men I killed had in their lives combined. I took the easy road. I don't know if that's because I was weak, or simply young and lost, but it doesn't change the fact that I took the easy road."

He shook the meat pointedly. "You don't get that choice, Carro. Your god wouldn't let you, Talo wouldn't let you, and *I'm* certainly not going to let you. Instead, you're going to eat. You're going to sleep. You're going to hurt and wallow and bear that pain until it becomes a part of you, a scar that adds to the beauty of the 'gift' of life you say Laor has given you. In the end, you'll be stronger for it."

There were tears in Carro's eyes now, as he looked at the meat, understanding what it was meant to imply. If he took it, he admitted a willingness to continue, a desire to go on. If he took it, he was accepting the weight that tore at him now, acknowledging that he would carry it until such time as it was a part of him.

Slowly, with staggered hesitation, the man reached out his good hand and pried the dripping venison free of Raz's claws.

"Good man," Raz told him. "Laor would be proud."

At that Carro gave a helpless, croaking chuckle, then brought the meat to his mouth and started to tear into it.

They spent the rest of the evening in conversation, talking as they had over the course of the earlier morning, speaking of nothing and of everything, resolutely staying away only from the topic of Talo and what was to be done about the mountain men now that he was gone. They spoke of Raz's family, of the mother that had given Carro to the faith when he was young, and even of Lueski and Arrun Koyt. They spoke more of the Citadel and its inhabitants, and Raz once again felt the budding excitement well in him as Carro told him more about how the furnaces worked, about the battlements that offered breathtaking views of the world on the rare clear days, and about the education of the acolytes as they grew from initiates into consecrated Priests and Priestesses. They spoke of old friends, Raz telling Carro more about how he had met Eva, now far behind them in Ystréd, and about the master smith, Allihmad Jerr, who to this day worked out of the shithole that was Karth. Carro talked to him of the former High Priest, Eret Ta'hir, of Jerrom Eyr, the last of that generation, and of Jofrey al'Sen, whom Talo had left in charge of the Citadel in his absence.

When Carro started to speak more of Syrah, though, Raz found himself suddenly hard-pressed to pay attention to the man, distracted once more by the inexplicable image of a white-haired girl dancing across his mind. He didn't notice Carro smile as the Priest watched him, examining the distance of his gaze and the calmness of his face as he listened to stories of the woman's youth, and more of her successes with the mountain tribes after she'd been granted her staff.

Eventually, an hour or two after night had fallen in truth, Carro began to yawn. The ward would tell them if anyone came along the path behind them, but all the same they agreed to split the watch, neither trusting in the fact that the Kayle's men weren't hunting them up the mountainside. Raz took first shift, bidding Carro goodnight as the Priest extinguished the flames in the center of the stone floor and made for his bedroll. His sheathed gladius in one hand, Raz moved towards the alcove's narrow entrance, settling himself against the right wall of the opening from which he could look back down along the path. Spreading his wings so that they wouldn't get pinned, he slid himself down the stone, coming to a seated rest at its base.

It had started to snow in earnest again. Looking up, Raz watched the thick tumble of flakes fall across the sky, further muting the already dim glow of the moon behind a ceiling of stormy clouds. He wondered, as he settled in for the night, if Talo waited among Her Stars now. Would his Lifegiver allow it? Would he, rather, already have been born anew to the world, as his faith decreed?

Raz smiled to himself, chuckling softly, and wished silent luck to the parents of whatever newborn had been gifted with the bright, fiery soul of Talo Brahnt, High Priest of Cyurgi' Di.

XXVII

"We are not a perfect people. We are perhaps considered as such by many, held in the highest regard by those who draw strength and inspiration from the Lifegiver and his Laorin, but we are not a perfect people. The faith is—like any congregation of different-minded individuals—rife with disagreement, dislike, and enmity. Laor knows that, despite all efforts to the contrary, such difficulties are an inevitable part of life. It is an unfortunate truth, but truth nonetheless: we are not a perfect people."

—Eret Ta'hir, High Priest of Cyurgi' Di

Reyn Hartlet watched in silent, seething anger as the pale glow of fire, muffled and discolored white by the falling snow, extinguished in a wink far below. As it did there was a rustle of shifting cloth beside him, and Cullen Brern got to his feet at his right, standing up from where he'd been crouched along the edge of the path, peering down the twisting, turning stairs.

Without a word, he motioned for the advance.

As one Reyn and ten other bodies straightened themselves up and fell in behind the master-at-arms, moving as quietly as they could. Ordinarily they would have cleared the way with fire and heat as they descended, but Brern had given the order that they would handle the stairs without such magic for the time being, in case a suspicious lack of snow unnerved possible envoys as they resumed their climb the following morning. That was the official reason, at least.

Reyn thought it more likely Brern wanted to save all the strength they could, in case the night culminated in a fight.

The wind was godsend, for once, the storm masking the sound of their feet and staffs crunching through ice and against stone as they took the steps in a careful line, one after the other. Reyn could barely hear his own footfalls, and very much doubted whatever waited for them below would make out their coming. Brern had mercifully allowed for the summoning of three small orbs of light, empty globes of white that floated through the group. It was barely enough to see by, the glow just enough to illuminate the path beneath their feet, but they made do. Any less would have made the descent precarious, and any more would probably have been visible from where the Kayle's men had settled in for the night, in the alcove far below.

It was a good problem to have. Focusing on where he had to place his feet forced Reyn to focus on something other than what he wanted to do to the men they were cautiously stealing down upon.

For a quarter-hour they descended, slowly winding their way along, back and forth across the mountainside. More than once one of them slipped and gasped involuntarily, and Brern would signal an immediate halt, peering down through the dark and snow, listening for shouts and watching for the flare of light that would have meant they'd been found out. Reyn found it odd that the fire had been extinguished in the first place, leaving the Kayle's men to the bitter cold of the altitude and night, but he brushed the thought away. As much as he hated to admit it, the tribes were more accustomed to nature's cruelty than he or any other Laorin could ever hope to be. Perhaps they'd simply chosen to suffer the assault of the freeze rather than risk their fire being seen from above after darkness fell.

Too late for that.

Eventually the group settled in, just a single turn above the alcove in which Reyn knew the mountain men had taken shelter for the night. Brern motioned for everyone to crouch down, and they did so, inching to the edge of the steps to peer down as the master-at-arms extinguished their lights with a wave.

It took a long time for Reyn to make out the scene below him through the dark and falling snow. When he finally managed it, though, he felt a rush of elation course unbidden through him.

Two! he thought, a harsh smile cutting across his face suddenly. *There's only two of them!*

The Kayle, it seemed, had sent a pair to make his demands, whatever that may be. Reyn felt the anger he had struggled with for the last weeks flare up as he took them in, eyeing the large form of one of the men—apparently asleep on a bedroll almost directly below them—then the hulking, indistinct outline of the other—keeping watch at the entrance of the alcove. Off to one side, the silhouette of a massive stallion stood in repose along the wall. Reyn found the presence of the animal queer, as no mountain tribe to his knowledge had domesticated horses, but he again ignored the momentary nag of incertitude. Most likely the beast was bounty from the sacking of Metcaf or Harond, and was simply being used as a pack animal.

Only two...

He turned hungrily to Brern, praying the man was seeing the same opportunity he was. He'd hoped to see an excited gleam in the older man's eye, the shine of anger and battle-lust Reyn himself felt trembling through his body now.

The look on master-at-arms' face, therefore, hit him like a fist to the teeth.

The man looked relieved! Of all the possible emotions he could have been experiencing, Cullen Brern looked *relievea*, gazing down at the pair of men below as though he were grateful they were there. He was watching them, eyes flicking from one to the other, then to the stallion, then about the rest of the scene, as though searching for the possibility of a larger force hidden among the rocks and snow.

When he found none, Brern sighed and smiled in grim content.

Then he raised a hand, and formed the signal to turn back.

Reyn felt his self-control chip, and as Brern and the others started to back away from the edge of the stairs he grabbed the arm of his superior's robe.

"What are you doing?" Reyn demanded in a furious whisper as the master-at-arms gazed down at him in surprise. "There are only two of them!"

"Exactly," Brern hissed back, tugging at his sleeve and looking annoyed. "Which means we fall back. If they're envoys, they'll show themselves tomorrow. If they're not... well... the wards will let us see them coming a mile off regardless."

"But this is an *opportunity*!" Reyn insisted. "There are twelve of us! We could capture them! Make them tell us what they know about the Kayle!"

The annoyance in Brern's face grew suddenly cold.

"Jofrey's orders were clear, Reyn," he growled, almost menacingly. "If they pose no immediate threat, we fall back."

"Jofrey's not the High Priest!" Reyn said furiously. "Not really! If Talo were here he'd tell us—!"

"He'd tell us to trust in the man he left in charge of the Citadel's safety," Brern spat. "Now *enough*. Get on your feet, Priest. This conversation is finished."

"But they could tell us everything!" Reyn's voice pitched dangerously loud as he felt his fury spike at the incomprehensible cowardice of the man before him. "They could tell us the size of their forces! Where they're camped, and what their plan is! They could tell us if they have prisoners! Where they are keeping Syr—!"

"Syrah Brahnt is *dead*!" Brern practically howled, his own voice rising to dangerously high levels as he lost patience. "Get that through your damned head, boy! She's gone, and your pitiful need for blood and vengeance is a stain on your robes. Elber was right. It *was* a mistake to bring you along. Now—for the last time, Hartlet—get on your feet, and get moving! We'll have words about your idiocy later!"

With that, Brern ripped his sleeve free of Reyn's insolent grip and stood up. For a second he looked down on the younger Priest, his gaze disgusted, and Reyn felt his own anger start to boil over in truth, rising to surpass the older man's fury.

Then Brern turned away from him, spitting bitterly into the snow as he climbed up through the quiet, shocked forms of the other ten Priests and Priestesses. Once he'd reached the head of the line again he repeated the signal for them to move out.

For several long seconds Reyn watched the men and women file upward, not one turning to meet his eyes as they left. He felt betrayed, deserted. Not a one among them spoke up. Not a one among them voiced concerns for Syrah, or shared the wisdom in his words.

Fools.

They had climbed high, taking the turn in the stairs and managing the steps until they'd reached the twist above, when Brern stopped the group. The master-at-arms peered over the edge of the path, glowering eyes meeting Reyn's. The old Priest motioned aggressively for him to fall into line, the furious promise in the gesture all too obvious.

Reyn, though, didn't move from his crouched place at the edge of the stairs. Instead, he turned his back on the men and women above him, looking down once more at the paired silhouettes of the mountain men below.

"Reyn…" he heard Brern's voice hiss warningly, weaving its way through the wind.

Reyn looked back up. For a moment he met the man's seething gaze. As though feeding off the emotion there, swelling under the pressure of his companions' cowardice and ignorance, Reyn felt the rage inside erupt, bubbling over and consuming him in a boil of hot, devouring hatred.

Without a word he showed Cullen Brern his back.

Then he leapt off the stairs, taking the sloped, snowy earth at a run, aiming for the open top of the alcove as he heard the older man curse and shout after him.

The crunching beat of booted feet over icy stone ripped Raz from distracted thoughts even before the attacker's howling scream broke the stillness of the winter night. Instinct and practiced skill kicked in long before his mind caught up to his actions, and the gladius flew from its sheath with a deadly *hiss* of steel as Raz leapt to his feet in an instant, already running into the alcove, towards the descending noise.

"Raz!"

Carro had woken suddenly, undoubtedly spurred from his slumber by the breaking of the ward. He yelled in warning while struggling to get up, weighed down in the layered leather and iron he wasn't accustomed to.

It didn't matter. Even in the limited light of the dim Moon Raz needed no assistance to make out the form of a man in the night, shapeless against the falling snow, leaping down on them from the outcroppings that surrounded their little shelter. There was the glint of metal in his hands, and Raz had just enough time to throw himself out of the way as the indistinct weapon slammed down into the stone exactly where Raz had been standing.

"BASTARDS!" the man screamed shrilly, sounding almost hysterical. "WHERE IS SHE? WHERE IS—!"

Whatever the next question was, though, it was cut short as the stranger turned to find that Raz wasn't where he'd expected him to be, off by the wall to the right. He froze, dumbstruck, staring at the spot Raz had vanished from.

"Too slow," Raz said in a hiss, launching himself upward as Gale whinnied in confused terror off to his left.

Raz had moved with all speed, using old skills and the uneven surface of the wall at his back to get above and halfway behind the man. Now he was in the air, plummeting down even as the attacker whirled in shock. Raz had the briefest glimpse of a handsome, fair-skinned young face beneath a hooded robe before the gladius point fell in a spearing stab, driven true towards the crook of the man's neck and left shoulder. Helplessly the stranger threw up a hand as though to defend himself from the falling steel, and Raz almost felt sorry for him.

Felt sorry, that is, until the gladius slammed into something thick and invisible, like molten glass, nearly all the momentum drained from the blow by the unseen force. It was so surprising that Raz's hand nearly slipped off the hilt, his body suddenly moving faster that the sword.

Adjusting reflexively, without really understanding what had happened, Raz used the suddenly transfixed gladius like a handle, swinging himself forward and down. The man had saved himself from being skewered, winning another few seconds of life.

Whatever he'd done, however, did nothing to stop Raz's steel-clad shin from whipping around with wicked force, using the suspended blade as a pivot point and catching the man a tremendous blow to the side.

There was the *crack* of breaking ribs, and even as he careened sideways the stranger gave a shocked gasp of pain. He tumbled and skidded across the slick stone and through the entrance of the alcove, the long weapon he'd been holding clattering to the ground. It ricocheted off the metal guard around Raz's left leg, spinning away as he leapt once more to finish the job.

Raz was practically in midair when his mind registered what the weapon had been. As he powered skyward, gladius poised for second attempt at a killing strike, the other details clicked into place. The white hood and the robes that accompanied them, making the man indistinct against the snow. The inexplicable barrier that had protected him like an invisible shield.

The steel staff now rolling across the ground...

"RAZ, NO!" Carro shouted out from behind him, trying to be heard over Gale's continued screams. "HE'S A PRIEST!"

Priest, Raz repeated to himself in silent understanding.

He dragged the gladius away at the last moment, the steel sparking against stone as it slammed into the steps upon which the Priest who had attacked them had come to rest. Raz landed atop him, absorbing the force of the jump on two legs and his free hand. Rather than leap away, though, he flipped the gladius over and brought the blade up under the man's chin.

"You move, you die," he snarled.

The Priest made little reply, his eyes shut tight and his face screwed up in pain as he clutched at the side where Raz's armored leg had connected. His breaths were coming in shallow, wheezing gasps, and Raz's anger turned abruptly to uncertain concern. The Priest probably didn't even notice the razored steel resting beneath the hook of a jawline.

Shit.

"Carro!" Raz yelled, standing up quickly and starting to haul the young man back through the slash in the wall. "He's ruptured a lung! I don't think he can breathe! Can you—?"

Before Raz could finish the question, though, there was a series of *thump thump thumps* as a number of white-robed figures fell into the nook of their campsite, jumping down from the rocks above, following the path of the young Priest now being towed along in Raz's one hand. About a half-dozen in all, Raz had time to register another five that had remained above, standing along the outcropping like sentries. Three of the ones who had jumped down surrounded Carro in a blink, the other three moving on Raz, steel staffs at the ready. Their aggressive press forced him to take a step back towards the sheer drop of the path's edge some seven or eight feet behind him.

"*Reh'las üi-meyn!*"

A man had stepped forward to lead the trio, staff raised aggressively. He had a heavy frame, about the same size as Carro, but there was a firmness to this Priest's body and posture that lacked in the healer, obvious even beneath the billowing edges of his white robes. He was stout and muscular, and held his staff in a way that told Raz that he very, *very* much knew how to use it.

"Stop!" Carro was trying to yell, waving his arms about in panic as the three robed figures drove him back against the wall. "Wait! You don't underst—*urk*!"

Carro's voice was cut short as he was shoved back into the stone, a steel staff pressed against his throat to silence him.

234

"*REH'LAS ÜL-MEYN!*" the large Priest at the head of the group bellowed, repeating the command as he advanced on Raz, flanked on either side by comrades in identical stances, one male and one female.

"I didn't understand it the first time, so I very much doubt it will come to me when repeated *at a louder volume!*" Raz growled back, rapidly losing his patience.

The Priest froze, looking suddenly hesitant.

"You speak the Common Tongue?" he demanded, sounding confused. "Both of you? What manner of tribesman doesn't speak the mountain speech?"

"I speak the Common Tongue because I'm not a *fucking* tribesman!" Raz roared, losing all self-restraint. "Carro and I were on the way to help you shits when this asswipe—" he swung his sword down to indicate the wheezing Priest he still held in his left hand "—decided to attack us in our sleep and—!"

Raz instantly realized the mistake he'd made. The sudden movement of the gladius towards the injured man at his side was the spark, igniting the tension of the scene. Even as the eyes of the large Priest in the middle grew wide in realization at Raz's words, the Priestess to his right reacted in panic. She yelled in alarm and, in a jerked, reflexive motion, punched out at Raz with a gloved palm.

It was a spell that Raz had never actually seen, but understood instinctively. As the air before him rippled, rent apart by some terrible, invisible force, Raz had just enough time to hurl his gladius and the injured Priest to either side of him. The concussion hit him just as he fell on all fours, digging claws and steel into stone, seeking desperately for a lip or crack. It overwhelmed him with a crushing, suffocating weight, and his legs flexed and strained, struggling to keep his body earthbound and prevent him from being hurled over the ledge into the void of the Moonlit mountain cliffs. Hind claws scraped against ice and metal, screeched against stone as he was forced back, foot-by-foot. His sunset wings flared out to their extent, tensing on either side of him as though instinctively trying to slow his perilous horizontal slide towards the edge. His hood was thrown back off his head and face as though by some hurtling wind, and his neck crest rose as Raz roared under the strain of the effort, feeling his back foot slip off stone and into nothingness.

"LYRA, NO!"

Just as he thought the claws of his other foot would fail him, Raz heard the large Priest's howled words, and the unrelenting magic vanished in a wink. For several long seconds Raz stayed as still as he could, gauging his precarious situation. One leg hung off the edge of the cliff, scrabbling for a foothold where there was none. The other barely held onto the rocky lip, and Raz could feel the time-dulled edge of the steps on the ball of his foot, not three inches back.

After he was sure he wasn't going to tip backwards and off into darkness, Raz slowly, inch by inch, eased his cramped body up, hauling himself onto the stone stairs.

"That's twice tonight, Priest," he growled as he found his feet before the big man standing ashen-faced a body-length in front of him. "*Twice*, that your people have tried to kill me. I don't find the irony *remotely* amusing."

The Priest, though, said nothing. He was staring, open mouthed, tilting his head back to watch Raz stand and rise to tower nearly a foot above his head. Behind him every other eye was turned in Raz's direction as well, glinting in the Moon's light as they took in the Monster of Karth, wings partially spread, crest still erect.

"Laor save us..." someone muttered from amid the group, half in awe, half in horror.

It was precisely at this convenient time, it seemed, that Carro, too, lost patience. There was a brief flash and a dampened *boom* of magic, and the three men and women that had pinned him to the wall cursed as they were thrown back off their feet.

"Cullen!" Carro bellowed, shoving his way through the dumbstruck group, all of whom were still staring at Raz. "Dammit, man! What in Laor's name possessed you to attack without reason? Has Jofrey gone mad?"

"Carro?" the large Priest standing in front of Raz—Cullen, it seemed—demanded in disbelief as he whirled and recognized Carro al'Dor. "Lifegiver's mercy. Why are you dressed like a damn mountain man? Where's Talo? Why is your arm in a sling? And who the *bloody hell*—" he pointed an unapologetic finger at Raz "—is that?"

"Raz is a friend," Carro told him angrily, and Raz didn't miss his obviously brushing aside of the other questions. "And a damn good one, at that! If it wasn't for him I would have been dead at *least* thrice over trying to get back to—!"

"Carro!" Raz snapped, interrupting the pair. "You can sing my praises later! Your man still can't breathe!" He pointed a finger at the shaking form of the first Priest who had attacked them, lying on his stomach off to the left where Raz had thrown him clear of the blast. "*Help him!*"

For a second both Carro and the newcomer, Cullen, gaped at the prone form of the younger Priest. Then they paled and rushed over, bending down over the man and yelling instructions.

As the others who had jumped down into the alcove hurried to follow the orders—one lighting a fire nearby as someone drew a slim knife from beneath their robes—Raz made his way carefully along the path in the opposite direction, eyes on the ground. He found the gladius in the snow building up just beyond the warmth of the ward, a dozen feet off. Plucking it swiftly from its own imprint in the fresh powder, he shook the sword clean, making a mental note to stop throwing his weapons away at every opportunity. By the time he turned around again the path beyond the alcove's entrance was narrowed by a dozen bodies, the Priests and Priestesses who had stood watch over the chaos having leapt down to lend a hand.

"Back up!" Raz heard Carro shouting. "Give us room! Back up!"

The group backed away immediately, one young man almost stepping right into Raz, who had moved forward to see if he could assist. The Priest yelped as the heel of his boot struck the steel of Raz's greave, promptly leaping aside to make room and gawking as Raz moved by him without so much as a glance.

The sound, though, reminded the others of his presence again, and Raz felt eyes raking him in combined dread and wonder as he shouldered his way into the group.

"What can I do?" Raz asked as he came to stand over Carro's shoulder, the old man having eased himself down to both knees beside the injured Priest. A bright ball of ivory fire was seething between Carro and Cullen, the blade of the knife someone had procured resting among the flames, already approaching white-hot.

"You can hold him down," Carro said in a hushed voice, glancing up at Raz. "I won't be able to, with this damn thing." He waved his left hand pointedly against his chest. "Cullen will take his legs. Can you manage his arms and body?"

Raz nodded, moving around the gasping form of the man at his feet.

"Carro, are you sure…?" Cullen began, trailing off meaningfully as he eyed Raz uncertainly. It wasn't a malicious appraisal, to be fair. In fact, it was a far warmer regard than Raz was accustomed to when meeting people who had never seen or heard of him.

Regardless, the implication of mistrust was there, and Carro put his foot down with deliberate force.

"*Yes*, I'm *sure*," he snapped, glaring at Cullen, "and that will be the end of any more pointless doubts. Now, both of you, get him on his side."

Cullen hesitated only a brief instant, then did as Carro said, starting to roll the young man—Reyn, Carro had called him—onto his left side as Raz knelt down to help. The Priest groaned and hacked as he was moved, and Raz saw with some trepidation that his face was turning slowly blue in the bright light of the summoned fire.

"Carro…" he said worriedly. Carro looked up at him, then followed his eyes. He cursed as he saw the man's darkening skin.

"I need to get at his ribs," he said anxiously. "Raz, can you—?"

But Raz was already a step ahead of him. Pulling up the cloth of the white robes beneath Reyn's armpit so that it was well away from the skin beneath, he gave the thick cotton a quick, careful slash with the metal claw of his index finger. The fabric parted cleanly and—ignoring the gasps from the other Priests and Priestesses behind Carro and Cullen as they noticed, for the first time, the steel gauntlets on each of his hands—Raz wrenched the opening wider, tearing the robes apart. The right side of the man's lithe torso was revealed, heavy with bunched, quivering muscle. Midway down his trunk his otherwise light skin became suddenly dark, blackening as a massive bruise crept outward before their eyes directly over the last grouping of his lower right ribs.

Without pausing to gape at the ugly sight, Carro rapidly began to poke and prod at the injured area, clinically ignoring the choked gasps of pain from his patient.

"Nothing broken away," he mumbled under his breath as he ran a palm quickly over the back, side, and front of Reyn's exposed torso. "No open fracture either. Good."

His fingers moved again, tapping along the outline of the ribs against the skin. Several times the sound struck dull, like he were hitting solid wood. Then, after a few attempts, it resonated differently.

Thunk thunk.

"There," Carro said in a rush. "Raz, can you keep a finger right on top of—yes, just like that! Perfect!" He reached around with his good hand and grasped the handle of the knife, its blade now glowing bright in the fire. "Alright, when I tell you to move your hand, I need you to hold him down. Cullen, you too. We don't have time to dull the pain. This is going to hurt. He will fight. Are you both ready?"

Raz and the large Priest nodded at once, Cullen bending over to get ahold of both Reyn's legs while Raz shifted so that he had one arm over the man and would be ready to get the other in position when Carro gave the word.

"Alright," Carro said again, as though readying himself.

Then he pulled the blade from the fire and brought it to hover carefully over the marked point, the metal smoldering an orange-white.

"Now," he ordered, and Raz snatched his hand away. He had just managed to get ahold of Reyn's arms, pinning them up over his head and bearing the man's body down into the stone in a massive, bear-like hug, when Carro drove the knife between the man's ribs with surgical precision.

Instantly, despite his condition, Reyn convulsed, every muscle in his body contracting with agony and shock as the super-heated metal cut through skin and muscle like they were water. Even Raz was hard-pressed to keep the muscular man still as he writhed and choked, trying to scream, and he heard Cullen curse behind him, clearly having difficulty controlling Reyn's legs. Raz's snout wrinkled reflexively at the smell of burning flesh and fat, his ears flattening against his head as best they could to muffle the sizzle and pop just behind him.

"Almost done," Raz said in a half-soothing, half-tense voice, still fighting Reyn's twists. "Almost done. Just a little more."

And then, as though on cue, the sizzling vanished as Carro retracted the blade, and there was a momentary *hiss* of briefly escaping-pressure.

Reyn gasped in a massive lungful of life-giving air, his eyes going suddenly wide as his chest expanded against Raz's arms. He'd barely finished inhaling when he started to howl in continued pain, screaming profanities the likes of which Raz had never heard, even in the dimmest corners of Miropa's dirtiest pubs.

"Keep holding him!" Carro shouted, dropping the cooling knife and bringing his right hand over the cauterized hole in the man's flesh. As Raz continued to fight Reyn's thrashing—growing only stronger now as color steadily returned to the Priest's face—he saw a now-familiar golden glow begin to play on the ground beside him. After a few seconds Reyn's convulsions seemed to lessen. Within ten he was barely fighting at all, and soon he stopped moving altogether, his eyelids fluttering sluggishly, his face slackening. Then the last bit of tension left his body, and the man went limp, eyes closed, breathing evenly against the side of Raz's chest.

"Alright," Carro breathed, sounding relieved. "He's asleep. You can let him go."

Raz extracted himself from around the man at once, hearing Cullen do the same. As he pressed himself back up onto his knees he saw that Carro was still weaving his one-handed magic, the slowly sweeping lines of golden lightning moving inch by inch over the great bruise against Reyn's side.

"Can you fix the breaks?" Raz asked, watching the spellwork, the yellowish light reflecting against his amber eyes.

Carro shook his head. "No such luck. If I could, I would have taken care of this already." He indicated his slinged arm with a shrug. "Our magics can only do so much. I can stitch the flesh more or less back together, and ensure he won't die of infection, but that's about it."

Raz nodded, subconsciously twitching his left shoulder as the now-healed scar along his spine seemed to throb at old memories.

"He'll be all right?" Cullen asked, looking down at Reyn in relief.

"He'll be all right," Carro confirmed, but he turned to glower at the larger Priest. "No thanks to you lot, I might add. What in the *blazes* were you thinking, Cullen, assaulting us like that? He's lucky Raz didn't rip him into a hundred parts!"

"Priest Brern didn't order the attack!" someone—one of the Priestesses—chimed in over Carro's shoulder, sounding defensive. "Hartlet charged in on his own, against orders!"

Carro frowned, looking to Cullen. "Is that true?"

Cullen nodded, a flash of anger wiping the worry from his face. "Aye. You two—" he indicated Carro and Raz "—triggered a ward when you started your climb. When Jofrey heard, he sent us to investigate. If you were a war-band we were to slow you down long enough for help to arrive. If you were envoys—or pretty much anything *but* an assault force—we were to gather information, send it to the Citadel, and make our retreat back up the path."

He blinked suddenly, as though remembering something.

"And speaking of," he said, raising a hand, "it's past time we let the rest of the council know what's going on."

As Raz watched the man begin to twist his finger in a small circle through the air, he felt an unbidden ping of curiosity.

The council, he thought privately. *Syrah...*

The notion was chased away at once, though, as something began to materialize in the space around Cullen's finger. Like light made tangible, the spell seemed to expel magic out, then pull it back in to weave into a slim length of what looked like thin, tattered silk. At once Raz knew what it was and—as Cullen sent it whipping up the path with a flick of his wrist—he turned to watch the pale glow of the messenger spell zip back and forth along the stairs above them until it vanished into the thickly falling snow.

"Now..." Cullen started slowly, as though encroaching on a sensitive subject. "Carro... what the hell is going on? Where is Talo? Why isn't he with you?"

For a long time, Carro said nothing. For a long time he didn't lift his gaze from his work at Reyn's side, the golden glow illuminating the lined face and aging it once again before Raz's eyes. After almost a half-a-minute he tried to speak, opening his mouth to reply, but seemed unable to. He tried again, and failed again.

As he looked about ready to give it a third attempt, Raz reached out and rested a clawed hand carefully on his friend's shoulder.

Carro looked up, and Raz saw tears building in the old man's eyes.

"Let me," Raz told him gently.

Carro hesitated, looking torn.

Then he nodded.

"Priest Brern, is it?" Raz said at once, letting his arm drop and looking to Cullen. The larger man looked at him quizzically, but calmly, any fear and uncertainly now replaced with more curiosity than anything else.

"Aye," he said by way of acknowledgment.

"Then, Priest Brern," Raz said, pushing himself to his feet with the dull *clink* of steel beneath fur, "I would appreciate it if you would follow me. It seems my horse requires calming, and I could use the help."

Indeed, Gale could still be heard whinnying in confusion and fright from inside the alcove, his hooves clacking against stone. Brern, to his credit, took the hint at once, and as Raz made his way through the other Priests and Priestesses—an easy feat, as each and every one seemed absolutely intent on staying well out of his way—the older man picked up his staff from where it lay beside him and made to follow.

Raz looked over his shoulder in time to see a few of the others start to tail them hesitantly.

"I would recommend," he said quietly, falling back to move with Brern into the carved shelter of the recess, "that we keep what I have to tell you between us until I've finished. After that, you can feel free to share what you see fit, as you see fit."

Brern frowned at that, but only paused briefly before half-turning and motioning for his group to stay where they were.

It took Raz a minute or so to calm Gale, and he used the time to gather his thoughts. As the stallion finally relaxed, ducking his head in his habitual request for stroking, Raz turned to speak.

"Talo Brahnt is dead, Priest Brern."

The effect of the words was instantaneous and expected. The Priest gave a sharp intake of breath, his already pale face losing all color in the darkness of the night as he absorbed Raz's news. For a long moment he just stood there, looking almost lost, one hand wrapped around the haft of his steel staff, the other hanging limp by his side.

To his credit, though, the man recovered quickly.

"How?" he asked shortly.

"He was killed by one of your Northern beasts—some form of bear, Carro tells me. It happened barely a day ago, now."

"A day?" Brern demanded in subdued disbelief. "So recently?"

Raz nodded. "Hence my preference that you would hear it from me. Talo was a friend, and growing rapidly in esteem in my eyes, but more to the point I believe you will understand why Carro doesn't wish to speak of it if it can be helped."

Cullen nodded slowly, raising an eyebrow as he did.

"You must be familiar with them, if you're aware of that," he said, almost as though admitting something to himself. "Where did it happen?"

"As we passed through the Woods," Raz told him, absently sliding his leather palm along Gale's snout as the horse huffed. "But the details aren't what's important. I can give you those, in time. For now, let's keep to the essentials."

"Starting with the obvious," Brern said, eyeing Raz. "I would still like to know who it is, exactly, you are...?"

"My name is Raz i'Syul Arro. To keep a *very* long story *very* short, Talo and Carro took me in after their undertaking to Azbar was abandoned for your more pressing threat, this 'Kayle' of yours. I shared a brief history with Talo, from when he was last in the South."

Cullen looked surprised by that.

"That was the better part of a decade ago, if memory serves. I admit I don't know much of your kind other than the name 'atherian', but I wouldn't guess you to quite be of the age to have had many dealings with Talo and his entourage while they were in the fringe cities."

"I was fairly young, you're correct." Raz nodded.

"If what you say is true, though," Cullen said, sounding incrementally uncertain, "then you would have seen Reyn Hartlet as well. He was with Talo—in Karth, I think it was?—on the same expedition. You didn't recognize him tonight, when he—?"

"The man who attacked us?" Raz cut in, surprised. "No, I didn't. I never met or even saw him. My encounter was actually mostly with Syrah Brahnt. Talo I only noticed in passing."

At that, Cullen's frown deepened.

"I'm sorry I didn't recognize your man, but how was I supposed to?" Raz asked, responding to what he assumed to be disbelief. "He attacked us without warning. Carro is right, he's lucky I didn't—"

"No, no, it's not that," Cullen said quickly, waving Raz's defensiveness aside. "You were well within your rights to defend yourself, Master Arro. If anything I hope it teaches Hartlet a lesson. Maybe the idiot will realize now that he's not invincible."

He paused, then, looking as though he wanted to continue along his original train of thought. Then he sighed, and seemed to think better of it.

"It's nothing of import, right now," he grunted. "Nothing that can be fixed, anyway. As you said: keeping to the essentials. Please, continue."

Raz nodded, choosing to allow the man his silence for the time being. He was sure they would all have a great many things to share, once they arrived at the Citadel.

Raz kept his retelling of the last month as short as possible, briefly explaining how Talo and Carro had rescued him from a group who had been trying to collect a bounty on his head, then how he had agreed—seeing few other purposes to give himself at the time—to accompany them back to their mysterious "Cyurgi' Di." He told Cullen Brern nothing of Azbar, or of the Chairman and the Koyts, keeping to "relevant" information only. He spoke only of his rescue, then of their trip northward, out of Ystréd, across the Dehn Plains, and through the Arocklen. When he got once more to events of the previous night,

242

succinctly detailing Talo's death and the breaking of Carro's arm under the ursalus' assault, the Priest once more demonstrated a strength of will and character as he set his jaw in anger and sadness, but did not interrupt. Only when Raz told him of the camp of five hundred or so mountain men they had discovered along the base of the path, in fact, did he speak up.

"Only five hundred?" he asked, suddenly tense. "You're sure?"

"'At least,'" Raz repeated pointedly. "Though there can't be more than a thousand, with no horses, and seemingly few archers."

"Yes," Cullen nodded, looking thoughtfully down at the ground. "I admit, I found it odd that you had a mount with you. I'd never heard of tribesmen being riders. Regardless... even a thousand... That could be a manageable number..."

He continued to stare at the stone for several seconds, and Raz could see the wheels turning in the Priest's head. He'd already guessed that Cullen Brern was a member with status in the Citadel, based on something he had said earlier about "the rest of the council," but he was rapidly starting to believe that Cullen had a much more distinct role.

And one of military significance.

"You would be hard-pressed to get past the path," Raz warned after a while. "It's a choke-point, and one I don't think you can avoid."

The Priest grimaced. "Unfortunately, it certainly seems that way. It's why we haven't made any attempt to escape already. The reality is we would need the assistance of the town to manage a force of that size, if we are limited to descending the path. On an even battlefield it would be an altogether different scenario, but as is..."

"Even without killing?"

"Aye," Brern said with a snort. "There are a myriad other ways to render a man unable to fight, Master Arro, and we know them all. Our vows hold even in war, despite all evidence to the contrary tonight..." He looked suddenly uncomfortable. "I hope you'll forgive Reyn and Lyra for that. They're among the greener of our company. Promising fighters when safe behind thick walls..."

"But it's a different world when the walls fall away," Raz said with a nod. "Don't strain yourself over it. I hold enough grudges as is, and I don't need more. Not to mention that's not the closest I've come to death, if you can believe it."

"Oh, I believe it." Brern eyed Ahna, all seven feet of her standing upright against the wall to his right, foreboding even with her blades covered in the leather sack. "And I get the feeling it won't be the last."

"Likely not," Raz grumbled, finally pushing Gale's head away gently. "But as you were saying: your vows only add complexity to your predicament, Priest. With Talo gone, I don't see many ways out of this situation that don't result in bloodshed."

Brern said nothing for a time, not looking away from Ahna, his face tense. He was still thinking, Raz could tell, his mind trying to fit all the information he'd just received into the game of war they were locked in, trying to place the pieces on the board as best he could.

"It certainly looks that way," he said after a while, and left it at that.

Raz gave him a few seconds to elaborate, but the Priest looked to have nothing else to say.

"What do we do now, then?" Raz asked. "You have the story, as best as I can give it in a short period. What's our next move?"

Finally Brern looked away from the dviassegai and turned his head toward the entrance of the alcove. The silhouettes of a number of younger Priests and Priestesses stood there expectantly, outlines cut against the black of the night by the blaze of magical flames Carro seemed to have kept alive.

Then Brern looked upward, peering through the storm and snow, following the trailing stairway as it snuck its way up, back and forth, until it disappeared into the night.

"Now," Brern said, "we get you both up this damn mountain."

XXVIII

"The ferocity of our rage is a gift, my son. Use it to your advantage. Play upon it wisely. Patience and a steady hand have their place in the crafting of the world, but in the end it is not patience that topples the greatest of trees, nor a steady hand which fells mountains. In the end, the strength of the Stone Gods is what will elevate our people back to the place of power they once held over all the North, and it is through our rage that you will see Them of Stone have lent us their vigor."

—Tarruk Baoill to his son, Gûlraht

"*AAAAAAAAARRRGGGHH!*"

Vores Göl howled in anguish as the point of Kareth Grahst's knife slit another diagonal cut slowly across the Kregoan's chest. He was on his knees, naked, strung between two poles that had been pounded into the ground before the great fire outside of Kareth's tent, arms outstretched and a wrist lashed to either side. All about him, standing as silent onlookers, a hundred men of the camp bore witness to the man's final punishment. Göl had suffered a long time now, the skin beneath his neck and collarbones a slashing mesh of bloody, pulpous lines. Red ran in a single broken sheet down his abdomen, around his genitals, and along his thighs.

If he were fortunate, the Stone Gods would weigh his strength and will to live over the disgrace of his flight from his command over the sentries along the mouth of the pass.

There were no more questions to be asked, Kareth knew. The Kregoan had answered every one a dozen times, holding to his recounting of the events even as the steel cut cruelly through his flesh, attempting to draw veracity when every word the man spoke seemed to be a lie. In the end, though, his story had been corroborated by the rest of the survivors—as well as the paired lookouts who had stumbled into camp in their underclothes—echoing the truth through the screams of their own interrogations. To a one they had babbled on about "dahgün" and "demons," each of them swearing on Them of Stone that a beast of legend had come from the Arocklen itself to feast on the lives of a half-dozen before the rest could even think to flee. A massive creature of wings and teeth, capable of breathing fire and possessing the strength and speed of an avalanche.

Kareth still wasn't sure what to make of the story, but he was convinced the remaining men would say nothing else, no matter how long they were questioned. They were set firm, held strong by their "truth" in a way that falsified stories would never have stood. Eventually deceit could be wrought out at the end of a blade, wicked lies drawn forth with spilled blood. On the three occasions that men had broken tonight, though, attempting to tell their interrogators whatever it was they wanted to hear, all three recountings had been completely different. One man had said the Priests had descended from their mountain fortress, while another had sworn it was a full contingent of valley town soldiers bearing the marks of Drangstek and Stullens. The third, meanwhile, had claimed it was half-a-hundred Sigûrth warriors, under direct orders of the Kayle.

The last man Kareth had killed himself, silencing his treacherous tongue with his fists, beating him to within an inch of death before cutting his throat open and leaving the body for the wolves, off among the trees.

The truth, it seemed—as puzzling as it was—was to be found in the first story. Kareth had heard it, repeated over and over again by the man now hanging limp and moaning before him between the poles. A dahgün, a dragon of the North, seemed to have materialized in aid of the Priests, appearing in time to assist a stranger on horseback pass the sentries. It had fought with the ferocity of its kind, tearing into bodies, breaking bones, and even shearing off limbs, all evidenced in the violent remnants of the fight that had been brought to Kareth's tent in a cart a few hours before.

A dragon had come, ripped into his men like paper, and scattered the pieces to the wind.

For a long time Kareth had pondered the conundrum of the reality, struggling to find an explanation for what the men unanimously swore they had seen. Kareth was no fool, of course. He didn't believe for a second that what had attacked the sentries along the bottom steps of the mountain stairs had been a *true* dahgün. For one thing, the dahgün were said to be gargantuan creatures, capable of draining a lake in one drink and curling themselves around a mountain to sleep. For another, the dahgün had long ago been razed from the world by the Gods themselves. The stories taught that the dragons had been the first of the Stone Gods' children, crafted in an image of strength and savagery, created as wild animals to entertain Them of Stone through eternity with endless war and battle. The tale went, though, that as time went on the dahgün grew tranquil, ending their wars in favor of peace. The dragons, forged of fire to rage forever across the face of time, became docile as they tired of fighting, tired of killing.

And so the Gods had wiped them from the earth and created new children in their own image, seeding them with the ferocity needed to please Them for as long as the world turned.

The dahgün were gone, their flame snuffed by the hammers of the Gods. Kareth was left, therefore, with few possible explanations, each even less likely than the prior. At one point he had considered sending for the Witch, intending to offer her a brief reprieve from her own torment if she could offer him clarity into what had happened. He'd thought better of it in the end, though. *If* the woman had any knowledge of the events, then revealing to her that someone had gotten past Kareth's guard would only feed the infuriating fire within her that seemed unwilling to be extinguished completely. With the Kayle expected to arrive within the next several days—Elrös of the Grasses had returned not three nights prior with the news—Kareth wanted to be ready to present his cousin with the Witch upon his arrival.

When he did, though, he intended her to be beaten and broken, not resistant and willful and spurned to new defiance by the news that the mountain men had lost this small battle.

It was as he had decided not to summon the woman, though, that the realization had finally come to Kareth. It struck him while he thought of the Witch, considering the atrocities of her faith and the feeble deity that was their false-god. He was wondering, perhaps, if the creature that had killed his men was some wicked creation of their "Laor," some golem summoned to wage war against the children for the true Gods. Then he realized, with sudden clarity, that no such creation needed to exist. Them of the corrupted faith had already been granted blasphemous gifts, meant to set man on a path of reliance and complacency, allowing him to use his powers as a crutch and to let weakness seep into his body and mind.

Magic.

Kareth had made the connection in a state of half-scorn, half-anger. The rider, he had realized, the one who had appeared with the creature out of the Woods, had been a wielder of the dark powers granted to him by his false-god. He must have been in disguise, indistinct without the customary robes of his faith. It would have made him unremarkable, unworthy of attention compared to the beast that had fallen among the men with ferocious, rabid brutality.

And it would have made it easy for him to maintain the spell that had conjured the beast in the first place.

It had been then, as he saw the truth behind the deception, that Kareth resumed Vores Göl's punishment, seething at the commander's inability to see beyond the simple trick.

"*Fool,*" Kareth spat, wiping the bloody blade on the Kregoan's quivering shoulder as the man fought to stay awake, his head hanging while tears of pain slipped unbidden down his ritually scarred cheeks. "*Fleeing in the face of a false-prophet. You allowed yourself—your MEN—to be deceived by common trickery.*"

"*G-Grahst,*" Göl pleaded in a hard, tired whisper, "*on the Gods, I s-swear it. The beast was of flesh and bone. I-I swear!*"

"*If he was of flesh and bone then it is only because you allowed him to be.*" Kareth bent down, bringing his blade up and under the man's chin, forcing his head up. "*You struck at shadows when you should have been trying to snuff out the light. Had you done so, had you been clever enough to see through the enchantment, you would have spared yourself this. You would have spared you and your men your honor, and your lives. Them of Stone have no use for the weak, Göl. They've no love for the craven, for those who allow themselves to be swallowed by fear and flee the field of battle. You are a coward, my friend.*" He dug the blade in, piercing the skin beneath the Kregoan's cheek so that blood ran anew. "*Shall I grant you a coward's death?*"

At that, the pain and fear reflected in Göl's eyes transformed into an altogether different kind of terror. Tension returned to his slackened body, knees slipping on the bloody dirt beneath them as he spasmed involuntarily at Kareth's words.

"*No!*" he shouted hoarsely. "*No! Please! PLEASE! Allow me to redeem myself! Allow me to show the Gods I am no coward!*"

Göl was struggling mightily now to hold himself up, his tired, broken body betraying him as he was unable to keep his head upright without shaking. Kareth, though, smiled cruelly at him, pleased with the man's resolve.

"*You wish for second chance?*" he purred, drawing the knife slowly down Göl's neck, across his shoulder, up his arm, and finally resting its point in the hollow of his palm, as though about to nail it to the wooden post. "*Is that your desire?*"

Göl's eyes widened in fear as they looked at the knife, hovering over his hand. He understood the implication. A coward's death was meant to force a warrior to suffer every scar, every wound they might have incurred in the fled battle. It started with the removal of a finger, then two, and continued thus inwardly along the arms and legs with careful, deliberate precision. It happened over days, sometimes weeks or months, allowing the condemned to recover from shock and lost blood as needed before continuing. Those with hearts too strong to give in were reduced to nothing but torsos and heads, and it was only if they managed this extraordinary feat of will that they were given the mercy of the ax.

It was a horrible, drawn out death.

"*Please,*" Göl was still begging. "*Allow me to prove myself before the Gods...*"

Kareth Grahst gazed into the man's watery eyes for a few seconds more, judging the will there.

Then, satisfied with what he saw, he moved his knife from the palm of the Kregoan's hand to the bindings around his wrist.

With quick cuts he set the man's right arm free, then his left. He stood and moved out of the way as Göl collapsed onto the ground, unable to hold himself upright, his lacerated chest and bloody thighs sticking to the earth and thin snow.

"*You are granted your chance at redemption, cowara,*" Kareth said imperiously, playing with the knife in his hands as he stared down at Göl's tortured form. "*Use it well, or I'll see to it that your death takes you until the end of the freeze.*"

Göl said nothing in response. Instead, like a newborn deer, he pushed himself painfully onto all fours, limbs shaking under the weight of his naked body. Dirt lifted with him, clinging to his skin and the cuts that crossed in a dozen directions across his chest. He groaned in pain as he slowly, agonizingly, turned himself around, lifting his head in search of the warmth and glow that was his goal. After a brief pause the man began to crawl, pulling himself forward inch by inch, through the silent witnesses on either side of him, towards the great fire in the center of the ring.

Vores Göl was no coward in death, holding his silence even as he burned.

XXIX

"It can take days to climb the mountain path, depending on the time of year, the weather, and the state of the individual attempting to manage the steps. For the Priests and Priestesses of Laor, it is a small thing to invigorate ourselves and our companions with simple spells along the way, alleviating fatigue and combating the toll the climb can take on the body. It is a difficult journey, but most do not realize the final test that awaits them upon reaching the apex of the stairs. There, standing on the flattened stone of the outer courtyard, one must take hold of their emotion, gathering up whatever fear or awe or shock they experience, and compose themselves as they take in the great wonder that is the High Citadel."

— *"Studying the Lifegiver"* by Carro al'Dor

They climbed in silence under the hesitant glow of an early Sun, heads bowed to watch the ground and hoods pulled over their heads to bar the buffets of a heavy wind that had picked up in the last hour. Raz knew, as they took each step one after the other, that they had to be getting close. He could feel a tension in the air, a pleasant, tempered excitement that manifested itself in a quickened pace and the occasional dull buzz of conversation among the eleven Priests that led the way. Carro followed behind them, pausing every twenty minutes or so to rid himself and Raz of cramping legs and the lightheadedness that came with the altitude. He had changed back into his Priest's robes shortly before they'd departed the alcove that morning, the white cloth making him at times hard to distinguish from the backs of the other faithful. Raz took up the rear, leading Gale carefully and ignoring the annoyed looks occasionally shot his way by a few at the front of the line, displeased with the plodding pace.

He was in too good a mood to care about the grumblings of men and women who had almost killed him not half-a-day prior.

He felt somewhat guilty for his high spirits when his eyes fell on the back of Carro's bowed head, but he couldn't help it. The painted picture his mind had crafted of famed Cyurgi' Di seemed to shimmer before him whenever he looked around, playing like some mirage out of the snow. He started thinking about all the wonders he had wheedled out of Carro, and Talo before him. He held in his mind's eye a great castle of ivory and gold towers, rising into the heavens as though in salutation to the gods. A hundred needles piercing the sky, encasing a world of warmth and light and magic, where night never fell and the cold never penetrated. Among the halls he imaged a thousand white-clad men and women, moving in devout perfection, going about the holy businesses they were charged with.

And—gliding among them like a single perfect flake in a winter storm—a woman with white hair danced about, her pale red eyes raised to meet Raz's as she moved.

He found, to his moderate—though fortunately private—embarrassment, that he was hard-pressed not to get excited.

There was a groan from behind him, and Raz looked around, shifting Ahna higher up onto his shoulder with one hand as he did. Slung across Gale's back—and propped slightly onto his left side by a bedroll so his healing ribs wouldn't be stressed by the weight of his own body—Reyn Hartlet was strapped over the saddle with rope, preventing him from sliding off. Carro had insisted the man remain in his suspended sleep, and so Raz had had to try to keep the aggressive stallion calm for nearly a half-hour that morning as the others did their best to get the man on the animal's back. They'd managed it, but had made the mistake of slinging Reyn's head over the *right* side of the saddle, the side which generally faced the wall of the path as they moved north and west up the mountain. While more often than not this had been something of a nuisance, forcing Raz to be extra careful when guiding Gale along the narrower parts of the steps, he *had* enjoyed himself a few times by deliberately knocking the young man's head into the lines of fragile icicles that occasionally hung over them, dangling from the outcroppings above.

Raz wasn't about to forget that Reyn had done his best to cave his skull in not ten hours before, after all.

"Halt!"

Raz barely made out the command over the howl of the wind, and he turned back to the front to see why Cullen Brern had stopped their climb. He gazed upward, over the heads of the Priests that crowded the stairs, frowning at the uneven, monolithic outline of the mountain that continued to tower upwards into the storm.

"How much further?" he called out to Carro, taking several more steps until he was only a few feet behind the old Priest. Carro turned and peered at him from between snow-caked lids.

"What did you say?" the man shouted back, clearly not having heard a word.

"How. Much. Further?" Raz enunciated, yelling still louder. "And what have we stopped for? What's Brern doing up—?"

Raz's question choked and caught suddenly as he looked up again to try to make out Cullen Brern's outline among the others at the front of the group. He found him easily enough, head and shoulders above the others.

And as he did, he realized he'd been wrong about the lumbering outline that hung, dark and foreboding, in the sky above them.

Slowly, second by second as the winds shifted and the snows fell in undisciplined patterns, Raz started to make out details of the great structures that hid beyond the veil of the blizzard. In an instant the fantastical rendition of the Citadel he had been keeping in his head was swallowed up and discarded, banishing the white and gold marble spires in favor of high, heavy walls, pointed stone towers with angled turrets, crenelated battlements that hung out impossibly over the openness of the mountain slopes, and wicked, leering arrow slits. The mystical marvel that was Cyurgi' Di suddenly transformed itself into the hulking body of some great, slumbering beast, resting eternally among the peaks. He couldn't see much more than the hints of what was directly in front of him, but as Raz's sharp eyes trailed the outlines through the snow he took in the vastness of the place, like a walled city built right into—and out of—the cliffs.

"Sun and Moon and all Her Stars…" he breathed, numbed even by what little he saw. The High Citadel wasn't a castle, or some transcendental keep built among the heavens.

The High Citadel was a fortress, carved right out of the mountain itself.

"Incredible, isn't it?"

Carro's shout almost made Raz jump, so unexpected was it as he lost himself in the massive shadow that was Cyurgi' Di, mostly hidden by the falling snow. The man had moved back to stand beside him, following his eyes upward as they trailed the dulled crenellations of those ramparts that he could see.

"It is!" Raz yelled back after a few seconds. "It's not exactly what I expected, but I suppose that's on me!"

"With time, it grows more friendly!" Carro responded sagely. "Initially… less so!"

"I'll say!" Raz's eyes now trailed the outlines of what he thought might be a pair of bastion towers. "This doesn't exactly look like a place I would expect to find your kind, Carro!"

"Precisely why it is so ideal!" the Priest yelled with the hint of a smile. "There are many layers to all things, Raz! A face of peace and goodness can hide twisted desires, while the façade of force and war—" he waved at the Citadel "—might be home to the greatest source of hope mankind can forge!" He smirked, looking back up at Raz, only one eye visible beneath the hood. "I think you know what happens when people take *you* at face value, hmm?"

"I do," Raz said quietly, but Carro didn't hear him. At that moment there was a *crack* and a static sizzling, and something seemed to fall away in the air between their small party and the Citadel. A moment later there was a second *crack*, and the same thing happened again, the air shimmering in falling geometries, like a shattering wall of clear crystal that one might not have even noticed was there.

"Brern's taken down the defensive wards!" Carro shouted in explanation. "The council will get them back up as soon as we've entered!"

Raz nodded, watching Cullen Brern motion that they were moving again. As one his group took the last steps onto what appeared to be some sort of flattened platform, and Carro moved to follow at once. Raz coaxed Gale into motion again, guiding him over one last patch of ice and onto the steep incline of the final stairs.

When he'd managed to get the horse safely up and over the last step, buffeted back and forth by the wind all the while, Raz stood straight and looked around. They were standing at the edge of a wide, semicircular plateau, a perfect half-ring buried under a foot of soft, powdered snow. To their right, the wall of the mountain rose in an incline overhead, while to their left the lip of the plateau fell off into the infinite white of the storm. The only mar in the scene was a slight indentation that led in a line directly ahead of them, along which Raz assumed Brern and his men had come the night before.

It was when he followed this hinted path with his eyes, trailing it as it led ahead and away from them, that Raz began to feel his fingers tingle in what could only be described as a reverent thrill.

The mouth of the High Citadel stood some twenty paces ahead of them, a dark, arched hole that tunneled for what looked like fifty feet through solid stone. The wall it breached towered upwards, fearsome in its silent breadth, its top ledge barely visible another fifty feet above them. On either side of the archway, like giant sentinels, the bastion towers Raz had indeed made out stood guard, jutting into the plateau like swords held before a shield. They hulked overhead, pierced by a dozen arrow slits each, as though daring anyone fool enough to step forward and claim entry.

Raz, for a moment, felt himself suddenly seized by the desire to turn around and march right back down the path. As Cullen Brern led his group forward, though, and Carro turned to give him a coaxing jerk of his head, he sighed.

Then he stepped forward, guiding Gale through the trampled snow, into the mouth of the beast.

Priest Dolt Avonair was slumbering at his post when a pounding knock shook the heavy main doors of the Citadel to his left. He'd been told there was no need for him to keep his watch, that the wards would warn the council if anyone was approaching. But Dolt had been gatekeeper for too many years to feel comfortable leaving his appointment unattended, especially in times such as these. He had insisted he be allowed to remain—had even brought his case to the interim High Priest himself, in fact—and Jofrey had eventually relented, muttering that he didn't see any harm in adding another pair of eyes to their defenses.

It was for this reason, therefore, that Dolt was seated in his regular chair, dozing off to dreams of rich meals and sunshine, when the heavy, booming knocks woke him with a jolt.

"Dolt!" the familiar voice of Cullen Brern called, muffled through the wood. "It's us! Open up!"

Dolt scrambled to his feet, cursing the stiffness of muscles and ache of bones from sitting in the cold by the door. "Just a moment!"

Rubbing his hands together for warmth, Dolt hurried over and quickly reached up to jerk at a slim slot of wood that was set just an inch or two above his eye-level in the door. It took a couple tries to break the snow and ice that had built up on the other side, but within a few seconds Dolt was able to slide the wood away and peer outside, squinting against the sudden blast as frigid air was sucked in through the hole. He saw a number of robed figures huddled against the wind and storm, then the bearded face of Brern himself, glowering down impatiently, clearly in no mood to be kept waiting.

Slamming the slot shut again, Dolt kicked the bottom lockbar up on its hinge, releasing the other two by hand. Then, with a grunt of effort, he threw his tubby body against the door, fighting the gale, layered snow, and the sheer weight of the timber as he got it ajar.

As soon as a crack showed, several gloved hands appeared to help, and a moment later the door swung wide.

"Hello, Brern!" Dolt said cheerfully, stepping quickly out of the way as the master-at-arms moved into the relative warmth of the hall, the men and women at his command following one after the other. "How was the descent? And the climb? What news do you bring us? Anything promising?"

"Cheerful even under siege," Cullen Brern chuckled, though he sounded oddly somber as he threw off his hood and started kneading clumps of snow out of his beard. "It's always good to see you, Dolt. As for news, it's nothing half so pleasant, but you'll hear all about that soon enough. For now, though, do you know what our stocks of straw look like?"

"Straw?" Dolt asked as what he thought was the last of the group stepped through the open door. "I'm not sure. Plenty, I'd have to say, what with needing it for beds and the birds and—" He paused, looking more closely at the last man to have entered the room, one arm in a sling around his neck. "Oy, is that Carro? Carro! Where did you come from, you old—?"

Dolt's rambling ended so abruptly, one would have thought he'd been struck dumb. He was staring, open mouthed and eyes wide, at the last figure to step out of the snow, breath billowing around its head in the cold. Like some monster come right out of a child's nightmare, the beast seemed to rise endlessly, standing an easy head over Carro and Brern both. Even before it raised a hand to pull down its pelt hood—the appendage encased in a steel gauntlet complete with wicked claws—Dolt saw the shine of long needled teeth protruding up and down along a black, serpentine muzzle. As the furs fell away, Dolt found himself stricken by golden eyes, vertically slit and quick, settling on him. Spined, webbed ears, strung with membranes that looked blood-red in the warm light of the hall, spread and extended on either side of the creature's head. Even as he noticed these, Dolt saw the flicker of more red, and his gaze moved slowly down to the hint of leathery wings folded beneath a thick mantle, then lower still to armored legs and long feet protected by heavy pelt boots from which black claws extended through slits in the fur.

It was only as he made out the slithering, snaking form of a dark, scaled tail, as thick at its base as a man's thigh, that Dolt heard himself make a sound.

"A-ah-a-uh-a," he stammered, his tongue failing him as he took in more and more of the *thing* that had appeared at his doorstep. The hand that had pulled down its hood now rested on the head of a long ax looped into the creature's belt, and Dolt finally noticed reins entwined between the steel fingers, leading back to a massive black horse that still stood outside, head turned away from the wind. A Priest was trussed up and tied down over the animal's saddle like a sack of potatoes, but Dolt barely registered this. His eyes were moving back to the monster, following his other hand, wrapped about the haft of some great, spear-like weapon, its bottom weighed down by a pointed steel tip, its top hidden by what looked to be an old leather bag.

"A-eh-aa-ah." Dolt tripped over himself again, unable to form even half a word. Brern, who had finished patting the ice from his beard and hair, looked up, his expression mildly amused.

"Dolt, meet Raz i'Syul Arro," he said with a smirk, indicating the creature. Then he gestured to Dolt. "Master Arro, this is Priest Dolt Avonair, the Citadel's primary gatekeeper since before he got his staff."

Dolt was still incapable of enunciating so much as a coherent sound. The thing—Arro—raised the steel-clad fingers of the hand holding the lance-like weapon over his shoulder in a casual salute.

"Hello," it said, the word rumbling from its throat in a dangerous, animalistic tenor.

There was nothing else to be done. As he heard the creature speak, opening its cruel mouth to reveal lines of wicked white fangs, Dolt felt the blood rush from his head.

Then the world went black, and Dolt Avonair knew only that he was falling.

"Oh dear," Carro said, hurrying forward as the gatekeeper—Dolt, Brern had introduced him as—tumbled to the floor before their eyes. The man crumpled where he stood, spilling to the ground in an awkward pile of robes and limbs.

"Ha!" Cullen Brern laughed out loud. "Has he gone and fainted? Poor fellow." He turned, revealing the first relaxed grin Raz had seen since meeting him the previous night. "I wouldn't take it too personally, Master Arro. Priest Avonair's a cheerful fellow, but he's not known for his constitution. I do believe he has a tendency to hyperventilate when the harvesters haul up slaughtered game every summer."

"No offense taken," Raz said with a shrug, peering down in concern as Carro eased himself to one knee beside the unconscious man. "He's not the first, though I admit it's usually women who faint at the sight of me…"

"Can't imagine why that might be," someone's voice muttered sarcastically from his left, among Brern's group. Raz slowly turned his head in their direction, eyeing the man he suspected had made the comment. The Priest refused to meet his gaze, though, as did several others among the men and women that surrounded him.

Brern, too, it seemed, had heard the remark. He lost his grin abruptly, as though remembering himself. Pulling off his gloves he began banging his boots against the ground, looking around. "Loric." One of the men behind him glanced up attentively. "Fetch Jofrey. I imagine he'll be in the High Priest's chambers, waiting for more news than I could send with the messenger spell. Tell him it's of the utmost importance, but say nothing else. Tell him he'll have the answers to any questions he might have. We'll be in the consecration room."

As the Priest nodded and began making his way left down the hall, Brern grabbed him by the arm. "And not a word of this to anyone else, you hear?"

Loric's eyes grew wide, but he nodded again, hurrying off as soon as Brern let go of him.

"Vance, Kahsta," he said, looking at the man and woman closest to him. "Gather the rest of the council. The same rules apply. Say nothing, not even to them. The consecration room. Clear?"

Each gave their indication of understanding, and Brern sent them off with a jerk of his head. Raz watched them leave, wondering which would be the one to find Syrah Brahnt first.

"The rest of you!" Brern called, speaking to the remainder of his group. "I know you're tired and hungry, but you'll have to bear the wait a little longer until after the council has sorted this mess out."

There was a grumbling of discontent, but no one seemed brave enough to voice any actual disagreement.

"Excellent," the master-at-arms said with a nod. "Then off to the room with you. We'll follow soon."

As one the men and women shuffled on down the right hall, opposite the direction the other three had gone, peeling themselves out of damp robes as they went.

"Is there a place for Gale?" Raz asked, feeling awkward in front of the open door, the horse snuffling in the cold behind him.

"None," Brern said without looking around, moving over to where Carro still crouched over Dolt Avonair. "At least nowhere you'd traditionally keep a horse, that is. There are a few chambers along the north hall that still have arrow slits." He waved in the direction he'd sent the majority of his subordinates. "They're warm enough, they'll have plenty of fresh air, and with some straw we'll make something work. For now, he stays with us."

Raz nodded at that, pulling Gale into the hall. The horse snorted and stomped, unsure in the sudden warmth, light, and dryness. As Reyn Hartlet's tall form barely made it through the opening, Raz heard Brern speaking quietly to Carro, on his knees by the still form of Dolt Avonair.

"Is he all right?"

"He'll be fine," Carro replied quietly. "Just hit his head on the way down."

"Serves him right, fainting like that."

"Cullen, the first time I saw Raz up close, I'm quite certain I nearly pissed myself."

Raz chuckled privately, listening to the old men discuss in hushed voices as he dropped Gale's reins and moved back to pull the heavy door closed behind the stallion. As he turned around again he allowed himself to bask in the comfortable warmth of the space, taking in the hall in detail for the first time.

It was less bright than he had imagined the interior of the Laorin's home would be, but there was no discomfort in the dimness of the light. Rather, the glow was hearty and welcoming, blue and white candles on shelves and tables, and still others tucked into tiny alcoves in the stone supplementing the torches that burned with familiar smokeless ivory flames every few meters along the wall. The ground beneath him, a puzzle of grey slate slabs, was warm even through his furs, and Raz recalled what Carro had said about the copper piping in the floors and walls channeling warmth and fresh air into the fortress. He tasted the hall with a flick of his tongue, then took in a deep breath simply out of curiosity. Indeed, there lacked a stuffiness to the space that one usually found in such constricted environments. It might have been because they were standing just inside the main doors, but Raz rather thought he could give credit to the ingenuity of the Citadel's builders.

This is going to be interesting, he thought, tilting his head to look up at the vaulted ceiling overhead.

"Welcome back, friend," Brern's voice said suddenly. "Nice of you to join us."

Raz looked around. Avonair was moving again, slowly pushing himself up onto his elbows between Brern and Carro.

"Wh-what happened?" the man was mumbling, clearly bewildered to find himself somehow on the floor. "H-how did I...? Why did I...?"

He continued to look confused, gazing down at the ground around him, before looking up. Instantly his gaze snapped onto Raz again, who hadn't moved from his place with Gale by the door.

"Oh, Laor's saggy b—!" the man began to shout, paling again and looking at once like he might faint for a second time. The master-at-arms, though, clapped a hand over his mouth, silencing him.

"Master Arro is travelling with Carro, Dolt," Brern said firmly. "For that reason, I would appreciate it if you would do him the respect of not announcing his presence *to the whole of Cyurgi' Di*. Now, on your feet! You're coming with us."

"C-coming with you?" Avonair stammered as Brern removed his hand from his mouth, though the man's eyes never left Raz. "Wha—No, I have to stay here. The gate—"

"Will stand an hour or two without you watching over it," Carro finished for him gently, using his staff to pull himself to his feet. "For the moment it's important we keep my and Raz's return quiet."

Avonair was still stammering his denials when Brern hauled him to his feet, spun him around, and started leading him to the right, along the north hall. Carro waited for Raz to retrieve Gale's reins, then indicated that they should follow.

"I take it I'm to meet the council, then?" Raz asked him as they fell into step beside each other.

"You are," Carro said with a nod, the steel of his staff *clinking* gently with every other step against the stone beneath their feet. "It seems the best course of action, and I have to assume Talo would have done the same." He looked momentarily sad, but shook it off. "Pilgrims and travelers aren't usually required to meet any of the Citadel's highest ranking Priests or Priestesses, but I hope you don't take offense when I say you don't fall under the 'usually'-category."

"The whole situation doesn't fall under the 'usually'-category, Carro," Raz muttered as, ahead of them, Brern turned Avonair with a firm hand and led him through a tall door along the left side of the hall. "Have you been thinking about what happens now? What happens next?"

Carro sighed. "It's all I've been thinking about."

"And?"

"And I have no more solutions than I did yesterday, or the day before. I'm hoping and praying the council will have something to add, once they hear our news."

Raz frowned, but said nothing. They'd reached the door through which Brern and Avonair had disappeared, but as Carro went for the handle he paused.

"Leave Gale here," he said, glancing back at the horse. "He won't be able to manage the steps down. Can you carry Reyn in?"

"The steps?" Raz asked with mild trepidation as he pulled Ahna off his shoulder to lean her against the nearby wall, then moved to start freeing Reyn Hartlet's sleeping form from the saddle.

I'm developing a phobia... he realized in half-amusement, thinking of the mountain stairs they'd only just left behind.

Carro nodded, but said nothing, waiting until Raz had untied the young Priest completely, sliding him off Gale's back and into his arms.

"I'll be back," Raz told the stallion gently. "Stay put."

Gale bobbed his head as though in understanding, bending down to snort at the wall and floor. Raz moved around him and nodded to Carro, who opened the door and walked inside, holding it wide behind him. Raz stepped in sideways, intent not to smash Reyn's head or legs into the frame or wall, and so didn't get a good look at the room until after the door had closed behind him.

When he did, he gaped.

For the first time, Raz glimpsed a hint of the wonders he had initially imagined the greatest of the Laorin temples would hold. While the comfort and warmth of the hall had done something to offset the sense of foreboding that had gripped him upon seeing Cyurgi' Di's high walls and looming towers, *this* room whisked what remained away in a blink.

The consecration room of the citadel was less 'room' and more 'theater.' As soon as Raz entered behind Carro he found himself on the top tier of a series of rectangular marble seats that dipped down and inward with every level, like a geometric funnel towards the very center of the chamber. It would have reminded Raz of Azbar's Arena, in fact, were it not for the brightness of the place. In the very middle, at the bottom of the seats, a large, flat platform of dark marble rose a half a foot off the floor. Gold lined its corners and edges, making the whole thing look like some ornate box, and atop it, towards the very back of the dais, a massive silver brazier, tarnished by time, was filled to the brim with white, boiling flames. Above their heads two identical braziers hung suspended in the air, supported by nothing at all, drifting and floating around each other in a lazy circle on the current of magic that seemed to keep them eternally suspended. The walls of the room were not stone, Raz saw, but carved panels of some dark wood, depicting sceneries and stories and portraits of half-a-hundred varieties. More gold lined the joints between these works, and as Raz looked up, following these lines as they crisscrossed each other over a perfectly domed ceiling, he was briefly reminded of the songbirds some of the nomadic families used to trade for in the port city of Acrosia, brought from the distant Imperium in little gold cages for the pleasures of the Southern aristocracy.

"Down this way."

Raz pulled his eyes away from the expanse of the ceiling in time to see Carro waving him along, already marching down the tall steps to the very center of the room. On either side of them the others were already seated, most of the Priests and Priestess stripped down to thin underclothes, their robes laid out over the stone to dry under the spells of warmth cast over them by their owners. Brern had marched Avonair to the bottom of the room and plopped him down right in front of the dais, upon which the master-at-arms himself was taking a seat, lowering himself with a sigh like a tired old man. He looked up, watching Raz descend with Reyn in his arms, sizing him up slowly—as Raz had noticed him doing several times over the course of the morning. He had the sense the Priest was attempting to witness in him what it was Carro—and apparently Talo—saw.

"Set him here," Carro said, indicating the empty slab beside Avonair. Raz obliged, bending to ease Reyn's still form down gently. As he did he saw the gatekeeper's eyes widen when he finally made out who the sleeping Priest was.

"Hartlet?" he demanded, sounding bewildered. "What in Laor's good name happened to him? Is he dead? What—?"

"Priest Hartlet bit off more than he could chew," Brern interrupted—something Raz was starting to understand happened frequently when it came to Dolt Avonair. "He picked a fight he couldn't win, and was lucky enough to make it out alive."

Avonair's eyes just grew wider, and his gaze rose slowly from Reyn to Raz, who still stood over the man. Raz saw him put the pieces together one at a time, and he turned away before the gatekeeper found the courage to start bombarding *him* with questions.

"What now?" Raz asked Carro, moving to take a seat beside the Priest who stood at the bottom of the steps, looking up.

"Now we wait," Carro replied, his eyes on the room's single door. He didn't sit, despite the weeks they had spent on the road. He looked anxious, as though he half-expected something terrible to come in after them.

Raz shrugged, then leaned back, resting his shoulders against the edge of the seats behind him, kicking his feet up onto the black dais. Crossing his arms over his chest, he decided to pass the time by studying the wood carvings that made up the walls and ceilings.

It was about ten minutes before the first knock came, and the sound pulled Raz away from an enthusiastic examination of what looked to be a battle between five armies beneath the shadow of some great mountain. He looked around just as Carro raised his voice.

"Enter!"

At once the door opened, and the woman Brern had sent off—Kahsta—poked her head into the room.

"I have Priestess Petrük and Priest Argo," the woman called down the stairs. "Should I have them enter, or wait for the others?"

Raz heard Carro curse under his breath, and glanced at the man in time to see that the expression on the Priest's face said very clearly that these were *not* the first individuals he was hoping to hear from. He had just started to reply—likely asking that they remain outside—when a tall, sour-faced crone of perhaps seventy brushed passed Kahsta.

"Out of the way, girl," the woman snapped, not even looking at the younger Priestess as she scanned the room. "Who are you to ask whether or not I have permission to enter? I received my staff in this very place thirty years before you were even a poor idea."

The woman caught sight of Brern, then Carro, and her brows shot up. As a short, heavy-set man with a kindly face stepped into the chamber behind her, the Priestess Raz assumed now to be Petrük started down the steps at a shockingly brisk pace for her age.

"al'Dor?" she demanded, sounding an odd combination of disbelieving and annoyed at the sight of him. "We didn't expect you'd be fool enough to climb the mountain. Where is Brahnt? Has he already gone off to relieve Jofrey of the High Priest's mantle?"

"Valaria," Carro said, his tone even, "if you and Behn could take a seat, all will be explained in time. We should wait until—"

"Until what?" Petrük demanded scornfully, still moving down the steps. "The others arrive? A dramatic demand to celebrate your return, summoning the council. And whose damn *horse* is that in the hall? What idiot would have led that animal all the way up—?"

She stopped moving so suddenly, for a moment Raz thought the woman might trip and fall headfirst down the stairs. She had, of course, finally caught sight of him, and her sallow blue eyes were frozen, transfixed by his own. Raz didn't bother standing up, or raising a hand in greeting. He'd decided at once that he didn't like this narrow, abrasive Priestess, and he hoped the black glower he gave her conveyed the dislike without doubt.

It must have, because when the woman regained her sense, she opened her mouth and shrieked.

"*Valaria!*" Brern's hard voice cut across her scream. "Control yourself, woman!"

Petrük's raspy screech cut short at once, but she still stood, pale and still, staring at Raz.

"What in Laor's name is *that?*" the man who had followed her into the room—Priest Argo, Kahsta had said—demanded, pointing unashamedly at Raz.

"*That*, Behn," Carro shot at the man angrily, "is Raz i'Syul Arro. He's a friend, and I highly suggest you stop pointing like some damn child."

"Or what?" Argo demanded, sounding deceptively hot tempered for his gentle features.

"Or you'll find yourself relieved of a hand, *Priest*," Raz growled, lifting his feet from the dais and leaning forward, flaring his neck crest slowly.

"It speaks?" Argo demanded, his offending hand dropping more out of shock than anything. "Lifegiver's mercy." He turned on Carro. "Is that a *sword* it's carrying on its back? What did you bring into our home, al'Dor? If you've welcomed a killer into our midst, I'll—!"

"You'll do nothing, Argo," Brern spat at him, getting to his feet. "Master Arro is a guest, as per my wishes *and* Carro's. It'll be up to Jofrey to cast him out, if it's to happen, and you certainly won't have shit to say when—!"

"Jofrey?" Petrük asked him shrewdly, tearing her eyes away from Raz to look at the master-at-arms. "Jofrey, you said. Not Talo?"

Brern stopped talking at once, seeing his mistake. Raz suddenly felt a lurch of distaste for Valaria Petrük that took a moment to place. She was clearly astute, intelligent and perceptive, and yet bore a distinctly cruel, pretentious air.

Tern, Raz realized suddenly, gritting his teeth at the thought. *She reminds me of Quin Tern.*

"Valaria, we will explain *everything*," Carro was saying, sounding increasingly impatient. "If you could just sit down and wait, the others can't be long behind you."

As though on cue, there was a second knock at the door. Kahsta, who had remained standing at the top of the stairs, turned and pulled it open at once. The two men Brern had sent off, Vance and Loric, strode in one after the other. They glanced about the room briefly, then moved to join their comrades among the stone tiers, leaving the group behind them to file in. Six in all, the men and women of the council each bore the white robes of the faith, making them look for a moment like a congregation of bright, flowing ghosts. Some carried staffs at their side, others nothing at all. One pair clutched a half-dozen heavy bound tomes between them, as though they had been interrupted amidst their studies. At their head, a small man with a grey beard that reached his collar stood taking in the room from behind a pair of clear spectacles with sharp, tired eyes. They flicked first to the Priests and Priestesses of Brern's group, then to Brern himself, Dolt Avonair, Reyn Hartlet's sleeping form, and on to Petrük and her companion, Argo. After this they paused and grew wider when they fell upon Carro.

Then they finally shifted to Raz, who finally decided it was time to stand up.

If this man registered any surprise at Raz's presence, it was well masked. Several of the men and women behind him weren't quite as composed, however, instantly breaking out into gasps and hisses of shock at the sight of Raz's massive fur-and-steel-clad form rising in what he assumed to be something of a sacred room. The Priest at their head, though, gave no hint of such disquiet. Instead, slowly, he began to descend the stairs, eyes moving once more around him before settling on the Priest waiting for him in the center of the room.

"Carro," the man said warmly, extending his arms and smiling an exhausted sort of smile that no less expressed the pleasure of one friend greeting another. "I'm glad to see you safe. I didn't think we'd come across each other for some time yet."

Carro smiled in the same weathered way, accepting the embrace. "It's good to be home, Jofrey. I wish I came bearing better news."

At that, the man—Jofrey—took pause. He looked around one last time, like he were searching for something, his eyes lingering on Raz only a spare moment.

"Carro…" he started quietly, as though afraid to know the answer. "Where is Talo?"

There were a few seconds in which Raz witnessed Carro fight mightily to control himself. He battled the emotions, but one after the other they played across his face like a story. He said no words, but as his features twisted into a mask of grief, tears began to spill from his eyes uncontrollably. Once again he couldn't seem able to get the words out, and Brern stepped forward, moving to stand beside the pair, putting his free hand on Carro's arm.

"Carro, let Arro and I explain," he said softly.

Raz saw Jofrey's blue eyes flick over to him briefly once again as he registered the name, but otherwise the man didn't move. For several seconds Raz watched Carro's heavy frame wracked by silent weeping, and he hoped the Priest would nod and let him step in.

He was surprised, therefore, when Carro shook his head stiffly.

"N-no," he said through his tears. "Not… n-not this time."

He paused and took a heavy, shaking breath, closing his eyes. For a moment more he stood there, obviously struggling to gain control of the grief. Slowly the shaking stilled, and he took another breath, standing tall.

When he opened his eyes again, he met Jofrey's gaze evenly.

"Jofrey," he said. "Talo Brahnt is dead."

XXX

It took a long time for the room to settle after that. There were cries and gasps of "No!" and "How?" and other various denials. Most of them came from the younger Priests and Priestesses who had formed Brern's group, while the older, more life-worn members of the council mostly just exchanged dark, mournful looks. Eventually Brern managed to calm everyone and get them seated about the dais, the council and Dolt Avonair in the front two rows, the others in the back.

Slowly, heartbreakingly, Carro told the story. He left out no details this time, introducing Raz after reaching his and Talo's arrival in Azbar, and allowing him to explain his connection to the former High Priest. The men and women before him listened in rapt stillness, drinking in Raz's words with alternating reflections of astonishment and unease as he spoke. Many were disconcerted by him, he could tell. Frightened, even, their hands twisting nervously, their bodies tense and quick to react with every move he made. And yet they listened, voicing no argument or disbelief. In light of the news he and Carro bore, the council of Cyurgi' Di chose to accept this strange character among them, at least for the moment, and by the time Raz's recounting trailed off the Priests and Priestesses were hunched forward on their stone seats, aching for the rest of the story. Carro resumed the tale as Raz sat himself once more upon the gilded stone, speaking of his and Talo's failure to end the violations caused by the Arena, their return to Ystréd, and how they had met up with Raz for the second time.

As Carro spoke, Raz examined the faces of the men and women before him. He felt an increasing unease as he studied them once, twice, and finally a third time, assuring himself that he was not incorrect. He knew he wasn't, of course. Raz was loath to admit it to himself, but his hope of seeing the woman with the white hair once again had led him to seek her out the moment the council had entered the room.

Syrah Brahnt, though, was nowhere to be found.

The unease turned into a prickle of something like fear, rising in Raz's chest as he forced himself to take in more about the men and women before him. Apart from Cullen Brern, Jofrey, the insufferable pair of Valaria Petrük and Behn Argo, and Carro himself, there were five strangers. Two women—one perhaps as old as Petrük and the other in her thirties—and three men—one wizened old Priest who looked to be defying death in his age, one who Raz thought had half-a-dozen years on Carro and Brern, and one perhaps in his late forties who shared not a few distinctive features with the master-at-arms, leading Raz to guess the two men were at the very least cousins, likely brothers. Each after another Raz studied with professional detachment, distracting himself from Syrah's absence by trying to make out what sort of characters the council of the Laorin's greatest temple was crafted from.

He was relieved, based on the reactions to Carro's story, that Petrük and Argo looked to be the only true bad apples of the bunch.

For nearly a quarter-hour the Priest spoke, pausing only on occasion to answer questions when they were posed, and to look to Raz for confirmation or assistance in the details. When he got to the evening of the wolves' attack he began to falter, and Raz feared he would fall apart again. Carro held himself together, though, and went on to explain in detail how they had fended off the pack together only to be assaulted by the ursalus not long after, and how Talo had been struck down shortly before Raz's slaughtering of the bear.

It was here, for the first time, that Raz was puzzled to hear Carro deviate from the story. As he recounted Talo's demise, there under the faint light of the Moon as he tried desperately to heal his lover, Carro made it sound as though Talo had passed on of his own accord, succumbing to his broken body peacefully, as though in his sleep.

He said nothing of the merciful death Raz had granted him, delivered in steel.

Raz didn't really understand *why* Carro had changed the story, but it was an important enough detail to omit that the Priest would lie about it, and so he kept his mouth shut. Eventually Carro completed retelling of their breaking through the sentries at the bottom of the stairs, catching up to where they'd met Brern along the mountain path.

"In retrospect, I should have assumed we would cross a ward," he said with a frown, "but my mind was preoccupied by other things as we climbed. Reyn went first for Raz, who'd taken watch." Carro allowed himself a small smile, the only one since he'd started speaking. "It wasn't a long fight."

"Apparently." One of the council spoke up—the man Raz thought to be a bit older than Carro and Brern—looking to the master-at-arms. "I *said* it was a bad idea to bring Hartlet, Cullen."

Brern grimaced, waving the comment away. "Aye, Elber, you did, and you weren't wrong. In light of everything else, though, I suggest we not waste time on my moment of folly."

Jofrey, sitting front and center in front of Carro, nodded his agreement.

"Indeed," he said slowly. "It wasn't Cullen's folly alone, to be sure, and we have other matters to attend to. Talo's death leaves the Laorin in a precarious position. It grieves me that we can't afford the time to mourn, much less retrieve his body for the Giving Grounds, but if we can no longer expect assistance from the valley towns then we have a great many things to consider."

"What options are left to us, if we can no longer rely on aid from the towns?" the bent elder sitting behind Jofrey asked in a frail, soft voice. "Our stores are limited, we have no High Priest, and we haven't the numbers to defeat the Kayle on our own."

"No High Priest?" Cullen Brern demanded incredulously, sounding almost angry. "Jofrey was left with the mantle by Talo himself. Jofrey is our High Priest."

Raz watched Jofrey look suddenly uncomfortable but—before the man could say anything either way—Valaria Petrük leapt to her feet to his left.

"Jofrey was cast as *interim* High Priest until Talo's return," she said haughtily. "He was never given the mantle officially. It is the responsibility of the council, therefore—"

"To vote in Talo's successor," the younger man Raz was nearly positive now had to be Cullen Brern's younger brother drawled sarcastically from over Jofrey's right shoulder. "Aye, we know, Petrük. And—as I agree with Cullen that we don't have time to waste on frivolous matters—I'll take the shortest route to ensuring your poisonous tongue doesn't fill a second more than needs be. Esteemed members of the council—" he said this with a dramatic roll of his eyes "—cast if you are *not* in favor of Jofrey retaining the High Priest's mantle."

Petrük glowered at the Priest, but raised her hand at once. After a moment's hesitation, Behn Argo followed suit.

There was an ugly pause as every eye in the room fell on them, waiting, not a single other motion breaking the stillness of the chamber. After several seconds the man who'd called for the vote chuckled, reaching an arm down to clasp Jofrey on the shoulder.

"Congratulations are in order, High Priest al'Sen."

Jofrey's face was flushed—though not quite to the extent of Petrük's, who was sitting down in seething silence once again—and he patted the man's hand.

"Thank you, Kallet," he said with a strained smile. "I hardly think we can call that a fair vote, though. I imagine Talo would have liked Carro to take his place if—"

"*No.*"

Every face in the room turned to Carro, who had almost shouted the word, and Raz watched as the Priest's face grew suddenly sickly, like the implications of becoming High Priest did nothing short of terrorize him.

Jofrey frowned, looking surprised. "The only reason *I* was asked to oversee the Citadel in Talo's absence was because you were leaving with him, Carro. I know he would tell you the same thing, if he were here…"

Carro turned sad at the man's words, but Raz noticed something else in his bearing as he stood over him on the dais. The hand of Carro's broken arm was clenched into a hard fist, half-hidden in its sling, and the one grasping his staff before him was gripped so tight that the steel was starting to shake against the black stone at his feet

Why is he angry? Raz wondered, perplexed at what about taking on the High Priest's mantle could possibly have thrown Carro al'Dor—the calm, level-headed right hand of Talo Brahnt—into such a quiet ire.

Eventually, whatever had taken hold of Carro passed, and he calmed.

"I have no interest in being High Priest, Jofrey," he said evenly. "Not now, not ever. I would appreciate it if you accepted the mantle, and allow us to move on."

Jofrey, too, Raz saw, seemed to have noticed Carro's momentary change. He was watching his old friend with genuine worry now.

Still, after a time, he nodded.

Carro sighed, and the last of the tension left him as the rest of the council—with the exception of Petrük and Argo—either exclaimed their enthusiasm and support or else reached out to extend Jofrey their compliments and felicitations. Jofrey, though, raised a hand for silence.

It fell at once, all eyes on the new High Priest of Cyurgi' Di.

"My thanks, all," he said in a tired voice. "We will revisit this, in time, but for the moment the Kayle knocks on our door and we've minimal means by which to defend our home. As things are, we are only condemning ourselves and every inhabitant of the Citadel to a slow demise if we do not devise a way to deal with Gûlraht Baoill."

"Baoill isn't at the pass," Cullen Brern said, shifting his weight more comfortably against the dark stone beneath him. "Not yet, at least."

Jofrey frowned and—to Raz's surprise—looked right at him. "So we've heard. You're certain of this? There are no more than a thousand men in the encampment you saw?"

Raz nodded at once, taking the opportunity to make himself of value. "At most, though I can't speak to if they are expecting reinforcements. If you're thinking of launching a counter-assault, I would highly recommend you do so soon, before—"

"A 'counter-assault?'" Behn Argo raised his voice scornfully, staring down his nose at Raz. "What do you take us for, lizard? Some sort of military outpost?"

Raz saw Carro bristle and turn to face the man out of the corner of his eye, but he reached a clawed hand up to stop him, grabbing him gently on his arm.

"Your infantile attempt to goad me aside, Priest," Raz said coolly, narrowing his eyes at Argo in the seat above, "I have no delusions as to the purpose and mission of your faith. Despite the poor example you seem intent on setting, I have seen the good this faith attempts with my own eyes, have witnessed the warmth and hope you spread. No, I don't take you for any kind of army or war-band or anything of the sort, but I think you would be foolish to discount that there are warriors among you, given your situation." He gestured at the form of Reyn Hartlet on the stone beside a—for once—quiet Dolt Avonair. "The only mistake your man made last night was picking a fight with *me*. I've spent the better part of the last decade of my life with a sword in hand, and have been in the company of Priests for long enough now to be familiar with the magics and skills you possess. The mountain men are battleworn and blooded, I'll grant you that, but they are also overconfident, ignorant, and superstitious, characteristics I have witnessed with my own eyes. They may have you under siege, may have claimed control of your only way on or off this mountain, but you still have advantages you could press. If you play the game right you could break the control they have on the mountain path and make for the relative shelter of the Woods."

"But how would we manage that, without killing?" the man Jofrey had called Kallet asked warily. "Because we of the faith are honor bound not to—"

"Not to take a life," Carro interrupted in an impatient huff. "Yes, yes, he knows. I've drilled it into him enough at this point."

"Then the beast is telling us to abandon our home!" Petrük voiced in disdain. "As if we would leave the High Citadel to the violations of tribal cretins like the Kayle and his men."

"The *beast*," Raz told her in an angry hiss, enunciating the word so the woman might know the line she was toeing, "is demanding nothing of you, nor suggesting that anyone should be ready to cast their vows aside. He is merely attempting to enlighten you on your options: relinquish your halls and fight for a chance at freedom and life, or stay and die a slow, stubborn death of starvation until you're all too weak to stop Baoill from marching right through the front gate and finishing the job at his leisure."

There was a long, leaden pause after Raz's words as everyone gaped at him. Even Petrük and Argo looked shaken, as though the ultimatum he had just presented was putting things into perspective all too painfully.

Eventually, Carro coughed and broke the silence.

"What does Syrah think of all of this?" he asked, looking to Jofrey. "I'm surprised she isn't here. Was no one able to find her?"

The effect his words had was immediate and terrible.

Like some invisible executioner's ax that had been hovering over the group was suddenly falling, the council seemed to shrink into themselves as one, drawing away from Carro's question as though they could keep it from reaching them. In an instant the seed of fear that had wedged itself in Raz's heart took root, and his eyes snapped to Jofrey.

The High Priest was staring up at Carro, mouth open and face white, and this time it was *he* who seemed unable to get the words out.

"What happened?" Raz demanded, rising to his feet like a boiling, furious storm, towering over them all. "Where is Syrah?"

Jofrey's blue eyes shifted to his. There was no fear there, as most men's eyes might have held if the Monster of Karth descended on them, horrible in his need to have his questions answered. Instead, there was only pain.

Pain, and unbearable, immeasurable sadness.

"Where is she?" Raz asked again, his voice rising rapidly. "Where. Is. *Syrah?*"

Still, though, Jofrey seemed unable to formulate a response.

It was Cullen Brern, in the end, who answered.

"Syrah Brahnt was killed at the base of the mountain path," the master-at-arms said softly while Raz whirled on him. "It was nearly two weeks past, now. She was part of a delegation, a group of Priests and Priestesses who went to seek terms from the mountain men." Brern swallowed painfully, but looked up to meet Raz's burning gaze. "I'm sorry. I wanted to tell you on the path, but..."

As the man's words trailed away, Raz recalled suddenly the odd hesitation the Priest had displayed during their conversation in the sheltering alcove. He had thought at the time it had to do with Reyn Hartlet's attack.

He understood, now, that that was not the case.

"How do you know?"

It was Carro who voiced the question, and Raz turned to see the man staring at Cullen Brern with livid intensity, body rigid, face tense and strained.

Brern blinked, surprised at the question. "What do you—?"

"*How do you know?*" Carro roared. "Did you see her? Did you see her body?"

Brern's features became suddenly ashen. "They sent up the heads of the delegation. They brought them to the gates, before we'd cast the wards. We couldn't even recognize some of them..."

An image, vivid and horrible, flashed across Raz's mind. A basket, bloody and frosted with snow, whose contents were hidden from view. He refused to look over the edge of it, refused to peer inside, but all the same he couldn't help but stare at the thing, taking it in with terrible fascination.

Especially the strands of white hair that tumbled out between the wicker weaving, fluttering over the ground, sad and limp in death.

Suddenly, for the first time in what seemed like years, Raz felt himself start to lose control.

"Syrah wasn't with them."

For a long moment Raz wasn't sure he had actually heard Jofrey speak the words. It seemed that they were part of some far-off dream, some fantasy. As he looked to the man, though, he saw that the newly appointed High Priest was gazing up at him intently, almost desperately.

"Wh-what do you mean?" Carro croaked, staring at Jofrey as well.

The High Priest hesitated, and Raz noted that most of the other council members were averting their eyes from him, clearly uncomfortable with his admission.

"Syrah's head," he said at last. "It wasn't among the others. They sent every single one, except hers. I don't—" He paused, looking pained.

When he spoke again, it was with confused, hopeful terror.

"I don't think she's dead."

The revelation of his words rocked Raz like a tidal wave, cracking his consciousness further as his mind ripped something else from his memory. The Woods. The light of fires and the sounds of men. The maddening, nerve-racking route they had taken along the outskirts of the camp.

The cruel decision they had been forced to make, there beneath the icy blue-green canopy of the Arocklen.

Slowly Raz turned, seeking Carro's eyes. He wondered if the man was thinking the same thing, wondered if the Priest was putting the same pieces together he was, forming an identical, horrifying picture.

The aged man's stricken, petrified stare, told him he was.

"Jofrey is the only one who continues to suffer from the delusion that Syrah Brahnt hasn't returned to the Lifegiver's embrace," Valaria Petrük chimed in, taking advantage. "If anything, I think it should be grounds to reconsider him as—"

"The woman," Raz hissed, punctuating the Priestess' vain prattling. "The woman from the tent."

Carro's face was bloodless, his eyes wide in horror.

"No..." he whispered. "Laor's mercy... No..."

"We heard her, Carro," Raz said, feeling something terrible start to crawl its way out of the deepest corners of his mind. "We heard her, and we did nothing."

"What are you talking about?" Brern's voice seemed to come from far off, trying to break into their conversation. "What woman?"

Raz ignored him. Before him Carro could do nothing, his sight far off, as though fighting the understanding now crashing down.

"We *left her*, Carro," Raz snarled, feeling the black descend, feeling the rage and fire boil upward. "We left her, and did *nothing*."

"It was a camp slave," the Priest choked out, sounding as though he were trying and failing to convince himself. "It had to—It was a slave!"

"It. Was. *HER!*"

Raz's roar ripped through the room, ringing high and cold against the warmth of the air. As it faded it left only silence, like the words had swallowed all other sound, leaving a ringing heaviness to the place. Raz sensed the tension shift at his back as the council began to fear him once more, his sudden fury palpable even to them.

"Raz...?" Carro began hesitantly, seeing the signs and taking a tentative step closer. "Raz... wait."

But Raz was already fading by the time the Priest spoke the words. The world seemed to twist around him, changing before his very eyes as he remembered the woman's muffled screams, remembered the men's laughter through the leather and canvas.

As he recalled the vile sounds of pleasure, Raz felt the cold rise up to swallow his mind.

His last thought was the final blow of some cruel hammer, shattering the last remnants of his control.

I did nothing.

"Raz...?" Carro started as he saw the change come over his friend, taking a cautious step forward. "Raz... wait."

But it was too late, and as he met the atherian's blank gaze Carro felt a thrill he had never experienced in the man's presence before, even upon their first meeting.

A light seemed to have gone out behind Raz's eyes. Like some spark had been snuffed, the glint of life that made the amber orbs shine with amusement, sadness, merriment, anger, and every other emotion, had suddenly vanished. In its wake something darker had appeared, hungry and pitiless. Raz's eyes, usually so lively and alert, had suddenly taken on an empty, wicked edge, sharp with intelligence but lacking all gleam of ego and being.

They reminded Carro of the eyes of a cliff hawk or falcon, of the great birds of prey that circled in the heavens of the North, keenly seeking the next meal among the leaves and the flowing grasses of the woods and plains.

They were the eyes of a predator.

"Raz...?" Carro tried again, though he found himself unable to brave taking another step further.

"I left her."

The voice chilled Carro to the very bone. It was Raz's voice, but there was a deadness to it, an utter lack of emotion that made it almost monstrous. Combined with the fathomless, empty gaze, the atherian became suddenly more animal than beast, and Carro instinctively prepared a defensive ward in his bad hand, readying the spell.

Instantly, he regretted it.

Behind Raz the Priests and Priestesses scattered about their seats sensed the magic, and it set them immediately on edge. Behn Argo was on his feet in an instant, followed swiftly by Petrük, Elber, and Forn. Most of the group Cullen Brern had led down the mountain followed suit, looking anxious. Even the members of the council who hadn't moved were suddenly tense, exchanging worried glances.

"Carro, what's going on?"

Jofrey's voice seemed to draw Raz's attention before Carro could answer. The atherian's head jerked to the side, ears flaring, and the rest of him turned to follow this leading motion as though in some lumbering trance. Carro watched Raz's hard, cold eyes sweep the room, taking in the council, then Avonair, Reyn Hartlet, and the Priests and Priestesses behind them.

Then they settled on the door at the very top of the room.

"I left her," Raz repeated, taking a step towards Jofrey, though Carro rather thought the man was utterly unaware of the men and women who stood between him and the steps leading upward.

It was Behn Argo who made the first mistake.

Whether or not it was his own life or the High Priest's he feared for would be the matter of much debate in the coming days, but whatever his reasoning, Argo's actions were remembered by all as the spark that lit the fire. With a yell of fear the man drew from the magics and summoned a handful of milky flames into the palm of his left hand, hefting his staff with his right.

In a mirroring cascade, the others followed suit.

"NO!" Carro, Cullen Brern, and Jofrey shouted together, but it was too late. Valaria Petrük was already on her feet, preparing what looked to be a complex warding spell. Old Jerrom's withered hands were suddenly aglow with twin orbs of blinding white light. Benala Forn and old Priest Elber matched each other, hefting staffs in both hands. Young Aster Re'het and Kallet Brern moved together, leaping down from their seats to get between Raz and Jofrey, she with stunning spells in both hands, he with steel filling his.

"No!" Carro heard Jofrey yell again, trying to press through the Priest and Priestess. "Stop this! All of you!"

Jofrey's plea for peace, though, was cut short as Petrük shouted in victory, flinging her completed casting down on Raz, who hadn't looked away from the door. The spell had the shape of a clear sphere while it lanced towards the atherian, like a large ball of swimming, shifting glass, but as it struck the ground beneath his feet it expanded, shimmering as it grew. Raz snarled in sudden anger as the spell swelled around him, swallowing his feet, then his legs, then his torso. He fought the pull of the magic, attempting to throw himself away from it, but the spell held him firm, gripping him like hardening mortar. He screamed in fury one last time as the ward warped and bent itself over his head, and suddenly the sound of his fighting became dampened, as though he were howling through water.

"Valaria!" Carro shouted, whirling on the woman standing above him among the seats. "Release him! Let him go!"

Petrük, however, gave him a cool, demeaning glance.

"*You* brought the animal into our home, al'Dor!" she sneered, smiling victoriously as her hands moved before her, maintaining the spell that encased Raz's twisting, thrashing body. "How are we to know what he's capable of? Even you were preparing yourself for an attack!"

"I was mistaken!" Carro insisted, looking back to Raz and feeling a sudden tightness as he watched the atherian's dark form begin to move faster and faster, lunging and smashing itself against the sides of the magic. "Please! Let him go!"

"Why?" she jeered, clearing enjoying herself. "To let him loose, like some hound of war?"

"Valaria, Syrah is alive! We heard her, as we were moving around the Kayle's camp! He just thinks he can get her back!"

"Delusional," Behn Argo snorted spitefully. "Even if she didn't die with the rest of the group, it's been almost a fortnight. By this time the mountain men would have—"

CRACK!

As one, everybody in the room stiffened in shock at the sound. It was one they knew well, one every consecrated Priest and Priestess had had instilled in them a thousand times over in the practice chambers as they trained and fought.

It was the sound of a breaking ward.

XXXI

All eyes fell on Petrük's spell, fluid and turning about the dark form of Raz i'Syul. The atherian, though, had stilled, calming in his writhing, rabid attempts to free himself of the confines of the magic. He knelt now, indistinct within his shimmering prison, arms above his head.

Indistinct, that is, except for the silvery steel claws of the hands that were forcing their way slowly through the very top of the spell, sending thin, shifting cracks over its surface as it began to fail.

"Impossible," Carro heard someone mutter from behind him.

But whoever had spoken didn't know Raz i'Syul Arro as Carro had come to know him. Any learned Priest would have quickly said that it would take a battering ram to break a detainment ward.

And Carro knew well—thinking of the bloody tales Talo had reluctantly told him of the Azbar Arena—that a battering ram didn't hold a candle to the destructive power of the Monster unleashed.

There was another *crack*, and the whole spell seemed to cave upward slightly, bending under the tremendous pressure of the atherian pushing himself up on powerful legs.

"Valaria, release him!" Carro shouted again, hearing the plea creep into his voice now. "Please! You don't know what you're doing!"

The old woman, though, seemed deaf to his cries. She was staring, pale and frightened, at the breaking spell, clearly numbed by what she was witnessing. The others, too, were silent in their horror.

Fortunately, there was one exception.

"Everyone out!" Jofrey bellowed, pushing himself between Aster and Kallet. "OUT!"

The man's words shook the shock from some of the more strong-willed members of the council. Cullen and Kallet rushed forward with Jofrey towards Raz, though Carro didn't know if they intended on breaking the ward or attempt to strengthen it. Old Elber whirled in the stands above, shouting at the younger Priests and Priestesses behind him to run for help. Even old Jerrom was attempting to struggle to his feet, hands still full of light.

Before anyone could really do anything, though, the magic failed.

BOOM!

The force of the shattering spell went off like a bomb, the built-up energy of the sorcery releasing all at once. Carro caught only a glance of the ward evaporating in a rush of silver and white smoke before the shockwave smashed into him, throwing him backwards like a rag doll to slam into the great brazier at the far end of the dais and send his staff flying. The trough of fire overturned under the force of his heavy body, spilling flames out over the ground as the wind was brutally knocked out of him. He might have broken his back if he hadn't still been holding onto the protective ward that had set everything off in the first place. As it was, he felt a spasm of pain in his left arm, and knew well that whatever healing his body and magics had managed to do to the broken bone over the last two days had just come undone.

All the same, Carro did his best to scramble to his feet, struggling for breath while pushing himself up with his good hand. As he looked up he saw that Jofrey, Kallet, and Cullen were all picking themselves up as well, having been thrown back by the blast. Aster was in a crumpled heap on the stairs, unmoving, one leg at an awkward angle and her face half-covered in blood from a great gash across her forehead. The others, further away from the breaking ward up among the stone benches, seemed to have only been knocked off their feet.

And in their center, towering upward like some hungry titan of flesh and shadow, Raz stood, wings outstretched around him, his scream of fury painful to the ears.

"Laor save us…" Carro breathed, taking in the beast that was all that remained of his friend. It was the first time he had ever seen the Monster in truth. The heavy furs that covered Raz did nothing to hide the lithe, twisting cords of muscle beneath dark scales, nor the terrifying sheen of membrane extending around him like a bloody cloak. For a solid few seconds Carro could only stare at the atherian, experiencing again the primal fear that made him feel like a lame rabbit at the feet of some ravenous wolf.

Then Raz's attention shifted, and Carro's suspended sense of terror broke as he realized the atherian was no longer intent on just the door.

Valaria Petrük shrieked shrilly as the eyes fell on her.

Before Carro could yell a warning, the Monster was moving, little more than a black and red blur streaked with silver steel and brown fur. Even as Carro started forward he saw Raz take the great stone seats two at a time, rushing Petrük with the still confidence of a hunter descending on easy prey.

Fortunately for the councilwoman, neither she nor Behn Argo, standing beside her, were actually that easy to kill.

Whereas Reyn Hartlet's single defensive spell had done little more than slow Raz down the night before, the combined sorcery of the man and woman—thrown up instinctively more than anything—did much better. The magics layered to form a thin, shimmering wall between them and the atherian, and Raz—with no time to slow down in his headlong rush—smashed into it with the force of a falling tree. The ward held, and the man ricocheted sideways off it, thrown away with a sizzle of burning fur. As a dozen voices began to shout in fear and anger, Carro adding his to the mix, Raz tumbled down to the base of the consecration room once again. He was on his feet in a blink, though, snarling as he rolled and rose, amber eyes taking in the chamber and the men and women standing above him in quick, calculated flicks.

This time they settled on the door again, and Raz moved like lightning up the stone once more.

"Let him go!" Carro heard himself screaming, and he thought he made out Jofrey and Cullen echoing the command from off to his right. "Let him go!"

Whether the words were lost to the shouts and cracking of summoned magic, or just ignored by a group of men and women frightened beyond rational thought, he didn't know. Whatever the reason, the faithful moved as one to close in on Raz, like they were penning in a cornered animal.

And like any cornered animal, the Monster became vicious in his desperation to escape.

The first to go down was the Priest Loric, part of Brern's entourage, who had seated himself at the edge of the stairs. He leapt up directly in Raz's path, intent on preventing the atherian from getting away. He howled his own battlecry as he flung paired stunning spells at the dark form barreling upward towards him, throwing them with calm, practiced efficiency.

Skill and talent only went so far, though, when facing off against the Raz i'Syul Arro.

The atherian dodged both spells with ease, ducking under one and leaping clear over the other. As Loric's face slipped from warrior's confidence into stunned fear, the man was on him. In a quick succession of moves the Priest was doubled over by a punch to the stomach, then knocked cold by a hard, chopping blow to the back of the head. He fell forward, unconscious down the stairs, coming to rest half atop the form of Aster Re'het, still sprawled on the steps.

The next pair, armed with staffs, did only slightly better. The Priest and Priestess, whose names Carro didn't know, moved from either side of the room, trying to take Raz in a well-timed pincer. The man yelled and pelted the atherian with a trio of flickering fire strikes, the white flames hissing through the air. Raz turned towards him in time to dodge these spells as well, dipping and weaving beneath the first two, then half-spinning, half-flipping under the third.

This final moved landed him right in front of the woman, coming from the other side, and she shouted triumphantly as she brought the full weight of her staff down on Raz's head.

Had she stayed silent, she might just have been the first person to ever take the Monster of Karth by surprise.

Instead, Raz reacted instinctively to her yell, twisting as he brought an arm above his head defensively. The staff collided with the bracer of his gauntlet with a crash, and the woman had barely enough time to register a gasp of shock before the atherian's hand shifted to rip the steel out of her grasp. Raz, armed with something of a familiar weapon now, moved like water, his movements ingrained in his body. One end of the staff came around to smash into the side of the woman's left knee, rousing a horrible howl of pain. It was cut short, though, as the other end whipped around to ram her full in the body, just below the center of her chest.

Had the staff been Ahna, the Priestess would have lost a leg moments before being run through by the dviassegai's wicked blades. As it was, the woman fell back with a pained inhalation as all the air rushed agonizingly from her lungs, the muscles of her chest momentarily paralyzed by the shock of the blow. Even as she crumpled, though, Raz was turning, the woman's staff moving like silk in his hands. The man who had caught his attention first was still charging him, joined now by two more, one on either side. Carro watched in horrified anticipation as the atherian's body tensed, his legs coiling beneath him, the supple body of a snake set to strike. He thought to shout out, thought to scream a warning at the trio so foolishly rushing into a fight they had no prayer of winning.

Then, seemingly out of nowhere, a line of light slashed across his vision, cutting through the air with the crackling buzz of angry magic. Like a whip the goldish-white stroke of thin fire slithered out, wrapping around Raz's right arm just as he started to pounce. The atherian roared as the spell pulled him down and sideways, throwing him off balance. His golden eyes shifted, seeking out the offending spellcaster.

They settled, cold and hungry, on the thin form of old Jerrom Eyr, shaking and frail on the steps below. The wizened Priest looked to be struggling mightily, all his limited strength having gone into first transforming the light he had been holding into the lash of fire, and now restraining just one of the atherian's arms. Raz, it looked like, was realizing this quickly, because even as Carro watched the Monster gave the magic a testing pull, forcing Jerrom to take a shaky step forward.

Before the atherian could do anything more, though, there was a flash, and another sizzle of boiling air.

The second lash, bright and white, slashed upwards from the left to snake around Raz's other arm. Carro turned in time to watch Behn Argo strain to hold onto the magic, his face going red under the effort when Raz roared in fury, pulling at this new restraint. Another flash, though, and a third tether joined the melee, Benala Forn's magic wrapping around the howling Monster's neck like a noose even as he screamed louder.

A fourth. A fifth. A sixth.

Within five seconds, Raz i'Syul was trapped in no less than a half-dozen magical snares, one around his throat, one around each leg, one around his left arm, and two around his right. It seemed, though, that the spells did little more than immobilize the man, the thin flames already starting to fail in places as Raz threw himself about, thrashing and straining against the bonds, snarling like a rabid beast.

"Someone PUT HIM *DOWN*!" old Elber yelled from up in the seats, straining with Jerrom to control Raz's right arm. "PUT HIM DOWN! BEFORE HE GETS LOOSE!"

Even Carro didn't find it in himself to argue, now. Aster and Loric were sprawled out at the bottom of the stairs before him, feet away from the cracked stone that bordered the crater from which the blasting magic of the failing ward had emanated. Above them, the unnamed Priestess had found her breath again, and was now using it to screech in agony as she rolled around, clutching what looked to be a shattered knee.

Madness, Carro thought in unbelieving sadness, his eyes falling on Raz again, watching him fight his bonds and remembering something Talo had once told him. *A taste of madness…*

Carro himself thought he could sense a hint of it in his own thoughts, thinking of the ravages he and Raz had left Syrah to at the hands of the Kayle's men.

Abruptly there was a blinding bloom of light, and Carro was forced to raise his good hand to cover his eyes as they burned and watered. It took a moment, but eventually he was able to peer through the glare to see Jofrey standing at the base of the stairs, hands moving before him as the High Priest summoned and pooled his magic. A great orb of shifting, swimming white built up in the space between his palms, growing and expanding outward as Jofrey crafted the spell. It took several short seconds—a testament to the man's skill with the gifts Laor had granted him—but when the sphere of combined stunning spells was about his chest-width across, Jofrey didn't so much as hesitate. With both hands he lifted the spell above his head, then flung it with all his might up the stairs.

The magic lanced upwards, over the steps, lashing out bolts of blue electricity at anything that got within a few feet. Like a lightning storm condense it boiled and raged as it flew, the air around it reverberating with pulsing power. Raz saw it coming, saw the end it spelled to his rage. He roared again, redoubling his fight against the bonds of flames. Valaria Petrük screamed as her lash broke, freeing his right leg. Jerrom's was next, and above him Elber cursed as he suddenly became the only one fighting Raz's right arm.

Before the atherian could completely free himself, though, Jofrey's magic struck him full in the chest.

Raz's scream of fury in his last moments of consciousness was cut abruptly short as the spell collided with him. The remaining four lashes all broke together, overloaded by the power of Jofrey's casting. Untethered, Raz's body was lifted clear off the ground, careening up the steps, his long arms and great wings trailing behind him like the grotesque tail of some bright comet.

He only stopped when the spell carried him all the way to the top of the stairs, smashing him into the heavy door of the room itself.

Meeting a solid object, Jofrey's shock spell finally dissipated. For several heartbeats Raz half-stood, propped up with his back against the wood, the carved portraits and scenes around him charred and blackened by the residual discharge of the magic.

Then he fell to his knees, and it was only a moment before he collapsed face first to the stone floor in a heap of dark limbs, brown fur, and red wings.

For a long time no one spoke. There was no shout of triumph, no call of victory. Even Petrük and Argo were silent in their fear, eyes fixed on Raz's still form. It was quiet, save for the groans of Priest Loric as he came to, and the continued pained wails of the Priestess up in the seats.

"Lifegiver's fat *fucking* arse," Kallet Brern finally managed to get out, and the world took life once more.

"Valaria, Behn, Jerrom," Jofrey shouted in a commanding voice, already moving up the stairs. "You three see to Loric and Grees. Kallet and Benala, get Aster and Reyn to the infirmary. Tell the healers the truth. No use in trying to keep this under wrap now."

Carro had to agree, looking around. While the members of the council were moving as quickly as they could to do as their new High Priest ordered, the other Priests and Priestesses in the room were standing rock still, eyes wide and mouths hanging open. Each and every one was staring without fail up the stairs, mesmerized by Raz i'Syul's prone form.

The story would be told and retold a hundred times before the evening meal, Carro knew.

"Carro!" Jofrey yelled from the top of the steps. "Cullen! With me!"

Carro jumped, shaking himself free of the residual shock of what he had just witnessed. Pausing only to retrieve his staff—and hissing as his re-broken arm shifted in its sling—he fell in quickly behind Cullen Brern, hurrying up the stairs.

They found Jofrey standing over Raz's prone form, staring down at the atherian, face pale.

"Could someone please explain to me," he said in a half-furious, half-desperate voice, "what in the *Lifegiver's name* just happened?"

Carro swallowed painfully as he felt Cullen's eyes move to him. Taking the hint, Jofrey's mimicked the motion, piercing Carro's with confused anger.

"Carro?" he pressed firmly.

For a moment, Carro could say nothing. He stood there, staring at his new High Priest, left arm throbbing against his chest, right hand shaking at his side.

This was going to be harder than telling them about Talo, he realized suddenly.

After a few seconds—and all the limited patience Jofrey seemed to have left—Carro opened his mouth. Slowly, painstakingly, he told the two men standing on either side of him of the horrors he suspected he and Raz had abandoned Syrah to, down there at the bottom of the pass, in the shadows of the snow and trees…

XXXII

"There is no shame in defeat, so long as the battle lost was one worth fighting…"

—Jarden Arro, Champion of the Arro clan

Raz woke to pain the likes of which he had only rarely experienced. It consumed him completely, an angry, bone-deep ache, like every inch of his body had been pummeled and kicked by a hundred men wearing armored boots. He groaned as he rolled onto one side, trying to get his bearings and figure out where he was.

As he did, he felt the unfamiliar touch of cold granite against his scaled skin.

Raz jolted up instinctively. He regretted the motion at once, feeling the aches intensify and wash through his body in one nauseating wave. It reminded him on the one hand of his first weeks training with Ahna, echoing the constant tenderness of brutalized muscles, and on the other of the time—some months back now—when a crossbow bolt had taken him through the side.

Neither were particularly fond memories.

Raz pushed the pain aside, forcing it out of his mind to make room for greater concerns. Chief among these: he was naked, or at least very much felt so. He had been stripped of every piece of his armor and weaponry, left bare save for the long pants he had taken to wearing under steel in order to add an extra layer of buffer between his already-cool skin and the bite of the Northern freeze. He couldn't remember the last time he hadn't been within arm's reach *some* part of his gear, usually Ahna, or his gladius at the very least. He felt, for half a moment, utterly helpless.

Then he decided he didn't like that feeling either, and shoved it aside as well.

He was in a cell of a sort, Raz realized as he looked around. He'd been laid out carefully on the flat stone "bed" carved into the back wall of a moderately sized room, the entire space about five paces wide by eight long. It might have been more spacious than he was giving it credit for, but most of the floor was taken up by a half-dozen tall, layered shelves, line up on either side of a narrow path that led to the room's reinforced timber and iron door, stacked high with any number of foodstuffs. Potatoes seemed to take up most of the space, piled wherever they fit, but there were roots, dried berries and other fruits, grains, spices, flasks of wine and ales, and a stack of barrels between the shelves on the left wall that had the distinct smell of salted meats.

Raz chuckled to himself, momentarily amused that the Laorin had so little use for their dungeons that the Citadel could afford to turns its cells into larders. Then he remembered *why* he had been thrown into this place, and all amusement fled, swallowed by the pit that ripped open in his stomach.

Syrah.

He had left her. He had left her to her suffering, to the savage treatment of Gûlraht Baoill's men and all their horrid pleasures. He had been so close to her for a moment, been practically within arm's reach. He had heard her, though the memory of her pained cries brought no pleasure to him. His gladius had been *in his hana*, half drawn and all too ready to spill the blood of the men taking their liberties in that tent.

But he'd sheathed the blade, and left her.

Abruptly, the rage returned. Raz felt his heart start to beat faster, thudding in his chest as a fire sprung up within him. His breath began to draw itself in in ragged, burning heaves. He barely noticed his clawed hands ball into massive fists, nor the twitching, threatening rise of his neck crest, flaring for no one in particular.

When the anger reached a boiling point, Raz opened his mouth and screamed.

He screamed and screamed, howling out in thundering, shattering roars filled with grief and fury. When the fire didn't die within him, Raz threw himself at the nearest of the shelves, shattering the wood with a single colossal blow, ignoring the pain that lanced through his unarmed fist and hand as splinters and potatoes and carrots and all manner of other fare tumbled through the air around him. Before the mess even had a chance to settle Raz had moved to the next shelf, crushing the horizontal slats with a heavy two-handed blow.

For another three or four minutes Raz allowed the Monster to rage once more, barely keeping a leash on the animal. He rampaged around the cell, unchecked and half-mad as he drowned in the emotions spilling out from within.

I left her, was the only thing his mind allowed itself to register. *I left her.*

By the time he had run the madness out, Raz had turned the larder-made-cell into little more than the aftermath of an earthquake. Not a single shelf remained standing, their fractured and broken remnants scattered about the ground like the bones of long dead enemies. Their broken forms mixed in with the mess, strewn up in the chaos, the potatoes and roots coming to rest in the grooves and cracks of the slate floor, the grains and other dry stuffs soaking in the wetness of spilled wine and spirits.

And in the center of it all, flat on his knees as he stared at the cuts and bruises of his hands, Raz sat defeated.

I left her.

And he had. He and Carro both.

For a long time Raz gave himself to the wallowing, allowed himself to flounder in that truth, that inconceivable irony. His interest in seeing Syrah again, in discovering what she'd become in the years that separated them, had swelled over the last weeks. Raz realized now that he *needed* to see the woman, needed to witness the one good thing that had risen from the ashes and butchery that were all that was left of his memories of Karth. She was, in so many ways, the only thing left that even remotely connected him to an old, coveted life.

Raz traced the twin scars that ringed both of his wrists, the paler flesh almost bright against the darkness of his otherwise scaled skin. It seemed an eternity since he'd last *really* looked at them, *really* remembered the feeling—that acrid, sickening sensation that never faded, no matter how old he got—of the chains that bound his hands.

And he had left Syrah to that bondage, abandoned the one true gleam of goodness to have risen from his past to those same irons, and renounced her to the horrors that came with them.

Once or twice, Raz tried to convince himself it wasn't actually reality, talking himself—as Carro had tried to—into thinking the woman he had heard was some camp slave, some battlewife taken in the Kayle's march of pillaging and death. For moments at a time he conned himself into experiencing a mixed sense of relief and grief, thinking it much more likely that the tormented woman he had heard had been some commoner, some unfortunate who'd fallen into the hands of the mountain men as they marched.

Every time, though, Raz returned to the truth. Reflecting back, he knew he hadn't heard any other women when they'd first found the camp. He hadn't made out the gossip of cooks, nor the grumbles of discontent washerwomen, nor the shouts of true wives yelling at their men. The contingent Baoill had sent to the pass were nothing but male warriors of the mountain clans. They had been sent ahead, untethered and unencumbered by women and families and all such other distractions in order to make all haste for the Citadel.

And there, they'd found Syrah.

I left her.

Raz continued to stare at the blood dripping from his fingers, smelling the iron scent in the air that swirled to mix with the odd, musky perfume of the smokeless magical candles set into the walls around him.

So what are you going to do about it?

Raz blinked, then grimaced. The question came from a different part of his soul than the softer, fragile portion that was allowing him to be so submerged in the desperate sadness of the situation. It was a colder, harder part, one honed by tragedy and a hard life.

And it was much, *much* stronger.

Raz felt himself lifted up and out of his melancholy slowly, steadily. It took him a long minute, but eventually he got to his feet, letting his hands fall to his sides as he gave his wings a shake to free them of the dust and splinters that had settled within their folds as he had taken his revenge on the room. Eventually a smile, unyielding and wicked, began to play at his mouth. Slowly it spread, bringing with it an odd, corrupt tingle of pleasure as Raz realized what it was that he was going to 'do about it.' It wasn't an elaborate answer. It was a brutal, bloody solution that took a simple, uncomplicated path, one that Raz had enacted too many times in his life already.

But for the first time, Raz thought he would rather enjoy showing the mountain men of the western ranges what *true* savagery looked like.

First, though, he thought, looking around himself before eyeing the chamber's single heavy door, *how to get out of this damn room…*

"Syrah Brahnt is *deaa,* you old fool!" Valaria Petrük was saying with a dismissive sneer, eyes on Carro. "And if she's not, then it's no mercy. Perhaps Laor is punishing her for fraternizing with practicers of untruths and worshipers of fraudulent divinities!"

Not for the first time in his life—nor indeed for the first time that morning—Carro had the abrupt and devouring urge to leap across the table and grab the old Priestess by her scrawny, mottled neck, and choke the life right out of her.

He tempered the desire, however, choosing rather to glare at the woman with as much malice as his nature would allow.

"She's *alive*," he said for what had to be the hundredth time in the last hour. "I swear it, and Raz will swear to it as well."

"That *thing?*" Behn Argo scoffed. "Swear to what? To family? To gods? Does it even understand the concept of gods?"

"That's *enough,*" Jofrey said, his voice a dangerous, impatient hiss.

At once, every participant in the argument fell silent.

They were standing in the wide, vaulted space of the great hall, everyone on their feet around the leftmost worn and food-stained table. Those still breaking their fast had been unceremoniously banished and told to finish their meals elsewhere. The benches that usually flanked the table had been slid out of the way, every single member of the council—

with the exception of Jerrom, who had retired to rest after the excitement of the morning—far too agitated to even think of sitting down.

They'd been there for two hours now, arguing themselves in a circle, half the time spent debating whether Syrah Brahnt was indeed alive, and the other half equally divided into disputes on what should be done if she was, what Carro was thinking in allowing a beast like Raz i'Syul Arro into their halls, and what use could be made of the news the pair of them had brought up the path with them.

And in those two hours they hadn't made so much as an inch of progress.

"We have been chasing our own tails long enough," Jofrey continued, the harshness of his tone spelling out all too clearly that his patience was at its end. "This pointless hounding is getting us nowhere. *I* choose to believe that Syrah is alive, and as you were all fool enough to cast me as High Priest, *that* part of this discussion is at an end. As for Arro—" he turned to Carro "—if you say you've never seen the likes of what we witnessed in the consecration room, then I believe you. However, that doesn't change the fact that it happened." He picked up a roll of parchment from the table before him, the letter having been delivered not ten minutes prior by a red-faced acolyte who looked like he had run flat-out from wherever it was he had been sent. "The healers say they had to set Aster's leg, and will be keeping her asleep until they know she hasn't suffered anything worse. Vora Grees is likely to walk with a limp the rest of her life. Bonner Loric has a concussion, broken ribs, and won't be allowed to move his neck for at least a week. And Reyn—"

"Priest Hartlet's injuries are purely of his own doing," Carro said, bristling. "He attacked Raz and I without provocation, going against direct orders, as Cullen has already explained *three times*." He paused just long enough to allow the master-at-arms to nod gravely from where he stood by Jofrey's left shoulder. "As for the rest, Raz was not in his right mind, and even in that state was only defending himself, and doing so with the utmost lenience, if I'm not mistaken."

"And what is that supposed to mean?" Elber asked, crossing his arms over his chest and narrowing his eyes.

"He means that the atherian could have ripped the lot of us to ribbons and then some, if he'd wanted to," Cullen Brern cut in before Carro could answer. "And I'll second that, too. I've seen him move, when Hartlet decided he'd rather preach war than peace. If Arro had wanted Grees or Loric dead, then we'd be scrubbing blood from the stone of the consecration room right now, not arguing amongst ourselves."

"Then the only thing you've proven is that al'Dor has brought a *killer* into our home," Petrük snapped pointedly. "What sort of beast is this 'Arro' if you can so calmly tell us that he would end life so easily?"

"He is a friend," Carro snapped. "Of mine, as he was of Talo's. If we were to shun every man in this world who did not walk the path of Laor's light, then we would be nothing more than sour old hermits bickering amongst ourselves up on our lonely mountain."

"Your 'friend' attacked me!" the old Priestess howled, slapping the table between them with both hands in anger. "With no cause or reason, he *attacked me*."

"While I'm not denying that he went after you, Valaria," Benala Forn said coolly from beside Carro, "it's a little brazen of you to claim that he had no reason. I seem to recall you caging him in a detaining ward before the man had so much as lifted a hand against us."

At that Valaria Petrük flushed and fell silent. Her lapdog, though, was quick to come to her aid.

"It was a preemptive measure," Behn Argo snapped. "The beast was going after our High Priest."

"He was after the *stairs*, you deluded IMBECILE!" Carro roared. "Raz realized—just as I had!—that we had left Syrah behind! We left her, when we had the chance to save her!"

"Syrah Brahnt is d—!" Argo began, but the retort choked off under the withering gaze Jofrey gave him.

Carro forced himself, then, to calm. He took a long moment, feeling the eyes on him. He had already explained to the group what he and Raz had borne witness to, as they snuck past the Kayle's camp, what they had been forced to ignore. There had been a few accusing glares, but most had borne looks of pity, both for the woman and for the hard choice Carro had had to face.

Now, though, he didn't need their pity.

Now, he just needed them to listen.

"Syrah Brahnt is alive," he said slowly, evenly, "and Raz i'Syul Arro is our *only* chance at getting her back."

There was a heavy, dead pause, as the council registered what he meant.

Then everyone started shouting at once.

"Blasphemy!" Behn Argo was hollering. "Blatant blasphemy!"

"Carro, you can't mean...?" Cullen began, but let the question hang.

"Madness," Kallet Brern and Benala Forn could be heard echoing each other.

It was just as Petrük opened her mouth, obviously all too ready to make sure she got *her* quip in, that Jofrey held up a hand for silence.

Once more, all talk ceased immediately.

"Carro," Jofrey started slowly, his voice kinder now as he looked upon his friend, "I understand what you are suggesting. I even understand *why* you are suggesting it. I can't begin to claim that Syrah means as much to me as she does to you, but I hope you know that she still means much to me and more. Despite that… releasing that man seems not only a gamble to me, but a clear breaching of our cardinal laws."

"He might not—" Carro started, hearing the desperation in his voice, but Jofrey cut him off.

"He *will*. He *will* kill, Carro. Of this I have no doubt. I'm still unconvinced that Arro is completely either the friend you claim he is *or* the animal he has proven himself capable of being, but of this I am certain. Beyond that… I think you are too."

At that, Carro stood silently, possessing no response. All he could feel was the crushing weight of the options laid out before him, just as he had felt when Raz had given him the choice to turn his back on the Citadel or accept the cost of climbing the mountain.

Lives will be lost, he realized once again, *no matter which path we take.*

"By leaving her down there, you are sentencing her to death." He met Jofrey's eyes evenly as he spoke. "You realize that, don't you?"

He expected the question to take some toll on the man, to exact some effect on him. All he saw, though, was a resigned sadness steal across the High Priest's face, subtle as the shifting of snow.

"Most likely," Jofrey said. "But I hold out hope. I've been going through every manuscript in the library that might give us an opportunity to negotiate with the Kayle, or at least whoever holds command at the bottom of the pass. There may be something they want more than Syrah."

"There won't be," Carro said, desperately now. "It's very possible Gûlraht Baoill is after her specifically."

Jofrey nodded. "I thought the same. She was the key in the leap forward Emreht Grahst took for the Sigûrth."

"Or the door that slammed shut on centuries of tradition, depending on how you look at it. The Kayle won't want anything more than Syrah, Jofrey…"

The High Priest nodded again. "I know, but I still hold out hope."

Carro felt his patience wear again.

"Raz could save her," he insisted. *"Trust me.* Let me go with him. I'll make sure he doesn't—"

"You'll do nothing," Jofrey said firmly, making it clear that this conversation, too, was one he would see end. "At the *very least* the atherian seems nothing more than unpredictable and uncontrollable. Until he proves himself otherwise, he will *stay where he is.*"

His face softened once again, falling as though pulled down by the exhaustion Carro now suddenly saw mixing with sadness there. "I'm sorry, Carro," Jofrey said quietly. "I will continue to search for another way, but as of now Arro stays put. I won't allow the discarding of our laws for the sake of one life. We took the vow. If death is the price we pay for holding true in the reverence of Laor's light, then it is a coin we must all be willing to produce when the time comes."

"But this isn't *our* life," Carro insisted angrily. "This isn't *our* decision. If Syrah were here—!"

"If Syrah were here, I have absolutely no doubt she would be standing by my side, echoing my words!" Jofrey responded just as fervently. "I'm surprised at you, Carro. To think you would have any other notion of what Syrah would wish concerns me. If you ever knew her at all then there should be no question as to what she would tell you to do in this situation."

He paused, the look he gave Carro now a strange mix of suspicion and concern.

It was the look of a friend suddenly realizing something wasn't right.

"What happened?" he asked slowly. "Carro... What happened?"

Carro—only a moment ago all too ready to smash aside the idea that Syrah would so casually nod her life away—felt himself go suddenly cold. He had the strangest sensation, like all heat were being stripped from his body, as he felt the blood go from his face. Unbidden, the hand slung across his chest began to quiver slightly, and he was thankful his fingers were mostly hidden within the cloth.

He didn't think he would have had the strength to worry about hiding their shake *and* fight the rush of horrible images that were clambering up to the forefront of his thoughts.

Talo. The bear. The tree. The blood.

Raz's sword, poised over the heart of the man he loved more than anything in the world.

Unable to handle the crushing wave of grief that ripped upward through him, Carro straightened up. Shaking bodily now, he reached down and lifted the staff from where it lay propped against the table.

Then he turned from the group, and slowly started making his way between them, heading for the arch of the great hall. He felt as though he were moving against the flow of some crushing river, fighting the current as it pressed back and down on him, redoubling with each new picture as they flashed across his mind.

Talo's broken ribs. His final words. Their last kiss.

And the soul-wrenching, world-shattering sound of the man's dying breath as steel slid home.

Carro barely noticed Behn Argo start to step in front of him, and Jofrey's snapped order of "Let him go!" sounded muted and dull against the thrumming of blood coursing through his ears. He pushed past the shorter Priest, making his way down the table, along the wall and through the archway, then into the relative dimness of the hall beyond.

Only one thought permeated the grief that Jofrey's pointed question had brought surging back. As he saw again the slick redness of Raz's gladius pulling slowly, almost tenderly from Talo's still chest, only one thing broke through the quickly-rising sorrow.

Not Syrah, too.

Jofrey watched his friend go with rising concern. When Behn Argo had made to stop Carro he had stepped in, ordering Argo to stand down. It had been an instinctual decision, one made as a man who shared a little of the wretchedness and despair Carro must be drowning in as Talo's death and Syrah's torment weighed on his shoulders.

Had Jofrey made the decision as High Priest, though, he wasn't so sure he would have been as quick to let Carro leave…

Something was wrong. Something was off. More than Talo's passing. More than Syrah's situation. Much more, surely, than Raz i'Syul Arro's incarceration. Whatever had happened somehow affected the Priest Jofrey had known, diminishing him.

No, not diminishing, Jofrey thought privately as Carro disappeared into the outer hall. *Warping.*

That was more accurate, he decided. Carro al'Dor had left the Citadel one kind of man, but appeared to have returned another. There was something bent now. Not twisted, per se—Carro certainly seemed to *be* there, somewhere buried beneath a layer of grief and sadness—just… off-keel. Unbalanced.

But Jofrey didn't have more than a moment to contemplate what it was that could possibly have unfooted the normally so steadfast Carro al'Dor. As he stood there, looking toward the last place he had seen the retreating back of his friend, Cullen Brern gave a soft cough, bringing the new High Priest back from his distracted thoughts.

It must have been apparent that he had lost his train of thought, because Valaria Petrük smirked and Benala Forn spoke up gently.

"Jofrey…" she said. "The pass … If we assume the Kayle's men are waiting for the rest of the army to arrive, this may be our only chance to act…"

Jofrey set his spectacled eyes at her for a long moment, collecting himself. Once he'd done so, he turned to the master-at-arms.

"Cullen, how many of the faith would you consider competent fighters?"

Cullen Brern frowned. "Two hundred? Maybe three, if we take into account promising acolytes."

"Do so," Jofrey said with a nod. "Every staff will count, if this is a fight we plan on taking down the mountain."

"We're going to attack *them*?" Behn Argo demanded, sounding shocked. "What madness is that?"

"The sanest sort," Jofrey said slowly. "Whatever else he might have done, the atherian was right about one thing: we can't stay in the Citadel. I for one can't see any other way around it. We leave… or we die."

XXXIII

"All men are destined to fall. It is only a matter of fate's interruption, the obstructing factor that is death, that prevents the darkening of the soul within the span of a lifetime. I—in some twisted logic that only a mind as old as mine is capable of conceiving—envy the youth we gave to the Giving Grounds on this day. He was less man than boy, not even twenty years of age, a victim of the perilous footing along the path and the sheer drop of the cliffs. He was a true bastion of the faith, I am told. Pious, humble, kind, giving... Naïve. I envy him that. He did not have time to discover the seeds of doubt, nor witness the ravages they reap as they grow..."

—private journal of Eret Ta'hir

Reyn awoke slowly, blinking away the ache as his eyes adjusted to a sudden, familiar brightness he did not expect to find as he rose from his slumber. He knew that light, knew that wavering, clean glow.

And he knew the familiar sensation of comfortable, humid warmth that surrounded him.

Rapidly Reyn came to, somewhat disoriented as he shoved himself up onto one elbow, intent to make out more of his surroundings. As he did so a jolt of pure, white-hot pain lanced along his left side, extending outward from the edge of his chest to shoot down his leg and up into his neck. He inhaled in shock, falling back down onto what he realized was a thin, feather-stuffed mattress, the blankets bunching up about him as he curled around himself, attempting to stop the agonizing throb.

There was a shout, followed by a hurried exchange of voices, and Reyn saw a number of figures in the white robes of the faith appear at the foot of the bed, moving to either side of him as he continued to groan.

"Easy, Hartlet," a man's familiar voice said gently. "You're going to ruin everything al'Dor managed to do for you if you're not careful."

Slowly, gingerly, Reyn eased himself over onto his back again, eyes shut tight against the shifting pain that tore at him once more with even this simple motion. When he opened them again, three faces were peering down at him, one from the end of the bed and another on either side. He recognized all, two men and one woman. He'd been in the infirmary enough times in his years working in the practice chamber to be on good terms with most of the Citadel's healers, after all.

"Wence," he grumbled, eyeing the man who had spoken, hovering at his feet. "What am I doing here? What happened?"

Priest Wence al'Kars grimaced in a half-amused, half-annoyed sort of way. He was a tall man, thin but paunchy, with a small gut that awkwardly contrasted with the rest of his narrow frame. He kept his long, brown-blond hair loose and wild around his shoulder, and his square jaw clean-shaven. All in all Wence had a gaunt, unsavory look about him, but Reyn knew him to be deceptively good-natured.

And one of the few healers in the Citadel that was better at his craft than Carro al'Dor.

"Apparently you bit off more than you could chew," Wence answered. "According to Kallet Brern and Benala Forn, your little expedition returned home early this morning with guests. al'Dor and some hulking lizard-kind come all the way from the Southern deserts. *You* were apparently trussed up across its horse's saddle. Beats me how in Laor's name it managed to get all the way here without freezing to—"

But Reyn was no longer listening. Wence's words had brought his memory back in a rush. His argument with Cullen Brern. His rush down the mountainside. His encounter with the atherian.

The confused realization, as he lay on the icy stone struggling to breathe, that Carro al'Dor was there, working quickly to save his life...

Reyn winced involuntarily, his left hand moving up his side slowly, looking for the spot where the blazing hot knife had slipped through his ribs. He remembered wanting to die, then, wanting anything that would make that incredible, unending pain stop.

"Don't you even think about it," the short, plump Emalyn Othel snapped from beside the bed, her hand moving like a whip as she closed her fingers around his wrist. "Your stupidity already cost you a punctured lung. I won't let you make it any worse."

"May as well let him do what he wants while he can," broad Vance Molder chuckled from his right. "When Cullen Brern hears he's awake, he's a dead man anyway."

Reyn flushed at that. Clearly the council had heard the whole story, and hadn't spared his healers any details. He felt like a fool, now. At the time he had allowed his rage to control him, hating the unnamed, unknown men below for whatever part they had played in Syrah's taking.

"What happened to Arro?" he asked, wanting to change the subject.

All three of them gave him a bewildered look.

"The atherian," Reyn said, lifting his head from the bed to meet the healer's gaze. "Arro. Isn't that his name?"

"We know who you mean," Wence said, sounding bemused. "But how did *you* know that was his name?"

Reyn sighed, letting his head hit the bed again. Quickly he told them of the mission he, Jofrey, Talo, and Syrah had taken to the Southern fringe cities some years back, attempting to spread Laor's light as far as they could. He couldn't remember the atherian's whole name—Talo had only briefed them briskly on why they had had to leave so soon, and only Jofrey more fully later—but it seemed too much of a coincidence that any *other* lizard-kind might have come across Carro al'Dor in the wilds of the North, not to mention one who spoke the Common Tongue to boot.

After he finished, it was the healers' turn to fill him in. Wence did most of the talking, but only Emalyn thought she remembered the atherian's full name confidently: Raz i'Syul Arro. It had sounded right to Reyn, and he nodded as they continued. They hadn't yet arrived to what had become of the atherian, however, before Vance let slip much more pressing news.

"Talo Brahnt is dead," the man said quietly. "Jofrey al'Sen has been voted in as the new High Priest."

For a solid five seconds Reyn gaped at him, head rolled to one side so he could look up at the healer.

Then he turned back to Wence. "Is it true?"

Wence was frowning at Vance, but he nodded. "Aye, it's true. Though I *prefer* that my patients not be burdened by such tidings whilst recovering."

Vance had the decency to flush with embarrassment, but it turned quickly into a willful glower.

"He was going to find out soon enough anyway," he said with half-a-shrug. "It's not like Cullen Brern wouldn't have told him about Talo, or about Brahnt."

That confused Reyn outright, his uncertainty only magnified as Wence's frown turned suddenly livid, mirroring Emalyn's hiss of anger.

"*Vance!*" she snapped.

Vance shut up at once, looking suddenly mortified.

It was the last straw, for Reyn.

"What?" he demanded, looking around at Wence again. "What's he talking about, 'Talo *and* Brahnt'? What does he mean?"

Wence, in response, only looked at him, almost like he were waiting for something. Reyn stared at him, wondering what was going on.

He was just about to turn to Emalyn and demand *she* explain, though, when it hit him.

"Syrah!" he gasped, and suddenly he was struggling to sit up again, ignoring the pounding pain that raked his left side. "Syrah! What happened? What do you know? Where—?"

"Reyn, stop!" Emalyn yelled, reaching out and trying to push him back down. "*Stop!* You'll only make things worse!"

"Get off me!" Reyn yelled, shoving the woman's arms away. "If Syrah's alive then I need to speak to the council. Get *OFF ME!*"

He could feel himself spinning out of control again, but he didn't care. Even when Vance's arms reached out to help Emalyn try to keep him down Reyn only yelled and fought harder. He was bigger, stronger than them, and they found themselves quickly hard-pressed to keep him on the bed.

Woosh.

There was a flash, and suddenly Reyn felt himself wrenched back, slammed down into the mattress. Like invisible iron hands had materialized out of the air, something was pinning him down, pushing through his shoulders and thighs and pressing his wrists into the bed. Reyn roared, attempting to thrash his way free of the magic, trying to writhe himself out from under the spell.

"Calm *down*, Hartlet!" Wence yelled, and Reyn saw that it was he who was holding the spell in place, one hand extended over the bed like he were controlling a many-stringed puppet. "Calm down! When you're ready, I'll release you, but you need to *stop* trying to get up. If you break off a piece of rib there's no telling what could happen!"

For almost a minute more, though, Reyn strained his considerable bulk against the spell, yelling and cursing at all three of them and continuing to demand where Syrah was, if she was alive, and what had happened to her. He fought and thrashed, feeling the mattress shift under him and stick to the skin of his back as it became slowly dampened by sweat. He howled and screamed, only barely noticing Wence shooing away healers and patients alike as they rushed over, the former to see if they could help, the latter just curious as to who was causing the commotion.

In the end, though, his recovering body exhausted quickly, and before long Reyn stilled again, forcing himself to calm, breathing hard and feeling his muscles wince and quiver involuntarily, unwilling to bear the strain and the pain in his side.

"Where—Where is she?" he said in a voice of forced calm, speaking between heavy breaths. "Where—is she—Wence?"

The healer didn't answer at once. For several seconds more he held the spell firm, watching with a careful eye as though suspecting Reyn were faking this sudden subdual.

Eventually, though, he let his hand fall, and Reyn felt the magic release him all at once, the arcane fingers slipping off his skin.

"We don't know," Wence said gently. "I'm sorry. The rumors reached us about midday. I don't want to give you false ho—"

"Tell me," Reyn snapped, looking up at him, though being careful not to make any sudden moves lest he be restrained again. *"Tell me."*

Wence, once again, hesitated. It was only after a small, encouraging nod from Emalyn, in fact, that he finally spoke.

"The word seems to be that al'Dor and the atherian—Arro, or whatever his name is—claim that Syrah is still alive. When they realized it, in fact, Arro apparently went insane. Tried to kill half the council, they say."

"Kill the—?" Reyn started, surprised by this. "Why? Why would Arro attack the council?"

"We're not sure," Emalyn said quietly. "There's a rumor that he was sent here by the Kayle to assassinate the High Priest Brahnt's replacement, and another that he's just some wild animal Brahnt and al'Dor freed from the Arena in Azbar while they were down there. I don't believe either of them, but it doesn't help that al'Dor won't speak to anyone. He's locked himself in his chambers and won't answer the door. Most of the council tried. I didn't even think he opened for Jofrey…"

She looked suddenly nervous, glancing at Wence before continuing. "We overheard a few of Cullen Brern's students talking, though, ones that were in your group on the pass. They stopped in to see how you and the others were doing."

"You weren't the only one Arro managed to take a chunk out of, in the end," Vance cut in eagerly, obviously attempting to rectify his earlier slip up. "Loric has enough broken ribs to match yours, and Grees is in worse shape than either of… of…"

He trailed off slowly, quailing under the look Wence gave him.

"As Emalyn was saying," Wence told Reyn, though his eyes didn't leave Vance for several moments. "We overhead talk that the atherian was actually trying to *leave* when the council stopped him."

"Leave?" Reyn asked, annoyed by his own confusion. "Why would he be trying to leave?"

For what seemed like the hundredth time, the healers paused, exchanging dark looks. Reyn was about to insist again when Wence finally answered.

"Apparently… he may have been trying to go back for Syrah."

For a long time after that, Reyn could only stare at the healer standing at the end of his bed, his head still wrenched up at an awkward angle. He wanted to scream again, wanted to shout, to howl and demand why *in fuck's sake* the council would want to *stop* a beast like the atherian attempting to save one of their own. He wanted to scramble up again, to shove past the three standing around him now like a guard, to hunt down his former Priest-Mentor and shake him until Jofrey explained himself.

But there was no need. After all, it wasn't hard to guess why the council would have strived to stop someone like Raz i'Syul Arro from leaving their sight. Reyn didn't know much about the atherian. He had not met him, some six or seven years ago now, back then in the dusty heat of the South. He knew only what he had learned in their ten seconds of brief, eye-opening combat, of which he had certainly come out the worse for wear.

Mostly, he suspected, because of the deadly, savage edge of murderous instinct he had seen in Arro's eyes, half-a-moment before the creature's kick had crushed his side in and sent him flying over the roughened stone.

There was a ruthlessness there, a hungry, unsettled coldness in that look that Reyn knew suddenly he would never be able to mirror.

It was the will of a killer.

Reyn couldn't even *begin* to guess as to why the atherian would bother with saving Syrah. He didn't think they could have formed much of a bond during their brief encounter in the South, nor did he think it was Arro who owed Syrah, rather than the other way around. But if the atherian *had* been intending to make down the mountain again and attempt to save her, Reyn understood all too well why the council had tried to stop him.

It was in this state of numb, hopeless shock that Wence and the others left him, giving Reyn his privacy. He would appreciate this later, though barely so much as noticed at the time. For longer than he knew, Reyn did nothing but lay on his back, staring at the greyish hue of the ceiling, cast in the white and blue light of the Citadel candles. The shadows moved across the mortared shale, reminding him of those that used to dance across the wall of his darkened room, cast from the single line of brightness that was the bottom lip of his doorframe. He thought of them now because he had only ever started to watch them after he'd noticed the flickering shimmer once playing across the soft, pale skin of Syrah's neck and back as she lay naked in the bed beside him.

Syrah...

He loved her. Reyn was all too aware of that, now. He had known it the moment he'd heard she hadn't returned from her attempts to negotiate with the mountain clan, had known it from the black fear that had pooled up inside of him like ice set aflame.

And now she was alone, abandoned by her peers and friends, left to die at the hands of savages that would see her—and every last narrow branch of her faith—burned to ash.

Reyn didn't notice the tears spilling from the corners of his eyes as he lay there, warm and comfortable in a bed that felt suddenly like a betrayal to the woman he loved. He was there, safe and whole, while she was likely curled up somewhere, shivering in the cold and snow. Slowly, steadily over a long time, his breathing became cracked and uneven, and all at once Reyn found himself sobbing quietly, his mind far, far away.

He still hadn't noticed the tears when Cullen Brern arrived. The master-at-arms entered the infirmary like a thundercloud, his mood already darkened by the events of a day he didn't think could get any worse. He was all too ready to vent some of his anger in Reyn Hartlet's direction, ready to rage and abuse the man until nothing was left of the fool's ego but charred cinders from which, hopefully, something better would rise.

When he found the Priest, however, Cullen felt all the fire sapped from him. He watched for a time, silently from the far corner of the wide room, as his student cried quietly, still on his back, eyes empty as they gazed upward, seeing nothing and everything all at the same time. It didn't take too many guesses to figure out who the man was thinking about.

After a few minutes, Cullen turned and left the infirmary again, quietly this time, feeling that in the coming night Reyn Hartlet would likely suffer enough punishment to last a lifetime.

XXXIV

"Mountains only fall when they rise too high."

—old Sigûrth proverb

Kareth stood beneath the faded blue glow of the Woods' icy canopy, lounging lazily with his back against the thick roots of a particularly behemoth ash wood. Its great branches were so high and so wide above them that the massive tree had formed a sort of pseudo-clearing all about itself, discouraging other life from growing where it could never reach the light. To one side a wide stream formed a thick stroke of ice through the forest, its steep sides dipping down like a scar in the earth. It was at the edge of this embankment that Kareth sat, waiting, immune to the cold as a dozen Sigûrth warriors moved nervously about him, their torches held high enough to illuminate the other side of the stream.

Kareth waited with less impatience than anticipation, eager for a sign of the men they were expecting. Elrös of the Grasses had been the one to bring the news of the imminent arrival, and what was expected of Kareth in response. The Kayle was legendary for his patience, among his enemies and allies both, but there was one thing which tested that restraint beyond its limits.

And the men they were waiting on were coming to collect proof for which Gûlraht Baoill apparently couldn't delay another night.

"They come," Elrös said quietly from where he was crouched beside Kareth, sharp eyes peering into the dark to his left, west along the stream bank.

At once the men all about them shifted, every eye turning to follow the Gähs'. For another minute or so there was nothing. Only the wind, distant through the sheet of snow and ice high above their heads, made a sound as they waited. Kareth forcefully tempered his excitement, willing himself not to look up until Elrös shifted at his hip, subtly indicating their guests had arrived.

When he lifted his eyes, he could make out little more than black ghosts melting out of the dark.

Before Gûlraht had given him command of the vanguard, Kareth had never seen the Goatmen move as a pack. In truth, in fact, he had always thought little of the clan, even scoffing privately at his cousin's penchant for using them as scouts and flankers. They had seemed weak, frail things, of little use except as hunters and foragers when game was scarce.

It was an assumption Kareth had quickly discarded.

The group of Gähs shifted out of the Woods as though they were a part of it, their mottled furs and bleached skulls all but indistinguishable against the brown vegetation, dark bark, and the thin layer of frost that patterned the ground in uneven patches. It seemed in one moment that nothing moved between the trees through which the Sigûrth's torchlight permeated, and then all at once the Goatmen were there, standing in a staggered half circle some thirty feet away, just at the edge of the clearing.

Kareth felt a chill of appreciation.

"Tell them to come closer," he told Elrös.

Elrös nodded, standing up and raising a hand. Slowly the Gähs moved forward, almost cautiously, as though hesitant to step within the revealing boundary of the firelight.

"Welcome, friends!" Kareth boomed, grinning wide but still not moving from where he lounged between the roots of the great tree. *"How fares my cousin?"*

"The Kayle wishes you to substantiate your claims, Kareth Grahst," one of the Goatmen said in response, ignoring the question. *"He wishes we tell you that he hopes you understand the vastness of the rewards you stand to earn should you speak the truth, and the horror of the punishments you face if you are found a liar."*

Kareth's grin slipped into a wide, crooked smirk, and he waved the comment away with a lazy hand. *"Whatever ideas of torment Gûlraht can weave will have to be saved for another man, I'm afraid. I know too well how my cousin would take false hope in this matter."*

"Then you have her?" the man asked, eager now, taking another step forward. *"You have the Witch in truth?"*

Kareth, still smiling, nodded once.

"Then bring her to us," the man said quickly. *"Bring her forward, that we might return to the march with news of this great victory."*

Kareth made a great show of hesitation, as though contemplating whether he truly wanted to show the Gähs anything. He pretended to study them, looking each one up and down with slow deliberation, enjoying the subtle shift they made as his eyes found theirs, as well as the building impatience that was almost palpably emanating from their leader. Kareth considered delaying even more with further questions after his cousin's health and wellbeing, but ended up thinking the better of it.

Lifting a hand, he flicked a finger, and there was the rustle of dead leaves shifting beneath booted feet.

The Witch didn't fight as she was dragged forward from around a tall weaving of roots on the other side of the tree. Two men pulled her along, one by each arm, carelessly trailing her legs and bare feet across the icy ground, uncaring of the torn cloth of her white robes, or the bloody state of her knees and shins.

They were the same two men Kareth had sent earlier to beat her senseless, ensuring her submission as she was tendered to the Kayle's envoys.

There was a collective inhalation from the Gähs pack as they recognized the woman. Though it was doubtful any of them had actually ever seen the White Witch before, there was no mistaking the pallor of her skin, nor the bone-pale color of her hair. Her hands, still shackled behind her back, were almost luminescent in the bluish rays pouring through the ice above, then ashen as they came into the light of the torches. Her bare legs were the same, though marred by bruises and cuts. As the Sigûrth dropped her unceremoniously to the ground at the feet of the Goatmen, rolling her over with a rough boot on her shoulder, her face was revealed, ivory skin smooth despite the weeks of abuse she'd suffered.

Kareth watched the leader frown as he looked down on the woman, now in a limp heap on her back before him, hands pinned beneath her.

"*Her eye,*" he said, bending down to trace the dirty cloth that ran diagonally across her forehead, covering the right top-half of her face. "*What happened to it?*"

"*We asked her to make a choice,*" Kareth said, his voice almost a laugh. "*It would be something of an understatement to say she chose wrong...*"

The Goatman's frown only deepened at that, but he said nothing else. He stayed kneeling over the woman for another half-minute, turning her head this way and that on a slack neck, opening her good eye to peer at the pink orb, examining the ugly scar of her right ear, and even checking for a pulse. As he did his own eyes traveled down her body, noticing the large tears in the robes and the feminine parts of her that might otherwise not have been exposed to the cold.

"*You've defiled her,*" he said plainly, reaching down to drag away what little modesty the woman had left, revealing the bruises and bite marks along the front and inside of her legs.

For the first time, Kareth's smile faltered.

"*And what of it?*" he asked defensively, suddenly questioning his assumption that Gûlraht would care little for the state his gift was in when he received it.

The Gähs, though, merely shrugged.

"*Just an observation,*" the man said, reaching down to draw a long, slim knife from his hip. "*The Kayle welcomes you to any amusement you can take until he arrives. He only requires that she be able to speak when you present her to him.*"

Then, quick as the wind, the Goatmen gathered a handful of the frayed braids of the woman's white hair and lopped them clean off with a single quick slash.

"*That being saia,*" he went on as he sheathed the knife and got to his feet, "*I recommend you allow her to keep her other eye, if only for the time being.*"

Kareth's smile returned with confidence, and he gave a small nod. *"I'll take the suggestion under advisement. I hadn't intended to claim anything else from her just yet, regardless."*

The Goatman smirked at that, but said nothing in reply. Only after he had torn a long piece of thin string from his chest piece, looping it quickly about the bunching of braids before stowing the whole thing carefully in some hidden pocket of his cloak, did he speak.

"The Kayle will be pleased with your triumph, Kareth Grahst. I imagine you have just gained yourself much favor in his eyes."

And with that he whirled about and vanished back into the Woods, the rest of his pack no more than a moment behind, their footsteps less than whispers before they were gone.

After the last hint of them had disappeared among the trees, Kareth breathed a quiet sigh of relief. Still smiling, he allowed his head to tilt back and rest against the rough root behind him. He had essentially just hand-delivered his cousin's greatest desire to his feet. Kareth had little doubt he had just made himself the favorite, had little doubt he had just won himself Gûlraht's ear.

In one move, he had forged himself into the second most powerful man in all of the North…

He couldn't help but grin even wider at the thought.

There was the sound of crunching snow, and Kareth looked around. The men who had brought out the unconscious Witch were picking her up again, turning to head east once more. They started back at once, towards the very edge of the camp where fear of her sinful magic didn't have quite the same effect as imprisoning her amongst his men had.

But this night, Kareth found he cared little for the weaknesses of the superstitious rabble.

"No," he said aloud, directing the command at the pair. Immediately the two men froze, half-turning as Kareth finally got to his feet, pulling himself up by the roots around him.

"No," he said again, lifting a hand to indicate a more southeast line. "My tent. Leave her atop my furs."

The two didn't so much as hesitate. Nodding together, they shifted course, making for the distant twinkle of firelight that was the Sigûrth clump, separate from the rest of the encampment.

Kareth felt a surge of anticipation as he watched them leave, dropping his hand down to toy with the pommel of the sword on his hip. He had much to do before his night's work was done. Elrös had assured him Gûlraht would be arriving before noontide the following day, and he had many things and more to prepare to ensure his cousin was impressed with the siege he found on his arrival. When that was done, though, Kareth would break a fast he had forced upon himself for nearly two weeks. He had allowed the Sigûrth free rein of the woman in that time, granted them their pleasures and their cruelties.

But, now, as the White Witch's last night pulled darkness across the ice and snow above them like a closing eye, Kareth wanted to ensure it was *his* face she cursed when the Kayle arrived to take her head.

XXXV

"I have often wondered, looking back, why we so easily criticize the rashness of youth, the impunity of immaturity and the imprudency of children. When I consider many of the things made to bear fruit by such 'ill-judged' acts, I cannot help but wonder if it is—rather than a growth of the mind and spirit—simply the innate fear and cowardice that is the unfortunate harvest of years that stops an old hag like myself from having the guts to do what boys and girls not even a quarter my age will do without doubt or hesitation."

—the Grandmother

The quarter-hour Reyn forced himself to wait after the infirmary attendant came around to extinguish the lights for the night felt like the longest fifteen minutes mankind had ever been made to suffer in all its history. He put a smile on his face and returned the niceties when the acolyte had nodded to him and muttered a hasty "goodnight," then settled in to wait. He listened to the boy move about the chamber, hearing the quiet puffs of his breath as he blew out each candle one after the other, and the hiss of dying magic when he extinguished the half-dozen torches on each wall with a wave of his hands.

When the room was dark and tranquil, and the boy had moved off to a different part of the ward, Reyn started to count.

When he reached five hundred he slowly, silently—and ever so painfully—eased himself up from the bed.

Reyn had made his decision in the hour after Wence and the others came and went. It was, in fact, Cullen Brern who had forced the choice for him, when the man had come and—believing Reyn hadn't noticed him—watched from the corner of the room. When the master-at-arms had left, Reyn had settled in his resolve.

If the councilman had had no words of comfort, no hint of hope to give and draw from all his stoic and strong bearing, then Syrah had well and truly been abandoned to her fate.

And that singular thought had been enough to convince Reyn to cast aside all other things.

He grit his teeth as he pushed himself up, refusing to utter a single sound of complaint when his broken ribs burned in protest. He already had trouble breathing, sitting at the edge of his bed, feeling his left side strain with every inhalation. He gave himself a minute there, in part to see if anyone had noticed his rising in the dark, but also to allow himself to get accustomed to the pain.

When the ache became a constant but manageable presence, and he heard nothing but the shallow breathing of the other patients all about him in their own beds, he eased himself down to the floor.

His feet found warm stone, and he stood up in full. The farther stretch of his chest made his side cry out again, but he pushed the throb away, feeling about carefully to his right. Another acolyte—a woman nearly half his age again, in fact—had deposited his cleaned and folded robes on the small table by his bed an hour before the lights went out, in case he was summoned by the council. There had been no summons—for which Reyn was grateful—and with a small, ironic prayer of thanks to the Lifegiver, he pulled the robes over his head, inch by inch.

When they fell over his shoulders, settling with comfortable, familiar weight around his ankles, Reyn began to move.

He knew his boots would be somewhere about the bed, delivered at the same time as his robes, but he wasn't sure where and he didn't have the time or patience to try and find them. Instead he took two careful steps to the side, then started making a steady line straight ahead, as slowly as he could convince himself to go. He knew the infirmary well enough, given the number of times he had visited as a patient after one of Brern's brutal lessons, but he had requested assistance to the latrine twice that evening just to memorize where *exactly* he was in relation to the nearest door. As he'd suspected, his little bed-space faced the back wall, curtained off from the other patients. If he was careful, and just kept a watchful eye out, eventually he would see…

The door, he thought in triumph, finally making out the faint outline of the arched doorway some fifty feet to his right. Feeling about himself and sidling sideways a little, he found nothing barring his way.

Picking up the pace, he made directly for the light.

It was a clear lane, he was sure, kept so by the healers in case they were needed for an emergency. He grew more and more confident as he got closer and closer, seeing the whitish outline grow in the dark before him, the stone around his feet becoming more distinct in the limited light. He arrived before it quickly, reaching out a hand to lift the handle and let himself out into the hall.

The latch rose, then struck a lock with a loud *clang* of metal on metal.

At once there was a grumbling rising of noise as several of the sick and injured closest to the door were roused from their sleep. Reyn felt his heart skip a beat as someone asked "Who's there?" in a loud, tired voice. Whether it was in his head or actually happening, he thought he made out the beat of boots on the stone, come running from another part of the ward.

Without thinking twice, Reyn drew as much power as he could into the palm of his right hand, then pressed it to the handle of the door.

BOOM!

The door latch blew outward in a deafening crash as the blast of magic tore it free of the wood. Without a moment to lose Reyn reached into the hole, ignoring the splintered timber that bit into his fingers as he used it to swing the door wide. Several shouts of fear and anger followed him out into the hall.

Then he ran as fast as the pain allowed.

Reyn knew now that he didn't have long. It wouldn't be more than a few minutes before the healers figured out who was missing, and another ten before the council was summoned and pieced together where he might be going. He had to move, and he had to move fast. Reyn took every turn he could, every passage and shortcut he could find and think of. Even at this late hour he passed a number of Priests and Priestess about their own business, some walking in groups or pairs, others on their own, turning to watch him curiously as he ran by. After the first few of these individuals grew wide-eyed at the sight of him, Reyn reached back and pulled the hood of his robes over his blond hair, keeping his head bowed as he ran. When he was half a mile from the infirmary, well away from any chasing healers wanting to make sure he didn't hurt himself further, Reyn forced himself to slow to a fast walk.

All it would take was a question as to what he was fleeing from, and curiousity might very well turn into suspicion.

He wasn't worried about his bare feet. Even in the middle of the freeze it wasn't uncommon for some Priests and Priestesses to walk about without shoes or boots, usually when they couldn't sleep, or between lessons in unarmed combat in the practice chambers. Indeed, the next few men and women he passed didn't do more than give him a polite nod as he hurried by, one older Priest not even bothering to look up from the great tome he had his long nose buried in as he moved languidly down the hall.

All the same, Reyn didn't relax until he reached his final destination.

It took him nearly ten minutes to arrive at the larders, the old halls that were second only to the furnace room in how deep they descended into the mountain. They were a ways from the kitchen, unfortunately, but the dark coolness did well for certain foodstuffs, and—more to the point—no one had ever been able to come up with a good suggestion on how better to use the Citadel's dungeons, relics of a bloodier part of Cyurgi' Di's history.

Relics, that was, until this day.

For a moment, as Reyn arrived at the top of the steps that led down into the underground prison, he feared suddenly that he had been mistaken. He had deliberated all afternoon, gone over every option he could think of, and in the end had always come to the conclusion: the council would lock Raz i'Syul Arro up in the only place that was—or had at least once been—designed to detain him. No one guarded the stairway, however, and as Reyn started down carefully, keeping one hand on the thick chain that served as a guardrail along the wall, he saw no sign of anyone else waiting along the stairs.

He had almost reached the bottom-most steps, in fact, before he discovered his guess had been on the mark.

Voices.

They belonged to two, maybe three people. A pair of men at the very least, but Reyn didn't discount that there might be others he couldn't make out, or who weren't talking. He descended the last steps slowly, ignoring the continued ache in his side that had only worsened during his hasty flight from the infirmary.

When he reached the landing, he snuck to the edge of the closest wall and peered around.

Two men, both of whom he recognized, stood opposite each other on either side of the larder's long, wide hall. They were leaning back, clearly bored, talking casually as one man thumbed the steel of his staff, tucked under one arm, and the other motioned excitedly with his hands.

His staff stood some ten feet away, propped up in the nook of one of the dozen iron-and-wood doors that staggered each other on either side of the hall.

Reyn found himself subconsciously noting that he would have to speak to Cullen Brern about putting some thought into how they instructed their sentries.

Like they'll ever let me teach again, after this.

Something caught the corner of Reyn's eye then, causing him to startle and twist only to find the flicker of shadows as some draft blew over the candles set in the stone walls that surrounded him. He cursed himself and his paranoia, but the anxiety built up, reminding Reyn of how little time he had.

Taking a breath, he steeled his resolve, then stepped out from around the corner.

The man on the right, opposite the edge Reyn had been creeping behind, spotted him first. Gane Trehl was a pudgy, heavy-framed youth of twenty-two, but he'd been born into the faith and had earned his staff after proving himself a deceptively quick and capable fighter. Reyn had helped train him, and knew what the boy was capable of.

"Hartlet!" Trehl said in surprise, coming off the wall, his staff in one hand. "What in the Lifegiver's name are you doing here?"

Reyn made a show of limping—which wasn't all that hard to fake, at that point—and raised a hand in greeting.

"Came to give the bastard that did this to me a piece of my mind," he said weakly, feigning a wheeze and pressing his other hand gingerly to his side. "The lizard tricked me. He's crafty, and I don't mean it as a compliment."

Trehl nodded sanctimoniously.

"Told you," he said, turning to the other sentry as Reyn continued to walk towards them. "Told you there was no way he's as good as they say. Dirty fighting, that's all it was."

The man shrugged, looking over at Reyn. Danon Hest was the opposite of Trehl, a tall, wiry convert nearing fifty, but he had a talent with spellcasting that had gotten him noticed by Cullen Brern despite his age.

"May'aps," Hest said in with his signature drawl that always made the educators amongst the faith wince. "May'aps not. I done heard he messed you up somethin' good, Hartlet. You and Loric and Grees. *And* one a' the councilwomen, too."

"Like Trehl said," Reyn replied, stopping between the two and trying to make it look like he were casually observing his surroundings. "Dirty fighting."

He'd intended to get the men to tell him what cell the atherian was in, saving himself the trouble of searching every one until he got lucky, but realized at once that it wouldn't be necessary. He had wondered—if Raz i'Syul Arro had indeed managed to create havoc in a room filled by nearly a score of consecrated Priests and Priestess—why the council had thought it wise to post only two sentries in the dungeon. It seemed a gross underestimation of the atherian's abilities.

Or his madness, Reyn had thought.

But Reyn understood at once why the High Priest and his advisors hadn't bothered with greater security. Though the magics weren't actually visible, they were palpable, a strong, binding essence that emanated from a singular door along the right wall, not twenty feet down the hall. Reyn cursed before he could stop himself when his eyes fell upon it, realizing the additional problem now cast at his feet. The ward was a strong one, emanating power about itself in ripples Reyn was sure even those not attuned to sorcery could sense. It seemed to have been bound into the steel *and* wood *and* stone around the door, essentially walling off the cell until such time as the council saw fit to release their prisoner.

It would take Reyn longer than he liked to unwind a spell like that...

"Aye, they're not fooling around," Trehl said with a jerk of his head, indicating the door as he mistook Reyn's frustration for admiration. "You'll have trouble giving the beast a piece of anything. The ward won't even let us see him, much less talk to him."

"You tried?" Reyn asked, raising a brow.

"*Trehl* done tried," Hest said, spitting into a corner sourly, as though he wanted to make it clear he had no interest in getting mixed up in the nonsense his younger comrade was about. "Earlier, when we traded out with Cayst Etber and Samis Jehn. They told him some damned wild tale 'bout the lizard tearin' up the place and howlin' like a banshee, and *of course* this idiot just *has* ta' try and see what the fuss is all 'bout."

Trehl had the grace to blush.

"Reyn came to talk to him!" he squeaked in embarrassment. "Why aren't you giving him shit, too?"

Hest chuckled, scratching at the dark beard around his neck.

"Cause *Reyn* got a chunk taken out a' him by that snake, so *Reyn* ain't just lookin' ta' chat him up out of stupidity—oh, I'm sorry. I meant 'curiosity.'"

Trehl blushed deeper, and was about to say something in response when Reyn cut across him.

"Can you take the ward down?" he asked, still eyeing the door, trying to make it seem as though he truly was intent on speaking to the atherian. "Even for a minute?"

For the first time, he saw more than casual intrigue on the faces of the two men, and he instantly regretted the question. Trehl's pudgy cheeks frowned in confusion, while Hest smartened up faster. The older man was suddenly looking at Reyn with distinct suspicion.

"No," Hest said slowly, pushing himself off the wall to face Reyn full on, his hands by his side. "We been told the ward stays up, no matter who asks. Why you lookin' ta'—?"

He never got a chance to finish the question.

Reyn took him down first. Hest's magic scared him more right now than Trehl's strength, and he was closest. With a quick step forward Reyn closed the gap between them suddenly, bringing himself within inches of the man. Hest reacted instinctively, throwing up a protective barrier, but too late.

Shielding wards only worked when your opponent was *outside* the shield.

Reyn allowed the magic to close in behind him, thinking it might buy him a couple of extra seconds if Trehl rushed from behind. Two quick blows caught Hest before the older man could even raise his arms in defense, one hard to the side of the head to daze him, a second to the gut, doubling him over. As he dropped, Reyn's knee came up, catching the man a devastating strike to the face.

He felt Hest's nose break against the tight muscle of his thigh.

The Priest's body twisted back as his knees went limp, and he collapsed awkwardly to the ground, out cold. Turning as quickly as he could, Reyn threw up his own protective shield as he heard the *crack* of breaking magic.

Good thing too, because Trehl's staff made short work of the remainders of Hest's ward.

Reyn managed to get himself around just in time to witness the steel slammed through the rapidly fading spellwork, shattering it in a rainbow of something like splintering glass. As Hest's magic broke, though, Reyn's ward caught the staff, absorbing the blow. Reyn could see Trehl's face now, though, all confusion gone from the chubby creases.

Now the man just looked *maa*.

"What are you doing, Hartlet?" he demanded, spinning the staff back under his arm and gathering light into his left hand. "What are you *doing*?"

Reyn didn't answer. Instead he pressed one hand out, willing the ward around him to expand. It weakened exponentially as it did, but it was still strong enough to disrupt Trehl's casting when it hit him, staggering the large man and forcing him back a step, yelling in anger as he did.

The sound was cut short, though, as the shockwave Reyn had been building up in his other hand hit Trehl straight on, disguised behind the expanded ward, using the weaker magic as a distraction.

Gane Trehl was thrown back a full five feet, his heavy body slamming into a cell door with a dull *thud*, his head snapping back to *crack* against the wood so loudly it made Reyn wince. The man's steel staff spun away with the tinkling clatter of metal on stone, and Trehl himself staggered, rattled by the blow. He had just finished taking a shaky step forward, clutching at the back of his head with one hand as he looked up, when Reyn's stunning spell hit him square in the chest.

He'd never been as good at throwing them as Syrah was, but at this range it would have been difficult for even a novice to miss.

Trehl collapsed where he stood, all will sapped from his limbs. He tumbled to the ground in a hefty, ugly mess of thick arms and white robes, his head only saved by a meaty shoulder as he tipped sideways.

Then the man settled, rolling half onto his back in front of the door, and lay still.

Reyn stood for several seconds, listening for any distant shouts of alarm, or the clap of booted feet come running. Hearing nothing, he looked from Hest to Trehl and back again. He hadn't had a chance to truly convince himself the fight was over before he was forced to let out a dull groan, falling to one knee and clutching at his side as his ribs screamed in agony, the pain of the motions dulled until then by the rush of the scuffle. For a good thirty seconds he stayed like that, hissing in every breath, fighting hard not to give in and pass out. He feared, suddenly, what would happen to him after tonight. Would the Laorin allow him time to heal before Breaking him and sending him out into the world? Would they cast him out as he was, pitting him against the freeze and the mountain men below?

No, Reyn thought, forcing himself up onto his feet, grimacing as his ribs protested. *More likely they'll just lock me up down here until they can figure out what else to do with me.*

With that uncomfortable thought settling itself in the back of his mind, Reyn limped over to Hest, checking to make sure the man was breathing. He was—if a little throatly through his swollen, lopsided nose—and Reyn moved on to Trehl. The larger man had a lump the size of a small egg where his head had hit the door, but there was no blood and his breaths came in the dull, low lull of unconsciousness the stunning spell brought on.

Relieved, Reyn looked around.

Then he started for the door, that solid slab of iron and timber behind which Reyn was fairly sure death incarnate sat impatiently waiting.

XXXVI

"It is a source of amusement to me, the irony by which the world works. It is inconceivable, for example, the places in which one might find their greatest allies."

—Ergoin Sass

Raz had run out of patience six hours ago.

He had tried everything, *everything*, to get the damn door to open. He had wrenched at it, thrown things at it, tried to pick—and then break—the lock with bent nails he'd recovered from the wreckage strewn about the room. He'd attempted to leverage the hinges with lengths of wood, had even done his best to bash it open with the stocks of salted meat that had been stacked along the right wall, using two of the heavy barrels as battering rams, one after the other. When that had failed—spilling salt and slabs of cured venison over the floor—he had screamed in fury and slashed at the door, leaving long, angry gouges that crisscrossed over the wood.

The thing hadn't so much as twitched.

He knew why, of course. He didn't know if he was sensitive to the magic—as he was to sounds and scents—or if the barrier cast about the door was just that potent, but Raz could literally *feel* the power radiating from the iron-bound wood and the stone around it, vibrating over him if he got too close. It wasn't an unpleasant feeling, at first. For a time it was like the song made by a distant waterfall, a dull, low rumble of noise that spoke of something both powerful and beautiful all at once. After the first hour, though, Raz had started to get irritated by the feeling, associating it with his frustration.

After he was certain half the day had gone by, he wondered if he would ever get over the acute, irrational rage the thrum brought on whenever he neared the ward.

He sat now—for this very reason—some ten feet away from the door in the center of the room, chewing mindlessly on a thick hunk of meat he had scooped up from the ground nearby for his dinner. The salt tasted good after weeks spent eating unseasoned game, his sharp teeth making quick work of the tough, fibrous flesh, and he sated his thirst from a few clay jugs of what had turned out to be ale and water he'd found intact among the mess. Eating distracted him, allowing him to sit back and think.

Unsurprisingly, no solution presented itself.

"Damn trims are going to keep me in here until I rot," he muttered through a mouthful of meat.

Great. Now I'm talking to myself even when Ahna isn't around.

Briefly amused by the thought, Raz smirked, his eyes never leaving the cell door. For the thousandth time that day he studied the thing, taking in every inch of wood, every line of hammered metal that shone in the glow of magical light and every flicker of shadow cast by the unevenly cut granite around it. He looked for any weakness, anything that might give him so much as a hint on how to escape. He wondered what would happen if he started talking to the door, rather to himself.

And then, as though in response, the door started talking to *him*.

Raz froze mid-chew. He was *sure* he had heard something, some muffled, garbled noise that sounded all too much like someone were calling his name. He sat there, tense and still, listening.

"Ar-o. Ar—Ar—ro."

Raz was on his feet in an instant, the remainder of his meal tossed hastily to one side, his aversion to the magic totally forgotten as he leapt for the door.

"Arr-o," the voice came again. "Ar—ro."

It was a male voice, sounding as though it were coming from everywhere and nowhere all at once, warped and echoed and faded, like a man were screaming at him from the other side of a very large cavern.

All the same, it was definitely real.

"Here!" Raz roared, pounding on the wood. "In here!"

The voice made no reply.

There were two slots in the door, one that slid sideways to form a peephole around Raz's chest height, and one at the very bottom that was meant to swing out of the way so food and drink could be delivered to the incarcerated. Raz had tried both of them before and found them magically sealed, but he tried again all the same now, first digging his claws into the wood and trying to pull the peephole open, then scrabbling once more at the feed slot, again finding no purchase for his claws. He howled in anger again, punching and kicking at the wood.

And, as he did, feeling it shake.

In half-a-day of struggling, not *once* had the door so much as shivered. Even when he'd struck the reinforced timber and iron with the heavy frame of the meat barrels, the door hadn't even creaked in protest. It had merely existed, like it were part of the wall itself, a silent and impassive witness of his distress. Raz had become sure, in fact, that even if he had used his claws to carve *through* the wood, eventually he would have been met with a solid, inviolable barrier of magic.

And yet now, as he'd pounded at the door with bare fists and feet, it had shaken.

Sizzle… crack…

At first the sounds took Raz by surprise, and he retreated a cautious step back. Then he recognized them, drawing them from his memory of that same morning, of the bitch woman's—Petrük's—ward breaking beneath his hands in the madness Syrah's absence had thrown him into.

It was the sound of spellwork being undone...

Eagerly Raz waited, then, knowing there was nothing and less he could do. Impatiently he shifted his weight from foot to foot, feeling he could guess *exactly* who it was behind the door.

"Come on," he muttered to himself, yellow eyes darting about, watching the latch and the hinges and peephole slot. "Come ooooon."

But there was no rushing the process, it seemed, and it was several minutes before a distinct *crack* came, and the dull hum of magic around Raz became suddenly much quieter.

Metal shifted, there was a *clunk*, and the wooden slot slid aside in the center of the door.

"Carro," Raz breathed in relief, bending down. "About damn time. I was wondering when you were going to—"

But he stopped, then, because the face looking through to him from the other side of the door was *not* that of Carro al'Dor.

Reyn felt his breath catch in his throat as Raz's i'Syul Arro bent down to peer through the hole. For the first time he became *truly* aware of how massive the atherian was, towering and lithe, corded muscle bunching beneath the black-scaled skin of his neck that gleamed in the firelight.

When Arro's eyes came into view, Reyn couldn't help but take a step back, and the man's words were entirely lost to him.

He had, for a moment, the impression of looking in on a caged beast, such as he'd heard some of the inordinately rich kept in private sanctuaries in the Seven Cities and Perce. There were several seconds of silence as the amber orbs drilled into him, glinting in the light, one second shining like a wolf's in twin disks of white, the next sharp and gold, with black, vertically slit pupils that held no warmth for him, no fondness.

Then the atherian spoke again, and this time Reyn heard him.

"What are you doing here, Priest?"

It wasn't an unkind, question, truth be told. If anything Arro sounded perplexed, as though Reyn were the last person he would have expected to find on the other side of the door that kept him from his freedom.

Which isn't all that surprising, Reyn realized, seeing his mistake.

"They say you know where Syrah Brahnt is," Reyn said, deciding to clear the air all at once. "Is it true?"

314

Arro watched him for a time, blinking slowly, but made no reply. He seemed almost wary.

"Is it true?" Reyn demanded, hating the desperation that was all too blatant in his voice.

Another pause.

"It is," the atherian said finally. "Why?"

"Can you save her?"

"Yes."

There was no hesitation to the answer this time, no moment of pondering or consideration. Rather, there was only calm, deadly confidence, and a coolness to the word that sent a chill down Reyn's back.

"You're Hartlet, right?"

Reyn startled as the atherian said his name.

"Y-yes," he stammered, feeling a fool for not having introduced himself. "I'm sorry for my behavior on the pass. I wasn't in my right mind. I—"

"Are you going to let me out of here, Hartlet?"

The question came in the same cold way, with the same hard conviction. Suddenly, Reyn was all too aware of what he was doing, what he was *about* to do. All at once it came to the forefront, closing in. As he looked into those golden eyes, seeing the bloody intent lingering behind them, he understood what it was he was about to release onto the world.

Reyn opened his mouth to speak, unsure, exactly, of what he was going to say.

He never saw the glint of the magic, nor flash of light as the stun spell streaked out of the darkness from the end of the hall by the stairs, catching him in the side.

Raz watched with ever-building confusion as Reyn Hartlet tumbled out of view. He'd seen the glimmer, recognized the casting, but hadn't even had a moment to give warning before the spell struck the Priest in the ribs. The young man's eyes had rolled up into his head, leaving him suspended like that for two solid seconds in front of the door.

Then he'd fallen sideways, out of view.

"Hartlet!" Raz shouted in half-desperation, half-concern, grabbing the peephole with both hands and shaking the door. "Hartlet!"

"*Quiet*, Raz!"

Instantly Raz shut up, the familiar voice strangling his cries.

There was the muffled rustle of footsteps, and Raz watched the slide of the shadows as someone made their way quickly down the hall. The steps got louder and louder, and eventually a man came into view, peering through the door at him.

This time the face *did* indeed belong to Carro al'Dor.

"Carro," Raz hissed, still holding onto the hole. "What's going on? What did you do to Hartlet?"

"Stopped him from destroying his life," Carro grumbled, taking a step back and examining the door. "They would have cast him out, if he'd managed to free you. He would have had nothing."

Raz paused at that.

"Then what are you doing?" he asked slowly, watching the Priest take in the door from the hall.

In the semi-darkness of the subdued torchlight, an ordinary man might not have seen the shift in Carro's face at the question. The grief, so plain to Raz's sharp eyes, might have gone unnoticed in the shadows, a twisted exposure of the raw pain that Raz had only seen glimpses of over the last few days.

"I've already lost everything," the Priest said quietly, his eyes settling on the center of the door. "Now get back."

Raz made no argument, and retreated several steps as Carro gathered light into his good hand.

Carro, it turned out, was *much* more efficient at undoing wards than Reyn Hartlet. Raz watched in silent wonderment as blinding white flashed in scattered patterns through the open slot, listening to the Priest's muttered incantations and occasional curses. Within a half a minute the dull thrum of the magic had faded beyond perception, and not long after Raz made out the creak of wood and metal as the door settled on its own weight.

Then there was a final blast of magic, and the entire thing wrenched open, the heavy latch tearing a chunk out of the wall and scattering stone across the floor.

After the dust had settled, Raz picked his way quickly over the rubble and out into the hall. Carro had already moved away, further down the corridor to the cell next to Raz's, and was gathering some spell into his right hand once more.

"What are you doing?" Raz asked, starting towards him.

Carro stopped him with a brief shake of his head. "Stay back," the Priest said. "As much as I'm loath to admit it right now, Jofrey isn't a fool. He elected to keep your things close by, in case they were needed."

And with that, he blasted open the second door.

As Carro clambered over the ruined iron and wood, disappearing into the room, Raz looked back around, down the hall. He took in the two unconscious men nearer the dungeon stairs, then Reyn Hartlet, passed out beside the broken opening of Raz's cell.

"Did you do all this?" Raz said, impressed, turning back as Carro reemerged, struggling to drag a familiar, massive cloth traveling bag behind him with his good hand. It clinked with the sound of steel on steel as he pulled it over the crumbled stone and broken timber slats.

"No," Carro said with a queasy frown, not looking towards the men he knew Raz was speaking of as he heaved the bag into the center of the hall. "It took me long enough to build up the courage to stun Reyn, much less the other two. He's a cretin, but I can't say I don't appreciate his idiocy. I figured the council would have a guard on you, and I'm honestly not sure what I would have done if Reyn hadn't taken care of them first."

Raz snorted, amused at Carro's continued distaste for violence, given the situation. Then he frowned down at the form of Reyn Hartlet.

"Why *did* he come?" he asked.

It took a while for Carro to respond, and eventually Raz looked around at him, assuming the man hadn't heard him. He found Carro looking at him oddly, though, and when their eyes met the Priest sighed.

"Because," he said slowly, "he's in love with Syrah."

That took Raz by surprise, and he looked at the Priest more sharply. "He's in love with her?"

"Raz," Carro said with exasperation, waving his hand at the bulging sack of gear at his feet, "I will be happy to fill you in on every *ounce* of gossip and drama that floods these halls on a daily basis, but not now! Please! We have to move!"

The desperation in the man's voice made it clear that it would have to be a story for another time, and Raz hurried over to him.

"Where is Ahna?" he asked, noting the distant protruding shape of a sword hilt in the cloth.

Carro waved into the room. "In there. You know full well she's too heavy for me, even if I did have both hands."

Raz ducked into the cell at once, stepping over the broken door. It didn't take him long to find the dviassegai, propped up against one of yet another series of tall, food-laden shelves, and he hefted her up quickly before returning back out into the hall.

As he did he made out the sound of running feet, far off in the distance, echoing louder and louder towards them through the tunnels of the Citadel.

"Someone's coming," he growled, snatching up the bag of gear and tossing it over his left shoulder.

Carro blanched, but turned at once and started hurrying down the corridor, towards the opposite end from the stairs.

"Dammit, Hartlet!" Raz heard the Priest curse as he made chase, following on the man's heels. "They must have figured out what he was about."

"What are we going to do?" Raz asked, catching up to the Priest quickly despite the added weight of Ahna and his gear, the claws of his feet *clacking* against the slate floor beneath him. "Where are we going?"

"Up," Carro said, pointing ahead. "There are stairs that will lead us out onto the battlements."

Raz thought that peculiar, but as he followed the Priest's finger he indeed saw a narrow archway set into the far wall, framing the bottom of a thin spiral staircase. As they got closer Raz made to let Carro lead, but the man pushed him forward.

"Go," he said, slowing as they reached the arch. "All the way to the top. Wait for me there."

Raz was about to argue when Carro started moving his right hand through the air, tracing out a series of complex runes in the space around them, crafting lines of colorless fire that hung, suspended by nothing.

He's slowing them down, he realized, watching as the symbols drifted swiftly to latch onto the walls on either side of them, burning themselves into the stone.

"Raz!" Carro cried. "Go!"

And he did just that, taking the short steps three at a time, his powerful legs carrying him up and up and up. For almost two minutes he climbed, each passing moment making him realize with a mix of awe and shock just how far down he must have been sequestered. Beyond that, there was something odd about the air as he ascended. Whereas one would ordinarily think it would get *warmer* as one rose from the bowels of the mountains, the temperature seemed to be dropping the higher he went. By the time Raz finally reached the top, arriving on a wide landing accented only by a heavy iron door along the right wall, he could see his breath again, watch it billowing out around his snout.

He didn't give himself time to start worrying about the cold.

Dropping the pack to the ground, Raz tore it open with the claws of one hand even as he leaned Ahna against the closest wall with the other. His things spilled out onto the worn floor in front of the door, his armor clattering about his feet and his gladius and ax tumbling out in a single bundle, wrapped in the heavy fur cloak the Laorin of Ystréd had gifted him almost a month ago now. With practiced efficiency Raz donned his gear, picking through the mess and strapping Allihmad Jerr's hammered steel into place over his body. By the time Carro joined him, huffing as he staggered up the last of the steps, Raz was in full armor. With a flourish he threw the cloak over his shoulders, feeling the warm weight of it settle about him.

The Monster of Karth stood tall once more, gladius slung over his back, ax on his hip, and Ahna lifted onto one shoulder by hands clad in familiar steel gauntlets.

"Outside," Carro said quickly, pressing Raz towards the iron door, not even pausing as he reached the landing. "Hurry. *Hurry.* The runes won't deter them for long."

Raz did as he was told, reaching out to lift the cumbersome latch that locked the door shut from the inside. He had to put a shoulder into the metal before it budged, but after a few seconds the whole thing shifted with a screeching whine of rusted hinges and Raz—straining with every fiber he had—pressed it open for what must have been the first time in over a hundred years.

As they spilled out into the night onto some part of slick, icy ramparts, the wind and snow resumed the relentless barrage that had hounded Raz and Carro all the way up the mountain pass not a day before. Instead of cursing the storm, though, Raz smiled into it, spreading his ears and wings into the blizzard, welcoming the freedom of the open air.

Then he looked around, and realized where they stood.

The door had led them out onto the wide ruins of some ancient stage of iron and dark marble, all remnants of wooden supports and flooring having long rotted to dust. They were some fifty feet above the courtyard, standing in a solid wash of snow that reached even Raz's knees, but despite this the skeleton of the long-forsaken contraptions loomed like cruel fingers closing up and over them through the dark. Immediately Raz understood why there were stairs at the end of the dungeon, and why the door he had just forced open seemed to have been shut for the entirety of several generations. The Laorin, after all, could make use of empty cells and the dark gloom of the prison.

But the faith would never have had need of gallows.

Abruptly, the weight of what Carro had done fell over Raz, heavy and terrible, and he turned to look at the man who stood behind him in the snow. The Priest, too, was staring up at the metal and stone scaffolds above them. There was no sign of regret on his bearded face, however. No sign of shame or self-hate.

Rather, it seemed something like a smile played on the man's lips, as he looked up at the haunting reminders of what his beloved Citadel had once been.

"Carro…" Raz started, taking half-a-step towards the man, unsure of what to say.

The Priest brought his eyes down to him, and Raz saw that he was indeed smiling. At the same time, he saw the glint of tears track against the man's flushed cheeks, illuminated by the dull hint of the Moon through the clouds above.

When he spoke, though, Carro's voice rose above the wind like the words of a man suddenly set free.

"Go, Raz. Bring her back to us."

Raz stood there, looking down at the man. He took in Carro's face, recognizing the sacrifice the Priest was making, understanding what he had just given up, and what he had given it up for.

Then he nodded, turned, and ran along ramparts, heading for the outline of the stairs he could see some hundred feet off, leading down into the courtyard below.

Tell her to hold on, he prayed to Her Stars as he moved. *Tell her I'm coming.*

When Jofrey barreled up the last steps of the Dead Man's Climb, he found the Last Door thrown wide, its rusted hinges flaking and cracked under a force he knew only magic or the atherian could have provided. His blood chilled at the sight of the great iron thing, shifted from its position for the first time since the Laorin had settled Cyurgi' Di, vowing the Citadel would never again suffer witness to such willing disrespect of Laor's gifts.

And now it lay open, symbolic of the betrayal of the man who stood quietly waiting just inside.

"Carro…" Jofrey said in a stunned voice, putting a hand out behind him to stop Cullen and Kallet Brern, Priest Elber, and the group of other Priests and Priestesses who had followed once they'd managed to break the rune traps laid out at the bottom of the stairs. "Carro… What have you done?"

Carro al'Dor stood silent for a long time, staring out into the wind and snow of the stormy winter night. When he finally moved, he turned to smile sadly at his old friend.

Jofrey saw the lines the tears had traced on his face.

"I'm sorry, Jofrey," Carro said, his voice shaking. "I… I couldn't lose them both."

Jofrey said nothing, stepping forward carefully to stand beside the aging Priest, joining him in the frame of the Last Door. He, too, looked out into the blizzard, noting the clawed tracks leading out and away through the gibbets, across the ramparts.

"Carro… Petrük will demand your head for this," he said, his eyes not leaving the last sign Raz i'Syul Arro had left as he escaped. "I won't be able to protect you…"

"And I won't ask you to," Carro said, his voice more firm now. "I've broken our only decree, Jofrey. I know the law."

"And Reyn?" Jofrey asked in a hushed tone, stepping closer and looking at the Priest again, afraid of the answer. "Did he help you? We found him downst—"

"Reyn Hartlet had no part in this," Carro said loudly, so that the councilmen and group hovering along the top of the stair behind Jofrey could hear. "This was my doing, and mine alone." Then, in a softer voice, he added: "I stopped him before he could undo your ward. He violated no law, whatever his intentions might have been."

Jofrey felt himself sag in relief. He wasn't sure he would have been able to sentence his former student to be Broken.

It would be hard enough to do once…

"Carro, will you come with us?" he asked gently.

Carro nodded, but didn't move away from the door. For several seconds more he continued to stare out into the night.

"Do you think he'll manage it?" he asked suddenly. "Do you think he'll reach her?"

Jofrey didn't respond immediately. Instead, he looked back out through the now open Last Door, looking again at the clawed footprints, their outlines already dulled by the ever-falling snow. He hadn't told the council what he knew of the atherian, what Talo Brahnt had told him of the boy Syrah had met, so many years ago. He recalled vividly the images his mind had conjured up as Talo had described what Syrah had witnessed, had told him of the bloody spectacle Raz i'Syul Arro had produced in just a few short seconds.

And as he thought of it now, all he could do was pray the Lifegiver would keep as many of the mountain men out of the atherian's path as possible.

"If anyone can manage it, he's the one, my friend," Jofrey said, stepping forward and taking Carro's arm lightly. "Now come on. Let's get you out of the cold."

XXXVII

"When the Scourge fought for himself, he was a terror. He made a bloody mess of anything that came within reach, eviscerating and butchering all that threatened him and his own. When he fought for the woman, though, he became something more. There was a feeling about the way he moved, the way he battled. It was as though the sword had evolved, become more shield than blade. When the Scourge fought for her, he became the wall between she and the rest of the world. His dance spoke the simple truth, told all who wanted to chance their luck one absolute fact: no one would ever touch her again."

—Born of the Dahgün Bone, author unknown

It was as though the Moon herself had blessed his descent.

Like the gods had heard his prayers, heard his pleas and understood his need for haste, the storm quailed within twenty minutes of Raz's clambering start down the pass. At first it was the snows that abated, clearing his view and making it easier to skirt the loose stone and leap over the icy patches. Then it was the wind's turn to die, stilling to a bare breeze that Raz hardly felt as he dropped from one section of the path to the next, ten, twenty, thirty feet at a time, wings spread wide to slow his falls.

Then, as though in final benediction, the clouds themselves thinned, allowing patches of true Moonlight to pepper the snow and rocks and cliffs about him as he plunged towards the forest far below with all the speed and urgency of an avalanche.

Raz didn't feel the burn in his legs as he moved, didn't feel the ache in his chest as mountain air flooded his lungs. He didn't notice it getting warmer, or his breathing coming easier as the atmosphere thickened. Nothing existed for him. Not the snow, not the icy stone beneath his feet, not the ledges he swung himself around and over, or even the cliffs he leapt and launched himself from into open air to land dozens of feet below. He became unaware of the world around him, unaware of the existence of more than a single thing beyond the mountain.

Syrah.

At first, as he'd started down the path once more, Raz had tried to make a plan, tried to steady himself and his rage. He had felt the tickle of an old, familiar terror in the back of his mind, but he'd beaten it back, trying to maintain control as he descended. With conscious effort he considered all the variables of the situation he was about to throw himself into, focusing with all his might on one factor at a time.

But, as though mirroring his own descent along the mountainside, reason soon began to fade, cracked by the memories of the sounds he heard as echoes inside his head. The laughter and pleasures of the man, the voices of his friends, and the muffled, pained cries that could only have come from the white-haired woman.

Syrah.

The animal, for the first time in Raz's life, rose slowly, steadily. As he dropped from bend to bend, leaping down entire flights of stairs, trusting his clawed feet to hold firm against the ice, Raz didn't realize he had lost the fight. His mind preoccupied by the face of the woman from his dreams, he didn't notice the darkness falling, the bloodlust rising up within him. In the end, it took him less than three hours to make his way down the mountain path, the evergreens appearing and growing thicker as he got lower and lower, the glare of firelight that marked the base of the stairs bright in the mercifully clear night.

And it was a long time before that that the scene around Raz became nothing more than contoured shades of red and black, highlighting the cool, calm sway of the pines.

Bjen al'Hayrd was not flush with pride at his new assignment as commander of the sentries along the base of the blasphemers' pass. He was not fretful, nor anxious or worrisome. Bjen al'Hayrd had been a warrior of the Kregoan clan for far too long to still be plagued by such weaknesses, such frailties that needed to be beaten out of boys before they could truly be considered men. His was a toughened spirit, sympathetic to the Kayle and his cause, and he had been among the first to take a knee as the giant that was Gûlraht Baoill began to demand fealty from the western tribes.

He had also been present when Vores Göl—the man whose position he had succeeded—had thrown himself into the fire in order to escape a coward's death.

And Bjen had no intention of echoing the man's failures.

"*Eyes* open, *goat*," he growled while making his rounds, cuffing a Gähs archer who looked to be nodding off at his post. The Goatman jerked and blinked around at him in fear, muttering something in the dialect of his clan before ducking swiftly out of the way, his bow held tight to his chest in both hands.

Bjen grinned at the man's retreating back, the movement twisting the scars on his cheeks that cut spirals through the brown hair of his beard and shifted the carved finger-bones that pierced the bridge of his nose between his dark eyes. Bjen was big, even for a man of the mountain clans, and had always enjoyed the command his height and breadth won him, especially from the more slender tribes like the Gähs or the Velkrin.

There is no place for the weak among the strong, he thought, turning and continuing his inspection.

Kareth Grahst himself had given Bjen command of a full score of men, picked for their skills and utility. Grahst, it was rumored, was the new favorite of the Kayle following his defeat and capture of the infamous White Witch, and so Bjen had seen this promotion as a good sign of his own advancement in the new order of man the Kayle would soon put in control of the North. He moved about the camp with confidence, giving orders and hefting his twin axes at any who looked in danger of dozing off. Men moved about him in pairs, some trading shifts with those posted along the bottom stairs of the path, others bearing armfuls of dry wood carried across the dark from the Arocklen for the half-dozen fires he'd had built in a wide circle around them. He kept them lively, kept his warriors on their toes and constantly moving, refusing to allow them to settle or get comfortable.

Bjen was not about to be taken by surprise, as Vores Göl had allowed himself to be.

Thinking of the tales he had heard, Bjen turned southward, looking towards the Woods. He could see nothing, of course, the night beyond the fires painted black to his eyes by the light, but he imagined he could make out the line of trees, watching them shift in the faint breeze. He wondered again—for the hundredth time, in fact—what magics the sorcerer must have woven to sneak so easily past the camp. He'd heard the tale of the beast over and over again, spewed in keening screams from the mouths of the last men who had stood sentry over this very spot. Kareth Grahst had explained to him, when granting Bjen the command, his suspicions of how he believed one of the Priests had conjured the demon to do his fighting for him. It was a thought that had made Bjen's blood boil, as any man not capable of fighting for himself didn't deserve to be called a *man* at all.

"*More wolves. You'd think they'd have learned to run off by now.*"

Recognizing the voice, Bjen turned away from the hidden tree line and looked around. A pair of men, one Kregoan and one Amreht, were standing a half-dozen feet away, peering west and north through the dark. They appeared to be scrutinizing the indistinct mountainside, searching the bluffs above their heads for something.

"*Dolf,*" Bjen said, moving towards the two and addressing the Kregoan, whom he knew, "*what's this about wolves?*"

Dolf Rohn was short for a man of his tribe, but half again as broad. He had the look of a wall, squat and thick, with a black beard and brows that were marred by carved lines that stroked vertically down his cheeks and forehead. His bottom lip was pierced by a pair of curved ribs that had been cut and filed into twin points, then braided into the hairs of his chin.

"Vahlen says he thinks he saw something coming down along the cliffs, from on high," Dolf told Bjen, looking around and shrugging a shoulder at the Amreht as his commander approached. *"I said it had to be an animal, if it came through the rocks."*

Bjen frowned, looking to Dolf's companion. He didn't know the Amreht—nor did he have any particular fondness for his kind, given they had practically had to be beaten into submission by the Kayle—but Vahlen's words concerned him.

Wolves didn't generally hunt in the mountains. There wasn't enough game to make it worth the energy.

"What did you see?" he asked the man, studying Vahlen as he did. The Amreht's skin was painted with traditional dyes, splitting his face down the middle. One side was clean and pockmarked, while the other was a solid shade of bright red, a feature believed by their tribe to strike fear into the hearts of their enemies.

To Bjen, it looked more like the foolish powders the women of the valley towns were sometimes known to wear.

But Vahlen, to his credit, struck no effeminate air as he spoke. He met Bjen's eyes confidently, nodding briefly in respect as he answered.

"Too big to be a wolf," he said simply. *"Came right off the path, through that clump of trees there."* He pointed upward, to a spot some thirty yards off and ten up, where a thicket of spruces stood, barely distinguishable at the edge of the casted light. *"More like a bear, if anything."*

Bjen studied the copses and the sheer cliffs around them. A bear was more likely, he thought, but bears tended to hole themselves up when the freeze came. Still, it was early enough into winter, so it was certainly possible, not to mention ursali were not known to hibernate as soundly as their smaller cousins…

Bjen decided it wasn't worth the assumption.

"Dolf," he said, speaking to the Kregoan but not looking away from the mountain, *"take four of the Goatmen and see what you can find. If it's a bear there'll be tracks, and the goats will sniff it out."*

He saw Dolf nod from the corner of his eye, then turn and lumber off, shouting to a group of Gähs sitting huddled by one of the fires nearby. Not long after, the five of them were pressing out beyond the ring of the flames, the Gähs moving easily despite the deep snow, Dolf huffing and cursing behind them, a broad, two-handed claymore drawn and bare over one shoulder as he struggled to keep up, a torch held high in the other hand.

Bjen and Vahlen stood at the edge of the camp, watching the group move. Others joined them, the half-dozen men not assigned to be on watch, and for once Bjen didn't shout at them to get back to work, too preoccupied was he with knowing what the Goatmen might discover.

It was a minute or so before the group of five reached the base of the cliffs, directly under the trees Vahlen had indicated. For several seconds Bjen could see them milling around, scouring the ground and rocks, illuminated in the glow of Dolf's single torch.

And then, so unexpectedly Bjen might have blinked and missed it, the light went out.

"*What the*—?" Bjen began as he heard confused questions being shouted by the Gähs in the distance, his hands dropping instinctively to the axes he kept on each hip.

Then the weapons were out and bare, because a single long, drawn out scream cracked through the dark, shattering the peace of the night.

"*WALL!*" Bjen roared, smashing his axes together like an alarm bell as Vahlen ripped a longsword and dagger from his hips beside him. "*TO ME! WALL!*"

At once the men around him responded, surging from all around to form a staggered, curved line along the edge of the ring of cleared snow as more screams hammered them from across the night. There were shouts, yells of horror, and another keening screech of pain that lingered, then ended abruptly. For several seconds Bjen and his wall stood silent, weapons held aloft, archers with arrows knocked and ready, aimed at the ground until it was time to draw. All around him Bjen could feel the men shifting nervously, and even he couldn't help his eyes from darting about the blackness, looking for a sign of *whatever* it was he should be expecting.

Then, as though on cue, he made out the rapid sounds of boots crunching through deep snow, approaching at a breakneck pace.

"*Hola*," he hissed as one of the archers began to lift his bow. He had just made out what sounded like hard, ragged breathing, coupled with whimpers of sheer terror.

If there was a survivor, he didn't want him accidently riddled with arrows before he could explain what had happened.

"*There*," Vahlen said, pointing with his knife. Sure enough, the ghostly form of a fox skull had just manifested out of the dark, the man whose head it helmed appearing shortly after. He was running through the snow as fast as he could, sending powder flying everywhere as he flailed and stumbled.

"*HELP!*" he screeched. "*HELP! DAHGÜN! DAH*—!"

His last cry was cut off though, as the night seemed to bend out of itself behind him, slamming the Goatman to the ground. The man screamed in terror as whatever *it* was dragged him backwards, back into the dark, his arms scrabbling at the snow as he vanished once more into the night.

There was a terrible tearing sound of ripping flesh, and the world stilled once again.

Bjen stood frozen, riveted by what he had just seen. It had all happened so fast, so suddenly, that he hadn't so much as had time to tell his archers to draw.

And the man had said "dahgün"…

Bjen al'Hayrd was not a superstitious man. He suspected, in fact, that this was one of the reasons Kareth Grahst had selected him to command the new sentries along the foot of the pass. He hadn't believed a word that the tortured men had screamed about a dragon appearing as though by magic from the trees, tricking them and decimating their ranks. He had seen the aftermath, seen the charred armor of the bodies that had been carted from the steps, but had chalked it up to the profane powers of the Priests and their false god.

And yet now, while the night held its silence as though intent on swallowing the screams of horror and pain that had just shattered its peace, Bjen al'Hayrd found himself doubting.

And it only made him angry.

"*Where are you?*" he growled, scanning the edge of the light, beyond which the unfortunate Goatman had just been dragged. "*Where are you, you conjured bastard?*"

This time, nothing responded.

Nothing, that is, until a warrior at the left-most edge of their wall howled in fear and agony.

Bjen and his men whirled only in time to see a shadow that seemed to have come from *behind* blow past in a blur of silver and black, impossibly fast despite the snow. The Velkrin who had screamed was on the ground, clutching at his left side where a massive, gashing wound seemed to have suddenly appeared, cleaving him half in two. He didn't take long to die, but even as Bjen and the rest of his sentries watched the man still, there was the wrenching sound of cleaved flesh, and a *thump*.

All turned once more to see the massive shadow careen past them yet again, from the opposite direction this time, disappearing into the dark beyond the fires before Vahlen's head had stopped rolling, the Amreht's body tumbling at their feet in their midst.

Bjen wouldn't have had a chance of keeping his sentries in line if he had been the Kayle himself.

It was *instant* chaos, the men howling about "*THE DRAGON!*" and "*DEMONS!*" as they scattered and spun, turning this way and that, attempting to guess where the *thing* would come from next. Bjen kept his head, but couldn't do more than bellow for order, attempting to shove the nearest men back into some sort of formation.

In the time it took him to gather even a small group of three about himself, the shadow struck thrice more.

Bjen watched in horrified fascination as his men fell around him, victim to some great blade he only caught glimpses of as flashes of steel and white wood. Again and again the creature struck, hurtling in and out of the firelight, claiming blood every time. The camp was pure bedlam, the attacks only slowing down when a few of the survivors chose to make mad dashes south through the dark, hoping to reach the safety of the front line beneath the trees.

None of them had disappeared into the night for more than five seconds before Bjen heard them die.

Slowly, though no one gave the command, Bjen and his three warriors began to back up the mountain pass, tripping and stumbling as the heels of their boots caught the hidden lips of the steps beneath the snow. They continued to watch, in disbelief, as the twenty men Bjen had started with became ten, then nine, then eight...

By the time only the four of them were left, they were some twenty steps up the pass, approaching the first curve in the stairs.

For a long while, nothing happened. The world was quiet, the brutal scene below illuminated in the warm orange glow of the fires still flickering around the ring of cleared snow. Bodies lay scattered, almost ten in all, only a few of them whole. Blood painted the earth and stone like a mad canvas, accenting everything in curved streaks of splattered red. A few of the men were still alive, one or two of them moaning and shaking as they died, another delirious in his pain, pulling himself along on his side as he laughed maniacally, crawling towards the better part of his left arm cast some dozen feet away along the base of the steps.

It was he who drew the shadow from the dark.

As the dying man drew nearer to his lost limb, the fabric of the night seemed to bend inward once more along its southern edge, directly across the firelight from Bjen and his survivors. A part of the black itself broke away from its mother, a massive, winged silhouette that made easy work of the snow on long, powerful legs. In one hand it held a straight sword of some queer kind, and in the other it hefted the most terrifying weapon Bjen had ever seen. It was a great, beautifully-crafted spear, with forked blades, a white handle wrapped with dark leather, and a cruel, pointed tip on its balancing end.

The four of them stopped abruptly at the creature's appearance, watching it move. Bjen took in the beast as it made its way slowly across the ring, calm and graceful despite its massive frame. As it moved the shadows twisted around it, splintering when it passed into the fires until six mirroring silhouettes reflected its every step, cast against the mountainside around them.

When it reached the dying man, who had finally managed to get within reach of his severed left arm, it paused. For a moment it waited, like some terrible raptor studying its prey, watching the laughing man grab his limb and roll onto his back, struggling to reattach the arm to the stump below his left shoulder.

Then, with the speed of a lightning strike, the great spear whipped skyward, then down, falling like an executioner's ax to take the man just below the chest.

Both halves of him were finally still when the beast stood straight again, gleaming eyes looking up the stairs, towards Bjen and his three feeble warriors.

Bjen heard one of the warriors to his left begin a death prayer.

He watched, as though in some horrible dream, as the beast stepped over the two parts of his most recent kill, making for the stairs. It took the bottom step slowly, then the second, then the third, climbing upwards with a quiet confidence that was more terrifying than anything Bjen had yet seen. One man lost his head completely, dropping his sword and turning to run, tripping and scrambling up the path as he tried to escape the inescapable. The other two were made of sterner stuff, but their war cries were still shrill with terror as they charged, one lifting a massive two-headed ax over his head, the other a sword and shield. Together they made for the creature, and Bjen saw his only chance. Lifting both axes, he bellowed his own roar of defiance as he plowed forward, intent on taking the monster down. It might have been a danger in the darkness of the night, but in the light of the fires no man had a prayer of surviving a three-on-one engagement with the weathered champions of the mountain tribes.

But the *thing*, it turned out, was no man at all.

The first of Bjen's survivors went down in a blink, the beast sidestepping the great overhead swing of the man's ax casually, as though he were politely moving aside to let the man pass. As the weapon completed its arc, the strange sword came around in a blinding horizontally slash, severing head from shoulders. The dance wasn't done, though, as the creature used the momentum of the strike to complete a spinning turn, lifting the great spear up as it did.

The second man didn't even have time to correct his shield placement before the heavy twin blades crashed into his side, cutting through his arm and into his chest, carrying through to slam him against the uneven stone along the side of the stairs.

It happened so fast, Bjen didn't have time to rethink his charge. As it was, though, even seeing his men snuffed out before him like candles pit against an ocean wave didn't shake the resolve of a trueborn Kregoan warrior. Bjen roared again, his cry stronger now as he embraced death, seeking only glory for himself and his Gods at his end.

Mercifully, the end came quickly.

Bjen barely glimpsed the blow that pierced his heart. All he knew was that whereas in one instant the winged specter was before him, weapons held lazily to either side, in the next it was beside him. In the same moment Bjen felt a searing, numbing pain through his chest, and his breath choked in his throat. As his axes fell from his hands, fingers going limp with the shock of the feeling, he took in the beauty of the craftsmanship of the hilt sticking out of his chest, the care that had been put into the weapon. He lifted his head, finding himself face to face with the sleek reptilian maw of the beast, and he looked into its dead, golden eyes for a moment, witnessing the animal behind them.

Then the blade was retracted, and Bjen fell forward down the stairs, tumbling along the steps, numb to the pain as his body died. He landed on his back, looking up the mountain face, and had only one last notion as he watched the creature continue to ascend the pass, hunting the last survivor.

Dahgün, Bjen al'Hayrd thought, just before the Stone Gods came and lifted him to their halls of laughter and plenty.

XXXVIII

"I don't know if the beast ever came back in truth, after that night. I believe that Syrah calmed the animal in Raz, that she managed to soothe the fire that had burned within him for so long. He will always be a killer, I think. It's in his blood, in his nature. He is made to fight, made to protect. But I think that was the night Raz i'Syul rid himself of what little of the Monster was left in him…"

—private journal of Carro al'Dor

Not here.

It was the first echo of conscious thought Raz had had in hours, but he didn't fight to regain control. He needed the Monster, right now. He needed the cruelty, needed the hunger. It was the wakened beast—usually curled up and asleep within him—that had so effectively cleared the mountain pass. It was the beast that had hunted the sentries down to the last, keeping their cries short and their deaths quick.

And it was the beast that had brought him to this place, drawing forth memories he didn't know he'd kept.

Raz sat crouched on the balls of his feet in the low overhang of a thin tent. All around him small boxes with provisions and baskets of wool and cotton were piled high, pushing out the cloth canopy and widening the space.

Things they use, he thought, not blinking as he stared down at the piled, dirty furs at his feet. *She was kept among the things they use.*

And she *was* here, or at least had been. Raz was sure of it now. He hadn't doubted in the true sense of the word, hadn't strayed from the belief that Syrah was alive, but he had wondered. He had wondered in the way a man of faith wonders at times, given no tangible proof of the existence of his gods.

But now, Raz was certain. He could smell her, could taste her presence in the air, heavy and recent. He hadn't known that he remembered what the woman smelled like until he'd gotten nearer to the tent, hadn't thought that he could recognize her in such a way. He'd prayed to the Moon and Sun that she would be where he'd left her, and hadn't given more than a moment to the fear that she might not be.

Now I know, though, he thought, lifting his snout to taste the air. *Now I can find you.*

There were a hundred scents and flavors to the room, few amongst them pleasant. Raz's eyes dropped again to the short chains, shackled to the center post of the tent. The woman seemed to have been secluded to the space, allowed reprieve only to relieve herself, though not always.

Instead of revulsion, though, Raz felt only rising, unbridled hate begin to build again, the conditions in which Syrah Brahnt had been kept feeding the wrath within him like tinder to a ravenous flame. He battled it back, though, closing his eyes and fighting to find the scent once more through the confusion that assaulted his senses. It took him a moment, but once he latched onto it Raz knew he would never forget it again. It was a clear, calm redolence, bringing to mind wind and dusk and living greenery.

It was the scent of the Garin at sunset, the sands of the desert lake, when a cool breeze would blow waves across the still waters and tease the leaves of shaded palm groves swaying along its shores.

Syrah…

Raz opened his eyes again. He found himself—having not moved his head—staring once more at the cold iron of the chains, limp on the ragged fur blankets she had left behind.

This time, he allowed the fire within to gain a little bit of a foothold, knowing he would need it soon.

Turning away from the space Syrah Brahnt had been kept prisoner for the last two weeks, Raz crept over and peered between the entrance flaps of the tent, taking in everything he could see. When nothing moved among the trees in his view he slipped outside once again, standing up and allowing the animal to move his head this way and that, tasting the air.

Within seconds, it had the scent.

Silent as a whisper, Raz moved west towards the glow and noise of the camp. He kept to the trees, darting from shadow to shadow and trunk to trunk, Ahna's gleaming blades held low and clear of the light. Before long the dull thrum of several hundred men became a true roar of noise to his ears, and the animal started being more cautious, peeking out from behind cover before moving.

When he reached the edge of the camp, he stopped, and cursed.

Syrah's trail led right into the lines of two hundred some-odd tents, staked out wherever there was space among the trees.

Without hesitating Raz moved north, around the camp, dashing through the underbrush. He saw men as he moved—though he made sure they didn't see *him*—patrolling about in pairs and trios. Despite the later hour it seemed most of the Kayle's warriors were still awake and active, and Raz cursed again, wondering if he might have been able to brave slinking *through* the tents if more had been asleep. He blamed the Arocklen for it, blamed the ice and piled snow overhead that had made it hard even for Talo and Carro to sometimes tell the difference between night and day as they'd steadily made for the Citadel.

Fighting back the fear that he wouldn't be able to get to Syrah before the massacre at the base of the path was discovered, Raz kept moving.

For a long time he made a wide circle west among the trees, keeping to what darkness he could find and pausing when he needed to. Three times Raz was almost caught, twice by camp patrols whose eyes he managed to avoid only at the last second, and once by a large man with red paint across his face that had been off among the Woods, relieving himself against a tree.

This one Raz had killed, coming up behind him and crushing his forehead against the trunk for no other reason than to relieve a little of the anger that was threatening to pour out of him every time he allowed himself to dwell on where Syrah might be.

It seemed, however, that the Moon was not finished in blessing him this night. About five minutes into circling the camp, Raz stopped dead, flattening himself against the tall roots of a great fir as the animal found what he was seeking. The scent of the desert shores caught him almost off guard, and he slowly eased himself down onto all fours to sniff at the ground. It was another fifteen seconds or so of scrounging around, backtracking and searching the snowy brush, before Raz found what he was after.

A trail—strong and no more than a few hours old—pulling him further west than the tents, back into the trees.

The woman had been dragged *through* the camp, then out the other side and into the Woods. Raz didn't allow himself to wonder as to what reason there might be for this odd occurrence, but he moved with all haste as he ran, faster and faster as he got further and further away from the dangerous light of the cooking fires.

With Syrah's scent, after all, had come the reek of at least a half-dozen men.

He didn't have to run long. Soon after, Raz found himself breaking through the greater body of the forest and sprinting out into a semi-open space, a wide, natural clearing crafted by the Sun-choking branches of the most massive tree Raz had ever seen. Even with only the dull light of the Moon coming through the canopy, he couldn't help but pause and stare up at the monolith, following the dark outline of its trunk up and up and up into the spidery branches far above.

But the Monster growled within, unimpressed by the scene, and took hold once more.

Her scent led Raz forward, over the frozen ground and dead leaves, directly up to the tree, where it was suddenly much stronger. Raz sniffed around the base, assuming she'd been kept there, among the roots for a time, though again he couldn't guess to what purpose. He followed the trail sideways, staying close to the ground, wincing as he came across the scattered hints of iron in the smell of moss and loam.

She'd been hauled over the ground, skin to frozen earth, without a care as to what it did to her body.

For a few seconds he continued in this fashion, paralleling the steep banks of a stream to the right. Eventually he overshot the trail, losing the scent and having to backtrack several steps before finding it again.

As he did, something caught his sharp eye, pale and distinct even in the dim Moonlight. Raz paused and knelt down, resting Ahna's point in the earth as he reached with his free hand to pluck something from the ground, lifting it close to his face.

There, pinched delicately between the steel tips of his thumb and forefinger, was a single strand of fine, ash-white hair.

Found you, Raz thought, lifting his eyes as the scent dragged his attention eastward once more, their amber glare settling wrathfully on a pocket of firelight that seemed separate from the rest of the camp, removed from the common foot soldiers.

Pulling himself slowly to his feet, Raz let the strand of hair fall from his hand.

By the time it came to rest among the dead, frost-tipped leaves, the Monster was no more than a deadly flicker among the trees, moving in the direction of the light.

Syrah had never been more afraid in her life.

When she'd come to an hour or so ago, the fear had taken its time to settle in. She'd been groggy, her head still muddled from the beating the men who'd come to fetch her from her tent had given her, pummeling her into unconsciousness. The confusion had since cleared slowly, replaced by a dull, deep ache between her temples.

And the overwhelming, all-consuming sensation of sheer, paralyzing terror.

She was on her back, her arms wrenched painfully up above her head, wrists shackled to a support post in the corner of the large tent she had found herself in. Thick furs muffled the roughness of the ground beneath her, and the air was warm, heated by a number of small, wood-fed braziers scattered about the space. Even through her grogginess and the headache it hadn't taken Syrah long to figure out where exactly she was.

Grahst's tent.

Syrah had wondered—for weeks now, in fact—why Kareth Grahst had never paid her a "visit." It had been part of the fear, part of the horror of every moment, wondering when she would hear boots crunching over snow and dirt, wondering when that entrance flap would be pulled open once more, and what cruel, bearded face she would see when it did.

Eventually, the wait and fear had become worse than the actual acts the Kayle's men had forced, one after the other, upon her.

And now, that terrified anticipation was layered tenfold.

She understood, now, why Grahst had denied himself her body. She'd wondered if the man was impotent, or perhaps preferred bed partners of a different sort. She'd gone through a hundred reasons, trying to convince herself that he wouldn't come, that she wouldn't have to bear the memory of him taking her, of his gruff hands pinning her down and stifling her screams, as a dozen had before his.

She blinked away a tear building in the corner of her good eye, brought forth from the unbidden, hateful pit that was her stomach bottoming out at the thought.

But Syrah had never screamed for help, despite the constant urge to do so. She had refused to cry out, refused to allow herself to be lost to fear and desperation and physical pain the men's abuses had inflicted. In the days that she had been held captive, Syrah hadn't once broken before the men who came to take advantage of her, hadn't once given them the satisfaction of seeing her bend to their cruelty. Half a week prior she'd had the meager pleasure of overhearing—from a Sigûrth who'd either forgotten, didn't know, or didn't care that she understood the mountain tongue—that this fact was slowly enraging Grahst. She'd taken pleasure in that knowledge, drawn strength from it. It had given her something to survive on, something that didn't let her die, even when she'd wanted to.

Now, though, her situation had stripped her of that strength. Kareth Grahst was coming, and Syrah knew with agonizing certainty that the man wouldn't be done with her until he had shattered her resolve completely.

This realization had driven her half mad, for a time. For several long minutes she had struggled with her bindings, fighting and pulling at the irons until her already-raw wrists bled once more and the muscles of both arms ached from the stress. In desperation she had tried heating the shackles with magic, hoping to soften the metal, but the results—repeated as they had been the ten times she'd tried before on other days—were only her seething in pain as the cuffs burned into her skin. She had then considered every other spell she knew, every attack and ward and rune. Nothing played in her favor, the possible results ranging from a benign waste of strength to the risk of blinding herself completely with wood shards and splinters if she tried to blast her way free.

Magic, in the end, fell short once again.

And so Syrah had taken a ragged gasp of air, her body shaking despite the warmth of the tent, and begun to pray.

She found comfort in speaking to the Lifegiver. It had been her only source of comfort, in fact. It had carried her through the worst of the last weeks, lifting her up when her mind drifted to the darkest places. Her relationship with Laor had changed, she knew, had shifted through the course of these trials, but her faith had remained unbroken. She'd prayed and made her devotions, doing her best to plead for the wellbeing of everyone she cared for as often as she begged for release from this gauntlet she was suffering through. It had leveled her, kept her earthbound and sane, forced her to draw up the faces of her loved ones, her friends, and others who'd driven themselves unforgettably into her life. Now, as she felt something terrible descending upon her, she drew up these faces once again, thinking of Talo, of Carro and Jofrey and all those others far above her, likely mourning her from the confines of Cyurgi' Di where the mountain men had them trapped. She prayed for their lives, for their happiness after she was gone, after Kareth Grahst—and then very likely the Kayle—were done tearing her down to nothing. She prayed for their safety, even if it meant the cost of her own life.

Then, when she was done with her prayers, Syrah conjured up one last face, one more monstrous and terrifying than any before, and settled into the old, comforting habit of studying the grace of his inhuman features, taking in the fierceness of his golden eyes that always made her feel safe, always made her feel calm.

The crunch of snow ripped that peace from her in an instant.

Syrah's good eye snapped open at the sound, and she gasped involuntarily, feeling adrenaline wash through her in an unbearable cascade across her back, arms, and legs. A few times she had heard men's voices about the tent, but they'd all been either grouped up or too distant to be of any relevance to her current situation.

This time, though, the approaching man spoke not a word.

It seemed an eternity then that she waited. Each of the man's steps rumbled through her mind, echoing in the cavern of terror that opened up once more within her. She tried not to listen, tried not to care as she made out the rustle of his armor and furs, then the light pant of his breathing. She failed though, the sounds warping together to pull at her, to bring her to a state of near panic as her own breath began to come in shallow heaves, her heart pounding in her chest like someone where striking her from the inside with a heavy club.

There was the bending sound of creasing leather followed by the chill of icy air pouring in from the outside, spilling around Syrah like some vile omen.

Then the man stepped into the tent.

XXXIX

Kareth Grahst stood over her for some time, leering down with a look of such inhuman anticipation that Syrah felt herself go numb. She was stiff with fright despite having known what was coming, unable to move or speak or even breathe. She took him in with her one eye, marking his worn leather and fur armor, the sword slung on one hip, and the beads and metal rings wound into his dirty hair and beard. She saw again the thickness of his form, the terrifying breadth of his shoulders and the wretched hunger with which his gaze sought her out. She saw again the demon who had butchered the Priests and Priestesses that had stood alongside her at the bottom of the mountain pass.

This time, though, his attention was directed wholly and undistracted at her, and his bloodlust had been replaced by simpler, raw desire.

At last the man spoke.

"*Welcome, Witch,*" he said, not moving and not taking his eyes off of Syrah. "*I hope you've been comfortable while you wait.*"

The way he said it made Syrah understand without a doubt, then, that Kareth Grahst had known all too well the sort of torment delaying the inevitable must have caused her. It was a tactic, a ploy to shake her, to start the final, gradual process of breaking her.

Instead, it just reminded Syrah of what sort of man—of what sort of *monster*—stood before her. Instead, it drove the terror and trepidation away, shoved it aside for something harder, stronger.

Fear was suddenly replaced with cold, shivering anger.

"Let's get on with this, Grahst," she said in the Common Tongue, shifting herself more comfortably up on the furs and spreading her knees in mockery of his lust. "I doubt you've ever lasted long enough to be entertaining, so the sooner you embarrass yourself, the sooner the real men can get about their business again."

It was only for a half-a-moment, but it was there. Grahst's face twisted, his smirk vanishing to transform into a furious grimace. In that time Syrah felt a thrill of victory.

Then Grahst smiled again, and the viciousness there, lying in wait like some half-starved wolf, made Syrah suddenly wish that she had kept her mouth shut.

In a flash Grahst's sword was in his hand, and he swung it down at her, striking at her leg. Syrah screamed instinctively, first in shocked fear as the blow descended, then in pain as the flat of the man's cold blade struck the inside of her exposed thigh, hammering into the bruised flesh. She had just enough time to close her legs, rolling her body to one side, when the blade fell again, this time striking her calf with such force she thought any more would have broken the bone. After that it fell a third time, then a fourth, then a fifth. Each time the steel connected with some fleshy part of her hips, thighs, and shins, but Syrah—after two weeks of being fed little and less—was not the fit, healthy young woman she had been in the High Citadel. She was too thin, too ragged, and the hammering metal sent waves of fire through her bones and limbs. She screamed with every strike, wailing in pain.

When the blows finally stopped, she laid there, awkwardly twisted on the furs, shaking as her legs spasmed, half-numb and half-burning below her.

"*Speak out of turn again, bitch,*" Grahst said, standing directly over her now, sword held by his side, "*and it won't be the flat of the blade when I strike you next. Do you understana?*"

Syrah said nothing, partially in defiance but mostly because she had no space to give thought to respond. She was dominated by the torment, trying not to cry out while struggling with the residual pain of the blows, her breathing coming in uneven, anguished inhalations.

There was a *thump* of a knee settling down beside her, and a hard, calloused hand clamped suddenly around her jaw, wrenching her face up again.

"*I saia,*" Grahst repeated in a low, threatening hiss that didn't match his smile, "'*do you understana?*'"

Given little choice, Syrah nodded.

Grahst smiled wider. "*Gooa.*"

Then he backhanded her, striking her across the face so hard Syrah felt her lip split as she gasped.

There were stars dancing across her vision as she looked back around at the man, her vision blurred. Grahst was busying himself by unfastening the loops of his armor, stripping out of the hardened leathers piece by piece until his torso was covered by nothing but a stained cloth shirt. She blinked up at him, still kneeling across her, and it took a moment for the horror to return as she realized what he was doing.

Grahst was getting undressed.

Suddenly overcome with panic, Syrah did the only thing that came to mind. The man was half-straddling her, a knee on one side of her, a boot on the other. Bucking herself up, Syrah drove a leg upward, aiming for his crotch, yelling vengefully as she did.

Grahst, though, was faster. Demonstrating all the speed and agility he had shown as they'd fought up the first steps of the pass, he blocked the blow by shifting his high knee down, shielding the fragile parts of his anatomy from her abuse. Then, before Syrah had so much as an instant to brace herself, he drove a gloved fist into her stomach, right in the center of her gut.

"*Pitiful*," Grahst said, watching Syrah retch and hack as the breath was driven out of her. "*You'll have to do better than that to save yourself. And if you can't even fight me off, imagine how little amusement you'll provide the Kayle on the morrow.*"

Syrah said nothing, trying to curl around herself as waves of nausea wracked her body. Grahst, though, wouldn't hear of it, and his smile only widened as she struggled against his touch, tears of desperation and panic forming unwillingly to trail down her left cheek while she fought to breathe. Syrah gasped and heaved, trying to free herself of the man's hands even as she felt them begin to wrench her legs apart. She fought him, this time, thrashing about even after Grahst settled his hips between her knees, preventing her from closing them again. Finally catching her breath, Syrah began to shriek, her composure broken, the beating having done its job.

Grahst just pulled off a glove with his mouth and shoved the leather between her teeth.

Syrah retched again, then, gagging on the taste and feeling of the hide against the back of her throat. She kept trying to scream, though, as she watched Grahst reach down with his other hand and shift his hips out of the thick cloth pants he was wearing. It took a moment, but soon he was free of them, the fabric falling about his knees. Syrah began to buck again as he revealed himself. He struck her once more, this time across the other side of the face, then moved his hand to pull at her robes, trying to hike them up and out of the way. As he did a wave of cold fear washed over Syrah, tingling across her skin and drawing gooseflesh to its surface. She looked around at him again, blinking as the blow and the braziers played tricks on her muddled mind, shifting the shadows so that it seemed Kareth Grahst became a demon in truth, dark wings blooming out to either side of him while he smiled, managing finally to get the torn cloth of her clothes out of the way. He laughed in wicked triumph, starting to press his hips forward. She could feel him now, feel him seeking the space between her legs where he could take his pleasure.

Schlunk!

Abruptly, Grahst's laughter cut short. In the same moment, he stopped fighting, his eyes growing wide, their gaze shifting slowly from Syrah's terrified face downward, towards his chest. It was only when they rested there that Syrah, too, looked to see what had drawn the man's attention away.

The leather glove muffled her howl once again.

Grahst's ragged shirt, originally loose and baggy around him, stood out from his chest in two twin points. Even as Syrah watched, the cotton around these tips grew steadily darker, spilling downward to form ragged, thick lines of uneven blackish red along his torso. Grahst started to make a noise, a bubbling rasp of agony and death, but before he could get it out in full it was swallowed by a different, much more terrifying sound.

A throaty, deafening roar that chilled Syrah to the core.

Grahst made a last "*urk!*" as he was lifted off his knees, pulling the glove from Syrah's mouth as he hung suspended three feet off the ground on the end of whatever strange device had impaled him. As the roar pitched higher he was whipped sideways, his body careening into the side of the tent to Syrah's left. There was the ripping sound of thread, and the cloth and hides split as the man's corpse tore through a section of the wall and tumbled over the ground to come to a rest, twitching, in the basking glow of the Sigûrth camp's main fire.

Syrah, though, didn't see the hole. She didn't see the flames, or the shadows, or hear the shouts of men come running to see what the commotion was about. The only thing she noticed, in fact, was the cold brought in from the night outside. The cold, mirroring the chill of Grahst's entrance into the tent.

And the cold moments before, which she'd thought was fear, but was in fact the winter air pouring through a great slash that had been in the back wall, behind the figure that stood over her now.

A figure she had never thought to see again, except in her dreams.

He was a massive, terrifying thing, far bigger than she remembered, all dark scaled muscle and worn steel armor. The membranes of his ears and wings glowed red in the firelight now, long matured from the sunset shades she had last seen. He had an ax on one hip, the hilt of a sword peeking over the opposite shoulder, and a massive, twin-bladed spear held in hands gloved in clawed gauntlets. His face had changed, too, the angles of his serpentine features having grown sharper, harder than she recalled.

And almost every inch of him, from the leather wraps about his arms and thighs down to the matted brown furs of the huge mantle that hung over his shoulders, was splattered with blood.

All these details, though, Syrah only vaguely registered, barely noting them as her gaze lifted, seeking the most striking thing she remembered about the man. She found what she was looking for at once, meeting his eyes even as they sought hers.

Those sharp, amber eyes, the color of burnished gold, warm—to her—as the rising sun.

For several seconds they just stared at each other, she drinking him in, he doing the same.

When she finally spoke, it was in a choked, sobbing whisper of unbearable relief.

"Raz?"

For an instant Raz i'Syul Arro's face changed. As she recognized him, Syrah witnessed a relief of equal measure wash over the atherian, dragging the anger and hardness from him. She saw, in that brief second, a glimpse of the boy she had met so many years ago, the boy who had thrown himself into the wolves' den to save her, the boy who had killed for her.

And the boy who hadn't, when she'd begged him not to.

Then there was a howl, and one of Kareth Grahst's Sigûrth came leaping into the room, closely followed by two others. In a blink the atherian's face settled into a beastly calm.

Then he was between her and the mountain men.

What Syrah witnessed in the minute that followed was something she would only ever be able to describe as terrifyingly beautiful. Too shaken to voice any denial, with sickened fascination she watched Raz i'Syul Arro dispatch the Kayle's warriors one after the other, never granting them so much as an inch in her direction. The great spear in his hands moved with the grace and speed of a bird of prey, twisting and turning and diving into the melee, joined by striking kicks, lithe lashes of a heavy tail, and blurred slashes of steel claws ripping through leather and flesh or else darting out to pluck swords from hands and wrench shields out of the way. In less than thirty seconds the three men were slain, then a fourth, delayed behind them, a fifth, and finally a sixth. After that it seemed all who had been nearby lay dead or dying at the atherian's feet. There were shouts in the distance, others who had made out the sounds of the fight, and for the space of a breath Raz kept his back to her, the red blade of his crest rising threateningly above his head, wings spread to either side.

When he turned again, though, his golden eyes finding hers once more, the menace died, the animal fled from his face, and the heartbreaking warmth returned. He approached her, dropping to one knee at her side, falling as though dragged helplessly down by the intense deliverance that painted his alien features, the spear *clunking* atop the furs beside him.

"Syrah," he breathed, the word choked by some mix of joy and misery. "Syrah. Thank the Sun."

Raz knelt beside Syrah Brahnt, deaf and blind to all but the woman before him, lying on her back on the layered elk and wolf pelts, chained up like some animal readied for the slaughter. He didn't know how to feel, how to *think*. All he could do was stare at her, taking her in, bathing in the realization that she was alive, that she was whole.

Or almost.

Raz, helpless in his growing outrage, stared at the woman's face. His eyes first flicked to the knotted remnant of her right ear, then to the rag, worn and dirty, wrapped diagonally over her right eye. He felt cold fire spring up within him once more when he saw the hint of a vertical scar above and below the frayed edges of the cloth.

The mark of a blade.

"What did they do to you?" he demanded with wrenching fury, ignoring the rumble of voices building up and approaching in the distance behind him. "Syrah, what happened?"

Syrah looked suddenly ill, turning her face away from him to hide the eye. As she did he noticed her shifting uncomfortably, trying to cover herself after the savage had hitched her robes above her hips. Raz made to help, reaching for the tattered remnants of the clothes in the hopes of saving what modesty she had left.

But before he could do so, he froze.

He saw the marks, then, all along the insides and outsides of her thin thighs, fiery welts that looked like the flat of a sword overlaying dozens of black and blue bruises. He saw the yellowed imprint of teeth—*human* teeth—in her flesh, marring the otherwise calm paleness of her skin. He saw the way her legs shook, and the way she spasmed when he took ahold of the bunched cotton around her hips. He saw the way she refused to look at him as he—slowly and with delicate, gentle care—finally covered her up.

It took everything he had not to drop into the pit that had ripped open inside of him at the sight of the damage that had been done.

More shouts gathered behind them, and Raz slipped.

"I need to get you out of here," he said hurriedly, getting to his feet, lifting his spear in one hand as he did. Syrah turned to look at him again as he took stock of the bindings around her wrists.

When he grabbed hold of them with one hand, she looked suddenly fearful.

"What are you going to—?" she started.

"Cover your face," he interrupted just as the sound of approaching feet, running towards them at full tilt, became clear over the snap and crack of the fire behind him.

Syrah, hesitated, then did as she was told.

When he was sure her eye was covered, Raz gave the post a single crushing kick.

The timber—despite being as thick as a man's arm—didn't have a prayer under the force of the blow. It snapped in two without so much as a fight, partially collapsing the tent around them. Raz started to haul Syrah up, intending to help her towards the slash he'd cut in the back of the tent. As he did, though, he realized with a heavy pitting in his stomach that the woman weighed next to nothing, her tall form almost pulled right off the ground by his assistance.

She's so thin, he thought, noticing for the first time the prominence of bone in her arms and legs, and the shallowness of her cheeks. Syrah groaned as she settled onto her feet, swaying dangerously.

Making a decision, Raz scooped her up in one arm, cradling her against his chest, and sprinted towards the back wall.

The other supports held, and they were outside in seconds, dashing into the trees. For half-a-minute Raz ran, driving straight north, towards the Saragrias. When he heard voices behind them, though, howling in fury and hooting as they gave chase through the dark, he slowed down, then stopped.

The Monster reared its head within him, snarling hungrily at their pursuers, and Raz felt the bloodlust rise once more.

Then something small and gentle came to rest against his chest, and he glanced down.

Syrah was looking up at him, her one eye bright and tired in the soft blue light of the Woods. She was watching him, her right hand resting against his heart, and it seemed in that moment she knew what was going through his mind.

When she spoke, it was in a quiet, comforting whisper.

"Leave them, Raz," she said, the broken, dirtied nails of her hand digging lightly into his skin in subtle supplication. "Please. For me."

There was a long moment as Raz stared down at the woman in his arms. He met her gaze evenly, feeling as though he were ready to fall into the depths of her one good eye. He remembered the last time he had listened to this same request, recalled the price he had paid for it.

Then, like her words had been a lullaby, the animal retreated back to where it had come, settling into sleep.

"If you're sure," he said softly, turning away from the sounds of approaching men. Syrah smiled at him as he did so.

The warmth behind that smile was all Raz needed to spur himself to new speeds through the Woods, out of the trees, and over the carnage at the base of the path before taking the wide stone steps of the mountain pass two at a time.

XL

"We are fortunate, in the end, that Raz's actions were not cordoned in with the facts of my own betrayal. He was an outsider, a man of the world, not of the faith. His choices—while still his responsibility—were not governed by the laws of the Laorin, and so he was not bound by the same restrictions, the same expectations and punishments. It is for this reason, I think, that his return to us that day was the first great step in earning the trust of the faith. Instead of running, instead of fleeing the men and women who had held him prisoner, he returned to us willingly, bearing with him proof that he was not the soulless contraption of mayhem and butchery so many have tried to paint him out to be."

—private journal of Carro al'Dor

Jofrey felt he had only just gotten to sleep when the summons came in the earliest hours of the morning, well before first light. It had been a late, restless evening, he and the rest of council having retired well after midnight had come and gone. Carro had been interrogated to every possible extent, half the council seeking some reason to forgive him his folly, the other half demanding he be Broken immediately and cast out into the snow. Valaria Petrük and Behn Argo had—of course—been particularly virulent, both of them raging the night away about the "madness" of setting an untamable brute like Raz i'Syul Arro free upon the world.

And all the while Carro had only smiled, looking—*For the first time since he returned,* Jofrey thought—at peace.

It was towards this troubling realization that Jofrey's mind had wandered as he fell asleep, the heavy series of poundings on his room door serving to rip him out twisted dreams of an old, bloodier life best left behind. Unused to the spaciousness of the High Priest's quarters—which he had been hastily moved into permanently the previous afternoon—at first Jofrey's groggy mind had been mostly convinced it was the sound of sudden hail hammering the wide window set beside the bed in the circular wall. When the pounding came again, though, he started up from his mattress, intent on shouting a tired "Come in!" as he made to swing his legs over the edge of the bed.

Before he could get the words out, though, the door was thrown open, swinging inward so hard it hit the inside wall with a *crash*, bathing the dark room with a wedged stroke of the brighter light of the hall. In its wake Cullen Brern practically tripped inside, looking desperately in all directions before finding Jofrey. Behind him Priest Elber did the same, rushing in as though chased. Both men's faces were white, their eyes wide when they fell on their new High Priest.

"He's coming back!" Cullen was the first to get the words. "He's coming back! He's got her!"

For a full five seconds after these words, Jofrey sat stunned, still halfway in and out of the bed. Slowly, eventually, his eyes went to Elber's, seeking confirmation of the impossible.

"T-two!" the older man gasped, struggling to catch his breath. "Two people! Coming up the pass! When the first ward broke we wanted to wait, to let you sleep. But now the second tells us there're two people and—!"

"He has her," Jofrey hissed in incredulous, disbelieving shock. "Arro found Syrah."

"It's the only explanation," Brern insisted. "If the Kayle were sending a response, it would be more than two. Jofrey, please! Let me take a group and meet them! Let me get to them and—!"

His words were cut short, though, as Jofrey scrambled the rest of the way out of bed, snatched his robes from where they hung on the corner post, and dashed right at the two men.

"Like hell," he half-snarled, half-yelled as he pushed past the pair, running in nothing but his nightgown in the direction of the temple gates. "Cullen, get your brother. Elber, find Benala. We're going to get them ourselves."

Not fifteen minutes later, in the dark of the early hour, Jofrey, Cullen, Kallet, Priest Elber, and Benala Forn were dashing across the Citadel's inner courtyard, taking turns to blast aside the piled snow and ice as they ran. They made their way through the outer wall quickly, the hammering of their boots echoing eerily in the tunnel, the light of the glowing orbs hovering above their shoulders shivering against the stone that curved overhead. After that, their course took them out over the plateau and towards the top of the stairs. Jofrey led the charge, now, his magic fueled by his hope and need, his spells blowing the path ahead clear thirty feet at a time.

For hours the five of them descended, sometimes yelling to one another to watch their footing, or else shouting concerns about what would happen if it wasn't Syrah and the atherian, or what state the pair might be in if it *was* them. Jofrey had no patience for doubts, at the moment, and so didn't deign respond to any such concerns thrown his way. He knew—he *knew*—that Arro had succeeded. In the same way he had felt—though told no one—a sense of calming relief as he'd watched the atherian's fleeing footprints fill with snow beyond the frame of the Last Door, so did he feel an absolute certainty that it was the man and Syrah fighting their way back up the mountain in the night. He could sense Laor's hand in that confidence, could sense the Lifegiver feeding that conviction.

And so for almost three hours Jofrey ran in focused silence, refreshing and warming himself only when he had to, leaving the others far behind more than once. *Around the next corner*, he kept telling himself. *Around the next one.*

And then, just as the sun began to make itself known over the distant eastern horizon, his anticipation bore fruit.

Whether it was coincidence or by some godly decree, they met in the same place Cullen Brern had first encountered Carro and the atherian. Jofrey had descended the winding path, back and forth across the mountainside, vaulting down and cutting every corner whenever he could. He had taken the bend, hurrying down the steps and past the entrance to the alcove he knew the two men had rested in only a few nights ago, when a shape came around the ledge in front of him, large and dark against the orange and purple of the new dawn. Jofrey felt a thrill wash through him as he made out the black silhouette against the backdrop of the sunrise behind it, watching it lumber in staggering, uneven steps, one after the other.

Then the figure caught sight of him, and it stopped.

Jofrey said nothing as he continued his descent down the last of the steps, rushing along the flat part of the path as he reached it and hearing the others hurdling along above and behind him. As he ran forward, the massive shape fell in exhausted relief to its knees.

When the High Priest finally came to halt before the man, he felt his heart stop.

Raz i'Syul Arro knelt, worn and beaten, half-hunched over the still, spectral, form of the woman curled up against him. The atherian was a terrifying sight, glistening and streaked with dark stains that looked almost black in the morning light. The dried and frozen blood clung to everything, from the great spear hanging limp from one hand on the ground beside him to the reddened teeth along the snout that hung wearily down, shielding the woman from the cold and the snow as it began to fall again. He was heaving, his eyes closed, his breath blowing out of his mouth and nostrils like smoke to rise and wreath his head. The man shivered, his body shaking even beneath the layered pelts of the crusted mantle hanging over his shoulders.

When the atherian spoke, though, his voice was firm, his words audible over the crunching sounds of booted feet coming to a halt behind Jofrey.

"Lead the way."

XLI

"Cruelty is, simply put, an accepted medium of interaction among the mountain tribes of the North. It is, in some ways, a limitedly quantifiable measure of power among a people who value strength above all else. A man who can be cruel is a man who must be strong, for cruelty requires a hardness of the heart and soul through which a man can stand firm even under the greatest of threats. It is for this reason, perhaps, that the Stone Gods were born, for if a man's strength can be measured by his cruelty, why not his gods?"

—*Legends Beyond the Border*, by Zyryl Vahs

For a long time Gûlraht Baoill stood silent over the shaking forms of the three Sigûrth warriors kneeling in a line before him. Their fear was palpable, like a stench they couldn't shake, emanating from their helpless shivering and the breaking pitch with which they'd spoken as they'd delivered their report. Any other time the Kayle might have had the men lashed for displaying such blatant enfeeblement in his presence. Any other time he might have just killed them himself, demonstrating once more that he would tolerate no frailty within his army.

As it was, the words they'd brought with them had stilled his heart, head, and hands.

And pointed his rage, with all distinction, in another direction.

"Take me to him," he told the three men simply.

The messengers jumped at the deep sound of his voice, but didn't pause. At once they clambered to their feet and turned to hurry east through the forest. Gûlraht gave nothing more than a small nod to the man beside him before following, his great ax held in one hand at his side. As he moved away he heard Agor Vareks shout the order to march, and the rumbling sound of twenty-five thousand men lumbering forward behind him chased the Kayle through the trees.

None of it reached him, in the frightening place he was descending to, the place of whirling darkness dragged forth by the news he'd been brought as soon as the camp sentries had made out their approach through the Woods. For several minutes he followed the messengers along their winding path through the underbrush, keeping his eyes on their backs. He didn't take note of them slowing down when they realized their Kayle was in no rush to keep up with them, nor did he notice the terrified glances they gave each other as they glanced curiously up into his face.

If he had, he might have measured the wrath he felt slowly building up within, consuming his heart and soul, leaking out to paint his features in violent detail.

It wasn't long before he started to make out the sound of men in the distance, then the glint of flames through the trees. A minute later the Sigûrth led him out of the forest into a circle of tents, and he felt warmth bathe him as they moved into the light of a great fire in the middle of the ring. All about, dozens of men from every tribe were standing, their voices an angry rumble, their faces rough and fearsome in the orange dance of the flames. At first, when the three messengers started to push their way through the gathering, warriors turned to snarl and challenge them, wondering who dared attempt cheat a glimpse of whatever it was the crowd encircled.

When they saw the towering form of their Kayle, however, their threats died in their throats and they slunk quickly out of the way.

Word spread through the men as a silent wave, washing ahead of Gûlraht like some spell across the ranks. Where a minute ago the air had been thick with the buzz of hard and curious voices, by the time he reached the center of the ring the only sounds that could be made out were the crackling of the fire and the whistle of the wind as it battered the tops of the trees far above them.

When the last line of men parted, the three who'd led him there quietly vanishing into the crowd, Gûlraht was left to stand over the proof of his first true defeat.

Of the bodies lain out before him, few were intact. They waited, mangled and ugly, in two curved rows of over a dozen each, wrapped partway around the fire. Gûlraht's sharp eyes took in their state as the shadows leapt about, and for the first time since his father had called him a man of the clans he felt something like fear prickle up inside him. He had been warned in the story he'd been told by the messengers, but the words and tally had been drowned out by the greater loss they had informed him of. As he stood now over the corpses of the fallen, he heard them again.

Then, as though to echo his thoughts, someone behind him whispered the one thing they were all thinking.

"*Dahgün.*"

As hard as he tried, Gûlraht couldn't find fault in the fear while he stood looking down at the dead. His men hadn't just been slain. They hadn't just fallen in battle, or been claimed by the sword. His men had been *ravagea*. They had been torn apart, limbs wrenched clean of sockets, heads twisted the wrong way, backs bent almost in two. Those that did bear blade wounds showed more familiar signs, but they were no less alarming. Arms and legs missing. Innards and gore emptied from opened cavities, the stench kept at bay only by the cold. Bodies cleaved almost in two—and one that *had* been cleaved in two.

To Gûlraht, it was these corpses that drew his eyes the most. The others he might have explained away, might have written off as a tale of cruelty of winter and Them of Stone. He had seen bears tear men asunder in much the same way, had seen wolves shred armor and flesh and drag off their prizes in pieces to scatter the bones amongst the cliffs.

But the wounds caused by steel, he couldn't ignore. Those bodies he couldn't take his eyes off of, couldn't look away from. They resonated within him, bringing to mind memories and images of a dozen bloody battles.

They dragged Gûlraht back, because they were the same sort of savagery he caused with the very ax he held now in his right hand...

For a long moment the Kayle wallowed in that realization, unwillingly wondering what sort of man—if it was a man at all—could have caused such devastation to his warriors. For a long time he stood and pondered what aid the Laorin's false-god had summoned for his people, questioning his knowledge of the faith and their vows of peace.

As his eyes shifted from body to body, though, they found a familiar face, and the doubts and questions whipping through Gûlraht's head were momentarily snuffed out.

Men did their best to leap out of the way as Gûlraht surged suddenly to the right, making a line for one corpse in particular, near the end of the first row. Those that didn't move in time found themselves shoved roughly aside or shouldered back into the crowd, but no one muttered so much as a sound of complaint. All there were members of the vanguard, of the advanced force the Kayle had sent with the purpose of laying siege to the Laorin and their cursed Citadel.

And all knew who Gûlraht had seen.

Of any corpse laid out before the great fire, Kareth's was perhaps the most intact. The man might have been asleep, in fact, with his hands folded over his chest, were it not for the uneven streaks of blood that stained the front of his cotton shirt black. He'd been run through, Gûlraht saw in an instant, and from behind nonetheless. The cloth he could see was intact, which meant the weapon had taken him through the back. Somehow, someway, Kareth Grahst had allowed himself to be taken by surprise. He had failed to put up so much as a fight, failed to face his death like a man.

And, in the process, had lost the White Witch.

This last thought brought the anger back to the surface of Gûlraht's mind, and as he stared down at his cousin's body he felt his face contort into a grimace. He continued to dwell on the enraging loss of his one absolute and most desired prize, and from somewhere the Kayle heard a sound like a building growl.

By the time he realized it was his own growl, Gûlraht had already lost control.

The ax moved of its own volition it seemed at first, coming up into his two hands to swing high above his head, then driving down with frightening force as he bellowed out his fury and frustration. It struck Kareth's corpse with the wet, cracking sound only sheared flesh and breaking bone can make. There were shouts of fear and horror all around him, but the Kayle ignored all, lifting his ax once more. It fell a second time, sinking into the body again, and was retracted even quicker. Before long Gûlraht's was grunting and yelling with every strike, oblivious to the thick blood that sprayed his boots and clung to his ax, oblivious to the gore that flew in every direction as it cut and struck at the body again and again and again. Soon the only sounds that could be made out over the flames were the sickening *thunks* and *cracks* of the iron striking the dead man.

It felt like hours before Gûlraht was finally too tired to continue. As he straightened up, chest heaving from the anger and strain, he realized that all around him silence had fallen once more, the men of his army staring up at their Kayle in equal parts awe and terror. He stood, a blood splattered, angry titan amongst lesser men, staring down at the grisly mess that was left of his cousin's corpse.

Then, in a final motion, he stepped to the side and brought the ax down one last time, striking at the one part he had avoided in his rage.

Schlunk.

Kareth's head rolled off, coming to rest against Gûlraht's boot as the ax sunk deep into the hard-packed earth.

Wrenching the weapon free with one hand, Gûlraht knelt and lifted the head up by its hair in the other. Bringing it to face-height, he glared at the thing for a long time, watching it revolve slowly in place, suspended before him.

"*In the end, cousin,*" he spoke to Kareth's closed eyes finally, his voice a black hiss, "*you were of even less use than your father.*"

Then, before any of the hundred men around him could think to protest, he spat in the thing's face, then swung the head around and tossed it into the blaze of the fire.

As the stench of burning flesh and hair filled the air, Gûlraht turned to face the crowd. He stood beside the ravaged remains of his cousin's corpse, a great shadow among the still forms of the dead.

"NOW," he thundered in a growling voice that carried over the crackle of the blaze, "*TELL ME WHAT MANNER OF CREATURE WAS FOOL ENOUGH TO STEAL THE WITCH FROM ME!*"

"*A dragon?*" Rako the Calm demanded, sounding none-too-convinced. "*They claim a dragon slew Kareth and took the Witch?*"

"*Whatever manner of creature, all say it was no man,*" Agor Vareks murmured, watching as Gûlraht—having taken a seat along the back of the tent—allowed his bloody hands to be washed in warm water by a pair of slave girls on either side of him. "*They say it had the head of a serpent, the wings of a bat, and claws and teeth of iron and steel.*"

"*Then they're maa,*" Rako said impatiently. "*That, or they have conspired to feed you a great lie, my Kayle.*"

There was a pause at these words, in which the Kayle glowered at the oldest of his advisors. They were in what was left standing of Kareth's tent, the still-burning braziers in each corner providing warmth enough while they waited for the camp slaves to pitch their own abodes. The generals had arrived not ten minutes after Gûlraht had brutalized Grahst's corpse, leading with them the rest of the army. After settling the affairs of getting the ranks in order and starting the lengthy process of setting camp, they had met with their Kayle here, in this place of his choosing, and listened to what it was he had discovered in their absence. Rako—as one might have expected—had immediately thrown himself into the usual meek tirade, claiming treachery and foolishness.

Gûlraht, though, wasn't so easily convinced. What was more, the tingle of fear he had felt when he'd first laid eyes on the remnant carnage of the dead had twisted and evolved as he'd stood among the fallen, waiting for his advisors. It had shifted, altering in the heart of a man who had met and vanquished every challenger in his life without hesitation or concern.

Now, rather than anything like fear, Gûlraht was beginning to feel only the emerging hint of excitement, bloodlust, and anticipation.

"*Have you examined the bodies, old man?*" he demanded, sneering at his aged general. "*Did you not see the marks and wounds that have turned more than two-dozen hard warriors of the clans into little more than shredded flesh and bone?*"

Rako flushed at that, though he knew better than to rise to the bait.

"*I saw the bodies, my Kayle, and I saw the wounds. I am merely suggesting that it is often the nature of man, faced with consequences, to cling to any story that will lessen his punishment.*"

"*And so they would craft some nonsense about a dragon?*" Agor asked testily from his spot leaning against one of the tent ribs behind Rako's shoulder. "*Of all the other plausible explanations? Unlikely.*"

"*A 'plausible' explanation is exactly what they would avoid!*" Rako spat, his temper flaring now, his eyes not leaving Gûlraht's. "*Your army knows that you do not treat failure kindly, my Kayle. Perhaps this tale is nothing more than an attempt to escape your wroth. I have told you before that you are too hard on the men. They have resorted to base story-telling and lying in order to avoid punishment!*"

"*Or,*" young Erek Rathst spoke from the far end of the tent, where he was examining a great slash in the leather wall that was letting the cold air in about their feet, "*they are telling the truth.*"

There was a long, heavy pause.

"*The truth?*" Rako demanded derisively, giving the younger man a scathing look. "*That a dragon has been set upon us? What foolishness is this?*"

"*Oh, it is foolishness,*" Erek replied without turning around, and Gûlraht saw him feel the edges of the sliced cloth between his fingers. "*Or rather, it is superstition and the product of weak minds and weak men. All the same, though, that is not to say that the story they tell is not the truth, at least to their understanding.*"

"*Erek,*" Gûlraht rumbled in warning, already tiring of the riddle. "*Speak plainly.*"

Erek turned around at once, bowing his head briefly to the Kayle in apology.

"*I mean simply that it may not be we who are misinformed, my Kayle, but rather those who are informing us. Did you know that this is not the first time this 'dragon' has made its appearance?*"

Gûlraht kept his face impassive, but out of the corner of his eye he saw Agor blink and Rako jerk in blatant surprise.

"*Not the first time?*" the older man demanded. "*Explain, Rathst.*"

Erek smiled, clearly enjoying his moment of power. "*It is indeed not the first, but the second. Two days past, the sentries posted along the base of the mountain stairs suffered lesser losses, but all claimed the same story: they were attacked by a dragon, a dahgün.*"

"*How do you know this?*" It was Agor's turn to demand. "*Who has told you this?*"

"*One man, and then a half-dozen more,*" Erek answered with a shrug, stepping away from the cold to warm his hands over the embers in one of the braziers. "*I overheard mutterings, and I followed the trail. Regardless, the facts stand: this is the second time this creature has attacked. More importantly, Kareth apparently had a theory as to where it came from...*"

He looked to want to pause dramatically, then, but Gûlraht gave him such a chilling glare that the man continued almost at once.

"*Kareth thought the beast had been conjurea,*" he said quickly. "*He believed the dragon was a thing of magic.*"

There was a collective silence, in which Gûlraht and the other two generals took this to mind. It resonated with them, bewildering them in its simplicity. Agor looked mildly appalled, while Rako looked nothing short of impressed.

The Kayle, though, felt something altogether different, as the budding hope of a fight worthy of his ax started to slip beyond his reach.

"Magic," Rako finally said in slow, thoughtful voice. "Yes... It would certainly explain much and more. I find it hard to believe such devastation could be caused by a single being, beast or otherwise. But a creature of magic..."

"'The head of a serpent, the wings of a bat,'" Agor followed up, repeating the quote. "What else but the wicked power of the false-prophets could conjure up such a beast...?"

The Kayle for his part, frowned, feeling his anticipation fade even further. He admitted to himself, then, that some part of him had hoped to find truth in the story the men of the vanguard had spun for him.

As it was, it was starting to look as though winning the glory of slaying a dragon was not a thread of his fate.

"Magic," he muttered, the word spilling from his lips as though it were a putrid, abhorrent thing. He said nothing more, letting it hang there, spelling out all too clearly his disgust.

"My Kayle..." Agor said finally after several long seconds of heavy silence. "If this 'dragon' is truly nothing more than blasphemy and spellwork, then it is of little consequence to the greater need. The vanguard has done as it was assigned. The Laorin have been kept to their temple. Even if the Priests can conjure beasts by which to protect themselves, it makes little difference against the power of your will, much less the strength of your army."

Gûlraht frowned further at that. He had little mind, at the moment, to dwell on anything other than the lost opportunity to fight a creature of myth, but the man had a point. They'd marched with all haste for more than two weeks now to catch up with the advance line, and now that they were here there was greater business to attend to.

Making up his mind, he looked around at one of the slaves still scrubbing diligently at his hands. At once she paled under his gaze, then hurried to stand. Grabbing the other girl by the hand, they bowed together to the Kayle and his advisors, then hurried from the tent.

Once the flap had rippled shut behind them, Gûlraht looked around.

"Agor," he said, putting an elbow on the armrest of the chair and leaning his cheek into his fist, "divide the contingents that would have been under Kareth's command between the three of you. Erek will take what's left of the vanguard in addition. Rako—" his cruel eyes fell on the older man "—find out everything you can about what has happened here in my absence, and report back to me, especially if you hear anything more of this 'dragon.' Erek—" his gaze moved to the last of his generals "—you're to see to the pass. As mere sentries aren't doing the job, I want the entirety of the vanguard camped along the tree line. No one, NOTHING, comes down those stairs, do you understand?"

354

Erek nodded at once, but Agor looked concerned.

"*Does this mean you intend to wait out the faith, my Kayle?*" he asked, sounding almost frustrated. "*Need I remind you that time is not on our side, and that if the freeze should end before we—*"

He cut himself short, though, as Gûlraht rose to his feet with all the fearsome power of a god. He stood, two-head taller than any of them, his wild, beaded braids brushing the fur-lined ceiling. His shadows whipped and shimmered about them in all directions, faded, monstrous outlines cast by the glow of the braziers. He stared down at Agor, eyes wide, as though challenging him to continue speaking.

When the general didn't, Gûlraht reached up, sliding a hand into the side of his leather breastplate.

"*I intend, Agor,*" he said in a voice of deadly calm as his fingers fumbled around in the space between the armor and the shirt beneath, searching, "*to not play the fool. I intend to allow my army to rest, to allow my men the reprieve they need after two weeks' hard march. I intend to revel with them as we prepare, to drink and fight and fuck until the battlefog descends, until every ax is honed and every arm is strong and ready again.*"

His fingers stopped moving, and he slowly pulled something from behind the leather.

"*Then,*" he continued, holding the thing up for all of them to see, cast in the orange glow of the embers, "*I intend to bring the wrath of Them of Stone down on the heads of the false-prophets, and to leave them and all their ilk as nothing more than a stain on the face of the mountains.*"

He watched as Agor's face, followed quickly by Erek's, broke into a slow, hollow and ravenous smile. He watched as Rako frowned, but said no word in defiance. He watched their eyes, following their gaze to what he was holding in his hand.

There, clenched so tightly between his fingers that its limp ends trembled as they hung down from the bottom of his fist, was a twined clump of bone-white, braided hair.

XLII

Syrah awoke slowly, rising from so deep a sleep that, as she cracked open her eyes, she couldn't be sure whether she was leaving a dream or entering one. All around her she felt warm softness, and she blinked as blue and white light shimmered overhead, playing against the ceiling above. Slowly, second by second, the world came into focus, and before long Syrah was staring up at a familiar pattern of uneven stone hanging comfortingly above her.

At once she felt tension build up in her lips and cheeks, and she swallowed, fighting the impulse to sob.

Laor have mercy, she prayed. *Let it not be a dream…*

In the end, she couldn't help it, and she began to cry softly, spilling small tears, each weighed down by heavy, almost desperate solace.

"Syrah?"

The voice, hoarse and tired, took her by surprise, and Syrah rolled her head to look beside her. There to her left, blinking away what seemed to have been weak sleep as he sat forward in the wide armchair that had been dragged up to the edge of her bed, was Jofrey.

"J-Jofrey," she said in a low, breaking moan that was mixed wretchedness and relief. "Oh, J-Jofrey. I'm so s-sorry. I couldn't-couldn't stop them. I—"

"Shh, child," the aged Priest said, leaning forward at once and reaching for her bandaged hand, laying atop the blankets that covered her. "Shh. It's all right. It's—"

But as his fingers settled atop hers Syrah gasped, wrenching her arm away. A wave of something very much like nausea ripped through her, and she felt—albeit unwillingly—the touch of a dozen other hands, warm and rough on her skin, pulling and pushing at her, forcing her down.

The tears started to come in truth.

"I'm so sorry, Syrah!" Jofrey said in a hurried whisper, his face a wretched picture of grief and pain as he pulled his hand away again. "I'm so sorry! I didn't think! I shouldn't have…"

But he let the words trail away as Syrah continued to sob quietly, clutching her hands to her chest. She turned her face away from him, intent on waiting out the stir of helpless dread that was coursing, unbidden and unwanted, through her.

But, as she rolled her head to the other side, Syrah suddenly felt all the fear drain away.

There, awkwardly slumped half over himself in another chair pulled up on the right side of her bed, was Raz i'Syul Arro.

He wasn't the terrifying, grisly form she remembered from Kareth Grahst's tent, now. Nor was he the ragged, shivering and wheezing man who had carried her up the mountain, whispering comforting words to her between gasping breaths as she faded off against the reassuring firmness of his neck and chest. Rather, the atherian was clean and still, his whole body rising and falling slightly with every slow, deep inhalation, the worn cotton shirt he wore looking tight and almost odd on him. His ears and wings twitched on either side of his head and shoulders as he moved, his big, clawed hands resting across his lap to reach out in a strange, pleading sort of way, lightly grasping the hanging lip of her blankets.

Sleeping, she realized.

And, for some reason, it made her smile.

"He's been like that since the moment you were put to bed," Jofrey said gently from her other side. "He raged and roared and threatened to tear off every one of our heads until we agreed to let him stay by your side."

Syrah saw, then, with a jolt of revulsion that tightened about her heart, the rectangular wood and iron bracket that encircled his wrists, shackling his hands together.

"You've chained him," she whispered sadly. "Why would you chain him?"

"It was at Petrük's insistence. She did her own ranting. Wanted to make sure we didn't 'let him loose' in our home. When Arro first arrived he... uh... to say 'made a scene,' seems a very mild way to put it."

"That bloody hag," Syrah mumbled, reaching out to touch the cold iron of the bindings with the shaking fingers. "She doesn't realize he could be out of them as soon as he has half a mind to be?"

Behind her, Jofrey chuckled.

"Fear is blinding, as they say."

Then, abruptly, his voice sobered.

"Syrah..." he said gently. "When I put that on him... The man has scars. There, on his wrists. They look like... well... I think he's giving up much of himself, to wear that thing now..."

Syrah nodded, but said nothing. She knew all too well what Raz i'Syul was giving up, allowing himself to be bound in such a way. The bandages around her hands encircled her palms and wrapped halfway up her forearms, hiding what was beneath, but she could still feel the pain, that thrumming ache that followed chafing and blistering. Despite this, she felt oddly as though she wouldn't be afraid of removing the cloth bindings.

Whatever scars I have, she realized, eyeing the hint of paler flesh about where the manacles were locked around Raz's wrists, *I won't be alone in bearing them.*

Her fingers trailed along the metal and wood, following the rectangular edge of the bracket downward. Then, after a moment's hesitation, she moved them slowly to rest atop the back of the atherian's hand.

His skin felt like silk made solid. There was a deadly softness to it, a firm smoothness that was cool beneath her touch. She had been frightened, for a moment, that she would be repulsed by the feel of his scales, as she had been by Jofrey's kindly touch. But no nausea came, no crushing weight of dread and sadness. Instead, Syrah felt an old sensation seep its way inside, reaching down and warming her in a way the bed and blankets and heat never would. As with the times when she had sought out his face in her recollections, pulling the memory of him forth to draw hope from and calm her nerves, so too did the feeling of Raz's hand beneath hers do the same. To an extent, in fact, it was a much, *much* stronger sensation. Syrah suddenly felt an odd sort of strength return to her, as she trailed the edge of the atherian's fingers with her own. It wasn't strength of body—despite however long she had been asleep, Syrah was still heavy-eyed and drowsy. Instead, it was rather as though something had reached down within to find the shivering, bruised spark that was her spirit, and pulled it lightly to its feet.

She smiled wider, feeling the will, the desire to live, return to her steadily.

"How did he get here, Jofrey?" Syrah asked quietly, not taking her eye off the sleeping atherian's face. "Where did he come from? Did someone call on him?"

For a long time, Jofrey didn't answer it. The silence had stretched for a good ten seconds, in fact, before Syrah rolled back over, looking at him in concern as she saw that his face bore a stoic look lined with sadness.

"That's a tale I think Arro had best tell you himself," Jofrey finally said, his gaze shifting to look at the man across the bed from him. "He's been dead to the world ever since he got you back up the path, but something tells me he won't mind if you wake him. First, though, Syrah"—he looked at her again, his face truly grief-ridden, now—"there's something you need to know. I would rather Carro be the one, but the rest of the council wouldn't stand for—"

"Carro?" Syrah demanded, almost forgetting herself as she felt a leap in her breast. "Does that mean he and Talo made it back? When? How did they—?"

358

But she stopped then, as she registered what the man had said. She barely noticed Jofrey's expression, in fact—a picture of sadness and heartbreak, now—as she realized the implication of his words.

"Jofrey…" she started slowly, knowing all too well that she didn't want the answer to the question she was about to ask. "Jofrey… Where is Talo?"

It took a very long time, then, for Jofrey to gather himself enough to answer, and far longer to tell her the story of Talo Brahnt's death. He talked with slow, heavy words that spoke to his own pain in the retelling, and he had to stop often to keep his voice from breaking. He told her as best he could of what had happened, of how Talo and Carro had received her letters and set out immediately for the Citadel, and how terror and tragedy had struck them on the road. He told her what he knew of Raz's role in the matter, of how he had slain the beast that had dealt the killing blow, but too late. He told her that her Priest-Mentor had died among friends, with his lover by his side, and that he had been laid to rest in the deep reaches of the Arocklen where Laor would certainly have taken him up into his arms and returned him to the eternal cycle of life.

By the time he finished speaking, Syrah felt as numb and hollow as she had after the first visit the Sigûrth had paid her in that cold, cruel tent far below them…

Somewhere, in a distant part of her mind, Syrah was grateful that her hand still rested atop Raz's. Had he not been there, had she not been able to reach out and touch him and draw from him the warmth his face had always inexplicably given her, Syrah thought she might have lost herself then, in the minutes that followed Jofrey's news. All of a sudden she remembered waking in the black of night, shivering in the icy air, feeling the hard ground beneath her.

And knowing, by some twisted means that was neither blessing nor cruelty, that somewhere, something terrible had happened.

Laor allowed me to be there, Syrah thought, the realization muddled by the heavy darkness filling her mind. *He allowed me to know, allowed me to share that loss…*

She wasn't sure if she was grateful for it, or if she suddenly—for the first time in her life—hated her god with every essence of her being.

She didn't notice Jofrey leave. She didn't see him watching her for several minutes, nor heard him call to her in a low voice, seeking to comfort her. She didn't even see him glance at her hand atop of the atherian's, or make out the scrape of his chair as he slowly stood, looked at her for a moment more, then made for the door.

It seemed a long time, in fact, before Syrah noticed anything. It might have been no more than a few minutes, or perhaps a couple of hours or even half a day. She was away, floating in the despairing realization that

Talo Brahnt—that the man who had been her father in every way but blood—was gone from the world. When Eret Ta'hir had passed some months back, Syrah had thought she understood what loss was. The man had been her confidant, her friend, and she had loved him as a girl loves her grandfather. But this...

Syrah felt a bitter taste in her mouth, and she came to the ugly understanding that—indeed for the first time—she *did* hate the Lifegiver. He who gives takes, and He had somehow seen fit to take everything from her, and all at once. He had allowed her body to be beaten and used, allowed her spirit to be trampled and cracked. Then, when all that was done, He delivered upon her the coup de grâce, this last great cruelty, this horrible understanding that she had long since said her final words to the man who had raised her, the man who had loved her as any father would love their child.

Eventually, Syrah found that she had run out of tears, and it was this odd awareness that brought her back to the moment. Her left cheek felt sticky and damp, and she rubbed at it and her eye with the sleeve of her left hand as she sniffed. This done, she looked back around, watching Raz's still-sleeping form, his shoulders rising and falling in a slow, mesmerizing rhythm.

After a time, Syrah found herself smiling again. It wasn't a happy smile, to be sure, but nor was it a sad one, as can be found on the face of one fondly remembering the dead. It was, instead, a smile of understanding, a smile that spoke to the fact that she had been delivered from misery and terror into grief, but delivered all the same. All of a sudden Syrah felt that she didn't want to be alone anymore. She had been alone for so long, with the companionship of the baskets and boxes and the cloth beneath her preferable to the touches and salacious words of the men who had visited her. She'd had enough of being without, of being without happiness or hope, without desire to see the next day.

Slowly, carefully, so as not to wake the man, Syrah eased herself up in the bed, lifting her hand from his for the first time since she'd touched it. She felt—as though his skin had been bonded with some strange sorcery—the lingering tingle of his cool smoothness along the tips of her fingers as she did so, and for a moment couldn't help but stare down at her hand, wondering at the sensation.

After she had bundled the blankets about her hips, making sure she was modestly covered, she paused, then reached out once more. Just before her fingers found his again, she hesitated, looking up into his face, and blushed.

A fine time to start wondering at what sort of mess I must look like...

Overcoming this, Syrah softly grasped two of his fingers in hers, feeling their supple strength, and squeezed them lightly.

"Wake up," she whispered, watching the atherian's closed eyes, wanting to see the shine of their gold again.

XLIII

"There is great value in dreams. Many wonders can be discovered among the worlds we visit as we slumber, wonders that seem intangible and unreachable to the woken mind. Take solace in those places, my child, and always seek to bring back what you find there..."

—Uhsula, Seer of the Undercaves, to Princess Shas-hana Rhan

Raz was dreaming of sand and Sun, which was strange in and of itself because Raz rarely felt he slept deep enough to dream. On this occasion, though, he found himself far gone from the humid warmth of the High Citadel, taken away from the cold grey of winter and the constant threat of snow and wind.

Raz was standing at the edge of the Garin, watching the Sun begin to set over the western edge of the lake's encircling dunes. He was alone at the water's edge, the surface a single clear sheet that didn't so much as shiver in the gentle desert breeze whispering about him, caressing the skin of his face and shifting about his wings. He took in a deep breath, realizing at once both that he was dreaming and that he would have been almost content not to wake.

Almost.

For some time Raz stood there, the claws of his feet digging into the warm sand, watching the washed colors of dusk sweep across the sky. There was no sound except the wind, but he felt, without turning around, that his family was nearby, waiting for him to return to the caravan.

Not yet, he thought. *Not yet.*

It was peaceful, in that place. Thinking this, Raz wondered all at once if he really knew what "peace" was. If he didn't, then what he felt now must have been as close a thing to it as he was like to get. He could be calm here, quiet, still of mind and body, not worried about living through the next day, or whose blood would stain his hands on the morrow. He could simply *be*, in that place, just exist without threat or need or desire.

Almost.

There seemed, somehow, to be something missing. Raz couldn't place it, but it was as though a part of everything about him were absent, as though the painter of the scene had forgotten the one last detail that would make the work complete. Raz didn't know what it was, but he didn't bother worrying about it. He had the odd feeling—in the same way he knew he was dreaming—that whatever was out of place would be there soon.

It was then that he felt a slender, delicate hand take his fingers in its own.

For a little while longer Raz didn't look around to see who it was that had taken hold of him. It reminded him, in a way, of how Ahna had once held his hand, toddling along beside him through the camp, keeping to herself and her dolls but never leaving her older brother alone. It was in the same moment, however, different. The hand was not Ahna's, to be sure. It was larger, but also more tender. It did not cling to him the way his sister's had. Rather, it rested about his fingers, holding onto them like they were fragile, priceless things it neither wanted to break, nor let go of.

As the last glint of the Sun began to vanish behind the dune, Raz finally turned to see who it was that stood before him. As he'd suspected, his sister was nowhere to be found. Instead, a woman stood beside him, tall and graceful, the top of her head reaching just about his chest. She didn't move to meet his gaze, the one pink eye he could see taking in the sunset, her braided hair, so white it might have been bleached by the desert, waving about her pale face in the warm breeze. She wore a thin gown of white, and as he looked closer, Raz realized he recognized it. It flowed about her, crafted of the silk mantle he had given her so many years ago to shield her from the cruel gaze of the Sun. She had grown, in that time, almost to the extent that he had grown, becoming a woman in truth.

It was just as night fell, arriving with the last fading flash of day, that she finally turned to look at him. Syrah Brahnt's eyes, both whole and wide and gleaming in the sudden shine of Her Stars far above their heads, looked up into his.

Then she smiled, and he remembered how he had wanted to keep that smile upon her face forever.

She opened her mouth to speak.

"Wake up."

Raz awoke quickly, as he was apt to do. He blinked once, twice, then the world returned, drawing itself into sharp focus all around him. He was sitting—rather uncomfortably, in fact—in a hard-backed chair that had been supplied only at the High Priest's insistence. The room about him was a small thing—at least to his mind—and at once felt cramped, tight and smothered in the limited space of the walls that seemed to press in on him from all sides. There was no fire, but the place was warm and kept lit by the candles set in alcoves in the surrounding stone, throwing guttering light over the bed before him.

And illuminating the Priestess, upright and smiling gently, seated atop it.

Raz grinned back slowly, his fingers tightening about hers as he realized that it was indeed *her* hand in his, and when he spoke he almost breathed the words, as though awed by what he saw.

"Syrah Brahnt."

"Raz i'Syul Arro," Syrah said by way of reply, laughing softly. "I'd say I'm surprised you figured out my name, but I think that would be shunning the hundred other things that are more surprising about your being here."

Raz chuckled. "No one has ever spoken a truer word." He felt his face fall, then. "Are you all right? How are you feeling?"

He regretted the questions immediately, seeing a little of the spark die in the woman's eye as she started to lose her brightness, but a moment later it was back, though she averted her gaze.

"Well enough, I suppose," she said quietly. "I-I should thank you, to say the least. If you hadn't come when you did—"

"Stop," Raz cut her off, squeezing her fingers comfortingly. "Enough. If you want to thank me, then do me the favor of not speaking of it, at least as of yet. I don't want to regret leaving those men breathing, back there in the Woods…"

Syrah turned to meet his eye again, and she looked grateful. "I promise," she said, her smile returning in full. "If we're to talk about something else, though, I think you can understand I don't even know where to start the questions."

Raz gave an understanding nod. "I can. And I won't leave your side until I've answered every one."

He might have imagined it, but he thought he saw the woman flush the smallest bit at that. To top this, her voice sounded almost teasing when she replied.

"Well in that case I'll be sure to keep a few for another day."

It was Raz's turn to blush, or would have been had he been capable of it. As it was, he felt a strange sensation in the pit of his stomach, as though someone had twisted it suddenly into a loose knot. He opened his mouth, intent on saying something clever, but found that the words wouldn't come. A moment later he felt a fool, sitting there gaping at the woman sitting on bed before him.

It appeared, however, that this might have been exactly the reaction Syrah Brahnt was looking for. Her bandaged free hand came up to cover her mouth, and she barely stifled a giggle. Raz grinned sheepishly at that, his eyes moving over her, taking her in.

She was frighteningly thin. That much wasn't like to change overnight. The bones of her shoulders were sharp and distinct through the thin gown they'd dressed her in before putting her to bed, and her fingers, still wrapped about his, felt thin and frail, one bent and crooked where it looked to have been broken and poorly set. Her ruined eye, too, was saddening, though at the very least it had been covered with clean bandages and cloth, and for the first time Raz noticed also that her hair, though clean now, seemed to have been unevenly cut. It hung long and loose, now, undone from the frayed and dirty braids he had found her with, and whereas it hung well past her right collarbone, barely hiding the twisted remains of her ear, on her left it looked to have been roughly sheared, and didn't fall far past her chin.

What sort of torment did they put you through? Raz pondered silently, his eyes lingering on this clean, uneven sheet of beautiful white hair. *What violence did they force you to suffer?*

As though she could read his thoughts, Syrah's fingers fell from her face, her eye meeting his. She reached down to take his one hand in both of hers.

"My questions for now," she said softly, looking at him with a sort of kind sadness. "Yours for another time. All right?"

Raz didn't reply, struggling with himself as he took her in once again, witnessing her wasted, bruised body, thinking of everything that he knew and wondered had been done to her.

Then he nodded.

"All right."

After that they spoke for what could only have been hours, no matter who was keeping track of the time. Raz told Syrah his story, initially starting upon reaching the North but going back to working with the Mahsadën and its šef at her insistence, then further back again at her continued urging. Eventually, Raz found himself at the very beginning, spending a great deal of time telling her of the Arros and the life he had lived as a child of the trading caravans. He spoke of how he had come to be among them, then of how he had come to be accepted. He spoke of his mother and father, of his sister Ahna and his uncle Jarden. He'd laughed, remembering the antics of he and his cousin, Mychal, telling her of how he had once rebroken his wing when the boy had convinced him to jump off his parents' wagon in an attempt to fly.

Before long, Raz realized he was speaking more of his family than he had ever done since that frightful night, nearly eight years ago…

Eventually, though, his tale grew dark. Syrah sat, quiet and attentive as he told her of the day they'd first met, when he'd saved her from the slavers. He tried to get around the truth, get around *why* his family had been torn apart and butchered, but there was no doing so. He felt Syrah's hand begin to shake as he described the events of that night, telling her of the fire and the bodies, and of how he had pulled Mychal, Prida, and the Grandmother from the flames.

When he spoke of how he had ruthlessly butchered the unfortunate slaver who'd been attempting to crawl away, then hunted down every one of the group who'd borne down on the Arros, she stopped shaking.

After that, Raz tried to tell his story faster. He spoke of Mychal's betrayal, of the Mahsadén's attempts to use him, and of the half-madness in the weeks that followed as he pushed himself to new limits in an attempt to eradicate them from Miropa, the Gem of the South. He told Syrah of his murder of the šef, then of his flight to the North. For the first time since starting he found himself having trouble continuing as he spoke of meeting Lueski Koyt in the woodlands around the Northern city of Azbar, and of how he had saved her and her brother, Arrun, from the bounty hunters who had been set upon them.

It was only her hands around his, tightening lightly in a reassuring sort of way, that kept him going. Even then, after he'd described his meeting Talo and Carro and their eventual departure from Azbar, he couldn't bring himself to speak of how Lueski and Arrun had died.

"They're... gone," he said simply, almost choking on the words. "They're just... gone."

Then, though, he'd taken great pleasure in describing for Syrah how he'd dealt with the man responsible for the children's passings.

It was at this point that the woman began to involve herself in the story. She started asking questions, occasionally pressing him for more details, especially when Talo and Carro were involved. She didn't interrupt often, and when she did Raz found himself wishing she would do so more frequently, if only to hear her voice. He guessed, by what she said and asked, that someone—likely Jofrey, whom Raz suspected by the lingering scent of the man had kept him company as he slumbered by Syrah's bedside—had given her their understanding of the story as best they could, and Raz found great relief in this, because he was rapidly coming upon the part of the retelling he was most greatly dreading.

He knew he had been right when he got to the night, not that many days ago, when the ursalus had set upon them in the Woods. He felt Syrah's fingers tense in his, and he got the distinct impression that she was steeling herself for what was to come. He had hoped to slip by this portion of the story as quickly as possible, sparing her what pain he could, but it was at this very part of the tale that Syrah began to demand more and more of him, practically begging him to tell her all he could remember.

Eventually he obliged, forgoing only the grisliest particulars.

She was dry-eyed as he told her of how Talo had died bravely striving to fend off the most terrifying creature Raz had ever—and hoped *would* ever—laid eyes on. As he recounted the battle, Raz felt himself slip back to that night, and once again it became difficult to speak. Together he and

Syrah sat there, holding each other's hands in the flickering light of the room, she listening and he speaking with slow, deliberate detail. When he came to his slaying of the beast he felt her hands tighten abruptly, and her eyes glinted with what looked to be righteous fire.

Then, though, he was at the moment of Talo's death.

"He asked me for mercy," Raz said, feeling almost ashamed, averting his eyes from hers. "He was in pain. He was broken, and he asked me for mercy. So... I gave it to him."

For the first time since he'd started the story, a stillness seemed to fall over the room. As though some of the warmth had been sucked out of the air, Raz felt a sudden chill, and he looked around. Syrah was staring at him, wide-eyed and mouth agape. She seemed paralyzed, almost horrified, and for a moment Raz was terrified that, in admitting this fact to her, he had doomed whatever closeness they might have had. He felt his heart sink as she began to pull away.

But only one of her hands left his, to come up and clench at the clothes over her heart. The other stayed within his grasp, and he understood then that whatever emotion it was that he had drawn from her, whatever anger or fear or sadness he had elicited, none was truly directed at him.

"Talo... Talo died by your sword?" Syrah asked him slowly. "And Carro was there?"

Raz suddenly understood why she appeared so surprised. By the way she asked, it seemed that this was *not* what she'd expected to hear following the story as had been told to her by Jofrey. He suffered several seconds of confusion, then remembered another similar instant he had been taken by surprise, regarding the exact same events.

That time Carro had been retelling of Talo's death to the High Priest and his council, and had made it sound as though Talo Brahnt had died of his injuries, rather than after asking for Raz's sword.

I've said too much, Raz thought, still watching Syrah as the woman continued to gape at him. *I've let something slip.*

"Raz!" Syrah hissed in a hushed tone, demanding an answer.

Raz hesitated, thinking fast.

Seeing no way out of it, though, he nodded.

In response, Syrah groaned, and seemed to collapse in on herself. Her thin form slumped forward, like a tree bending under the weight of snow.

"What's wrong?" he asked, starting forward as he made to catch her. "Syrah! What happened? What did I do?"

"Not you," Syrah moaned, her face hidden from him for a moment, bent down towards the blankets. "Not you, Raz! *Carro!* Carro's broken the law of our faith! He allowed you to take a life!"

All at once, the understanding came to Raz in full, rushing over him in a terrible wave.

"That's why he refused the High Priest's mantle," he said aloud, though he was speaking to himself as he gazed emptily into the silky folds of her hair. "That's why he let me out of the cell…"

"Cell?" Syrah asked him, looking up from the bed, her left eye red and wide with worry and confusion. "What cell?"

Raz turned all the information he had over in his head, struggling to make sense of it. When he thought he had everything in place, he looked back at Syrah.

"Syrah… I think Carro broke your law more than once."

XLIV

"There is an abundance of evidence, throughout all the great realms of the world, of the existence of the religions that influenced our own modern concepts of gods and deities. The Southern tradition of worshiping the Sun and Moon have their base in a belief system in which the desert itself was considered a god, and of which carvings and depictions have been found scrawled across sana-smoothed stones among the dunes, or in caves within the crags. In the North, it can be assumed that the Stone Gods of the wild men of the mountains derive from the elements themselves, drawn from simpler minds put in awe by the sheer power and terror of the winter storms. Laor, too, has his roots in bygone beliefs, as echoes of him can be found in the old tales passed from a time in which the earth and woods and sky were prayed to for rain and game and health. Religion, though, is a living thing in many ways. Ana—as many of these antiquated faiths seem to have gone—like a living organism, it can either adapt... or die."

—from the libraries of Cyurgi' Di, concerning archaic religions

"You aren't going to let me see her, are you?"

The man's question almost broke Jofrey's heart. The Priest sat, stripped of his robes and his broken arm still slung across his chest, on the stone bed at the back of the very cell he freed Raz i'Syul Arro from not twelve hours prior. He looked somewhat diminished out of the familiar clothes and colors of the faith. The old cotton shirt he wore was loose over his bulk, and the worn cloth of his wool pants seemed almost dirty in the dim light of the room. His beaded and braided hair, usually so iconic of him, looked tangled and wild over his thick blond beard. His feet were bare, resting on the floor before him, now cleared of the mess Arro had left the room in.

And yet, despite all this, Carro al'Dor seemed more himself now than he had at any point since his return to Cyurgi' Di. His blue eyes were bright and clear, his back erect as he sat, straight and proud, to face Jofrey and the council, who had come to inform him of the atherian's success.

And to demand, one last time, that he explain what foolishness might possibly have possessed him to so callously transgress the laws of his faith.

"No, Carro," Jofrey said with a shake of his head, looking down on the Priest as he answered the man's question. "I'm not going to let you see her. Not yet. You stand accused of breaking the cardinal law of Laor, and know damn well you'll be found guilty of it unless you can provide this council with information that would incline us otherwise. You won't be allowed more than food and water until then."

"Murderer," Valaria Petrük muttered under her breath from Jofrey's left, though she kept her tongue after he gave her a sharp look.

Carro, though, heard the accusation clearly.

"Murderer?" he almost chuckled, looking at the woman without so much as a hint of regret or even anger. "Aye, maybe. Maybe in your eyes, and maybe in mine. And for longer than you know."

"You admit it, then?" Behn Argo demanded, taking half a step forward from behind Petrük. "You admit to your crime?"

Jofrey was about to snap at him, to tell him to mind his tongue, when Carro's reply stopped him.

"If I do, will you let me see her?"

There was a shocked pause, and fortunately it was Jofrey who recovered first.

"Carro, your admission is only half of what that will cost you," he said slowly. "We *know* you let Arro free. Even the atherian didn't deny it when pressed for his side of the story." He gave his friend a long, hard look. "What we want to know... is why?"

In response, Carro met his eyes coolly. "Do you know how Talo died, Jofrey? Do you know how the man whose mantle you now wear was killed?"

There was a collective murmur from the others as Talo's name was spoken, but Jofrey ignored them.

"A bear," he replied steadily. "You told us you were ambushed by an ursalus, and that the animal—"

"Talo died on the end of Raz's sword."

In an instant, the council erupted.

"WHAT?" Behn Argo could be heard yelling.

"The beast?" Elber howled, looking suddenly livid.

"Laor's mercy..." Benala Forn whispered from the back of the group.

Jofrey actually had to put a restraining hand on Cullen Brern, who looked as though he had just been stabbed in the back.

"I'm assuming," he said loudly, his voice carrying over the confused shouts of anger and horror, "that as Carro didn't tell us this before, he has good reason to do so now."

The words had the desired effect. Over several seconds the council settled, though none looked too pleased to do so, and all eyes found Carro again.

"I was never one for the world," Carro began slowly, for once not looking up at them but rather down at the ground, between his bare feet. "Ever since my mother gave me to the faith, I rarely left the Citadel. Talo asked me to, often enough. When he went on missions to the South, or to the western valley towns. He always asked me, even though he knew I would almost never go. The long trips up and down the mountains stairs during the foraging season were enough for me, and I thought I needed little else but Laor and my friends and the walls of my home." He paused, searching for the words before continuing. "I wish I had gone, now. Maybe if I had, I would have had a better understanding of the world…"

He looked up, meeting Jofrey's eyes once more. "When Talo told me he had asked Raz i'Syul Arro to join us, I was appalled. Raz was a beast to me, a killer I'd heard the commoners of Azbar cheer as 'the Monster.' I was *furious* with him, and it was a sensation that lingered for a long time. I couldn't understand what would possess him, the *High Priest* of Cyurgi' Di, the greatest of Laor's temples, to wish to bring such a brute under his wing. I couldn't fathom what had come over him, and pushed it all aside merely as the musings of an old man that saw a reflection of his former life in a creature living the same violence he once had."

Carro took a breath, sitting back to lean against the wall behind him, wincing as his arm shifted uncomfortably. "But Raz, it turns out, is not a *creature* at all. He's not a beast, or an animal. In fact, he's a man that has gained a better understanding of life in his twenty-something winters than I think I have in my sixty."

There started to be another angry outburst at this, but Carro carried on through it.

"We have allowed ourselves to assume, whether by the grace or folly of our god—I'm honestly not sure which—that the world beyond these walls exists in a way that can be balanced by our beliefs. Life is precious. Death is avoidable, save for with great age. Peace over war. Kindness over cruelty. We have allowed ourselves to be ensnared in the artificial peace projected by Laor's light, and even as we fight the dim border of the shadows that flicker at the edge of that glow, we are blind to the world beyond and the darkness that exists there, real and caustic and harsh."

His eyes hardened, and swept over the group. "Talo's injuries were not something out of a tale of heroism and glory. He was not dying peacefully, as knights do in the stories we tell our children in their beds. He was a broken man. His chest was crushed, caved in from the blow the bear gave him. His ribs were shattered, edges tearing out of his flesh to cut at his skin and leak his life away into the snow. Blood was in his mouth, in his throat, in his lungs. He was in torment, well beyond the help of magic. He was lingering, and among the few words he was able to say before he passed, the ones I remember most clearly are those he formed when he asked Raz to fetch his sword."

The council was utterly still, hanging on to every word.

"Laor—or at least the Laor we claim we know so well—would have demanded I allow the man I loved to suffer and remain, to bear the agony of his broken body until his injuries saw fit to claim him. *That* Laor would have demanded I stay by his side for those seconds, those minutes, those hours, and fight with him using prayers and kind words and sorcery to ease what pain I could."

Carro grimaced, and it was an ugly look. "I worship a god of light and kindness," he snarled, "not the hateful Stone Gods of my father. I worship a god of mercy and love. So—when Arro returned with his blade—I allowed him to thrust it through Talo's heart."

Only Valaria Petrük hissed at that. When she realized she was the only one to make a sound, however, she shut up again.

"Raz gave my love a mercy I would not have been able to, a mercy *none* of us would have been able to. He took Talo's pain away in a moment, even though the act took a great toll on him. I watched a man end the life of his friend, and it was the single greatest act of kindness I have ever witnessed. I don't think Raz could have sacrificed more than he did in that moment, to save Talo a slow, miserable death."

Carro took a deep, shaking breath then, and was silent for some time. The council allowed him his reprieve, partially out of understanding that this story must be a hard one to tell, and mostly out of being unable to say anything themselves. When the Priest started speaking again, they listened all the more intently.

"I think the world was a new place for me, after that," Carro said quietly. "Reality set in, and I could see the darkness again. Raz proved it for me once and for all not long after."

"How?" an anxious voice, possibly Kallet Brern, asked helplessly from behind Jofrey.

"By showing me that choices often present themselves only in lesser variations of evil," Carro replied, seeking whoever had asked the question with his eyes, but seeming unable to find them. "We found the Kayle's men laying siege to the mountain pass. The only way to reach you was through the sentries they'd posted along the base of the stairs."

"You could have turned back," Behn Argo began angrily. "You could have returned to Ystréd and—"

"It would have taken you weeks to get back to the town," Jofrey interrupted quietly, understanding. "The same to return once more, not counting whatever months would have passed while Ystréd sought to gather help."

"*If* they sought to gather it," Carro spat. "By which time you would all have been dead, as I don't think the Kayle is fool enough to let time slip idly by."

"You chose the mountain pass," Jofrey continued, seeing the whole picture now. "You chose to make for the Citadel."

"And to bring you what news we could," Carro said with a nod. "And in doing so... I condoned the death of as many of a score of men Raz needed to kill in order to get us up the stairs in one piece. I traded the lives of a few for the hope of saving the lives of a thousand. Any other decision would have only been choosing *my* life over all of yours…"

There was a long, drawn out silence as Carro's story came to an end. Finally, after almost ten seconds of allowing the words to sink in, Jofrey found his voice again.

"When I asked you to take on the High Priest's mantle…"

"I couldn't take it, knowing full well I'd already twice broken the law of our faith," Carro confirmed with a shake of his head. "That knowledge also made it easy to choose to set Raz free."

"All else aside," Petrük snapped, "that *was* a foul action. How many men did your lizard kill in his rescue of Syrah Brahnt? In his rescue of *one woman?* Hmm? One? Ten? A hundred?"

"You'll have to ask *him*," Carro growled right back, narrowing his eyes at the woman. "I will admit I let Raz out for selfish reasons. For that alone I know what the price is. But for *half-a-moment* clear your minds of your blind naivety and see what else my and Raz's actions have brought you. Syrah is alive. The woman who understands the Sigûrth best of all is *alive*. If there is a way to bring down the Kayle, or even just to outsmart or appease him…"

"Syrah will be the one to know it," Jofrey finished, the realization hitting him in full. At the same time, the idea seemed to register with many of the others, because they started talking in muttered pairs and trios.

Carro smiled grimly, and said nothing more.

XL V

"He will be the speaker of his people.
To leave and then return,
bearing a woman of ice and snow on his arm."

—Uhsula, Seer of the Undercaves

In the time it took to finish his story, Raz thought he had watched Syrah go through almost every possible emotion. Surprise, grief, horror, fear, anger, sadness. She had fallen back into silence again, and didn't so much as flinch until he admitted to her that he'd lost control when he'd discovered that she'd been taken captive. Then she'd only gasped in response when he described how Carro freed him from the warded cell the council had sealed him in.

After that, he trailed off. Syrah knew all that came next. She had seen most of it herself, and had borne witness to the ghastly remnants of the rest.

For a long time afterwards they sat in silence, Raz watching Syrah as the woman absorbed the entirety of the tale. The distress had long faded from her face, but she still looked pale, the understanding of Carro's betrayal clearly taking its toll.

Small wonder, Raz told himself. *And it must have taken its toll on Carro, too...*

He was thinking, as he allowed Syrah her time with her own thoughts, of how the Priest had seemed and acted in the days following Talo's death. Raz had believed, at the time, that it had been purely the passing of his lover bearing so heavily on the man, especially as they'd made their way up the mountain pass. Looking back, though, he realized that there had been other moments where Carro could very well have been perturbed about something altogether different.

Like committing the most absolute of blasphemies...

Raz grimaced at the idea. When he'd forced Carro's hand in order to get them past the mountain men at the base of the stairway, he had known it was a hard decision. He'd laid out for Carro two impossible choices, pointing out that death waited behind either of the doors to be taken at that time. He had thought the Priest would be able to come to terms with this, come to understand that sometimes there really *was* no peaceful, bloodless option.

But not for a second, in the moments before or in the days after he had committed the act, had Raz even considered the means by which Talo had passed could be a betrayal all on its own.

"You would just let him suffer?"

He hadn't meant to ask the question aloud but—whether because it bothered him so much or because he wanted to spark more conversation—it slipped out. Syrah started at his voice, shaken from her own thoughts. She blinked and looked at him, for a moment seeming not to understand what he was talking about.

Then it dawned on her, and she looked stricken.

"I-I don't know," she said, sounding like the answer was a hard truth to cope with. "Sitting here, in the heart of the faith, it's easy for me to say that the Laorin law would hold me firm. But... I don't know, Raz." Her face tensed. "Was Talo... was he in so much pain?"

Raz clenched his jaw in frustration. He could let loose, could tell Syrah every gruesome detail of the scene that he had managed to spare her. He could tell her about the hollow that had been Talo's chest before he died, and the ribs that had protruded from torn and bruised flesh. He could tell her of the blood dribbling from her Priest-Mentor's lips, and how it bubbled as he practically pleaded with Carro to let Raz retrieve his blade from the body of the bear that had so brutalized him.

And then the impulse vanished. Raz looked into Syrah's eye—that rose-colored warmth—and understood his own wickedness. He could see her bracing herself again, see her preparing for the worst. Like a lit match tossed into water, his anger winked out.

He shifted the manacles to bring his free hand up, placing it atop both of hers as they clung to his other. He struggled to find the words, working hard to weave at least some kindness into an answer that was ultimately cruel.

"Talo would have had a hard passing, if he hadn't asked for the sword..."

Syrah nodded at this, though it was a shaking, uncertain motion. She seemed in some distant place, her thoughts pulled aside to some dark corner inside her head. Raz was about to draw her back from it, had just started to think of reaching up for her face, intent on lifting her chin to meet his gaze, when she seemed to rise from the misery of her own accord.

"Thank you."

Raz blinked, uncertain he had heard her right.

"Thank you," Syrah said again with a sad, broken smile. "I don't know if Talo had the chance to say it, nor Carro the will to. So... thank you."

Raz watched carefully for a moment, almost expecting to see a hint of resentment layered in amongst the woman's gaunt features.

When he saw none, though, he nodded slowly.

Then he remembered, her words sparking memory like a blaze.

"He-he asked me to tell you something," he started, stumbling over his words as the recollection came back in a rush. "Talo… Right before he passed. One of the last things he said."

He paused, making sure he had the words exactly right as Syrah tensed before him.

"He told me to tell you," he said in a slow, careful voice, "'I will always be there'…"

A stillness came over Syrah then, so absolutely it was several seconds before Raz realized he couldn't hear her breathing anymore. She watched him, her eye burning into his, taking in these last words from the man that had been nothing less to her than a father.

And then the eye began to glisten, and shortly thereafter her cheek was wet once more with a steady stream of tears.

She didn't wail, as some might have been prone to do. Syrah Brahnt, it turned out, was made of stiffer stuff than most. Instead she just sat there, silent as she cried, holding onto Raz's hand so tight it almost hurt, meeting his gaze until she could no longer fight the quaking of her own body and dropped her head as her shoulders shook. Raz sat in silence with her, letting what he could only imagine was a maddening confusion of grief and joy work its way in and out. Soon Syrah's tears had started to splotch the clean white sheets of the bed bunched about her hips, and when he saw this he instinctively tried to reach up, hoping to wipe her cheek dry and tell her it was going to be all right.

The motion, though, only resulted in the sudden, harsh scrape and clank of metal on wood as the manacles he'd forgotten about—if only for a minute—wrenched his wrists firmly together.

"Damn thing," he snarled at it. "Your council can count themselves lucky I'm keeping my word about keeping this—"

Before he could finish, though, Syrah had pulled her hands from his, grabbed the paired padlocks that clamped it closed on either side, and made a motion like she were tearing it apart.

Several things happened at once. The first Raz's mind registered was the heat. It blasted in a single shocking wave from the Priestess' hands, chasing a violent flash of white light and almost searing the scales of his arms nearest her fingers. At the same time, whatever magic the woman had summoned seemed almost to backlash, the power thrusting outwards from her arms and causing the bandages—and the fringes of the sleeves of her gown, which ended around the elbow—to curl, burn, and tear, the cloth falling away.

Their charred remainders settled to the floor at the same moment the scorched halves of Raz's bindings hit the stone with a *crash*.

"I'm sorry," the woman said, dropping the padlocks and the twisted handfuls of blackened wood the magic had burned through, though she still didn't look at Raz as her hands fell back to the bed. "I just couldn't bear to see those on you anymore."

Raz, though, didn't reply. In fact, he hardly registered that she had said anything at all. Two thoughts occurred to him at the same time, each of equal and opposite weight. First, like an echo from the past, a great emotion welled up in Raz as he looked at his freed hands. Something clicked, an understanding that the woman had just thrown away some part of herself to give him back a part of *himself*, had cast aside the desires of her own people and the command of her elders to allow him his freedom. It was a strange, breathtaking realization, which might have seemed negligible to most men, but is of great magnitude to one that remembers the feeling of being bound in iron.

Sadly, it was tempered by a horror Raz realized he should have expected.

As the seared bandages fell from Syrah's wrists and hands, they revealed the damages that had been hidden beneath. Raz had seen the bruising and marks on and between the woman's legs, could see even now the hint of the cut that had claimed her eye, and the ugly scar of the half of her ear that had been cruelly sawed away. He noticed again the uneven, rough chopping of her hair, and the thin frailty of her body.

But he had not been by her side when they'd removed the manacles from her wrists.

Raz knew there were limits to Laorin magics. Carro had been unable to heal his broken arm, nor do much of anything for Talo as he lay dying. If he had thought about it, though, Raz would have certainly assumed whatever the rough metal of her bindings had done to Syrah's wrists would have been mendable.

It turned out, though, that two weeks of rubbing metal and weeping sores left scars that not even magic could resolve...

Syrah began to shake as Raz, slowly and tenderly, took her hands in his again. She seemed at first to want to pull away, but he made sure, gripping them firmly, that she knew he wouldn't allow it. She surrendered, her breathing coming a little faster as he turned her hands over, studying the marks. They were a little narrower than his, but no less pronounced, the angry, blotchy red standing out against the white of her skin. *Some* sort of spellwork had certainly been spun, Raz was sure, otherwise the wounds would still have been raw and scabbing

But not one strong enough to rid her of the reminder...

"I thought I wouldn't be afraid to see them..."

Raz blinked and looked up. Syrah was gazing down at her wrists as well, eye red but dry, turning her hands over herself now, flipping them slowly in his.

"I thought I wouldn't be afraid," she repeated. "I thought, after seeing yours, that I wouldn't be ashamed or saddened by them."

At that, Raz looked down again. Like a shadow, his wrists mirrored her injuries, reflecting the painful stories there. Her red rings about white skin, his pale over black.

"You will always be saddened by them," he told her, reaching with his clawed thumbs to rub the line of her blemishes lightly. "You will always be ashamed of them, in a way. But they will become a part of you, just as everything does eventually. In time, they will become nothing more than a reminder of something that shaped you, something that has served to make you into what you've become…"

He ended at that, unsure if he wanted to draw Syrah's mind to what it was that *he* had become.

Once again, the woman seemed to know what he was thinking. She brought a hand up slowly, hesitating only a moment, then rested her fingers against the side of his face. Raz nearly closed his eyes at the warmth of her touch, feeling himself melt into it.

"If these help me become half as strong as you, then they'll be well worth the pain," she said quietly, her eye boring into his.

Raz snorted.

"Maybe then you could convince your council to forgive Carro for letting me out."

Syrah frowned, pulling her hand from his face. "I would count it victory enough if I could convince them to just listen to *you*. They should. They *must*. If Carro had no other way—"

"He *didn't*," Raz insisted, growing frustrated again. "Your law infuriates me, Syrah. It's as though none of you have ever seen the world. Your faith seems to exist with a skewed concept of the states in which the world—the *real* world—exists. Your god leaves you no place for certain mercies, or even self-preservation."

"Laor's gift is the greatest treasure one could possibly hope to—" Syrah began, responding in reflexive defensiveness, but Raz interrupted here.

"If you're talking about *life*, then I *agree!*" he stressed. "But it is a gift that you have the right to defend, as well as one you have the right to protect when it comes to family, to friends!"

Syrah said nothing, and Raz continued.

"Maybe I should try to make them see sense," he muttered. "How do they plan on defeating the Kayle's men without killing? By punishing Carro for seeking to help? What sort of idiocy is that?"

"They'll say there is another way," Syrah said after a second. "That there *was* another way, in Carro's case. They'll insist on it, in fact."

"They can insist all they want, right up until the moment Baoill's axes fall upon their necks. Your law may have held your faith firm since the beginning of time itself for all I care. It's about to get every one of us killed and cast to the vultures."

"And they'll Break Carro long before that," Syrah groaned, hanging her head and clutching at the cloth about her chest again.

"Break him?" Raz thundered, outraged. "They would go that far? They would cast him out?"

Syrah blanched. She looked at him, and Raz only had time to register the odd sort of fear that was there, swimming in her eye.

Then they heard a shout of surprise from the hall.

Both of them looked around. Whatever happened, the commotion was kept short. There were more yells, what sounded like a brief scuffle and grunts of effort, and then the door to the room flew open with a crashing *bang* as it smashed into the wall.

Through it, in a flurry of white cloth and blond hair, ran a young man Raz recognized immediately.

"Syrah!" Reyn Hartlet cried out, seeing the woman and rushing towards her even as two other figures in the robes of the faith chased him in. "Syrah! Thank Laor!"

What occurred in the next few seconds happened so quickly, Raz's speed became the subject of impressed and fearful rumors alike within the hour. Syrah's face shifted first, her eye going wide in horror as they took in Reyn's paired hands, reaching for her, seeking to embrace her. For Raz, this was enough. In a blink he was over the bed, his great form vaulting across the mattress to land nimbly between Reyn and the woman. In the same motion his left hand snapped around the closest of the Priest's wrists, his right catching him about the throat.

Then, with a snarl that made the two men chasing after Reyn stop in their tracks, Raz lifted the Priest clear off his feet and slammed him into the wall behind him.

"YOU NEVER LEARN, DO YOU HARTLET?" he raged into the man's face, neck crest flaring over his head as Reyn grabbed at his arm with his free hand, choking for air. "THAT'S THE SECOND TIME YOU'VE ELECTED TO BARGE IN ON ME UNANNOUNCED! HAVE YOU ALREADY FORGOTTEN HOW THE FIRST ENDED?"

The Priest didn't respond, his breathing coming out in spluttering hacks as Raz's fingers tightened.

"Raz, no!" came Syrah's voice over his shoulder. "Let him go! I'm sorry! I didn't mean to let him frighten me like that!"

Raz only hesitated briefly, then did as she asked. Reyn tumbled to the floor, hacking and wheezing, one hand rubbing at his throat, the other clutching at his side where his broken ribs could only have just started healing.

"Idiot," Raz grumbled, not moving from between the prone Priest and Syrah. "How you haven't gotten yourself killed already is a mystery to me."

"Our apologies!" one of the Priests—who was now standing over Reyn as he coughed and hacked at their feet—said with a fearful glance at Raz. "We told him the High Priest gave orders you weren't to be disturbed, but he wouldn't listen!"

"I just-just came to see Syrah!" Reyn managed to croak out, getting his knees under himself and pushing up to kneel with his shoulder against the wall. "They said—in the infirmary, they s-said you'd returned, that the lizard had—had rescued you!"

Raz's crest twitched again at the slur, and he let a deep growl build in the back of his throat.

It died, though, as he felt Syrah's slim fingers grasp his forearm lightly from behind, calming him.

"I'm sorry, Reyn," the woman said from the bed as Reyn got to his feet in front of Raz. "You just gave me such a fright, and Raz was just—"

"Trying to kill me?" Reyn demanded, glaring up at Raz with a shocking amount of defiance for a man who had just been partially flattened against a wall. "After what I did for you?"

Raz frowned down at him. "As far as I know, you did just enough to keep yourself from being tossed out of the faith. If Carro hadn't been there to stop you I doubt you'd be free to have this conversation right now."

Reyn went red at that, but seemed to think better of responding. Instead he peered around Raz to Syrah again, who was looking confused.

"Syrah," he said again, his voice awash with relief, and he acted like Raz was nothing more than a pillar in his way, moving around and reaching for the woman once more. "I was so worried. I knew you were alive. I knew you couldn't have—"

"DON'T TOUCH ME!"

Syrah's shrill scream took them all by surprise. Raz snapped around, turning just in time to see the woman—her face contorted in horror again—recoiling from Reyn's seeking hand as it made to reach for hers, scrambling back to the very head of the bed. He started to move forward at once, planning to grab the man by the collar and throw him back into the paired Priests still standing uselessly by the door.

Syrah beat him to it.

As Reyn, taken aback by the outburst, started to ask her what was wrong, the Priestess panicked. She was already as far away from the man as she could get, her eye staring at his outstretched hand, her back pressed against the mortared marble.

When it didn't stop in its approach, she broke, throwing her scarred arms up in panic as she screamed again.

The crackling blast of magic was so strong it slammed Raz into the wall at his back. Reyn, who was closest to her, was thrown completely off his feet, falling once more to the floor and skidding back over the stone until he collided with the shins of one of the Priests still lingering by the open door. The chairs that had been set on either side of the bed were tossed up and tumbled in the air, and it was only via the quick reflexes of the other Priest that the one Raz had been sitting in split in two over the man's casted ward rather than crashing into him.

"SYRAH!" Raz roared, throwing his arms up in front of his face as the magic continued to rip about him, snapping through his ears and wings like a windstorm. "ENOUGH!"

At his words, the storm died.

When Raz brought his arms down again, he found Syrah still huddled against the very back edge of the bed, one shoulder against the wall, her arms wrapped around her legs as she pulled them to her chest. She was shaking, her eye wide and staring at Reyn through the white hair that was falling across her face.

"I'm sorry," she was whispering into trembling knees, not looking away from the man as Raz heard him get up behind him. "I'm sorry. I'm sorry. I'm so sorry."

"Syrah…" Raz said again, gently now, easing himself towards the woman. At once her gaze snapped to him, but she gave no hint of further panic as he approached. On the contrary, as he started to crouch down beside the bed, she scrambled forward, away from the stone at her back.

Before he had a moment to think on what he was supposed to do, the woman had thrown her arms around his neck, pulling herself up onto her knees on the bed, and buried her head into the smooth, scaled skin above his collar.

She clung there, for a time, as Raz stood half-crouched. She wasn't crying now, he could tell, but she was still shaking, her body jerking and shivering against his, her breathing coming short and fast.

Deciding there was nothing else for it, Raz carefully brought his arms around, encasing her in a firm, comforting embrace.

"It's all right," he said into her ear quietly, one clawed hand brushing through her uneven hair slowly. "It's all right. We're fine. Everything is fine."

Syrah, in response, only nodded into his shoulder.

It was a while, it seemed, before her breaths became steady again and she looked up once more. When she did, she dropped back to sit on her heels on the bed, and Raz let her go. She didn't move far, one hand still resting against his chest even as she turned to look at Reyn and the other men.

All three of them were staring at her and Raz with open mouths, the Priests red in the face while Reyn just looked as though he had been kicked in the gut.

"Reyn, I'm so sorry," Syrah said to him once more, though the grief in her tone told Raz she was apologizing for something much more than just her lashing out a minute before. "I... I can't... What they did... I... I just can't..."

Whatever her desired effect might have been, Syrah's words certainly had *some* impact on the young man. Reyn's face went from pale to green, then almost grey. He gaped at her, his mouth moving silently, seeking and failing to find the words that would deny what she was trying to tell him, his eyes moving between her face and the hand that was crumpling the loose cloth of Raz's shirt.

When he finally managed to speak, his voice was like the hoarse moan of someone who'd just been told to expect their own death.

"B-But, Syrah," he started, stumbling on the words, "I need to—I came to tell you..."

He trailed off and, with what seemed like a great effort, swallowed.

"What happened?" he asked after another moment, his eyes pleading, seeking answer in hers. "Please. I need to—I need to understand. Your hair. Your eye..."

Raz felt himself tense at the question, but Syrah's fingers curled softly against his chest.

"I'm s-so sorry, Reyn," she choked, the words not coming easy now. "I can't. I just ca—"

"What *in Laor's name* is going on in here?"

Every head turned, then, as a threesome of men hurried into the room through the open door. At their head was Jofrey al'Sen, looking furious as his gaze took in the small space, the broken and knocked over furniture, the Priests still standing meekly along the front wall, and Reyn, pale and shaken between them. Behind him came Cullen Brern and the one Raz only knew as "Elber."

"Priest Hartlet," Jofrey seethed, his tone even despite the wrath all could tell was upon him as his eyes settled on the man. "You are clearly under the delusion that your misdeeds in the past days have gone unnoticed. It's my understanding that you were to be confined to the infirmary until such time as you were in a fit enough condition to stand before the council and address the allegations made against you."

For all Jofrey's importance and eloquence, his voice might have been the buzzing of a fly on the ceiling for all the notice Reyn took of it. The

Priest was still staring at Syrah and Raz, his cheeks rapidly recovering their color. Even as Raz watched, the man's face shifted, transforming over several seconds from miserable realization to something very different, hateful and embarrassed. He made no response, his eyes fixed on the hand Syrah still had resting over Raz's shirt.

He was quiet for so long, in fact, that Jofrey started to snap at him again. Just as the High Priest began, though, Reyn turned on his heel and limped out the door, one hand on his ribs as he shouldered his way between Brern and Elber.

"Hartlet!" Jofrey bellowed, turning to watch the man go. "Who gave you permission to leave? You'll stay and—!"

"Let him go, Jofrey," Syrah interrupted him quietly, her face mournful when Raz looked down at her. "I-I think he's had enough punishment for the moment."

Jofrey, too, looked around at the woman's words. He still appeared irate, but much of the heat left his face as he took Syrah in again, seeing her kneeling on the bed beside Raz.

His gaze dropped behind his spectacles to eye Raz's freed hands, loose on either side of him.

"I thought we had an agreement, Master Arro," he said in a slow, calm tone that said he wasn't at all in the mood to deal with another situation at the moment. "I allowed you to remain with Syrah without restriction, and you stayed bound."

"He didn't free himself," Syrah said, and a good amount of the anger that seemed to have just left Jofrey looked to have found itself abruptly in her tone. "*I* did. I don't have much of a taste for chains at the moment, least of all around the wrists of the man who freed me from them."

There was no accusation in her tone, but all the same the three men looked suddenly somewhat ashamed of themselves, exchanging quick glances before meeting her eye once more.

"All the same," Priest Elber said, "if Valaria finds out Arro is walking about the Citadel unbound..."

"If the viper has something to bitch about, tell her to take it up with me," Syrah snapped, her hand finally leaving Raz's chest as she eased herself down to sit more comfortably along the side of the bed. "It's about time I give her something to choke on, I think."

Raz might have imagined it, but he thought he saw the barest hint of a smile dart across both Jofrey's and Cullen Brern's faces.

"As...uh...*delightful* as that confrontation might be to witness," the master-at-arms said following a fake cough to hide the amusement, "I'm afraid it will have to wait. Carro is asking for you."

At that, Syrah looked stunned. "You'll let me see him?" she demanded, her tone something between delighted and suspicious. "When? Why?"

"We will," Jofrey said with a nod. "He's being kept in the larders. In the same place he freed Arro from, as a reminder of his offense." He nodded briefly to Raz, though more so in acknowledgement than any unkindly fashion.

"A reminder?" Syrah demanded, looking suddenly furious, but Raz cut her off pointedly.

"You didn't answer the question," he growled, his eyes set firmly on Jofrey. "She asked you *why?*"

It was Elber who answered.

"In exchange for the truth," the man said with a frown. "Carro has admitted to his crimes, admitted to the betrayal of our laws. He allowed Talo Brahnt's life to be ended before it was due, condoned the killing of tribesmen in order to clear a path to the Citadel, and played his part in the murder of however many *Master Arro—*" he said the words with what was almost disgust "—had to cut down in order to retrieve you from the Kayle."

Raz's spine tingled as the man finished, but it was Syrah who spoke first.

"Jofrey," she said, looking to the new High Priest. "He had no choice. Have you spoken to him? Has he explained the circumstances?"

"He has," Jofrey said gravely, and for a brief moment he looked mournful. "All the same, Syrah, the law is clear. Whether by choice or by design, Carro knowingly stole away Laor's greatest gift."

"He stole *nothing*," Raz snapped, gnashing his teeth. "Carro only acted as was necessary for the preservation of *your* lives. *I* am the killer. If you seek to punish someone, punish me." He smiled, then, grinning nastily at Elber in particular. "Or give it a try, at the very least."

"You are not of our faith, and therefore are not bound by our law," Jofrey said evenly, not even blinking at Raz's underhanded threat. "Beyond that, we won't pretend we are not grateful to you for returning Syrah to us."

Cullen Brern nodded at that, and the distaste across old Elber's face actually faded somewhat.

Raz, though, just frowned, turning his back on the men and extending a hand to Syrah.

"If you're so grateful," he said, not bothering to look at them as he helped the woman shakily to her feet "then we'd like to see the only man who seems to have any sense among you."

XL VI

The path down to the Citadel's dungeons-turned-larders was brighter than Raz might have imagined. He'd had an image in his head of what "dungeon stairs" should have looked like, fed by a childhood of stories and years spent coming to understand the evil the darker half of the world was capable of. Rather than a dark and gloomy descent into cold misery, however, what Raz found was a steep, well-lit flight of stairs that led down and down into the earth, as warm and clean as any other part of the Citadel he'd seen, replete with chains fastened in iron loops at hip height to act as railings. Syrah walked between him and the wall, one hand following the chain as they took the steps, the other firmly looped under his right arm. No one spoke as they drew further into the mountain, just as no one had spoken since they'd left the room.

When they reached the bottom of the stairs, Raz found himself in a more familiar setting. He hadn't recalled the way there—having been unconscious at the time the council had had him incarcerated—but as they turned right and left into the main hall of the dungeons he gained his bearings. The unconscious forms of Reyn and the two Priests who had been guarding his cell were obviously gone—replaced by half-a-dozen stern-faced sentries—and the rubble Carro had made of the two doors had been cleared from the floor. In addition, at the very back of the wall, the shadows seemed to have deepened, and it was a moment before Raz realized the heavy darkness was actually an illusion caused by scorch marks blasted into the stone.

Looks like Carro's runes did their job, he thought with a smirk as Jofrey led him and Syrah forward through the line of guards, Brern and Elber trailing behind them.

The High Priest took them straight to the door Raz expected him to, or at least the great hole in the wall that had been a door. A pair of tough-looking older Priests nodded respectfully to Jofrey when he passed between them, their eyes following Raz and Syrah curiously as they stepped into the cell after him, Raz ducking under what was left of the granite overhang. Here, too, he saw that the mess he had made of the larder had been mostly cleared away, what refuse remained having been shoved along one wall of the large room. In its place, a group of men and women stood to either side, faces set as they turned to see the group arrive.

Between and beyond them, seated on the stone bench that Raz had first woken up on when he'd come to in this place, was Carro al'Dor.

"Carro!" Syrah gasped in relief, pulling her hand free of Raz's arm to hurry forward as quickly as she could on unsteady legs. Raz, staying with Jofrey, Elber, and Cullen Brern a little ways back from the rest of the council, saw that Carro looked little worse for wear. His robes had been taken from him, making him appear somewhat less clean and regal than he might have, and his hair was a bit more tussled than usual. His left arm was still slung across his chest, and his right was secured to the wall behind him by a short iron chain, ensuring he wouldn't slip away.

When he made Syrah out in the dim light of the candles, Carro smiled broadly.

"Hello, child," he said warmly, getting to his feet as best he could to meet her. "To say I'm pleased to see you would be the understatement of a lifetime."

Syrah, for a moment, looked as though she wanted to throw her arms around the old man's thick neck. At the last moment, though, she seemed to think better of it, coming to a foolish stop just out of his reach. Her hands were open, like she wanted to reach out and touch the Priest, but something, some invisible force, was holding her back. Raz wasn't at all surprised when Carro frowned in confusion, scrutinizing the woman.

The confusion, though, was almost instantly thrown aside in favor of shock.

"Your eye," Raz heard the Priest exclaim. "Syrah, what—?"

"It's nothing," Syrah told him quickly, leaping on the opportunity to shove aside the awkwardness of the moment and simultaneously ignoring the mutterings from behind her as some of the others—who must not have seen her since she'd returned—noticed her injuries as well. "I'll count myself lucky that this was most of what I left behind. Are you all right? Have you been treated well?"

"Of course he's been treated well," came an impatient drawl Raz recognized at once. "What do you take us for, girl? Beasts?"

"No," Raz growled before Syrah had time to reply, his eyes finding Valaria Petrük in the group. "Fools. Dunces who have locked up the only man to have done anything useful towards the goal of pulling you out from under the Kayle's boot."

"When your opinion is wanted, creature, we will *ask for it*," Behn Argo spat, turning to face Raz and looking abnormally sure of himself. "I imagine you've just finished cleaning the blood from your claws. Disgusting. How do you feel, knowing y-you—?"

He spluttered to a stop, eyes dropping down to where Raz's arms rested, crossed over his chest.

"He's *free*!" Argo practically howled, taking a step back. "Laor save us! The lizard has freed himself!"

"Jofrey!" Petrük seethed, she too shrinking away to half-hide behind Benala Forn and a bandaged Aster Re'het. "What is the meaning of this?"

"You've already chained one of my rescuers to a wall, Petrük!" Syrah snapped from behind her, turning away from Carro to face the woman. "I wasn't about to let you fetter Raz just because your prejudices won't allow you sleep soundly while he walks free!"

"You?" Petrük demanded, whirling on the Priestess. "Are you insane, Brahnt? This thing *attacked* me! How dare you—!"

"QUIET!"

Carro's roar took everyone—except Raz, who had seen the man's face twist in anger as the old woman spoke—by surprise. Many jumped, turning to face him.

"Your jabs and insults aside, Valaria," Carro snarled, easing himself down to sit upon the stone bed once more, "I am *tired* of your poison. We had this argument half-a-dozen times after the consecration room, and I can only imagine how many occasions you've brought it up since I've been down here. Furthermore—since Raz has *not* been thrown back into a cell since his return—I also assume your accusations have been met with the same fatigue by the rest of the council. Therefore: SHUT UP!"

His words seemed to vibrate through the room, and Raz was fairly sure he was the only one who could see the pink tinge that had crept into Petrük's withered cheeks. All the same, the Priestess puffed herself up, all too ready with her reply.

Jofrey cut her short.

"That's enough," he said in a firm, tired voice, stepping forward, into the group. "Valaria, your opinions will have more weight regarding other matters we must discuss. And Carro—" he frowned at the Priest "—until such time as you have been sentenced per the council's ruling, I recommend you keep yourself in check."

Carro, in response, merely shrugged.

"I've admitted my crimes," he said in a voice that was just as worn down as Jofrey's. "Sentence me, and be done with it. I knew what I was doing the moment I sent Raz into the snow."

"Gladly!" Behn Argo said with a harsh laugh, but Syrah's shout overcame him.

"No!" she yelled, and Raz could see her hands spasm into fists where she still stood just beyond Carro's reach. "You've heard what he has to say! Raz will tell you as well! He had no *choice*!"

"There is always a choice," Elber said firmly. "Had he taken the time to contemplate this, Carro would have seen this as well."

"There are situations in which time is not a commodity one has in abundance," Raz chimed in gravely. "There are occasions in which the swiftness of the decision is paramount."

"There is *no* situation in which the most important factor to consider is *not* the upholding of the gift of life!" Elber retorted. "Had Carro taken the time, he would have found a way."

"If I had taken the time, Talo would have left for the Lifegiver's embrace knowing me as a man unable to grant him the mercy he had to beg me for."

Carro, it seemed, had more fight left in him than his previous statement implied.

"Had I taken the time," he said, his voice rising now as he looked to Elber, "then Raz and I might have lost the opportunity to reach you. Had I *TAKEN THE TIME*—" his voice raged, now "—THEN SYRAH MIGHT BE DEAD. HAD I TAKEN THE TIME, ANY HOPE OF ESCAPING THIS HELL THE KAYLE HAS PUT US IN MIGHT BE LOST!"

"There is ALWAYS ANOTHER WAY!" Elber howled back, going purple in the face. "You have betrayed the faith, Carro! The laws are clear!"

"I wonder how your laws will hold up for you when the choices Carro has had to make are set at your feet, rather than his," Raz said calmly from behind the group.

The effect his words had was instantaneous. Every man and woman in the room froze, turning slowly to look at him. A few looked angry, some confused, but most had identical, stricken expressions.

As if Raz had just taken something horrible they all knew hovered, invisible above their heads, and shoved it under their noses…

"Arro," Jofrey breathed warningly from beside him. "Ease into it…"

Raz blinked and turned to stare down at the man. The High Priest wasn't looking at him, almost refusing to meet his eye.

All the same, by the way he stood by expectantly, Raz wondered suddenly if this wasn't *exactly* what Jofrey had expected to happen.

Or planned… Raz thought, suddenly impressed.

"What is it?" the feeble, sickly voice of Jerrom Eyr, bent over beside Kallet Brern, spoke up. "What are you two whispering about? Explain yourself, Master Arro."

Raz didn't look away from Jofrey for a few seconds more, waiting to see if the High Priest would catch his eye, would give him some indication of what he wanted.

When the man did nothing, Raz decided to speak his mind.

"Syrah told me," he started, looking back at the group, "that I wouldn't be able to give you an impossible choice. She said you would insist there is another way, a better way, a way to resolve anything without death, without breaking your 'law,' as you call it."

He paused, wondering if anyone would voice a disagreement, but no one spoke up.

"What would you say, though, if I proved you otherwise?"

"You won't," Behn Argo grumbled, sneering at Raz.

Raz nodded. "I thought that might be your response. And yet Talo once told me that 'Until the day comes when He sees fit to end all wars, the Lifegiver is not unaware that violence will exist among His flock.' Is this false? Is this an opinion not shared by the faith as a whole?"

"That's different," Kallet Brern said crossly, folding his muscled arms over his chest. "War is war. Even the Laorin cannot be expected to keep the peace everywhere, at all t—"

"You *are* at war, Priest," Raz interrupted him coolly.

There was another pause.

"Stop your lies, creature," Valaria Petrük spat out at last "We are a faith of peace, not conflict. We are as much at war as you are likely to throw yourself off a cliff."

"If you don't start *listening*, Valaria," Carro barked from where he sat, "then it will be the death of you."

"Is that a threat?" the woman demanded, giving him a sour look.

"Valaria," Syrah interrupted the argument, speaking in a calm, solemn voice Raz would never have expected from her given the individual she was speaking to, "do you recall how many went down the path with me?"

At that Valaria Petrük hesitated. She seemed to sense something in the question, some trap.

Curiosity got the better of her, though, and she eventually answered.

"Ten. Why?"

"Do you know what happened to them?"

A low, dark grumbling started up among the group again, and Raz watched them turn to each other, muttering in what sounded like alarm.

Haven't heard this part of the story yet…

"They were killed," Petrük answered once the excitement had subsided somewhat. "Again, though, I ask, wh—?"

"And do you know how they were killed?"

This time, the alarm was palpable. Eyes went wide, hands clenched, and old Jerrom began a coughing fit he tried to stifle with a withered hand.

"They were butchered," Syrah said before Valaria had the opportunity to respond. "I watched it happened, was in the *middle of it*. The Gähs fell on us from the cliffs above, cutting us down as we stood beneath a flag of truce. After that the Sigûrth charged, crushing those that were left beneath iron and steel. By the time I fell, what was left of those ten was nothing more than flesh and blood, corpses so ravaged that the snow turned red as it fell upon them."

Syrah narrowed her eye at the old Priestess, who stood watching her in horrified silence. "Does that sound familiar?" she asked her. "Does that strike a chord with you, in any way? Do you recall, perhaps, what happened to Harond? To Metcaf? Do you remember what they did to the men living within? To the women? And the children?"

The old woman stiffened at this, taken by surprise.

Then she stuck her nose in the air. "I see no comparison," she said haughtily. "Those were cities teaming with the faithless and blasphemers. You have no right to compare them to the likes of us, who live our lives in devotion to—"

"Those were a people the Kayle set himself against," Syrah cut her off, her lips curling in anger. "They were victims of siege, of rape and murder and poisoning and torture. They were left to carnage, in the same way I was left to see what remained of the men and women who came down the pass with me. They were victims, trapped inside the shell of their walls, and I can't help but wonder how long it took *them* to grasp the danger they were in."

These last, final words, drove home. The point may have gone over Petrük's stubborn head, but it seemed to strike others with the force of a lightning bolt. As he watched, Raz saw most of the faces before him grow suddenly still, comprehension sinking in. Whatever they might have thought their situation was, whatever delusion or denial they had been under, it was being rapidly swept away as they finally understood the truth of the situation.

"Laor's mercy," Kallet Brern muttered under his breath.

"You *are* at war," Raz said again, his voice as harsh as the falling blade of an executioner's ax.

XLVII

"What are we going to do?"

It was Aster Re'het, her head still swaddled in cloth and a crutch under one arm, who asked the question. It was a thought that had been hovering over them, omnipresent and frightening, suspended in the silence after Raz had spoken.

"We fight," Cullen Brern said, his firm voice betrayed by a slight tremor in his hand. "If we don't, we die."

"Yes, but *how?*" Benala Forn asked, her wrinkled face pale. "It's one thing to take on five-hundred. Even then we would be bottlenecked by the pass. If the rest of the Kayle's army arrives—"

She was stopped abruptly, though, as Syrah cried out from her place beside Carro.

Raz snapped around to look at her, fearing something had happened. As it was, Syrah was merely gaping at Forn over a hand now covering her mouth, looking as though she'd just had some terrifying realization.

"Syrah, what is it?" Carro demanded, looking her up and down. "What's wrong? Are you hurting?"

Syrah shook her head.

"I-I've just remembered," she moaned, starting to shake again. "Oh no. Oh no, no…"

She looked around slowly, and Raz could feel his own apprehension building up as she met his gaze.

"Grahst…" she began, seeming to be struggling to put everything together. "When he—before he…"

Raz understood why she was so shaken, then, putting two and two together. Grahst, it seemed, had been the man he had killed and ripped off of her. Raz waited, holding her gaze. He wanted to go to her, to take her in his arms and hold her again. He knew, though, that this would draw nothing good from the council, and he couldn't take the risk of damaging whatever headway they'd managed to make.

And so he just waited, doing his best to silently tell her with his eyes that she had it in her to overcome the memory.

Shortly after, Syrah spoke again.

"Gûlraht Baoill will arrive today, if he hasn't already."

The sentence was barely out of her mouth before the council was in an uproar.

"WHAT?" Behn Argo demanded, furious.

"Syrah, are you sure?" Raz heard Carro ask her.

"How do you know this?" Priest Elber shouted over the noise.

"I-I was told," Syrah answered this last question shakily. "I… I didn't recall until now. I didn't remember…"

"You *'didn't remember'*?" Valaria Petrük nearly shrieked in disbelief. "You expect us to believe that? That you *didn't remember*?"

At that, what little color she had left Syrah, and Raz saw in her face a hint of the horrified expression it had held as Reyn Hartlet reached for her in the bed. She seemed to crumple in on herself, her eye going wide, the fear there growing by the moment.

Raz decided it was time to intervene.

"Priestess Petrük," he snapped, his every word laced with lethal assurance as his amber eyes fell on the hag of a woman, "I will say this once, and once only: believe her. Syrah has her reasons, none of which she should feel the need to share with the likes of you. More importantly—" Raz let a growl build up behind his words "—if you continue this line of questioning, you will shortly find yourself absent a tongue. And yes—" he dropped his arms to his sides, flexing the powerful limbs and spreading his clawed fingers in promise "—that *is* a threat."

The air itself almost grew cold, as though Raz's voice had drained the warmth from the room. No one spoke, all eyes on him as he stood, still staring at the old woman. The Priestess, for her part, appeared to have been struck utterly dumb, and just when Behn Argo looked to have found his voice, Kallet Brern stopped him with a hand, jerking his head towards the back of the room as though to soundlessly say "Don't. Look."

Argo did so, and Raz saw his face fall.

There, in the direction Brern had indicated, Syrah stood with her head bowed, her uneven hair falling in lopsided sheets to hide her face. She was shaking again, leaning with one shoulder against the wall of the cell and hugging herself with both arms. Raz felt his stomach bottom out as he saw her, and he didn't notice as even Valaria Petrük—for perhaps the first time in years—looked suddenly heartbroken as each of the council members came to have some inkling of an understanding as to what, perhaps, the "reasons" Raz had just spoken of were.

"Go to her, Arro."

The words reached Raz from what seemed to be a faraway place as he stood helplessly, watching at the woman. When he registered them, though, he stirred and turned his head.

Jofrey was still not looking at him, his blue eyes on Syrah now, but it was unmistakably he who had spoken.

"Go to her," the High Priest said again, firmly this time.

Raz didn't hesitate.

In four broad strides he was through the council, over the dusty floor, and in front of the Priestess. There he hesitated, towering above her as she shook, watching the quiver of her thin shoulders through her shirt.

Then he reached out, wrapped his long arms around her, and pulled her into his chest.

Syrah gasped when he first touched her, starting and making to pull away. When she realized it was him, though, she stopped fighting, stumbling into Raz and pressing herself against the hardened muscles of his trunk and torso. There were inhalations of surprise and outrage from behind Raz, but he ignored them all. As he pulled her in as tightly as he dared, still hugging herself as she buried her face into his shirt, he saw only Carro, sitting a little off to the left. The Priest had, until then, generally maintained the expression of concern and worry that had settled into his face when Syrah hadn't moved to hug him, or at least reached out to touch him. He'd had questions, Raz could tell, and had perhaps been planning to ask them if the council left him in peace with the woman long enough to do so.

Now, however, by the distinct look of sad understanding overcoming the man's bearded features, Raz thought most of those questions had been answered.

It wasn't long before Syrah's episode subsided. Her shaking ended within a few seconds, and in another ten she was breathing easy again. Eventually she lifted her head from Raz's chest, looking up and pulling her arms from where they were pinned to rest her hands on each of his forearms.

"Thank you," she said.

Raz nodded, then let her go. At once Syrah turned back to the council. Making neither comment nor apology regarding what had just happened, she continued as though they had never been interrupted.

"As I said—" she met everyone's eyes steadily, now "—the Kayle is likely to arrive today. We should assume, therefore, that the rest of his forces will join the advance line, and prepare accordingly."

There were a few grumblings at this. Some, Raz thought, were unsatisfied mutterings regarding what they had just witnessed, but fortunately the next question brought them around to the matter at hand.

"Prepare?" Aster Re'het asked faintly, taking a halting step forward on her crutch. "Prepare how? Baoill has tens of thousands at his disposal, Syrah. We have less than a handful of capable men and women in comparison. How do we prepare?"

"My fighters and I are ready and willing to do what is necessary," Cullen Brern said resolutely from the front of the room. "Should it come to an attack, we will ensure as many escape as possible."

"Escape to where?" Re'het asked shrilly, turning awkwardly to face to the man. "Where are we to run to? The mountains? The Woods? Most of us wouldn't last a week in either place."

"*If* the tribes don't hunt us down first," Benala Forn groaned. "Escape isn't an option."

"What other choice do we have?" Cullen Brern demanded, glaring at the women. "If the Kayle has indeed reunited with his vanguard, we've lost any small advantage we might have had with numbers. We can defend the pass, as discussed, but even *if* we manage not to be flanked from the cliffs our stores won't last us more than the freeze, at which point we're dead regardless. So—unless you two have some brilliant suggestion on how to convince Baoill to send away the greater part of his army again and meet us on an even playing field—I say again: we have *no choice.*"

Beside him, Raz felt Syrah stir suddenly, and he looked around.

The woman looked abruptly to have been pulled away, her mouth slightly open as she stared at Brern's back. While the council started falling into disarray again, the Priests and Priestesses snapping at each other in annoyance and tempers born from fear, Raz gave the woman a minute or so before allowing curiosity to get the better of him.

"What is it?" he asked under his breath. "What are you thinking?"

Syrah didn't respond immediately, and Raz could almost see the ideas coming together behind her blank gaze.

"There's a way," she told him finally, keeping her voice low while the others continued to bicker. "At least... I think so."

"A way to what? Escape?"

"No." Syrah shook her head. "A way to force the Baoill to meet us on an even field, like Cullen said."

Raz's felt the skin along the back of his neck tingle as she said this. "What? How?"

Syrah was quiet for a few seconds more, looking for the words. Finally she reached up, grabbing Raz by the elbow and pulling him down as she stood on tiptoes.

"By cutting the head off the snake," she whispered into his ear.

Then she told him her plan.

When she was done, Raz suddenly found that he, too, was staring off at nothing in particular. He considered her idea, contemplated its implications. It was a reach, but not *too far* a reach to be discounted outright. If there was even just a sliver of likelihood that Baoill could be so goaded... it might just give them a chance.

If I survive my part in it, Raz thought privately, though he didn't tell Syrah this.

Instead, he glanced over at Carro, who was watching them— completely ignoring the arguing council members—with a combination of intrigue and suspicion.

"Do you think he would agree, though?" Raz asked Syrah. "Come to think of it, do *you?*"

At this, Syrah looked nervous. "I-I'm not sure. I..."

She paused, then took a breath and looked up at him. "I've... I've been struggling, Raz. It took losing Talo to shake Carro, and it took losing these—" she indicated her ear and the bandages covering what was left of her right eye—"and other things to shake me. If you can imagine another way, I would beg you to tell me. But if my only options come down to the death of fewer over the death of more... then the answer is easy to make, if difficult to swallow."

The words rang familiar to Raz, and after a moment he couldn't help but smile despite the morbidity of the conversation. "Talo told me something similar, once," he said to Syrah in reply to her inquisitive look. "Very similar, in fact. I don't know if he would be *proud* of you, given the nature of the situation, but I can tell you he would have made the same choice in your place."

Syrah blinked at that, but didn't look displeased.

Then she sidled away from Raz, making for Carro.

Raz watched the pair of them lean close together for a minute, listening to Syrah whisper to the old Priest everything she had just told him. As Carro grew more and more pale, though, Raz decided it wasn't his business what the man had to say, so he distracted himself by turning back to the infighting still ongoing within the ranks of the Citadel's council. Cullen Brern had been joined by his brother, and the two of them were arguing with Benala Forn and Aster Re'het. Priest Elber was bending low in hissed conversation with the withered Jerrom Eyr, while behind this pair Valaria Petrük and Behn Argo had their heads together, muttering to each other and every now and then casting dubious glances in Raz's and Syrah's directions. Only Jofrey stood apart from the group, arms crossed, his body outlined against the broader light of the hall outside.

And, for once, he was looking right at Raz.

Raz met his eyes, watching them disappearing and reappearing behind the flash of his spectacles. The High Priest didn't move towards him or indicate that he had anything to say, but something tugged at the corners of his mouth as Raz watched him. The man's eyes flicked, then, moving to where Syrah sat with Carro, then back to Raz.

Then he raised an eyebrow, and the question was plain on his face.

What are you planning?

Raz had just taken a step towards him—thinking Syrah wouldn't mind if Jofrey had *some* idea of what it was that she and Carro were discussing—when Carro himself suddenly gave a loud cough. Raz turned to him, as did Jofrey, but they seemed the only ones to have made out the Priest's polite attempt to interrupt the heated conversations happening about the room. The rest of the council continued in their mutterings, oblivious of Carro's call for their attention. The man tried again, then once more, each cough becoming louder and more obvious than the previous.

Finally, he lost patience.

"OY!" the aging man bellowed, cutting across the general rumble of the others. "SETTLE DOWN!"

The noise died away almost at once. Syrah stayed where she was, seated beside the Priest, carefully set several inches apart from him so that they wouldn't touch, even inadvertently. As Raz watched, she looked around, met his gaze, and gave a quick, sharp nod. It was not an excited motion, or a happy one, but it spoke to the desperateness of the situation.

Carro agreea, Raz realized, and the tingling sensation returned, sweeping across his whole body now.

At the same time, he felt a knot tightening in his stomach.

"There is an avenue we have not explored," Carro told the gathered men and women about him. His voice was coarse, and he had the ashen look of a man following a path he very much did not want to take. "One that could play greatly to our advantage. Not to mention—" he glanced over at Raz briefly "—Laor has seen fit to deliver onto the Citadel all the pieces we could need to win this particular game."

"Explain yourself, al'Dor," Priest Argo said testily. "This is no time for riddles."

"I will," Carro promised with a nod, reaching up to tug nervously at his braided beard, "but before I can, I must first have an answer from you." He paused, and looked to be steeling his resolve for the question that was to follow. It was a long few seconds before he found his voice again.

"Would you allow a Priest of the faith to condemn the life of one, even if it meant saving the lives of a thousand others?"

The rumblings began again at once, the council's faces ranging from extreme agitation to borderline nausea to outright anger. Raz watched them all, feeling his heartbeat quicken in his chest as he waited for their answer. His eyes trailed across the ensemble, settling once more on Jofrey.

The High Priest looked suddenly ill at ease, as though he sensed trouble on the horizon.

"The law is absolute, Carro," Priest Elber spoke up finally after a minute or so of discussion. "Whatever doctrine Talo might have instilled in you, and whatever good you perceive might have come from your actions, a man of the faith who knowingly plays a part in the death of another is no Priest."

From the corner of his eye Raz saw Carro nod slowly, as though he had expected the answer. When the Priest started to get to his feet, though, it was still Jofrey that Raz watched.

Jofrey, who looked suddenly horrified, his mouth open and his hand half-outstretched, almost as though he wanted to cry out and stop the madness that he suddenly understood was about to occur.

"In that case," Carro al'Dor, Priest of Laor and the High Citadel, said in a hollow, hard voice, "I confess to the full extent of my crimes, to the betrayal of the Lifegiver and His light as a whole, and beg of you to remove me from the ranks of the consecrated faith while time is still on our side."

XL VIII

Carro was Broken at dusk of the following day.

Raz, not being of the cloth, was allowed to accompany the old man and Syrah to the entrance of the consecration room, but barred from entering the chamber itself. He had been of a mind to challenge the paired Priest and Priestess who'd informed him of this, stopping him at the door, but Carro himself had put a big hand on Raz chest, his face tense as he looked up. There'd been a sadness to his blue eyes that Raz had never seen before, something separate from the depths of loss that had overtaken the man after Talo's passing.

"This isn't something I want you to see anyway, lad," he'd said simply.

Then he had given Raz a forced, pained sort of smile, and allowed the man and woman to lead him into the room, starting down the stairs towards the black dais Raz could just make out at the bottom of the steps, looming ominously beneath the wooden carvings and floating braziers filled with white flames. Syrah had lingered a few moments longer, torn between desiring to stay by his side and wanting to be there for Carro as the ceremony began.

Raz had told her to go.

As the door closed behind the woman, slamming shut on the glance back she gave him, Raz stood stoically in the hall, suddenly alone in the dim glow of the candles and torches, each alight with magical fire. For a long time he told himself he would stay, told himself he wouldn't move from that place until the ritual was at an end.

Then the crackle of spellwork began, and Carro began to scream.

It was a sound unlike anything Raz had heard in his life. It was strange to him, in some ways, and yet all too familiar. There was pain, there, true, miserable pain, but there was also much more. More than the physical agony that the man seemed to be suffering, the nature of the scream reverberated with the notes of loss and sorrow, like a man who had just been told about the death of his child. Carro screamed and screamed, howling unintelligible words of denial and pleas to the men and women Raz could just imagine surrounded him, standing about and above him in the rising stands that lined the room's four sides.

After a minute had passed into two, then three, Raz found he could stand it no longer.

He turned his back on the door, moving along the long outer hall of the Citadel, looking for the companionship of a friend who wouldn't weigh on his weary mind with needless conversation and questions.

Raz found Gale settled down in the wide room he'd been shown only the evening before, after he and Syrah had been all but forcibly removed from Carro's company. It was a large space, warm enough despite a number of narrow arrow slits that looked over the harsh edges of the Saragrias and the grey and white of the mountainsides below and around them. A substantial amount of yellow straw had been poached from somewhere and laid out thickly over the greater part of the room's stone floor, and a large wooden trough, filled with the clear, clean water the Laorin collected from melted snow, took up much of the uncovered surface. The day before, the room had been brightly lit with a single floating orb of blazing magic, its white light chasing away any shadow apart from Gale's. Today, though, the magic seemed to have run its course, for which Raz was grateful.

He was in the mood for the peace and quiet of the dark, rather than the bright cheer of light and sorcery.

Gale—as good horses sometimes do—seemed to sense Raz's mood before the room door had so much as clicked shut. He snorted and ambled slowly over, dipping and bobbing his head as he moved, shaking his neck so that his black mane fell unevenly to either side. Reaching his master, Gale thrust his nose right into Raz's clawed hands. As might occur if a favorite dog did much the same, it wasn't long before Raz found himself almost smiling despite himself, stroking the horse's head absently as he looked out at the wisps of clouds one could discern through the nearest balistraria. He wondered, briefly, what the room would be like in the middle of a storm.

Then, as though this hollow query were the key to the quieter place in his mind, Raz allowed his thoughts to wander, desiring even just the smallest taste of escape from the echoes of Carro's screams he convinced himself he could still hear. For half an hour he stayed like that, absently brushing Gale's black hair, the huge horse occasionally stepping this way and that and lashing at his flanks with his long tail. All the while, Raz willed himself to be elsewhere, anywhere that was not there, in that place, in that moment.

Only the eventual groaning sound of the door opening behind him brought Raz back in the end. Even then, it wasn't until he heard it creak shut again, the latch clunking roughly into place, that he looked around.

Syrah stood just inside the room, her back pressed against the wood of the door. She said nothing, her white hair—which had been cut evenly to her chin only that morning—moving gently about her face as a thin breeze snuck its way in through the arrow slits. Her robes had been replaced, her hands re-bandaged, and as he took her in Raz was so vividly reminded of the first time they'd met that for the space of a heartbeat he felt almost a boy again.

Then his eyes met hers, and the present returned.

Syrah had not cried, he saw at once. Her left eye, pink and bright even in the gloom of the room, was dry, and her jaw was set. Despite this, her arms shook by her sides, and Raz could see the weight of what she had witnessed bearing down on her. Whatever morbid curiosities he might have had about what had occurred in the consecration room banished themselves from his thoughts, and he turned away from Gale to face her in full.

She did not lunge, or run at him, despite however much he thought she might have wanted to. Instead, Syrah stepped towards him slowly, the hay crunching delicately beneath her new boots as she walked. He made no move as she approached, doing nothing more than watch her come steadily closer, here and there her face brightening with the natural somber glow of the Sun outside.

When she reached him, she didn't hesitate. She just reached out, wrapped her arms around his waist, and pulled herself tightly into him.

Raz returned the embrace gently, saying nothing as he brought one arm around her shoulders, his other hand drawing clawed fingers carefully through her shortened hair. Behind him Gale huffed and moved away, satisfied that his job was done.

They stood like that in the hay, beings so different from one another that they might have been almost eerie to witness in the same room. They spoke not a word, and only when Syrah began to shiver did Raz move, gently bringing his wings around and wrapping her in them like a pair of leathery blankets. She didn't flinch as they settled around her, and only held him tighter until her quivering subsided.

Together, desiring nothing more at that moment than each other's company, they shared in mourning the sacrifice a friend had made for a people he was no longer a part of.

XL VIX

"It would take the spirit of war itself to best a man who fights already as though he were half-a-god…"

—camp whispers, regarding the Kayle

Gûlraht Baoill's heart hammered in his chest, his spirits soaring so high it was as though he had remembered what it meant to be alive. Snow crunched beneath his boots, settling between his heels and the rough stone beneath. The wind, singing the song of approaching storms, blew his hair and beard about his rough face. As he climbed the air seemed almost to harden, sharpening to cut at the bare skin of his shoulders, growing colder and harsher with every passing hour.

And to his left, stretching out far below him and shrinking until it seemed a world he could practically hold in the palm of his hand, the white and green blanket of the Arocklen extended to the horizon beneath a veil of low-hanging clouds.

As he led his army upward, into the vastness of mountains much like the ones they'd left behind only months ago, Gûlraht couldn't stop himself from smiling towards the slate-grey of the heavens above. It was more than just the four-day that had passed since his rejoining with the vanguard, time which he had largely spent venting his suppressed impatience and anticipation on unfortunate sparring partners, often to the point of unconsciousness. It was more than just the weeks he and his men had spent sunken in the murk and gloom of the cursed Woods and its world of great shadows and even greater trees. From the moment he had descended from the Vietalis, leaving the lands and villages of his ancestors behind to march south and east on the weaker men of the valleys, Gûlraht was realizing he had left some part of himself behind.

Now, as cool mountain air filled his lungs once more and the coming squall blew drifts of powdery snow across the icy path before him, Gûlraht found that lost sliver of his soul again. The higher they went, the more he reclaimed, and by the time half the climb was behind them the Kayle felt what could only be described as the will of Them of Stone coursing through his veins. It was an enthralling excitement, the sort of thrill that usually came only before battle.

When the shapes in the clouds above them changed, suddenly becoming something more than jagged cliffs and the outline of the path crisscrossing along the mountainside, the thrill spiked.

"*Hola,*" Gûlraht said calmly, bringing his left hand up into a fist as he quit his endless climb. At once he heard the word repeated behind him, borne down and along the path a thousand times like some strange echo.

"*You've seen it, my Kayle?*" Agor Vareks asked, coming to stand beside Gûlraht. The older man was dressed for battle, as was every member of the Kayle's entourage. He had matching swords strapped to each hip and a round shield thrown over his shoulder. In the true tradition of the clans he wore no helmet, but a studded leather band had been wound tight about his head, keeping the beads and metal in his greying hair out of his face. Like Gûlraht, the upper half of his arms were bare, hardened and worn by a lifetime spent in the elements, and—despite his age—beneath the hide-like skin, thick muscle pulsed and flexed as the man moved.

"*I've seen it,*" Gûlraht answered, not taking his eyes off the shapes that vanished and flickered in the shifting sky above their heads.

Nature did not breed straight lines…

"*Are the Gähs still above us?*" the Kayle asked at last, still not looking down. Out of the corner of his eye, he saw Agor nod.

"*Elrös and his clan are likely to be in the outcroppings there, further west.*" Agor pointed upward towards a jagged line of jutting, snow-covered stone. "*They were to get as close as could be dared without being seen.*"

Gûlraht nodded. "*Send a runner to call them back. Tell them to meet us along the path.*"

Agor stepped away at once to do as instructed. As Gûlraht heard the man give orders to one of his subordinates, he finally took his eyes off the outline of the Laorin's High Citadel far above, turning around.

The mountain below appeared almost afire, shifting and flickering with the writhing darkness of twenty-five thousand souls.

Since dawn Gûlraht and his generals—along with a small party of a hundred or so more—had led the slow ascent along the worn stairs that had been carved like a scar up the faces of the mountains. Others had followed behind when space and opportunity permitted, but the mere fact was that most of the path did not allow more than one or two abreast, much less what it would take for the army as a whole to climb in a timely fashion. As a result, the greatest part of the common warriors had been left to devise their own paths.

The result was a sea of steel and dark fur, seething and rumbling above and below where Gûlraht now stood, strong hands and a life among the cliffs making steady work of terrain the men of the false-god would never have dared attempt.

After several minutes a lone figure could be seen breaking off from the army's edge above them. By the way it moved, dashing and vaulting through the crags as though the bluffs were nothing more than a precarious ladder, Gûlraht could tell it was one of the Goatmen. He watched until the Gähs vanished among the layered edges of the bluffs.

Then he turned back to where Agor, Erek Rathst, and Rako the Calm stood awaiting his command.

"Start the drums."

Not long after, the army was on the move again, pressing ever upward. This time, though, they were accompanied by the slow, rhythmic beat of half-a-hundred heavy wood-and-hide drums, each slung about the thick neck of a Kregoan warrior.

Gûlraht did not call for another halt when Elrös of the Grasses dropped down from the snow banks above them half-an-hour later, landing on all fours some twenty feet before his Kayle as a dozen others fell similarly around him. The chieftain of the Gähs stood and waited for the march to meet him, the greyish-white pelts slung about his shoulders for camouflage flourishing in the wind as he fell into step beside Gûlraht.

By the graveness of his face, it was easy to guess that the man did not come bearing good news.

"Speak, Elrös," Gûlraht said quietly, not bothering to look at the man as he moved.

"My Kayle," the Gähs started up at once, his voice hoarse from the dry chill of the air. *"A figure awaits you, at the top of the path. Behind him, a hundred men of the fortress stand along the gates. They prepare for us, I think."*

Gûlraht was surprised by this, though only mildly. He had guessed the hateful powers the Witch and her ilk wielded would have a way of informing the Citadel of his coming. It was why he had started the drums. If surprise was of no advantage to them, fear might as well be.

On the other hand, he had expected the false-prophets might retreat behind the relative safety of their walls, not prepare to meet his army in open battle. Unless he was misinformed, there couldn't be more than two or three thousand within the keep, and only a fraction of them men and women capable of defending the place.

"Perhaps they seek to meet us along the path?" Elrös asked, falling in behind Gûlraht as they started up a narrow set of carved stairs. *"They hope to gain the tactical advantage, assuming we will only be able to launch our attack from the steps."*

Gûlraht shook his head, his brow creasing as he thought. *"Were that true, then they would send their men as far down the mountain as they could, so as they were pressed back they would still hold the advantage. Meeting us at the top defies that purpose..."*

He considered the possibilities, for a time, shifting his ax to his other hand so he could balance himself against the wall to his right as the stairs grew slick.

This struck him with a thought.

"*Elrös*," he said sharply, looking back at the man as soon as he was on sure footing. "*Tell me of the terrain. What sort of place is it that they wait for us?*"

The Gähs' sharp eyes peered up at him from beneath his wolf-skull helm. "*A plateau, my Kayle. An outer courtyard, like a flattened half-circle, clearly carved out of the mountain by man. It is the space before the walls of the fortress itself, one edge—the north's—walled in by stone, the other sheer as a cliff.*"

"*How large is it? Is it snow-covered, or has it been cleared?*"

Elrös squinted as he made to recall.

"*It is of great width, and what little snow covered the stone seems to have built up since a recent clearing. In fact—*" he sounded suddenly surprised "*—several of the men were set about doing exactly that…*"

Gûlraht nodded, but said nothing more, thinking. After a minute or so of further contemplation he dismissed the man with a word, listening to the Gähs scamper back along the path to where the rest of his pack likely waited.

Agor joined him again almost at once.

"*What news?*" the older man asked under his breath, as though he didn't want the others to hear. Gûlraht rather thought it was Rako's ear he was avoiding, and didn't disapprove.

Despite this, as he answered, he kept his private thoughts to himself. "*They wait for us at the top,*" he told the man truthfully. "*Tell the men to prepare for an ambush, but* do not *attack without my command. If it is words they wish to share, I would hear them.*"

Agor looked surprised at this.

"*Words?*" he asked in a tone that bordered on frustration. "*What words could blasphemers have that would sway your judgment?*"

"*None,*" Gûlraht told him, fixing the man with a burning glare to put him back in his place. "*But we can ill afford to risk spending the next few months wasting time on a siege while the valley towns strengthen their defenses and bolster their armies. If words allow me even a few minutes more to surround the fortress without resistance, then I. Will. Have. Words.*"

He injected every enunciation of this last statement with a fierce promise meant to tell Agor all too clearly that he was toeing a line with his questioning. In truth, Gûlraht cared little and less what terms the Laorin might present him, because he had other suspicions as to why he was being met at the fortress gates. If he shared them, though, he suspected his generals would do their best to convince him of the folly falling for such a trap could mean, and he was in no mood to be hounded as the Citadel became more and more distinct with each passing step.

Agor, for his part, did as he was commanded, falling back to relay the orders. As the general did this, Gûlraht reached into the side of his leather breastplate—like he had every few hours for the last four days—and wrapped his gloved fingers around the silky bundle of braids he kept there, close to his heart.

He smiled, fingering the hair in anticipation, feeling the bloodlust begin to rise within him. Not long after, Gûlraht couldn't help but allow a shiver of pure excitement work its way up his spine, because he'd taken a bend in the path and found himself looking up, towards a flat edge not far above.

With rising exhilaration, he started up the last of the path's steps.

L

The High Citadel, to the eyes of a man of the mountains, was nothing short of a wonder worthy even of Them of Stone. It was a castle carved from the living rock of the cliffs, suspended in many parts—by what Gûlraht could only imagine was both man's ingenuity and the devilish magics of the place's current residents—over open air and slick bluffs. Towers and walls jutted from the mountain in layers, until the fortress looked almost a city lost among the peaks. Gûlraht had been—to his chagrin—impressed by the mass and breadth of the valley towns he had descended on over the first weeks of his campaign, taken aback by the truth of their size as he saw them up close for the first time. In comparison, the home of the Laorin was a small thing.

And all the more magnificent for it.

It existed, like some great beast, almost untouched by the endless assault of winter and wind. Here and there light could be seen against the grey and white of the carved granite and mortared slate, peeking through narrow arrow slits like dozens of fiery eyes. Its mouth lay below these, directly across from where Gûlraht and his generals stood at the top of the stairs, a gaping entrance to a long tunnel, flanked by paired bastion towers that loomed almost like arms overhead. For a moment the crenellations of the walls seemed claws, and the Kayle could just imagine the Citadel as a whole rising up to crush him like he were nothing more than a flake of snow amid ten-thousand others beneath its paws.

When the fleeting vision left, Gûlraht found himself swearing by his life, his army, and the Stone Gods themselves that he would have this place for his own.

The figure that awaited the Kayle was, in comparison, a disappointing sight. Gûlraht had anticipated a regal reception, likely the richly dressed form of whatever master this fortress might currently suffer, or perhaps even the White Witch, come to goad him within safe reach of her friends. After a moment he realized that the Witch *was* indeed present, but stood some twenty yards away, glaring at him with one pink eye from the front of a group of some two hundred men and women all armed with silver staffs, their white robes whipping about them in the wind.

Gûlraht stared the woman down as she met his gaze, turning to the figure before him only after the Witch had paled and looked away.

The man standing no more than ten feet in front of them was a strange sight. He carried no staff, and his robes were grey and ratty. One sleeve was loose and flapping, and by the bulge along his chest the arm looked to be strapped about his torso, like a healing break. A dark cloth covered the lower half of his face, hiding his nose and mouth, and a wide hood billowed and cut low over his forehead, almost blocking his eyes from view.

When Gûlraht finally made them out, though, he knew there was more to this man than his worn clothes let on. These were eyes that did not fear him—or at least not nearly as much as they should—their clear blue shining against the somberness of the cloth about them. They took the Kayle in with something less than respect, but more than hate. They took him in with confidence, despite having to look up into his face to meet his gaze, and did not flinch away even as the Kayle took a step forward.

"*My Kayle—*" Rako the Calm started from behind Gûlraht at this motion, his voice almost lost to the growing wind, but Gûlraht stopped him with an aggravated wave of his hand, not looking over his shoulder. He had eyes only for the man before him, and was peering down at him carefully, trying to make out the detail that had made him curious enough to approach even a little.

Then he saw it again. An odd scar, formed by two smooth, straight lines crisscrossing over the man's right eye, disappearing beneath the hood and mouth cloth. Gûlraht had no idea how such a wound could be suffered, and had only enough time to gauge that the lines were far too perfect to be made by any blade, when the man spoke. His voice thundered out in practiced mountain tongue from behind his wrappings.

"*I seek audience with he who is Kayle of the mountain clans!*"

Gûlraht snarled, then replied in the rough Common he had had his slave girls instruct him in every night over the last few months.

"Cease butchery of mountain language, little man. Befouling the tongue of the Gods, you are."

The figure before him—who by any accounts but Gûlraht's was not at all "little"—looked surprised, then almost impressed.

"I seek an audience with the Kayle of the mountain clans," the man repeated, reverting to his own speech. "Are you Gûlraht Baoill, of the Sigûrth tribes of the Vietalis Ranges?"

At that, Gûlraht smiled wickedly.

Then he looked over the stranger's shoulder. Syrah Brahnt had gathered courage from somewhere to meet his stare now, and her scowl did not flinch away this time even as his eyes settled on her.

"Better to trust one of your own to tell you, you would like?" he asked in a playful tone. "Bring the *Wyth* within my reach and ask *her* who stands before you, you should."

The man didn't bother acknowledging the words, only repeating his question. "Are you Gûlraht Baoill?"

Gûlraht frowned, seeing that this was a character unwilling to play his game. He set his face into a searing glare that would have withered any of his own men to nothing.

"Gûlraht Baoill, I am," he said fiercely, taking another step forward so that he was practically towering over the man. "Chieftain of the Sigûrth, conqueror of the Gähs, the Kregoan, the Amreht, and the pitiful tribes of your own mountains. Slayer of Emreht Grahst, who was chieftain before me. Son of Tarruk Baoill, who was chieftain before Emreht. Born of Them of Stone, carved of the winter storms, and your end, bringing behind me."

At this he stepped partially aside, indicating the mountains east of him with his ax, along the path he had been climbing since that morning. Like a black flood his army overran the cliffs, blotting out the snow and ridges as they moved to surround the Citadel. The drums continued their endless beat, their hammering echoing ten-fold with every strike.

The grey-robed man before him didn't so much as blink.

"You seek to bring war down upon the faith," he said calmly, his eyes following the dark mass of the army edging its way north and west, surrounding them. "The Laorin are a people of peace, of sincerity. By seeking their destruction, you move against those that have never sought you ill will."

"Seeking their destruction, I move to wipe false-god from the stories of past and future," the Kayle snapped back, flexing his powerful arms as he stood looking down upon the stranger. "Your ilk are blasphemers, heretics and prophets of wickedness. Your *Wyth* alone—" he raised a hand to point a finger at the woman near the back of the courtyard "—spits on old ways and tramples tradition under boot."

"She sought only to save your people," the man said, still eerily calm. "She sought only to better your lives through peace, to strengthen your weak and allow your children to grow old."

"No place amongst the mountains for the weak, there is!" Gûlraht thundered. "No place for children not strong enough to survive the storms on their own. You and your kind are frail kind, dependent on vile sorceries and strength of others to survive. Blight on this world, you are."

The man's scarred face twisted into a grimace. "Then you will not parley for peace?" he demanded. "You will not allow us to seek terms, that we might avoid the madness that is this war you so desperately seek?"

At this, Gûlraht began to laugh. It was a heavy, fierce laugh, thick with amusement at the man's offered prospects. Truth be told, Gûlraht was impressed. Had this stranger been one of his own men, he didn't know whether he would have sought to flay him for his cheek or promote him for his gall.

"No," he finally said, looking back down and hefting his great ax with one arm, thrusting it forward, under the man's nose. "No *parley*. No *seek terms*. Your time you waste, and mine. Declare yourself, and end foolishness of yours."

"*I AM A MAN WHO WOULD SEEK TO CHALLENGE YOU, GÛLRAHT BAOILL, IN FORMAL COMBAT!*"

The words, shouted out in perfect, practiced mountain tongue, rang clear over the wind, echoing across the mountainside. Though the army around them and in the distance might not have made it out as they marched, the challenge was audible enough to Gûlraht, his generals, and the entourage that had followed behind them. In an instant the rumbling of a hundred voices could be heard, building up second by second as more and more men caught and spread the words. Behind him the Kayle made out Agor and Erek snort in derision, and Rako gasp in surprise.

Gûlraht, though, only grinned.

It was as he had suspected, and his heart quickened with excitement.

"*Arrogant dog!*" Agor's voice suddenly shouted out from behind him, apparently meant for the grey-robed man. "*Is this your plan? You have been blinded by your own hope. Only a man of the clans may call for a—!*"

Agor's voice faltered and cut short as the stranger reached up with his one hand and pulled free the cloth about his mouth. As it flew off, whipped away by the wind, he reached up and pulled down his hood.

Gûlraht felt his heart sing.

He saw now the extent of the scar. It extended without end, a perfect X over the man's right eye, marring his skin in an almost surreal fashion. He looked to be of an age, older than Agor but not quite of Rako's years, and there was a graveness to his face that spoke of sadness, will, and an understanding of the cruel realities of life. Gûlraht, though, registered all of this in an instant, his attention fixed more on the other details, the ones that made him want to roar in pleasure.

Blond, braided hair danced wildly about the man's head, wooden beads *clacking* together and metal rings glinting in the dim glare of the sun through the thick clouds above. His beard whipped about, plated and decorated in similar fashion, his mouth a tight line behind the yellowed hairs.

Were it not for the robes, the stranger could have practically counted himself among the ranks of the Kayle's armies and none would have been the wiser.

"*I am Carro al'Dor, of clan blood by my father's seea,*" the man said once more in the rehearsed tongue of the tribes, still loud enough for all nearby to hear. "*I am as much a son of the Stone Gods as any of you might claim to be. I therefore claim my birthright and challenge you, Gûlraht Baoill, to formal combat.*"

The rumbling of men's raised voices redoubled as Carro al'Dor's claims were repeated again and again and again, passed back and upwards through the ranks pouring about the Citadel. Gûlraht knew, even if he had wanted to, that it was too late to refuse now, and he took a moment to appreciate how well this robed stranger had played the game, forcing his hand. The challenge had been made, and whether or not al'Dor's declarations were true or merely some last-ditch effort to grant the Laorin even the barest sliver of hope, it didn't matter.

If Gûlraht refused on grounds he could not disprove, he would shame himself.

And more importantly, the Kayle thought, meeting the man's queer, scarred eyes levelly, *here is an opportunity to break the Laorin's spirit in an instant...*

"*I accept your challenge, Carro al'Dor of clan blood, and will grant you the duel you seek.*"

And like that, the deed was done. A stillness settled over the mountain, spreading like water poured over dry stone. The Kayle of the tribes had acknowledged this strange man's claim, and had accepted the challenge

Carro al'Dor inclined his head.

Then for the first time, he asked something Gûlraht had not anticipated.

"Will you be selecting a champion, Kayle of the tribes?"

Gûlraht stared at him for several seconds, finding himself somewhere between infuriated and amused. al'Dor had the right to the question, of course, but any who had ever seen Gûlraht Baoill stand beside even the next greatest of his warriors would have known it was a foolish inquiry.

Gûlraht was about to laugh and mock the man—had even opened his mouth to retort—when he paused, realizing what the man was after.

Right then, Gûlraht's excitement became almost intolerable. He had assumed this man before him, who stood tall and strong despite his age and apparent injuries, would be the one he would fight. He didn't dress in the manner of a Priest, so perhaps he was precluded from the ridiculous rule the Laorin held regarding the taking of a life. If he was skilled in wielding the black powers of their corrupt deity, then he might just prove a worthy opponent, one whose death would garner great glory for both Gûlraht and the Gods. Gûlraht had never had the chance to battle magic before, and the sweet taste of the opportunity was almost palpable.

But if there was a stronger warrior among the false-prophets that the faith would allow to fight...

And then, all of a sudden, Gûlraht felt a dead hope flame up within him. A word came to his mind, one that had spread like fire throughout his men, whispered in hushed tones or else only spoken of around the evening fires, in the comforting presence of companions. He could barely contain himself as he finally answered al'Dor.

"No champion will I claim, old man," he said, smiling widely and bending down until he was practically nose-to-nose with the former Priest. "And you?"

al'Dor did not move for a long time. He didn't flinch away from Gûlraht's gaze—though it looked as though he might want to—nor did he speak. After several seconds, though, he took a step back, then another, then turned and made his slow return towards the group near the mouth of the Citadel, his boots leaving distinct prints in the thin layer of snow that had gathered in the time they had been speaking.

Then, as al'Dor joined the ranks of the Laorin, a different figure rose, stepping out from where it had been hidden behind the White Witch, and began to move towards the Kayle.

It seemed, in that moment, that the drums themselves faltered in fear.

Gûlraht didn't hear the hissed gasps of shock and awe from the men behind as he watched the creature approach, nor did he make out Erek's curse or Rako's hasty prayer to Them of Stone. He watched, through a veil of bloodlust and excitement, as the thing left clawed prints, moving parallel to the path Carro al'Dor had taken back to the Laorin.

Only when it stood not ten feet in front of him did Gûlraht finally make out some of the mumblings going on in the group behind him. His heart felt as though it skipped a beat every time he caught the word he had so desperately hoped for, repeated again and again as it chased itself through his army.

"*Dahgün*," came the whispers.

Dragon.

In all his life, Raz had never imagined he would have to look *up* to a man. It was a foreign concept to him, a thought that he'd never so much as paused to contemplate. If someone had asked him that morning to consider it, he suspected he might have laughed at the idea.

Now, though, Raz found no humor in the notion.

Gûlraht Baoill, Kayle of the mountain tribes, might have done better to consider himself more giant than man. He stood well over seven feet tall, the top of his head some inches above Raz's, and his shoulders and hips were half-again as broad. His arms, their top halves bare to the storm that was building steadily around them in gusts and heavy flurries of snow, were as thick as a large man's thighs, the muscles beneath their weathered skin bunching like rolling, vein-covered boulders. His legs, planted slightly on either side of him in a confident stance, looked more like the trunks of trees than limbs. Hardened leather settled about his form in thick iron-studded plates, and grey and black fur tufted about his neck, shoulders, gauntlets, and boots. The heavy brown pelt of what appeared to be some kind of bear was thrown about his shoulders, and in his right hand the Kayle held a massive double-headed great ax that looked to be of a weight comparable to Ahna's. He bore no other weapons, but there was an air about the way Gûlraht Baoill held that ax that said all too well he'd never had need of any other blade.

It was the same sort of deadly confidence with which Raz carried the dviassegai, slung over his right shoulder.

This man, Raz thought with a silent thrill of realization and anticipation, *might just be the death of me.*

In kind, he had the impression, as he stopped less than a dozen feet before the Kayle and took in the odd, excited expression on the massive man's face, that Baoill was having the exact same notion.

They squared off with each other then, both silent and both staring, each taking in all there was to behold about the other. For almost half a minute there seemed to be a holding of all breaths, during which they acknowledged one another as something more than the lesser men all about them, and respected each other for it.

Gûlraht Baoill broke the silence first.

"You speak, beast?"

Raz narrowed his eyes at the man.

"I speak, Kayle of the clans," he said, growling over the wind. "As well as any man you have cause to discourse with."

The Kayle looked surprised at that. "Hard to believe, it is then, that you are creature of sorcery…"

Raz snorted. "Is *that* what you've been told?" He eyed the men behind Baoill. "That I'm some summoned *thing* brought down on your heads by the Laorin?"

"Is, yes," the Kayle responded, surprising Raz. "'Demon' and 'dragon' you are called among men of mine. They tell stories, how you have been birthed of snow and shadow, how bear you such strength and speed only witchcraft could carry you to life." He smiled at this, his blue eyes growing hungry beneath the thick, beaded brown hair lashing about his face. "Hope, I admit I do, that you prove them wrong."

Raz said nothing, taking in the man a while longer, pondering him. After a time he reached up and put a steel claw against his cheek, one of the few places not covered in leather or fur or steel.

Then he drew the razor edge across his skin, splitting the thick scales before flicking the blood out to pattern the snowy stone between them with splattered red.

412

"I am of flesh and bone, as you are," Raz snarled at the Kayle, whose eyes had fallen to watch the blood freeze. "I am born of sand and Sun, not sorcery and spellwork. Your men died by a living hand. They were not slain by a conjured blade. They took something from someone I care for, so I took something from them."

At this, the Kayle grinned. It was an ugly look, twisting his shaggy, cruel face.

"Blood for blood," he chuckled darkly. "Done well among my kind you would have, dragon, had you been born to the tribes."

"To be molded by cruel gods into an even crueler man?" Raz retorted, bringing Ahna down slowly from his shoulder as he saw the minute flexing in the man's ax-hand. "I'll take my chances with the foolish peace of gentler divinities."

"Long way seeking death, you've come," Baoill said even as he undid the fastenings of his bearskin, letting it fall to the ground before settling into an aggressive stance. "If make it you do to the halls of Them of Stone, will have you tell me such a story, I think."

"If I make it," Raz agreed, taking Ahna in both hands. "In the meantime, save me a seat."

The Kayle grinned at that, the look one of such utter, ravenous hunger it shot a shiver down Raz's spine.

A man came forward then, one of the Kayle's generals by the look of him, moving around his master to stand between and beside Raz and Baoill as they faced off. He was older than Baoill by some years, his black hair streaked with silver and grey that patterned well with the shine of gold rings and baubles braided into it. For a second the Sigûrth eyed Raz, then turned to Baoill.

"*Al'Kayle*," he spoke in hushed tones, addressing the massive man in the guttural tongue of their people, clearly questioning the situation, "*dü sen—?*"

"*Agor*," the Kayle responded harshly, cutting the newcomer off. "*Stea.*"

Despite the difference in languages, Raz understood this last statement clearly, as it had been given not as reply, but as a command.

Agor, the Kayle had said, speaking to the man. *Enough.*

And the Sigûrth did as ordered, turning to face them equally again.

"*Sen ül Karyn-Des!*" he bellowed, raising his arms to either side, his voice echoing over the mountains as the wind faded momentarily. "*Da brán ed brûn, dü'vren ist micht!*" He looked to Baoill.

"*Da brán ed brûn*," the Kale responded, inclining his head reverently.

Agor—if that was indeed the man's name—turned to Raz.

"Under eyes of Stone Gods," he repeated in broken, accented Common. "By blood and bone, this challenge yours will be met." He paused, watching Raz meaningfully.

Raz had an idea of what was expected of him.

"By blood and bone," he repeated, hoping he had caught the translation correctly as he inclined his head respectfully, if not as deeply as the Kayle.

The general gave him what could almost have been an approving look. He then turned from the pair, facing the mountains beyond and around, where Raz realized Baoill's armies had come to stand still, like a monster suddenly frozen and holding its breath. Agor began to shout in his native language, and Raz didn't bother trying to understand what the man said. He suspected it to be part of the ritual, perhaps the announcement of titles or the stakes of the fight. Whatever the reason, his eyes never left the Kayle's for the full minute Agor yelled himself hoarse to the men of their army.

The Kayle, too, never looked away.

At last Agor turned back to them. With only a short pause, he raised a hand, like the starter at a horse race.

Then the hand fell, and whatever words the man shouted to commence the duel was lost to the winds as Gûlraht Baoill launched himself forward with a howling war cry, and Raz lunged to meet him.

LI

If Raz had had any lingering illusions about the balance of the fight, they were whisked away in the first handful of engagements. He had expected his first impressions to be of the man's strength, of the power of his blows and the firmness of his parries and blocks. He had expected Baoill to bull into him, to use his mass and size to his advantage. In the end, the Kayle did exactly this.

But not before Raz gained the abrupt—and painful—knowledge that, above all else, Gûlraht Baoill was *fast*.

It was as though the great ax he alternated between wielding in one and two hands weighed nothing more than a child's toy hatchet. It blurred about the man, slashing this way and that as the pair of them danced over the courtyard ground, the snow crunching beneath their feet as they moved. By the time they separated for the first time, Raz had almost lost a limb on three separate occasions, was bleeding from a shallow gash where razored iron had cleaved through the leather wrappings about his thigh, and was half-nursing his left shoulder where the ax had left a sizeable dent in his steel pauldron. Gûlraht, too, was hurting, blood welling out of a narrow puncture in his left bicep, his lip swollen where Ahna's wooden haft had caught him a blow across the face, and his chest plate askew from when her blades had severed the strapping holding them in place over one of the man's shoulders. Both men's breaths billowed out, hovering like smoke about their faces as they edged a rough circle around each other, eyes flicking this way and that looking for an opening. From above the wind Raz just made out the roar of the Kayle's army, soldiers cheering on their lord, as well as the nearer shouts and bellows of the Laorin.

From their enthusiasm, it sounded as though neither group had come to the understanding Raz—and he was quite sure Baoill—already possessed.

They were evenly matched.

For the first time in many years, something happened to Raz, then. As fear bubbled up within him, taking hold in the subtle way it does in brave men, something else rose as well. It was an alien feeling at first, a twisted sort of rush that was less than bliss but more than excitement.

He was enjoying the fight.

And with that understanding, Raz leapt at Baoill, Ahna coming around in a massive two-handed sweep from the side, aiming to take the man in the ribs as her master's face creased into a terrible, serpentine smile.

Baoill leapt clear of the blow, then forward again, raining strikes with his ax down on Raz's head and shoulders. Raz dodged and darted, blocking some and even punching one out of the way that cut too close to his collarbone. He moved back all the while, trying to lengthen the gap between him and the Kayle and get to a place where he could use Ahna's length to her full advantage. When he managed it, he put the dviassegai to rapid use, and suddenly it was Baoill who was on the defensive, the man cursing and grunting with every reverse step he was forced to take.

By the way the Kayle was suddenly frowning, Raz thought it might have been the first time in his life the giant had ever been beaten into any kind of retreat.

Baoill recovered rapidly, though. As Ahna swung above and down at his head, the man stepped nimbly aside and forward, bringing Raz within reach again. The ax shrieked as it aimed to sever Raz's neck, but he ducked and twisted, bringing a steel-clad fist around to punch at the Kayle's face. Baoill shifted and brought an arm up to accept the blow, and the sharp edges of Raz's knuckles cut black and blue furrows down the man's shoulder. Baoill gave as good as he got, though, taking advantage of the brief opening to throw his own punch.

The haft of the man's ax caught Raz in the chest, knocking the wind of out of him.

It was Raz's turn to retreat, wheezing and struggling to catch his breath as he danced away from a pursuing Baoill. The man seemed unwilling to release his advantage, hounding Raz about the courtyard, bellowing his war cry as he swung and cleaved at the air, his strikes only ever barely missing as Raz ducked and weaved. By the time he got his wind back, Raz was bleeding from two more wounds across his chest and upper arm.

Slowly and steadily, the ground about the two men was turning from white to streaked and splotchy red.

As soon as he was able, Raz went on the offensive again. Ahna lanced out abruptly between Baoill's strikes, her points finding their mark but becoming fouled in the thick plating of the man's lopsided chest piece. The Kayle responded instantly, grabbing the dviassegai about the neck below her blades and holding her firmly to him. As the ax fell once again, one-handed this time, Raz dodged sideways before returning and vaulting *over* Ahna's haft as he kicked.

The top of his foot connected with the side of the Kayle's face, and Raz felt the *crunch* as at least one tooth came loose of its socket.

Baoill grunted in pain and staggered back, releasing his hold on Ahna. As she came away she took the loose leather platings with her, tearing the other straps and dragging them off the man's shoulder. More blood fell to the ground as the white shirt beneath was revealed, the pale cloth marred by two thick points of crimson where the dviassegai's tips had apparently managed to work their way through the armor. When Baoill found his footing he stood straight, spitting out blood and a pair of broken teeth before touching the fingers of his free hand to one of the red splotches, staring as they came away wet and sticky.

Then he looked over to Raz, who was busy kicking the leather chest piece free of Ahna's points, and began to laugh.

A second later he was charging in headfirst again, the roar of the man's army spurring him forward like the thunder of hooves leads a stampede.

For longer than either might have believed, the pair fought. Neither felt the fatigue that attempted to weigh them down, each too entranced in the battle. Pain was non-existent even as they cut and slashed each other's skin and flesh, the sting of the wounds melting together with the bite of the wind as the snow began to fall harder about them. When one part of the courtyard became too precarious, slick with blood and packed ice as they stomped and darted over the ground, they would move to another area, then another. Eventually it seemed to onlookers that not a square foot of the massive semicircle was untouched, but before long the snow was falling so thick and rapid that the red evidence of the titans' vicious passings was obscured by the even more powerful force of the squall rising around them.

Raz, though, was as unaware of the storm as he was the lacerations that cut across his chest, arms, and thighs, or the burn in his shoulders as he brought Ahna around faster and faster. He had eyes only for the Kayle, whose dark form shifted in and out of the snow as they met and retreated, then met and broke apart once more, over and over again. Ahna slashed. The ax fell. Claws arced though the air. A massive fist hurtled forward. Wings and tail whipped out. Heavy boots kicked up.

There seemed no end to the pattern, but even of this Raz was oblivious to. He was gone, taken away from the world in a way he had never been before, not even within the oppressive wall of Azbar's Arena. It wasn't the animal that had overcome him, for once. The scene before his eyes was white and grey and dark and bloody, not the frightening shades of black and red that descended as the Monster rose. His mind was clear and whole, his own in its entirety.

And it was focused on the single, obsessive need to kill the man towering before him.

They had made it to the edge of the courtyard that opened up to the endless emptiness of the heavens. On a clear day the pair might have looked out, over the edge, to bear witness to the splendor of the green and white lands laid out for them by whatever gods of creation truly reigned supreme. Instead, there was only a solid ocean of swirling, cold grey, the snow falling so thick and fast now Raz could barely make out the shape of the Laorin party standing some fifty feet away, their backs to the wall of the Citadel.

It was here, at the edge of the world, that Raz's strength failed him.

Ahna flowed around him like liquid metal, whirling and spinning and striking out at every opening the Kayle offered him. They traded ground for the better part of three minutes, back and forth along the edge, each unwilling to disengage and step away for fear of leaving themselves vulnerable. Their weapons crashed and cracked against each other, shrieking as only metal screaming over metal can. Sparks flew, flashing in their eyes, but not once did either give the other enough of a gap to go for a killing blow. Every opening was a trap, every feint readied with a counter attack. They were matched so evenly, Raz a little faster and Baoill a little stronger, it seemed for a time nature would decide the winner as both men blinked away snow and wind, fighting to keep their vision clear.

But Baoill, in the end, proved the more enduring of the two.

It happened as Raz decided it was time to chance a change in his patterns. The Kayle was too good a fighter, too skilled with his ax to allow himself to be beaten with moves he'd seen a dozen times. Until that moment Raz had kept as far from the man as possible, using Ahna's greater reach to his advantage as often as he could. The tactic had been his saving grace often enough, but it had also been his bane, as the Kayle was always just quick enough to react to the strikes and lashes.

He had to get closer.

Raz made his move in the same moment he came to the decision, hesitation having long been cut from his mental state as he fought. As Baoill knocked aside yet another overhead cut from the dviassegai, Raz twisted and lunged forward, bringing Ahna's pointed bottom end around with momentum the Kayle's parry had provider her, driving the steel forward. For half-an-instant he tasted victory as the man's blue eyes went wide, seeing the mistake he had made.

Schlunk!

Ahna's point buried into flesh, and Raz went cold.

Blood followed the edge of the dviassegai's steel, dripping to the ground and freezing to the metal. Baoill had brought up his right arm, using the limb like a shield. The dviassegai's tip had run it through, driving between muscle and bone, but the sacrifice of the limb had saved the Kayle's life.

And cost me mine, Raz realized in horror as the ax came down on Ahna's haft, the inside curve of the iron blades catching the wood and steel like a hook. There was a massive tug, and Raz felt his fingers, numb and weak from the cold and fight, give way.

Ahna was torn from his hands, the dviassegai clattering and rolling over the stone deeper into the courtyard, disappearing into the falling snow.

As the ax came down again Raz did his best to react, dodging back and reaching for his ax and gladius. With the understanding of his sudden disadvantage, though, awareness seemed to rush into his body, as though his mind were screaming at him that this was a fight he was going to lose. His legs suddenly felt sluggish, his hands and arms thick and heavy. He managed to pull his ax free of its loop at his hip, but his right hand slipped off the sword hilt as it stuck firm in its scabbard, frozen shut by the snow and ice that had built up as they battled. Baoill's great ax came around, unrelenting, and Raz spun to cross his ax and armored forearm in a desperate block. Iron hit wood and steel. There was a *crunch*, and splinters flew about Raz's face as the shaft of his ax shattered, leaving only the bottom half in his hand. The blow carried through, barely dampened, slamming Raz sideways.

His claws, finding purchase at the last moment beneath the snow, were the only reason he didn't slide right over the edge of the cliff.

Raz stood himself up precariously, his right arm numb and throbbing beneath its steel bracer after accepting the blow, the splintered shaft in his other hand. Behind him, maybe a foot away, the edge of the plateau waited, the endless gaping mouth of a terrible leviathan come up the mountains to claim him.

And before him, looming like a shadow against the backdrop of falling snow, stood Gûlraht Baoill.

The Kayle of the mountain tribes was not the erect, powerful man he had been a quarter-hour before. His hair was wild and matted with freezing sweat, his face bruised and his mouth bloody. He panted, grimacing in pain as he held his right arm to the stained cloth of his torn and cut shirt. Red ran down the weathered skin, dripping off his elbows to trickle about his right foot. His armor was a mess, little of it left unscathed and much of it punctured and torn completely off as more blood seeped here and there from between iron-studded plates. All in all, the man looked more dead than alive.

And yet, Raz knew as he waited for the inevitable killing blow, it was he who had won this fight.

As he watched, Baoill toed at something in the snow, kicking it up and over the edge of the cliff. Raz saw the glint of the head of his war ax plummet down to vanish into the tumbling grey of the storm.

Baoill spat, splotching the ground with yet more red.

"My admiration you have, beast," he wheezed, edging forward as he brought the great ax up in his good hand. "Not lightly given. I would have the name of yours, so seek you out in the afterlife I might, when time comes."

"I have many names," Raz responded, playing for time as his mind whirred. "Which of them would you prefer?"

As he spoke he looked around, seeking a way out. He still had his sword, but he didn't trust himself to be able to pull it free in time when he had already failed once. His claws wouldn't reach the Kayle before the ax fell, and the same went for his teeth. He had to find another answer, had to find a way to survive.

Then Raz's eyes fell on the dull outline of the Laorin, huddled under the looming silhouettes of the Citadel's walls, and he saw something that made his heart stop. As he looked, he thought he saw a portion of the group shifting and moving. He couldn't make them out through the snow, but it looked as though several people were holding back another.

There was the barest glimpse of white hair, and Raz's suddenly remembered a smile he had told himself he would fight for, no matter what.

Even if survival wasn't an option, in the end…

"I would have all," he heard Baoill answer him, as though from a far-off place. "Names you have won. Name your father placed upon you, and name of his, so tell him of the strength of his son I might."

Raz's eyes didn't leave the Laorin. For once, he didn't care what the Kayle was doing. He sought the hint of that pale hair once more, seeking the warmth it brought his soul.

When he saw it again, clear for a moment as the woman struggled with the men that held her back, he began to find the courage he needed.

"I am Raz i'Syul Arro," Raz thundered, turning back to the Gûlraht Baoill and standing tall as the mountain man continued his slow advance forward. "Son of Agais, son of Aigos. I am heir to the masters of the Arro clan. I am the Monster of Karth, the Scourge of the South. I am demon and dragon, a child of the Sun and Moon, watched over by Her Stars." He raised a hand, pointing a steel claw at Baoill. "You can tell my father that, whenever you meet him."

Gûlraht Baoill nodded his approval.

"I shall remember your name, Raz i'Syul Arro," he said, stopping some four feet away. "And my men. They call you dragon, as well they should. I doubt I will ever meet a more worthy opponent." He set his feet, preparing for the final blow.

"So…" he said quietly. "Until we meet again, dragon."

Then he lunged.

And Raz met him.

He did not leap forward, as if to collide with the man and knock him off balance. He did not strike at his face, for he didn't have space to get his hands up. Instead, Raz darted forward just enough to get inside the arc of the weapon, wrapping his arms around the Kayle's body as he felt the great ax's haft slam into his side. Baoill, understanding his mistake in an instant, roared and wrapped his left arm about Raz, ax and all, pinning him to his body in turn.

Then Raz set his feet, said a small prayer to the Sun hiding somewhere above the storm overhead, and strained backwards.

Under the momentum of his pull and the Kayle's lunge, they tumbled, entwined together, into nothingness.

LII

"It was with this great act that the Dragon of the North was born. As a man he had proven himself, driving the Kayle of the clans—who many among the mountain tribes had begun to suspect was perhaps some bastard of the Stone Gods themselves—to the brink of death. As a beast he had shown his character to be more human than animal, demonstrating himself capable of sacrifice and abandonment of desire for others. But only as the Dragon could he have been responsible for what came next..."

—*Born of the Dahgün Bone*, author unknown

"NO!"

Syrah's barely heard her own scream reverberate over the howl of the storm. She stared, still struggling against the powerful arms of Cullen and Kallet Brern on either side of her, at the empty spot along the edge of the plateau.

The empty spot where, only a moment before, she had watched the dark outline of Raz drag Gûlraht Baoill down with him over the edge of the cliff.

"NO!" she shrieked again. "NO! RAZ! RAZ!"

"He's gone, Syrah!" someone bellowed in her ear, though she wasn't sure who. "Please! He's gone!"

But she wouldn't believe it, *couldn't* believe it. From the moment they had seen the great spear Ahna skitter by them across the snow, Syrah had felt dread consume her entirely. She had tried to intervene, tried to get to the shadowy shapes lingering in the snow at the edge of the precipice, but *Carro* of all people, standing beside her, had shouted for someone to hold her back.

And so the Brern brothers had taken her under the arms—their touch only driving the building panic within her—and kept her from rushing to Raz's aid.

And now he was gone...

At once, Syrah stopped fighting, all will ripped from her. She fell to her knees in the piling snow, shivering and shaking. Cullen and Kallet released her as they realized she had given up, the younger of them crouching down beside her.

"Syrah," Kallet said quietly. "I'm so sorry. But please, we have to move. *Please.* They're coming."

There was the sound of bodies in motion, and Syrah realized that all about her the Laorin were retreating, rushing back for the relative safety of the Citadel's walls. She looked up, seeing a score of men and women moving forward before her, forming a wall between the others and the

422

dark mass that was blooming through the snow towards them across the courtyard, the rough outline of a hundred bodies pressing forward through the storm. Light bloomed in complicated tendrils through the air as the Priests and Priestesses before her began crafting a line of interlacing wards, sealing Cyurgi' Di's entrance from assault, at least for a time.

"We failed…"

Syrah looked around. Carro stood beside her, staring with sadness through the weaving magics at the coming line of mountain men. His scarred face was heartbroken, that of a man whose last hopes had just been snuffed out.

"We failed," he said again, and then Syrah understood. Carro's sacrifice had been in vain. Raz had not won the fight. The Kayle was dead, but no champion stood to claim his title. It would pass on to the next in command, to the generals of his army.

Generals who seemed to have wasted no time in pressing their advantage.

Syrah felt hot tears build in her eye, stinging in the wind, and yet they were not tears of grief. Watching Raz fall had torn her apart, ripping away a part of herself she hadn't realized had become so entwined with the atherian, but it wasn't sorrow that claimed her now. As she watched the coming onslaught of men, men who had chained her, defiled her, stolen away her body and her freedom and now the very man who had pulled her from their clutches, something scorching billowed up from within.

Wrath took her by force, and Syrah's quivering turned suddenly into spasms of fury.

Before anyone could stop her, she was on her feet again, barreling towards the mountain men with a raging scream.

The three Priests directly before her, still weaving their sorceries, started and looked around at the sound. One reached for her as she charged by, but she was too quick, her eye set resolutely on the distinct shapes of the men she could now make out clearly through the snow. As she passed through the unfinished magics she thought she might have heard someone shouting her name, thought she might have heard shouts for her to stop, but she would have none of it. Fed by her anger, the spells she gathered in either hand crackled and snapped audibly, erupting from her palms in twin balls of blinding flame.

When she was ten feet from the front line, she leapt as high as she could, then slammed the magic into the ground.

Fire, true, raging fire, bloomed outward across the stone from where her hands splayed over the rough slate. It arched like lightning over the courtyard, crisscrossing and cutting through the legs of the tribes before her. Steam blasted upward in a gushing cloud, ice and snow vaporizing in the explosion of heat. The fire spread, dragging back and forth across the plateau until it found the wall and the cliff's edge to her left and right respectively.

In the same instant, the men before her began to scream, and Syrah felt satisfaction course through her.

She might not know how to kill, but fire is painful, no matter how it is born into the world.

Her victory didn't last long, however. Men were moving before her, leaping over and around the lines of flames, avoiding the magics as they charged. They came, bellowing their war cries, axes and swords raised, and Syrah suddenly realized she was all alone in the no-man's-land, facing a flood of steel that threatened to crush her.

Then, abruptly, men stood on either side of her.

"Dammit, Brahnt!" she heard Cullen Brern curse from her right as he sent a shockwave into the very heart of the mountain men, blasting the first dozen over the heads of their companions behind them. On her left, his brother did the same. "Don't be a fool! Get back!"

But Syrah ignored him. The fire within her hadn't even begun to run dry yet, and she had always had a talent for combat. Before Cullen could say anything else she was casting stunning spells into the crowd at a frightening rate, howling her defiance as men fell like toppled statues about them. Anyone who managed to get too close was knocked back again, either by her or one of the brothers, and before long the forms of the unconscious and injured were piled about their feet. Eventually they found themselves surrounded, and Syrah heard Cullen continue to curse as he shifted to protect her flank, Kallet muttering under his breath as he continued to hurl spells from her left. They were being pressed now, though, every man they knocked down or aside replaced just as quickly by two more. Syrah summoned a ring of fire up about them, willing it to rage and roar, but it only slowed the mountain men down as they stomped out the magic and pressed forward. Like a churning ocean of grey and brown, the tribes tightened the circle. Syrah could see the gleam of the blades, see the hunger in the eyes of the men, fixed upon her. Her rage began to falter, replaced by something darker as she saw what a fool she had been, how selfish and thoughtless. Fear began to take her over as the hungry faces grew nearer, her spells wavering when images flashed before her of the last time she had been so near their savagery.

Her courage was just about to give out when a thundering wave of a hundred shouting voices rose up from behind, and the mountain men at her back broke and split, many tossed aside and into the air on the ripples of a dozen different spells.

The others had joined them in their final stand.

Goaded on by her charge, it hadn't taken much for the Priests and Priestess of the Citadel to find their own courage. Where a minute ago they had been fleeing inward, making for the safety of the fortress, now they poured out in all directions from the wall, wards and spells leading their rush, steel staffs flashing in the dim light of the day. Bloody and dirty snow was trampled to slush beneath their feet as they pressed the enemy, struggling to push them back.

But push them back they did.

Syrah felt a thrill as she realized the line before her was staggering. The tribesmen were being forced off the plateau and onto the path again, giving way foot by foot under the onslaught of spellwork and steel. They were winning, gaining ground and reclaiming the outer courtyard. If they could take back the semicircle of stone, then they might have a chance to get the greater wards up again, which would make it ten-fold more difficult for the tribes to assault the—

There was a hiss, the wet sound of metal burying into flesh, and Kallet Brern tumbled to the ground before her in a tangle of white robes and thick limbs, an arrow through his eye.

Before she had time to do more than gape at the body of the man that had been her friend, there were a hundred more twangs of arrows let loose, and instinctively Syrah cast a protective ward upwards, above her head. As she felt the heavy strikes of the projectiles against her shield she looked up, feeling her heart drop at the sight above her.

Along the cliffs above their heads, sliding down like an avalanche of leather and steel, the rest of the army had come to the aid of their brethren on the plateau.

In an instant, the tide of the battle turned again.

Syrah saw Goatmen standing along the ridge overhead, bows drawn and firing at any white robes they could distinguish through the snow. Kregoan and Amreht and every other tribe tumbled and leapt down upon them to join the thick of the fight, managing the bluffs with ease. They poured forth, a never-ending cascade of bodies, and within seconds the Laorin found themselves no longer fighting for ground but rather struggling to survive long enough to make it back to the relative safety of the Citadel. Priests and Priestesses were falling now, their magics and staffs failing them as the one man they had been dueling became two, then five, then ten. Soon the ground was equal parts trampled snow and still forms, the mountain men unconscious or screaming and clutching at their injuries, the Laorin dead or dying.

"BACK!" Cullen Brern roared, not even blinking down at the body of his brother. "BACK TO THE WALL!"

But it was too late.

The Laorin were crushed, pinched here against the bastions and the outer wall of the Citadel and there with their backs to the drop of the plateau along its southern ridge. Some managed to make it to the tunnel, funneling in as quickly as they could, but not fast enough to compensate for the constant, violent push of the tribes. More men and women fell, more screams echoing over the mountain tops to join with the clash of steel and hiss of arrows. All around Syrah death reared its ugly head, and the Lifegiver carried his servants off one after the other to return them to the cycle of life. Soon Syrah herself began to wonder if she would be allowed the honor of glimpsing the face of Laor as she died, or if she would simply be born squalling back into the world to taste life anew.

But then, in the moment she thought this, a very different face loomed out of the battle towards her, and fear ripped through Syrah like a sword.

Between the writhing mass of tribesmen before her, each fighting the other for space as they clashed, a man was making his way in her direction, his blue eyes fixed on hers. She recognized him in an instant, noting the black, silver-lined hair and the paired swords he held in each hand, as well as the way the army seemed to separate before him. This was a man she had heard of, but never seen with her own eyes until today. He had been banished from Emreht Grahst's council before the chieftain's death, his ambitions too bloody and his will unyielding. He had aided Gûlraht Baoill to power, then stood by his side as the man rose higher still. He had led the sacking of Metcaf beside his master, and she had heard rumors during her imprisonment that it was *he* who had had the idea to poison Harond's waters with the corpses of slaves.

More frightening still, Agor Vareks had only minutes before performed the *Baresk oi-Sayra*, the Blessing of Blades, marking himself as the right hand of the Kayle.

Syrah knew then, without a doubt, that the greatest of Baoill's generals was after her head. He would hold it aloft, proclaiming himself the slayer of the Witch, and demand the crown his master had died with.

And he'll have it, too, she thought in a panic, watching the man advance on her.

He was less than than ten feet away, now, barely three or four bodies separating him from Syrah. Not once, as he began shoving aside the battling men on either side of him, did he look away from her. Even as he ducked under a stunning spell she threw at his head, then stepped nimbly over a line of fire that still burned smokeless beneath the feet of the army, he never glanced away. Syrah prepared herself, watching the general manage finally to break through the front line of his warriors, steeling her body and gathering a protective ward about her, summoning a fistful of fire in her free hand.

"*Wyth*," Vareks snarled, raising a sword to point at Syrah while the men about him pulled aside to leave their general within a small circle of space. "*Ûi-mys.*"

Witch. *You are mine.*

Then he brought the swords into a readied stance, his muscled frame tensing in preparation for the charge.

A sound reached Syrah's ears then, a strange, thrumming note, like the snapping of a banner in high wind. Even as a part of her mind pulled away, wondering at what it could be, something like a shadow flickered overhead, and suddenly the noises of the battlefield changed. Battle cries and shrieks of pain still wound their way within the snap and fizzle of magic and the crack of blades and staffs, but from within these came other sounds. There were gasps of awe and shock from behind Syrah, then wails of horror and dread before her. She had only enough time to glimpse Vareks' face as it went pale, his eyes flicking skyward, before something slammed down upon the stone in the few feet of space between the two of them, dark and massive and terrifying. It took a moment for Syrah to see more than dented steel armor, to see more than the bloody two-headed great ax held in one clawed gauntlet, or the ugly object that hung by its hair from the other.

Then she saw the wings, flickering and folding themselves along the figure's back, moving like they had a life of their own as he stood tall, thrusting his right hand and the thing dangling from it into the air.

Syrah felt as though her legs would give beneath her, a thousand different shades of joy blooming in her breast at the sight of the man.

"ENOUGH!" Raz i'Syul Arro rumbled in a pitching roar that drowned out the battle all around them, echoing a hundred times across the cliffs as Gûlraht Baoill's severed head swung aloft.

427

LIII

As though time itself had taken pause, the world froze. In the cliffs above their heads Syrah could still hear the continued shouts and bellowing cries as more men came down from the mountain in the hopes of joining the fight, but even those began to die away as the seconds ticked by, until they were only distant sounds to be soon drowned out by the storm.

Syrah's eye, though, was fixed on the scaled, lithe shoulders of Raz, her heart hammering so hard she thought it might leap from her chest.

"YOUR KAYLE IS SLAIN!" Raz bellowed, so loud the words continued to carry over the wind. "IF YOU DESIRE PROOF—" he dropped Baoill's head at the feet of Agor Vareks "—THEN TAKE IT!"

Vareks gaped down as the thing settled in the slush a foot from his fur-lined boots, struck dumb by the unmistakable sight. Behind him, cries of denial began to rise up from the tribes, muddled by a resonant murmur as those learned in the Common Tongue translated Raz's words for their less knowledgeable comrades.

"ANY WHO WOULD CHALLENGE THIS CLAIM," Raz continued, hefting the Kayle's great ax above his head with one hand now, "ARE FREE TO STEP FORWARD!"

Not a soul moved. The scene as a whole looked almost like it were holding its breath. For a long few seconds Syrah waited, still standing behind Raz, watching for the twitch from the dark crowd before her that would mean someone was stepping forward to take the atherian at his word.

No one came, though. Only the wind, blowing in their faces, seemed willing to make itself known.

And then Vareks knelt down, his eyes on the ground, falling to one knee before sheathing a sword and reaching for the former Kayle's head with his free hand.

For a long time the general studied it, turning it slowly this way and that, taking in the eyes and nose and ears and the beads in its brown hair with wide eyes. He had the look of a man searching for something—anything—that would show the lie for what it was, the look of a man for whom the truth weighed too much, was too painful to bear, and who needed another explanation for the facts laid out in all their bloody glory before him.

Finally, reverently, he set the head aside and looked up to Raz. Without getting up from his knee, Vareks took his other sword and brought it up to hold lengthwise in both hands.

As he set it gently down on the ground at Raz's feet, Syrah understood what needed to be done.

428

Forcing herself to look away from the scene—away from the inexplicable miracle that was the atherian—she turned and pushed her way through the Laorin behind her. Quickly people caught on to her same thought, because soon they were moving for her, murmuring a name as she sought the man out, praying to the Lifegiver he still lived.

When she found Carro, she almost sighed in relief to find him whole and well.

The former Priest looked shaken, his scarred eyes wide when he met Syrah's gaze. His grey robes were torn and singed, and he held a Priest's staff in his good hand—something the Broken were forbidden from ever touching again—that looked as though it had seen some use. Ignoring this, Syrah reached out, thinking to pull him along with her, to coax him forward.

Finding herself unable to touch the man, though, she paused, let the hand drop, and gave him an uncertain smile.

"Come on," she said quietly, turning to lead him through the crowd.

The Laorin parted before them again as they walked, eyes wide and mouth agape. No one spoke a word now, all eyes on the pair, the gravity of the moment weighing too heavily for something as trivial as their victory to be of any importance. Together Syrah and Carro moved through the lines of men and women, heading for the outline of Raz's head and shoulders standing tall above the rest.

When they reached him, the sight took their breath away.

In suit of Varek's submission, others had followed. Even as they watched, men were kneeling by the hundreds, easing themselves down onto one knee in the snow and ice. It looked as though the Saragrias themselves were sinking and settling before them, the army falling one after the other in a wave across the mountainside, bowing their heads respectfully in Raz's direction.

No, not Raz anymore, Syrah thought, seeing dozens of blue eyes glimpse up in amazement as she and the former Priest came to stand beside the atherian.

And so it was. Like a ripple across a field of black and grey and brown, heads lifted while voices rose to spread the news that Carro al'Dor had arrived. More eyes came up, seeking the man, drinking him in.

Carro al'Dor, whose champion had slain their master, delivering onto them the head of the most fearsome warrior the men of the clans had ever known.

Judging the moment right, Syrah stepped forward, gesturing back to Carro theatrically with one hand as she drew a rapid rune in the air with the other, touching her fingers to her neck.

"GRA! GRA DUSTEN YS-KEHN!" she screamed, her voice magically amplified so that every word shrieked above the wind, making all nearby jump. *"GRA DUSTEN YS-KAYLE!"*

Then she stepped back, out of the way, and willed herself not to cover her ears as the mountain tribes responded with fervor.

The sound was like the building rumble of a rockslide, distant at first, but growing with frightening speed. It swelled, growing with every passing second, rising as new voices picked up the roar. Before long Syrah thought she could feel the ground beneath her feet shake, and soon after that she was sure of it.

Twenty-five thousand men, before and above them along the face of the mountain, roared in tremendous unison, their combined voices merging together until the air itself vibrated.

At that moment, Syrah felt a heavy hand settle on her shoulder. She had to battle the desire to look around, had to push down the flush of disbelief and joy that touch flared within her, firm and comforting in its weight. She refused to look away, refused to break her gaze from the bowing army that blotted out the land and cliffs before her.

"What did you say to them?" Raz asked from behind her, just as Carro stepped forward, coming to stand tall before the kneeling form of Agor Vareks.

For a moment, Syrah hesitated.

Then, unable to help herself, she reached up and across herself, grasping the atherian's clawed fingers in her own.

"Bow," she responded as Carro al'Dor began to address his people, her voice returning to its normal pitch. "Bow before your master. Bow before your Kayle."

LIV

"It does not take a lifetime of seeking and research to imagine that the years following the Battle of the Pass were turbulent for the clans of the Saragrias and Vietalis Ranges. There were some, pockets of resistance within each tribe, which still clung to their old ways, to their iron devotion to the savage Stone Gods. The Peacekeeper did not press the mountain men to convert, of course. If anything, what can be gleaned from the entries in his journals point in another direction, to a personal struggle with a faith that took much from him, then forced him from their company. He did, however, pick up the work where Emreht Grahst left it, and this time there was no—or at least no successful—coup. What attempts were made to seize power by the remaining radical aspects were hammered down at once by the rest of the tribes, most holding to their new Kayle's side as they came to understand the prosperity that peace could bring. It would be naïve to think, however, that all stood by the Peacekeeper out of love and respect. There were elements, it can certainly be assumed, that supported him purely out of a desperate desire to save themselves from the potential wrath of his monstrous champion…"

—*The North: Ancient Tradition and Culture*, by Agor Kehn

The Giving Grounds of the Cyurgi' Di, Raz thought sadly, had never in the history of the faith borne witness to so much pain.

The dead were laid to rest alongside each other, every body lovingly set one beside the other in a curved line that filled much of the innermost circle of the Grounds. Had he been in better spirits, Raz might have found himself taken by the morbid beauty of the place, a massive, perfectly flat circle at the highest point of the mountain within which the High Citadel had been carved. All about them, in dozens of wide, meticulous rings, the corpses of the dead were set out in the old fashion of burial, for the elements to claim. The loops closest to where he stood—Carro and Syrah on either side of him among hundreds of others of the faith—were occupied by the most recent of the lost, their desiccated corpses already marked by the Sun and winds and storms. The outermost rings, though, held little evidence of the men and women they had once held claim to, marked if anything by nothing more than bits of bone or old, tattered cloth that shifted in the cool breeze.

Despite this, however, no soul would ever be forgotten within the boundaries of the Grounds. In the top corner of each space where a body had been carefully laid, the silver of a Priest's or Priestess' staff stood erect to the heavens, magically hammered into the stone, shining like a thousand steel trunks in a forest of memories.

And fifty-three new trees had been planted, on this day…

All about him, Raz could hear the moaning cries of denial, the shuddering, choking sobs of those left behind. Now, even as the ceremonies came to an end and the faithful began their slow return back to the Citadel, the loved ones of the departed lingered, unwilling to let go of the hope and dreams they had had with those that would no longer exist as a tangible part of their lives.

Raz knew that wretchedness well, and he shared in their grief.

Tilting his head back, allowing himself a reprieve from the sad scene before him, he looked to the sky. The Sun shone, bright and clear against a heaven of clear blue. It was an exquisite day, a day worthy of the men and women who had fought and died in brave defense of their home, and Raz sent up a brief prayer to his family somewhere above, hidden among Her Stars behind the curtain of the day, asking that they look after the lost.

Then he looked earthward again, watching the Laorin take their leave in groups of twos and threes and fours.

He could feel Syrah shaking beside him, her hand in its now-familiar place in the crook of his bandaged arm. She did not cling to him as she had a four-day ago, but rather stood firmer and taller at his side, taking in the scene. Her chin-length hair fluttered in the gentle wind, and for a few moments he sought her gaze, but for once she was too preoccupied to look up at him. Her eye was on the families of the dead, and he knew what she was thinking. He had told her a thousand times in the last two days that it wasn't her fault, that her stand had been the Laorin's last desperate chance, but Syrah wouldn't believe him. She blamed herself for the blood that had been spilled.

Raz had decided she would find her own truth, eventually.

On his other side, Carro al'Dor stood a changed man. His now-marked face still held that calm, sage quality that Raz had come to know well over the last weeks, but aside from that he was practically unrecognizable. His robes had been exchanged for leathers and fur, hammered iron and studded plates. His steel staff was gone, taken from him at his Breaking, and instead he carried a carved stave that had been gifted to him by the chieftains of the Amreht as he had released them from their forced indenturement to the Kayle's army. It was a queer object, and yet beautiful, sculpted from white ash so that the detailed faces of the Stone Gods that had been meticulously whittled into the top quarter of the wood looked wise and somber in the light of the day. It was a new take of the fierce deities Raz rather thought he liked. He'd heard whispers that Carro had already begun to earn himself a name amongst the tribes. "Peacekeeper" they called him, which Raz found terribly amusing. In addition to Gûlraht Baoill, the Dragon—as Raz himself was known among the mountain men, now—had had to overcome his injuries to slay six others over the last four-days who had had a change of heart, thinking themselves worthy enough of the Kayle's crown to challenge Carro for the seat.

Erek Rathst, one of Baoill's old generals, had been the last of these unfortunate fools, putting an end to the needless butchery.

He suspected Jofrey and the council were already at their wits' end, having seen true war for the first time, and more blood spilt over the steps of their home would only drive them further from the lessons of the last week.

Out of nowhere, Carro sighed.

"It wasn't going to end any other way, was it?" he asked darkly, his eyes on the backs of the last of the departed's families as they clung to the limp hands of wives, husbands, brothers, sisters, fathers, and mothers.

"No," Raz said, following his gaze. "And if it had, it wouldn't have been for the better."

He felt Syrah's fingers tighten around his arm at his words.

"Why was he so bent on bloodlust?" she asked quietly. "What did Baoill have to gain for it, in the end?"

"Freedom for his people," Carro answered with a shrug, watching a woman and her two children pass them to make for the Grounds' steps, all three faces tear-streaked and stricken. "Or freedom as he understood it, at least."

"*I* don't understand it," Syrah said. "I don't understand what could have driven him to this, what could have driven *all of them*. What sort of men speak only in bloodshed? What sort of men need a *dragon* to fall from the heavens on their heads in order to convince them to take a knee?"

Raz smirked at that. It had been an amusing moment, in the hours after the battle, explaining to Syrah, Carro, Jofrey, and the surviving council what had happened after he'd fallen from the cliffs with Baoill. He'd intended for the mountain men to believe he could fly, of course, intended to strike terror into their hearts as he plummeted from the sky amongst their midst, but he hadn't considered the Laorin would think the same.

They had fought even as they fell, like birds of prey clawing at each other during an earthward dive. As gravity ripped at them, pulling them through the grey gloom of the falling snow, neither had known or cared when the rocks of the mountain would rush up to meet them. They'd been consumed, conscious only of the other, battling with fists and claws and the great ax as they held on to one another, refusing to let go. It had felt like an hour—though it must really have been only seconds—before Raz found a way to gain the advantage. He'd had one clawed hand in Baoill's hair as he tried to wrench back the man's neck and bite at his throat, the other wrapped about the haft of the axe. The Kayle's free braids whipped about his face, the loose edges of his cloth shirt flapping in the wind.

That was what had given Raz the idea.

An instant later his wings had exploded outward, extending to their limit, pushing against his fall. As Raz's own speed was cut short Baoill had continued downward, howling in rage as the ax had been torn from his hand, Raz lifting away unexpectedly and taking the weapon with him. The howl turned to a roar of pain as the fistful of hair Raz still had in hand snapped the Kayle's head back, dangling him for half-a-second over the emptiness of the abyss below.

Then, using every ounce of strength left to him, Raz had brought the great ax back to its extent, screaming his victory to the storm around them before the iron blades whipped around with terrifying force.

Gûlraht Baoill, Kayle of the mountain tribes, had died mid-fall, his decapitated body dropping away to vanish into the twists of snow as Raz's descent continued to slow.

In comparison to this, landing had been almost easy.

Raz—whether by luck or skill—had just managed to guide himself precariously towards the cliffs moving by him now at a much more manageable rate. His back strained and spasmed as unused muscles tried to control his flight, but it had been all he could do to get close enough to swing the great ax out again, slamming its double head snuggly between two outcroppings that came so close they'd almost taken his arm off. From there Raz had hung for a moment, catching his breath and centering himself.

Then he'd begun to climb.

It had taken him nearly ten minutes to manage what couldn't have been more than fifteen seconds of falling, and he had done so in a desperate rush. The great ax looped securely in his curled tail, the braids of Baoill's head foul between his teeth, he had ascended the snow cliffs with all haste, summoning every ounce of speed he could muster, drawing on old skills honed on the roofs of Karth and Miropa and every fringe city the Arros had ever set foot in. The wind had howled around him, doing its best to rip him from the stone. The icy edges were slick beneath his fingers and feet, and not for the first time Raz wondered how, by the Sun, man survived without claws.

By the time he made it to the top, the growing sounds of battle driving him ever faster, Raz felt as though every one of his limbs was likely to fall off from fatigue

Initially he had cursed to find he hadn't managed a straight path, ending up beneath the bowed lip of the Citadel's outer wall. The mortared granite proved easy to manage, however, and he'd found ample foot and handholds in the eroded joints between the stones. In thirty seconds he was vaulting—or rather tumbling weakly—over the crenellations and onto the ramparts. He'd forced himself shakily to his feet, his breath coming in misty bellows as he looked out over the plateau beneath him, the battle raging like a mad ocean across its edge.

His vantage had allowed him to find Syrah, her hair distinct along the front lines of a Laorin force that looked to be rapidly losing. At the sight of her, Raz had found the strength to pull himself up onto the top of the wall once more. Taking the ax from his tail and the Kayle's head from his teeth, he'd spread his wings.

And leapt.

"Arro."

Raz blinked, pulled back to the present as a familiar voice spoke his name. He was surprised to find Jofrey al'Sen standing before him, flanked on either side by Benala Forn and Cullen Brern. The High Priest looked worn and exhausted, and Raz couldn't blame him. As new as he was to the mantle—which now hung over his shoulder, the single black stripe cresting the hood that was pulled over his greying hair—Jofrey had just been forced to handle the single most violent event to have ever fallen upon the Laorin.

And it was clearly already taking its toll.

"High Priest," Raz said in greeting, nodding his head respectfully to the man. "It was a splendid ceremony. Her Stars will shine with new lights tonight." He then turned to Brern. "You have my condolences for the loss of your brother. I did not know him well, but he seemed a strong, good man."

Cullen Brern said nothing—indeed, he seemed unable to speak, his jaw clenched and his eyes red—but he nodded in thanks.

"I've come," Jofrey said in a tired voice, and Raz thought he could sense uncertainty behind the man's word, "to give you our thanks. You are a true friend of the faith. We knew that the moment you leapt from the cliff."

Raz said nothing, feeling that there was more to come. Syrah, too, seemed to perceive something foreboding, because he felt her hand tighten against his arm.

Jofrey sighed, reaching up to rub his eyes with thumb and forefinger. "I've also come to tell you that, come the end of the freeze, you will no longer be welcome within the walls of Cyurgi' Di."

Raz felt Syrah spasm beside him. On his other side, Carro took half a step forward, enraged.

"What?" the former Priest spluttered. "Jofrey, how could—?"

"I understand."

Raz's firm words cut Carro off, and the man froze, then whirled.

"You *understand?*" he demanded, slamming his stave on the stone in anger. "What do you mean, you *understand?*"

Raz didn't look at him, his eyes on Jofrey as he spoke. "The Laorin and I tread different paths. It would not do for a place of faith to shelter a killer. It would send the wrong message, encourage a poor image of Laor and his followers."

Jofrey, for his part, looked almost relieved, and he nodded. "We have suffered a great loss. We are hurting. What aid you have offered us has been unorthodox to begin with, and I won't be surprised if my name is struck from the faith's history for allowing it. I *must* preserve what dignity Cyurgi' Di has left. You will be welcome through the end of winter. Additionally, our healers—" he indicated Raz's dressings "—will continue to be at your disposal until such time as you are no longer in need of them, as will any other facilities you might require. When the snows melt, however…"

"I'm to take my leave," Raz finished the man's trailing words. "I will, and I thank you for your hospitality."

Jofrey gave him a small smile, then turned to Carro.

"Carro…" he started hesitatingly, and this time it was obvious what he intended to say was painful.

Carro, though, stopped him with a wave of his left hand, still strapped to his chest. "I know," he said with something between regretful glumness and a glower. "I have the same thanks, and the same conditions." He shrugged. "I'll be spending most of my time among the clans that haven't left anyway. There's a man—Rako the Calm, they call him—who seems to have been sympathetic to Emreht Grahst's agenda. He seems eager to have my councel, and teach me the ways of the Sigûrth."

"I'm sorry, old friend," Jofrey said with a sigh. Then his eyes sharpened. "That being said, once things are settled amongst the tribes, count on the aid of the Citadel as you need it. You have my pledge of unconditional support." He paused, then stepped forward, placing a hand on Carro's shoulder. "Thank you," he said quietly as a tear fell from Benala Forn's eye behind him. "We will not forget what you have done for the faith, Carro."

Again, Carro shrugged, though he looked a little flushed.

Giving them a last nod, Jofrey and the councilmembers took their leave.

"Bastards," Carro grumbled once they were out of earshot, though he didn't sound like he meant it.

"They're only doing what they must," Raz said, watching the backs of the retreating trio as they took the steps down from the Grounds.

"Maybe," the man grumbled, moving as though to follow, "but they're still bastards."

436

When he passed in front of Raz and Syrah, he paused, and looked around. He scrutinized Raz for a long moment, the X-shape scar on his face distorting as his features shifted, becoming something like pride mixed with grief.

"Talo would have been proud of you, lad."

Then he left, trailing Jofrey and the others, leaving Raz with Syrah at his side and a lump in his throat.

For a time Raz and the woman stood in silence, watching the final stragglers say their goodbyes to the dead before taking their leave. Raz knew Syrah would not be able to go until she was ready, just as she knew he would not leave her on her own in this place, full of lives she believed lost by her own foolishness. And so, in silence they waited, her hand in the crook of his arm, his hand on hers.

When they were the last living souls within the boundary of the Grounds, Syrah finally looked up at him.

She had kept her peace as Jofrey had said what he'd come to say, which Raz had found distinctly odd. He would have expected her to jump in, more so even than Carro, and certainly to have had harsher words for the High Priest about his decision to banish the men who had bled and sacrificed for the Citadel. When she'd held her tongue, he'd grown curious, wondering what was on the Priestess' mind.

Now, as he looked into a face set in resolute desire, he understood why. Her right eye was covered as always, now by tight black wrappings wound about her hair and diagonally across her cheek and forehead. Her left took him in fiercely, her mouth set. He could see a hundred things in that face, experiences and emotions and desires she hadn't spoken of, but that he suspected. He saw anger, lingering and unquenched and vengeful. He saw confusion, a mix of uncertainty and need that drifted about her features every time she looked at him. He saw doubt, the same doubt he made out every evening as he sat outside her door, listening to the hesitation in her prayers.

And he saw fear, saw the same terror that ripped at her as she woke up screaming every night, thrashing and kicking until he came running to sooth her and hold her until she fell back asleep.

He knew what she was going to say before the words left her mouth.

"When you leave," she told him, not as a request or question, but almost rather as a demand, "take me with you."

Raz said nothing for a time, looking down at her, considering. After a while he reached around her and pulled her to his chest.

Then he bent his head down, pressed the end of his reptilian snout against the top of her head, and answered.

EPILOGUE

"The greatest empires in the history of any world have always been built by bound hands."

—Azzeki Koro, Third Hand of Karesh Syl

"AAAWWOOOOAAAHHH!"

Karan Brightneck woke to the sound of Abir's moaning scream as one wakes when falling in a dream, jolting and shuddering. At once she pushed herself up onto her hands and knees, scurrying with a clatter of iron on iron between the bodies laying and curled up on the worn wood around her, ignoring their muttering and groans as they, too, were pulled from what little sleep they were allowed.

"Abir!" she hissed in a hushing tone, reaching the old man's spot along the far wall of the shack and seeking his hand in the half-darkness of the room. "Abir, hush! Hush now!"

But there was no helping the man. Sweat sheened his face as he lay on his back, dripping along the tanned skin of his bearded cheeks and balding head. His eyes were shut tight, and he squirmed and writhed in the thralls of the dream. He had claimed, when Karan had first met him some dozen-years ago, that he had been a seer in another life, a fortuneteller that men of wealth and prestige once called upon from all over the realm. He had said that he had made the mistake of giving a Tash a fortune he did not like, and that his punishment had been the stripping of his name, home, and freedom.

But in all the time she had known him, Karan had come to realize that Abir's "fortunes" were nothing more than the ramblings of an aging man clinging to sanity, and that more often than not they just led to nightmares that kept the rest of them all awake at night.

"Abir!" she said more urgently as angry voices began to rise behind her, shaking the man. "Wake up! Wake *up!*"

Finally the man's shuddering quit, and he opened his eyes.

His gasps and groans, though, only barely lessened.

"He comes!" he moaned, his maddened, fevered gaze falling upon Karan. "He comes! He comes!"

"Who?" Karan asked him in a whisper, trying to sooth the man. "Who comes?"

"The dragon!" Abir hissed, his body beginning to shake again. "From sand then snow then sea, the dragon comes! He comes to rip the irons from their pegs, to free those who have been shackled! He comes from fire, then from ice!"

"*Enough!*" someone grumbled from behind her in a different, harsher tongue, and Karan felt a thrill as she recognized Brahen's throaty growl. "*Shut him up, female, before I do.*"

"Abir," Karan pleaded, starting to panic. "Please! You're waking the others! Please!"

At last, the old man began to calm. Much less than hearing reason, though, he looked rather to be fading back into delirium, dropping once more into sleep as his words faded away.

"He comes," he said in a wavering voice, his eyes fluttering. "He comes with a one... who wields the power of the gods... He comes... The... dragon..."

And then he was gone, fallen back into the peace of dreams, his breathing coming soft and slow.

Karan sighed in relief, still kneeling beside the man, one hand on his chest. Light, clear and bright, fell down upon her from an open window set in the wall above Abir's section of the floor. It shined off the iron manacles that had encircled her wrists for almost as long as she could remember, glinting off the scrapes and blemishes in the chains that ran between them. Checking one last time to make sure the man was asleep, Karan got slowly to her feet, intending to return to her own space.

Before she did, though, she looked out over the sprawl of the city beyond their little room, taking in the glow of the roads and the noise that echoed up at them even this late at night. She pondered, for a moment, what Abir had said, wondering at the life she would have if she was allowed to walk free among the shops and quarters and raised palisades.

Wouldn't that be something, she thought, turning her back on the light of Karesh Syl, her clawed feet clacking lightly against the dusty wood as she returned to her little corner of the floor.

Note From the Author
[aka: The Plight of the Writer]

I once again find myself at the point of disbelief, staring in something between awe and delirium at this final draft of *Winter's King*. It is such an incredible feeling to see your characters come to life, and yet the prospect of releasing them out into the world is also terrifying. Release them we must, though, and we do so with the hopes of getting them in front of as many eyes as the world will allow.

It is with this note that I move on to a more personal plea, a cry for assistance from all of you who got to the end of the book and were even just a little bit sad to have to put it down:

Please, *please*, consider rating and reviewing *Winter's King* on one or two major bookselling or book group sites.

Even better, *please* consider supporting me directly on Patreon, and get early access to chapters and books, art, cool stuff, and much more. Find me at:
patreon.com/bryceoconnor

Many people don't know that there are thousands of books published every day, most of those in the USA alone. Over the course of a year, a quarter of a million authors will vie for a small place in the massive world of print and publishing. We fight to get even the tiniest traction, fight to climb upward one inch at a time towards the bright light of bestsellers, publishing contracts, and busy book signings.

Thing is, we need all the help we can get.

Your positive input into that world, whether it's a review, a follow on social media, or financially supporting your favorite authors, makes the climb just a little bit easier. Rating and reviewing books you enjoy and following a writer's journey gives your favorite authors a boost upward.

With that all out of the way, thank you again so much for picking up *Winter's King*. If you'd like to give me feedback directly, have a question about Raz and his adventures, or just want to chat, drop me a message any time on Facebook, or on my website.

It has been a pleasure entertaining you, and I vigorously hope you continue to follow *The Wings of War* series to see what becomes of Raz i'Syul Arro.

Bryce O'Connor

CPSIA information can be obtained
at www.ICGtesting.com
Printed in the USA
FFOW01n0851080618
47058287-49402FF

9 780998 810638